CARREÑA 2:

Lamina

BY

K GERARD MARTIN

Shouldercat Books

Contents

CHAPTER 1

Awake!

2110 Dec 28, Sun Morn. 376 Grey Road, Hamilton, New Zealand.

"Do you remember the way to her house?" Kristi Fernandez asked.

"Of course I remember," Margaret McAleese replied. "It was at the end of Grey Road. There's a dirt road somewhere around here—yes, there it is!"

Margaret wheeled the Channel-A television news van onto the dirt road, which was in fact Dr. Jonara Carreña Pindus's driveway.

"Even though we've been here before," Kristi said, "it still feels like we're going back in time."

Margaret pulled the van up to the house and parked. Kristi helped Margaret with the equipment in back, and the two approached the front door. Similar to the day before, Kristi pressed the doorbell button and knocked. The door opened slowly with the chainlock preventing it from opening wide.

"Yes?" Jonara asked, not recognizing the two.

"Mamma Maffet, it's us—Kristi and Margaret," Kristi said.

"Mamma Maffet?" the elderly Jonara asked. "There's no one here by that name. Go away before I call the police."

The door closed. Kristi looked back at Margaret, and Margaret shrugged her shoulders.

"Try again," Margaret said.

Kristi pressed the doorbell button and knocked on the door. Jonara opened it as before but did not recognize the two from a few moments earlier.

"Yes?" Jonara asked.

"My name is Kristi Fernandez, and this is Margaret McAleese. We're from the Channel-A television station. We spoke the other day about doing your biography."

"Did you say Fernandez and McAleese?" Jonara asked.

"Yes, you remember us!" Kristi said.

"The heads of state for Argentina and Ireland," Jonara said. "One moment while I let you in."

Jonara closed the door slowly and spent several seconds undoing the chain.

"She doesn't remember us from yesterday," Margaret said. "We'll have to do the introductions all over again."

"I hope we don't have to restart her story from the beginning. If so, we'll never get through to the end," Kristi said.

Jonara opened the door slowly.

"Come in, come in," Jonara said. "Watch your step. I have a little bit of mail I need to clean up."

Margaret followed Kristi through the front door as before. The lobby area had remained unchanged since the previous day. Indeed, Jonara had not changed her clothes either. The two followed Jonara down the hallway as they walked past the tables of mail.

"I've been meaning to catch up on my mail," Jonara said like the day before. "One of these days, I'll get 'round to it. I place all my mail on these tables."

The three reached the living room. Kristi did not wear a sweater as she did the day before, and so her abdominal bulge was more noticeable than previously.

"Dr. Pindus," Kristi asked.

"Please call me...oh, you're expecting a baby," Jonara said. "You're due any day now."

"Yes, we are," Kristi said as she gave Margaret a smile.

Margaret returned the smile.

"You're the parents?" Jonara asked. "Congratulations. Oh, that means I'm your Mamma Maffet. Come give me a big hug!"

Kristi and Margaret gave Jonara a hug much like the previous day.

"Wait a moment. I think I know you two. You're the television crew from Channel-A," Jonara said.

"Yes!" Kristi said.

"You were here yesterday interviewing me about my life. I remember you two. See? My mind is as sharp as ever. Never forget a thing," Jonara said without realizing her earlier lack of memory.

Kristi and Margaret exchanged knowing looks.

"I also remember that you like juice and coffee," Jonara said. "Ah, Joni, you still have it. And Kristi—don't try to help me. A Spanish woman should never be without her legs."

Jonara left the living room and returned with the platter of orange juice and coffee, much like the prior day. Margaret and Kristi set up the equipment, but Margaret was concerned about drinking the coffee—was it leftover from the prior day? Margaret took a sip, and to her relief it was not.

"Whew!" Margaret said.

"What's 'whew' about?" Jonara asked.

"I thought the coffee would be old, I mean stale, I mean left-over from yesterday," Margaret said, but Kristi nudged her all the same.

"I make fresh coffee every day," Jonara said. "It should have an excellent taste."

"It is good coffee, thank you," Margaret said.

"The juice is good too," Kristi added while sipping orange juice.

"You're welcome. Now then, what may I do for you young girls?" Jonara asked. "Did you come to sell me something?"

"No, we're here to finish the interview from yesterday," Kristi said.

"Oh, that's right," Jonara said. "You're Kristi and Margaret from the television station. Silly me. But I'm not much good until I get at least one cup of coffee under my belt. Now then, if you could let me know where we left off, I'll be happy to continue."

Kristi read the last bit of her notes from the prior day to Jonara. Jonara then went on to explain what followed, and here is how Kristi narrated it:

2023 Oct 4, Wed Late am. Corpus Christi, Texas.

It was dawn when Jonara stood by the bedroom window. She didn't know how long she'd been watching stars ascend above the horizon in her great-grandmother's house. The arrival in Corpus Christi and the visit to her pregnant mother in the hospital with Davino and Cerafina seemed years ago. She was tired, horribly tired, but she was afraid to sleep.

A hand touched her on the shoulder. She knew it was her father and did not jump. He stared out the window as the breaking dawn obscured the last of the prior night's stars.

"It's morning," said Johnny Pindus.

"Yeah," Jonara replied.

"You're up early," he said.

"I know," she replied.

"Would you like some breakfast?" he asked.

"All right," she replied. "Daddy?"

"Yes?"

"Do you ever look at the stars and feel they are speaking to you?"

"All the time," he said.

"They seem to have their own stories," she said.

"They do."

"Daddy?"

"Yes, Jonara?"

"Do you think the stars know about us?"

"They may."

"Daddy?"

"Yes, dear?"

"I love you."

After a moment's pause, Johnny said, "Let's get some breakfast."

"What about Grandma? And Anna?" Jonara asked.

"They're asleep. I'll leave a note," Johnny replied.

Johnny scribbled a brief note and left it on the refrigerator door. He led Jonara outside Geneva's house and into one of Geneva's cars where he had Jonara fasten her seatbelt before driving away. Johnny drove onto Nueces Bay Causeway bridge across the bays into Portland—Portland, Texas.

"Welcome to Portland," said Jonara.

"Funny, isn't it?" Johnny said.

"But it's not the same Portland," Jonara replied.

"No, it isn't. There's a quiet restaurant next to the bay...hardly anyone visits...it might be out of business already...we'll see," said Johnny.

Johnny and Jonara were in luck. The restaurant had not yet gone out of business. Johnny led Jonara into the restaurant where the owner recognized Johnny and showed him and Jonara to a table outside on a deck with an excellent view of the bay, yet it was shielded from the wind. The owner left two menus at the table.

"Coffee?" the owner asked.

"Not me," said Johnny. "And Jonara is too young—"

"I want some coffee," she replied.

Johnny's eyes opened with surprise.

"You've never had coffee before," said Johnny. "Are you sure you—"

"Yes," said Jonara.

"Better start her off with decaf—the one with orange—"

"No, I want it black," said Jonara.

"Honey, I...you..." Johnny stumbled.

"And I'll need some fresh creamer—these old ones are like balloons and are ready to explode," said Jonara.

Johnny lifted an eyebrow several times as Jonara handed a bowl of old creamers to the owner. The owner took the creamer bowl from Jonara and poured coffee for her. He looked at Johnny and asked:

"And you?"

"Root beer," Johnny said.

The owner poured Jonara's coffee, left, and returned briefly with Jonara's creamer and Johnny's root beer.

"Are you ready to order?"

"I'll have a cheese omelet," said Jonara. "And a side of fruit."

"Steak and eggs," said Johnny, "with wheat toast."

The owner took the order and passed it on to the cook. Jonara stared across the bay while early-morning shadows shrank and orange flickers of the sunrise changed to amber.

"You didn't sleep well, did you?" Johnny asked.

"No. I had nightmares all night," Jonara said.

"Were you thinking of your Great-Grandma Geneva?" Johnny asked.

"It was more than that," she said. "Much more."

"Like what?" Johnny asked.

"I don't know how to start," said Jonara.

She watched several fishing boats troll by. Two sailboats in the distance faded in and out of the humid air.

"What's the last thing you remember?" Johnny asked.

"Stars. Stars with bright hopes fading. The sunrise. The starlight disappearing into the blue sky."

"That really happened," said Johnny. "I stood next to you. You were frozen by the window."

"Mommy went to prison. Mommy was in court. Mommy hurt her legs. Mommy—" Jonara said, but her voice choked in sadness, and she could not speak well. "Did it really happen?"

Johnny paused for a moment and sipped his root beer. Jonara stirred creamer into her coffee along with a packet of sugar. She took a swig, held her mouth open, panted to cool the hot coffee, and swallowed it.

"Is it what you expected?" Johnny asked. "The coffee?"

"No. It's bitter. How can adults drink it?" Jonara asked.

"Adults drink many bitter things," Johnny said.

"Daddy, I read some of Great-Grandma's diary," said Jonara. "I really did."

"Did the diary have a symbol on the first page—a symbol that looked like this?" Johnny asked.

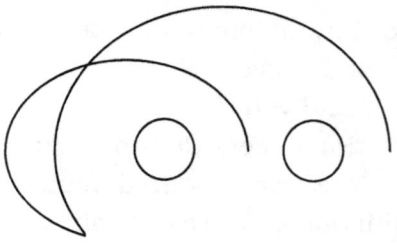

Johnny produced a stone hanging around his neck on a small chain. The stone had a symbol on the front side resembling the upper-half of a face with two circles for eyes, the upper curvature of a nose, and one ear.

"Yeah—that's it," said Jonara. "What does it mean? The diary, the stone, and the symbol? I have so many questions."

"I bet you do," he said. "But I can't answer all of them. The diary was special to your great-grandmother. But it's more than a diary. How? I don't know, but I think it has to do with the symbol, this stone, or something else."

"Let me see your stone," Jonara said. "You never showed it to me before."

"You were never old enough, but I guess you are now," said Johnny.

"It's strange. It's black and shiny, like volcanic rock," Jonara said. "No wait, now it's clear. Now it's cerise. It changes colors."

"Igneous rock?" Johnny said as if repeating Jonara's speculation.

"Is it?"

"No, I don't think so," Johnny replied. "I had it analyzed once. It looks like a stone, but it's mostly a mixture of different metals with a few other elements—aluminum, oxygen, silicon, boron, nitrogen, and carbon. There are other trace elements, but there's also phosphorus. There shouldn't be any phosphorus—it doesn't make sense, but it's there—embedded inside the rock."

"How come I wasn't old enough, Daddy? This stone—is it special?" Jonara asked.

"It's very special. It has power, I think. I was never superstitious, Jonara. I don't have a rabbit's foot. And no four-leaf clover. But the stone. It...well...hold it up to the sunlight!"

Jonara held the stone up in the morning light. Depending on how she rotated it, it was either shiny and black or shiny and clear. She moved the stone around in front of her and placed it between her and the sun. Sometimes the stone blocked the sun, but other times it allowed light through—pinkish-purple light.

"You see, it is not always opaque," Johnny said. "Light gets through."

"Is it glass?" Jonara asked. "And where does the color come from? And why wasn't I old enough?"

"Glass is made of quartz. Quartz is made up of silicon and oxygen. And I thought the same as you, maybe it was glass or even amethyst—which is also composed of silicon and oxygen—like glass. But the lab said no."

"A ruby?" Jonara asked.

"That was my next thought. Rubies are composed of aluminum oxide. But the lab also said no—because rubies don't have silicon or carbon," Johnny said. "Then there's the boron and nitrogen—alone it forms boron nitride, which can be as soft as graphite or nearly as hard as diamond. But it can't be just that—there are those other elements."

"Then what?"

"The lab suggested some sort of moissanite," said Johnny.

"Mois-a-what?" Jonara asked.

"Moissanite. It's like nothing in this world. And that's because it isn't. Moissanite comes from outer space and lands as a meteorite. But moissanite is usually silicon carbide. So that didn't explain the boron nitride, aluminum oxide, or the phosphorus," Johnny explained.

"Maybe it's a half-ruby, moissan...moisten, phosphorus... um, let's see...moisten, wet, water...I know, a water ruby!" Jonara laughed.

"That's pretty good!" Johnny said. "The lab called it a Moissan Ruby. But Water Ruby is fine too."

"How hard is it? Will it scratch glass? And why wasn't I old enough?" Jonara asked.

"It's harder than glass, rubies, moissanites, and diamonds. Probably 11 or 12 on Mohs scale. The lab couldn't be sure—it seemed to change its structure slightly during testing," said Johnny.

"Huh? What do you mean? It's solid, how could it change?" Jonara asked.

"Hold it up to the sun again," said Johnny. "Look closely—do you see a swirling pattern in the stone?"

"No," said Jonara.

"Hold it for ten seconds and look slightly to the side. Let your peripheral vision see the stone—don't look directly at it. Just relax and let the stone be...well...just relax."

"Okay. Hmm. Yeah, there is something. Like a swirl. I'll look—oh drat, it stopped swirling," Jonara said.

"That's because you stared directly at it. But you did see it swirl, right?" Johnny asked.

"Yeah. Is there water inside?"

"It's a solid—straight through," Johnny said. "Acceleration and deceleration tests proved that in the lab."

"Then what is it?" Jonara asked.

"No one knows, at least no one on this planet," Johnny said.

"Huh?"

"I told you it was from outer space. Could be from another planet. You never know. I took it to a geo-astrophysicist. She said a supernova most likely created it. But she said there were other possibilities. Space probes are revealing all sorts of new things every day. It could have been created any number of ways—ways that we don't even know about."

"Another form of life. People on another planet," said Jonara.

"I doubt it," said Johnny. "If there were intelligent people on another planet, at least one close enough to send this stone to us, we would have known about it. Radio telescopes have been scanning the sky for decades. The SETI project, for example—"

"But you just said there are ways we don't even know about. Ways of other people," said Jonara.

"Not other people. Maybe geological forces. Not people. Men can't make this stone," said Johnny.

Jonara paused in thought. She stared at the stone again in the sun and moved her line of sight to the stone's side. The stone swirled. Jonara was stuck—she couldn't make any understanding of the stone. She stared back at the water and watched the sailboats sail closer to her in a zigzag fashion.

"Here we are," said the owner. "A cheese omelet and steak with eggs. Can I get you two anything else?"

"Extra napkins," said Johnny.

"I'd like some hot chocolate," said Jonara.

"Very good," said the owner, and he returned shortly with napkins and hot chocolate.

Jonara sipped her hot chocolate. She enjoyed the taste better than coffee. Taking a bite of her omelet, she continued asking her father questions.

"What makes the swirl pattern in the Water Ruby?" Jonara asked. "And why wasn't I old enough?!"

"I thought you'd forgotten the age question. Anyway, the lab thinks small bits of phosphorus interact with oxygen in the aluminum oxide—the ruby portion of the stone. The silicon conducts the phosphorus light in one-way directions—this is the swirling pattern," said Johnny.

"And the boron nitro-what was it?"

"Boron nitride. The lab thought it gave structure to the Moissan Ruby."

"Is the lab right about the—the light and swirls and structure?" Jonara asked.

"I don't know," said Johnny. "It's the lab's theory."

"What's your theory?" Jonara asked.

"I'm not sure I have one," said Johnny. "At least not a scientific theory. But one thing I've noticed—the stone reacts the most to ultraviolet light—and human aura."

"Did the stone give you your gift? The stone?" Jonara asked between bites of omelet and fruit.

"My gift?" Johnny asked. "Well, I guess."

"You never told me," said Jonara. "How did it all start? Where did you find the Water Ruby? How did you learn to use it?"

"I, uh, yeah, well, hmm," Johnny replied. "How much did the diary tell you?"

"Only about what happened in 2006—how you could read women's thoughts and how you found Mommy in the hospital. The sander on the back of your neck. Cerossi Café. Shocking yourself in the hospital to wake Mommy from her coma," Jonara said. "I also know about Aunt Valeria's funeral. Oh Daddy!"

"That was a very difficult year," Johnny said.

"Did the Water Ruby help you connect? In Mommy's trial, someone said you could only read women and not men," said Jonara.

"It's true," said Johnny. "The stone is like an amplifier, or maybe a tuner. It's a radio to the environment, but it doesn't read everything. It needs ultraviolet light to energize it, and it must be near the bay to absorb that energy."

"Energize? What bay?" Jonara asked.

"The one formed by Ross, Hardtack, Toe, and East Islands in the Willamette," Johnny said.

"Do you put it in the water or something?" Jonara asked.

"At first I did," Johnny said. "But it's tricky. At one time, the islands were owned by a gravel company, and they didn't like trespassers. Some of it was donated to the City of Portland as a wildlife refuge. Portland also doesn't like trespassers. Anyway, yes, I put it along the top of the waterline so it could get some ultraviolet light from the sun. That process would take hours to get it a little energized."

"Are there other ways you can reenergize the stone?" Jonara asked.

"There are only two other ways that I discovered. Whenever I ate in the Cerossi Café, the Moissan Ruby reenergized, and very quickly," Johnny said.

"Wow!" Jonara said.

"Yeah. I went back there quite often with your mother. The other way is to dip it in Corpus Christi Bay—yes, that bay out the window there."

"But this bay is so far away from Portland," Jonara said.

"I know, I know. Also, the stone seems to draw energy from people, but people don't reenergize it."

"Huh?"

"When I place it inside my shirt, it feels cold. I think it draws heat from my chest, and when it does, I can use it to read things around me, and women. Girls too. But not boys and not men. I don't know why."

"Where did you find it? Are there more?" Jonara asked.

"I found it in the Willamette River—in the other Portland— our home in Oregon," Johnny explained, "when I was younger— maybe eight years old. What year was that? It was 1989, I think. I remember now—it was just before I started going to MacNessi Dental and before your Grandma Eva got pregnant with your mother. I swam along the shores of Ross Island. I'm trying to remember why. I think it was because I kept having dreams I would find something there. Children dream all sorts of things, and I thought there was sunken treasure off of Ross Island. So I swam and swam with my facemask and snorkel when something bit me. It was a fish, and I tried to brush the fish free, but it wouldn't let go. I had to swim ashore and get a stick to pry the fish off my arm."

"I pried the fish off. It fell onto the beach and flapped like mad," Johnny continued. "I knew it wanted back into the river, so I pushed it back in with the stick. It struggled to get swimming again, and I thought it swam off, but a minute later while I was nursing my wound, I saw it floating at the top of the water. It dove back down. Then it floated again, as if it were dying."

"It finally quit diving down and stayed on top of the water," Johnny said. "It floated back to shore, about twenty yards down the shoreline from where I was standing. I walked down to see if I could help it, but it was too late—the fish was beyond hope. I touched it with the stick, and in a last gasp, it convulsed and pushed something out of its mouth. It died right there, and the waves took it back out into the river where something grabbed it and pulled it under."

"And the Water Ruby came out of its mouth?" Jonara asked.

"Yes, it did," Johnny continued. "I picked up the Moissan Ruby and looked at it, but when I did, the bite in my arm burned like fire. The fish must have caught my muscle, because reaching down for the stone made it hurt. My arm burned and burned, and I wished I had an ice pack, but then I realized that the more I held the Moissan Ruby in the sunlight, the colder the Moissan Ruby felt. I put the Moissan Ruby on my bite wound. My burning muscle immediately cooled, and the pain subsided."

"But something strange happened," Johnny continued. "The stone made me cold, and I shivered. My legs, my feet—I felt something. I was connected to the water, like watching a movie at a drive-in theater. And the movie was about the fish that just bit me. It was now at the bottom of the river being eaten by other fish. It was a horrible sight, and it terrified me. I took the Moissan Ruby off my arm and nearly threw it back in the river."

"But you didn't. What changed your mind?" Jonara asked.

"I thought maybe, maybe I could learn to tame it. I know that sounds corny," Johnny said. "But I thought maybe something good could come of it if I worked hard to figure out how the Moissan Ruby worked."

"So did you?" Jonara asked.

"Not at first. I put it away in my closet for a week and almost forgot about it until my mother was rearranging clothes in my closet, and the stone fell out. She thought I stole it," Johnny said.

"You never talk about your parents," Jonara said. "What were they like?"

"I don't remember much," Johnny said. "They were always fighting over money. Dad kept losing his job at one factory or another. His job kept getting outsourced overseas. Mom didn't work, but she was quick to spend Dad's money on trinkets. I was afraid to do much of anything at home. Everything had a cost it seemed, and I was always in the wrong. Mom was atheist, and Dad was Jewish. Mom got mad every time Dad celebrated the Sabbath or anything Jewish. She refused to watch me while he went to the synagogue, so he took me along. Dad talked about his service in the military when he was in Vietnam. Lots of awful stories. I don't like to think about it."

"Why would your mommy think you stole the Water Ruby?" Jonara asked.

"I don't know. She just wanted to punish me. She hit me with a rubber hose—" Johnny started.

"Why a rubber hose?" Jonara asked.

"It leaves no marks. She didn't want to be accused of child abuse," Johnny said. "I told her the truth. I told her the same story I told you. She didn't believe it, and she kept beating me with that hose to the point where I would say anything to get her to stop. I confessed I stole it from your Aunt Valeria's workplace. Mom believed it and gave it to Valeria. Valeria wasn't sure what it was, but after I told her about my story and the beating, she understood."

"The next day, Mom went crazy. She yelled and screamed about my path to deceit and how it was my dad's fault. He tried to get her to stop screaming, that his heart was giving him pain, and he needed to go to the hospital. She accused him of lying just like me. She got paranoid and thought we were ganging up on her," Johnny said.

"Was he having a heart attack?" Jonara asked.

"Yeah, he was. He slumped over. Mom thought he was faking and left him there. She stormed out of the house. I ran to a neighbor for help, and the neighbor called an ambulance. It was too late. He was dead," Johnny said.

"Mom rushed everyone through the funeral. She went through Dad's things and sold almost everything except for two items: an old scroll of the Torah—which Mom gave to Valeria, and something else," Johnny said.

"What?" Jonara asked.

Johnny pulled a necklace from his pocket. An elliptical-like wooden object with two holes on one side and letters on another was attached to the end, and Johnny showed it to Jonara.

"My old man carried this keepsake with him all the time," Johnny said. "His first name was, 'Aromani,' and his previous last name was 'Pindos.' Story goes that his mother lived in the Pindus Mountains in Greece back in the early 1940s before he was born. She moved to Palestine and later to New Zealand with him. My dad served in Vietnam with the New Zealand Army. That's where he met Mom. She was a nurse. They got married, and he returned to Portland, Oregon with her. Valeria says she was the sweetest mother until I was born. Then she changed. She cried a lot and hardly slept. No one knew what to do at the time, but today we know she was undergoing post-partum depression. She never sought treatment. It's too bad, because I think she would have been okay if she'd gotten help before it was too late. Well, that's the past."

"What about the keepsake?" Jonara asked.

"I think Dad used it to celebrate the Sabbath," Johnny said. "The two holes are just large enough to hold birthday candles."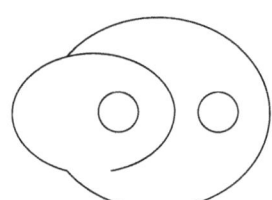

"Then it's a candleholder," Jonara said.

"Yes. Here—take a look."

Johnny passed the keepsake to Jonara. She stared at the back of the wooden block.

"These are funny letters," she said.

"It's Greek," he said.

"What does it say?"

"The big words say *Aromani Pindos*. The little words say *son of Fantina from*. So it can be read two ways—*Aromani Pindos*, and *Aromani son of Fantina from Pindos*. That's why I think my dad was from the Pindus Mountains."

"One of the letters looks funny—the 'D' in Pindos," Jonara said.

"That 'D' is the letter 'delta'. I've always wondered about the extra delta inside the delta. It could be a secret symbol," Johnny said.

"Secret for what?" Jonara asked.

"Secret for the Star of David," Johnny said.

"The Star of David doesn't look like that," Jonara said.

"I know. The Star of David consists of two overlapping equilateral triangles. But the 'D' in Pindos has a small triangle inside. I'm guessing this candleholder was made for my grandmother, that she was Jewish, and she wanted Aromani to know who his mother was, where he was from, and her religion. Being Jewish was difficult in those days. There was always some sort of hatred toward Jewish folk. I'm not surprised the Star of David was modified to a delta-inside-a-delta."

Jonara passed the candleholder back to Johnny. She paused for a moment before asking her next question.

"Daddy?" Jonara asked.

"Yes?"

"What was Grandma Pindus's name? You know, the one with depression."

"My mother's name? Deladi Sweets," Johnny said.

"Is she still alive?"

"Yes," Johnny said. "But she's catatonic."

"What does that mean?" Jonara asked.

"It means she can't do anything on her own or respond to things. She's physically alive, she awakens and sleeps, but she's like a zombie. Doctors say she went crazy because of encephalitis. That's an infection of the brain. They say her depression weakened her immune system, and the encephalitis gradually took hold. Anyway, it made her catatonic. Do you remember her?"

"A little. Didn't she visit us when I was little?" Jonara asked.

"You were five years old at the time," Johnny said. "And it was a mistake. I shouldn't have agreed to it."

"Was that when she gave me that awful thing to drink?" Jonara asked.

"Paregoric," Johnny said. "Jonara—she was catatonic, but the hospital convinced me they could perform electroconvulsive therapy on her and make her normal. I reluctantly agreed. The hospital started shock treatment, and at first she seemed normal—normal enough to live outside the hospital. So I agreed to let her live with us. She did well the first month or two, and she continued getting shock treatments, but then she got hold of the paregoric—from where I don't know. And she gave it to you so you'd sleep—just like she did when I was a boy. I confronted her, and her mood went sour. Not long after, the shock therapy failed to help her, and she went catatonic again. I visited her after that and tried using the Moissan Ruby to help her, but it was no use."

Jonara paused for a moment.

"Do you remember the first time you used the Water Ruby? I mean after you found it. What was it like?" Jonara asked.

"I remember the first time I used it—not counting when I first found it. It helped me. Your Aunt Valeria didn't show up from work one night," Johnny explained. "I knew she was in trouble. I paced around the apartment. I had a sense of the apartment structure, but I felt trapped. I worried, and I didn't know what to do. So I took a hot shower."

"A hot shower? How strange," Jonara said.

"Back in those days, a hot shower was the only thing that would help me relax. And I needed to relax to think clearly," Johnny explained. "Then it happened."

"Then what happened?" Jonara asked.

"I had my first long-distance vision of another human. It was your Aunt Valeria, and she was being held against her will at her boyfriend's apartment. I called the police, and she got away. He wasn't her boyfriend after that, but she was surprised I knew where she was, so I had to explain it to her—about the Moissan Ruby."

"I got to see Aunt Valeria last night in my dream," said Jonara. "It was sad. She was in her casket and all."

"She was a special sister. She took care of me when I was little. Dad was dead, and Mom was put away. Valeria took me in to her apartment and gave me all the comforts of home," Johnny said.

"How did you figure out a shower helped—what's the secret to using it?" Jonara asked. "I want to try it."

"You must be very careful, Jonara. It shows you things that exist—in great clarity—but exist in truth nonetheless. Lots of people don't like seeing the truth—it can be overwhelming and painful," Johnny warned.

"I know. I slept with Great-Grandma's diary. Was that the truth?" Jonara asked.

"From what you've told me, yes," Johnny said.

"So tell me, how do you make the Water Ruby work?"

"You must find a way to make your skull vibrate at a high frequency," Johnny said.

"Huh?" Jonara asked.

"When I shivered, my skull shook. When I took the shower, my skull shook," Johnny continued.

"That doesn't make sense," Jonara said.

"Have you ever been to the dentist—" Johnny said.

"Lots of times," said Jonara.

"—when a tooth is getting drilled, and suddenly the drill catches your tooth a certain way and your skull shakes too fast for you to think straight?" Johnny asked.

"I think that happened once," said Jonara.

"Well, when I shivered on the riverbank, my brain went kinda numb—I couldn't react to what I saw or heard through my eyes and ears. But when that happened, I felt the Moissan Ruby—I felt and saw images from it. Once my shivering stopped, images and sounds from the real world overpowered the weak images from the stone," he explained.

"Kinda like the stars this morning when the sun rose? The stars disappeared," said Jonara.

"Yes, that's exactly what it's like," Johnny said. "The sun is powerful, and the atmosphere is dense enough to scatter the sunlight around so you can't see the stars. But when the sun is blocked out at night, you can see the stars. That's what the Moissan Ruby is like—a star in the night."

"Can you teach me how to use it?" Jonara asked.

"I'm worried," said Johnny.

"About what?" Jonara asked.

"What it will do to you. Because of what it's done to me," he replied.

"Huh? How?" she asked.

"Have you ever held a power tool like a sander or drill for too long, and it shook your arm to the point where your arm itched and hurt afterward? And it itched from inside out?" Johnny said.

"No, you never let me use the power tools," said Jonara.

"Or a lawnmower with an old engine that doesn't run well? The shaking it does—the hands and arms—they hurt so badly," Johnny said.

"No, you never let me mow the grass either," said Jonara.

"Every time I use the stone, my skull itches and hurts afterward—and I can't scratch the inside of my skull. Over the years, it just keeps hurting. And there are the nightmares. I wish I never found the Moissan Ruby," Johnny said.

"I know," said Jonara. "My three-wheeler—when I went down the gravel hill in our back yard—that shook me real bad. It hurt, and it itched like you said. Like when I was playing out in the cold and forgot my gloves, and I came in to warm up my hands—they itched too."

"Yes, that's right," said Johnny. "So now you understand."

"But you use the stone for good," said Jonara. "I was just goofing around on my three-wheeler."

"I know, honey, but sometimes doing good causes the greatest pains there are," said Johnny. "Look at your mother. She's going to bring another person into the world. It's a wonderful gift. But she's suffering for it, too."

Jonara looked at her fruit plate and finished the last bit—a small strawberry. She placed her empty plates at the side of the table where the owner picked them up shortly thereafter. Johnny also finished his breakfast and waved the owner down for the bill. The owner returned after a moment with the bill and thanked the two for dining at his restaurant.

"Are you ready to go?" Johnny asked Jonara.

Jonara stared out into the bay at the sailboats that had once zigzagged toward her. They had turned around and were now sailing directly away from her. She looked at a flagpole next to the restaurant and noticed the flags were flapping in the same direction as the sailboats were now traveling.

"Daddy?" asked Jonara.

"Yes?"

"The sailboats—do you see the sailboats?" Jonara asked.

"Yes, I do."

"They're sailing away," she said.

"Yes."

"The wind is pushing them along," she said.

"Yes, that's how sailboats travel—they use the wind to push them along," he explained.

"But Daddy," she continued.

"Yes?"

"They sailed over here just a few moments ago," Jonara said. "They sailed into the wind."

"They seemed to," Johnny replied.

"Did the wind push them?" she asked. "How can wind push a sailboat into the wind and not away?"

"It's difficult to explain—there are pressure differences. The sails and the boats must be configured a certain way," Johnny said.

"But they did it; they sailed into the wind," she said.

"Yes, they did. Seems impossible, doesn't it?" Johnny asked.

"Yeah. I *believe* they can sail into the wind—I saw them do it," she said.

"Can't argue you there," he said. "C'mon, honey, let's go home."

Jonara kept talking as Johnny paid the bill and escorted her to the car.

"But I didn't think they could sail into the wind," she said.

"Lots of people thought the same thing, until the first sailboat did it," Johnny said.

"I bet there are other things in the world that can be done, but people don't believe," she said.

"Most things have been discovered already," said Johnny. "With modern computers helping people solve big problems and with the easy way we communicate, it's unlikely people will stumble across something that hasn't been thoroughly examined and tested already."

"But people have to know what to examine. They have to know there's something else to look at, don't they?" Jonara asked.

"Yes, but everything has been looked at. There's—" Johnny started.

"How can that be true? What about the Water Ruby? Does everyone know about that?" Jonara asked.

"No, but it's just a matter of time before someone creates a device and writes a computer program to unravel the inner workings of this stone," Johnny said.

"I don't think so, Daddy, I think the stone was meant for you to find and for me to use. I believe this, Daddy, I believe," said Jonara.

"Oh honey! Some day you'll grow up and realize how silly you sound right now," Johnny said.

"I'm the star, Daddy, I'm the star, and I don't want the morning sunrise to wash me out. I don't want to grow up and see how silly I am. Daddy, you learned how to use the stone when you were little. Did anyone else try to use it?" Jonara asked.

"Your grandmother. I tried to show her how to use it, but it didn't work," Johnny explained.

"How old was she when she tried it? Was she an adult?" Jonara asked.

"Oh heavens yes," he replied.

"Who else?"

"Your mother. When she was sixteen. At the Elrod 402," Johnny said.

"Did it work?" Jonara asked.

"Yes, it did. And it almost killed her. It was too much stress, and I promised her I'd never lend it to her again," Johnny said.

"But she was not an adult yet. You weren't either when you first used it. It worked for you and Mommy. It didn't work for Grandma—she was an adult. Don't you think I should use it before I'm too old?" Jonara asked.

Johnny did not reply immediately. The two traveled back across the Nueces Bay Causeway bridge, and he stared at the bay.

"What's the Elrod 402?" Jonara asked, breaking the silence.

"Didn't you dream about that in the diary?" Johnny asked.

"No. Mommy was taken to the...to the...some juvenile center," said Jonara.

"The Portland Juvenile Detention Center?" Johnny asked.

"Yes," Jonara replied.

"So you didn't dream about the transfer to the Elrod 402?" Johnny asked.

"No. The dream ended. I was staring at the stars in my dream, and then you were standing next to me," Jonara said.

"Hmm."

"Daddy—how does Great-Grandma's diary work? It has the same strange drawing as the Water Ruby. They must be related," Jonara said.

"They seem to be. Your great-grandmother's family made the paper from cotton and flax grown in northern Spain. The paper is very strong and durable—much like paper vellum of today. The front cover is made of Norway spruce, the side binder of lignum vitae, and the back cover of Norway maple. These woods are finished with a mixture of linseed oil and beeswax," Johnny explained.

"Then the diary is magic," said Jonara.

"Magic? Um, not really," Johnny said.

"It must be magic," said Jonara.

"Honey, magic is just an illusion, performed by a magician. It isn't real," said Johnny.

"Was my dream real?" Jonara asked.

"No."

"But it happened, right?" Jonara asked.

"Yes, but—"

"You said magic isn't real. But magic happens. My dream wasn't real, and it happened. My dream was magic. The diary is magic."

"This is getting complicated," said Johnny. "Someone once said if technology is too advanced for us to understand, it will look like magic."

"Great-Grandma's diary is advanced technology?" Jonara asked.

"It must be," said Johnny.

"Like the Water Ruby," said Jonara.

"Maybe. Who knows?" said Johnny.

"It must be. Someone made the symbols—they're the same. But how? And whose technology?" Jonara asked.

"I don't know," said Johnny.

"'All things have been discovered'—that's what you said," Jonara said. "Doesn't anyone know?"

"I don't know," said Johnny.

"Outer space. People from outer space know the answer," said Jonara.

"I already said 'no'," said Johnny. "There are no little flying saucers. UFOs are a myth."

"Somebody must know somewhere. I'm going to find them," said Jonara. "I will, I promise."

The two arrived at Geneva's home. Anna and Eva were now awake and enjoying biscuits with tea.

"Well, where did you two go off to?" Eva asked. "You're missing some nice biscuits Anna made up. There's tea and homemade preserves. Jonara, if you'd like some milk, there's plenty in the fridge."

"We ate already," said Jonara.

"Really," said Eva.

"I told you, Miss Eva, I saw them go out," said Anna.

"We went for a little drive over to Portland and had some breakfast," said Johnny.

"You're up early, Jonara. I would have thought you'd want to sleep in," said Eva.

"I couldn't sleep," said Jonara.

"Oh, that's too bad," said Eva. "I'm sure Anna won't mind if you need a nap later in the morning. She'll be here to take care of you while your father and I go over to the hospital to see your mother."

"I want to see her," said Jonara.

"I don't think that's a good idea. Your mother is very ill, and I don't think she should—" started Eva.

"Should what?" Jonara asked.

"She needs her rest," said Eva.

"And I'll upset her? That's not true," Jonara said, getting a little belligerent.

"Listen here, young lady, if I say you will stay here with Anna, you will stay!" Eva said. "I'm a medical professional and your grandmother—I know the situation far better than you. Now be a good girl and let Anna take care of you!"

"It doesn't matter," Jonara said, speeding out of the dining room (away from Eva) and into the living room by herself. "I already saw her last night at the hospital!"

Jonara threw her face into the couch and cried. Eva shot Johnny a startled look. Anna followed Jonara and comforted her.

"Johnny, what is she talking about?" Eva asked.

"I'm not sure," said Johnny with a quiver.

"She knows something, and you know half of it. What's going on?" Eva asked.

Johnny slipped into a shell of silence.

"Johnny, answer me!" Eva demanded.

Johnny motioned Eva to follow him. He went upstairs into Jonara's guest bedroom with Eva in tow. Johnny drooped his head and pointed at Geneva's diary. Eva let out a heavy sigh.

"I thought I got rid of this thing years ago!" said Eva. "What's Jonara doing with this black magic? No, it's my fault. Mother was dabbling in the occult. I should have disposed of her dark trappings before I let you and Jonara fly down. I just had too much on my mind. Don't worry—we'll get Jonara straightened out."

"I'm...sorry," muttered Johnny.

"It's not entirely your fault," said Eva. "I'm just not used to dealing with two generations of tragedy. Now it's three generations—not counting my own. When will I ever get a break? No, don't answer that."

"Is Jonara in trouble? It's just a diary," said Johnny. "I thought she would be okay."

"Okay?! Nothing is okay, Johnny," said Eva. "My mother is dead, my only daughter is dying, and my granddaughter has just taken the first step of corruption that I hoped my family line would be spared. But no, it starts all over again. All over! Well, it's time to put my foot down. I'm going to get rid of this diary and all the other sentimental black-magic items my mother left behind to trap us. Here, get a box out of the basement. We'll take the worst items to the dump on the way back from the hospital. Well, what are you waiting for? Don't just stand there."

"The diary—it's important," said Johnny.

"Not you too!" said Eva.

"It has a symbol—the same symbol as my Moissan Ruby," said Johnny.

"You didn't bring that with you, did you? I thought you kept that evil thing locked away," said Eva.

Johnny pulled the Moissan Ruby from inside his shirt and showed Eva.

"Good God Almighty!" said Eva.

"I told her about it. I explained how it worked," said Johnny.

"Why now? Couldn't you have waited until she's eighteen? At least until after the funeral!" said Eva.

"She needed to know. After last night...the dreams she had ...she knows," said Johnny.

"How much?" Eva asked.

"Most of 2006," said Johnny.

"Including the factory fire?" Eva asked.

"Yes."

"And the trial?"

"Yes."

"And detention too!? Is nothing sacred?" Eva asked.

"No, not detention. Not the Elrod 402," said Johnny.

Eva breathed a sigh of relief.

"Well at least that's something. Any other years? 2006 is only the second worst year after 1989 or 1990," said Eva.

"She knows nothing of Marc—" Johnny started, but Eva placed her hand on Johnny's mouth.

"Don't say that name," said Eva. "What else did Jonara tell you about Evanita?"

"That's it. She saw her mother in her dreams," said Johnny.

"No, that's not what she said. She said she saw her mother at the hospital last night," said Eva.

"Maybe when Evanita was in the hospital in 2006...maybe that's what she meant," said Johnny.

"But why single out the hospital? Did she see her mother in other ways in her dream?" Eva asked.

"Yes, but—" Johnny said.

"Where did you find her?" Eva asked.

"What?"

"When you woke up this morning, Johnny. When you saw your daughter for the first time this morning—where did you find her?" Eva asked. "Was she sleeping in bed? No, that's not how the diary works. Where did you find her?"

"Standing by the window," said Johnny.

"Of course. She ended the night as she started it," said Eva.

Eva walked over to the windowsill. The old paint seal had been freshly broken. Eva opened the window and looked straight down at the shrub next to the house on ground level. Several twigs were broken.

"Oh she definitely saw her mother last night, but it wasn't a dream," said Eva. "That little sneak went out after bedtime! I bet she climbed down the rainspout, walked to the hospital, and wormed her way in. Why, when I get my hands on her I'll—"

"Leave her alone," said Johnny.

"And you," said Eva, returning her gaze from out the window to inside where she focused on Johnny. "You're encouraging her. She doesn't need—"

Something was different. She looked around to find the diary but could not.

"She doesn't need—" Eva repeated.

She stared at Johnny, and he had a canary-swallowing grin. He attempted to distract Eva from seeing his hands behind his back.

"Hand it over," she said.

"Hand what over?" he feigned.

"Geneva's diary. I know you have it. Give it to me," said Eva.

"Uh, it's not necessary to—" Johnny started.

"Give me that diary!" she demanded.

"Nope," said Johnny.

"Mr. Pindus. This is Carreña family property. You have no jurisdiction over my mother's personal writings. Now I ask you —politely—hand it over to me."

"No," Johnny said. "You'll destroy it. It shouldn't be destroyed."

Jonara heard Eva's and Johnny's raised voices echoing through the heating vent. She pulled free from Anna's comforting arms and dashed upstairs to her guest bedroom. Anna followed closely behind. Jonara rushed into the bedroom in time to see her father holding Geneva's diary above his head and behind him as far from Eva's reach as possible. Eva had Johnny pinned in a corner and used her strength and agility to advance her hand toward the diary.

"Jonara," said Johnny. "Catch!"

Johnny tossed the diary to Jonara. Jonara caught it.

"Good girl," said Eva. "I'll take that now. Anna will give you some milk and coffeecake, won't you Anna?"

Jonara held the diary behind her back and nodded no.

"Jonara? I'm your grandmother," said Eva. "Don't make me force it from you."

Anna passed behind Jonara, and in the same motion (obscured from Eva's view), Jonara handed the diary to Anna. Anna walked in the bedroom in such a way that she, Jonara, and Johnny formed a triangle around Eva. Johnny stood in a corner to one side of the bed, Anna on the other side, and Jonara near the doorway.

"Jonara—give me that diary!" Eva commanded.

Eva grabbed Jonara's shoulders and twirled her around to reveal the diary, but to her surprise, Jonara exposed her empty hands.

"What diary?" Jonara grinned.

"Okay, no one leaves this room until I have the diary in my hands. Jonara, where is the diary?" Eva asked.

Jonara shrugged her shoulders as if she didn't know, and while Eva faced Jonara, Anna tossed the diary over the bed to Johnny behind Eva's back. Eva heard the pages rustling through the air and spun in time to witness Anna's carry-through motion, the diary's path through the air, and Johnny's catch.

"Keep away!" Jonara yelled like a happy child at school recess.

"This isn't funny. Johnny," said Eva as she reached for him, but he tossed the diary to Jonara.

"Your grandmother is losing patience," said Eva as she dove for Jonara.

Eva had overcompensated her dive in expectation of Jonara throwing it to Anna, but Jonara threw the diary back to Johnny. Johnny threw the diary to Anna before Eva could reach him. Eva walked around the bed calmly in such a way as to block Anna from throwing the diary to Jonara. Anna tossed the diary to Johnny, but no one expected Eva's next move. She leapt over the bed and tackled Johnny while he was catching the diary. He didn't have a chance to throw the diary to Anna or Jonara.

"Help, help!" he laughed while Eva struggled with him for the diary.

Anna leaned over the bed and cheered Johnny to toss the diary to her while Jonara approached the two and urged Johnny to toss the diary to her. Jonara jumped on her grandmother's back like a monkey and tried to pull her off Johnny—all in fun. Only Eva wasn't laughing.

"Dog pile on the rabbit!" Jonara said, waving Anna to come over and "help".

"It's just a diary," said Johnny.

"I'm going to throttle you if you don't give me that diary!" said Eva.

Eva clasped her hands around his neck—half in fun and half in frustration—and shook Johnny in hopes he'd release the diary to her. She shook, and shook, and shook Johnny. The diary came loose and lodged between his back and the floor. Eva shook once more, and Johnny closed his eyes.

"You're choking him!" said Jonara.

Johnny's arms shook, and he placed a hand over his mouth. He opened his eyes with a grave expression and with his free hand pointed at Eva.

"There, I have it!" Eva said triumphantly as she pulled the diary out from under Johnny's back.

Johnny stood up but felt lightheaded and sat down on a chair. He bit his finger and tried to speak.

"You," he said referring to Eva. "You!"

With his free hand, he removed the Moissan Ruby from inside his shirt and flipped it to the shirt's outside. It gave off a reddish-purple swirling glow.

"What is it, what's wrong?" Jonara asked.

Jonara placed her hand on the Moissan Ruby, but it was ice-cold, and it froze her fingers. She recoiled and shivered.

"You didn't," Eva said. "You didn't. How could you? You promised sixteen years ago you'd never use that thing again."

"I couldn't help it. It just happened," said Johnny. "And it's not the first time."

"What do you mean?" Eva asked.

"When you had the flat tire on the bridge, I used it to find you," Johnny said.

"How could you!" Eva said.

"It was an emergency. Evanita needed to find you. The news of Geneva was serious. I had to use it," Johnny said.

"Like now, is that it? Vices come all too easy. Well you've done it this time, haven't you?" Eva asked.

"Yes, and I'm sorry," he said.

"But you read me. You read my body! Johanidan Reginald Pindus, how dare you? I have been violated!" Eva said.

"It's too late. And I know, I know what you have," said Johnny.

"What? What does he know?" Jonara asked.

Anna placed her hand over her eyes to shield herself from the surfacing knowledge she already knew.

"And you knew too, Anna. You should have told us," said Johnny.

"She promised to keep it quiet—as you should now do," said Eva.

"Keep what quiet? Grandma, what do you have?" asked Jonara.

"I'm being treated with methimazole," said Eva. "That's all that matters."

"But...it's..." Johnny stumbled.

"Yes! It's thyroid cancer! I have hyperthyroidism. Let's announce it to the world. There, is everyone happy? Now all four generations of Carreña are under fire—all of them."

"Grandma, I don't want you to die!" Jonara cried as she rushed into hugging Eva.

"No one's going to die—not yet," said Eva.

"You should be in the hospital," said Johnny. "It's advanced. It's ready to spread."

"I can't, not yet, not until I make sure Evanita gets through her pregnancy. She's having a hard enough time without everyone burdening her with their problems," said Eva.

"You'll die if you don't," said Johnny.

"That's enough. No more discussion," said Eva.

"Grandma!" Jonara cried.

Anna fell into quiet tears and hugged both Eva and Jonara. A dark shadow fell onto Johnny's face. He looked horribly tired. He rubbed his temples and neck to relieve his post-Moissan symptoms.

"The cancer can't be silenced away," Johnny finally mustered after listening for a moment to quiet sobbing from Jonara and Anna.

"Let's go downstairs and have a little chat," said Eva finally. "We'll just sit down in the living room and work this thing out. Anna—we'll need coffeecake, tea, and—"

"Hot chocolate," said Jonara between sobs.

"Yes. Hot chocolate. Come now, it won't be that bad."

The four returned downstairs and sat in the living room. Anna brought fresh coffeecake, tea, and some hot chocolate for Jonara. Jonara sipped the hot chocolate and thanked Anna—it was better than the stuff she drank at the restaurant earlier that morning. Anna sat with them and shared in consuming the sweets.

"Grandma," said Jonara. "In my dream, Daddy used a shocker to bring Mommy out of a coma. Can't we do that again?"

"No, we can't," said Eva. "There are too many issues—the baby, Evanita, me, Johnny's health, and the hospital rules—we just can't."

"He used the Water Ruby before, though," said Jonara.

"Water Ruby?" Eva asked.

"She means the Moissan Ruby," said Johnny. "She called it a Water Ruby at the restaurant this morning."

"Oh," said Eva. "Dear child—your father has suffered greatly from the grip of that Moissan Ruby. I made him put it away sixteen years ago after...after your mother's Coming-Of-Age ceremony. Not the first one she ran out of, the second one after she finished...sigh...after she was released from detention."

"From the Elrod 402?" asked Jonara.

"Yes, the Elrod 402. The strange circle of airplanes by the Portland airport. Your mother used the stone without my knowledge," Eva said.

"Used it for what?" Jonara asked.

"Jonara—let your grandmother finish," said Johnny.

"It's all right. She used it—how I don't know—to learn about her past. Well, not her past, more like my past and my mother's past. Family history, I guess. But some things are best forgotten. I've worked hard to shield her and you from the ugly past. Why relive it?"

"I want to know," said Jonara. "I want to know where my family came from."

"I wish it were that easy," said Eva. "The things people do to get from one part of life to another—it isn't an easy swim in the pool. But you can't convince the youngers this—they feel compelled to know their own family history."

"But," started Jonara.

"Look at your father, Jonara," continued Eva. "He's a wreck. Do you know why? Because he's seen too much. That Moissan Ruby has forced him to see and endure multiple facets from multiple people. He is hounded every night with memories and experiences too real and oppressive to ignore."

"What does 'oppressive' mean?" Jonara asked.

Eva sighed. Jonara didn't seem to understand. Eva knew all too well.

"You're not hearing a word I'm saying. You think the world is a playground ready to explore," said Eva.

"It is," Johnny blurted before realizing his mistake. "Sorry."

Eva shot him a glance to silence him.

"Don't you want to have a normal, happy life, honey?" Eva asked Jonara. "You want to be a doctor, right? Don't worry about these little things. You know how much your family loves you. We've set aside a college fund for your education. And there's plenty of money for your first car and house when you're old enough. You don't have to worry about the little things of life like the less fortunate. Enjoy your youth, Jonara, enjoy it before it's taken from you."

"But...I...want to know where the Water Ruby came from, Grandma. I want to know about my family," Jonara said.

Eva sighed again.

"There's no way out, is there?" Eva asked Johnny, not expecting him to answer.

"There is," he replied.

"No safe way," she replied. "Without injury to the family, to Jonara."

"No safe way," Johnny agreed.

The four were interrupted by a knock at the front door. Anna rose and greeted the visitor.

"Cerafina!" Jonara yelled as she ran and hugged her new friend. "Everyone, this is Cerafina. Cerafina, this is Anna, my father—you can call him Mr. Pindus I guess—and my grandmother."

"You can call me Ms. Carreña," said Eva.

"Nice to meet everyone," said Cerafina.

"You make friends quickly in Corpus Christi, Jonara," said Eva. "How did you two meet?"

Jonara and Cerafina accidentally spoke over each other. Cerafina tried to say they met on the sidewalk while Jonara tried to say they were both friends of Almarita.

"Our stories don't match, do they?" asked Eva.

"No ma'am, they don't," said Cerafina.

"Shh," said Jonara.

"I know you snuck out last night, Jonara," said Eva. "Did you meet Cerafina on the street?"

Jonara and Cerafina looked down sheepishly.

"Just as I thought. Well, Cerafina, where were your parents last night when you and my granddaughter were gallivanting around the city?" Eva asked. "Or should I say, gallivanting around the hospital?"

"We were with my father," said Cerafina.

"It's not her fault," said Jonara. "Almarita helped me find a friend down here."

"A friend who would sneak you into the hospital?" Eva asked. "Why else would your father be with you, Cerafina? It's not every girl who wants to gallivant with a parent. Especially not two girls."

"I admit, ma'am, my father took us to the hospital. Poor Jonara—" Cerafina started.

"—was confined to her bedroom," said Eva.

"She just wanted to see her mother," said Cerafina.

"It's okay, Cera, you don't have to explain," said Jonara. "I guess I'm restricted for the rest of our visit. Is that right, Grandma?"

"I would say 'yes'," replied Eva.

"You can't do this, Mummy Eva," said Johnny. "She's my daughter. As her parent—"

"You should know better," Eva finished. "But that was always handled by Evanita. Cerafina, you're welcome to keep Jonara company here at the house. But Jonara must stay here and not go out for the rest of today. If I feel any better about things, I may reconsider."

"Yay!" Jonara and Cerafina chimed in.

"I said, *may*. That wasn't a definite thing. Anna will watch after you, Jonara," Eva finished. She turned to Johnny and said, "To make sure things don't go awry, I want you to nail Jonara's bedroom window closed—from the outside."

Johnny gave her a puzzled stare.

"Don't fight me on this, Johnny. I'm now the decision maker when it comes to running this house," said Eva.

Johnny left the living room, went into the garage, and retrieved nails and a hammer along with a fiberglass ladder. He climbed the ladder and tap-tap-tapped the nails through the window frame into the sill. The job itself didn't take long, but he didn't like the idea of imprisoning his daughter, though he didn't know why this bothered him. He temporarily removed the Moissan Ruby from around his neck and placed it on the sill to relieve his neck and chest from chafing. But when he finished nailing the window shut, his frazzled and confused mind was too distracted by the morning's events to remember he'd removed the Moissan Ruby from his neck. It was the first time he'd ever made this mistake, but a mistake he made. He returned to the living room in time to see Eva holding Geneva's diary in her hand and informing Jonara that there'd be no more black magic with the diary.

Eva tossed the diary in the trunk of Geneva's car with every intention of throwing it into a dumpster or perhaps even the ocean. That could wait. She had pressing business at the hospital, and bringing Johnny with her was a way of keeping Jonara and him from getting into trouble with, "all these Moissan relics," as she was fond of repeating. She also went on a rant about men like Cerafina's father who had no understanding of cause and effect on a child's psyche when it came to privilege and discipline.

Johnny did the best he could to endure the ride, but he was beginning to wonder about Eva. Was she obsessing and overworking herself over Jonara's antics? He did agree with her—it seemed the entire Carreña clan was under attack. He felt a need for action—that he hadn't done enough to help. True, he did answer some of Jonara's questions and showed her the Moissan Ruby, but did he do more damage than good?

CHAPTER 2

Music

2023 Oct 4, Wed Morn. Corpus Christi, Texas.

"I'm glad my grandma didn't ask," said Jonara to Cerafina, "but how did you get out of school today?"

The two sat in Geneva's living room enjoying the last bits of coffeecake while Anna cleaned up in the kitchen.

"There's a teacher's strike," said Cerafina. "They want better benefits and more pay. Oh yeah, they want evacuation pay, too."

"Evacu-what?" Jonara asked.

"You know. When a hurricane blows in and everyone evacuates. They want to be paid for lost work days plus travel and motel expenses."

"Wow! Forget being a doctor. I wanna be a teacher," said Jonara.

"What would you teach?" Cerafina asked.

"I dunno. Something," said Jonara.

"That's no good. You have to specialize in something. Math, English, Science, Music—something," Cerafina explained. "You were pretty good with music last night."

"Oh, well, I don't know. It was just something I heard once," said Jonara.

Cerafina looked around the living room at the pictures on the wall. Many were of musical instruments, people playing those instruments, and people dancing. Especially common were pictures of couples dancing.

"Someone likes music," said Cerafina.

"What do you mean?" Jonara asked.

"These pictures," said Cerafina.

"Yeah, I know. Great-Grandma Geneva likes that Spanish dance stuff."

"Well, you can't dance without music. You need a beat, rhythm, and notes to sweeten the dance," Cerafina explained. "I bet your great-grandma has some records we can listen to."

"What are records?" Jonara asked.

"Those black vinyl disks with grooves. They were popular until the 1990s. You put them on something called a turntable, or was it a record player? I don't remember. Anyway, you placed a needle on it," Cerafina said.

"A needle? Like when I get a flu shot?" Jonara asked.

"Not that kind of needle," said Cerafina.

"Wouldn't the needle scratch the record?" Jonara asked.

"Not too much. The ancient ones did from a hundred years ago, but I think they improved a little. Something about going from 78 records to 33 records. Anyway, that's what I read. I've never seen a record. But your great-grandma was around in the old days—maybe she has some."

Jonara was excited for a moment, but her enthusiasm waned into disappointment.

"I can't," said Jonara. "I'm restricted."

"You're restricted from leaving this house," said Cerafina. "Did your grandma restrict you to the living room? What if you're thirsty, can you go to the kitchen?"

"Anna can bring me something."

"How do you go to the bathroom?" Cerafina asked.

Jonara scratched her head and thought for a moment.

"I guess Anna can't bring the toilet to the living room," said Jonara.

"I hope not!" laughed Cerafina.

"Let me ask," said Jonara.

"Do you really need to?" Cerafina asked.

"Yeah, I really should," Jonara said. She cupped her hands to her mouth and called, "Anna!"

The dishwasher's swish-swashing sound blocked Anna from hearing Jonara's calls. Jonara walked into the kitchen followed by Cerafina. Anna was now vacuuming.

"Anna," Jonara said in a quiet voice, but Anna had her back to Jonara and didn't realize Jonara was calling her.

"Anna," Jonara said again, and she tapped Anna on the back.

Anna jumped with a start.

"Oh, I didn't see you there," said Anna.

"What?" Jonara asked.

Anna turned off the vacuum cleaner and led the two from the kitchen to the living room.

"You startled me," Anna said.

"Does Nanna Geneva have old records we can listen to?" Jonara asked.

"She does," replied Anna, "in music room. I keep it locked, but if you promise to be careful and not break records..."

"We promise," said Jonara.

"Okay, I show you," said Anna.

Anna led Jonara and Cerafina from the living room down a side hallway and past the laundry room. She opened the door to a room containing a piano, bookcases, tables, chairs, a window, and a windowseat.

"I'm sorry. I haven't dusted in a while. Nobody goes inside," said Anna. "And I'm not sure I should let you inside. Miss Geneva was protective of this room."

"We'll dust for you," said Cerafina.

"We'll what?!" Jonara grumbled, but Cerafina elbowed Jonara to shut her up.

"You will? There are so many little books and music sheets to dust—I just wouldn't know where to begin," said Anna. "Wait, I get dusters."

Anna left the music room for a few moments in search of two dusters.

"Why did you say that? I don't want to dust," said Jonara.

"Don't you see? If we offer to help her, she'll let us play records. She hesitated at first. But now we're bribing her," said Cerafina.

"Bribing her. Is that like lying to her?" Jonara asked. "I hate lies. You're just like Almarita—pushing me into lying. I don't like it."

"We're not lying. We're exchanging—we help her and she helps us," said Cerafina.

"Something doesn't feel right about it," said Jonara, "but I can't put a finger on it."

"Don't worry about it," said Cerafina.

"Okay, here we go—a duster for you and you," said Anna, handing each girl a duster. "Now I show you the record player. Over here!"

Anna opened what appeared to be a window seat. It was a wooden, rectangular box the size of a casket on the floor next to the window. One could sit on the box or open the lid (which Anna did). Inside the box was a turntable for playing 33, 45, or 78 rpm records. Records were stored in the same box, protected individually in cardboard sleeves. Anna pulled out a 45 record, attached a small adaptor to the large hole in its center, and placed it on the turntable. She powered up the turntable and placed the needle on the record. The record came to life. The girls were surprised to hear a woman singing about a dog in the window, and how she hoped it was for sale.

"Do you like the song?" Anna asked. "Your Nanna Geneva loved it. Song is by Patti Page."

The girls laughed.

"It's from the olden days," said Jonara.

"No one sings like that," said Cerafina.

"It's funny," returned Jonara.

"Okay, okay. Record is funny. But you know how to play records. Don't forget to return record to sleeve and put away. Don't forget!" Anna warned. "Now I leave you to music and dusting!"

Anna left the music room.

"There must be something else," said Jonara. "Look—Spanish dancing tunes—let's try this."

Jonara placed the 33 record onto the turntable and lit the needle onto the outer groove. The music started after a few seconds, and the girls found themselves dusting and dancing to Spanish rhythms and melodies.

"I could dust all day to this music," said Jonara, who started by dusting the window seat.

Cerafina laughed.

"What's so funny?" Jonara asked.

"You didn't want to dust a minute ago. Now you can dust all day," Cerafina replied.

"Yeah, but the music makes me want to do something," Jonara replied.

"That's the mambo for you," said Cerafina.

"It's like...it makes me dance...it makes me want to dance," said Jonara.

"Intoxicating, isn't it?" asked Cerafina.

"Intox-a-what?"

"Like drinking too much wine," said Cerafina.

"I'm not allowed to drink wine. Or beer. Not that I want to," said Jonara, who was now dusting the piano.

"What's wrong with beer and wine?" Cerafina asked.

"You mean you like them?" Jonara asked.

"Only if they're good enough," said Cerafina.

"Who lets you drink? You're too young."

"Mamma does," said Cerafina. "I'm her little girl, her favorite daughter."

"You're her only daughter," said Jonara.

"You didn't answer my question—what's wrong with beer and wine?" Cerafina asked.

"They're disgusting. Beer tastes like soap, and wine tastes like vinegar. They taste worse than paregoric," Jonara said.

"You had paregoric? That was outlawed years ago," said Cerafina. "Who gave you that opiate?"

"What's an opiate?" Jonara asked.

"You know, opium? From the poppy plant. Heroin, morphine, and codeine for starters. They're addictive painkillers. Paregoric had morphine. So who gave it to you? Some old relative?" Cerafina asked.

"Yeah, my daddy's mother, Grandma Sweets, when I was five. I only saw her that one time. I told my daddy about it, and we never saw her again. She didn't seem to think it was so bad, especially after she added the honey. Said she gave it to my daddy when he was a boy so he'd sleep."

"Asian Indian Whiskey in a baby bottle is what they gave my dad," said Cerafina. "Had a molasses taste to it."

The record reached the end, and the music stopped. Cera-fina walked over to the window seat and placed the Spanish dance tunes record back in its sleeve. She dug around and found a 33 record of classical music by Haydn. Cerafina placed the record on the turntable and lit the needle on the outer groove. To the girls' delight, a piano-cello duet filled the room with gladness.

Jonara finished dusting the piano and proceeded to dust several small tables at the non-keyboard end of the baby-grand piano. She enjoyed the music so much that she lost track of Cerafina's whereabouts. She knew Cerafina was still in the mu-sic room, but as to what she was dusting and where, Jonara didn't know or care. The record carried through its piano-cello rendition and appeared to finish, but the piano music lit up again sans the cello. Jonara thought nothing of it at first—just a piano solo moment or whatever. The window above the small tables vibrated ever so slightly. Jonara thought it odd.

"Did you turn the volume up?" Jonara asked without turn-ing around.

"No," said Cerafina.

"But the window is shaking. What did you do to the turnta-ble?" Jonara asked.

"I didn't do anything."

"Then why is it shaking the window?"

"It isn't," replied Cerafina.

"What?!" Jonara asked.

She turned around and placed a hand on the piano. It shook. Jonara walked around from the back of the piano to the front where she saw Cerafina pressing keys with her fingers.

"You're playing the piano!" Jonara exclaimed.

"Do you like it?"

"I thought the record was still playing!"

"O no, I thought I'd check out the piano here. Seems to be in tune," Cerafina replied, still playing.

"I'll say! It's like being in a music hall or something. You're a pro!" Jonara said.

"Well, I dunno. I practice a lot," said Cerafina, who stopped playing.

"Why did you stop?"

"That's all I know of that song," said Cerafina.

"Can you teach me to play?" Jonara asked.

"I can try. But I've been practicing for many years now. It isn't easy, especially playing with two hands."

"It looks easy. C'mon, let me try," begged Jonara.

"Okay. Sit on the bench with me," said Cerafina.

Jonara sat next to Cerafina, who took Jonara's hands and placed them at the center of the piano keyboard with both thumbs on middle C.

"Curl your fingers a little—do not rest your palms on the piano," Cerafina instructed. "Now your thumbs are at middle C. Starting with your thumb, each finger on your right hand goes to C, D, E, F, and G. On your left hand starting with your thumb, each finger goes to C, B, A, G, and F."

"What are the black keys for?" Jonara asked.

"Those are flats and sharps. They add or subtract half a step to or from each note. From one white key to the next is a whole step, except between B and C, and between E and F. Now—"

"Wow, how confusing!" said Jonara.

"Now on the right hand, play the notes C, D, E, F, G—then G, F, E, D, C."

Jonara started with her left pinky and pressed F.

"No, that was F. Start with your other right hand—the thumb, and go up the scale," said Cerafina. "Each finger is a number—your thumb is 1, your index finger is 2, all the way up to your pinky which is 5. So on your right hand, do 1, 2, 3, 4, 5."

Jonara did as instructed. With each finger on her right hand, she called out the numbers and played the notes from 1 to 5—from C to G.

"Good. Now play C, E, G," said Cerafina.

"Um, how?" Jonara said.

"1, 3, 5."

"1, 3, 5," repeated Jonara, and she played C, E, and G.

"Now move your right hand over so your thumb touches E. Now play E, G, B," said Cerafina. "1, 3, 5."

"One," Jonara called, but she played C with her left thumb. "Three," she called, but she played E with her right thumb. "Five," she finished by playing G with her middle right finger.

"No, no, no. That's not it," said Cerafina.

"I did 1, 3, 5—just like I did before," said Jonara.

"Those numbers are for your fingers, not the notes," said Cerafina. "The numbers and notes change relation as you play."

"Well how can anyone keep track of that? It's too confusing. I want to play the piano, not do a math test," said Jonara.

"Hmmm," said Cerafina.

"The piano is too hard."

Frustrated, Jonara got up from the bench and brooded around the music room. She picked up the duster and lightly dusted books and furniture with less intent to clean and more intent to gather her thoughts. Cerafina searched through the window seat and retrieved a book of sheet music. She opened the book on the piano and played one of the pieces.

"It just takes a little practice and patience," said Cerafina.

"I don't have time," said Jonara.

"Huh? You're thirteen years old. You have your entire life to practice," said Cerafina.

"No, there may not be much left to live for. Not with Mommy in the hospital, Grandma being sick, and Great-Grandma's funeral coming up," said Jonara.

"Oh, cheer up! Pull yourself together," said Cerafina.

Jonara stopped talking and continued brooding. Cerafina finished the song, turned the page, and played another musical piece. Jonara tapped the duster around as if searching for something new. Cerafina started singing words to the music:

Oh, what shall we do with the drunken sailor
What shall we do with the drunken sailor
What shall we do with the drunken sailor?
Erlai in da mor-nin.

Put 'em in the longboat until he's all sober
Put 'em in the longboat until he's all sober
Put 'em in the longboat until he's all sober
Erlai in da mor-nin.

Wey-hey and up she rises
Wey-hey and up she rises
Wey-hey and up she rises
Erlai in da mor-nin.

Stick him in the John and call him Suzie
Stick him in the John and call him Floosie
Stick him in the John and give him a swirly
Erlai in da mor-nin.

Birch him in the butt until he sings soprano
Birch him in the butt until he swims to Alabama
Birch him in the butt O sweet Suzanna
Erlai in da mor-nin.

Keelhaul him under until he's all sober
Keelhaul him under—over and over
Keelhaul him under and call him Suzie
Erlai in da mor-nin.

Wey-hey and up she rises
What shall we do with the drunken sailor
Make him shave with a rusty razor
Erlai in da mor-nin.

"That's not how it goes," said Jonara. "You made up some of that."

"Oh, you know that song," said Cerafina. "I didn't think anyone knew it—it's so old."

"And it's a horrible song," said Jonara.

"I like it. But maybe you'll like this better," Cerafina replied while turning ahead several pages. "This piece is by Chopin and is called 'Military Polonaise'. It's one of the hardest pieces I can play."

As Cerafina played the piece, Jonara felt invigorated, as if she were some swashbuckling musketeer or pirate. She wielded her duster like a sword and slashed the air.

"*En garde,*" Jonara said.

She danced around the piano and slashed the air until she reached Cerafina. She poked the duster into Cerafina's back and said, "Ha, I gotchya!"

Cerafina was startled, her concentration failed, and her fingers flattened the keys and spoiled the song.

"Okay, funny, but I can't play and play fight. Here, take my duster and pretend you're fending off two bandits," said Cerafina.

Jonara took the dusters and slashed through the air again while Cerafina resumed the Chopin piece. Jonara danced through the room like a true Robyn Hood. But she slashed too far and caught a large cabinet door—almost tall enough for her to hide inside. The door popped open just a little bit. Jonara nudged it with her elbow to close it, but the door opened again. Something inside kept the door from closing.

"Do you like this piece?" Cerafina asked.

"It's cool!"

Jonara checked the cabinet and saw that a stick had fallen down and blocked the cabinet door from closing. She dropped her dusters, removed the stick from the cabinet, and slashed it through the air like a sword. Closing the cabinet door behind her, she slashed and danced as before. She danced behind Cerafina's back, so when Jonara poked Cerafina in the back with the stick, Cerafina was startled again, stumbled with her finger, and landed her forearms and elbows on the keys.

"I told you not to poke me while I'm—" she started to say as she turned around, but the stick immediately caught Cerafina's eye.

"Do you like my sword?" Jonara asked.

"That's not a sword. It's a bow," said Cerafina.

"Maybe there are arrows nearby. I wonder if Nanna Geneva has target practice in the backyard."

"It's not that kind of bow, Jonara. And it has a crack in it. Let me see it," said Cerafina, reaching out her hand to accept the bow.

"No. It's my bow, I found it," Jonara said, and she smugly held onto the bow.

"Okay, keep your bow. But where did you find it?" Cerafina asked.

"Over there. Behind that door. Maybe there are arrows too," said Jonara.

"It's too small for a violin," Cerafina mumbled about the bow. "It could be—"

Cerafina and Jonara opened the cabinet door fully and exposed a large case—a case belonging to a musical instrument.

"A guitar!" Jonara said.

"That's not a guitar case," said Cerafina.

"Then what is it?" Jonara asked.

"It's a cello case," said Cerafina.

"Let's take it out and see!" said Jonara, excited to find something.

"Do you think your grandma will mind? It looks expensive. We don't want to hurt it," said Cerafina.

"She's not here. And she didn't restrict me from anything in the house. Let's open it and see," said Jonara.

Cerafina placed a protective cloth over a nearby table and placed the case atop the table. Opening the case revealed a six-stringed instrument similar to a cello—but its face was whitish-light gray instead of the more traditional amber- or brown-stained color.

"A white cello!" Jonara said.

"Wait!" Cerafina said. "It's not a cello. It looks like a viol."

"A what?" Jonara asked.

"A *viola de gamba*—and a bass viol at that. Instead of 'F' holes it has 'C' holes. It has six strings. But there are no frets on this instrument. A viol is supposed to have frets. And there's a place to attach an end piece, but again—a viol isn't supposed to use an end piece—it's to be held between the legs. And the viol is white! It's white! Not a painted white, but a natural one with grains. Let's take it out of the case—carefully! Okay, put it on the cloth—don't drop it. There."

"It's not completely white," Jonara said. "Look—the sides and back are crimson."

"And the neck is dark brown," Cerafina said.

Cerafina drew her fingers across the different wood grains.

"Do you know how rare this is? These woods are not normally used in cello or viol making," Cerafina said. "Funny—I don't know what to call this instrument."

"Why don't you call it 'Viola de Carreña'," Jonara suggested.

"That's not a bad idea," Cerafina said.

"What kind of wood is it made of?" Jonara asked.

"Do you have a flashlight?" Cerafina asked.

"Huh? Why?" Jonara asked.

"To look inside," Cerafina replied.

Jonara hurried around the room and found a flashlight in a drawer. When she returned to the table, she found Cerafina expressing content and bliss while sweeping her hands over the viol's surface.

"It's like Heaven," said Cerafina. "It doesn't look like it has a finish, but it must. It's so very smooth. Must be highly refined linseed oil. And it's definitely not made of plywood. I would say it's Norway 'Crimson King' maple on the back and sides, and Norway white spruce on front—the layers of deep low tones and crispy upper tones. It's the ultimate musical lamina. Listen!"

Cerafina knocked on the viol in various places, and it resounded with deep warmth.

"What about the—what did you call that long-pole section?" Jonara asked.

"You mean the neck? Hmm."

Cerafina knocked on the viol's neck.

"It's very hard. I'd say it's lignum vitae. That's the wood used in Merlin's staff. 'Wood of life.' This must be worth thousands," said Cerafina. "Give me the flashlight so I can look inside."

"How can you look inside?" Jonara asked, passing the light.

"Through the C-holes," Cerafina replied. "Mmm-hmmm. Unusual. The inside seems to be finished too. I don't understand. I didn't think viols were finished on the inside. I could be wrong. But what's that—there's a strange marking on the inside."

"Let me see!" Jonara said.

Jonara grabbed the flashlight from Cerafina and shoved her aside.

"Hey, what was that for? You must be more careful. You could've hurt the viol if you'd shoved me into it," said Cerafina.

"I want to see what's inside the viol," said Jonara.

"I told you," said Cerafina. "Finishing and a symbol."

"That symbol," said Jonara as she shined the flashlight through the C-hole. "That symbol could be...it is! Omigosh! It's the one from the diary, the one from the Water Ruby. It's the half-face symbol!"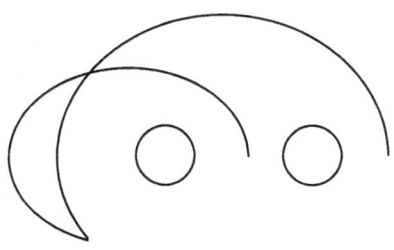

"Huh?"

"Half-face, half-face!" said Jonara.

"What are you talking about? What is 'half-face'? Whose diary? A water ruby? What's that? Jonara, what's going on?" Cerafina asked.

Jonara started to say something but stopped herself. She reached for the viol as if to play it, but Cerafina blocked her.

"Wait a minute! What are you doing?" Cerafina asked.

"I want to play it. Just a little. Can you teach me?" Jonara asked.

"Hold on there, Jonara. The viol is not that easy to play."

"But it looks easy. Just six strings. What's so hard about that? The piano has hundreds of keys, and they all look the same," said Jonara.

"Um, no, the piano has only eighty-eight keys," corrected Cerafina.

"Still—this cello guitar only has six strings," continued Jonara. "And I have ten fingers."

"It's not a cello guitar, it's a modified bass viol. And all beginners should be taught by an expert professional or—" Cerafina explained.

"Or what?"

"They'll develop bad habits," answered Cerafina.

Jonara laughed.

"You sound like my mother. 'Develop good habits. Brush your teeth before going to bed. Make your bed for the day. Clean up your room. Don't put off homework—do it every day.'"

"I mean it, Jonara. I've heard stories—"

"What stories? Anyway, I don't care, I'm just going to try it out," said Jonara.

"What about your grandma? What if she finds out?"

"She won't find out, not unless you tell," Jonara shot back.

"I won't tell. But maybe you better tell me," said Cerafina.

"Tell you what?" Jonara asked.

"About the half-face symbol, the Water Ruby, and the diary," said Cerafina.

"If I tell you, do you promise to teach me how to play the viol?" Jonara asked.

"I'm not an expert teacher, so I can't give you the best," said Cerafina.

"Do you promise?" Jonara repeated.

"I promise."

"Cross-your-heart, hope to die, stick a needle in your—"

"I won't stick a needle in my eye," said Cerafina. "I promised already. Now you start—tell me everything—and don't leave anything out."

Jonara recounted the events to Cerafina—beginning with the moment the two said their goodbyes the previous evening and concluding with Cerafina's arrival that morning. The diary, the dreams, her mother's ordeals, Johnny's gift, and the Moissan Ruby were all explained. By the time Jonara finished telling her tale, the morning was late, and Anna stopped in to check on them.

"Lunch will be ready soon," said Anna.

"That's incredible," said Cerafina. "And I wouldn't have believed it except for what Pappa's old ex-girlfriend used to tell us."

"Huh?"

"You know Marina is my mother, right?" Cerafina asked.

"Yeah."

"Well, Leo—that's my half-brother—he has a different mother. I think her name was...hmm...I can't remember. But she divorced Pappa because of the affair he had with Sheila," Cerafina explained. "That's the Sheila from your dream. I had a chat with her once, and she told me about the trial. Her story matches what you just told me, except she didn't know much about Evanita's side of the story."

"Did she say anything else about my mother?" Jonara asked.

"Not much," Cerafina said. "Sheila said she had broken off the friendship back in 2006. Said your mother was a jailbird and a few other things."

"So how come you live down here?" Jonara asked.

"Pappa was working hard at the factory in Portland," Cerafina said. "Remember, this was before he met my mamma, so he wasn't my pappa yet. The divorce took all of his savings. And he lost his factory job. He was depressed and couldn't continue racing cars. Sheila lost faith in him and dumped him. It was a bad relationship anyway—she was underage. Davino could have gone to jail for the relationship, and he almost did. Before formal charges were drawn up, he skipped town and moved down here to Corpus Christi."

"What about Sheila?" Jonara asked. "What happened to her?"

"She started dating a guy in the Air Force. I think his name was Adrian Cracbern," Cerafina said.

"Did your dad get jealous about Sheila's new boyfriend?" Jonara asked.

"No, not really," Cerafina replied. "He was so busy, so focused on his job that he forgot about her. He got promoted at the oil refinery, and his promotion became his new relationship—at least until he met my mother."

"Where did he stay in Corpus Christi?" Jonara asked. "Did he live close to your mother?"

"Here. In this house. Your great-grandma rented a room to him," Cerafina explained.

"I didn't know they knew each other," said Jonara.

"It's another long story, but the short version is this—they knew of each other through your grandma and Sheila's mother—Eva and Sharon," Cerafina explained.

"I don't understand. I never thought my Grandma Eva would go out of her way to help a man," said Jonara.

"She wouldn't, of course, but Sharon convinced her and convinced Geneva. I told you it's another story," Cerafina said. "Anyway, Anna will be in here soon to tell us lunch is ready, so I gotta hurry up this story. Pappa got custody of Leo after Leo's mother divorced Pappa. Sheila stayed up in Portland. Pappa lived here for a couple of years before he met Mamma. And that's the most bizarre story yet!"

"How did they meet?" Jonara asked with anticipation.

"Lunch is ready," called Anna. "Come in you two and get fed."

"Wait a minute," called Jonara to Cerafina. "Tell me what happened."

"No say, 'Wait a minute'. There will be *nada* for lunch if you do not come now," Anna called.

"C'mon, let's eat lunch," said Cerafina. "We have all day to tell stories."

"You go first," said Jonara.

"Nah-uh, you go first," said Cerafina. "I know you—you wanna stay here and play the viol."

Jonara rolled her eyes, but the two knew Cerafina was correct. They sat down at the breakfast table in the kitchen where Anna had prepared lunch—soup, bread, sandwich meat, and tea. Cerafina had a bit of everything including tea, but Jonara substituted a soft drink for her beverage.

"The music was *bueno*," said Anna.

"Thank you," said Cerafina.

"You can come over any time," said Anna with glee, but a grave expression removed the happiness from her face.

"What's the matter?" Jonara asked.

"It's *nada*," said Anna.

"The house is for sale," said Cerafina. "You didn't see the sign in front, Jonara?"

"No, I didn't," said Jonara.

"Don't worry. I find new job somewhere," said Anna.

"Maybe you can come with us to Portland," said Jonara.

"My family is here," said Anna. "Eat your soup before it gets cold."

Anna left the kitchen to clean upstairs.

"I can't imagine someone else living in this house. Maybe they'll let Anna stay," said Jonara.

"That would be nice," said Cerafina, "but I doubt it will happen. The world isn't nice."

Jonara dipped bread in her soup and chased it down with her soft drink. Cerafina finished off a turkey sandwich.

"So how did your mom and dad meet?" Jonara asked.

"Out in the Gulf," said Cerafina. "Mamma was fishing—"

"You're kidding," said Jonara.

"No, I'm not. We come from a big fishing family on my mother's side. Grandma ran a fishing business off the coast of Italy. Business was a little bad one year, so she decided to pack up the family and move here. Grandma runs a cargo business now. Mamma still goes out fishing now and then, though not as much as she used to," Cerafina explained.

"I don't get it—your dad came down to work at a refinery and your mom was what—working on a fishing boat? How did they meet?" Jonara asked.

"Yeah, Mamma was working on the fishing boat. Pappa was inspecting an oilrig when there was an explosion and he was thrown off the rig into the ocean. He didn't drown, but by the time help arrived, he'd already floated miles away from the rig. He was lost at sea. But Mamma's fishing boat came across him by chance. Actually, her boat almost plowed over him. She had to steer the boat sharply to avoid hitting him with the hull or chopping him up with the propeller."

"Wow!"

"And that's not all. She hauled him out of the water! Can you believe that?"

"No," replied Jonara, "I can't. She doesn't seem strong enough. Maybe she made that part up."

"Made-up nothing! It was Pappa who told me that part. She pulled him out, changed his clothes into something dry, and took care of him until her boat returned to port. He was cold, dehydrated, and sneezing like a drowned raccoon. Can you imagine? A big, proud man reduced to a shivering wimp? But that's how it was. He took her out to eat afterward to show his appreciation, and they got married about six months later."

"That was fast," said Jonara.

"Yeah, they had to. I was 'cooking' inside of Mamma," Cerafina grinned. "And they've been married ever since, except—"

"Except what?" Jonara asked.

"I think Pappa wanted more children, but for some reason it didn't work out. Mamma never told me why, but I think there was a medical problem. I wanted a younger sister, too, but it wasn't meant to be. Anyway, that's the story of how my parents met."

"I told you how my parents met at my grandma's dental office," said Jonara.

"Yeah, that's unusual," said Cerafina.

"But I want to know more about my family history. I want to know who my grandpa is—my mommy's dad, and I want to know about Nanna Geneva. She grew up in Spain, you know," Jonara explained.

"Yeah, I figured that."

"But Grandma took the diary away," Jonara said. "Then there's the Water Ruby, but that's my daddy's, and...well...even if he let me use it...would it let me look into the past? Now that viol—"

"Do you really think the viol is magical?" Cerafina asked.

"I don't know," Jonara replied. "And I don't know what magic is anymore. I think the diary, Water Ruby, and viol are all part of advanced technology that we don't fully understand. And I want to understand. I don't have to be a great violer."

"A great viol player," corrected Cerafina. "Don't say 'violer'. It's rude."

"Oh, okay. I just want to see what the viol can do—will it let me learn what happened to my mommy in prison? Will it tell me who my mommy's dad is?"

"Hmmm."

"You promised to teach me how to play. I'm done with lunch, how about you?" Jonara asked.

Cerafina stirred what was left of her soup. She took a last sip of tea and placed her dishes onto the counter by the sink.

"Okay," Cerafina replied. "I'm ready to teach you a little bit. But I'm not a magician."

Jonara placed her dirty dishes by the sink as well, and the two girls returned to the music room. Cerafina reached for the viol, but Jonara protested.

"I'm just going to tune it before we start," said Cerafina. "That means I have to—"

"Wait! Don't touch it!" Jonara commanded.

"Huh? You can't play an out-of-tune viol," said Cerafina.

"I want to be the first one to play it," said Jonara. "If you play it, the magic might be broken."

"I thought you didn't believe in magic," said Cerafina.

"You know what I mean," replied Jonara.

"Well, it must be tuned. How can you play a viol if it's not in tune? You can't tune—"

"Why not? Tell me what to do, and I'll tune it," said Jonara.

"Hmm, it could take a little while," said Cerafina.

"Grandma restricted me to the house, so I'm not going any-where," Jonara pointed out.

"Okay, okay. Pick up the viol from the table," Cerafina start-ed. "Good. Now sit down on this chair and put the viol on the floor—careful! Don't drop it."

"I just lost my balance for a moment," said Jonara. "I'm okay now. Wait a minute—it's too short."

"No it isn't. We haven't attached the endpin yet. I want to see how long we need to set it. Hold it like this," said Cerafina, and she motioned Jonara to move the viol's neck toward Jona-ra's left shoulder.

Cerafina gauged the distance and searched through the viol case.

"Okay, hmm, this is good. Your great-grandma—"

"Nanna Geneva," Jonara interrupted.

"Nanna Geneva. Yeah, she has several endpins—I wonder why? Usually a cello gets one—maybe two. But there are three here. Then again, this isn't a cello—it's a viol. Hmm. Okay, this one looks good. You don't mind if I attach the endpin, do you?" Cerafina asked.

"No, as long as you don't pluck a string or something," said Jonara.

"I promise. Okay, here," Cerafina said.

Cerafina attached the endpin and adjusted its length.

"Now, hold the viol like this."

Cerafina directed Jonara to hold the viol with the body between her knees and the viol's neck to the left of her own neck.

"You'll hold the neck with your left hand and use your right hand to play the strings. Here's the hard part—we have to tune it. Now this can be tricky. If the viol is badly out of tune...hmmm...there's also the question of how to tune it—*just intonation* or *mean temperament*. I think the common tuning today uses mean temperament—it's close to a cello—what was the cello? C2, G2, D3, and A4. I think the bass viol starts a full tone higher at D2 but it doesn't go up in even fifths...hmm, I think it uses fourths and a third, then—"

"Just get on with it," said Jonara.

"Maybe the easiest way to do this is if I—"

Cerafina walked over to the piano and pressed a key.

"That's D—two octaves below middle D. Pluck the string closest to your right shoulder. Good. Hey! The first string is in tune. Could we be lucky with the others? Here, I'll play the next note—G. Now pluck the next string over. Wow! It's also in tune."

"I'll pluck the third string over," said Jonara.

"That's C—an octave below middle C," Cerafina replied.

Cerafina played C on the piano, and the tones matched.

"All right! Now pluck the next string. It should be E."

Jonara plucked it as instructed.

"Also in tune. This is going to be easy," Cerafina said. "Now pluck the fifth string. It should be A—one octave below middle A."

Jonara plucked the string, but the tone did not match the piano's.

"Hmmm. Pluck it again," Cerafina said. "Hmmm. We'll skip that for now. Pluck the last string—it should be middle D. Hmm. Try again. Hmm again."

"What's all the humming about?" Jonara asked.

"Well, four out of six ain't bad," Cerafina said. "The last two strings are a little flat. You'll need to tighten them."

"By turning these two knobs?" Jonara asked. "Okay, I'll turn them really quick-like."

"Wait! You have to be careful," Cerafina called.

Too late. Jonara turned the tuning pegs for the upper two strings, the strings tensed up, and she plucked them. The strings vibrated much higher than they were meant to. As they vibrated, the strings slackened, and the tones crashed downward until the frequencies, volumes, and string motions failed completely into blubbering slackened wires. Ka-pop-pop!

"Don't move," said Cerafina.

"I didn't mean to break them!" said Jonara.

"Just don't move," Cerafina repeated.

Cerafina took the flashlight and shined the beam all about the viol's head, neck, bridge, and body. She feared finding one or more cracks, but none presented themselves.

"Okay, I think the viol is undamaged," Cerafina said.

"What happened? What made the popping sounds? I was only tightening the strings. Did I break the strings?" Jonara blurted.

"Shhh. Let's just work through this. Think, Cerafina, think!"

Cerafina paced back and forth in the music room.

"We must tighten the last two strings as I originally intended—slowly and with care," said Cerafina.

"But I—" Jonara started.

"Don't talk—listen. When, and only when I tell you to, tighten the A string's tuning peg," Cerafina said.

Jonara reached for the tuning peg, but Cerafina blocked Jonara's hand from advancing.

"I didn't say *when*," said Cerafina. "You have to turn it in a special way to keep the string from loosening up. When you turn the peg, push inward. This will lock the tuning peg in position and keep tension on the string. Also, you won't be turning and tuning the peg all at once. I want you to turn the peg until there's some tension. Then we'll test the string."

"Okay already," said Jonara. "I've waited long enough."

"Turn the A string's peg a little bit and push the peg inward," Cerafina said.

Jonara did as instructed, and the A string tightened a little.

"Good," said Cerafina.

"What happens if I play the other strings like this?" Jonara asked while she plucked the other four strings. The strings sounded a trifle sharp.

"No, no, no! Please, don't play the other strings, don't breathe, and don't touch any other part of the viol unless I tell you."

"But we need to fix the other strings," said Jonara.

"Don't fix what you don't understand. We'll check those after tuning the A and D strings. Don't be distracted!" Cerafina urged.

"Okay, okay, I'll be more careful. Whew!" Jonara said.

"Whew is right. Now where were we?" Cerafina mused.

"Tuning the A string," Jonara prompted.

"Yes. The A string. Does it have enough tension to pluck?" Cerafina asked.

"No."

"Okay. Slowly—and I mean slowly—turn the A string's peg until there is tension on the string. Remember to push in the peg," said Cerafina.

"I'm remembering, I'm remembering," said Jonara.

Jonara turned the tuning peg, and the A string acquired a tension.

"Now pluck it," said Cerafina.

"It makes a sound," said Jonara.

"Good, it's holding a tone. Now listen," Cerafina said, and she played the A key on the piano. "That's our goal. We want to get closer and closer without shooting over. If we shoot over, we should back off a little bit and reapproach the tone. But there's a catch. We also want to tighten the D string without overshooting too. But if we tune the A first and then tune the D from lax, the A could get overtuned. We don't want that. We must add tension to the A, then the D, then the A again, and so on until both are in tune. And don't get sidetracked. Now adjust the D tuning peg just a little bit until you get tension. Pluck it. Can it hold a tone?"

"Yes," Jonara said after tightening the middle D string.

"Good. Now tighten the A string again—just a little bit!" Cerafina directed.

Jonara did as Cerafina instructed. In this way, Cerafina and Jonara worked the tuning pegs until the A and D strings matched the piano's A and D key frequencies.

"I guess we have to tune the other strings now," said Jonara.

"Wait—don't touch those other tuning pegs. Just pluck each string in order—D, G, C, and E. I'll play the notes on the piano. Check before changing, okay?"

"Okay," replied Jonara.

Jonara plucked each string in order, and Cerafina played the corresponding piano notes. The frequencies matched. Jonara was shocked.

"I don't understand—they were out of tune, but now they aren't," said Jonara.

"Yeah, they were out of tune. When you loosened up the A and D strings so quickly, the tension on the neck changed. The other strings took up more of the tension load. The popping sound probably came from the strings changing load or something. The increased load tightened them and made them sound a little higher than normal. If you tried to retune them at that point, we'd have to tune them again after getting the A and D strings tuned. Fortunately, this is a viol, and the working string tension is not too high. Things are much worse on the cello with its higher tension. See how hard things can get?"

"Yeah, I never thought it could be that bad," said Jonara.

"But we're lucky—the viol is in tune, so I can show you a few things," said Cerafina.

"You're going to teach me to play?" suggested Jonara.

"Yes, yes, yes, I'll do my best as I promised," Cerafina continued. "Okay, let's see—you need a bow, and some rosin, and—"

"I don't want to use a bow," said Jonara.

"Not use a bow?"

"Plucking works fine," Jonara said.

"Plucking works fine," Cerafina echoed while thinking about what to do next. "Okay, we'll start you off with plucking the strings. Should be easier anyway."

"Good!"

"Yeah, good. Okay, you remember the six strings—D, G, C, E, A, and D? The notes run from A to G like this—A, B, C, D, E, F, G. There is no H. Also, there are sharps and flats—these are half steps between many of the notes. This gives twelve different notes—A, A sharp, B, C, C sharp, D, D sharp, E, F, F sharp, G, and G sharp. C sharp is the same as D flat, and so on with the other sharps."

"Wait a minute! Slow down! This is like math again, like on the piano," said Jonara.

"Notes are the same no matter what instrument you play," said Cerafina.

"But—on the piano you're forced to play the same notes because the keys are fixed. But these are just strings," said Jonara.

"Yes, you'll have to learn the proper places to put your left fingers to get the notes just right. There are no frets, but come to think of it, the frets might have forced us into just intonation, so maybe this is for the best," Cerafina instructed.

"But there can be more than twelve notes, right? I mean, there can be millions!" Jonara said.

"That's another topic for another day. Most modern music uses the twelve-note system. There are other systems...but...well...I can't teach you that," Cerafina explained. "Anyway, an octave higher than D is the next D, and the next."

"A funny name. Octave," said Jonara. "But it's another one of those tough words to learn. How do I do an octave?"

"The easiest way is to press your left finger halfway down the string," said Cerafina.

Jonara pressed her index finger down slightly on the lower D string (closest to her right shoulder), but her finger didn't touch the neck.

"Not that kind of halfway down," said Cerafina. "Look at the length of the string from the head to the bridge. Now figure out where the halfway point is, you know, imagine cutting the string in half—where would you cut? Put your finger down on that spot and pluck the string."

Jonara did as instructed and plucked the D string. The string returned with a D one octave higher.

"That's an octave? That's almost the same note!" said Jonara.

"It's the easiest musical relationship to understand," said Cerafina.

"Relationship?" Jonara asked.

"Yes, music is full of relationships. Without relationships, it would just be noise. An octave is a two-to-one relationship. The next one is a three-to-two, and those two relationships make up the very basics of music theory."

Cerafina continued to show Jonara the other fractional relationship between notes and eventually explained how all twelve notes were related to each other, and the meaning of equal temperament versus just intonation. She explained how the roots of modern western music came from ancient Greece and how music changed over the years.

"Whew!" said Cerafina. "That's a lot to explain. No one explained that to me when I started music—I just learned to play the notes from sheet music. But I gave you the history behind music."

"I'm glad you told me," said Jonara. "I don't want to play from sheet music anyway."

"You don't? Then how do you expect to play?"

"The way I want," said Jonara.

Cerafina laughed.

"What's so funny?"

"Every beginner gets this grand idea that she can play whatever she feels like, and it will come out sounding like the best concerto ever performed," said Cerafina. "But go ahead—you'll have to learn the harsh truth sometime."

Jonara played string D, an octave of D, string G, an octave of G, string C, an octave of that too, and the same for strings E,

A, and the upper D. Jonara plucked two strings at once and was stopped by Cerafina.

"Not too bad," said Cerafina. "But one more thing—let me show you how to hold your fingers."

Cerafina stood in front of Jonara and tried positioning Jonara's hands, but everything was backward, and it was an awkward moment for Cerafina and Jonara.

"I can't show you like this," said Cerafina. "If I could play the viol, I could show you—maybe you'd learn."

"No, I don't want you to play it," said Jonara.

Cerafina sighed.

"Okay, stand up and place the viol's endpin on—here, I'll pile up some books—put them on the books," Cerafina said as she piled up some books.

Cerafina moved the chair out of the way and stood behind Jonara. Cerafina's longer arms allowed her to reach around Jonara's back and hold Jonara's hands with her own. Cerafina directed Jonara's left fingers onto the viol's neck and her right fingers onto the strings. In this way, Cerafina guided Jonara in playing the viol. Jonara played her first song—Twinkle Twinkle Little Star.

It was a simple tune, and Cerafina didn't expect much from it, but Jonara felt odd. Cerafina was guiding her hands to play the viol, but Jonara discovered stronger feelings—the warmth and comfort of someone hugging her—someone who was non-threatening, roughly her age, and capable of understanding what she was experiencing in life. Someone who was willing to help her and guide her in learning. Someone who in wrapping herself around Jonara gave Jonara a sense of protection and calm, of expressivity and acceptance.

It was odd, to be sure. Was this what it was like to have a sister? Jonara wasn't sure, but the feelings were too strong all at once. Jonara wasn't sure if so much comfort and loving was natural, if it could be acceptable to social norms. She broke off the embrace from Cerafina and placed the viol to the side.

"What's wrong?" Cerafina asked in a thoughtful tone.

"I...don't know," said Jonara.

"You did well with Twinkle-Twinkle," said Cerafina. "You took over at the end of the song. Is the song too boring?"

"No," said Jonara. "I just feel funny."

"Funny as in 'hah, hah'?"

"No. Strange. I don't know if I should tell you," Jonara said. "Something feels strange here."

Jonara patted her abdomen.

"Oh, did lunch give you an upset tummy?" Cerafina asked with concern.

"No. It's not lunch," Jonara said.

Jonara walked around the room for a minute and returned to the viol.

"Okay, I feel better now. I want to try the bow."

Cerafina's eyes lit up with surprise.

"Wow, and I thought you didn't want to play with the bow," said Cerafina.

"I know. Something changed my mind. Can you show me?"

"Okay," said Cerafina. "There are several bows in the case. Hmm, this one looks nice. I just need to tighten it...ugh... shouldn't be that hard to tighten. Okay, I'm ready. Maybe you'd like to sit down and try it, if you're feeling okay."

"I'm okay."

Jonara took the viol and sat on the chair as before. Cerafina explained how to hold the bow, and Jonara complied. She moved the bow along the strings and attempted to play Twinkle Twinkle Little Star, but the notes were off, and the bow made a horrible scraping sound against the strings.

"Ugh," said Cerafina. "What happened? You were doing so well when you plucked the strings."

"I don't know," said Jonara. "Can you...no wait."

"I think we'd better do like before—I'll hold your hands and show you how to use the bow," Cerafina offered.

"I'm not sure that's a good idea," said Jonara.

"Why not? It worked before."

"Because...I'm not sure I'm ready," Jonara replied.

"I promise—I won't bite," Cerafina laughed.

"And you promise not to laugh or make fun of me?" Jonara asked.

"Make fun of what? Oh, come on—don't worry about a thing. I promise I won't laugh or make fun of you," Cerafina reassured.

"Okay."

Jonara stood up from the chair and placed the viol's endpin on the books as before. Cerafina stood behind her and wrapped herself around Jonara again. She placed her left hand on Jonara's, and with her right she held Jonara's right hand and a little bit of the bow, although Jonara held most of the bow's weight.

"We'll make slow, even strokes," said Cerafina.

With Cerafina's guidance, Jonara played the viol. The feeling returned—a funny sort of anticipation and warmth in her abdomen, as if she were to receive some sort of special gift. The warmth spread around her abdomen to her sides, around to her lower back, and up her spine. She didn't shiver. Instead, she savored the song's smooth and melodic waves, sounding like one of Chopin's piano pieces, yet she played it on the viol.

"Isn't that a pleasant sound?" Cerafina asked.

The light in the room seemed to dim a bit, and Jonara wasn't sure, but she thought she saw two people dancing in the middle of the music room. They were older girls—perhaps eighteen or nineteen, and they were holding hands and waists while doing some sort of waltz or slow-step or something. It was very graceful—the kind of charming classical ballroom dance one might see performed by a man and woman. The music wasn't too fast and wasn't too slow—it was just a nice, relaxing, fun bit of show. The music and dancing made Jonara think of a music box, and behold! The two older girls stopped dancing, and the taller one showed the shorter one a music box with a ballerina twirling inside with tinkling music rippling outward.

Cerafina continued helping Jonara play the viol, but Jonara had an out-of-body experience. She felt as if she'd stepped away from her corporeal body and walked over to the music box. She turned around to see Cerafina and a copy of herself continuing with the viol. She turned back to look at the music box, and she heard the older girls speak—they sounded like an older Cerafina and Jonara. Jonara looked at the girls more closely—yes, they did look quite a bit like Cerafina and herself at nineteen and eighteen respectively. The older girls set the music box aside and resumed dancing together as a couple.

The viol's music increased in volume and depth. Cerafina the cellist was drawing Jonara the viol player into stronger bow strokes and more dramatic finger movements on the viol's neck. Jonara the observer felt a strong force pulling her toward Jonara the eighteen-year-old, and in the next moment, she was in the body of Jonara the elder. She felt taller and stronger, but she also felt a sudden depth of understanding, that there was more to life than toy dolls and paper mâché. She looked into the eyes of the nineteen-year-old Cerafina and sensed years of defining experiences together. Jonara also sensed a stronger understanding of Cerafina—a woman with a beautiful mind and heart who so often was the target of male drooling, a woman who had a sense of the universe through fine music and dance—a characteristic men would rather subvert to satiate their lustful appetites.

An odd rattling carried through a windowpane as the bow completed each stroke. Jonara thought nothing of it at first, but the rattling grew in intensity and in harmony with the bow strokes. The rattling caused little statues and ornaments on the windowsill to vibrate and hop along until one fell from the sill onto the floor just as eighteen-year-old Jonara and nineteen-year-old Cerafina kissed each other on the cheek.

Smash!

Cerafina the cellist jumped back with a start, breaking her grip from the bow and Jonara's hands. Jonara lurched forward in astartlement but caught her step and managed to continue holding onto the bow while refraining from falling over and trampling the viol. The viol music stopped, the rattling on the windowpane stopped, and Cerafina stood motionless in bewilderment.

"Did you see them?" Jonara asked. "The two dancing girls and the music box?"

Cerafina walked a little around the room with her hand touching a spot on her cheek.

"I—" Cerafina started to say.

Cerafina avoided glancing at Jonara but instead stared at the wall as if working out a problem.

"Did you see them?" Jonara asked again.

"I did. I was one of them," Cerafina replied in shock.

Cerafina turned to the wall and spoke to reassure herself:

"I like boys, I like boys, I like boys!"

Jonara fell silent.

"I don't understand. I like boys," said Cerafina to Jonara after a moment. "What just happened here? I mean, I showed you how to play the viol. No big deal, right?"

"Yeah," replied Jonara.

"But...that feeling that you had in your tummy, Jonara. I had one too. More like butterflies. But I only get the feeling when I'm around cute boys," Cerafina said. She turned away and spoke to the wall, "This isn't right. I must like boys. I must. What's going on?"

"It was the viol," said Jonara. "It must be. It has the mark."

"Did you feel this way with the diary?" Cerafina asked.

"No. Sometimes I felt sad, other times I felt nothing. It was like watching the news on TV," said Jonara.

"And your dad—the Water Ruby?" Cerafina asked.

"He's a tired, nervous wreck after using it," Jonara replied.

"Then each thing does something different to the user," said Cerafina. "I have an idea—try playing the viol by yourself. I'll play some notes on the piano to Yankee Doodle, and you repeat them. Let's see what happens."

"Okay," Jonara replied.

Cerafina played musical phrases of Yankee Doodle, and Jonara repeated the phrases. In this way, they played the entire song. However, neither Jonara nor Cerafina had the abdominal feelings nor did they see a vision of two girls dancing. They didn't see a vision of anything. There was no inspiration—none.

"Anything?" Cerafina asked Jonara.

"Nope," said Jonara. "Wait, there is one thing."

"What's that?"

"The rattling stopped," answered Jonara.

"What rattling?" Cerafina asked.

"The windowpane. It was rattling. It shook the sill. See that broken thing on the floor? It fell off. The sill shook it off. But that was when we were playing together."

"This is the strangest viol I've ever seen!" said Cerafina.

"And it has a power," said Jonara.

"But it's hard to understand," said Cerafina. "It seems to require two people to make it work. The diary and Water Ruby— they need only one person."

"The viol sees the future," said Jonara.

"Does it? How can we be sure?" Cerafina asked.

"We saw ourselves when we are older," said Jonara.

"I don't trust it, Jonara. It makes me feel different," said Cerafina.

"I felt it too," said Jonara. "I fell in love with you."

"But...it...it can't be the future. You like boys, right?" Cerafina asked.

"Yeah."

"So do I."

"Maybe we like both boys and girls," Jonara said.

"But I don't," said Cerafina. "I only like boys. I like all kinds of cute boys—it's not just one. If I liked girls, wouldn't I like lots of them too? That's what I don't understand. And I only get the feeling when we're both playing the viol. When that stops, you're just my friend again."

"I felt that way too," said Jonara. "I didn't know how to tell you. That's why I had you promise not to laugh."

"And I didn't. I understand now," said Cerafina.

"What if the viol does tell the future, Cerafina? What then? Do we use it to find out stuff?" asked Jonara.

"It could be dangerous. These relics—" Cerafina started.

"What's a relic?" Jonara asked.

"A religious artifact. Something with religious power."

"You think the diary, Water Ruby, and viol are religious?" Jonara asked.

"They must be."

"What religion?" Jonara asked.

"Good question. What religion was your Nanna Geneva?"

"Catholic."

"Then these must be Catholic—probably left over from the Middle Ages," said Cerafina.

"I don't believe it," said Jonara. "They don't seem Catholic to me. Where's the...the...the letter 't'?"

"You mean the cross? Also known as the crucifix? Yeah—there's no crucifix on these relics."

"Then they can't be relics," said Jonara. "Cerafina?"

"Yes?"

"Are you religious?" Jonara asked.

"Sort of. I mean, yes, my mother's side—the Italian half—is Catholic. Pappa converted over several years ago. I'm Catholic by birth, I guess you could say, or by having Catholic parents, well, one Catholic parent when I was born. I was baptized a Catholic when I was four weeks old, I was confirmed in the first grade, received the communion host in the second, and had my first confession in the third grade. Yeah, I did it all backward, but that's how things turned out. I had no control over it."

"Do you believe?" Jonara asked.

"I believe in spirituality and maybe God," Cerafina said, "just not the Catholic God. And now things are different—or could be different. I mean...the Catholic Church says being a lesbian is a sin. I never thought I would be a lesbian—not sure if I really am. I mean, I still like boys. But if the viol is right...Jonara, you must not tell anyone about us, about what happened here—not until we're grown up and moved out from our parents."

"Yeah, I know. The other kids in school would call us queer," said Jonara.

"Worse than that, our parents might do something to us. I don't know about you—maybe you'd only get sent to a shrink, but I'd have to endure the wrath of the Church, too. Confession, penance, and punishment—I don't know if I want to go through all that suffering for the sake of a little honesty," Cerafina explained. "I could get excommunicated—not that that's a bad thing, but my family might stop treating me like a person. I don't want to be known as a freak."

"Then it's for sure. The viol can't be a relic, and it can't be religious," said Jonara.

"Why not?"

"Because...because...you know why," said Jonara.

"I think I know what you mean. Because it brought us together. And most religions would not want us to be happy like that," Cerafina said.

"Yeah, that's what I mean," said Jonara.

The girls paused in thought for a moment. Finally, Jonara spoke.

"Why us?" Jonara asked.

"Huh?"

"Why us? Why did the viol choose us?" Jonara asked again.

"I don't know."

"Well, it's driving me crazy. I want to know. And I think using the viol is the only way to find out," Jonara said.

"And here I thought you wanted to find out about your family history," laughed Cerafina. "Jonara Pindus—you are very curious."

"I like being curious," Jonara said. "Whaddya say? Wanna play the viol again? See what we can find out?"

"You'll have a hard time learning about the past if the viol shows the future," said Cerafina.

"Gotta start somewhere," said Jonara.

"Okay. This time I'll stand next to you and touch the viol while you play. Maybe that will make a difference."

Cerafina did as she suggested and stood next to Jonara while she played Yankee Doodle on the viol. Cerafina had a hand on the viol, but there was no vision, no window rattling, and no result.

"I think you have to touch me," said Jonara.

Cerafina stood next to Jonara and put her arm around Jonara's waist with her left hand, and placed her right hand on Jonara's right shoulder. Jonara played the viol, and something happened. Both Jonara and Cerafina felt warm comfort from each other as one feels when snuggling under warm bedcovers on a cold winter's night.

"There," said Cerafina. "Something's happening."

The windowpane rattled again. Jonara and Cerafina saw the Water Ruby falling outside the window onto the ground. Jonara continued playing notes, but slowly. The two girls felt themselves leaving their bodies and walking outside the house to retrieve the Water Ruby, bring it inside, and place it in a clear bowl of water. This bowl they placed on a table in the music room in front of the playing viol. Jonara picked up a duplicate of the white viol and began playing it with Cerafina while Cerafina held Jonara's waist. In this way, there were two sets of girls and viols playing in concert. The Moissan Ruby glowed with blends of violet, pink, and red before projecting modern images of the hospital and Johnny leaning over to kiss Evanita.

Cerafina in the original girl-pair leaned over and kissed Jonara on the right cheek. The window stopped rattling. The projections of Jonara, Cerafina, the extra viol, the bowl of water, and the Water Ruby vanished. Cerafina released her grip on Jonara, and the two girls gasped with a start.

"You kissed me," said Jonara. "You kissed me for real. Not in the future, but now."

"Yeah, I know," said Cerafina. "I'm sorry. I feel guilty, like I did something wrong."

"Don't be," said Jonara. "Maybe it's okay."

"I've been taught it isn't," said Cerafina shamefully. "And I'm sorry. I don't know if we should do that again."

"Do we love each other?" Jonara asked. "Is this what love is like between girls?"

"Like I said, I don't have a sister, so I don't know what it's like to love a sister. But this seems stronger than sisterly love. That's what scares me."

The girls fell silent for a moment and happened to be staring out the once-rattling window when the Moissan Ruby rained down outside the window.

"Look!" Jonara exclaimed. "It happened like the viol predicted. The Water Ruby! Did you see it zip down the window? It's on the ground outside. C'mon, we have to get it! Hurry, before a stray dog runs off with it!"

Jonara set the viol aside, and the two girls rushed outside to find the Moissan Ruby. It was a fine autumn day with a cool but not cold breeze rustling through the trees. Scattered cumulous clouds dotted the blue sky and mixed shadows with sunlight on the Corpus Christi landscape. Leaves had not yet begun to turn in Corpus Christi as they had in Oregon, but Jonara felt as if they were turning. Her anticipation for the Moissan Ruby and its perceived interaction with the viol was much the same reaction one experiences when enjoying the multitude of floral color changes on a clear autumnal day.

"There," said Jonara. "In the grass. See how it sparkles?"

"It's dark, and yet it sparkles," said Cerafina. "How strange."

"Yeah, my daddy showed me how ultraviolet light can make it sparkle," Jonara explained. "But look, the chain is gone!"

"What chain?"

"There was a chain on it. Daddy had the chain around his neck, and it held the Water Ruby. But it's gone. I wonder where it went," Jonara mused.

"The Water Ruby fell, right?" Cerafina asked.

"Yeah."

"So look up along the house—it must have fallen from somewhere."

The two girls looked up and saw the chain dangling from the upstairs window—the same window Jonara had climbed out of and Johnny had nailed shut.

"That's my bedroom window," Jonara said. "I climbed down that spout last night."

"Your bedroom window is nailed shut," said Cerafina.

"Yeah, Grandma made Daddy nail it like that so I can't sneak out tonight. He must have left the Water Ruby up there on the sill by mistake," said Jonara.

"The window rattling, the...Jonara, your viol playing loosened the Water Ruby," said Cerafina.

"The vision was right. They have a relationship," said Jonara.

"But only when you play the viol," said Cerafina.

"We should get this inside—ouch!"

Jonara picked up the Water Ruby but dropped it with a start.

"I don't understand—I held it this morning. But now when I pick it up, it feels like a thousand needles jabbing me," Jonara explained.

"The viol may have caused it to do that," said Cerafina.

"I think you're right. Here—I'll watch it. Go inside and get something to grab it," Jonara said.

Jonara "guarded" the Moissan Ruby while Cerafina rushed into the kitchen, grabbed a few cooking utensils, and rushed back outside to Jonara. Out of breath, she handed the first utensil to Jonara.

"Here," Cerafina said between breaths. "Salad tongs."

Jonara took the scissor-action metal tongs and lifted the Moissan Ruby, but she jerked back again in shock and dropped both the Moissan Ruby and the tongs.

"OW! It got me again!" Jonara grimaced.

She shook her hand several times and held her injured fingertips to her lips to nurse them.

"Metal. I should have known better," said Cerafina. "Here are some plastic tongs. Maybe they'll insulate you."

Jonara took the plastic scissor-action tongs. She tapped the Moissan Ruby twice to test for any shock-like reaction. There was none. Slowly and carefully, she lifted the Moissan Ruby using the tongs. All was safe.

"Whew!" Jonara exhaled. "Who'd have thought this thing would be so much trouble!"

The two returned inside the house—Jonara to the music room, and Cerafina to the kitchen. Cerafina returned the extra utensils and prepared a clear bowl of water. She carried the water into the music room and placed it on the table—the same table where the viol case once rested.

"Thanks for moving the viol case," said Cerafina.

"No prob."

"Okay, here's the water. Ready to drop it in?" Cerafina asked.

"Yup."

"On three—one, two, three!"

Jonara dropped the Moissan Ruby from the plastic tongs into the clear bowl of water. The two girls expected a big splash followed by smoke, fireworks, or some other extravagant display.

"Whew! Okay, I thought it would jump out at me or something," said Jonara. "I guess we're ready."

The girls took their positions as before, with Jonara playing the viol, and Cerafina placing her one arm around Jonara's waist and her free hand on Jonara's shoulder. Jonara drew the bow across some strings, and the Moissan Ruby reacted by rippling the water with random currents. Jonara went through a learning period where she tried different notes, different bow techniques of pulling the bow, pushing the bow, using short strokes, long strokes, heavy strokes, light strokes, and plucking to see how the Moissan Ruby reacted. In this way, Jonara learned how to interact with the Moissan Ruby and influence it to move water and display light in such ways that she was able to connect to the world outside Geneva's home.

This connection to the outside world had a profound effect, and it was this—Jonara and Cerafina found themselves in an out-of-body experience where their corporeal bodies were left behind in Geneva's music room, but their psychic energies or spirits saw the music room's walls give way to the outside sunshine, the trees, and the birds. They effortlessly followed the road down to the hospital where in brief fashion they witnessed Johnny tending to Evanita, and Eva sitting in a nearby room where Johnny had convinced the doctors to hold her for thyroid examination and treatment.

In the traces of Eva's mind, the girls learned the diary was in the trunk of Geneva's car—in the hospital parking lot. The girls swiftly left the hospital and reached the car. There was no need to unlock the car or force the trunk—the girls in their Moissanized state passed through the car's steel frame and found the diary tossed under old newspapers.

"This is the diary," said Jonara.

"How did you use it before?" Cerafina asked.

"I read it before going to sleep. But I want us to go back in time together," said Jonara.

"Then we must both read the diary—together—and at the same time. Do you know where we should start—the page?" Cerafina asked.

"I think so. Let me thumb through it," Jonara said.

Without thinking, Jonara picked up the diary, but something unusual happened. The diary seemed to bifurcate into two books. The one in Jonara's hand was heavily textured with tree and plant fibers, and bits of berry skin and seed mixed into the ink. Remaining in the car's trunk was an incredibly bleached version of the diary with smooth-white pages, faded-gray ink, and a slim-flat gray cover.

"Did you see that?" Cerafina asked. "The diary—you took its soul!"

Jonara returned a smile of acknowledgment. She opened the diary to the page where it first described Evanita's sentence at the Portland Detention Center.

"Are you ready to read together?" Jonara asked.

"Yes."

"This is where we start," Jonara said, pointing to the passage with her finger.

Jonara inhaled deeply, and Cerafina took this as a cue to synchronize her breathing and speech with Jonara's. The two girls then read the following passage from Geneva's diary:

"November 14, 2006. My dear granddaughter Evanita has been admitted to the Portland Detention Center. Eva has not been allowed to visit her, and I'm worried about the both of them. I know in my heart I should let my Eva stand on her own feet and deal with this crisis, but it saddens me to see my girls suffering so much. I'm taking the next flight up to Portland to see what I can do. The worst Eva can do is send me back here to Corpus Christi.'"

Jonara closed the diary and held it to her side. The winds picked up and encircled the girls, loose debris, and the first autumn leaves. The sun faded behind a cloud, the clouds blurred overhead at dizzying speeds, and the girls found themselves on an airplane with a younger Geneva of 2006. The airplane passed over the High Cascades mountain range—the same mountains Jonara had crossed a few days earlier in October 2023.

"It's funny," said Jonara.

"What is?"

"The mountains—they look almost the same in 2006 as they do in 2023," Jonara replied.

"Almost," Cerafina replied.

"But something is a little different. I don't know what. Little things all over I can't describe. But I know it's the same," Jonara said.

"Your Nanna Geneva looks almost the same, too."

"Yeah. Younger, but the same. She's like the mountains, Cerafina. Strong and always there. I know she's gone in 2023, but she's here now! I feel like she'll be with me forever."

"She will, Jonara," Cerafina replied. "Just like the mountains."

"I'm going to name a mountain after my...my...what do you call your female ancestors?" Jonara asked.

"Just that—female ancestors," said Cerafina.

"There must be a better name—something like family female loved ones," said Jonara.

"Yeah, there should be."

Jonara stared out the window and saw the Three Sisters. She named each sister mountain after a female ancestor. As she named them, she felt a sense of how each mountain extended her roots into the countryside, giving that countryside protection and fresh water.

"Evanita..." Jonara said.

Cerafina felt sleepy.

"Eva..." Jonara continued.

Cerafina's eyelids anchored themselves closed.

"Geneva..." Cerafina heard faintly. She slipped into a strange dream of two ballerina groups dancing around an overlap of canoe and circle.

"Cerafina," whispered Jonara as her voice carried across the ages.

CHAPTER 3

Elrod 402

2023 Oct 4, Wed Afnoon. Corpus Christi, Texas.
2006 Nov 18, Sat. Portland, Oregon.

"Wake up, Cerafina," Jonara called.

Cerafina opened her eyes and found herself in the back of a cab with Jonara. Geneva sat in the front, and the driver pulled into Eva's driveway.

"Here you are," said Geneva as she paid the driver. "Thank you."

The three exited the cab and walked up to the front door. Geneva rang the doorbell and knocked three times.

"Oh, it's you," said Eva indifferently as she let her mother in.

"Well," Geneva said with a light huff. "Don't act happy to see me or anything."

Eva walked back to her exercise room.

"Aren't you going to offer me the guestroom or anything?" Geneva asked.

"You know where it is," Eva motioned without turning around to face her mother.

"Do you need anything, Eva?" Geneva asked before taking her own luggage to the guestroom. "Do you need money? Would you like to go out to eat?"

Eva ignored her and continued walking to the exercise room. Before she left earshot of Geneva, Geneva shouted.

"How about a swift kick in the butt?" Geneva said with the utmost affection.

"You see? They argue too," Jonara said to Cerafina.

"Shhh," said Cerafina.

"Don't worry. They can't hear us. Sometimes my daddy can, but no one else can," said Jonara.

"Are you sure?"

"Sure! Try yelling as loud as you can," Jonara suggested.

"Hello!" Cerafina shouted, but neither Geneva nor Eva reacted.

"See? We can say or do almost anything. C'mon. Let's see what Grandma Eva is doing," Jonara suggested.

Jonara and Cerafina proceeded to Eva's exercise room and watched her put away the photo of Roberta, turn off the music player, and hide her ballet equipment.

"Why is she doing that?" Cerafina asked.

"I don't know," Jonara replied. "I saw her do it before, when Ms. Zyla came over. Grandma Eva did ballet stuff in front of Roberta's picture, but when Ms. Zyla came over, Grandma pretended nothing happened and started lifting weights."

"Who's Roberta?" Cerafina asked.

"I don't know that either. I think her name is Roberta because it's written on the photo," Jonara replied.

Jonara and Cerafina observed Eva switch to weightlifting just in time for Geneva's entry into the exercise room.

"One, two, three, four, five—" Eva puffed as she exercised her legs on the weightlifting apparatus.

"You don't have to be cold with me," said Geneva. "I spared you the bother of picking me up at the airport, after all."

"Fifteen, sixteen, seventeen," Eva continued.

"Why didn't you tell me you were having problems with Evanita? I only happened to find out through Sharon. She was shocked you hadn't told me. As am I," Geneva continued.

"Twenty-eight, twenty-nine, thirty," Eva puffed.

"How long are you going to keep up this wall between us, Eva? Look at you exercising away while I'm talking to you," Geneva said.

"Yes, you're talking to me, not with me. Forty-one, forty-two, forty-three!" Eva said.

"We used to have lovely talks when you were a girl. Then you grew up, and we grew apart," Geneva said.

"Fifty. Whew! Time for some bicep work," Eva said.

"Why don't we talk like we used to?" Geneva asked.

"I became aware of the world, Mother. Six, seven, eight!"

"You chose obsession over courtesy," said Geneva.

"I chose rationality over crazy talk! Thirteen, fourteen!"

"You seem to think I don't know anything. That I'm just this little woman who's stuck in her Catholic world," said Geneva.

"You are, Mother. And don't launch into the usual tirade about how bad things were under Franco to make me feel guilty or sorry for you. Twenty-seven!" Eva sweated.

"Can't you stop for a moment and talk to me?" Geneva asked.

"No, I won't stop exercising. That's what you want—for me to stop everything and bow down to what you want, what your religion wants. Thirty-eight, thirty-nine, forty!"

"Don't you think that's a little harsh, dear?" Geneva asked.

"No, I don't. That's how the military does it, and that's how the Church does it. Strip down the psyche, and force-feed the agenda. Forty-nine, fifty! Now for abs," said Eva.

"What are you talking about? The Church isn't the military," said Geneva.

"They are both emotion predators. Six, seven."

"Now who's doing the crazy talk?" Geneva asked.

"They feed on emotions, just as you are doing right now. Fourteen."

"That's outrageous," said Geneva. "I'm only trying to help."

"Those are the first words of an emotion predator. Nineteen, twenty."

"Just this once," continued Geneva.

"The next words of an emotion predator. Twenty-four. It never is 'just this once'. There's always more predation. Like an addiction, the predation doesn't stop. Twenty-nine, thirty."

Geneva held her tongue and walked around the room.

"We don't have to stay," Jonara said to Cerafina. "My grandma doesn't like the Catholic Church, and she'll say so. I know you're Catholic and—"

"It's okay," said Cerafina, "I don't much care for the Catholic Church either—especially now that...now that..."

Cerafina's voice trailed. She looked deep into Jonara's eyes, and Jonara exchanged the look. Their faces approached slowly in a tender moment, but the embrace was startled by Geneva's voice.

"You still love her, don't you?" Geneva asked, motioning to the facedown photo of Roberta.

"What?" Eva said just as she finished exercising her abdominal muscles.

"Roberta. And I see your ballet shoes in the corner here. They've been freshly used," said Geneva.

"See—that's the next part of emotion predation—looking for tender spots and applying downward pressure," said Eva who picked up a jump rope and started jumping.

"That was horrible how they treated you two in 1990," Geneva continued. "We should talk about that, for your own good."

"And so it continues—stirring up old wounds from the past," said Eva.

"You shouldn't keep things bottled up," continued Geneva.

"Wounds I managed to forget. I've moved on, Mother. You're only bringing up the past in hopes of getting me emotionally upset."

"You've moved on?" Geneva asked as she held up the ballet shoes and photo of Roberta.

"Yes, I have. How I've moved on is my own business. I'm not an exhibitionist. Whew. Time for a run on the treadmill."

Eva powered up the treadmill and started jogging.

"You seem to be an exhibitionist to me. All this macho exercising is for show, on my account."

"More crazy talk," said Eva between breaths. "I exercise every day whether you or anyone else is here. But there you go with the daggers. My workout has nothing to do with machoism. You're looking for a wedge to pry into my inner psyche."

"Oh, so you have one. You could be open about everything and not stuff yourself away in an 'inner psyche'. I have no inner psyche to hide," said Geneva.

Eva stopped running for a moment, looked squarely at her mother, and said, "Damn you and your manipulation games!"

Eva resumed running.

"I seem to have struck a nerve accidentally," said Geneva.

"It's no accident. You searched for the nerve to strike, and with all your might drove the phallic ice pick into my back—precisely where you meant to."

"Don't hide in riddles. Don't bury yourself in layers," said Geneva.

"If there are layers, it's because you refuse to understand the little bits of honesty I dole out. And I dole out what I think you can handle—sometimes more than you can handle—which motivates you to attack. So I put the layers back on. Layers are all that keep us from tearing each other apart," Eva said.

"I've never heard you talk like this before. So much pent-up anger. But there's an answer, there's—" Geneva started.

"Oh, now it comes. This is the moment you've been working toward. Work the psyche, work the psyche. Either push it into the depths of despair or to the peaks of irritation. Then pounce on it and deliver the verbal vomit your conditioning has commanded of you. You're addicted mother—you've reached the peak opiatic craving point. And once you deliver those words— the words your religion has commanded you to deliver, you'll achieve euphoria—at my expense! But only then will you stop, and only until the next time you need to feed!"

"—the Roman Catholic Church. Through the repetition of prayer, devotion, and penance—"

"There, you see? The power of the opiatic response to block out anything that threatens the euphoric moment. You accuse me of walls. I ask—who's the hypocrite here?" Eva asked.

"—you can achieve peace from your strife. Bind to Christ and let nothing challenge salvation. The Church will give it to you for free," Geneva continued.

"For free? The first one is free—that's what the pusher claims. Nothing is free, Mother. The price is paid—the price of addiction and giving up one's liberty to the pusher."

"You think too much, dear. Let go, and don't analyze too much," Geneva urged.

"Yes—don't think, don't challenge—you might find out things are better when you do. And we'll lose oppressive mind-control over you. Isn't that right, Mother? I know the truth, Mother. I first became aware of the world when I was eight years old—the world of trickery and deceit to extract the desired emotional response from the young and innocent! But who would have believed me back then? And how much I would have suffered from the onslaught of brainwashing tactics had I told this to you or anyone. I had to grow up in my own way until I could interact with freer-minded folk—free from religious persecution!"

"I knew I should have sent you away to parochial boarding school after I returned to the Catholic faith," said Geneva. "The nuns would have kept you straight. Oh how I've failed as a parent."

"And now you want sympathy? If you can't 'comfort' me in the emotionally upset state you had hoped to create, am I required to 'comfort' you in your own forced despair? No, Mother, no! Stop the cycle of abuse!"

Eva stepped off the treadmill and powered it off.

"I'm taking a shower," Eva said as she left Geneva in the exercise room.

"Wow! I've never heard anyone talk like that!" said Cerafina. "Is your Grandma Eva like this all the time?"

"She doesn't usually go on this long. But she has a sharp tongue," said Jonara. "I didn't know she talked like this to Nanna Geneva. Cerafina—did anything my Grandma Eva say make sense to you?"

"What do you mean?" Cerafina asked.

"About the Catholic Church tearing someone down like the military?"

"I don't know. I just zone out when I'm at Mass—I ignore as much as I can. When everyone else kneels, I kneel. When they stand, I stand. When they go up for Communion, well, so do I."

"You mean—you're a Catholic but you fake it?" Jonara asked.

"It's too painful trying to learn it. And none of it makes sense outside of church. So I ignore it. I don't know what your grandma means about the tearing down games."

"Hmm, I wonder if I should ask her," Jonara mused.

"I'd be careful, if I were you," said Cerafina. "The more I learn about the Catholic faith—especially the history—the uglier it gets. You might not like what you see."

"So what?"

"So what? Then you spend too much time thinking about it. Maybe that's the game your grandma is talking about—at least maybe one of them."

"Huh?" Jonara asked.

"The Church shows its ugly side—so ugly it gives you nightmares. You want to forget, but you can't. But that's the whole point—the Church doesn't want you to forget. The Church is always in your mind. And that's when they have you. I understand it now, Jonara, I understand!" Cerafina exclaimed.

Cerafina ran out of the room, up the stairs, and into the bathroom where she attempted to hug Eva. Jonara ran after her, begging Cerafina to wait, but to no avail. Cerafina swept her arms around Eva, but her arms passed right through. No hug was possible.

"You can't hug most people in the past," said Jonara as she ran up to Cerafina. "I've already tried."

"Most people? Did you hug someone?" Cerafina asked.

"Just my daddy. But I think I know how that worked. He was wearing the Water Ruby, and I think that gave him some ability to let me hug him. I think it also let him hear me," Jonara explained. "C'mon, let's go downstairs."

Jonara grabbed Cerafina's hand and led her back downstairs. Yet Cerafina didn't feel like someone was yanking her along against her will. Instead, she felt the warm hand of a girl whose grandmother was willing to stand up to the Catholic Church. In this way, Cerafina's handholding walk downstairs felt more like a welcoming rite into Jonara's family, a family named Carreña. When the two arrived downstairs, Cerafina inhaled and exhaled deeply. She pulled Jonara slowly toward her and kissed Jonara on the forehead.

"I feel...I feel like I could love your family," said Cerafina, but she blushed and felt embarrassed. "That sounds sappy, I know."

Cerafina turned away to hide her blushing face.

"No, it's okay," said Jonara. "Look at me."

Jonara turned Cerafina around and stared into her eyes.

"It's okay to love my family. In fact, I think it's cool. But if you go kissing my Grandma Eva, I might get jealous," Jonara laughed.

"Okay, I promise I won't go kissing your grandma!" Cerafina said.

Cerafina gave Jonara a big hug. In fact, the two hugged each other and touched each other's hands.

"Your mother should have kept her maiden name," said Cerafina. "Then you would be Jonara Carreña."

"Yeah, I've wondered about that too," said Jonara.

"Maybe you can change it when you're old enough," said Cerafina.

"To what? Jonara Vagatti?" Jonara joked. "What about your mother's maiden name?"

"It's Ancona. Funny thing, it's also *my* grandma's last name. She never took my grandpa's last name."

"So I can be Jonara Ancona? And you can be Cerafina Carreña," Jonara said.

Cerafina lightly hit Jonara on the shoulder.

"Brat," Cerafina said playfully.

Eva returned downstairs. She was cleaned up and wearing fresh clothes. She sorted through her purse for something before pulling out her keys.

"Are you going somewhere?" Geneva asked.

"Yes. They're transferring Evanita today. From the Portland Detention Center."

"Oh?" Geneva said. "Where is she being transferred to?"

Eva looked down with disappointment, up for strength, and directly at her mother to deliver the grave news.

"The Elrod 402."

The lighting flickered. Jonara and Cerafina sank through the floor and landed in the basement.

"What happened?" Cerafina asked.

"I don't know. Let's go back upstairs and see," Jonara said.

The two returned upstairs. Empty. Jonara and Cerafina looked out the window in time to see Eva and Geneva entering Eva's car. Eva started the engine and placed the car in Reverse.

"Hurry!" Jonara urged. "We'll have to run for it!"

The girls ran out to the front yard and dove into the backseat of Eva's car in time to catch her backing out of the driveway.

"No," Eva seemed to continue. "They won't let me visit her unless I attend a group session for parents. They want to counsel me on my parental skills. Of all the nerve!"

"Did you go...will you go?" Geneva asked.

"Of course not! No one tells me how to raise my daughter," Eva replied.

The lighting flickered again. Eva's and Geneva's speech seemed to fluctuate in the background. Jonara and Cerafina felt themselves sinking down through the back seat. They fell through the floorboard yet tried to stay with the car by hanging on. Their hands stretched overhead to the floorboard, but their heads were "submerged" below the pavement level, as if they were skiing in water, had fallen, and were being dragged in the water by a towrope. Concrete and steel rebar whizzed past them, and with each bit of steel passing through their bodies, Jonara and Cerafina sustained electrical shocks.

"I can't hold on," said Cerafina.

"Me neither," Jonara replied.

Both girls let go. They fell to the floor in Geneva's music room—Jonara one way with the viol and bow, and Cerafina the other. The viol music stopped. The girls regathered themselves, stood up, looked around the room, and were amazed to see the mess on the table before them.

"Look," said Jonara.

"The water got out of the bowl," said Cerafina. "It must have splashed out. There's water on the table, on the floor—everywhere."

"The Water Ruby is still in the bowl, but the bowl is dry," said Jonara.

"It must have forced the water out," said Cerafina.

"We'll have to keep the water from splashing out," said Jonara. "Maybe a casserole bowl would work."

"With a lid," said Cerafina.

"I know where one is in the kitchen. Let's go. We'll get towels, too," said Jonara.

Jonara found a clear casserole bowl with lid. She filled the bowl one-third with water and carried it into the music room. Cerafina scooped up kitchen towels and wiped down the table and floor in the music room. Jonara placed the casserole bowl on the table and dumped the Moissan Ruby from the first bowl to the casserole bowl. The Moissan Ruby—which was dark and seemingly opaque in the dry bowl—now glittered and visually vibrated in the casserole bowl's water. Jonara placed the lid on the casserole bowl quickly for fear the water might escape before the two could resume exploring the past.

"I don't think you have to worry," said Cerafina. "The water only splashes around when you play the viol."

"I want to be sure," said Jonara.

The two returned to the viol, but instead of standing, the girls placed two chairs together and sat down.

"This will be more comfortable," said Cerafina.

The chairs had no armrests. This allowed Cerafina to sit close to Jonara—close enough to wrap her arm around Jonara's waist as before. Jonara took the bow and began playing. The Moissan Ruby reacted by swirling the water and filling it with soft hues and transcending light patterns. As before, Jonara adjusted her viol playing to navigate through the Moissan Ruby—navigate to find the diary as she had before. Fortunately, she remembered the strokes needed to reach Geneva's car trunk at the hospital where the diary remained. In this way, the two girls reentered their out-of-body experience and appeared at the car close to the diary. Jonara lifted the psyche of the diary into her hands as before while leaving the bleach-base of a diary in the car's trunk.

"Let's read it together," said Jonara.

"Okay."

The two girls read aloud the following passage from Geneva's diary:

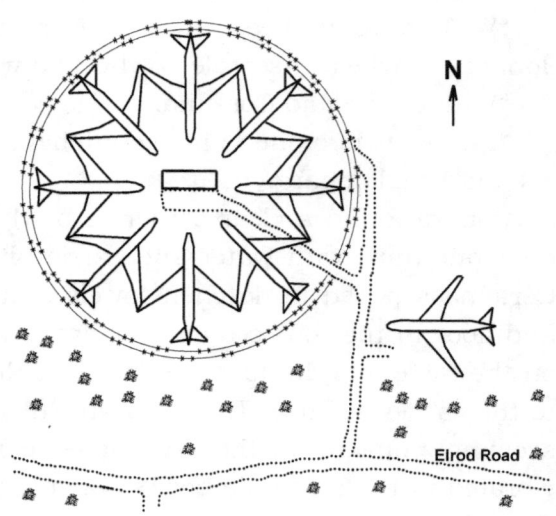

"Despite Eva's protests, I accompanied her to the Elrod 402 facility, a collection of nine jumbo jets parked on the north side of Elrod Road west of Portland International Airport. Eight airplanes face each other in a circle with their wingtips touching. These airplanes are surrounded by two circling layers of barbed-wire fence. A ninth airplane sits outside the barbed wire. This is the airplane Eva and I visited, the administrative office of Elrod 402, the airplane where Eva and I met Ms. Fronka Nordekter.'"

The girls switched from standing next to Geneva's car with the diary in 2023 to sitting in the back seat of Eva's car in 2006. Eva had just turned from Elrod Road onto a gravel road leading north. As described, eight airplanes to the left formed a circle, and one airplane stood alone to the right.

"What is this place?" Cerafina asked.

"I don't know. It looks like an airport," said Jonara.

"But there's no runway," Cerafina said.

"This is it," Eva said to Geneva. "Evanita should be arriving soon from the city detention center. Mother—please be on your best behavior. I don't want things getting worse than they already are."

"Of course, dear," said Geneva.

Eva parked the car. The two women were escorted up the stairs into the aircraft.

"A very unusual arrangement," said Eva. "Using airplanes for...for...come to think of it, what are they being used for?"

"Good question," replied a voice. "Please—let me introduce myself. I'm Ms. Fronka Nordekter—Chief Administrator of Elrod 402. Welcome aboard! You must be Ms. Eva Carreña."

"Thank you. This is my mother, Ms. Geneva Carreña," said Eva.

"Nice to meet you. Please, come this way! I'd like you to join our main group of parents in the lobby who are also registering their children," Nordekter said.

"What was her name?" Jonara asked.

"I think she said, 'Fronka Nordekter'," Cerafina replied.

"Fronka *Nordekker...Nordetter*...that's too hard to say," said Jonara.

"Nor-dek-ter," said Cerafina. "Like Nor-doctor."

"Whatever," Jonara said, giving up.

Nordekter led Geneva and Eva down a short hallway to a large open area where several expecting parents were waiting.

"Did you see the pendant she's wearing?" Cerafina asked Jonara.

"Yeah—it has the same shape as the eight jets," said Jonara.

"And all connected at the wingtips like the real ones," said Cerafina.

"We might as well get started with the tour," Nordekter said. "We are in the lobby of the administrative jet. All jets have names—the one you're standing in is Whalejet. In case you didn't notice, the outside of this jet is painted in the whites and blacks of killer whales."

"I wonder if that's an omen," said Jonara.

"Think positively," said Cerafina.

"Over here you can see a scale-model layout of the entire campus," Nordekter continued. "Go ahead—walk around it. You'll see the campus is made up entirely of Boeing 747-200 jumbo jets. They are at the end of their service life and were scheduled to be scrapped. But we at the Elrod 402 facility got hold of them just in time and have recycled them into buildings."

"Amazing!" said Geneva.

"Hmm," muttered Eva.

"That's unbelievable!" Cerafina said to Jonara. "Can you believe such a fantastic thing?"

"It doesn't seem as fantastic as some of the other things I've seen," Jonara replied. "Saint Stellan had a flying bench and a falling cage-like fence. Barnseed Baptist Church looked like a hunting lodge. And the factory fire—"

"I wonder what it would be like to live here," said Cerafina.

"You don't want to know," said Jonara.

"The management makes it look special. Look at how all the jets are painted and arranged in the model. Look outside—you can see the jets for real," Cerafina said.

"I get the feeling this place is bad," said Jonara.

"Why?" Cerafina asked.

"Just the way Grandma Eva and Johnny were talking about it this morning back in 2023, like it was the worst prison ever invented."

"In these modern times?" said Cerafina.

"I guess we'll have to find out," said Jonara.

"Eight jets form a circle—wingtip to wingtip. To prevent unauthorized entry into the campus, a double layer of fencing encloses the main campus for the protection of our residents," Nordekter continued.

"But a fence works both ways—to keep people in, too," said Eva.

"We don't want our residents sleepwalking over to the airport runway, do we?" Nordekter said.

Others nearby laughed in agreement.

"You'll notice each jet has a specially painted design," Nordekter said. "This design identifies the jet. The red one with white nose and wing tips is called 'Redjet'. This dormitory houses the girls tagged as violent. I assure you, they are as tame as pussycats once they complete rehabilitation."

"Meow!" mimicked one of the parents.

The crowd laughed in response.

"Next to Redjet," continued Nordekter, "is a two-toned coloring of orange on the upper half and white on the lower. That's

Oranjet—and it houses the substance abuse and mentally disabled cases."

"Do they get free Sunshine Orange?" called another voice.

"You got the words backward," said a third.

"Come now. LSD is a banned substance as you all well know," Nordekter continued. "We treat our resident patients with the utmost care—all FDA approved and certified. Even if begged, we would never consider experimental or illegal treatment methods."

"If you have to bring it up, you're probably doing it," muttered Eva.

"I heard that," whispered Geneva. "And you wanted me to behave. Hmph."

"The next jet—the two-tone with yellow on the upper and black on the lower is—"

"Yellow jacket," offered one of the parents.

"Sunshine Yellow," offered another.

Nordekter laughed it off.

"Oh no, no, no. It's the Aldojet," said Nordekter.

"What kind of strange name is that for a yellow and black jet?" Eva asked.

"It was named by our chief architect—Ms. Arfella Beffenstein. The Aldojet also houses substance abuse and mentally disabled cases. In fact, Ms. Beffenstein designed all of our jet layouts and décors."

"What about this green one?" called a parent. "Is that for the rugged outdoor type?"

"Grenjet is currently being renovated," said Nordekter. "The completed portions are used as temporary residence when the other dorm jets are full."

"What a bunch of crazy names," said Jonara. "But I wonder what this LSD is? I heard it mentioned at my Mommy's trial."

"An illegal drug. It makes people hallucinate," said Cerafina.

"Hallucinate—is that like seeing things that aren't there?" Jonara asked.

"Yeah."

"We have a diary and viol for that already, don't we?" Jonara asked.

"Sure do!" Cerafina replied.

"Maybe we'll end up staying in Aldojet," Jonara joked.

"I hope not!" Cerafina laughed.

"Bloomjet (the crisscrossing blue- and white-striped jet) and Violijet (the crisscrossing violet- and white-striped jet) house the young homeless girls of Portland until permanent homes can be found," Nordekter explained.

"Seems odd that you need two jumbo jets for homeless girls," said Geneva.

Eva nudged Geneva to be silent.

"Unfortunately, young people see Portland as the runaway haven of America. We do all we can to get girls off the street before they fall into lives of crime. Here at least in safety, we can take care of them and re-educate them. You must be from out of town, Ms. Carreña?"

"Yes, from Corpus Christi," said Geneva.

"Most folk from other cities aren't used to seeing so many young homeless people," Nordekter continued. "But in Portland, it's a very real issue. Elrod 402 is equipped to help the homeless girls—who are most vulnerable to abuse and stand the most to lose."

"What does Elrod 402 stand for?" asked one of the parents. "Yeah, why four-oh-two?" asked another.

"Well, the facility is on Elrod Road—that much is plain. The '402' refers to resident capacity. We can house 402 young girls," Nordekter explained.

"What about the other two jets?" Eva asked.

"Yes. The white jet with red crosses is known as 'Cafederijet'. Cafederijet contains the cafeteria and infirmary. The last jet is Patriojet. In Patriojet, the girls find schooling and church services. You'll notice Patriojet is painted with the American flag wrapped around its fuselage and wings."

"Mixing a cafeteria with infirmary doesn't seem very sanitary," said Eva.

"I assure you—our jets are certified to the highest standards of safety and cleanliness. The FDA, OSHA, the juvenile corrections board, and the fire department all make regular inspections of our campus," Nordekter said.

"It looks safe to me," commented one parent.

"What's wrong with a cafeteria and infirmary in the same jet?" commented another parent. "Seems like a good idea to me."

"Yeah," added a third.

"My thoughts exactly," said Nordekter.

"I think we'd best not say too much," said Geneva to Eva.

"Wow!" Cerafina said. "First your Grandma Eva was telling Nanna Geneva to be quiet, and—"

"Nanna Geneva is telling Grandma Eva the same thing. Funny, isn't it?" Jonara added.

"I don't think your grandma likes this place," Cerafina added.

"If you'll come this way," Nordekter motioned, "I'll show you the model bedrooms."

Geneva, Eva, Jonara, and Cerafina followed at the rear of the group. Fronka Nordekter first showed a model bedroom with bunk beds.

"This is a double bedroom. You'll see the room is well furnished with bunk beds, two closets, two desks, a television, and a bathroom."

"Nice," said Cerafina. "But who gets to sleep on the bottom?"

"Whoever is stronger," joked Jonara.

"Hah!" Cerafina laughed.

"Next," Nordekter continued, "we have a single bedroom. You'll notice it's practically the same as the double, but a little smaller. Just one desk and closet instead of two. Yes, it has a bathroom. We prefer to bunk residents in a double, but the more difficult cases must start off in a single."

"Did you see the bolts on these doors?" Jonara asked.

"No, I didn't really look," Cerafina replied.

"Look at the bolts—they're huge. Wonder why?"

"They are big," Cerafina replied. "I can't believe they need such large bolts to keep people from breaking in."

"Or breaking out," said Jonara. "Like Grandma Eva said about the barbed-wire fence."

"Continuing our tour," said Nordekter, "you'll see the model laundry room. Each girl is taught responsibility, and part of this is doing her own laundry. Plenty of washers and dryers to go around."

Several parents clapped.

"Yes, I know, kids these days don't take care of themselves like they should. You'll be amazed at how much your daughter matures once she completes her stay at the Elrod 402!" Nordekter bragged.

"Doesn't that sound like a motel name?" Jonara asked Cerafina. "The Elrod Motel. Vacancy with 402 rooms."

"Shhh," Cerafina replied. "Your grandmother is saying something."

"My Evanita never had to be told. She always took care of her clothes and things," Eva muttered.

"But think how much more helpful she'll be after her stay," said Geneva.

"Mother—something's not right here," Eva said. "It's almost too easy. More likely Evanita will want to go for a run to work off her frustrations. I wonder where a girl can go for a run around here—cooped up in a jumbo jet?"

"And the last room on our stop is the model rec room. This one is a little smaller than the real ones, but you get the idea. Plenty of activities to keep a girl occupied—crafts, ping-pong, and billiards for starters. Plus lots of jigsaw puzzles and board games. No card games are allowed, I'm afraid. Too many girls abuse the privilege with poker and blackjack."

"No card games?" Jonara remarked. "Not even Rummy or Crazy Eights?"

"Interesting," remarked Cerafina. "But who needs cards with all the other games? Looks like a lot of fun."

"We believe each girl should earn her free time," Nordekter said. "Once she completes her duties for the day and has maintained good behavior, only then is she granted rec time."

More applauding from parents.

"Is there a place to jog here?" Eva asked Nordekter. "What about sports?"

"Ah, we have outdoor facilities for basketball, volleyball, and yes—a track under the jets for running," Nordekter said with a wink toward Eva.

"That would seem to answer your question," said Geneva. "This place doesn't seem so bad after all."

"Still," Eva remarked. "I wish I could be sure."

"This concludes the tour," said Nordekter.

"What about religion?" Geneva asked.

"Mother!" Eva blurted.

"Patriojet holds services for several denominations—Jewish, Christian, Muslim, and others as needed," Nordekter said. "Each girl is provided religious material according to her faith."

"What about Catholic?" Geneva asked.

"No, Unitarian Universalism," said Eva.

"All Christian faiths are represented," Nordekter said. "Now if there are no more questions, it's time to break up our happy little group. Your daughters are waiting for you at the intake center. Just follow me down the hallway a short ways and register. An Oxian will lead you to your daughter."

"What the heck is that?" Cerafina asked.

"I don't know," said Jonara.

"Did she say an ox will show us?" Geneva asked Eva.

Other parents rumbled with whispered questions.

"Oh, my apologies! I neglected to introduce my staff!" Nordekter explained. "Each department person has a role name. Isn't that clever?"

"Oh, wonderful!" Eva muttered sarcastically with only Geneva to hear.

"Our security department is known as Oxi. Our security chief is the Oxia, and security personnel are known as Oxians. If you look closely at an Oxian's badge, you'll see the role name for that person—Ox-One, Ox-Two, Ox-Three, etc. Please call your staff escort by that name. Thank you!"

Eva rolled her eyes at Geneva.

"Be patient, dear," Geneva whispered back.

"Unbelievable, and cool!" Cerafina said.

"That's crazy!" Jonara said.

"Each department has role names like that. Our health department is known as Bari, our health chief is Baria, and health personnel are Bar-One, etc. Education is the Daz department. Sanitation is Dialytik, but the sanitation personnel are Diali-One, etc. Oh, the chief of sanitation is Dialytika. What am I forgetting? Yes, the cafeteria department—Macro, of course! The lead is Macron, and cafeteria personnel are known as Mac-One and so on. Whew!"

"May I see my daughter now?" an impatient Eva asked.

"Of course, Ms. Carreña the younger. Your escort is Ox-Three," Nordekter said.

Nordekter continued assigning Oxian security personnel to other parents.

Eva, Geneva, Jonara, and Cerafina were nearly out of earshot when Fronka Nordekter announced to everyone that she had a role name too:

"I'm O Grammeni!"

"You're Ox-Three?" Eva asked a tall, husky woman.

"That's me. Parents to see Eve Carson—follow me," said Ox-Three.

"Wait—we're here to see Evanita Carreña," said Eva. "I don't know anything about an Eve Carson."

"Evanita Carreña?" Ox-Three mused. "Hummm. Let me flip through the chart here. Yes, here it is in the back—'Original Name: Evanita Carreña'. Same girl. Follow me, please."

"You can't just change her name," said Eva as the Evas and young girls followed the Oxian.

"It's part of therapy—role name assignment," said Ox-Three.

"That's not therapy—it's brainwashing!" Eva said

"Here she is—in W218. I'll be waiting outside the door. You have thirty minutes," Ox-Three said, ignoring Eva's comment.

"Evanita!" Eva called.

"Mommy!" Jonara shouted with only Cerafina to hear.

Evanita stood with the help of her crutches. Both legs were in casts, and her face held a blank stare. Both Eva and Jonara rushed up to hug Evanita. Jonara's arms passed through Evanita of course, but this fact didn't stop Jonara's yearning to hug her mother.

"Mama," said Evanita coldly.

Evanita hugged back weakly but did not show emotion.

"It's your mother," said Eva, concerned about Evanita's lack of recognition. "Don't you know me, Evanita?"

"Yes," Evanita said just as distantly as she'd said, "Mama."

"Is she in shock, Eva?" Geneva asked.

"I'm not sure."

"What's wrong with your mother?" Cerafina asked.

"I don't know," Jonara replied.

"Can't you ask the Water Ruby?"

"You know we're using the diary to be in the past," said Jonara.

"I know, but isn't there a way to bring the Water Ruby back in the past with us? Then you could use it to read your mother's thoughts," Cerafina suggested.

"I don't know—it sounds complicated," Jonara replied.

"Maybe you could find the Water Ruby in this time and connect through it," Cerafina suggested.

"My daddy has it, I mean, my daddy before he was my daddy. But that would mean leaving Mommy here. I don't want to miss out on what's happening," said Jonara.

"I could stay here," said Cerafina.

"I don't think that will work. We need to stay together just to make the viol work with the Water Ruby back in the music room," said Jonara.

"Ms. Eva Carreña," said Ox-Three. "I have some papers for you to sign."

"All right," said Eva. She took one look at the papers and reacted badly. "Say, what's this in the fine print?"

"Sorry, I can't answer that question," said Ox-Three.

"It says I agree to waive all rights to necessary medical treatment. What defines 'necessary'?" Eva protested.

"You'll have to see Baria—the health chief," said Ox-Three.

"I demand to see her right now!" Eva said.

"Barian needed at W218 for nonemergency," Ox-Three radioed. She turned back to Eva and said, "One of the Barians will take you to Baria, Ms. Eva Carreña. I would, but procedure requires me to stay here."

"Yes, of course," said Eva. She turned to Geneva and said, "You'll watch over Evanita, won't you Mother?"

"Of course, dear!" Geneva replied.

While Eva exchanged a few last words with Ox-Three, Geneva put her back to the guard, faced Evanita, and spoke.

"Here child, put this around your neck. It will give you luck."

Geneva retrieved a necklace from her purse and placed it over Evanita's head. A dark, nearly opaque stone gave off a faint glitter as Evanita robotically placed the stone under her blouse.

"The Water Ruby!" said Jonara.

"How did your Nanna Geneva get hold of it?" Cerafina asked.

"I don't know!" Jonara replied.

"Your good friend, Johnny Pindus, asked me to give you this necklace," Geneva said to Evanita. "He gave it to me at the airport and would have come along, but he knows the compound has strict rules against non-family visitation. He hopes it will help you remember your family, Ms. Zyla, and him. Don't forget us, Evanita."

Evanita drew a hand to her heart over which the Moissan Ruby lay. Her eyes moved slowly from side to side. She closed her eyelids, opened them, and her distant expression melted into instant recognition and fatigue.

"Oh Grandma!" she said weakly.

Evanita leaned into her grandmother, and Geneva wrapped her arms around her granddaughter. Holding Evanita felt like hugging a snowwoman.

"You're so cold, my child!" Geneva said.

"I'm numb," Evanita replied.

"Let's get that circulation going."

Geneva held Evanita with one arm and used the other to sweep arm-strokes and circles across Evanita's back. Evanita sobbed a little as her emotions surfaced through her numb exterior.

"There there, everything will be better soon," Geneva promised.

As Evanita regained her strength, her numbness faded.

"I feel cold," Evanita said.

"Going from feeling numb to cold—that's an improvement," Geneva said.

Evanita's body shook with goose bumps in response to her need for warmth. Geneva continued hugging her and rubbing her back, but the shivering triggered a reaction in Evanita's Moissan Ruby. While there was no external evidence of the Moissan Ruby in action (at least not to anyone in 2006), Jonara and Cerafina noticed a low humming sound from the Moissan Ruby—growing and fading in strength.

"What's that sound?" Cerafina asked.

"Sounds like a vacuum cleaner," said Jonara.

"A vacuum cleaner one floor above," said Cerafina.

"And it's vibrating through the ceiling," added Jonara.

The air contorted like a fluid, and with each growing ultralow hum from the Moissan Ruby, Jonara and Cerafina felt heavy beats on their sternums, as one might when standing too close to a woofer loudspeaker.

"It's getting worse," said Jonara.

"It's only affecting us," said Cerafina. "We have to get out of here. It's hurting me."

"How?" Jonara asked, and as she did, the low beating vibrated her voice box.

A low-frequency squeal grew in volume—a squeal much like the feedback from a microphone and speaker coming together, only lower in frequency like two huge steel I-beams clashing and torsing under duress.

"We have to let go," said Cerafina.

"What?" Jonara asked.

Jonara couldn't hear Cerafina over the loud distorted humming from Evanita's Moissan Ruby.

"Let go of the viol! Let go, let go!" she shouted to no avail.

The two slipped back into Geneva's music room in the year 2023. Cerafina and Jonara were locked in position, unable to move as if being electrocuted with high-voltage direct current. Jonara's left fingers remained pressed against two strings on the viol's neck, and her right hand held rigid with the bow partway across the strings. Cerafina's hands and arms were locked on Jonara's waist and right shoulder, and all the two could do was stare at the lidded casserole bowl and watch— watch the Moissan Ruby bubble and churn the water increasingly stronger with bluish-red bursts of light shooting through like lightning. They watched as the lid skipped and hopped and leapt little bits at a time in defiance of the increasing pressure below—hopping like a lid on a boiling pot—hopping while bits of freezing water sprayed out the side into the room on the piano, the bookcases, the window, and onto the girls—hopping madly until the cycle of growing and dying deep-vibrational sounds with groaning squelches burst the water directly upward— shooting the casserole lid up toward the ceiling where amazingly it did not shatter but instead dug its knob-for-a-handle into the ceiling's sheetrock and lodged itself in place.

The water exploded in all directions at high pressure, but in doing so it depressurized and lost heat quickly. As the super-cooled water landed around the room, it froze immediately on contact. In this way, nothing in the room was actually wet. Extremely cold ice abounded everywhere, and it reacted with room temperature with a frosty-glazed appearance while emanating wispy clouds of sublimation.

Jonara and Cerafina lost their grips on each other and the viol. They fell apart in opposite directions, caught themselves, turned around, and looked at each other. Their hair and eyebrows were full of ice.

"Jonara, Cerafina!" Anna pounded on the other side of the music room's locked door. "What is going on?"

"Quick—we gotta get rid of this ice!" said Jonara.

"Out the window," Cerafina said as she threw the window and adjoining screen open.

"You want me to jump out the window?" Jonara asked.

"No, silly. Throw the ice out the window."

"You girls okay?" Anna called.

The two girls rushed around the music room gathering ice and throwing it out the window. Pieces froze to their fingers, and they shook their hands violently to get the ice off. Amazingly, they cleared out the ice within a minute or less, but they could not remove it from their hair and eyebrows.

"Open the door!" called Anna.

"We're fine!" Jonara called back.

"Then why the door be locked?" Anna called. "I heard something go boom, now open the door. I have the key somewhere, and I will open it if I have to. Jonara—your grandmother will be unhappy if I tell her about this. You gonna open the door?"

"Okay, okay," Jonara called back.

Jonara opened the door despite being unable to remove the ice from herself and Cerafina. Cerafina rushed to close the window as Anna entered the room.

"What on the living Earth are you girls doing? And what is in your hair?" Anna asked.

"We were just—" Jonara started, but Anna touched Jonara's hair and spoke.

"This is ice. Ice in your hair," Anna said to Jonara. "Cerafina, come over here. Yes, you have ice in hair too. What is this mischief?"

"We were, uh, we were..." Jonara trailed.

"And what you be doing by the window, Cerafina?" Anna asked.

"Nothing," Cerafina lied.

She stood in such a way as to block the window from Anna's view.

"Let me see," Anna said, but as Anna stepped to the side around Cerafina, Cerafina counter-stepped to block Anna again.

"Do not be difficult, Cerafina. I know your mother and where you live. Now stand still!" Anna commanded.

Anna grabbed Cerafina's shoulders and moved her to the side. Anna stepped to the window, opened it, and looked outside.

"Where did all that ice come from?" Anna asked. "Did you girls get into the basement freezer? Well?"

"We...just...were playing music...and..." Jonara started.

Anna's wonderings about the ice faded when she saw Geneva's viol leaning next to a chair.

"What is Miss Geneva's viol doing out? That should be locked up! No one is allowed to disturb it!" Anna said with a fit.

Anna walked partway from the window to the viol and in doing so stood next to the table with the casserole bowl.

"Which one of you girls was using it?!" Anna demanded with a stern finger—a finger that alternated between pointing at Jonara and pointing at Cerafina.

"I did it," said Cerafina.

"No, you can't take the blame," said Jonara.

"Then you're both in trouble!" Anna said with a mighty fist-pounding into the table.

The casserole bowl jumped up in response.

"I just wanted to learn to play it!" said Jonara, who was hiding behind Cerafina a little.

"The viol," Anna pounded with her fist, "is not to be touched," she pounded on the table again, "or played," she pounded more, "or disturbed in any way!" she finished with an especially forceful pounding on the table.

The vibrations carried through the room, shook the casserole lid loose from the ceiling, and sent it crashing down on Anna's skull. The collision rendered her unconscious, and she fell limp to the floor. Jonara and Cerafina rushed to catch her as best they could. Jonara missed Anna but managed to catch the lid as it careened off Anna's head. Anna's body trapped Cerafina against the floor.

"Help, help!" Cerafina called to Jonara.

"Okay, okay," Jonara replied.

Jonara set the lid on the table and helped free Cerafina.

"Is she hurt?" Jonara asked.

Cerafina took a look at her and checked her pulse.

"No, just unconscious," said Cerafina.

"We can't leave her here," said Jonara. "Help me drag her to the couch."

The two girls did just that—they dragged Anna to the living room and struggled mightily to place her on the couch, doing so by first lifting her head, her torso and arms, and following with her legs. Bits of ice fell from the girls' hair in the struggle, and they picked up the fallen ice on the way back to the music room.

"What happened to our connection with the diary?" Jonara asked as the girls tossed the ice out the window and worked the rest of the ice free from their hair.

"You're asking me? I don't know. I didn't invent these magic gadgets," Cerafina replied.

"Nanna Geneva gave Mommy the Water Ruby," said Jonara.

"Yeah, the one in 2006," Cerafina added.

"And we were using the diary to travel into 2006," Jonara continued.

"Along with the viol and Water Ruby," Cerafina added again.

"The Water Ruby of today—2023," Jonara said.

"Could have been a bad mix," said Cerafina.

"Then we can't use the Water Ruby again, at least not for going back in time," said Jonara. "Look what it did with everything!"

"Yeah—that was like an explosion!"

"It was an explosion!" Jonara said.

"We can use it if we don't come in contact with the other Water Ruby of 2006," said Cerafina.

"But how can we do that? Nanna Geneva gave it to Mommy in the Elrod 402. How can I find out what happened in the Elrod 402 if she has the Water Ruby? It'll mix badly with the Water Ruby here," Jonara explained.

"I guess we're out of luck—unless we can skip the Water Ruby—"

"—and use the viol with the diary only," said Jonara.

"How can that work? The viol only works with the future," said Cerafina.

"I know, I'm trying to think," said Jonara.

"The Water Ruby was our little road between the viol and the diary, because the diary isn't here," said Cerafina.

"Then we need to get the diary and bring it back here," said Jonara.

"Except you're grounded," said Cerafina.

"I know."

"I could ride my bike over there and get it, but I'll need the key to the trunk," Cerafina offered.

"Maybe Anna knows where a spare is—" Jonara started.

"Too late, she's knocked out!"

"Oops, you're right. Help me look for the key! Where would it be, I wonder?"

"In the kitchen most likely. At my house, we keep an emergency set of keys in a drawer," Cerafina replied.

Jonara and Cerafina searched through the kitchen cupboards and drawers.

"I know there's a set somewhere," said Jonara.

Anna stirred in the living room. She did not get up, but she moaned—half-consciously—about staying out of the cookies.

"That's it!" said Jonara.

Jonara removed the head of a duck-shaped cookie jar. Inside, she found a variety of items—paperclips, golfing pencils, golf tees, string, and at the bottom she found it—the extra set of keys.

"Here," Jonara whispered to Cerafina. "Don't let anyone see you."

It was this way then. Cerafina tied one of the strings to the keychain such that it formed a necklace. Around her neck she threw this keychain necklace, kissed Jonara on the cheek goodbye, and exited Geneva's house. She jumped atop her bicycle and rode off to the hospital parking lot where she had visited less than twenty-four hours earlier. Cerafina pedaled with what speed she could muster, dodged a few cars on the way, and arrived in the hospital parking lot—badly out of breath.

Finding Geneva's car was not difficult. Images from the journey with Jonara through the Moissan Ruby to the car trunk burned fresh in her mind, and in a quasi-daydreamish state, she applied the brakes on her bicycle and stopped short of running the front wheel into the car's left rear corner.

Cerafina jumped off her bicycle and engaged the kickstand. She removed the keychain necklace from around her neck and sorted through the keys in search of the correct trunk key, but which one to choose? Before she could try one, something electrocuted her outside left thigh. She jumped with a start. The electrocution stopped. She looked around—nothing. The electrocution repeated. She swatted the shock point on her thigh and realized there was something in her pocket causing the discomfort. Reaching into her pocket, she retrieved a little black plastic device. With relief, Cerafina laughed at her senselessness.

"Hello?" she said as she flipped open her cell phone.

"Are you there yet?" Jonara said on the other end.

"Yeah. Hey you, you scared me," said Cerafina.

"Huh?"

"My cell phone was on vibrate mode. I thought something was shocking my leg."

"That happens to me all the time," said Jonara. "Did you open the trunk?"

"No. I'm looking for the right key."

"Try them all," said Jonara.

"I will if I don't get any more interruptions!" Cerafina said. "Wait a minute."

"Is this your car?" an approaching security guard asked Cerafina, knowing full well she wasn't old enough to drive or own a car.

"No, it belongs to—"

"Breaking into a car is a serious crime," he said.

"I'm not breaking in. I left something in the trunk. This is my...my...mother's car," Cerafina blurted.

"Way to go," Jonara said sarcastically on the cell phone.

"Who's your friend?" the guard asked.

"Friend?" Cerafina asked, hiding the cell phone behind her back. "What friend?"

"The one on your cell phone," said the guard. "Give that to me."

Cerafina closed the phone to terminate the call before the guard was able to grab it from her.

"Very clever closing the phone like that," he said.

"Can I have my phone back?" Cerafina asked.

"Not until you explain what you're doing here," he said.

"I told you, I left something in the trunk. I'm looking for the right key to open it," Cerafina said.

"Shouldn't you be in school, young lady?"

"My school is closed—there's a strike. I left my book in the trunk."

"You're here with your mother then?" he asked, looking suspiciously at her bicycle.

"No. I live around the block. I biked over to get my book."

"What is your mother doing here?" he asked.

"She's visiting her daught...my sister. Yeah, my sister is having a baby," Cerafina said.

"Oh really! And is your friend also your sister?" he asked.

Cerafina grinned in nervous laughter, but before she could spin more tales, her cell phone rang.

"I'll get that," she said, but the guard prevented her.

"Hmmm. Someone named Jonara Pindus is calling. What do you suppose she would say if I asked her the same questions?" the guard asked.

"Ah...uh...oh..." Cerafina stumbled.

The security guard flipped the phone open to make the connection with Jonara. Jonara's voice carried through the air.

"Cerafina, Cerafina? Why did you hang up on me? Did you open my great-grandmother's trunk yet? Hurry up! Cerafina Vagatti, you answer me right now!"

"Cerafina can't answer you now," said the guard into the phone.

"Who's this?" Jonara asked. "Where's Cerafina?"

"She's going to be a little busy," he said and closed the cell phone.

"So what does your friend call you? Grandma Cerafina?" the guard asked Cerafina.

"I, uh, wait! I can explain everything," Cerafina said.

"Maybe you can explain everything inside!" he said.

The security guard dragged Cerafina and the bicycle into the hospital security office. Jonara called Cerafina's cell phone, but the guard responded by powering off the phone.

"Cerafina!" Jonara called into her unconnected cell phone.

Jonara looked around in the living room. Anna awoke, wondered what happened, and asked why she couldn't remember anything that day. Realizing her good fortune, Jonara said she didn't know, claiming that she, Jonara, walked into the living room and found her there sleeping. Anna felt badly for sleeping on the job but wondered where the bump on her head came from. Jonara promised not to tell Eva that Anna had slacked off, and Anna thanked her.

But Jonara wasn't satisfied with her current situation. Everyone around her was in trouble—her mother, grandmother, and now Cerafina. Should she try to help her friend? Should she attempt to retrieve the diary? Would Anna let her? There were too many questions to answer, and too little time to think about what to do. Jonara sat on the couch, buried her chin in her hands, stared at a painting on the wall across the living room, and pondered her future.

CHAPTER 4

Calico Shepherd

2023 Oct 4, Wed Afnoon. Corpus Christi, Texas.
2006 Nov 18, Sat. Elrod 402. Portland, Oregon.

"I'm all alone," Jonara said to herself. "Who can I turn to? Mommy is in the hospital, Daddy is with her, and Grandma is sick in the hospital too. Cerafina—oh why did you have to get caught? What about Allie? No, she's still in school. Anna, can you—"

But Anna was no longer in the living room. Jonara left the living room and found Anna sitting in her bedroom with an ice pack on her head.

"Anna, can you help me? I need to—" Jonara started.

"Oh child, don't you see I have a headache? Ow, my head hurts!" Anna said.

"But Anna, I just need you to—" Jonara said.

"Shh," Anna said. "It throbs so much. Someone with a little hammer is beating my head when you speak. Please—shush."

"Anna, please!" Jonara begged.

"Go do something, Jonara, and do it quietly. Oh my poor aching head!"

Jonara left Anna to her misery. She walked back to the music room and looked at the viol and Moissan Ruby. Perhaps she could make the connection to the past without Cerafina. She had wanted to make the attempt with Anna, but Anna wouldn't hear her out.

"Maybe it's better Anna doesn't know—she might not understand," said Jonara.

Jonara filled the casserole bowl with water as before, placed the lid on (which had not shattered), and played a few notes on the viol. The water remained calm, and the Moissan Ruby emanated no light and gave no hint of activity.

Jonara felt no feedback from the Moissan Ruby. She angled the viol away from the ruby and reattempted to see the future as she had when she and Cerafina first played the viol together.

The notes came out awkwardly. The room filled with the squawk- and scraping-sounds of two cats fighting. Jonara's ears were annoyed by her suddenly bad viol playing, and she had to stop.

"It's impossible," she said. "Even the viol and Moissan Ruby have left me."

Jonara felt the entire world had abandoned her. Trying to hold onto the present with memories of the past, she thought of her dreams—dreams of her mother: going from church to church in search of her faith, in a special friendship with her father, in a stressful relationship with Sheila, and invoking her ultimate tool for dealing with problems—running.

In an effort to follow her mother's running steps, Jonara burst from the music room, through the back door, and out of the house into the yard. She paused for a moment and looked around—did anyone see her? No, even Anna didn't know she'd broken the restriction and left the house.

"This is it," she thought. "I'll run just like Mommy. Maybe then I'll find the answer."

Jonara sprinted down the sidewalk toward the hospital. She thought back to her mother's jogs in 2006 and imagined she was with her. But somehow, Jonara couldn't connect with the earth, the sky, or the surroundings as her mother had done. Jonara looked around and wondered if anyone noticed her. Did anyone know or care what she was doing?

Sprinting caught up with Jonara's heart and lungs. Her legs slowed as her oxygen-deprived body cried in pain. Jonara exhaled heavily against the surrounding air, and her heart beat too quickly to be happy. She tried to pace herself into a regular jog, but it was too late—every muscle was too overworked to continue. Her gait slowed to a labored walk, and on seeing a park bench, her adrenaline levels dropped. Her walk became a desperate hobble to the bench where she plopped down in frustration, exhaustion, and despair. With no energy left to contain herself, she broke into tears.

The world continued its business, though Jonara didn't realize it. Despite passerby pedestrians, joggers, birds, and cumulus clouds, Jonara remained on the bench with blurry tears and sore muscles as her only companions. She did not notice, but something wet touched her leg. Then it sniffed. She turned to look, and a small dog on a long leash barked at her as if she were some invader from another world.

"Easy boy," said the owner.

Jonara scooched along the bench to avoid the small yapper, but the canine jumped and barked vigorously—jerking its master toward Jonara with each tug of its leash.

"No, leave that kid alone. Over here!" the owner said, but the dog did not obey.

The owner yanked on the leash, the dog yelped, and the crisis ended with owner and dog moving along. Jonara watched as the dog continued leading the master along the sidewalk. As the two passed nearly out of sight, the dog sniffed a tree, lifted its leg, and urinated on the trunk.

"That's all I am to the world, a kid to be barked at," Jonara whispered to herself.

She buried her face in her folded arms and reached in her mind to those images of her mother when she was young— running freely in the woods without exhaustion, without restriction, and without some yapping dog disturbing her.

Tap, tap, tap!

Jonara looked at the other end of the bench and saw a squirrel breaking open a nut. She held out her hand to the squirrel. It gave her a suspicious look, placed the nut back in its mouth, and scampered to the ground. In doing so, the nut fell from its mouth. Another squirrel came along and fought for the nut. The first squirrel regained the nut in its mouth and ran around in circles while the second squirrel followed. After a few go-rounds, the squirrels disappeared up a tree.

Bits of outer layers from the nut remained on the bench. Jonara brushed them off and caught a fingernail on old, peeling, bench paint. The flake cut under her nail a bit before detaching from the bench and falling over the edge to the concrete pad below, where it fell into a crack. Jonara looked at the concrete pad, the rusty iron-wrought bench frame ascending from the pad, the warped wooden seat and backboard attached to the frame, and the layers of peeling green paint on the bench. Jonara felt the entire bench construction from concrete to peeling paint was a failing—much as her family was undergoing—a failing. The solid concrete foundation of Great-Grandmother Geneva, the iron strength of her Grandma Eva, the natural support of her mother Evanita—all of these things formed the basis for Jonara's life. But now in this moment of solitude, she felt abandoned by the failing family. She was the peeling paint, and she was falling into the cracks of failure—forces she did not fully understand. It was a wild idea to be sure, and Jonara knew it, but the images were there nevertheless, and she buried her head in her crossed arms to shake the image from her mind.

Jonara's face remained lost in the time and space of her arms. More tapping on the bench. Jonara ignored it. She was tired of squirrels, dogs, peeling paint, and everything.

"Aren't you interested in this?" a familiar voice asked.

Jonara looked up and saw someone tapping a book on the bench.

"Cerafina!" Jonara leapt up to say.

Cerafina had been tapping the diary on the bench. She had a big grin on her face in response to Jonara's excitement.

"Oh Cerafina! I missed you!" Jonara said with hugs, cheek kisses, and a little impromptu dancing.

"I missed you too!" Cerafina replied with a laugh and song in her voice. "Were you going to rescue me?"

"I was, I was! I didn't know how I was going to do it, but I wanted to get you away from that mean person who answered your phone. Where's your bicycle?"

"It's over there behind the tree, silly! I rode back as soon as the security guard released me," said Cerafina.

"So that's what happened!"

"Yeah. He caught me breaking in...well, not really breaking in...trying to open the trunk to your Nanna Geneva's car. That was him on my cell phone. He was going to hold me all day! I finally decided I had to get help from either your grandma or dad," Cerafina explained.

"I hope you didn't tell Grandma Eva," said Jonara.

"Of course not. I know she doesn't want you to have the diary. But your dad is cool. I told the guard about him, and your dad stopped by and told a story about the book being important for your school. He kept explaining and explaining with all kinds of expensive words the guard didn't understand, so the guard gave up and let me go. Your dad showed me the right key—he even opened the trunk for me. He couldn't drive me back or anything. He said something about having to stay with your mother and making sure your grandma would stay in the hospital and get her thyroid treated."

"Wow!" Jonara said. "Wow!"

"Is that all you can say? I'm tired from all this," Cerafina laughed.

"You're tired? I ran all the way...I couldn't decide what to do...hey, gimme a ride back to Nanna's house," Jonara begged.

"Okay. Luckily my bike has a banana seat. Hop on and we'll go back together."

With that, Cerafina pedaled Jonara back to Geneva's house. Anna had not noticed Jonara's absence but was instead watching a soap opera in her bedroom with an ice pack soothing her head injury. The girls returned to the music room with the diary and anticipated an easy return to the past.

"How did water get in this bowl?" Cerafina asked. "Did you try connecting like we did before?"

"Yeah."

"Did it work?"

"Nope. Just a bunch of bad viol music."

"Well okay, now we have the diary. And I bet we can connect from the viol to the past without using the Water Ruby," said Cerafina.

"And then we won't have to worry about Water-Ruby feedback," Jonara added.

"We better do something with the Water Ruby to make sure it doesn't interfere," said Cerafina.

"I'll empty out the water," Jonara said.

"Better than that—can we put it somewhere out of sight—maybe even in a different room? It might pick up vibes from the viol," said Cerafina.

"Maybe it picked up vibes from before, and that made it fall from upstairs," suggested Jonara.

"Then where are we going to hide it?" Cerafina asked without expecting an answer.

"So it won't get in the way?" added Jonara.

"Exactly!"

"Hmmm. Well, it seems to need light and vibration," said Jonara.

"So we need to find a dark place with no vibrations," said Cerafina.

"But how do we block vibrations?" Jonara asked.

"Fight fire with fire," said Cerafina. "Give it other vibrations to keep it busy."

Jonara's eyes opened wide, and she grinned.

"You have an idea?"

"Yeah," Jonara said.

She left the music room and returned with a king-sized pillow.

"A pillow doesn't have vibrations," said Cerafina.

Jonara picked up the Moissan Ruby but dropped it immediately.

"Ow!" Jonara said.

"What's wrong?"

"It shocked me!" Jonara said.

"Like before?" Cerafina asked.

"Yeah," Jonara said.

Using the plastic tongs, Jonara took the Moissan Ruby and placed it inside the pillow stuffing. Cerafina followed as Jonara went into the basement, squeezed the pillow into the dryer, set the dryer to air-only mode with no time limit, and pressed the Start button. The dryer spun with the pillow inside. There were no sounds to indicate anything was in the dryer as one might hear with loose coins, but Jonara and Cerafina knew what was in there.

"I hope this works," said Cerafina.

The two returned to the music room. Cerafina returned the casserole bowl, water, and lid to the kitchen. Jonara sat with the viol and placed the diary over her right thigh like a dish-towel. It was time. Cerafina took her place in the chair next to Jonara as before and pulled part of the diary onto her left thigh to spare the binding from stress. She placed her hands on Jonara's waist and shoulder, and Jonara drew the first bow stroke across the viol. The two girls read:

"'We said goodbye to Evanita in the Elrod 402, assured by Ms. Fronka Nordekter that my granddaughter is in the best of care.'"

Jonara drew the bowstring across the viol. Her recent failure at playing the viol by herself left her with a taste of anxiety and concern. That taste soon faded as Cerafina's warmth and affec-tion melted away any last worries. As the viol strings vibrated, the surroundings blurred. Jonara learned to adjust her left fin-ger position on the neck and coordinate this with bowstring placement and movement to guide Cerafina's and her journey back in time. The result was not as immediate as with the inter-cession of the Moissan Ruby. When the Moissan Ruby was em-ployed, it possessed a more direct link to the girls' thoughts—relaying immediate feedback and so allowing Jonara to jump quickly back into time precisely where she meant to go.

The connection between the viol and diary was not so easy. The viol had a tendency to mix multiple images together, some-times all in the past, sometimes part past and part present. Jonara's and Cerafina's first experience with this phenomenon took the girls back to the restaurant where Jonara had eaten with her father earlier that morning. Yet the girls jumped to an-other restaurant in Portland where Jonara and her father ate two weeks prior. Several seconds later, the girls witnessed older versions of Jonara and Cerafina eating breakfast with Jonara's father. Jonara stopped the bow and paused.

"I don't understand," Jonara said to Cerafina back in the music room. "Last night I dreamt everything with the diary, and I didn't need the viol."

"But you were dreaming," said Cerafina.

"And now I'm awake, is that it?" Jonara asked. "But I want us to go back to the Elrod 402 like we did before."

"Maybe we need to be dreaming, or almost dreaming," said Cerafina.

"Huh?"

"Like before, when we first played the viol and saw ourselves older," said Cerafina. "If the music is good enough, then maybe—"

"Hey! My viol playing isn't that bad," said Jonara.

"Jonara. I like you a lot. But that viol playing of yours—unless it comes with a lot of help—either from me or the Water Ruby—well—it won't let anyone relax or fall sleep!"

Jonara threw the bow across the music room in frustration.

"Jonara!"

"Well?" Jonara said. "It's the bow's fault. It must be."

"Jonara Pindus—you gotta take care of musical instruments and equipment," Cerafina explained. She retrieved the bow and sat next to Jonara again. "This bow is made of pernambuco. That's wood from a special tree in South America, sometimes called brazilwood, but this is from the heart of a brazilwood tree."

"So?"

"So?! You can't even buy bows like this anymore. The tree is endangered. It's illegal to cut down or sell brazilwood. Most bows today are made of carbon fiber. This bow is an antique—it might be worth more than the viol!"

"If it's so great, how come it doesn't work?" Jonara asked.

"Hmmm. Okay, I think we need to do like before. Now I know you want to direct the journey, but until you improve... here, hold the bow. Good, now I'll put my right hand on yours, I'll put my left on your waist, and the diary stays on our legs. Just relax as we did before, Jonara. We're like sisters, remember? Relax, Jonara, relax."

Cerafina placed the bow across the diary. Jonara reached for it, but as she placed her right hand on the bow, Cerafina clasped Jonara's hand and bow. She held them flat against the diary.

"Sisters. Think sisterly love," Cerafina said.

Cerafina did not release her hand until Jonara's jittery anxiety slowed, shrank, and melted into an inner peace. From this inner peace, her muscles and flesh felt slightly numb and warm. Her warmth grew and seemed to exceed her bodily boundaries where it intersected with Cerafina and the diary. Cerafina felt Jonara's warmth and reciprocated. She gave Jonara a squeeze around the left waist, which in turn squeezed the last of Jonara's frustration from her body. The two lifted the bow to the viol and while drawing the first notes read the next diary passage:

"'Evanita is rooming with an experienced resident who will act as her big sister and mentor in campus life. Her legal name is Fiori Sheppe, but her Elrod name is Calico Shepherd.'"

Jonara and Cerafina appeared on the Elrod 402 campus next to the front wheels of Whalejet. As Cerafina reacquainted herself with the surroundings, Jonara observed Eva's car leaving the campus for Elrod Road.

"There," Jonara pointed.

Cerafina turned in time to see the last of Eva's car departing.

"They must be moving Eve Carson from intake to her assigned jet," Cerafina said.

"Please, call Mommy by her real name," said Jonara.

"Your mommy, I mean."

"Evanita is her name," said Jonara. "But how do you know what 'they' will do next?"

"My older brother was in juvenile once," Cerafina said. "And every juvenile has an intake unit. That's where they first go. It's temporary. Then they get moved. That's permanent. Well, sort of permanent. Until they get released. Anyway, that's how I know."

"What did he do? Your brother?"

"He stole a boat from Mr. Chuck Harbuck. Mr. Harbuck is one of Mamma's competitors in the shrimping business," Cerafina explained. "And he had a drinking party on the boat. Everyone was underage. Him too. Oh yes, one of his 'friends' was smoking something illegal. But that's how parties are— everyone's a friend until everyone's in trouble. Then the one holding the party gets all the blame."

"Bummer!"

"Look," said Cerafina. "There's your mother—Ms. Evanita Carreña. See, I know your mother's name. I was just kidding with the Eve thing."

"I don't like the Eve thing," said Jonara. "And no jokes about this being the Trap of Eve."

"I would never," Cerafina said. "But we better jump in that van—they're leaving!"

The two girls ran after the moving van but had trouble boarding it.

"What's the matter?" Cerafina asked. "Run faster!"

"I can't. And I'm getting tired!"

"You can't be. This isn't real."

"It's real to me! I gotta walk," Jonara said.

"No, you're almost there. Reach for the van!"

Cerafina urged Jonara to reach for the back bumper, in fact, Cerafina pushed Jonara. Jonara reached out but missed, fell into the gravel dirt, and tripped up Cerafina, sending both girls into a tumbling roll. Both girls sat up coughing out dust and dirt.

"That was mean!" Jonara said.

"I don't understand! This is supposed to be a dream," Cerafina mused. "We should be able to do whatever we want, like goddesses."

"Well we can't. I got split into two girls back at Barnseed Baptist—Victorian and Modern, remember? And I had to spin my two parts back together," Jonara explained.

"Strange."

"We'll have to be careful," Jonara said. "And don't push me in the back again."

"I won't, I won't," Cerafina promised. "Look—that van is going through the doublegate."

The girls stood up and first walked then jogged down the gravel road to the doublegate—a gate for each of the two barbed-wire perimeters. The van had stopped briefly for an inspection but not long enough to allow Jonara and Cerafina to catch up. The two were able to see, however, the van driving to Oranjet.

"I wonder if Mommy will go into that orange jet?" Jonara asked Cerafina as the two approached the doublegate.

"She was convicted of manslaughter, right?" Cerafina asked between breaths.

"Yeah."

"She'll probably get Redjet."

The van dropped off a security guard and two girls before driving to Aldojet.

"Now the van is at the yellow one," said Jonara.

"We're almost at the doublegate," puffed Cerafina.

"Another two girls and a guard," said Jonara. "Now it's going to that striped jet—the blue one."

"Bloomjet."

"And another two girls and a guard," Jonara continued.

"An Oxian. Look, here's the doublegate," Cerafina said.

The doublegate was closed, but the girls found they could pass through it, though with some difficulty.

"That wasn't easy," Jonara said to Cerafina on the inside of the doublegate.

"The steel wire...I thought it was going to strangle me," Cerafina said.

"Me too. Look, the van is at Redjet."

Redjet. It was the last passenger stop for the van. A security guard helped Evanita hop from the van to the ground. She stood there on crutches while the guard had some last words with the van driver.

"Quick—we can catch up with Mommy," Jonara said.

The girls made a run for Redjet. Evanita hobbled up the stairs to the main door, and as she reached the top, Jonara and

Cerafina caught up with her. Jonara tried to speak to Cerafina, but Jonara was too out of breath to make sense.

"We...have to...don't...ok?" Jonara puffed.

"Huh?" Cerafina puffed back.

"The Ruby. Mommy. Don't touch her," Jonara gasped.

"Wait a minute. Gotta catch my breath," Cerafina said.

Jonara and Cerafina followed Evanita and Ox-Three into Redjet and along the hallway. Evanita was greeted with suspicious stares from some girls and hostile stares from others. She shook a little in fear, and her Moissan Ruby scanned around her. Jonara and Cerafina could see the effects of the Ruby distorting the air like a lighthouse. They maneuvered behind Ox-Three and ducked several times to avoid being detected.

"Did you see that?" Jonara asked, now that she had caught her breath.

"Much better," said Cerafina.

"What?!"

"No squeal or feedback. We're safe," said Cerafina.

"Safe?!" Jonara replied. "That thing might see us."

"What's wrong with that? You never worried before when your dad had it."

"That was before. Somehow this is different," Jonara said.

"I think you're afraid," Cerafina said.

The two continued following Ox-Three and Evanita to the dorm rooms.

"Afraid? Me?" Jonara asked.

"Yeah you," Cerafina said.

"Of what?"

"Of connecting with your mother."

"That's ridiculous!" Jonara said.

"Then go hug her," Cerafina said. "I dare you."

"No, I shouldn't," Jonara said.

"Chicken."

"It might scare her! Maybe later."

"Humph! Maybe I'll hug her," Cerafina grinned.

"You better not. I get to hug my mommy before you do," Jonara warned.

"Jonara Pindus—you're so easy to tease. Of course you should hug your mother first."

"Don't tease me like that. I'm already teased out!"

"Okay, okay," Cerafina assured her.

"This is your dorm room, Eve," Ox-Three said to Evanita while placing Evanita's luggage on the floor. "As you can see, the room numbers are posted outside the doors. Yours is R201. You were trained at intake, so you know the rules and schedule. Dinner is at six—if you forget, you're out of luck until breakfast. You have the rest of the afternoon to yourself, but you're restricted to Redjet until dinner. Clear?"

"Yeah," Evanita sighed. "I understand."

"Good. Stay out of trouble, and you'll do fine. Good luck!" Ox-Three said, and with that she checked with a few other residents before leaving Redjet.

Evanita stood in the doorway on her crutches. The room was disorganized with random bits of clothing, newspapers, and books scattered about. One corner held a wooden stand with a coffee machine on top and various coffee supplies below. Evanita used her crutches to clear a path for her to hobble.

"What a mess!" Jonara said. "No wonder Mommy is always making me clean up my room."

"I've seen Leo's room this bad," said Cerafina. "You remember my brother, Leo?"

"When he was in juvenile?"

"No, I never saw his room there. But at home he lives like a pig," said Cerafina.

"Look—the others are coming this way," said Jonara.

"The other residents? Yeah, but why are they walking so slowly?"

"They're moving at sneak speed," said Jonara.

Evanita did the best she could to pull her luggage into the room. She looked for a place to sit and rest her legs, but the room was simply too cluttered for her to make much sense of where to sit. She looked at the bunk beds—the upper bunk was the only clean spot, and the bed was made.

"I can't climb up there," Evanita muttered.

Evanita looked at the lower bunk for a place to sit. She picked up a newspaper from the lower bed and placed it on a nearby desk. Next, she picked up a book. With passing curiosity, she opened the book and thumbed through the pages. She gasped when she realized every page had been doodled upon. Strong, forceful and repeated lines circled words and connected them together as if some mad person had become overly obsessed with connecting seemingly random words together.

Evanita set the book aside and proceeded to move some clothes out of the way when she came across a multicolored dust mop, but the mop was not attached to a pole.

"Some old mop head," she said.

Unknown to Evanita, an audience had gathered around the doorway. Cerafina and Jonara were forced to enter the room to maintain their view of Evanita as the crowd quietly pushed its way in—not caring about whose view it blocked.

Evanita yanked at the mop head and attempted to throw it aside, but it was attached to something heavy. A loud squawk filled the room and startled everyone in attendance. Evanita jumped back, and to her amazement, a large person wearing the mop head jumped out of bed, dove at Evanita, and pinned her to the wall with one arm across her torso and the hand from her other arm planting Evanita's head against the wall.

"A mop head am I?" said the large woman who'd been resting on the lower bunk.

The crowd cheered. Several chanted things like "Beat her up," "New girl needs a whupping," and "Go, Calico, go."

"You're hurting me," Evanita grimaced with her eyes closed.

"Mommy!" Jonara screamed, and she moved to help Evanita, but Cerafina held her back.

"No, wait! Remember, this has already happened. If you interfere..." Cerafina cautioned.

"Oh I'm hurting you?" Calico teased. "She says I'm hurting her. Hurting her!"

"You are!" Evanita mustered.

"Who was hurting me? Going through my things? And pulling my hair!" Calico said.

"I didn't know it was you," Evanita said.

"That's right, honey, because you don't even know me. And you don't want to know me," Calico said.

"I'm sorry!" Evanita pleaded.

"Whatchya gonna do, Cal?" one of the girls asked.

"What's your name, little rabbit?" Calico asked Evanita.

"Evanita...Carreña."

Calico thumped Evanita on the forehead.

"Then you must be in the wrong room," said Calico. "I'm expecting a new roommate, and her name is Eve Carson. Never heard of a Carreña before."

"It's a little town in northern Spain," Evanita tried to say, but Calico put her hand on Evanita's throat.

"We have a comedienne," said Calico. "Let's give a round of applause to our jokester."

Some clapped, others jeered, still others booed and emitted the raspberry sound.

"We don't like comediennes around here," said Calico. "Now before I kick your broken legs and skinny butt to the floor, do you want to restate your name?"

Evanita tried to speak, but she couldn't breathe.

"Hey Cali," said one of the girls, "she can't choke and talk at the same time."

"Well what is this world coming to?" Calico joked. "They don't teach girls like they used to. When I was a kid—"

"She's turning blue, you know," said another girl.

"Humm, so she is. Whatdya think, girls, should I let her breathe?" Calico asked.

One girl clapped.

"Don't get excited or anything," said Calico sarcastically.

More girls clapped.

"I don't know," added Calico. "Seems there isn't much mandate around here—or should I say womandate?"

The girls resounded with strong applause.

"What's your name?" Calico demanded from Evanita while permitting her to breathe a bit.

"Eve...Carson!" Evanita grunted.

Calico released Evanita. Evanita fell to the floor, massaged her neck, and gasped for air. Jonara ran to her mother and hugged her. Jonara was happy that she didn't pass through her mother but disturbed that her mother had been victimized.

"Show's over," Calico announced to the crowd. "Go on now, guess I gotta clean my roommate off the floor."

Calico pulled Evanita to her feet, and now that Evanita's vision returned from being oxygen-deprived, she took a good look at her assailant. Calico had a medium height yet wide stature, a shield-shaped chest, and clubby arms. Her skin was covered with unusual pigment patterns as if someone had brushed on swirls of brown paint. Her face was wide and square. She had one blue eye and her other eye was half green, half yellow. Her hair was full of cowlicks with shocks of white, black, blond, and red hair growing every which way. Calico had a webbed neck—thick cords of flesh running down the sides from her skull to her shoulders.

"There," said Calico as she helped Evanita to her feet. "Well, what are you looking at?"

"Nothing," lied Evanita.

"You got a problem with the way I look?" Calico snapped.

"No, no," Evanita lied again.

Evanita lurched for the door and attempted to hobble down the hallway.

"Guard, guard! Help!" she yelled.

Calico yanked her back into the room, slammed the door shut, sat Evanita in a chair, and dictated to her.

"There'll be none of that here," said Calico.

"You leave Mommy alone," Jonara yelled.

Jonara lunged at Calico to shove her away from Evanita, but Jonara simply passed through Calico's body without interaction.

"Guard!" Evanita yelled again.

Calico slapped Evanita across the jaw.

"Ow! That hurt!" Evanita said.

"That's right—a slap to the jaw hurts, don't it?" Calico said. "Now settle down a minute before you go stirring up this entire jet. We don't need no stupid fights around here."

"When my mama finds out—" Evanita started.

Calico slapped her across the jaw.

"I wanna go home," Evanita whimpered.

"So this is the 'tough' girl I've heard so much about," Calico mused. "Eve Carson. Man killer."

"I'm not Eve Carson. My name is Evanita. Ow!" Evanita cried after receiving another Calican slap.

"This can be a long day or a short day," said Calico. "And it all depends on how well you cooperate. Now do you wanna start cooperating, or are you gonna sit there and keep blabbering nonsense?"

Evanita was going to say something, but she held her mouth closed.

"That's better," Calico said. "Let's go over some ground rules. You follow?"

Evanita nodded her head, "Yes."

"Good. My role name is Calico Shepherd. Yours is Eve Carson. Agree?" Calico asked.

Evanita nodded again.

"Good. You're learning. This is my room. You're my new roommate. I sleep on the bottom bunk, and you sleep on the top."

Evanita looked at her legs and looked back at Calico as if to say something.

"You're wondering how you're gonna climb up the top bunk with those bum legs. There's a ladder. See? We're all friendly around here," Calico grinned.

"What kind of freak is this?" Jonara asked.

"I've never seen someone like that before. Maybe it's a costume," Cerafina said.

"No wisecracks about my looks, see? And I know what you're thinking, that I'm some sort of freak. There," Calico said, slapping Evanita across the jaw. "That's for thinking I'm a freak."

"I'm not, I'm not," Evanita sobbed, and she fell into tears.

"Better get used to tough girls around here, O Man Killer," said Calico. "All the tough girls are in Redjet. But as for my looks, I'm what you might call a hybrid Turner girl. The Barians call it mixed Turner's syndrome."

"What's that?" Jonara asked.

"Beats me," Cerafina replied.

"I got mixed chromosomes—some are XX, others are XO. Look it up sometime when you get library time. The way I figure, I'm blessed. I got the body of a woman with the power of a man. Someday I'll have kids, and if they give me trouble, I'll beat the snot out of them 'till they're old enough for the nursing home."

"Does it...hurt?" Evanita asked cautiously.

Calico laughed.

"Does what hurt? I'm better than a straight XX woman. I've got cellular genetic diversity—when I catch a cold, only some of my cells are affected. Takes a day to get over it. My skin is thick and tough to cut. My bones don't break easily. Where a straight XX woman is like concrete, I'm like concrete and steel. I may crack, but I don't shatter. My XXs and XOs are woven in with each other—where one fails, the other takes over. When XXs go bad in a straight woman, they all go bad. Ever been on a frozen pond?"

"No," said Evanita.

"You get a freshly frozen pond, half an inch thick, and step on it. What happens?" Calico asked.

"It breaks?"

"You get a loud pop. Then you realize a long crack has developed clear across the pond quicker than you can see. And you're sinking in the pond. Ever been on a pond where an ice flow is frozen together?" Calico asked.

"No."

"A crack forms in one little place. Doesn't travel across the pond. There's no uniformity to multiply the failure point. And no one goes sinking in the pond. I'm an ice flow. You're virgin ice. Get it?"

"Yeah," Evanita said slowly. "Is that why your name—"

"You making fun of my name?" Calico asked.

"No, but no," Evanita said quickly.

"Calico. Like a calico cat. Don't I look like a calico cat?"

"Yeah, a little," said Evanita.

"Is a calico cat a freak?"

"No."

"Of course it ain't. If you can like a calico cat, you can like Calico Shepherd. Shake?" Calico said, offering her hand to Evanita in request of a handshake.

"Yeah, okay," said Evanita, shaking Calico's hand.

Calico had a strong handshake and squeezed Evanita's hand into pain.

"Ow! Let go!" Evanita begged.

"Heh, heh, heh," Calico grinned.

She released Evanita's hand. Evanita pulled her hand to her mouth and soothed it.

"What do you want from me?" Evanita asked.

"First, never—and I mean never—interrupt me when I'm taking a nap. This is my first day off in three weeks, and I intend to enjoy it," Calico explained.

"I was just—"

"Second—I ain't the sympathy department! Save it for the army. But if you've got an issue, I'm the complaint department. I settle problems quickly—usually with my fists," Calico said.

"This is awful," said Jonara.

"Next—one of those desks is yours. Not the one with the books and coffee supplies. And no free coffee. If I'm in a good mood—which today I ain't—I might offer you a cup."

"Coffee tastes bad anyway," said Jonara.

"Calico seems to like it," said Cerafina.

"Well Calico is weird," returned Jonara.

"Good thing she can't hear you."

"I'd teach her a lesson," bragged Jonara.

"Hah!" Cerafina said.

"Hah yourself."

"I like coffee," Cerafina said. "I wonder what kind she has?"

"Terrible, I'd imagine," Jonara said. "All coffee is terrible, including Calico's."

"You know, she could stuff you in a hamper while clipping her toenails," said Cerafina.

"I bet she needs pruning shears for that," said Jonara.

"Girl! What a mouth you have," said Cerafina.

"The empty closet is yours," said Calico. "Better put your clothes away. I'm not going to spend my afternoon tripping over your suitcases."

"Even though she has books and newspapers on the floor everywhere," said Jonara. "What a brat!"

"Careful!" said Cerafina. "Your vibes might carry into the past."

"When you're done putting your clothes away, you can start cleaning the bathroom," Calico said.

"I just got here!" Evanita protested.

"You questioning me?" Calico asked. "Do you want a long day or a short day?"

"Short day," said Evanita.

"Then do as I say," Calico said. "After you clean the bathroom, you can pick up stuff off the floor and vacuum. Don't worry, I'll pick up the books and put them away. I don't want you messing that up. Just pile the newspapers in the corner and put my clothes in the hamper. When you're done, you can rest until dinnertime. See how nice I am? I'm not gonna make you do my laundry this week—unless you back lip me again. Got it?"

"Yeah," Evanita said reluctantly.

"After dinner, we gotta go over your schedule for tomorrow and the rest of the week," Calico continued. "You do what I say, and you'll have no problems with the staff around here. Yeah, the staff. Did you think I'm giving you all this work just for me? I ain't running the show, dearie!"

Calico exited the dorm room and locked Evanita in. Evanita shook a fist at the closed door and looked up.

"Someone help me," Evanita said in despair. "Please, I need help. Help me through this."

Evanita took a tissue and wiped her wet eyes.

"Mommy, I'm here," said Jonara.

Jonara hugged her mother, and Cerafina soon followed. Both girls felt Evanita's body and how scared she was.

"Is someone here?" Evanita asked, feeling the sudden warmth from the girls.

Evanita's body had been shaking in fear, and the Moissan Ruby activated.

"Mommy, it's me—Jonara. I'm here with my friend, Cerafina. We're here to help."

Evanita wasn't sure, but she thought she heard, "Here to help."

"God? Is that you?" Evanita asked the air.

"No, Mommy, it's me—your daughter—Jonara."

"And me, Cerafina."

"Who are you?" Evanita asked.

Jonara and Cerafina realized Evanita could hear them.

"I told you, Mommy," said Jonara. "It's Jonara and Cerafina."

"That's not funny. Did Calico put you up to this? I'm going to clean the bathroom as soon as I can stand on my crutches," said Evanita.

"It's not a joke, Mommy. We're not prisoners. Calico doesn't know about us," said Jonara.

"Better not push it too far," said Cerafina. "You might scare her more."

"Go bug another new prisoner," said Evanita.

"Find out what Calico is doing," Jonara said to Cerafina. "I'll stay here."

Cerafina agreed and left dorm room R201 in search of Calico.

Evanita stood on her crutches and hobbled to the bathroom. She started by cleaning the sink. As she ran the faucet to rinse the bowl, she dipped her hands in the stream. As she did so, she sensed pipes and water pressure flowing through the Elrod campus. She pulled her hands out of the water, and the extra-sensation left her. Dipping her hands in the water again, she felt the water extending outside the campus to a nearby water tower. For a brief moment, she enjoyed a view of the Portland skyline.

"Mommy, I want to help you," said Jonara.

"The voice has followed me," said Evanita, now feeling a little paranoid.

Evanita looked around but found no evidence of heating vents or speakers that might project these voices. She pulled out the Moissan Ruby and looked at it suspiciously.

"It's how Johnny acted at Page Clinic," Evanita said. "He heard that girl. And at the hospital—he was in my dream. Was this the reason?"

"Yes, Mommy, it's the reason!" said Jonara. "Keep the Water Ruby on—keep it on, and we can talk!"

"I don't know this Little Voice," said Evanita. "It keeps calling me, 'Mommy'. And the water pipe takes me outside. But this little stone doesn't help me remember Mama or Johnny or even Ms. Zyla. It's not working right!"

"I hear talking in there!" bellowed Calico's voice through the door. "That means you're not working. Better hop to it, gimpy, or I'll give you a better reason to limp around."

Evanita cast the stone through the bathroom doorway and across the room where it landed in a mixture of Calico's things. Evanita didn't watch where it landed, but it bounced off bits of junk until it settled at the bottom of a coffeepot.

"Mommy!" Jonara called.

She put her arms around her mother but slipped through as if Evanita weren't there. Jonara called again, but Evanita did not respond. Instead, Evanita returned to cleaning the bathroom.

"You've got to see this," Cerafina said, bursting into the room.

"What?"

"C'mon, you'll see."

Cerafina led Jonara to Redjet's recreation room. Inside, Calico was chatting with two security guards—Ox-Two and Ox-Three.

"Some of the girls like sneaking into the lower storage compartment to escape," Calico said to the guards.

"How?" Ox-Two asked.

"Uh, uh. I don't rat for free," said Calico.

"What's it worth to you?" Ox-Two asked.

"Ten pounds of tobacco," said Calico. "And five pounds of dark chocolate."

"You know tobacco is forbidden," said Ox-Three.

"So is escaping out a jet after hours," said Calico. "Which is the lesser of the evils? And you might as well throw in four pounds of coffee."

"Your terms are going up?" Ox-Two asked.

"Yup. I call it interest on the goods. The longer I wait, the higher the price," Calico said.

"Okay," said Ox-Two. "You'll get your precious tobacco and chocolate."

"Plus the coffee," added Calico.

"And the coffee," Ox-Three said.

"Now where is this escape door?" Ox-Two asked.

"Follow me," Calico replied.

Jonara and Cerafina followed Calico down a hallway to a small utility room.

"There's no door in here," said Ox-Three.

"You have to know where to look," said Calico.

Calico moved a table aside, landed her heel into the corner part of the flooring, and the flooring square popped up.

"There's your door. You'll find another door in the storage compartment that leads outside. That one isn't hidden," Calico smiled.

"You'll have your reward tomorrow," said Ox-Two.

"Tonight," said Calico. "I'm fresh out of tobacco leaf, and I'm gonna enjoy my Sunday morning by the window."

"We don't have to do as you please, you—" Ox-Three started, but Ox-Two held an arm out to Ox-Three to shush her.

"You'll have it. A pleasure doing business with you, Calico," said Ox-Two.

"Likewise."

"We've got to warn Mommy," said Jonara to Cerafina.

"About Calico?"

"Yeah, she's a real narc!"

"Then let's tell her. She has the Water Ruby on. Let's go!" Cerafina urged, dragging Jonara down the hallway in a running speed.

"Wait, wait!" Jonara called, leaning back against Cerafina's run.

"What's the matter?"

"She took the Water Ruby off," said Jonara.

"What?!"

"Yeah, she did it. Threw it across the room."

"Then how do we—" Cerafina started.

"I don't know. Maybe she'll...maybe someone...I don't know," Jonara said.

Jonara and Cerafina made several more attempts to communicate with Evanita, but none succeeded. Evanita resigned herself to cleaning the bathroom. The job took two hours in her condition, and yet Calico never returned during that time. At moments while cleaning, Evanita stood motionless while the sounds of a human herd thundered past the dorm door. Jonara and Cerafina looked outside the room and watched as a group of prisoners ran up and down the hallway with a guard on each end. Jonara and Cerafina realized why the girls made such a ruckus while running—Calico chased them, and whoever she caught at the back of the stampede became her next victim of roughhousing—Calico style. The guards stood around and chuckled as they enjoyed the misery of Calico's catch.

"She's in cahoots with the guards," said Jonara.

"The Oxians. The guards are Oxians," Cerafina said.

"I don't care who they are," Jonara said.

"Well there's nothing we can do. Unless your mother wears the Water Ruby—" Cerafina started.

"Or someone else wears it," Jonara added.

"I didn't think of that."

"What if someone else steals it?"

"They can't. Somehow it stays in your family until 2023," said Cerafina.

"But how does it stay in the family? Will we help get it back in the family?" Jonara asked.

"Or could we cause it to be lost from the family?" Cerafina added.

For the moment, it didn't matter. No one noticed the Moissan Ruby in the coffeepot. Evanita completed the bathroom cleaning assignment and moved on to cleaning the bedroom carpeting. Despite Calico's warning to leave the books for Calico to pick up, Calico never returned to pick them up, and Evanita decided to pick up everything. She placed the books and newspapers in their own stacks on Calico's desk. Finishing up with placing Calico's clothes in the hamper, Evanita vacuumed the carpet using the upright cleaner. It was an awkward maneuver with Evanita doing the best she could to balance herself on crutches while wielding the cleaner. She had just finished the last bit when Calico unbolted and opened the dorm door.

"Just put it on my desk," Calico said to Ox-Three.

"Well hello, Eve!" Ox-Three said to Evanita while carrying a box to Calico's desk. "Are you behaving? Hey Cali, there's no room on your desk!"

"What?!"

"All these books are in the way," said Ox-Three.

"I told you not to pick up the books!" Calico said to Evanita.

"I...I...needed to vacuum...no place to put them," fumbled Evanita.

"Put the box on my chair for now," Calico said to Ox-Three.

Ox-Three dropped the box of coffee, tobacco, and chocolate on Calico's desk chair.

"Doesn't matter what kind of jam you're in, if you break the rules, you face the punishment," said Calico. "And in this case, it's one book at a time."

Calico took the first book from the pile and clonked it over Evanita's head.

"Ow! That hurts!"

"It better," said Calico.

Calico tossed the book into a corner and reached for the next book.

"Need any help?" Ox-Three asked. "I'm good at swatting inmates with books."

"Naw," said Calico. "This is personal. I'm the one to do this. But stick around for a minute."

"Ow!" Evanita replied to the second book whacking across her head.

"I told you not to pick up the books. Receive your punishment," Calico said while slapping the third book over Evanita's head.

"Well she hasn't hung herself yet," said Ox-Three.

"Or cut her wrists," said Calico while moving the fourth book to slap Evanita over the head, but Evanita held up a crutch to block.

"Belligerence, Cali!" Ox-Three said.

"You take your medicine like a good girl!" Calico demanded.

Calico took the offending crutch and clunked Evanita in the forehead with it before tossing it aside. Calico completed swatting Evanita with the fourth book and picked up a fifth.

"It's only been four hours," said Ox-Three.

"Another forty-four and she'll pass the suicide watch," added Calico while clunking Evanita with the fifth book.

"What makes you think she'll pass? Your last roommate hung herself off the wing after only twelve hours," said Ox-Three.

"I made a mistake with that one," said Calico, clunking Evanita with book six. "I attempted reason with her."

"Talk therapy, what a joke!" laughed Ox-Three.

"That wasn't my idea, trust me," said Calico while clunking Evanita with book seven.

"Whose was it?"

"One of the new nurses—Bar-Seven," said Calico.

"There is no Bar-Seven," said Ox-Three.

"Not now, but last week there was before she was fired," said Calico while wielding book eight. "One of those 'advanced' therapists. Bet she doesn't come cheap."

"That's why she was fired, if I recall," said Ox-Three.

"Because she was too expensive? And here I thought it was her treatment style. You know, that consideration-for-the-patient plan?" said Calico while swatting Evanita with book nine.

"That was the second reason. Everyone knows treatment is based on what's good for the rest of the group," said Ox-Three.

"Well this one ain't hanging herself and making my group look bad," said Calico while swatting Evanita with book ten.

"You know what gets me? Most suicidals make a big stink about how they're going to kill themselves," said Ox-Three.

"For attention?" Calico asked.

"Of course! If a girl is really serious about suicide, she should just do it and get it over with," Ox-Three said.

"Well I'm not gonna let this one go on that road," said Calico. "I'm gonna keep her busy."

Calico ran out of books and started swatting Evanita with newspapers.

"I heard other cut-rate centers are following the KEB plan— Keep 'Em Busy," said Ox-Three. "Hey, I thought you said your roomie *was* supposed to pick up the newspapers."

"Yeah, I know," agreed Calico.

"So why are you swatting her with them?" Ox-Three asked.

"I ran out of things to hit her with, and I'm not done talking yet," said Calico.

"Okay, that's fine," laughed Ox-Three.

"Now I'm out of newspapers," said Calico after striking Evanita with the last one.

"Can you believe some centers actually treat their suicidal inmates with anti-depressant drugs?" Ox-Three chuckled.

"And it always backfires, doesn't it?" Calico said.

Calico had run out of things with which to swat Evanita. As a substitute, Calico swatted Evanita across the head with her hand as a means of punctuating each of Calico's statements to Ox-Three. Evanita kept her head down and gritted her teeth. She was angry at Calico and would have kicked her, but Evanita's legs were in no condition for such an act.

"Of course!" replied Ox-Three. "They don't take the pills. They pretend to take them but hide them instead. And then they either take them all at once to kill themselves with an overdose, or they sell them to a suicidal friend."

Evanita had tolerated as much pain as she could. Unable to remain standing, she fell to the floor on her knees.

"Are you going to keep hitting your roomie?" Ox-Three asked. "You might get bored!"

"I gotta keep her busy until dinner. How can she think of suicide when I'm keeping her brain busy with pain and a well-seeded hatred for me?" Calico pointed out.

"Of course," Ox-Three agreed.

"But I never get bored of hitting people. It's a good way to let off stress!" Calico added. "When I can't hit anyone, that's when I start going nuts."

A loud siren shook the room and Evanita's nerves. Ox-Three and Calico were not surprised and responded predictably to each other.

"Dinnertime!" Ox-Three said. "Need any help with the Soosie?"

"Naw," Calico said. "The Sooie-cidal will just get cleaned up. We'll be along any minute. Go on and get the best eats."

Ox-Three left Calico with Evanita. Jonara ran up to Calico and swung her arms into her, but the attack failed as before—Jonara's arms passed through Calico.

"C'mon, gotta get you ready for the march," Calico said.

Calico lifted Evanita to her feet on her one nearby crutch. Calico had turned her back to Evanita while fetching the tossed crutch when Evanita's hatred expressed itself with an explosive dive into Calico's back. Evanita wrapped both arms around Calico's neck and squeezed as hard as she could.

Calico's sturdy, webbed neck resisted any serious choking threats, but Evanita's efforts did create one effect—annoyance. Calico reached over the top of her shoulder, grabbed one of Evanita's arms, and performed a spinning maneuver too quick for Jonara and Evanita to see. In a split second, Evanita was no longer choking Calico but instead was being held by Calico, who was holding Evanita's right arm behind her back and applying upward pressure. This hammerlock hold pinned Evanita's face and front torso against the wall, and from this position she cried out in pain.

"I'm barely applying pressure," said Calico. "So stop your whining."

"It hurts!"

"I suppose you thought you could out-fox the Calico with a stupid move like that. My neck is unchokable, or didn't I explain all that? You remember—the body of a woman and the strength of a man?"

"I remember," said Evanita.

"Let me help you remember," said Calico as she applied additional upward pressure while shoving Evanita farther into the wall.

"OW! STOP!" Evanita shouted. "You're crushing me."

"There's no room for getting out of line around here," said Calico. "I've been extremely patient with you for now. But another outburst like that will not be tolerated. The staff isn't as forgiving as I am. I'm trying to help you adjust to life at Redjet, and you turn around and choke me behind my back? Some thanks I get."

Calico dropped Evanita to the ground. Evanita gasped for breath and moved her right arm back around slowly to her front side. She rubbed her shoulder with her left hand and shot Calico a fiery stare.

"Good solid hatred," said Calico, pleased with her work. "We form our strongest bonds with hatred. You'll make a good roommate yet. Now c'mon—let's get some dinner."

"All right," called Ox-Two from outside the room. "Everyone line up in the hallway for the dinner march."

"That's it. On your feet, Eve Carson, or you'll go hungry 'till breakfast," said Calico. "And no talking during the march."

Jonara and Cerafina were surprised to see Calico help Evanita to her feet with her crutches. Jonara and Cerafina followed the two as the inmates assembled in singlewide formation in the outside hallway. Calico was first in line followed by Evanita. The remaining residents fell in line behind Evanita. Ox-Two blew a whistle twice and called out cadence steps. The line marched to this call and proceeded out Redjet, down the steps, across the grounds, and up steps into the white jet with red crosses, known as Cafederijet.

Evanita did her best to keep up, but the tall Russian girl behind her repeatedly pushed Evanita to speed up her progress. Evanita nearly fell during one of those attacks, but Calico quickly spun around and yanked Evanita up by the arm without losing stride.

The Redjet girls passed through the food line with little issue and sat at assigned tables for dinner. Calico and Evanita sat with the Russian who had antagonized her, and a German. Evanita later learned these two girls stayed in the dorm room across the hall from herself and Calico.

There was no opportunity for socializing or entertainment during dinner. The other residential jets had already eaten in the cafeteria—leaving Redjet for last. Extra security guards patrolled the cafeteria to ensure no violence—a special measure not necessary for the other jet residents. The meal ended as quickly as it started, and in thirty minutes the girls were marched back to Redjet.

"I'm told you've been exempted from the games this evening," Calico said to Evanita once the two returned to their dorm room. "I, of course, am never exempt—I'm a referee."

Evanita lifted her hand and waved it as a request to speak.

"Yes?"

"Before dinner, you said something about a schedule," said Evanita.

"Yeah. We'll do that tomorrow morning. Don't worry—you'll be fine. I've kept you busy enough today, I think. I'm sure you'll behave and spend the evening resting, right?!"

Calico's question was more like an order, and Evanita hesitated to answer. Calico normally had a good humor after dinner, but Evanita's hesitation irked her.

"You're not going to do something stupid like hang yourself are you? I'm sure I've given you enough pain to keep your mind off that nonsense. But if you need a refresher, just cross me now. I'll haul you down to the games and throw you in a ring. I won't care who beats you up. And you'll need four crutches instead of two for the broken arms they'll give you. So I ask you— no, I'm ordering you—you'll behave and REST, RIGHT?!"

"Yeah. I'll rest," Evanita answered.

"Good. I'll be back late," Calico said, and with that she left the room and bolted the door behind her.

"Mommy, Mommy—pick up the Water Ruby!" Jonara shouted.

Evanita sat in her desk chair, stared at the desk surface, and breathed deeply.

"She can't hear you, Jonara," Cerafina said.

"There must be some way we can reach her," said Jonara.

"It doesn't look like we can."

"How can we help her?" Jonara asked.

"We can't. We'll have to wait," Cerafina replied.

After sitting for a few minutes, Evanita changed clothes and pulled herself up the ladder into the upper bunk bed. She rolled back and forth several times before finding a comfortable position facing the wall.

"Someone help me," she whispered. "I'm all alone. Alone."

Evanita drew the outline of a crucifix on the wall.

"Come to me, Jesus," she whispered. "Take my hand to the promised land."

Evanita drew the outline repeatedly and kept her finger on the wall between line endpoints. In this way, her drawing of the cross gradually changed into the drawing of a fish.

"Lead me to the fish," she continued, "the fish and bread you have multiplied for your flock. Talk to me, Jesus. Sing me a song asleep."

Evanita hummed a tune she'd heard in Johnny's Barnseed Baptist Church. She repeated the tune with a tired, croaky voice until she fell asleep.

For Jonara and Cerafina, the room faded into darkness, and the two floated above the room, outside the jet, and up into the air where the Elrod 402 increasingly shrank into an outline resembling the pendant Fronka Nordekter wore during Eva's and Geneva's introduction to the campus. The girls floated higher and higher as dusk fell into night. Wispy clouds and twinkling stars accompanied them on their brief journey to the dawn.

CHAPTER 5

Geneva Vallan Carreña

2023 Oct 4, Wed Afnoon. Corpus Christi, Texas.
2006 Nov 19, Sun. Elrod 402. Portland, Oregon.

Jonara and Cerafina lost their orientation in the twinkles of night. They were high up from the ground—that much they knew, but they were puzzled. The sun had just set below the horizon, and the clouds floated away from the sunset. Without warning, the clouds and sun ran in reverse. The clouds floated into the sunset, and the sunset rose into the sky.

"Something's wrong," said Jonara. "The world is running backward."

"And we're sinking back to Earth," said Cerafina.

"This never happened before," said Jonara. "Time always runs forward."

The two fell to Earth but not back to the Elrod 402. Fingers of sunlight converged onto orange flames of a burning building. Jonara and Cerafina felt completely disoriented—they weren't sure the time or place—only that they were now descending rapidly into a burning building, in a section yet to catch fire. Upon landing in a room, they jumped back in surprise when they realized Evanita was sitting in a corner. Evanita was of the same age as she was in the Elrod 402—sixteen years old—but she had no leg casts. She had been resting in a chair, but smoke filled the room, and Evanita choked.

"I have to get out of here," Evanita said.

"Mommy, this way, we'll help you out," said Jonara, but Evanita wasn't aware of the girls' presence.

"I'm choking!" Evanita yelled.

Evanita jumped to her feet and bolted through a door into another room. Jonara and Cerafina followed. This was the first time Cerafina had seen Evanita run, and though Jonara had seen her mother run, it was never this fast. The room the three had left was small and empty except for the chair in the corner, some empty bookcases, and a desk.

"Are we in the factory again?" Jonara asked.

She didn't need an answer. The three rushed into a shallow yet wide room with fake wood-paneled walls, long tables with pop-up metal legs on each end, and metal fold-up chairs. There were many young children and a few adults sitting at the tables with cone-shaped birthday hats. A pile of paper plates and plastic utensils waited on one end of the table. Evanita and the two girls continued running through the room past everyone as one woman carried in a birthday cake with six candles a-lit. Smoke from the candles fogged the ceiling. Evanita, Jonara, and Cerafina wasted no time in exiting the room to the next.

"That's your mother's kindergarten birthday party," Cerafina said to Jonara.

"How do you know?"

"The little girl with the presents looks like your mother, and I saw a tag on a gift that said, 'To: Evanita Carreña, Love: Grandma Geneva.'"

There was no time for a lengthy discussion. Cerafina had barely completed the explanation when the three entered a hospital hallway. Many patients were lying on gurneys alongside one wall. Evanita and the girls had to dart out of the way of a fast-moving wheelchair. Evanita paid no attention, but Jonara and Cerafina recognized the patient.

"That's Grandma Eva," said Jonara. "She looks so young—maybe in her twenties or thirties."

"She's pregnant too," said Cerafina. "How many children did she have?"

"Just Mommy," said Jonara.

Evanita did not stop. Her legs carried her through the hallway into another room—or was it? No, it was a very peculiar stairwell. They were on a landing with ornately carved granite steps running down inside a room, up to another floor, and down another end to some outside doors. Evanita ran down to the outside doors, but a big-link chain around the door handles kept it closed.

"Can't get out," said Jonara.

"And there's lots of smoke on the second floor," said Cerafina.

Evanita avoided going upstairs and instead descended the granite steps into some sort of finished basement. It was a wide room but empty. She ran along a windowed wall in hopes of finding an opening to the outside world. All windows were closed, but Jonara and Cerafina did see cannon-fire, shotgun exhaust, and the torching of trees and houses filling the shadows of a dawn in a land across the Atlantic Ocean. Smoke gave the sun a hazy appearance, and instead of the sun being too bright to observe, it appeared as a white circular pill ready to ingest.

Evanita ran to the other end of the basement and found a cramped stairwell leading up. Jonara and Cerafina followed her up the stairs to a rusty door, but it was hot. Evanita stood as close to the hinges as she could while she pulled the door open. Just a little open. As Evanita opened the door, an orange and yellow fireball powered through the opening. The door slammed itself shut as a backdraft wrenched the door handle from Evanita's hand. Evanita opened the door again—farther than before. Another blast flamed through the door opening, but Evanita fought with both hands to keep the backdraft from slamming the door shut again. She climbed around the door and wedged it open with her shoe and ducked. The flames poured over her head, yet she pushed on into the fire—knowing that going back into the building meant going through rooms of memories and other lives that did not belong to the Evanita of the moment.

"I cannot go back," Evanita said, "to when I was a child or a fetus. My legs won't let me rest, won't let me stay trapped in one room of my life. There is no choice for me. I can escape, but only by subjecting myself to the cancers of smoke and deformities of flame."

"I don't understand!" Jonara said. "What is she doing?"

"This is a strange place!" Cerafina said.

"She's going to go into that fire?" Jonara asked. "There must be another way out!"

"We must be in a bad dream," said Cerafina.

"Or a nightmare," said Jonara.

"But whose?"

"I don't know," Jonara replied. "I don't know."

Evanita crawled on her knees into the room filled with burning pressure-treated wood.

"Now we're in the factory," said Jonara.

The heat was tremendous. It singed Evanita's hair. Jonara and Cerafina were, however, unaffected. Evanita continued crawling on her knees. She screamed in pain as the hot floor melted her flesh. Jonara and Cerafina were sickened by the smell of burning flesh. Evanita choked on the smoke but continued fighting her way through a scrap chute.

The three reached the outside, but instead of reaching the River Wood and Battery grounds, the three were on the edge of a mountain pass between Spain and France. Airplanes flew over and fired upon the line of peasants clogging the pass. Many peasants broke into a run to avoid the flying death machines.

"I know this place," said Evanita. "Grandma Geneva told me. It's the end of the Spanish Civil War, and this is the road from Spain to France. These are the people of Spain. My God—these are my people. But where does the road end? Will it end?"

Without warning, a bomb landed on the pass. It obliterated some people and sent others flying through the air. One landed near Evanita—a young girl—and her legs were now missing. She stared at Evanita, and Evanita stared back. Both had difficulty breathing and choked. The smoke hazed up the air. Jonara and Cerafina had trouble seeing Evanita and each other. Evanita choked and coughed more strongly than ever—so much that Jonara and Cerafina were sure Evanita would cough up her stomach.

A bright light pierced through the haze and blinded the three. Evanita's legs hurt. She couldn't stand, much less walk. She rolled as best she could to hide from the sunlight, but she couldn't. Between the pain in her legs and the burning in her lungs, Evanita felt dead and unable to stop the multiple assaults on her body.

The surroundings turned blindingly white. Evanita stopped choking only because she stopped breathing. She blinked her eyes several times and stared at a distant figure sitting in the light. The smoke coalesced into a single stream emanating from that figure.

Evanita blinked again, and she was lying in her upper bunk bed in Redjet of the Elrod 402. She opened her mouth and breathed tobacco smoke. By the window sat Calico Shepherd smoking a pipe. She took a puff from her pipe, held it in her lungs, and exhaled slowly into the morning sunlight. Calico set the pipe on a holder and sipped freshly made coffee. Calico smiled with bliss and received the pleasure the tobacco and coffee had bestowed upon her body. She dipped fresh tobacco in her coffee and rubbed the leaves on her arms—back and forth and in circles—as much as she could to absorb the tobacco through her skin.

Evanita coughed.

"Oh, you're awake," said Calico in a quiet voice. "Would you like coffee and a smoke?"

"That stuff will kill you," said Evanita as she struggled to climb down to the floor.

"Which—the coffee or tobacco? Don't worry—I don't get sick like straight-X girls. And I ain't gettin' cancer."

"Damage to your lungs—damage to my lungs!" said Evanita.

"Can there be such a thing as diversified damage?" Calico grinned.

"Huh?" Evanita said, now standing on the floor with her crutches.

"I don't expect you to understand. But you might be right. Tobacco ain't good for you. You can't help being a straight-X. But I make good coffee. Ever had any? Try this," Calico offered.

"Coffee is awful," Jonara said to Cerafina. "I had some this morning."

"I think you said that," Cerafina said. "But *this* is the morning."

"I mean the morning back in 2023. Hot chocolate is much better," Jonara clarified.

"Blech," Evanita said in response to the offer.

"That's how I reacted," Jonara said to Cerafina.

"Ain't no one hated my coffee," said Calico. "And no one better start now."

"I can't drink it," said Evanita.

"You mean you won't drink it? Belligerence again? Go on— try it. It'll help you get through the day."

Evanita took another sip but had the same foul reaction. She gagged on the coffee and returned the cup to Calico.

"It's awful. How can people drink this?" Evanita asked.

"I guess I figured you all wrong. I thought you were this tough girl with a fire in her eyes. Can't even drink coffee? What good are you?" Calico asked.

"I'd rather have sewer water," said Evanita.

"I won't sit here and have my coffee called 'sewer water'. Now you sit here and stay until you drink my coffee. It's the best stuff in all of Elrod 402!" Calico bragged. "But maybe you need something to soften the taste. How about a mocha coffee?"

"Mocha coffee?" Evanita asked.

"Yeah—some chocolate in your coffee. I know, it sounds strange, but you'd be amazed how many girls love it," said Calico. "What kind of chocolate do you like?"

"Dark," Evanita replied.

Calico opened a bar of dark chocolate and dropped it into Evanita's coffee. Within seconds, the bar melted and sank into the coffee. Calico stirred the new mocha coffee with a stir stick and presented it to Evanita.

"There. One dark mocha coffee. Enjoy," said Calico.

Evanita sipped the dark mocha coffee and was impressed.

"It's good," she said, taking a much larger sip. "Do you ever use M&Ms?"

"Naw—they take too long to melt. Gotta use a regular chocolate bar," Calico replied.

Evanita slugged the dark mocha coffee down her throat and exhaled a sigh of satisfaction.

"Whoa! You switch sides quickly—from one who doesn't like coffee to a gulper," said Calico.

"More?" Evanita grinned as she extended her coffee cup out to Calico.

"Yeah, sure," Calico replied.

Calico poured more coffee into Evanita's cup and added another bar of dark chocolate. Calico handed the stir stick back to Evanita, and Evanita mixed up her second dark mocha coffee.

"I propose a toast!" said Evanita, who for some reason was willing to forget the pain Calico had been causing her.

"Well! This is a surprise," said Calico.

"A toast to a good morning," said Evanita.

Evanita held her coffee cup in the air toward Calico, and Calico clacked her mug against Evanita's. The two took slurps from their coffee and exhaled with contentment.

Without warning, the daylight fragmented into many colors before Evanita. Evanita's eyes darted back and forth to understand what was happening to her vision.

"Whoa there," said Calico. "There's something in this coffee. Must be. For a moment I thought I saw a rainbow."

"You too?" Evanita asked.

"What do you mean by that?" Calico asked. "You saw the rainbow?"

"Not exactly," said Evanita.

"Well either you did or you didn't. Which is it?" Calico demanded.

"I saw lots of colors, but not a rainbow," said Evanita.

"Something must have gotten in the brew overnight," said Calico, who was now checking her coffee maker for contaminants.

"What are you doing?" Evanita asked.

"Checking the coffee machine. Nope, it's clean. Now I know I cleaned out the pot yesterday morning. Hey, what's this?" Calico asked.

Calico swirled the half-filled coffeepot around and felt something strange in its weight. She probed the inside with a stir stick and detected the Moissan Ruby.

"What the devil is this?" Calico asked.

Calico fished out the Moissan Ruby with a fork and dropped it on a paper napkin, the paper napkin already being on Calico's desk.

"Someone put this in my pot. Is this yours?" Calico demanded.

Evanita paused for a moment, but Calico didn't give Evanita much time for thought. Calico pulled on Evanita's hair and asked again.

"Yes!" Evanita replied. "It's mine. I threw it across the room yesterday. I didn't know—"

"You didn't know it was in the pot? What a careless brat! And here I was being nice and all with mocha coffee," Calico said.

"Dark mocha coffee," Evanita corrected.

"I know what it is, Miss Brat! I ought to whup you right now, just to get the day started right."

"I'm sorry," said Evanita.

"You're sorry. Sorry doesn't fix anything. What's in that thing, poison?" Calico asked.

Calico wiped the stone and chain dry and held the stone up to the sun.

"Oh there's something in this thing, all right!" said Calico. "What is it, some glow-in-the dark thing? Is it tritium? Better not be radium—that stuff killed Marie Curie."

"It's safe. A friend gave it to me," said Evanita.

"My dear," Calico laughed, "the most dangerous things in this world are passed from one friend to another. Yes, thanks to the almighty trust factor, friends don't challenge the failed wisdom of a gift until it's too late."

"I don't understand," said Evanita.

"I don't expect you to. But see here—I ain't got any friends, and I don't plan to. So I don't trust you or your outside friend. I'm gonna have to turn this in and get it checked out—it could give all the girls in Redjet radioactive poisoning. How did you get this thing past security?"

"It's not a thing," Evanita said. "It's a keepsake to remember my family."

"Don't care," said Calico.

"You must care," said Evanita.

"Nope."

"Well at least check it by yourself," said Evanita. "You don't want people to find out about it."

"Huh?" Calico asked.

"I mean, well, you know, if it's dangerous—it could cause a riot, and if it has power, others would fight you for it," said Evanita.

"Honey, this thing ain't got no power that anyone would fight for. But you might be right about the riot thing. I'll check it out myself in the infirmary. They got a Geiger counter there," said Calico.

"And you'll give it back when you're done?" Evanita asked.

"Never no promises," said Calico. "That's my motto."

"But at least, at least—" Evanita begged as she grabbed Calico's hands in a desperate plea.

"Let go," said Calico.

"No," Evanita continued to beg.

Calico held firm, but Evanita kept pulling and straining. Evanita's muscles shook as their effort exceeded their strength. Both Calico and Evanita were surprised by a vision—detailed knowledge of every woman and girl in every jet on the Elrod 402 campus—where each was and what each was doing. The vision stopped after Evanita let go of Calico.

"Ah, humm, now what was that?" Calico mused. "Some sort of hallucinogenic trip? Is there *acid* in this stone? Oh man, are you in trouble."

"No LSD, no radium, no tritium—just a special stone from outer space. It's a meteorite. And it's for me—to remember my family and friends," said Evanita.

"Oh humm again," Calico said. "Maybe I should be your friend. But you'll have to show me how this works. Let's see...I hold it like this...and...no, that didn't do anything. I hold your hand and...no, that didn't do anything either."

"Only I can use it," said Evanita.

"Oh we'll see about that. But not now. You get showered and dressed. There's mandatory religious service in an hour over at Patriojet," said Calico.

"Patriojet?"

"Can't remember anything, can you? The jet with the stars and bars—that's Patriojet. You'll see it soon enough—church on Sunday, and school during the week. Now get in that shower!"

"What about—" Evanita started.

"Never mind about me," Calico said. "I already took a shower this morning while you were sleeping. Now scat!"

Jonara and Cerafina remained with Calico while Evanita took a shower. Calico made several more attempts to harness the Moissan Ruby's power but was unsuccessful. Calico gave up and placed the stone on her desk. She changed clothes herself in preparation for church—a blazer and slacks suitable for office attire. Evanita finished her shower and dressed in the bathroom. When she stepped out, Calico's eyes lit up.

"O whoa! You're going to church in that dress?" Calico asked.

"I've worn this to church before," said Evanita, who was wearing a long, black dress with ruffles.

"Looks like you're going to a party. You better be careful around here, someone might think you're looking for a date!"

"I like this dress!" Evanita insisted.

"Okay, but remember—I warned you," said Calico.

Evanita noticed the Moissan Ruby on Calico's desk. She reached for it but paused when she feared Calico might object.

"Go ahead, take it. I can check it later," Calico said.

Calico continued staring at Evanita and her dress.

"Why are you staring?" Evanita asked.

"I just can't get over you in that dress," Calico remarked. "I may have to protect you from the other girls. They may start rumors about you and me, but I got a thick skin. Besides, I find out things quick enough, and I'll put out the little gossip fires as they sprout."

An alarm sounded off much like the one for Saturday's dinner. The girls lined up in the hallway as before, but the Russian and German girls fought for who would follow behind Evanita. Calico settled the matter by placing Evanita ahead of her. In this way, Evanita led the march from Redjet to Patriojet.

Evanita drew attention from more than just the Redjet girls. Girls marching from other jets also took notice of her. She was on crutches, yes, but the long dress covered her casts. The other girls simply saw an elegant girl using crutches instead of two casts hobbling along.

The girls piled into Patriojet—a jet that had been gutted and opened into a wide space on the inside. There were no side rooms to take up unnecessary space. Patriojet was configured to hold large people-gatherings. Rows of chairs filled the highly configurable jet, and at one end there was a single stage with three podiums and an altar.

The Redjet girls were assigned seats in back. Oxia (the chief of security) whispered something into Ox-Two's ear, and Ox-Two relinquished Evanita and Calico to Oxia's custody. Oxia led Evanita and Calico to the first row—reserved for top staff and selected guests.

"You are my guests," said Oxia to Calico and Evanita. "Next to me is Baria—our health chief—and her two guests."

Calico and Evanita waved, "Hi," to Baria and her two guests.

"The service will be led by O Grammeni, Dazia, and Daz-One," Oxia explained. "Dazia is our chief of education. The other Dazians help out in the service. Look—here's Daz-Two with your headset, Eve Carson."

"I don't understand," said Evanita.

"Everyone in the audience—that's us—wears headsets," Oxia explained. "There are three different services you can pick up. O Grammeni leads the Catholic Mass, Dazia leads the Protestant service, and Daz-One the Jewish prayer. There are other services too, but those are prerecorded and broadcast over the campus radio. You can tune into any of the three here or any of the others from the radio."

"I don't understand. If I want to listen to a service by, say, Dazia, why do I need a headset?" Evanita asked.

"They all preach at the same time," said Calico. "They each have their own mikes."

"Huh?" Evanita asked.

"That's quite correct. It allows us to service all religious needs for the girls," said Oxia. "Eve—what faith are you?"

"I...I'm sort of not sure," said Evanita.

"Were you brought up in any particular faith?" Oxia asked.

"Unitarian Universalism," answered Evanita.

"Yes, the Type-O of religions. Well, you could listen to any of the broadcasts, I suppose. Your headset has a dial—setting one is for Catholic, setting two is for Protestant, setting three is for Jewish, and the others are on setting four plus the fine tuner," Oxia explained.

"If you're not sure, you can pick setting one. Ms. Nordekter leads the Catholic—" Calico started.

"Calico, you know we don't use formal names here," Oxia warned.

"Yeah—O Grammeni leads the Catholic Mass," Calico explained, "but she also adds news and stuff you might find interesting. Plus she runs the Elrod 402, so it might pay to listen to her first."

Evanita dialed the headset to setting one and placed it over her head. Within a few minutes, O Grammeni, Dazia, and Daz-One walked down the aisle to the strum of church music and took their places on the stage. Each spoke for their own church services in their own microphones.

The headset gave Evanita a peculiar feeling. There was some sort of humming or buzzing sound, like an old-fashioned ungrounded amplifier, and it gave her queer goose bumps.

1939 Feb 4. Girona, Spain.

Evanita was no longer in the Patriojet but instead was in a small apartment. Jonara and Cerafina were with her, and while they could see and hear Evanita, Evanita could not see them. In a chair rested a pregnant woman, due any moment.

"What's going on?" Jonara asked.

"I don't know," said Cerafina.

"Are we still in the Elrod 402?" Jonara asked.

"It doesn't look like the Elrod 402," Cerafina replied.

"The voice—I heard the voice," said Evanita. "But what is this? Johnny's stone is supposed to connect me with family and friends. I didn't know it could go back in time. This is Great-Grandma Margene back in the late 30s."

"Back in time?" Jonara whispered to Cerafina.

"The Water Ruby must be connecting through us—through the diary," Cerafina answered back. "Why are we whispering?"

"Because I don't want Mommy to hear us," said Jonara. "Remember the last time? She took the Water Ruby off. I don't want to scare her."

The woman (Margene) shuddered from each thundering blast outside the window. Airplanes dropped bombs onto the distant countryside, but each explosion grew nearer. The woman feared for her life but had received word her man would arrive soon. She wondered if too much time had passed for his safe arrival. A knock disturbed the quiet between bomb blasts. The woman walked slowly to the door and spoke through the crack.

"Who is it?" she asked.

"It's your beau," replied a male voice. "François Vallan has returned to you, Margene Carreña!"

Margene opened the door, and the two lovers embraced.

"I was told you were dead," Margene cried, "while fighting against the Nationalists."

"No, my sweet," François replied. "I'm sorry, but I could not contact you over the last eight months. Franco's spies are everywhere. When I received word of your condition—" he said, patting Margene's extended abdomen, "I rushed here as soon as I could."

"We must get married, François," Margene said. "I want my baby born in the Catholic Church."

"Soon," François replied.

"It must be now," Margene said. "I'm due any day."

"Look, my sweet, we must leave Girona. The Nationalists are closing in. It isn't safe in this city. Do you trust me?" François asked.

"You know I do," Margene replied.

"We must make for my homeland, for France. There we'll be safe," he said.

"I can't make the journey," she said. "I'm afraid I'll have the baby in the cold mountains. It's February, you know. And my baby won't be born in the Church. What if something happens and my baby dies?"

"Our baby," he said.

"Our baby. I don't want our baby going to Limbo."

"He won't," François replied.

"My baby could be a she," said Margene.

"It's a he, I can feel it," said François.

"It's not good for a new mother to travel on foot. I'll bleed too much. I could die!"

Margene panicked.

"Don't panic," said François.

"Then marry me!" Margene insisted.

"Here? Now? We haven't announced the banns," François said.

"I made arrangements in a little church just down the road. Do you remember Father Mendez? I drew up the license with him. We can get married today. We can go now!" Margene urged.

"Now? Why I've just arrived!" François said.

"And we must go! You said so yourself! The town of Girona will be under attack soon!" Margene said.

"This is so sudden. We should leave the town and be safe. We should—" François started, but Margene had already started preparing to leave.

Margene got her things together and pushed François out the door. She led the way, holding his hand and pulling his arm. François was not in a great hurry to get married, but Margene was mortally afraid for her baby's soul.

Evanita followed the couple with Jonara and Cerafina following Evanita. The group entered Saint Christopher's Catholic Church just a few blocks from Margene's apartment as she had told François.

"This church is huge!" Evanita said. "No, that's not right. It's not wide, but it's very tall. The ceiling is very high and domed. The columns are like ancient Roman or Greek columns. And the statues of Jesus and Mary—they're tall! The decoration is incredible! Everything is sculpted or painted. And look at the windows—they're of different colors and decorated with images."

"Father Mendez, Father Mendez!" Margene called.

Father Mendez was tending the coin-operated devotional candles when the couple burst into the church.

"My child! What is all this? You shouldn't be out in your condition," Father Mendez said. "And why are you pulling this man up the aisle?"

"Father Mendez," said Margene. "This is my fiancé, Señor François Vallan. He's the one I told you about."

"Nice to meet you," said Father Mendez.

"We want to get married now. I had to drag him to the altar," Margene said.

"We?" François said.

"Yes, 'we'!" Margene said.

"No witnesses. Can't get married," François said.

"There must be two witnesses," said Father Mendez. "Did you bring any?"

"No, but—" Margene said.

"And there's no time to get any," said François.

"If you had given me some advanced notice, I could have arranged—" said Father Mendez.

"I'll find some witnesses," said Margene.

To Evanita's, Jonara's, and Cerafina's surprise, Margene hobbled down the aisle, out the front door, and pulled in two people from the street. She hobbled them up the aisle and to the altar.

"Not only must I drag my fiancé to the altar, I have to drag witnesses too," said Margene.

"Your name?" Father Mendez asked the first witness, a man with dirty old clothes, a long unkept beard, and a foul odor.

"Garcia Delgato," the man said.

"What is your profession?"

"I am a homeless drunk," he said. "When do we get to drink the Blood of Christ? I ain't had a drink since—"

Father Mendez rolled his eyes and turned to the young woman.

"And you Señorita, what is your name?" Father Mendez asked.

"Chalina Darconejo," she said.

"And your profession, Chalina?"

"I am a waitress," she said. "What's this all about?"

"We're getting married!" Margene said.

"Who's the unlucky guy?" Garcia asked, but no one paid him attention.

"That's wonderful!" Chalina said in response to Margene. "But where's your maid of honor?"

"I don't have one."

"I'd love to be yours," Chalina said.

"Really?" Margene asked.

"Yeah, really!"

"That would be wonderful!"

"Awww!" Chalina celebrated.

Chalina hopped and danced over to Margene, hugged her, and stood on her left side. François, standing on Margene's right side, rolled his eyes in disbelief.

"I guess this means I'm your best man," said the drunk. He spat on his right palm and offered a handshake to François, saying, "Put it there, drinking buddy."

François took a look at Garcia and shuddered.

"I'm not your drinking buddy, and you're not my best man," said François.

"Be a good sport and shake hands," said Margene.

Garcia's handshake was stronger than François expected. When Garcia finally let go, François instinctively put his hand to his mouth to nurse it, but on touching his lips, he remembered the spit and wiped his hand on his pants while spitting his mouth clean.

"I've got a flower for the bride," said Garcia.

Garcia produced a crumpled flower from inside his coat.

"No thanks," said François.

"It's a wonderful gift," said Margene. "Accept it, François, and give it to me as a sign of our love."

François gritted his teeth. He took the crumpled flower from Garcia using just the tips of his fingers to minimize contact with anything the drunk possessed. François in turn gave the flower to Margene, who accepted it.

"We are ready, then. Would you like to be married as part of a Mass?" Father Mendez asked.

"Yes!" Margene and Chalina answered.

"No!" François and Garcia said at the same time as Margene and Chalina.

"There's no time for a full Mass," said François.

"Our wedding can't be a quickie," said Margene. "We must be married in the Church."

"We are in the Church. Father—can't you shorten the ceremony?" François asked.

"We're in a Catholic Church, but we must be fully married as Catholics, and not in some stripped-down civil ceremony bereft of the Blessed Mother's approval," said Margene.

"Amen!" Chalina chimed in.

"I didn't say, 'Stripped down'," said François.

"Yeah, bring on the strippers!" Garcia said.

Everyone stared at the drunk in disapproval (including Evanita, Jonara, and Cerafina).

"What?" Garcia feigned.

"We will begin without further argument," said Father Mendez, "so that François and Margene may receive the Sacrament of Matrimony before their child receives the Sacrament of Baptism!"

"Amen!" someone shouted.

Evanita was surprised to find herself shouting the "Amen". Jonara and Cerafina giggled in agreement, and Evanita heard their voices. While Evanita could not see them, Jonara and Cerafina took positions on each side of Evanita and held hands. For the first time while using the Moissan Ruby, Evanita felt comforted. She trusted these holding hands, and her anxiety eased.

"In the name of the Father and of the Son and of the Holy Ghost!" Father Mendez said while performing the sign of the cross in the air.

"Amen!" everyone replied.

"May the grace of the Lord Jesus Christ, the love of God, and the fellowship of the Holy Spirit be with you all," said Father Mendez.

"And also with you," the marriage party of four and Cerafina replied.

"We are gathered here at Saint Christopher's Catholic Church in Girona, Spain, in the Year of our Lord, February 4, 1939, to unite François and Margene in holy Catholic Matrimony," Father Mendez said. "May the Lord Jesus Christ bless and accept Garcia Delgato and Chalina Darconejo as witnesses to this most holy union unto God. Do you, Garcia, and you, Chalina, submit yourselves to the Roman Catholic Church, to God Almighty, and to his Community of Saints, to execute faithfully the humble role of witness, so that François and Margene may lawfully, legally, morally, spiritually, and sanctimoniously enter the union of marriage, founded on the love of Jesus Christ, the love he gave to his new Catholic people, unto his new Church as ordained by his rock, Peter the Apostle, and continued through an unbroken line to your priest, Father Mendez, the love of the Everlasting God who is, was, and shall be forever and ever?"

"I do," agreed Chalina.

"Huh?" Garcia asked.

François laughed and said, "Just say 'I do'."

"I trust you, drinking buddy," Garcia said to François. He turned to Father Mendez and said, "I do."

A bomb blast broke through a small window high up.

"We don't have time for the full Mass," Margene said. "The Nuptials, Father."

"Wait," Garcia said. "I was looking forward to the Eurcharist and the Blood of Christ. Can't we skip to the blood part?"

"No!" Margene and Chalina said.

"Do you, Margene Carreña, come before Christ's Church of your own free will, to give yourself in Holy Matrimony to the Roman Catholic Church, our Lord Jesus Christ, and to François Vallan?" Father Mendez asked. "Answer with 'I affirm' or 'I do not affirm'."

"I affirm," said Margene.

"Do you, François Vallan, come of your own free will—" Father Mendez started before François interrupted with a cough, no, it was more like a gag.

"Oh be quiet!" Margene said as she whumped him on the back.

"—before Christ's Church," Father Mendez continued, "to give yourself in Holy Matrimony to the Roman Catholic Church, our Lord Jesus Christ, and to Margene Carreña?"

"Can't I just give myself to Margene alone without the other stuff?" François asked.

"Sounds good to me," said Garcia.

"No!" Margene said. "To marry me you must marry the Church. Affirm it, François!"

"Answer with 'I affirm' or 'I do not affirm'," said Father Mendez.

"Give it up, drinking buddy, the Church is gonna get its hooks into you," said Garcia.

"Quit calling me your drinking buddy," said François. "And the Church isn't—"

François wanted to say more, but Father Mendez, Chalina, and especially Margene stared him down into submission.

"Answer," Margene said to François as she whumped him over the back again.

"I affirm," said François.

"There goes the drinking party," said Garcia.

"François and Margene—please join hands for the Solemn Promise," said Father Mendez, "so that you may declare your consent to marry before the Holy Mother, the Catholic Church."

Margene grabbed François's reluctant hands and joined them to hers.

"Do you, Margene Carreña, take François as your lawfully wedded husband, according to the rite of the Roman Catholic Church, as founded by Jesus Christ on the Apostle Peter, to have and to hold, in the name of the Father, the Son, and the Holy Ghost?"

"I, Margene Carreña, take as my husband, François Vallan, in the bonds of Holy Matrimony, by the grace of the Holy Trinity, inspired by the Holy Ghost, for better or for worse, for richer or poorer, until death do us part, and with...with this...r—"

"Do you have the ring?" Father Mendez asked François.

"Ring? Ring! We can't get married without a ring!" François grinned.

"I have a small keyring in my pocket," said Garcia, who produced it for François.

François pushed Garcia's keyring away.

"I forgot about the rings! How could I forget such a thing?" Margene panicked.

"I guess you're off the hook," said Garcia.

"No, wait," said Chalina. "Let Chalina come to the rescue. Here," she said, removing two rings from her purse. "These were left as a tip by two women who'd recently lost their husbands. Strange—they seemed happy to lose them."

"We can't ask you to give us—" François started.

"Oh yes we can!" Margene shouted with glee. She ripped the rings from Chalina and handed one to François. "Now put this on my left finger so I can finish my vow!"

"Tough luck, drinking buddy," said Garcia.

François shot Garcia a sour stare before proceeding to place the ring on Margene's finger.

"With this ring," continued Margene, "I thee wed, and accept your troth until death do us part, in the eyes of the Holy Mother, our Catholic Church, in the name of the Father and of the Son and of the Holy Ghost, Amen."

"And do you, François Vallan," continued Father Mendez, "take Margene Carreña as your lawful wife, according to the rite of—"

"I know the rest," interrupted François. "The Church and the Apostle part. Yes, I do."

Margene placed the other ring on François's left finger.

"With this ring," said Margene, "I pledge thee my troth. Do you, François, pledge your troth to me until death do us part according to the grace and laws of the Roman Catholic Church?"

"I do," François said.

"Good, short answer," said Garcia. "But she hooked you with the Church thing, buddy."

"Shut up!" Chalina and Margene said simultaneously.

"The Church blesses these rings as symbols of this couple's deep faith," Father Mendez said. "May the love of Jesus Christ bring peace and happiness to Margene and François as the exchange of rings promises their unconditional love and fidelity to each other. May they have many long years together and a bountiful family. Please—sign the marriage license."

Father Mendez passed a pen and a certificate first to Margene, and then to François. Both signed it.

"Uh, oh, we gotta know how to read and write?" Garcia asked.

"Just how to sign your name," said Chalina, who signed as a witness. "There's one blank line left. It's just for you, Garcia."

"Yeah, all right," Garcia said, writing some chicken-scratch of a signature on the license. He returned the license to Father Mendez.

"Margene and François—by the powers vested in me by the Roman Catholic Church, I now pronounce you as married— husband and—"

Without warning, all windows imploded from an outdoor explosion. Glass rained from the air. The wedding party and priest ducked, while Evanita, Jonara, and Cerafina watched the glass pass through themselves.

"They hit the church," Father Mendez said.

"It's the end of the world," said Garcia. "Father—give us the Last Rite and some Blood of Christ for the road."

"Garcia!" Chalina yelled.

"My dear, are you hurt?" François asked Margene.

"Just a few cuts," she replied. "I'm fine."

The church people were regaining their composure when another blast struck the church's roof. Timbers scattered down—one of which struck Margene. She fell lifeless to the floor with blood pouring through her dress.

"Margene!" François yelled. "Lord in Heaven! Spare my Margene!"

Father Mendez administered the Last Rites to Margene and her unborn child.

A man burst through the main church door and yelled, "They're here, they're here!"

"Who, the beer party?" Garcia asked, oblivious to anything but his own needs.

"No, the Nationalists! They're attacking the city!" the man replied.

"My wife is dying," François yelled to the man. "I need help! Get a doctor!"

"It's every man for himself!" the man yelled, and he returned to the street where chaos reigned.

"I must get help!" François said to Chalina and Father Mendez.

"Then you'd better hurry. I'll stay here with Margene," said Father Mendez.

"So will I," said Chalina.

François dashed out the main door and ran down the street while yelling for a doctor.

"Garcia, Chalina—help me take Margene to a small room in back. It's heavily protected and should be safe from bombardment," Father Mendez said.

"Well, only if you save a little of that Blood of Christ for me— I know it isn't grape juice. What do you say, Father?"

"Get out of here!" Chalina yelled.

"You'll find all the wine you want in the storage room in back. Now help us!" Father Mendez ordered.

"In the storage room, eh?" Garcia said.

Garcia strolled toward the back storage room, and before he left their sight, he thanked the priest.

"Chalina—take her right side, and I'll take her left," said Father Mendez. "Careful—we don't want to injure her any more than is necessary."

With Margene's arms over their shoulders, Chalina and Father Mendez walked Margene from the main worship area down a few steps into what initially appeared to be a utility room but in actuality was a small sleeping/worship room. Chalina and Father Mendez guided Margene to the bed where they reclined her onto her back. Evanita and the two girls followed.

"We must stop the bleeding," said Father Mendez.

Chalina handed him a clean, white cloth from a counter, and he tied it around Margene's shoulder and neck.

"I felt something when we walked her over here," said Chalina.

"What?" Father Mendez asked.

"It felt like a contraction."

"The shock must have sent her into labor," Father Mendez said.

Margene's water broke and sent Chalina scrambling for equipment.

"My Lord, she's having the baby!" Chalina said.

"Open the cupboard," said Father Mendez while he held pressure on Margene's neck-and-shoulder bandage. "There's string, a knife, and many clean towels. Also, look under the sink for a wash bowl—we may need that."

Chalina did as Father Mendez instructed and found the supplies. It was this way then—Father Mendez continued applying pressure to the bandage and supporting Margene's neck while Chalina delivered Margene's baby. Margene was losing blood pressure and had little strength—not even enough to scream from the pain. In fact, the labor pains were the only thing keeping her blood pressure up.

"Hey, I found the wine, I mean the Blood of Christ. You got a nice booze locker here," said Garcia while he strolled in.

Garcia leaned against the doorway like a mischievous elf.

"Garcia—can you help us? We need you to—" Father Mendez started.

"Man, oh, man! This is what having a baby is like?" Garcia asked.

"Stop yapping and help us!" barked Chalina. "Make up some hot water, will you?"

"That's woman's work," said Garcia.

"Garcia, in the name of the Virgin Mary and the Saints, be a good servant of Christ and help Chalina," said Father Mendez.

"With this disgusting female act? No way, man! You got more booze? Something harder than the Blood of Christ?" Garcia asked.

"No!" Father Mendez said.

"Well, you don't mind if I look, do you?" Garcia asked.

"Father, the baby is stuck!" Chalina yelled, who had her hands full with keeping Margene clean and dry while working the baby out.

"The contractions aren't strong enough," said Father Mendez. "They'll both die if we don't do something."

"Garcia, get your foul breath over here and push high up on Margene's abdomen—but only when I say!" ordered Chalina.

"Ain't no woman gonna push me around!" Garcia yelled back. "But just to make sure the Church ain't holding out on me, I'm gonna take a look at the cupboard in this room. Gotta be some strong liquor around here...wait," he said while finding a bottle in a cupboard. "What's this? Whiskey!"

"By the grace of God, put that back!" Father Mendez ordered. "That whiskey is for medicinal purposes. We'll use it as an antiseptic to prevent infection!"

"Oh I agree with you, Father—it's medicinal. But I'm the one in need of medicinal help. Bottoms up!" Garcia grinned while pouring the whiskey down his throat.

"Get out, get out!!" Father Mendez ordered.

The priest stood up in fury and struggled for the whiskey bottle, but Garcia was too powerful. He maintained his grip on the bottle and withdrew just outside the room and outside of Father Mendez's reach.

"Here, kitty, catch a whiskey mouse!" Garcia teased while swinging the bottle high up—back and forth.

"There is no time for games," said Father Mendez. "You're condemned of this action. Save your soul now or face the wrath of Hell!"

"Yeah? Forget it!" Garcia said.

"In the name of the Roman Catholic Church, you are condemned to Hell!" Father Mendez said while making a casting-out motion with his right hand.

"You don't scare me!" Garcia said.

Garcia lunged at Father Mendez, but the priest was too quick for Garcia. The priest slammed the door and locked it tight a fraction of a second before Garcia bounced his ramming head off it.

Father Mendez returned to supporting Margene's head and bandage. Garcia pounded on the door and yelled for the priest to open up or face his own wrath. The priest ignored him. Meanwhile, Chalina pressed on Margene's abdomen during contractions to assist in delivery.

"Hey Father, I'm sorry," Garcia said with a sudden mock contriteness. "I wanna make a confession. C'mon, open up. I'll confess my sins and help."

"Don't do it, Father," said Chalina. "It's a trick."

"It's no trick," Garcia lied. "I mean it. Please, open up."

"I'm a servant of the Church," Father Mendez said to Chalina. "I must heal the sick."

"But who is more important—a dying mother and a newborn, or a drunk man who should know better?" Chalina asked.

"God loves all his children," Father Mendez said, who felt conflicted inside and made several false starts to open the door.

"No, Father, I implore you. This poor woman who did everything to bring her baby into the Catholic Church under the protection of the Virgin Mary and God deserves our help," Chalina said.

"I heard that," said Garcia. "Men come first, Father. Adam, the Pope—even you, Father. Jesus was a man, Father, so was the first Pope, Peter. Are you going to let this woman fool you like Eve did to Adam? Let me in so I can receive Absolution!"

"Margene and the baby will die if you do!" Chalina warned. "Don't listen to him, Father! It's the booze talking!"

Father Mendez stood up, walked to the door, and pushed a smaller, skull-sized sliding door open that was attached to the main door. The opening was at eye level. Father Mendez was able to see and speak through the opening.

"I can hear your confession in this manner," Father Mendez said.

"Bless me Father," said Garcia contritely, "for I am about to sin!" he shouted while thrusting his arm through the opening.

Garcia caught Father Mendez by the throat and expended his mighty effort to choke the priest. Chalina screamed, and the priest gasped for air.

"Unbolt the door, or I'll kill you!" Garcia shouted.

Father Mendez attempted to pull Garcia's hand off his throat, but he failed. The priest quickly lost air and the strength to resist.

"Don't let him in!" Chalina shouted again.

"This is your last chance, Father. Unbolt the door, or I'll suffocate you!" Garcia demanded.

Chalina was in the midst of what she hoped was Margene's final contraction. She didn't want to leave Margene in this absolute moment of need, but she couldn't allow Garcia in. Father Mendez's spirit weakened, and he groped to unbolt the door.

Chalina lost patience. She grabbed the knife and lunged at Garcia's arm, hacking and slicing it until he loosened his grip enough to allow Father Mendez to escape the hold. Father Mendez did escape, but Garcia grabbed the knife from Chalina and slashed it through the air madly in hopes of catching one of the two.

"I'll kill you. I'll kill you both if I have to!" Garcia flailed.

Father Mendez and Chalina remained out of Garcia's reach. Chalina attempted to help Father Mendez get his breath back, but he waved her off. Not able to speak, he motioned for her to help Margene again, which Chalina did.

"Wah, wah!" cried a small baby.

Chalina tied off the umbilical cord but realized she had no knife to cut it.

"Father—I need the knife," Chalina said.

Chalina helped Margene by wrapping the baby in towels and pressing on Margene's abdomen to push out the afterbirth. Garcia continued shouting and waving the knife about. He groped the door's inside to unbolt it—using the knife as an extension of his own arm to undo the lock. Father Mendez shook his head a few times and finished massaging his throat. Then out of sheer anger, Father Mendez picked up a nearby glass vase and smashed it against Garcia's arm. Garcia dropped the knife and pulled his arm back through the door, cursing and howling at the priest for delivering glass shards into his (Garcia's) arm. Father Mendez closed the sliding door and secured it.

"My baby," a weak Margene called while Garcia went running around the church yelling and moaning in pain.

"Yes, Margene," said Father Mendez.

"Is my baby well?" she asked.

Father Mendez washed the knife and handed it to Chalina, who took it and cut the umbilical cord. The baby continued crying, and Chalina cradled the girl and placed her next to Margene to hold. The baby girl immediately calmed down and cooed.

"Yes," said Chalina, "you have a healthy baby girl. She'll grow up to be a strong, happy person."

Chalina returned to cleaning up the afterbirth and finishing the delivery.

"I wish to name her, Father," Margene struggled to say. "And she should be baptized. Please—baptize my baby now—while I am still here."

"You're going to be fine," Father Mendez lied to her, though he could barely wipe the grave expression off his face.

The priest poured water in another vase, blessed it, poured it over the baby girl, and spoke the proper words to baptize her. He appointed Chalina as the Godmother, to which Margene and Chalina agreed.

"What name do you give your child?" Father Mendez asked.

"Geneva Vallan Carreña," Margene said. "Father. The keys to my apartment are in my pocket."

"Shh," Father Mendez said. "Rest while I finish the baptism."

"No. You must give two things to the baby. First, a diary of my family. It is under a pillow on my bed. Second, a *viola de gamba* in my bedroom closet. It's important. Promise me you will give these to little Geneva."

The priest promised, completed the baptism of Geneva, and produced a baptismal certificate. Father Mendez signed as Officiant, and Chalina signed as Godmother. The priest gave the certificate and a pen to Margene. With the last of her strength, she opened her eyes, lifted the pen, and placed her signature on the document. Her energy expended, she heaved a final breath, dropped the pen, and expired.

"Margene, Margene, don't die!" Chalina yelled.

Father Mendez said a prayer over Margene's body, commending her spirit unto God and the Lord Jesus Christ. Chalina sat motionless and in shock.

"As Godmother, you are now responsible for Geneva," he said.

Father Mendez pulled keys out of Margene's pocket.

"Take these," he said to Chalina. "We must see about—" he started to say before falling fearfully silent.

Garcia had been moaning in pain, with his echoes carrying through the church—sometimes near, sometimes far, but always with the same consistency. Unexpectedly, he let out a sharp yelp, like a dog that'd been run over by an automobile. Thundering, heavy footsteps paraded through the church while deep, vulgar voices soiled the air.

"Franco's Nationalists are here," Father Mendez whispered. "They've just killed Garcia. You must keep quiet in here until they leave."

The baby sensed the hostile air and started to cry. Chalina swept Geneva into her arms and rocked Geneva into passivity.

"I must go out into the church," Father Mendez said. "The Nationalists will expect a priest to be here. And well, I must answer them."

"Father, no!" said Chalina. "You will be killed."

"I took a vow long ago. I'm in the Church's hands, not mine," he said. "But don't worry. It's more likely I'll be too busy performing Last Rites on the dead to be noticed as a threat."

"If they catch you giving a Republican the Last Rite, it could be your last Last Rite," Chalina said. "Stay here and be safe."

"No. I will go out. And I must find out what happened to François. He should have returned by now. Chalina—stay here with the baby. You'll be safe for the present. I'll come for you soon."

"Don't leave me, Father!" Chalina said.

"You are never alone in God's Church," he said, and with that, he unbolted the door and said, "Lock it behind me."

Chalina did as instructed. Evanita decided to leave with Father Mendez and find out where he was going. Jonara followed her mother, but Cerafina stayed behind with Chalina and baby Geneva.

"There he is," said a Nationalist soldier, referring to the priest. "You're the priest of this church?"

"Yes," said Father Mendez. "Peace be with you."

"Never mind that. We need to borrow the church for a few days until Girona is under control," the lead soldier said. "Is there anyone else here besides you?"

Father Mendez paused for a moment and thought about how quickly he could give himself Absolution to clear up the lie he was about to tell.

"No one. I am here alone," he said.

"He lies!" another soldier said. "How do you explain this?"

The soldier dragged Garcia's body to the priest.

"What happened?" Father Mendez said, feigning ignorance.

"He was here in the church, desecrating the pews with wine and his foul stench," said the soldier.

"I thought you said there was no one here but yourself. How do you explain this dead drunk?" the lead soldier asked.

"He must have come in while I was in back," lied the priest.

"With this in his hand?" the lead solider asked, referring to a bottle of church wine. "Who else is here?"

"I believe I answered that already. Now if you'll forgive me, I am needed—" Father Mendez said, but he was cut short.

"Another Republican," said a soldier now entering through the main door. He dragged with him the dead body of François.

"Did you know him, Father?" the lead soldier asked.

"Why do you ask?" the priest asked.

"You may have a clever tongue, but the rest of your face belies your true intent. You knew this man. It sickens you to see him dead."

"It sickens me to see any of God's children die in such a manner," Father Mendez said. "Yes, I knew this man. His name is François Vallan."

"I bet there are more of these Republican maggots hiding here," said the solider (Garcia's soldier) who'd brought Garcia forward earlier. "Let's clean them out!"

"Father," said the lead soldier. "You can help us and live a lot longer, or you can join your conspirator Republicans in the afterdeath."

"The Lord is my light and my salvation, whom shall I fear? The Lord is the stronghold of my life, of whom shall I be afraid?" Father Mendez said, reciting Psalms from memory.

Garcia's soldier struck the priest across the face and said, "Do you fear us now, Father?"

Several soldiers laughed. Father Mendez fell to the floor, stared down for a moment, looked up with fresh blood across his face, stood up, and continued.

"When evil men advance against me to devour my flesh, when my enemies and my foes attack me, they will stumble and fall," Father Mendez said.

François's soldier stepped forward and kicked out the priest's legs. Father Mendez fell again.

"So we're your enemies, are we?" the lead soldier asked.

"Who's falling now?" Garcia's soldier mocked.

The soldiers laughed again.

"One last time, Father—where are they?" the lead soldier asked.

Father Mendez expended all his effort to stand again.

"Lord, do not deliver me to the desire of my foes, for false witnesses have risen against me, breathing out violence," the priest recited.

"You're wasting time," said another soldier. "A priest takes a vow of silence."

"Then let him be silent," said the lead soldier.

The lead soldier throttled Father Mendez and dragged him along the hallway and stopped—close to the room where Geneva was born.

"Look," said the François soldier. "Broken glass."

"Yeah—like the glass I found in the drunk's arm."

"Do you wish to help us now?" the lead soldier asked Father Mendez while releasing his grip on the priest's neck.

Father Mendez gasped for breath and struggled to speak.

"Who are you hiding in there?" the lead soldier asked.

Father Mendez spoke the last words of his life, "The Lord is my shepherd, I shall not want. Though I walk through the valley of the shadow of death, I will fear no evil, for you are with me, your rod and your staff—they comfort me. You prepare a table before me in the presence of my enemies. Surely goodness and love will follow me all the days of my life, and I will dwell in the house of the Lord forever."

With that, Garcia's soldier slit the priest's throat. The lead soldier looked at Garcia's soldier with mock surprise.

"His voice was chafing my nerves," Garcia's soldier said.

The other soldiers chuckled in a low murmur.

"Let the fun begin," said the lead soldier. "Open the door."

Garcia's and François's soldiers lunged at the door and broke the lock. The door burst open, revealing an empty room with no traces of Margene or anyone else inside. Evanita and Jonara stared in disbelief—where were Margene, Chalina, and baby Geneva? Jonara had another question—where was Cerafina? Jonara knew that Cerafina was physically with her back in the 2023 music room. Yet she had no idea where to look for the daughter of Davino and Marina.

"Cerafina!" Jonara shouted.

Evanita heard the shouting and was startled.

"Don't worry," said Jonara while she held Evanita's hand. "The girl who held your other hand should be with Chalina and Geneva."

"Little Voice, I wish I could see you. You frightened me before, but nothing could scare me now—not after what I've seen here. The suffering, the killing—this is all so terrible. I thought I had it bad with the factory fire and prison. But these people—they're dead. Father Mendez knew he was going to die, but he spoke against these wicked soldiers to the end. I don't know if I could do that."

"He was a brave man," said Jonara.

"My mother hates all men," said Evanita, "but how could she hate someone like Father Mendez? He gave up his life to protect my family."

"She hates Catholics too," said Jonara. "She would hate Father Mendez for that."

"Yes, she would. Oh why must this world be filled with so much hate?!" Evanita lamented.

Evanita was both sad and irritable.

"Cerafina!" Jonara shouted again.

Jonara held her hands to her mouth and shouted one last time:

"Cerafina!"

"Don't shout in my ear!" Cerafina replied.

Jonara shook her head and realized she was back in Geneva's music room in the year 2023. In lifting her hands to her mouth, she dropped the viol and bow. Cerafina grabbed both from Jonara before they hit the floor.

"Where are you?" Jonara asked, a little dazed from the journey back to 2023.

"I'm next to you, as I've been all this time," Cerafina said. "I was about to answer you when you dropped the viol and bow. Now the journey is broken."

"We must go back—to Girona, no...wait...to the Elrod 402...no...what happened back in the church? No wait, they were both churches...Patriojet...what was the name of Margene's church? Saint Christopher...yeah...back to Christopher's," Jonara finally mustered.

"Girl!? I am pooped! And I need to go to the bathroom before my bladder explodes. That was stressful!" Cerafina replied.

"Tell me what happened," Jonara demanded, but her words weakened, and she was in dire need of water to spare her parched mouth. "Okay," she relented, "when you get back...you promise, don't you?...You'll tell me what happened...you know... with baby Geneva and the others...you'll tell me, right?...And I'm going to get some water...Cerafina...are you listening?...Where did you go?"

CHAPTER 6

Waltz

2023 Oct 4, Wed Afnoon. Corpus Christi, Texas.
2006 Nov 19, Sun Afnoon. Elrod 402. Portland, Oregon.

"Cerafina!" Jonara called.

"What is it?" Cerafina replied as she returned from the bathroom.

"Hurry. We must play the viol again. Hurry," Jonara urged.

"Jonara," Cerafina called. "Look at my hands."

"You have blisters," Jonara said.

"Now look at yours."

"I have blisters too. And one of them is broken open," Jonara said.

"We're not supposed to get blisters from a viol," Cerafina said. "And I'm terribly tired. I need to go home and rest."

"No, wait!" Jonara said. "We can wear gloves...there's lotion somewhere in the house. C'mon, Cerafina, we can't quit now."

"We can try again later," said Cerafina. "I'll see if I can come over after dinner."

"The viol, the viol!" Jonara replied.

"Jonara, be careful—you're getting obsessed with this viol. It could mess you up."

"I want to play it, but I need your help!" Jonara continued.

"Give it a rest! I know it's fun to learn a new instrument, but you have to know when to say, 'Stop'," Cerafina urged.

"I can't stop," said Jonara.

"Hmmm, what am I going to do with you?" Cerafina laughed. "If only you weren't grounded—we could visit your mother in the hospital."

"But I am grounded. I have nothing else to do," Jonara said. "And you never told me what happened at Saint Christopher's."

"Yeah, I didn't, did I?"

"Nope. You owe me that much, Cerafina!"

"Okay, I have an idea," Cerafina said.

"Does that idea include telling me what happened?" Jonara asked.

"Yes, it does. But I'm afraid of one thing."

"What's that?" Jonara asked.

"That after I tell you what happened, you'll get a bigger craving for the viol than you have now," Cerafina explained.

"I promise, I won't have a bigger craving," Jonara said.

Cerafina laughed.

"What's so funny?"

"How can you promise not to have a craving?" Cerafina asked.

"I just did," Jonara said. "I made the promise."

"I know, I know. Yeah, you made the promise. But how do you stop the craving? No, I don't think you have that much power yet. But I'm going to help you with your craving. I'll give you something to take your mind off the viol."

"I don't want to quit," said Jonara.

"I know. Trust me, Jonara, and I'll tell you what happened back in 1939. Can I get your trust?" Cerafina asked.

Jonara paused. She fidgeted with her hands, she lightly bit her lip, and her eyes darted around the room for a moment.

"Okay, I'll trust you," Jonara said at last.

Cerafina walked over to the record player and put on a waltz.

"I'm going to teach you the waltz," Cerafina said.

"But you are supposed to—" Jonara started.

"Listen, don't talk. Trust me—this means you must listen and follow," Cerafina explained. "The waltz goes in beats of three—one-two-three, one-two-three, one-two-three. Now I'll be the man and you be the woman. Put your hands like so, and I'll hold you like this. Good. Follow my lead and imagine your upper body is gliding through the air. Let your legs do all the work. Don't take little nervous steps—do as I do—long, gliding, graceful steps. Follow my gradual up and down motion—don't bob up and down like an apple in water. Good. You're doing just fine."

Cerafina led Jonara through the waltz while the record continued playing. Each time Jonara opened her mouth to say something, Cerafina shushed her.

"Shhh. Feel the waltz, Jonara. Feel the waltz. Do you feel it? Don't speak, just nod," Cerafina said.

Jonara nodded in affirmation.

"Good. One-two-three, one-two-three, one-two-three. Say that to yourself and nothing else. Good."

Jonara had started the waltz with a nervous shake, but Cerafina gradually worked most of it out of Jonara. To set Jonara completely at ease, Cerafina briefly stopped the waltz and kissed Jonara on both cheeks—one at a time. Both girls felt giddy and strange. Cerafina resumed the waltz, and Jonara followed with better nerves.

"Now I'll tell you the story," Cerafina said. "Father Mendez left the room. We were inside, but we could hear everything. Chalina got very nervous when she heard that both Garcia and François were dead. She knew the end had come. Baby Geneva picked up on Chalina's nervousness and started to cry—just a little, and she wasn't very loud—but it was enough that Chalina started looking for a way out. She tapped some of the walls and cupboards. I think she was looking for a place to hide. She didn't find anything."

"Chalina turned off the lights and started to climb under the bed, but she stopped. Next to the bed along a low place in the wall was a crack of light. Chalina pushed on the wall, and it moved a little. She figured there was a secret door there, and she was right, but she couldn't get it open. She did her best to force it in without making too much noise, but that didn't work. Then she thought to use her long fingernails and pull the door open. It came out a little, but not too much."

"Chalina was ready to give up when the door opened! A nun or sister came through the opening and waved Chalina into the tunnel. Chalina took baby Geneva and went in. Two more sisters came through the opening. They carried Margene's body into the tunnel. Another freshened up the bed and room, and I followed that one in the tunnel just as she closed the secret door and bolted it."

"The tunnel went on for a long ways—I don't know how long—but we ended up in some sort of crypt. We met with other sisters. I couldn't believe how many sisters were helping! Some were tending to Margene—placing her in a casket and all that. Another took baby Geneva and gave her bottled milk, and another sat Chalina down and gave her something to drink."

"Chalina worried about baby Geneva, but the head sister said everything was going to be fine, that Chalina could hide out there or could go back to her waitressing job. Chalina decided to stay there. The last thing I knew, Chalina went through Margene's purse and talked about getting Margene's apartment things and bringing them back to the sisters for the baby to have. Then you shouted at me and the visit ended," said Cerafina.

"They escaped," Jonara said with a calmer voice than before.

"Yes. They're safe. And you're safe too, Jonara. Just think about the waltz. One-two-three, one-two-three."

The record reached the end of the music. The two stopped and exchanged kisses on the cheek.

"It's almost dinnertime. I have to go," said Cerafina.

"I know," Jonara replied.

"I'll see if I can come back," Cerafina said.

"Okay."

"Are you going to be fine?"

"Yeah."

"Let's put the viol away before I go," Cerafina said.

They returned the viol and bow to the case and placed the case behind the small door where Jonara first found it.

"There," Cerafina said. "The viol deserves a rest too."

"I love you, Cerafina," Jonara said.

Cerafina smiled and winked at Jonara then said, "Our little secret."

Jonara walked her to the door and let her out. As Cerafina mounted her bicycle, Johnny Pindus drove up.

"Hi, Mr. Pindus," she said.

"Hi, Cerafina. Staying for dinner?" Johnny asked.

"No, not today. I gotta get home," she replied.

"Okay. Well, you're always welcome. Jonara can use the company," he said.

"I like her very much," she replied, and she turned back to Jonara with a giggling expression.

The two girls exchanged knowledge of their special affection for each other while enjoying the fact Johnny didn't know or pick up on the body language.

"Thank you for staying with her. Come back soon!" he said.

"I will!" Cerafina replied, and with that she rode away.

Johnny walked inside with some papers under his arm.

"Is Anna making dinner?" Johnny asked as Jonara met him at the front door.

"Anna!" Jonara said. "I completely forgot about her. She hit her head. She's resting on her bed. What are those, Daddy?"

"Papers from the hospital. Test results mostly, and some pamphlets on preeclampsia and thyroid cancer. But let's not worry about that now. Come—let's check on Anna."

Jonara and Johnny walked into Anna's bedroom, but her bed was empty and made up.

"Anna?" Johnny called.

"Over here," she answered from Jonara's guestroom.

Jonara followed Johnny into Jonara's guestroom where they found Anna straightening scattered books and things leftover from Jonara's sleep.

"I'm sorry, Mr. Johnny. I had such a headache from this afternoon. I got behind in my cleaning," Anna said.

"Let me see," he said.

Johnny touched his hand to her skull but was surprised when he realized he couldn't read her body structure.

"That's odd," he said.

Johnny reached for the Moissan Ruby around his neck, but it was gone!

"My stone—where did I leave it?" he asked aloud, not expecting an answer. "Let's see—I last had it—I know—I placed it on the windowsill this morning—it should be over here—no, it isn't. Did it fall to the ground?"

"Daddy," said Jonara. "I found it outside."

"Oh good," he replied. "What did you do with it? I'd like to have it back, so I can see how badly Anna is injured."

"It's...wait, what did I do with it?" she mused.

"Tell me you didn't lose it, honey," Johnny urged.

"I had it, and then I put it somewhere," Jonara said.

Jonara had been so preoccupied with Margene in 1939 that she'd forgotten about the Moissan Ruby. She walked around the bedroom and tapped various things—the bookcase, books, the dresser, the bed frame, the bed, and the pillow.

"A pillow. It's in a pillow!" she said.

"What pillow? Where?" he asked.

"In the dryer!" she said, and she ran into the basement to retrieve it.

"Of all the—" Johnny started to say. "Anna—are you doing laundry today?"

"No sir, and I sorry sir, I was sick and had no—" Anna started.

"Don't worry," Johnny said. "I'm sure Jonara can explain what's going on."

"Here it is, Daddy," Jonara said, but she stopped herself from reaching into the pillow.

"What's wrong?" Johnny said.

"Every time I touch the Water Ruby, it shocks me," Jonara said. "It didn't shock me at the restaurant."

"What about now?" Johnny said.

Jonara reached inside the pillow and retrieved the Moissan Ruby. She held it in her hand without issue.

"It's not shocking me. But it was before," Jonara said.

Johnny took the Moissan Ruby and held it to the light.

"It's in a lower energy state, that's why," Johnny explained. "When it has too much energy, it will shock you. Now then— how did my Moissan Ruby end up in a pillow, and why was the pillow in the dryer?"

"The Water Ruby...it fell from the window...I found it...I tried to see if it would work...it didn't...it got in the way...I had to put it in the dryer," Jonara stumbled.

"I'm not sure I understand. But I'm glad it's not lost. Jonara—in the future, maybe just don't do anything special with the stone," Johnny said.

"Okay," Jonara sighed in relief.

"Let me make something quick for you, Mr. Johnny," said Anna.

"Are you up to it?" Johnny asked.

"Yes sir, I am," Anna replied.

Anna whipped together spaghetti with meat sauce and garlic bread. For Johnny, she presented a beer while Jonara received chocolate milk.

"This is good," Johnny said to Anna.

"Will Miss Eva be here for dinner?" Anna asked.

"No, Anna. She's staying at the hospital," Johnny replied. "She's in extreme pain, and the doctors have her on morphine. The cancer is serious. I was right, unfortunately. The stone doesn't lie. Which reminds me, I was supposed to check on your headache, Anna."

"Oh don't worry about Anna, sir," Anna said.

"No, I insist. Here—let me check. Hmmm, just a slight concussion. You'll be fine, except for a sinus headache," Johnny said after touching her skull temples.

"*Muchas Gracias*," Anna said.

Dinner finished as quickly as it started. Johnny helped Anna clean up while Jonara sifted through the pamphlets he'd brought from the hospital. After the clean-up, Johnny broke out a deck of fifty-two cards and dealt them to Anna, Jonara, and himself at the dining room table.

"What game, Mr. Johnny?" Anna asked.

"Rummy," Johnny replied.

The game started, and the three took turns picking cards and performing melds of three-of-a-kind and sequences.

"Daddy?" Jonara asked.

"Yes honey?"

"I read through the pamphlets. Does Mommy have it?" Jonara asked.

"Yes, she does."

"What she have?" Anna asked.

"Preeclampsia," Johnny said. "The urine test for excessive protein came back positive. She has the other symptoms too—high blood pressure and excessive swelling in her face, hands, and feet. Your grandmother was right, Jonara. Last night, she pressed her lips into your mother's cheek and left an indentation behind."

"Is Mommy going to die?" Jonara asked.

"She can't. I won't let her," said Johnny.

Anna patted Johnny on the shoulder.

"How can you keep her from dying, Daddy?" Jonara said.

"He can't," said Anna. "Our Father in Heaven decides our time on this earth."

"Anna!" Johnny said.

"It's true. You don't want to lie to your daughter."

"Evanita is not going to die," Johnny insisted. "Not while I'm around."

"But she could die, couldn't she?" Jonara asked.

Johnny paused, inhaled deeply, and exhaled to clear his mind.

"Yes, she could die," Johnny replied.

Jonara broke into tears.

"Now don't cry. I told you I won't let her die."

"Can they help her, Daddy? Can the doctors help Mommy?"

"They're treating her with magnesium sulfate and steroid injections," Johnny said. "The magnesium will prevent seizures, and the steroids will develop the baby's lungs. There is another way to save Mommy's life—the baby will have to be born."

"Poor Evanita! She's not very far along," said Anna.

"I know. The baby is not quite mature enough to live on his own. That's why the doctors are giving him steroids—to speed up his development, especially with the lungs."

"What can we do?" Jonara asked.

"Pray," Anna replied.

"I once helped your mother out of a coma," Johnny said. "And I know how her body works on a physiological level."

"Her what?" Jonara asked.

"From using the Moissan Ruby, I know how every organ, every bone, and pretty much every system of her body works. I know why she has preeclampsia, but I'm not sure the best way I can help her."

"How...what...you know?" Jonara asked.

"Yes. It was that fiasco at the River Wood and Battery factory when she injured her legs. She suffered metal poisoning, and it damaged her immune system. Her immune system is supposed to protect against foreign agents like poisons—now it sees the poisons as self and other life as foreign," Johnny explained.

"Mr. Johnny, speak in English!" Anna said.

"Her metal poisoning is causing the preeclampsia. And it's all concentrated in her leg bones. To get rid of the poisoning, she'd have to have her legs amputated. She'd never run again. But even if she wanted to do that, it's too late for this pregnancy."

"Miss Evanita never had problem with Jonara," said Anna.

"I know," said Johnny. "Jonara—when you were inside your Mommy's tummy, your Mommy had no troubles at all. Well, maybe she had a little morning sickness, but she didn't have preeclampsia. We never even thought of her having problems—who does?"

"I don't understand," said Anna. "She was poisoned before, but only now she has the sickness."

"There is one difference," said Johnny. "We're expecting a boy. I know it's true—I've scanned Evanita. Somehow, his gender has triggered this reaction. Evanita was at the very edge of having preeclampsia during her first pregnancy. Because Jonara is a girl, her hormones did not push Evanita over the edge. But the new boy has."

"I've never heard of such a thing!" Anna said.

"I won't bother explaining it to the doctors. They'd think I'm crazy, so what's the use? Also, I don't want to tell your grandmother, Jonara."

"Why not?" Jonara asked.

"Because it will give her more reason to hate men," said Anna.

"But it's her grandson!" Jonara said.

"I'm afraid Anna is right," Johnny said to Jonara. "Telling your grandmother that she may lose her only child and daughter to a male fetus would push her over the edge. She's struggling badly enough with the cancer."

"Oh Blessed Virgin Mary! Save the Carreña family!" Anna prayed. "I can't play cards anymore—I'm too worried. I can't think."

"Try, Anna," Johnny said. "It'll help settle your stomach. No one cares about winning or losing."

"Rummy on the board!" Jonara called.

"Children always bounce back better than adults," Anna said, reacting to Jonara's attention to the card game. "The innocence of youth."

"I'm not so sure," Johnny said with a quizzical look aimed at Jonara.

Jonara won the Rummy game. And the second, the third, and fourth games. Johnny and Anna had played enough despite Jonara wanting to start a fifth game. Anna retired to book-reading in her bedroom while Johnny spoke with Jonara.

"Your hands have blisters," Johnny said.

"I know," she said.

"What were you doing?" he asked.

"Something," she replied.

"What kind of something?" he asked.

"A nothing something," she said.

"And then? What kind of 'nothing something' blistered your hands?"

"A blistery nothing something," she replied.

Johnny laughed.

"Was it the diary?"

"What?"

"Cerafina told you, didn't she? I gave it to her for safekeeping. It's here, right? Don't worry—I don't want it destroyed," he said. "The diary gave you blisters, didn't it? You held it too in-tently, didn't you?"

"Well, not exactly. I wasn't holding the diary, it was on my lap," Jonara said.

"Then what was the blistery nothing something that gave you the blisters if it wasn't the diary?" Johnny asked.

Jonara cringed.

"The truth?" she asked.

"You know I can just touch your forehead and find out. I thought I'd let you tell me first," Johnny said.

"Okay. It was Nanna Geneva's viol," Jonara grimaced. "Don't be angry."

Johnny's eyes lit up.

"I didn't know she still had it," said Johnny.

"Then you knew about it?" Jonara asked.

"Of course!" Johnny replied. "Nanna Geneva helped me learn how to harness the Moissan Ruby with the viol. She played it while I scanned the viol."

"Huh? I don't understand. I thought the Water Ruby only let you scan human girls and women," Jonara said.

"I can scan some objects—if they have a feminine quality to them," Johnny said. "The viol is one of them. But you must be very quiet about the viol. Your mother doesn't know about it, and your grandmother has forgotten about it, I hope. I need to find a way to bring it back to Portland without her knowledge. I never figured out how to operate it."

"I did. This afternoon," Jonara bragged.

"Really? How?" Johnny asked.

"I played it," Jonara said.

"I didn't know you could play," he said.

"I can't, not really. Cerafina helped me. We played it togeth-er," she said.

"Of course," Johnny said. "Why didn't I think of that? But then, how was it Nanna Geneva played it by herself and made it work? I tried several times...Nanna Geneva and I never tried playing it at the same time...it is confusing."

"Maybe it's 'cause I'm a girl and you're a boy," Jonara said.

"Could be, could be. Your Nanna Geneva could see into the future with the viol. I was able to see bits of the future too by touching the viol—but only if I had the Moissan Ruby around my neck. I couldn't see anything without it. But Nanna Geneva could see into the future without my stone."

"The viol can do something else, too," Jonara said. "It connects with these other objects—the Water Ruby, and the diary. Cerafina and I connected with the diary and went back in time."

"Where did you go?" Johnny asked with a grave expression.

"The Elrod 402," Jonara replied.

Johnny sighed.

"And to Saint Christopher's," Jonara added.

"I don't know that place," Johnny said.

"That's where Nanna Geneva was born."

"You went there!? Oh Jonara, how could you! That will give you nightmares," Johnny said.

"I didn't mean to. Mommy went back in time too. I was just going with her," Jonara explained.

"Huh? How? Your mother is in the hospital," Johnny said.

"Not that Mommy. The Mommy at the Elrod 402. She was in church, and she had this headset on, and well, you know, O Grammeni started the Catholic part of the service, and Mommy listened, but something buzzed in her headset, and...oh yeah, she was wearing the Water Ruby...and the next thing I knew, the three of us went back in time to 1939—to Margene's apartment in Girona, Spain."

"That's a mouthful," Johnny said. "Your mother told me about some strange things like that at the Elrod 402."

"Daddy?"

"Yes?"

"Did Mommy go back in time again? I mean, while she was at the Elrod 402?" Jonara asked.

"Yes, she said she did. I never understood why. The Moissan Ruby by itself only sees things as they are, not as they were."

"But I helped her see it...I mean...Cerafina and I helped her see it...the past, I mean...when we went back in time through the diary...she connected with us."

"If that's true, you will have to go back in time with the diary again so your mother can complete her journey," Johnny said. "She said she saw more than just Nanna Geneva being born. There was the other side of the family...oops, I shouldn't have said that."

"Shouldn't have said what? Tell me, Daddy!"

"Hmmm, I suppose you'll have to find out eventually," he said.

"Is this about my grandpa? Mommy's daddy?"

"Something like that," Johnny said.

"Last night when I went back in time to 2006, Mommy always wanted to know who her father was. Grandma Eva would not tell her. And no one ever told me. Do you know?"

"Yes, Jonara, I do," Johnny replied.

"Does Mommy?"

"She used to before the accident," he said.

"Huh? Grandma never told Mommy before the River Wood accident," Jonara said.

"Not that accident. Another accident."

"What accident? Tell me, Daddy, tell me!"

"I can't explain it in a few words. If I try, it will all come out wrong. You'll get the wrong ideas. You'll mistakenly hate certain people."

"Then you'll have to show me," Jonara said. "There's only one problem."

"What's that?"

"We have to put the Water Ruby in the dryer," Jonara explained.

"Oh?"

"Yeah. Well, it's a long story, but when we used the viol to connect with the Water Ruby to connect with the diary and went back to the Elrod 402...and Mommy had the Water Ruby back then...well...everything exploded into ice," Jonara stumbled.

"Whoa. Slow down. Exploded into ice? I don't understand."

"We put the Water Ruby in a casserole dish that had water in it. It seemed to be the only way to make it work without hurting me. The diary was in Nanna Geneva's trunk. We played the viol. It connected with the Water Ruby, the water bubbled a little, and we used the Water Ruby to connect with the diary that was in the trunk at the hospital. It was the only way we could go back in time. The viol only goes into the future, and the Water Ruby only goes in the present. Anyway, we ended up going back to 2006 when Mommy entered the Whalejet. She had the Water Ruby of 2006 around her neck, and then, I don't know how, the two Water Rubies connected. The casserole lid blew up into the ceiling, and the water sprayed everywhere, but it froze whatever it touched. And when Anna came in, the lid fell on her head. That's how she got her owie."

"Another mouthful!" Johnny said.

"So we had to connect without the Water Ruby, but we had to get the diary back. That's when Cerafina went to the hospital. Well, you know that part. She brought the diary back, and we didn't want the Water Ruby to connect, so I put the Water Ruby in a pillow and put the pillow in the dryer. And I ran the dryer. That stopped the connection. So we have to put it in the dryer again," Jonara explained.

"Now I understand," Johnny said. "But I think we should try it my way first. I'll wear it around my neck, and we'll see if we can go back in time together. Remember, Jonara, I've worn and used the Moissan Ruby for many years. I know how to use it. I know its limits. C'mon, let's go to the music room."

Johnny and Jonara entered the music room. Jonara reached to open the door to the viol, but Johnny waved her off.

"I don't think we'll need that," Johnny said. "We'll try this with the Moissan Ruby and Nanna Geneva's diary. It's been many years, but I think I remember how to do it."

"You mean you've gone back in time before? With the diary?" Jonara asked.

"Yes. When I was younger, before you were born."

"Really?" Jonara asked.

"Really! But that's another story."

"Tell me that story too, Daddy!" Jonara demanded.

"So many stories to tell, so little time to tell them all. Can anyone tell all the stories of the universe? Isn't the telling of the

story a story itself?" Johnny asked without expecting an answer.

"Sounds like philosophy," Jonara said.

"It may be," he said. "But there's no time for philosophy
now. Shortly after I found the Moissan Ruby, Nanna Geneva
showed me her diary. She'd been keeping it since she was a girl.
Funny thing, though—she added pages to the diary as she got
older."

"You mean she added more pages of writing, right?" Jonara
said.

"No—she added more physical pages. She'd get paper from
somewhere, cut open the diary's binding, add the paper, and
stitch it back up with catgut," Johnny explained. "Some of that
paper she made herself. She found some strange reeds growing
on Ross Island and made a kind of papyrus paper. She added
that to her diary. I think I told you—did I tell you? That I met
Nanna Geneva shortly after I started getting my teeth done by
your Grandma Eva. Nanna Geneva was up visiting, and she
stopped by the dental office—Page Clinic. That's when I showed
her my Moissan Ruby. I asked her what she thought."

"What did she say?" Jonara asked.

"That it was special. She agreed it was from outer space.
And she recognized the symbol on it. It was on the inside cover
of her diary. When I touched the diary, I saw myself being born.
It scared me so badly that I wanted to run out of Page Clinic,
but Nanna Geneva settled me down and invited me to your
Grandma Eva's house for the afternoon while Grandma Eva
was still at the clinic. That's when Nanna Geneva showed me
the viol. She showed me how to see the past and future without
fearing it. For the past, she used the viol to connect with the
diary, for the future, we just needed the viol. I put my hand on
her shoulder each time. The Moissan Ruby connected me with
her, the viol, and the diary. That's how I learned to use the
Moissan Ruby. Anyway, she knew these relics had nothing to
do with the Catholic Church, but she did believe that God had a
part in placing them on this earth, that we were meant to find
them, and they would reveal a purpose to us. She said it was

up to us to discover this purpose and fulfill it. That's why I don't want your Grandma Eva to destroy them. I don't think we've discovered their purpose yet, and destroying them would be a great tragedy, I'm afraid. I think your Grandma Eva hates them because they remind her of when she was pregnant with Evanita. Those were tough days for her."

"But how can we use the Water Ruby to go back in time without getting hurt?" Jonara asked. "Cerafina and I tried before, and there was a loud squealing noise between the two Water Rubies. It was really bad."

"That was feedback," he said. "Like a microphone coming too close to a speaker. But if we're careful, I think we can avoid that."

"I really want to see Mommy again; I want to help her get through the Elrod 402. Can you help me, Daddy? Please?" Jonara begged.

"Yes, I'll help you. We'll spend a little time there, but then you must go straight to sleep for the night. You look very tired," Johnny said.

"I am tired," Jonara yawned. "Very tired."

"Okay. Get the diary, and we'll sit down," Johnny said.

Jonara fetched the diary, and the two sat next to each other in the very same music-room chairs as Jonara and Cerafina had occupied earlier in the day.

"Open the diary. Do you remember where you left off?" Johnny asked.

"I can find it," Jonara replied. She thumbed through the pages quickly and found the right place. "There."

"Read the passage, Jonara," Johnny instructed. "No, wait. Don't start with the Elrod 402. Look—there's a section on Eva. That would be a safer place to start. We won't have to worry about the Moissan Ruby interacting—at least not at first."

Johnny placed one hand on her shoulder and another over his chest atop the Moissan Ruby. Jonara and Johnny read the passage Geneva had written:

"Eva needed my mothering more than ever, though she never admitted it. She was frustrated with the Elrod 402. They would not allow her to visit unless Eva attended their parental workshops, and Eva refused to attend. I can only hope my little family does not fall apart.'"

The music-room surroundings faded and blended into Eva's house of Sunday, November 19, 2006. Jonara and Johnny stood in the dining room. Geneva sat at the dining room table while Eva jittered back and forth between kitchen, dining room, and living room.

"Eva, sit down," said Geneva. "Relax a minute."

"I can't," Eva said. "Too many things to do. This flower needs repotting. Must repot it."

Eva threw newspapers on the dining room table in preparation for repotting the plant.

"I'm here for you, Eva. Your mother—Geneva Carreña—I'm here. Sit and talk."

"There's too much talking in this world, Mother. Not enough doing. Wow, no wonder. This spider plant is root bound."

Eva separated the roots from the old soil and massaged the roots in preparation for a larger pot.

"Evanita needs you too," said Geneva.

"I know what my daughter needs," said Eva while trimming away some of the roots.

"She needs a mother and a grandmother," said Geneva.

At those words, the knife slipped and cut Eva's finger.

"Ow!" Eva said as her finger bled.

"Wash that out and disinfect it," said Geneva.

"Just stop it, will you? You've been telling me what to do since I can remember," said Eva. "I'm a doctor for Chrissakes, Mother! I can take care of my own body!"

"You're a dentist. You only know teeth," grinned Geneva. "And your body belongs to Christ. Treat it like his tabernacle."

"Don't tell me what I know. Only *I* know what I know," said Eva. "And that body-tabernacle stuff doesn't apply to me. I don't believe in physical subservitude."

Eva grimaced while pouring hydrogen peroxide on her wound.

"You don't keep Mercurochrome in your house? I have some in my purse. It'll just take a second to apply. Here, let me help," Geneva offered.

"Mother, no!" Eva said while blocking Geneva's advancing Mercurochrome treatment. "That was banned in 1998. It's ineffective, and it has mercury."

"Don't tell me what doesn't work. I've used this for years!" Geneva bragged. "Besides, a little metal in the wound keeps the baby sleeping 'till noon."

"Stop pushing your mala-remedies on me!" Eva barked.

Geneva retreated into a wrinkled frown. She returned to her seat and let out a huff before the conversation resumed.

"There. Disinfected and bandaged. Good as new," said Eva as she returned to trimming the spider plant.

"Why don't we visit Evanita? Today? It will give you something better to do," Geneva said.

"I have plenty to do," said Eva.

Eva placed the spider plant in a larger pot and filled the pot with new soil.

"Repotting plants? You have plenty of time for that," said Geneva.

"Not when they're all root bound. They can't keep...argh!" Eva grated while the unbalanced pot tipped to one side, fell over, and spilled dirt onto the newspapers and floor.

"You see? Mother knows best. Your nerves are frazzled. Come then—give up your nervous hobbies and accompany me to the Elrod 402."

"We were just there yesterday, or don't you remember?"

"I remember. I remember many things. I remember my only daughter when she was young and happy, not older and a nervous wreck. I remember when my young daughter trusted me, and we enjoyed life. And I remember my granddaughter before she injured her legs. A Spanish woman—"

"—should never be without her legs. I know, Mother, I know," Eva said.

Eva dropped the bag of potting soil onto the floor in frustration and plopped into a dining-table chair. She wiped her hands clean, placed a hand over her eyes, took a deep breath through her nose (which was partially plugged), and exhaled. Eva combed her fingers back through her hair and looked up with a biting lip to regrasp her composure.

"They won't let me see her," said Eva. "Not unless I attend their parental workshops."

"What?"

"It's true. When she was at the Portland Detention Center before the transfer, I went to visit her. But they started this blaming tirade, as if I were at fault. I'm not a bad mother, Mother."

"I know," Geneva reassured.

"They said I had to attend the workshops. They were going to 'straighten me out'. Invasive people—that's what they are. Making me attend an eleven-step workshop before I can see Evanita. You should have heard them, Mother, they say the root of all teenage delinquencies is marital problems. That's just not true—it's not! And get this—they want to know all about my finances and say I should pay to attend the workshop. And the fee will be based on my annual income! I have a mind to call the American Civil Liberties Union and file a lawsuit permitting free access to my daughter."

"Oh no, no, no, Eva," said Geneva. "Don't drag them into this. You don't want to make a spectacle of our family. Let someone else suffer instead."

"That's exactly the attitude that drives me crazy. And I'm sick and tired of it," said Eva.

"Be practical, Eva. By the time you drag the ACLU into this, file a lawsuit, and get a verdict, Evanita will be out of detention. You've already been through one trial—do you want to go through another? Will there be other lawsuits after that? When will it end?"

"I don't know, Mother. Evanita's murder trial was murder on me. I feel ten years older now that it's over," said Eva.

"Trust me—you'll feel another ten years older if you go to court again," Geneva warned.

"Why must life be filled with so many unfair traps!" Eva lamented.

"Eva," Geneva called.

Eva sat in silence and stared at the spilled potting soil.

"Don't fight the roots of the plant," Geneva said. "Clean up and move on. Play along with the Elrod 402 workshop game. Visit your daughter. Salvage the family."

Eva heard her mother but did not pause to consider her words. Instead, she picked up the pot and plant, reclaimed the soil, and completed repotting it. She returned the spider plant to its living-room position and cleaned up the potting-soil mess.

"So you're going to ignore me, is that it?" Geneva asked.

Eva did not reply. She threw out the newspaper, wiped off the dining table, swept the floor, and mopped.

"Stubborn. You're too stubborn for your own good," said Geneva.

Eva left the room for a few minutes and returned. She was cleaned up and dressed for going into public.

"Well? Are you going to sit there or are you coming with me to the Elrod 402?" Eva asked.

Geneva smiled and nodded affirmatively.

"She's going to go!" Jonara shouted. "Go, Grandma Eva, go!"

Johnny, Jonara, and Geneva followed Eva to her car. Johnny and Jonara sat in back—Johnny behind the driver and Jonara behind the passenger—while Geneva rode in front with Eva.

"Yes," said Johnny as the car pulled into the road. "Your grandmother put up with parental workshop just to visit your mother. She swallowed her pride for the first time ever. I never understood what led her to do it, but now I do."

As Eva drove down the road, Johnny and Jonara experienced a sinking feeling.

"Something's wrong," said Johnny.

The left side of the car lost its integrity for Johnny's weight. He tilted to the left.

"We're sinking again," said Jonara who was now listing to the right.

"Again?"

"Yeah—it happened before with Cerafina—but we fell straight down. This is different."

"The middle of the car is holding up, like a dividing wall," said Johnny, "but the rest is giving way. Hold onto the middle, Jonara."

"I'm trying," she said.

Jonara and Johnny faced each other while holding onto the middle of the back seat. Their legs dangled through the floorboard into the pavement below. The scene was much like watching two people hanging off opposite sides of a wall.

"I feel like my legs are being electrocuted," said Jonara. "Every bit of steel going through my legs is stinging me."

"I know the problem," he said. "I'm not shaking enough. I need to focus more."

Johnny shook his head like some nervous Parkinson's patient. Slowly, the floorboard regained its cohesion, and the two regained their comfortable seats in the car.

"Whew!" said Johnny.

"That was close. Can you hold up?"

"I'll have to," he replied, but Jonara was doubtful.

Johnny continued shaking his skull. He sweated profusely.

"Daddy, you can't keep going on like this," she said.

"I can...have done this before...just takes concentration... can relax a little when car stops...always have problems with moving machines," he struggled to say.

It was nearly one o'clock on Evanita's first Sunday afternoon at the Elrod 402. Eva and the three arrived at the facility in time to begin the one o'clock workshop—held in Whalejet. The four exited Eva's car and proceeded up the steps to the jet's open door where an Oxian directed Eva and Geneva down a hallway to room W213. A placard hung next to the doorway and read, "W213: Parental Orientation".

"Please, Eva, sit here," said Dazia—the education chief. "And this is your mother, Geneva, I believe?"

"Yes, I am. Impressive," said Geneva.

"We try to learn the names of all our girls' parents, grandparents, and family," Dazia said.

"Are we late?" Geneva asked.

"Oh no, not at all," Dazia replied. "We'll wait a few more minutes before starting. It looks like we'll have a small turnout today. It's not surprising with the upcoming Thanksgiving holiday—parents are busy with turkeys and other preparations."

There were two other pairs besides Eva and Geneva—a middle-aged couple who'd gone all gray and looked like they had too much to drink and smoke over the years, and a younger couple who didn't look old enough to have a teenage child.

"I think that will do it," said Dazia. "Let's begin. My role name is Dazia. I'm the chief of education here at the Elrod 402 facility. Welcome to Parental Training Orientation."

"So far so good," said Johnny.

"With Grandma?" Jonara asked.

"No, with me. I don't have to focus as hard," he said.

"Yeah, you're right. You're not shaking your head and sweating like in the car," Jonara said.

"Don't have to," Johnny said. "Sitting down to human speech is easy—very little work needed. As I told you, the Moissan Ruby doesn't do well with machines. It works much better with people."

"The purpose of orientation," continued Dazia, "is to give you an overview of the program and to take your first steps toward rehabilitating your child."

"This is the brainwashing part," Eva whispered to Geneva.

"Shh," Geneva whispered back.

"I'm sorry, is there a problem, Ms. Carreña?" Dazia asked Eva pointedly.

"No," Eva replied, biting her tongue.

"Good," Dazia said. "It's very important we concentrate on completing the orientation and moving you all along to the next phase as soon as possible. We all have busy lives and don't want to dwell on any particular subject too long, do we? Please refrain from talking out of turn during the orientation. Periodically, I will ask for questions at which time you may raise your hand for permission to speak. At other times, I will ask you directly to answer. Is this clear to everyone? Good. Let's begin."

"This is worse than school!" Jonara said.

"Fortunately, no one can hear us," said Johnny.

"Mommy heard me the other time," Jonara said.

"Yes, the Moissan Ruby helped her do that," Johnny said. "We'll have to be careful around her, but here at least we can speak freely without worry."

"There are eleven phases to the parental portion of your child's rehabilitation. These phases are: marital problems, anger, rebellion, self-mutilation, divorce, anxiety, grief, depression, victimization recovery, parenting skills, and the teen-adult post follow-up support."

Geneva listened with intrigue while Eva rolled her eyes in disbelief.

"I can see why your Grandma Eva flipped out over these sessions," said Johnny.

"Why?"

"They seem to have come up with a formula to describe every parent with a so-called problem child. They'll probably try to convince your Grandma Eva that she fits into this scheme," Johnny said.

"To help you remember, I've prepared these handouts for your reference," Dazia said.

Dazia handed out packets listing the eleven phases and how parents should relate to them.

"Every one of us has fallen into one or more of these phases from time to time," Dazia explained. "But when a child goes bad, we as the parents must take the responsibility and admit our failings. We may not always see ourselves in these phases, but they happen, and others see us going through them. My job is to help open your eyes to the phases you are in and to prepare you for the following workshops. These workshops will show you how to move on to the next phase. Ultimately, you will reach the final stage—the post follow-up program. By that time, you will have the parenting skills needed to receive your child from the Elrod 402 and take her home."

"Grandma is a little jumpy," said Jonara.

"She's very disturbed by what she's hearing," said Johnny. "I can read her thoughts. She thinks this is propaganda, psychobabble, and a manipulation tool to rope in the parents."

"At this time, I want to touch on each of these phases with you all. It's not necessary to go into deep discussion—that will happen in your later workshops. What we want to do here is identify some of the major issues that have forced these phases upon us," Dazia explained.

"Your Grandma Eva is really fuming now," Johnny said to Jonara. "She doesn't like the use of the word 'we' as if she's automatically agreeing with whatever Dazia says. She also wants to say that the Elrod 402 is the major issue forced on her, not anything else."

"I can't believe she's keeping quiet, like Nanna Geneva told her to do. I'd tell that Dazia a thing or two," Jonara said.

"Your grandmother doesn't want to ruin the workshop. I don't know how she's keeping her anger buried, but she's desperate to visit Evanita," Johnny said. "Let's listen to more."

"You, Ms. Carreña—give me an example of a marital problem that has affected Evanita," Dazia said.

"I don't have any mari—" Eva started, but Geneva jabbed her in the ribs.

"I'm sorry, Ms. Carreña, I didn't catch that," Dazia said.

"I'm a single parent, with occasional help from my mother here," Eva said.

"Your grandmother is playing into the game," Johnny said. "She doesn't believe being a single parent has caused problems for Evanita, but she knows Dazia will accept it as an issue."

"But isn't it a problem?" Jonara asked. "Mommy kept asking about her father. I think it bothered her."

"It's complicated," Johnny said. "Let's listen more."

"Very good, Ms. Carreña," Dazia said. "Statistics show a child of a single parent is three times more likely to have problems than a child with both parents in the home. Did you marry and divorce the father then?"

"No. Evanita has no father," said Eva with a shaky voice.

"You must feel a lot of anger toward Evanita's father. You've rebelled against him by never marrying him and by denying his existence to me. And I can feel the anxiety in your voice. Good—you've just expressed five of the phases—marital problems, anger, rebellion, divorce, and anxiety."

Eva flicked her finger against her temple in disbelief.

"Self-mutilation, that makes six. You're over halfway through orientation already," Dazia said with satisfaction.

Dazia questioned the two couples—the younger and older—on their marital problems, and each gave examples of fights over money, work, and responsibility. Dazia worked them a bit harder to get examples of the other phases such as rebellion and self-mutilation, but they could not think of additional examples.

"Ms. Carreña, so far you've been quick to express your shortcomings in the form of the first six phases. Let's talk about your shortcomings in the other phases," said Dazia.

"Let's not," said Johnny.

"What?" Jonara asked.

"Sorry, I was repeating what Grandma Eva was thinking."

"It's a sad thing seeing our cherished children growing up and falling into the vices of life. I'm sure you've had many evenings where you wondered if it was worth getting up the next day," Dazia said.

"No, I keep active," said Eva.

Geneva elbowed Eva and said, "Why just this morning after you cut yourself, Eva, you were brooding over Evanita."

"Mother!" Eva muffled with a grimaced expression.

"Ah, yes!" Dazia said. "Brooding is an expression of grief. And you cut yourself—more self-mutilation, but in this instance, it's a means to pull yourself out of grief. Studies show that people who cut themselves do so as a means to release opioids from the body to reduce the pain of overwhelming grief. This is their way of crawling out of depression. It's unhealthy, but it works."

"I didn't cut myself on purp—" Eva started to say, but Geneva kept elbowing Eva's ribs and wouldn't let her speak.

"It's all right, Ms. Carreña the senior—she's just mixing her anger and rebellion with her grief and depression. It's quite common to get lost and confused in the phases," Dazia explained. "Good, Ms. Carreña the junior. You've admitted to the first eight phases. The last three—victimization recovery, parenting skills, and teen-adult follow-up—are things we don't expect you to have coming into this first workshop. We'll help you complete these phases in time for your child's release from the Elrod 402."

Dazia moved on to discussing the other couples' examples of grief and depression.

"Your grandma keeps repeating a phrase in her head," Johnny said to Jonara.

"What's that?"

"'She's wrong, she's wrong.' Oh wait, she's thinking other things, 'What a crackpot...more psychobabble...when will this nonsense end?'" Johnny said.

"There must be something we can do for her," said Jonara. "I'm going to give her a hug."

Jonara approached Eva and made a hug attempt, but her arms passed through Eva. It was an all too familiar result, and Jonara was tired of it.

"It seems the only people I can hug in the past are wearing the Water Ruby," Jonara said.

"I know."

"Very good—all of you," Dazia announced. "You are all victims of social pressures that have threatened the loving bonds you cherish in your families. Television, the internet, and other outlets of vice claw at us like nothing before. Your recovery begins here with orientation, and I have certificates for each of you so that you may go on to the next step—marital reconciliation. Please—stand with me now and take the Elrod Oath of Parental Affirmation so I may hand you your certificates."

Geneva and the two couples stood. Eva remained seated, but Geneva pulled her to her feet.

"Rebellious to the end, eh Ms. Carreña?" Dazia grinned. "This won't take long."

"She can't believe she's participating in this hypocrisy," Johnny said to Jonara. "And she's wishing she never came here. Look, she's biting her fingers."

"Why?" Jonara asked.

"Nervous tension," Johnny said. "She's trying to release it. Wait, she stopped abruptly. She realized Dazia is watching her, and Dazia is probably thinking, no, she *is* thinking Eva is participating in self-mutilation. Eva doesn't want to do anything that supports Dazia's claim. Hmm, did Eva think that? Yes, she did."

"What?" Jonara asked.

"Eva thinks Dazia is at least a high-ranking demon if not the devil herself," Johnny said.

Dazia recited an oath one line at a time so that the Carreñas and couples could repeat them. Johnny and Jonara had difficulty hearing the oath. Something was interfering—a buzzing sound that rippled through the airwaves.

"What's happening?" Jonara said.

"I don't know. I can't seem to keep my focus on this room," Johnny said.

The room would remain clear and still for a few seconds and shift to a vibrating distortion for another few seconds.

"We're drifting," he said.

Jonara and Johnny drifted to the floor's edge where it met the outside wall. They attempted to walk back into the room's center but lost grip with the floor.

"It's like slipping on ice!" Jonara said.

The two slipped off the floor's edge into the outside and fell to the ground. The ground shook like an earthquake, and despite Johnny's attempts to vibrate the Moissan Ruby into a more controlled state, the two lost grip with the Elrod 402 and slipped back to Geneva's music room in 2023.

"Oh!" Jonara said with a start. "I'm being electrocuted!"

Jonara reached for the offender inside her pocket and realized someone was calling her cell phone. The cell phone was in vibrate mode.

"Your cell phone broke the link," Johnny said.

Jonara answered the call.

"Oh hi, Cerafina," Jonara said. "You can't? Why not? Oh, okay. Yeah that's important. Yeah, you're having company—a business party for your dad. What's that? Yeah, he's fine. He's right here with me...We found a way to go back. Yeah, we did. Okay, I'll call you tomorrow. Kisses. Bye."

"You need to place your cell phone over on the table or something. Or maybe turn it off," said Johnny.

"Okay, Daddy," Jonara said.

Jonara powered down the device.

"Let's try again. What's the next passage in the diary?" he asked.

"'Eva swallowed her pride and took the Elrod Oath of Parental Affirmation. Dazia gave her the certificate. This allowed Eva to visit Evanita that Sunday afternoon. Evanita was taken from her Redjet dorm room to Whalejet.'"

Geneva's music room swirled. Jonara's and Johnny's surroundings changed to the intake section of Whalejet where Eva and Geneva waited patiently for Evanita.

"I've been here before," said Jonara. "Cerafina was with me. This is where it happened—where the two rubies met. Be careful, Daddy!"

As Evanita was led into the room by an Oxian, Johnny positioned his body such that his left side faced Evanita. In this way, his Moissan Ruby was at a ninety-degree angle to Evanita's. There was no feedback—Johnny and Jonara were able to attend the visitation without pain of feedback.

"What a lovely dress," said Geneva as Evanita hobbled to them and sat down.

"Thank you, Grandma. I wore it to church," Evanita said while setting her crutches next to her in a neighboring chair.

"How are you, Evanita?" Eva asked while giving her daughter a hug.

"I'm holding up, I guess," Evanita replied.

"What kind of church did you go to?" Geneva asked. "Was it Catholic? Protestant?"

"Unitarian?" Eva asked.

"Mostly all," Evanita said. "They held several services at the same time in Patriojet. It's hard to explain. We had headsets and could listen to whichever one we wanted."

"Which one did you listen to?" Eva asked.

"The Catholic one," Evanita replied.

"Good girl!" Geneva said.

"Evanita! You could have picked a more suitable one," Eva said.

"I couldn't, well, I didn't know what to pick. There were no Unitarian services, and I guess it didn't matter. Calico said I should pick the Catholic one since O Grammeni was running it," Evanita said.

"Who's Calico?" Eva asked.

"My roommate," Evanita replied. She lowered her voice, leaned close to her mothers, and whispered, "You have to get me out of here. It's a torture camp. Calico beats me and makes me clean up after her."

"Report it to the authorities," Geneva replied.

"But who?" Evanita asked. "Calico and the security guards are good friends."

"This is outrageous. I'm going to see Fronka Nordekter myself and file a complaint," Eva said.

"I'm scared," said Evanita. "It could get me into more trouble."

"It's only fair," said Eva.

"Maybe you should let Evanita file the complaint," Geneva said to Eva. "If you file it, Eva, they may think you're biased toward your daughter. And they might attribute your complaint to a form of rebellion. This would violate your oath you just gave."

"What? What oath?" Evanita asked.

"It's a long story," Eva said.

"Your mother took the Elrod Oath of Parental Affirmation," Geneva said. "She promises to follow their plan for parent-daughter rehabilitation."

"Huh? You, Mama?" Evanita asked.

"Yes, me!" Eva huffed. "Now let's skip this oath nonsense stuff and file a complaint."

"If you break the oath now, Elrod might not let you see Evanita until she's released," Geneva warned.

"I can't believe they'd do that," said Eva.

Eva called the Oxian (it happened to be Ox-Two) into the room and inquired about filing a complaint. Ox-Two delivered a form and pen to Eva and explained what parts the detainee could fill out and what parts were reserved for office use.

"Good. I'll fill out all the detainee sections. Evanita—give me the details."

"Uh, no," said Ox-Two. "You're not allowed to fill those out."

"Let's turn the other way," said Eva, motioning Evanita to turn her back on Ox-Two.

"Uh, that's a no-no," said Ox-Two. "I'm going to ask you to return that form. You can't break policy."

"No, I won't return this form yet. Not until it's filled out so my daughter can receive fair treatment. Now I'm going to fill this out, and there's nothing you can do about it."

"Extra security to room W218," radioed Ox-Two.

"Mama, just give the form back," Evanita pleaded.

Extra Oxians arrived and awaited Ox-Two's orders. The three Evas stood in defense.

"Give them the form!" Evanita shouted.

"They'll have to force it from me," Eva said.

"As you wish, Ms. Carreña," said Ox-Two, who motioned two Oxians toward Eva.

"Stop, stop!" Evanita screamed.

"Brutality! I'm a taxpaying citizen!" Eva called while she wrestled with the Oxians for control of the form. "You'll hear from my lawyer about this."

"Oh please, Eva, try to settle down," Geneva suggested.

It was no use. The scene turned ugly and violent. One Oxian struck Eva with a rubber hose while the other grappled for the form. Evanita continued to scream, and the Moissan Ruby around her neck harmonized with her waves of anxiety. The form crumpled between the grips of Eva and the grappling Oxian. Evanita screamed again, and the Moissan Ruby thrust out away from her chest and spun violently, like an unbalanced washing machine. Waves of electrical energy flew out in random directions from the centrifugal force. One such wave struck Johnny Pindus. He shielded his own Moissan Ruby by twisting his body (as if surfing the ocean) in an attempt to minimize contact between the rubies.

"Daddy—hold on," Jonara urged as she realized he was struggling to maintain control.

Johnny's sweat and shaking only added to the control problem. His own Moissan Ruby took to life and sent out its own electrical waves. A shock wave formed in the empty air between them. However, the shock point did not remain steady. Evanita's Moissan Ruby—feeding directly off the violence in the room—overpowered Johnny's Moissan Ruby and downtracked its way to Johnny's.

"Daddy!" Jonara shouted as a final bolt of bluish-white energy struck Johnny in the chest.

Johnny fell to the ground motionless. The wave from Evanita's Moissan Ruby encircled the room. Jonara's vision of the Elrod 402 faded, and she found herself back in Geneva's music room of 2023—but her father was still on the floor, and he'd slipped into convulsions.

"Daddy," she said while shaking Johnny. "Daddy, wake up."

The Moissan Ruby glowed through Johnny's shirt. Jonara removed the stone from Johnny and tossed it across the floor. In the short time she'd touched it, the stone fed electrical shocks through her forearm, like a thousand ants crawling inside her muscle tissues. She returned her attention to Johnny. His convulsions ceased, but he remained motionless. Jonara put her hand to his mouth to sense Johnny's breath—nothing. She searched for a pulse on his wrist—none.

"Daddy, you can't leave us now!" Jonara said.

Jonara pushed on his lungs, but nothing. She pushed on his heart—no better. She sat on his chest—no help.

"Stop this insanity!" she yelled.

Jonara beat her fists on his chest in rapid succession as if she were beating a rock-and-roll rhythm on a drum. Jonara checked for a pulse. She felt one—maybe two—heartbeats followed by nothing.

"Get up from that floor!" Jonara yelled.

She kicked her father in the ribs and continued yelling for him to get up. Johnny remained motionless. Without warning, Anna burst into the room.

"What are you doing?" Anna cried. "Stop kicking your father!"

"He's hurt badly," Jonara said while Anna pulled her away from Johnny. "He's not breathing, and his heart stopped."

Anna knelt beside Johnny, used one hand to feel for a pulse, and with the other lifted his eyelid open.

"Arrrg!" Johnny shouted as he sat up suddenly.

"Eeeeeee!" Anna screamed as she ran out of the music room.

"Daddy! Daddy!" Jonara jumped in glee. "Daddy! Are you alive!?"

Johnny blinked his eyes wide-open several times while he stared into space. He shook his skull once and turned to Jonara.

"Jonara," he said. "Hmmmm, wow, that was tough!"

"Don't you ever do that to me again!" she cried.

Jonara jumped into Johnny's arms and gave him a big hug while her tears soaked into Johnny's shirt.

"That wasn't supposed to happen," he said. "Boy do I have a headache!"

"I bet you do!" Jonara laughed between tears.

"What happened to the Moissan Ruby?"

"I threw it over there," she said.

"I better take a look at it," he said.

"I'll help you get up," Jonara offered.

Jonara helped Johnny to his feet, and the two walked over to the Moissan Ruby. Johnny leaned over to pick it up but quickly returned to an upright position.

"Whoa! Dizzy!" he said.

"I better pick it up," she said.

"Careful. Pick it up by the necklace—don't touch the stone directly."

Jonara did as instructed. She handed the Moissan Ruby to Johnny. He studied it, touched his finger quickly to it as a test, and was glad the stone didn't shock him as before.

"It seems to have calmed down," he said.

"I knew this would happen. I knew it!" Jonara said.

"Something's different about the stone," he said.

Johnny held the Moissan Ruby to the lamplight and fell into disappointment.

"It's not sparkling like it normally does," he said.

"Is it dead?" Jonara asked.

"You speak as if it were alive," Johnny said.

"Isn't it?"

"I don't know," Johnny replied. "But it does look dead to me. I'll test it tomorrow morning in the sunlight. Meanwhile, I think you should get some rest. I know I need to. Whew! That was a workout!"

"Are you going to be okay?" Jonara asked. "Should you go to the hospital?"

"No, no," Johnny said. "This happened once before when I first used the stone. Wow, that was over thirty years ago. My body isn't recovering like it did when I was younger."

"Then we should go," Jonara said.

"No, I'll be fine. Besides, who will take care of you if everyone's in the hospital? I'll just get a good night's sleep. Be a good girl then, Jonara—it's time for sleep."

"Okay."

Jonara retrieved her cell phone and returned it to her pocket. She walked up the stairs to her guestroom while leaving the diary in the music room. She was a bit jittery from the ordeal with her father's electrocution.

"He could have died," she whispered. "His heart and breathing stopped. Wait, he was dead!"

Jonara sat on the bed for a moment, hoping to settle down. She could not. She sifted through books in the bookcase. Books on the Catholic Church, works of fiction, and inspirational books filled the shelves. Jonara picked up one book and thumbed through it, but she couldn't sit still long enough to read it.

"I can't settle down," she whispered.

Her cell phone vibrated, and it startled Jonara out of her scalp.

"I am way too wired!" she said while regaining her breath.

Jonara placed the cell phone to her ear and pressed the answer button.

"Hello?"

"Joni! My best of friends. How are you doing down there in Texas?" a familiar voice said.

"Almarita Foster! I'd forgotten all about you!" Jonara said.

"You forgot about me? I just talked to you last night! How could you forget me so quickly?" Almarita said.

"Oh Allie, you just don't know what I've been through. It's too much to explain, just too much!"

"Oh try, Joni. I have all kinds of time for storytelling," Almarita said.

"They aren't stories—they're true—all of them. Everything that happened in 2006 and 1939 is true," Jonara said.

"2006? 1939? Huh? Are you okay?"

"Don't you believe me?" Jonara asked.

"What about the hospital? Did you get in last night?"

"Yeah," Jonara replied. "Davino took me, and Cerafina came along."

"Cerafina? Your new girlfriend?" Almarita laughed.

Jonara blushed and paused a moment.

"Davino is her dad," Jonara said. "You know that."

"You sound different, Joni. What's going on?"

"I told you—a lot has been going on," Jonara said.

"What kind of things?" Almarita asked with a more serious voice.

"I don't like your tone," Jonara said.

"What's up with you?"

"Cerafina is not my new girlfriend," Jonara insisted.

"I was kidding. Can't you take a joke?"

"It's not funny," Jonara said.

"Whatever. So have you met any cute guys down there?" Almarita asked.

"No, I've been too busy," Jonara said.

"Too busy for guys?"

"Yeah."

"You're in the perfect hunting ground. You can have a quick boyfriend—anyone you want. No worries about attachments. When you come home, you automatically dump him."

"That's not fair," Jonara said.

"That's life. You just gotta work the system," Almarita said.

"What about love?"

"Take love where you can get it," Almarita suggested. "But keep the leash short and firm on the guy—whichever guy you're walking at the time. Remember—you're the pack leader."

"Whatever."

"Don't 'whatever' me, Jonara Carreña Pindus. This is our future."

"Is there a mouse in your pocket?"

"Our future—as in you and me. And don't give me that wanna-be-a-doctor talk. You can be a doctor if you want, but you still have to rope a guy on a leash," Almarita explained.

"That will never happen to me," Jonara said.

"Don't fall for that relationship-based-on-love routine. It always ends up in divorce. And you'll be broke—no money. Love doesn't pay the bills, but a guy on a short leash will."

"I'm tired of hearing your short-leash crap," said Jonara.

"It's no crap. You'll find out sooner or later."

"Yeah, right."

"Yeah, right," Almarita mocked. "But you're too busy doing things," she continued with sarcasm. "Too busy to find cute guys. What have you been doing that's so important?"

"Seeing my mommy!" Jonara stated as fact.

"Seeing your mommy. Okay, when was that?"

"Last night."

"And how is she?"

"She has preeclampsia," said Jonara. "Her blood pressure—"

"I know what that is. My mom had that with me. I almost wasn't born. They treated her with magnesium sulfate and gave her steroids. I made it. So will your mom. That was last night. What about today? Did you see her today?"

"No. I'm grounded. Had to stay in all day today," Jonara admitted.

"Bummer! That explains why you haven't flirted with any guys. But couldn't you just sneak out today like you did last night?" Almarita asked.

"I did sneak out, but it wasn't to see guys," Jonara said.

"Oh? Who did you see?"

"What makes you think I went out to see someone?"

"Because you've been acting strangely since last night. I can hear it in your voice," Almarita said.

"I went out to help Mommy, sort of."

"Huh? How? You went to the hospital? You said you didn't see your mom."

"I didn't make it to the hospital, but that's where I was going, sort of."

"Sort of? You can do better than that! Who did you meet? What was her name?"

"There you go again, Allie!"

"If you're not out hunting guys, you're out making new friends. Figures. First time away from me, and you start dumping me. I see where I stand now!" Almarita said.

"You're making this bigger than it really is!" Jonara said. "I can't explain in easy words—it's too hard."

"Try. Where did you go, and who did you meet?" Almarita pressed.

Jonara paused.

"Well?"

"I walked halfway from Nanna Geneva's house to the hospital. And I gave up. I sat on a bench. And there was no one there to meet. I sat there alone," Jonara explained.

"Until?"

"Until?"

"Yes, there's always an until," Almarita said.

"Until Cerafina showed up with—"

"Aha! Cerafina!"

"She had a diary with her—my Nanna Geneva's diary. It was taken from me this morning, if you must know. Cerafina got it back from the trunk of Nanna Geneva's car. And that's all!"

"No it isn't," Almarita countered. "Nothing is simple when a diary is involved."

"What do you mean?" Jonara asked.

"You know what I mean, or you should know. There are two things people do with diaries—write them and read them. Since it was your Nanna's diary, she wrote it. So how much did you read with Cerafina?"

"Not too much. We read...hey, wait a minute. I never said we read—"

"You just did."

"But not before."

"You didn't have to," Almarita said. "Girls read diaries, especially diaries of female ancestors. It's the best kind of reading there is. So did you kiss her?"

"What!? Almarita, how dare you?" Jonara said.

"How dare me? How dare you! You never said anything to me about a diary until now. You held out on me. What other secrets are you keeping?"

"Nothing," said Jonara.

"So did you kiss her?" Almarita asked again.

"I told you I didn't."

"No you didn't, you didn't say anything. I think you kissed her."

"Kissed who?"

"Now Jonara—you can't play games *and* get away with them—at least not around me. I think you're experimenting."

"Allie!"

"And I thought we had no secrets between each other, because best friends are like that. But I guess if there are secrets between best friends, they aren't best friends anymore, are they?" Almarita said.

Jonara paused again.

"I'm right, aren't I? Your Almarita can read people like a book."

"I'm not holding out on you. It's just—"

"Just what?" Almarita asked.

"I'm confused. Too much is going on. Cerafina has been helping—"

"Because your Allie can't, is that right?"

Jonara sighed.

"Triangles don't work," said Almarita.

"What makes you think you're so smart?" Jonara asked. "You think you're some kind of adult who's been around the world and knows everything!"

"I don't know everything," Almarita said. "But I know a lot. I watch people. I read books, and I learn stuff on the internet. You know it's true. In fact, I don't know why you're asking. Wait, yes I do know—you're trying to distract me."

"Yeah?"

"Yeah! Triangles don't work. Best friends are one-two, one-two, one-two. Like a pair of fighter pilots. That's what we are, Jonara, a pair of fighter pilots. I'm the leader and you're my wing woman. There's no room for another plane—it'll just get in the way."

"But I like Cerafina. We're good friends," Jonara maintained.

"Triangles don't work. One-two-three—it's odd. Who's one and who's three? I'm your one and you're my two. Cerafina should be a three, but she's older than you, isn't she?" Almarita asked.

"Yeah."

"And more experienced."

"She did teach me how to play the viol," Jonara admitted.

"So! You're making music with her. What's the pecking order now? If you're two, who's one? Cerafina? So that makes me three, is that it?" Almarita asked.

"Why all the questions, Allie?" Jonara asked.

"Because I see my best friend being ripped away from me!"

"You're jealous!" Jonara said.

"Jealous?"

"Yeah, jealous!" Jonara repeated.

"Hold on now. You used the 'J' word. But that only works for a boyfriend-girlfriend thing," said Almarita.

"Not always. People get jealous of other people's things," said Jonara.

"But we're not talking about things. We're talking about friends, or are we?"

"What are you talking about?"

"You know what I'm talking about, Joni. About Cerafina: she's not just a friend, is she? You kissed her. Experimenting?

You played music with her. Did you dance with her? Who played the man?"

"Stop asking questions!" Jonara stammered.

"I'll stop, Joni, I'll stop. You've already answered them in your own way. Just remember, Joni—a woman can't have children unless she has a boyfriend. You want a family someday, right? Of course you do. You think a guy will fall for you if he knows who you really like?"

"I can like whoever I want," said Jonara.

"You can, but he can't. Better get used to saving your money for a visit to the sperm bank when you're older. I, on the other hand, plan to have a family the old-fashioned way—with a husband when I'm old enough."

"I'm only thirteen! I'm too young to think about a family," said Jonara.

"You're never too young to plan. Just be careful, Joni."

"It's getting late," said Jonara. "Allie?"

"What?"

"I don't want to lose you as a friend. Don't hate me."

"I don't hate you, Joni."

"I need friends. I need people."

"I'll always be there for you, Joni."

"Thanks."

"I'll call you tomorrow," said Almarita. "Goodnight!"

"Goodnight. Bye."

"Bye."

Almarita's conversation rattled Jonara's nerves. How could Allie know about Jonara and Cerafina?

"It doesn't matter," said Jonara. "Everything's falling apart anyway."

Jonara plopped into bed and pulled the sheets over her. She rolled over. And again. To the other side. Onto her stomach. No, her back. Switched pillows. No good.

"I can't sleep!" she said. "How can I sleep? Maybe if I read the diary, that will help me sleep. No, Cerafina said I'll get a craving. But I do have a craving. No, Cerafina danced with me. We did the waltz. One-two-three. Almarita says triangles don't work. One-two-three. Oh why must it be so complicated?!"

Jonara made for the bedroom door. She turned back. She went for the door again. And back.

"I'm like a pendulum. Stuck. Can't decide which way to go," Jonara muttered. "Caught between sleep and the diary. Caught between friends. In the middle of a sandwich."

Jonara continued like this for several more strides, but she was tired and lost balance. She struggled to regain her balance and in doing so reached for an umbrella to steady herself—an umbrella in the corner of the room. Jonara imagined the umbrella was Cerafina. Jonara waltzed with the umbrella, channeling her compulsive pacing into the dance Cerafina had shown her earlier.

"One-two-three, one-two-three, one-two-three," Jonara whispered as she continued her waltz.

Jonara felt at ease, and her troubles melted away.

"I'm sorry, Almarita," Jonara whispered to the air. "I can't stop the triangle. One-two-three...one-two...three. One...two... three."

Jonara's words and waltzing slowed. Her eyes and skull felt incredibly heavy. Her steps slowed and grew smaller. She miniwaltzed her way to the side of the bed and slipped in between the layers of sheets, placing the umbrella next to her.

"One...two..." she whispered as her mind carried her thoughts into the threes of sleep.

CHAPTER 7

Wielding A Stick

2023 Oct 4, Wed Late pm. Corpus Christi, Texas.

Jonara dreamed she danced the waltz in a threesome with Cerafina and Almarita. They held hands in a circle, and the entire circle rotated and revolved around a central cerise-colored light. Jonara could not see, but something inside the light generated waltz music. Jonara looked back from the light to her dance partners and was surprised to see her mother and grandmother instead of Cerafina and Almarita. They smiled at Jonara, and she smiled back.

"One-two-three, one-two-three, Grandma-Mommy-and-me," Jonara dreamed.

Without warning, the light went out, and the music stopped. She lost grip of her mothers and groped around in the dark. She sought relevance and direction but found none. Jonara trembled herself into consciousness. She sat up in bed and realized the dream was over, she was awake, and she couldn't get back to sleep. The umbrella remained next to her in bed. She glanced at it while trying to think of what to do next.

"I could sneak out of the house and see Mommy," Jonara first thought. "No, what good would that do? I can waltz again like Cerafina said."

Jonara took the umbrella and waltzed with it in her bedroom, but she lost inspiration. No music, no passion—just an empty, shaking nervousness.

"Maybe I'll get some hot chocolate and crackers," she said.

Jonara slipped down the stairs quietly to avoid waking Johnny and Anna. She walked past the music room on the way to the kitchen. She stopped. She walked back to the music room's door, reached for the doorknob, and stopped herself.

"No, I shouldn't," she whispered.

Jonara took a step to the kitchen and a step back to the music room's door.

"No. Cerafina says 'no'."

Jonara pushed herself into the kitchen where she sat down to a cup of hot chocolate and crackers. But in sitting there alone, Jonara had plenty of peace and quiet. Her thoughts jumped into the quiet, but she tried to suppress them with food. She ate a cracker and chased it down with hot chocolate.

"Think about crackers and hot chocolate," she reminded herself, but already her mind drifted to the diary.

"We're not stuck on the diary," she said. "Crackers—we can do many things with them. We can dip them in a drink," she said as she dipped a cracker in her hot chocolate and ate it, "or we can break them in half," she said as she broke one in half and ate it. "Crackers—think about crackers."

But Jonara's mind wouldn't stop. She went from breaking one cracker in half to breaking several crackers—in halves, quarters, and eighths until in a mad frenzy she crumbled her crackers into her hot chocolate and downed her beverage as if it were her last.

"I can't stand it!" she muttered.

Jonara placed her empty mug in the sink and began a march to her bedroom, but in her distracted state, she lost cadence and tripped on the first step of the stairway.

"Stubbed toe. Ow, that hurts. I'll just sit here for a moment."

She couldn't. The stairs were uncomfortable.

"No, the living room couch," she said, and she went to the couch.

"Too dark and lonely. Back to the kitchen."

Jonara never made it to the kitchen. She paused at the music room and couldn't stop herself from entering. She sat on the very chair where she had played the viol earlier with Cerafina.

"My toe...it doesn't hurt anymore. I'm getting...like before...butterflies in my stomach...Cerafina...I miss you."

Jonara half fancied an attempt at the viol, but consideration for her father and Anna got the better of her. She saw the diary and couldn't stop looking at it.

"I don't have to read it. Maybe if I bring it with me to my bedroom...maybe I won't worry as much...it's just for safekeeping," she said.

Jonara took the diary and snuck up the steps to her bedroom without incident. With diary in hand, her anxiety dissipated. She placed the diary under her pillow where she could be sure nothing unfortunate would happen to it.

"Grandma Eva wanted to destroy it," said Jonara. "Now I must protect it."

Jonara slipped into bed and stared at the ceiling.

"Maybe just one sneak peek," she said.

Jonara retrieved the diary and read the next passage.

"'After fighting with the guards over the complaint form, Eva was thrown out of the Elrod 402 and barred from seeing Evanita. We appeared in Multnomah County Court in Portland and petitioned the judge to permit visitation with Evanita. Fronka Nordekter appeared in defense.'"

Jonara placed the diary under her pillow and fell fast asleep. The sun and moon circled backward around the earth several times before slowing to a near stop. The circling lights blinded Jonara's eyes.

2006 Nov 20, Mon. Multnomah County Courthouse. Portland, Oregon.

Jonara's vision cleared, and she was in the Multnomah County Courthouse—not the same room as the one for the murder trial, but the judge was the same—Judge Gregory—and Mr. Manis represented Fronka Nordekter—who sat at the defense table.

"This hearing is now convened," said The Court. "Prosecution—I've received your complaint. Would you begin, please?"

"Your Honor," said Ms. Haughf. "In item one of the complaint, my client's daughter, Evanita Carreña, is subject to physical abuse."

"From the complaint, she is asked to perform cleaning duties, is that right?" asked The Court.

"Yes, Your Honor, but it is more than that. Evanita's legs are in casts. She cannot move around easily," Ms. Haughf explained.

"Yes, I remember that from her court appearance here," said The Court.

"Your Honor," said Mr. Manis. "The Elrod 402 prides itself in teaching self-sufficiency and discipline. Cleaning duty is a part of this. These girls are not at a resort—they're at the Elrod for rehabilitation—to teach them responsible lifestyle habits."

"Your Honor—the plaintiff's daughter has sustained injuries to her head from beatings," Ms. Haughf said.

"I don't see medical records in the complaint," said The Court. "Has she seen a doctor to evaluate her condition? Did she suffer concussions?"

"Yes and no," said Ms. Haughf. "However, her scalp shows redness where she was beaten."

"Redness that could be caused by the dry weather or an allergic reaction to Elrod shampoo," said Mr. Manis. "Your Honor, there is no proof the plaintiff's daughter has been beaten on the head."

"Ms. Haughf, do you have anything further on complaint number one?"

Ms. Haughf paused for thought but reluctantly answered, "No, Your Honor."

"Proceed to complaint number two," said The Court.

"Your Honor, my client is being denied visitation rights of her daughter," said Ms. Haughf.

"She was permitted a visitation with her daughter," said Mr. Manis.

"Yes, but only after being required to attend a workshop," said Ms. Haughf.

"The Elrod 402 values active parental participation in a child's rehabilitation. The workshop gives parents that participation," said Mr. Manis.

"The workshop is demeaning to parents," said Ms. Haughf. "It requires them to admit to some eleven-phase plan of failed parenting and recovery."

"The workshop is meant to illustrate areas a parent may wish to examine and ways to improve upon those areas," said Mr. Manis.

"Parents are required to sign a form and take an oath, admitting to these supposed failings," said Ms. Haughf.

"The oath and signature show attendance and completion of the workshop—nothing more," said Mr. Manis. "I would like to point out that the plaintiff completed her orientation workshop successfully after which the first visitation was scheduled and completed."

"Ms. Haughf—I fail to see the significance of the workshop regarding visitation rights. It appears your client has no issue with the workshop. She completed it without delay and took an oath," said The Court.

"Your Honor, the defendant requires workshop attendance before allowing visitation rights. The Elrod 402 has denied future workshops to my client. Direct visitation rights are not allowed," said Ms. Haughf.

"Rehabilitation requires cooperation from all parties," said Mr. Manis. "The child must see positive role models. We argue that children enter the Elrod 402 because of one or more parental failures. To reexpose the child to this failure means setbacks."

"Yes, Mr. Manis. But what is the harm in allowing a child to see her mother?" The Court asked.

"Your Honor—the plaintiff took an oath to follow Elrod's rules of conduct—this oath was taken during the parental orientation workshop," Mr. Manis explained. "The plaintiff violated policy by filling out a complaint form meant for the detainee. The plaintiff was asked to cease and desist from filling out this form, and she refused. The plaintiff was asked to return the form, and she refused. Further, the plaintiff fought with several security guards over this form. Your Honor, this disregard for authority was displayed in front of her daughter, Evanita Carreña, the detainee the defendant is attempting to rehabilitate. Now I ask The Court—why should good tax money be spent to rehabilitate a child under conditions such as these?"

"Ms. Haughf, do you wish to comment?"

"Your Honor, my client was attempting to file a complaint regarding physical abuse imposed on her daughter. My client was following Elrod procedure in obtaining a form. While it's true Elrod procedure states the detainee must fill out the form, my client was simply providing help to her daughter," said Ms. Haughf.

"Your Honor, the Elrod 402 has security videotape of the visit. We wish to submit it as evidence," said Mr. Manis.

"Let's see it now," said The Court.

"Prosecution states the plaintiff was providing help to her daughter. Let this video demonstrate the plaintiff's form of 'help'," said Mr. Manis.

The Court, Mr. Manis, Fronka Nordekter, Ms. Haughf, Eva, Geneva, and Jonara watched as the videotape projected onto a large screen portraying Eva as a defiant and passionate woman engaged in petty fighting over a piece of paper.

"Your Honor must understand the circumstances of this video," Ms. Haughf said.

"I understand full well the nature of this video," said The Court.

"Your Honor, if I may continue," said Ms. Haughf.

"Please."

"A mother should not be denied visitation rights of her daughter. And her daughter deserves fair treatment—not physical abuse—"

"That has not been proven," said Mr. Manis. "Further, the video shows the plaintiff demonstrating impulsive behavior toward a perceived abuse that does not exist. Instead of calmly seeking clarification through the Elrod process—a process approved by the district—she unilaterally takes what she perceives as an issue into her own hands. Your Honor, I submit the plaintiff is a vigilante. At a minimum, she should seek psychiatric counseling. Once a psychiatrist certifies her fit to participate in the Elrod process, we will be happy to re-admit her to the parental workshop process and reinstate visitation rights."

"Your Honor—this is a hearing to decide my client's rights as a plaintiff. Defense is out of order to propose to The Court—"

"Ms. Haughf. I will decide what is in order and what is not. Mr. Manis—do you have anything to add to this hearing?"

"No, Your Honor," said Mr. Manis.

"Ms. Haughf?"

"No, Your Honor."

"Very well. I'm ready to rule. There is not enough here to go to trial. Further, I'm upholding Defense's recommendation for the plaintiff's visitation rights. She is to seek a psychiatrist of her choice. Doctor-patient privacy will be maintained, however, the psychiatrist will inform the Elrod 402 when the plaintiff is fit to resume parental workshops. The Elrod 402 is, of course, free to relax these requirements at its discretion. This is the ruling of The Court. Case dismissed."

"Your Honor, may I approach?" Ms. Haughf asked.

"Yes. Counsel?" The Court said, beckoning Mr. Manis forward along with Ms. Haughf.

"Your Honor," Ms. Haughf whispered to Judge Gregory, "perhaps a psychiatrist isn't the best option for my client."

"Your Honor," whispered Mr. Manis, "a psychiatrist is the only viable treatment option for Eva Carreña."

"Your Honor, if you would hear me out," said Ms. Haughf.

"Mr. Manis—your observation is noted. Allow Ms. Haughf to present her point."

"Thank you, Your Honor. I recommend community service as a means of demonstrating my client's good faith," Ms. Haughf said.

"Community service? Your Honor, her client is—" Mr. Manis started, but Judge Gregory held a hand up and stopped Mr. Manis from continuing.

"What sort of community service?" The Court asked.

"Volunteer dental work through her church—the Broadway Unitarian Universalist Church," said Ms. Haughf.

"It's a trick. Ms. Carreña already does volunteer work through her church," said Mr. Manis.

"Mr. Manis is right. Ms. Haughf—I'm beginning to doubt your sincerity," said The Court.

"Then through Barnseed Baptist Church," said Ms. Haughf.

"That church is surrounded with controversy," said The Court.

"Again—counsel seeks to subvert your decision. You must not—" Mr. Manis started.

"Mr. Manis—control yourself. You are not The Court. Ms. Haughf—while your general recommendation for community service is admirable, your specific examples are weak. Since you cannot come up with a noble community service, my original ruling will st—"

"Your Honor, Your Honor," Geneva rushed in to say. "I could not help but overhear."

"You were not called to the bench," The Court said.

"I know, Your Honor, and I beg forgiveness," Geneva said. "But this community service idea—I have a good one. It occurs to me the Catholic Archdiocese of Portland is building a new church to replace Saint Stellan."

"Good God!" Mr. Manis said. "That's just another—"

"Wait, Mr. Manis. Ms. Geneva—continue," The Court said.

"Well, there are plenty of projects that need doing at Saint Eugene—that's the new church. And money needs to be raised to pay for everything. There are lots of things Eva can do—bake cookies for the bazaar, sew garments for the priests," Geneva explained.

"Your Honor, are you going to let this hearing slide by the wayside for some baked cookies and patchwork quilts?" Manis asked.

"Ms. Geneva—I'm sorry, but this—" The Court started to say.

"She's also an excellent ballerina," said Geneva.

"Really?!" Mr. Manis asked with excitement.

"Really?" The Court asked with equal anticipation.

"Really," Geneva answered.

"That I'd love to see," said Mr. Manis. "The reputed man-hating dentist dances in support of the ultimate pro-male institution—the Roman Catholic Church! Your Honor—I would be more than happy to drop my request for psychiatric treatment in exchange for this new proposal."

"Ms. Haughf?"

"Your Honor, in light of Mr. Manis's interpretation of this community service, I request the service be performed at a less patriarchal institution," Ms. Haughf said.

"Nonsense, the Catholic Church is fine," said The Court. "Besides, your client's own mother suggested it. I amend my ruling—"

"Your Honor," interrupted Ms. Haughf. "I wish to confer with my client."

"Do not interrupt my ruling, or I'll hold you in contempt! All of you—you may leave the bench. I will issue my new ruling. Well? Return!" The Court instructed.

Mr. Manis returned to the defense side while Ms. Haughf and Geneva returned to the prosecution side.

"Eva—I'm sorry. I'm afraid I've made things worse—" Ms. Haughf tried to explain.

"It is clear that Ms. Eva Carreña is beyond conventional psychiatric treatment," The Court said. "Therefore, as a sign of good faith, Eva must perform community service for the new Catholic Church—Saint Eugene—in the form of a ballet routine as part of a fundraising effort."

"What!?" Eva burst out.

"Silence!" The Court gaveled. "Upon completion of this fundraising activity, the Elrod 402 agrees to re-admit Ms. Eva Carreña to the parental workshop series. This hearing is adjourned."

Judge Gregory gaveled twice. The hearing ended, and while others exited the courtroom, Eva remained in her chair, shocked.

"What happened?" Eva asked Ms. Haughf. "We're supposed to be the plaintiff. We're supposed to receive rights under the law. Now suddenly I'm dancing for the Catholic Church so I can visit my daughter? Jan! You've let me down!"

"Eva, please, try to calm down. We'll work something out," Ms. Haughf said.

"There's nothing left to work out," Eva rattled. "Everything gets worse and worse. Have I no friends left?"

"You have your mother," said Geneva.

"I trust you least of all. Somehow you're behind this—I know you must be—what else could you have been discussing at the judge's bench. Jan? Say something!" Eva commanded.

"I tried to get you community service instead of psychiatric treatment," said Ms. Haughf. "It seemed harmless enough. I went for our church, but that was rejected. I went for community service at Barnseed. That was also rejected. I was running out of options."

"That's when I stepped in," said Geneva. "I volunteered you for a fundraising dance at Saint Eugene's."

"How dare you—both of you! Making deals behind my back!" Eva said.

"We stood right in front of you," said Geneva. "No one stood behind your back."

"It was wrong. I admit it," said Ms. Haughf. "I'm sorry. You're not legally bound to do the fundraising. We'll just have to work with the Elrod 402 to find another way. They were set on the psychiatric treatment option—"

"Which I would never do," Eva interrupted.

"Well there we go," said Ms. Haughf. "It may take a few weeks—maybe months."

"She'll be out by then," Eva said.

"Oh honey," said Geneva, "think of this as your opportunity to make peace with the Catholic Church. We welcome you with open arms."

Geneva held out her arms to Eva, but Eva returned a cold shoulder.

Jonara felt a tug on her right arm. She looked but did not see anything pulling it. Wanting to stay in the courthouse, she resisted, but the pull was too strong. Amazingly, the umbrella appeared in her left hand. She beat at the invisible force, but the force pulled her through the ceiling and into the atmosphere. Jonara continued to beat at the force pulling her right arm. The clouds and sun moved quickly through the sky, and Jonara descended into the Elrod 402 as the sun set below the horizon.

Jonara entered Patriojet.

"Mommy!" Jonara yelled.

Jonara rushed to hug Evanita, but Jonara's arms went through her mother.

"Mommy—can't you hear me? Don't you have the Water Ruby?" Jonara asked.

Jonara looked closely at Evanita's neckline and saw no necklace.

"It's gone! Where is it, Mommy?"

Evanita could not hear Jonara. Jonara watched her mother struggle with mopping the floor where so many Elrod girls had spent the day in school.

"Did you call me here, Mommy? Did you pull my right arm?" Jonara asked.

Evanita finished mopping a section, rinsed out her mop bucket, and proceeded to fill the bucket with fresh soap and water.

"Your time is up. Mopping should be finished. You'll have to stay and finish, but this delay cannot go unpenalized. In addition to mopping, tomorrow you will clean out the bathrooms in this jet," said Oxia, who tapped her security stick on Evanita's shoulder.

"It's too much!" Evanita complained.

"Are you complaining, Eve Carson? I need some cleaning done in Cafederijet. Are you volunteering for that too? Complain, and you'll volunteer."

"No, Oxia, I'm not complaining," Evanita gritted.

"Good. You know, Eve Carson, there are ways to reduce one's workload," Oxia said.

Oxia stroked Evanita's cheek while conveying a more compassionate tone. Evanita did not look up but instead continued to prepare the mop water.

"One doesn't have to work in solitude. One doesn't have to suffer. You can barter your skills—one type of work for another. I have a warm cabin with good food and clean air. There are no ammonia fumes from mopping, no dirty toilets to clean."

"What are you saying?" Evanita said.

Oxia moved closer to Evanita and spoke in her ear.

"I'm just asking you, Eve, to keep me company in my cabin tonight," Oxia said. "You won't get into trouble for being out late—I'll escort you to your dorm when we're done. I'm very gentle, Eve Carson. Don't be nervous—I'll guide you through everything."

"I have a boyfriend," Evanita said.

"Is he here? Would he know? He might enjoy being a voyeur—most guys do," whispered Oxia. "You're a beautiful young woman. Beautiful young women should not waste their time cleaning up after others."

Jonara swung her umbrella in a downward motion at Oxia, but the umbrella passed through her. Jonara didn't care. Oxia needed to be beaten off her mother, and Jonara had no reservations about repeatedly clubbing through Oxia. Jonara lifted the umbrella for another clubbing stroke when the force pulled her right arm from Patriojet into Redjet. Jonara was now in her mother's dorm room with Calico.

"What are your secrets, little stone?" Calico said while holding the stone.

Calico shook the stone like a bottle of pepper. Each time she shook the stone, Jonara felt a force squeezing her arm. Calico removed the stone from the necklace chain, set the chain aside, and tossed the stone in the air. As the stone returned to Earth, Calico took a rolled-up newspaper and smacked the stone across the room into the wall where it lodged.

1943 May 30. Lake Front Stadium. Kenosha, Wisconsin.

It was early Sunday evening on Memorial Day in Kenosha, Wisconsin. Through Geneva's diary, Calico and Jonara traveled back to 1943 where the Racine Belles women's ball team played against the Kenosha Comets. Calico did not see Jonara, but Jonara saw Calico. The two sat in the stands next to two women who had been sitting in the rain for hours waiting for the delayed game to begin.

"Grandma?" Calico said. "Grandma Trudy, is that you?"

"So what do you think of the stadium?" Trudy asked.

"Great—if it had a roof. How are we supposed to watch a game with all this rain?" Jane asked.

"It'll stop. I know it will."

"So much for the inauguration ceremony. Wasn't that supposed to start at three-thirty?" Jane asked.

"And the first game at four," Trudy added.

"It's after supper. What did you bring in the lunch bag?" Jane asked.

"Your favorite—a corned-beef sandwich," said Trudy. "Here."

Jane took the sandwich from Trudy and removed the wrapper. She took several bites and relished the taste.

"Mmmm. Nothing like corned-beef hash," said Jane. "It needs washing down. Good thing I brought my canteen with me."

While holding the sandwich in one hand, Jane pulled out her canteen with the other, placed it between her knees, and opened the top.

"Ahhh," Jane said after taking a swig of water. "That'll wash it down. I just thought of something—maybe I can hold my canteen out and refill it for free."

Jane held the canteen out in a meager attempt to catch raindrops.

"You'll never catch rain that way," said Trudy.

"What a way to spend Memorial Day!" Jane said.

"I hope my Wilton isn't spending the night in a trench where it's raining and miserable."

"Better to have him in a trench than in the warm arms of a French barmaid," Jane said.

"Jane! You take that back about my husband. Maybe there is someone over there looking out for him," Trudy said.

"Get a clue, Trudy. Men will look for any port in a storm."

"What about your husband? Do you wish the same for Jack?" Trudy asked.

"He knows what'll happen if I find out he's cheated on me. I'll simply beat him up."

"You'd never do that," Trudy laughed. "You always cave in to him."

"And I can do it, too," Jane continued.

"Maybe you can," said Trudy. "You're a tall woman, but I'm just a petite woman. I can't tell Wilton much of anything."

The rain stopped. Players for the Kenosha Comets and Racine Belles took to the field for warm-ups.

"Look—they're practicing," said Trudy. "So what do you think now, Jane? Can women play ball?"

"I always knew women could play softball," Jane said.

"But this isn't normal softball," said Trudy. "The rules are different. The game is somewhere between softball and baseball."

"The ticket says 'All-American Girls Softball League'," said Jane.

"I know, but this is different. Look how good they are in warmup."

"But how well can they play?" Jane asked.

"We'll see, won't we—well?" Trudy said.

"I'm glad I caught the first day of this new league. This is exciting! Thank you for inviting me," Jane said.

"What else? We're friends, aren't we?"

"Yes," said Jane. "We are."

The two exchanged hugs.

"Grandma, can't you see me?" Calico asked.

"No, she can't," said Jonara.

"Who was that?"

"Evanita—the one you call Eve Carson—calls me the Little Voice. You can't see me, but I can see you," said Jonara.

"This is a dream?" Calico asked Jonara.

"In a way. But everything you see really happened," Jonara said.

"Then this is my grandmother. And she really did watch the first game between the Racine Belles and Kenosha Comets. This must be May 30, 1943," said Calico. "I remember the date from newspaper clippings. Why are you here, Little Voice?"

"I'm here because you dragged me here. You used the stone to connect with me. But only I have the means to go back in time. So you're going back in time through the stone and then through me," Jonara explained.

"This is impossible," said Calico.

"See? Nothing is impossible," said Trudy. "Women can do anything. We play ball, we work in factories. Say, what are you looking at?"

"Everyone's warming up except for one girl," said Jane.

"You mean the one over by the fence signing autographs?" Trudy asked.

"Yeah. Who's that?" Jane asked.

"Don't you recognize her from the 'Kenowhere' Evening News?" Trudy asked.

"I never liked Kenosha being called 'Kenowhere'. I'm somewhere," Jane said.

"Yeah, you're in Kenowhere," Trudy laughed. "But c'mon—that gal's photo was in the paper. A good write-up on her too."

"She has many fans. Look at them all clapping and cheering for her," said Jane.

"That's because she's popular," said Trudy.

"I want to be her fan," Jane murmured aloud without realizing it.

Jane stood up and stared at the young outfielder with the light, golden hair.

"Are you all right?" Trudy asked.

Jane said nothing but instead stared at the outfielder. "Where does she live?"

"She's from Kenosha," said Trudy. "Sit down, Jane."

Jane remained standing and motionless.

"Hey you, do you mind?" yelled a man from behind.

"Come on, Jane, sit down!" Trudy urged while pulling on Jane's arm.

"Yeah, you make a better door than a window," yelled another.

"You're embarrassing me," said Trudy. "Quit staring. People will think something's wrong with you."

One of the men from behind left his seat, walked to the aisle, and walked into Jane's row. He confronted her.

"Hey buddy, do you mind sitting down?" he said, tapping Jane on the shoulder.

"I'm not a buddy," said Jane, and she hardly budged.

"My man, do you mind? We want to watch the young ladies on the field. So be a sport and sit down!" he said.

"I'm not your man," Jane said while keeping eye contact on the outfielder.

"Well you ain't no lady!" he laughed, and his friends sitting behind laughed with him.

"Yeah? Maybe this woman needs to dummy you up!" Jane said, now turning toward him.

"Oh look fellows, Tomboy here is going to dummy me up. Oh, I'm shaking in my boots!" he said sarcastically.

Jane lifted her fist and started into a motion to punch the guy, but Trudy jumped up and grappled Jane from behind.

"No!" Trudy commanded. "Don't do it. You'll make a scene."

Trudy urged Jane to sit down. Jane agreed reluctantly while Trudy remained standing.

"That's better," he said to Trudy. "Good to see you and Tomboy know your places." He turned to Jane and jeered, "And you know yours!"

The man leaned over uncomfortably close to Jane's head and laughed. In his laughter, his diseased breath plumed around Jane's face, and his acrid odor ate through her sinus passages. Jane bit her lip to repress her discomfort, but the man simply would not stop laughing and breathing on her. When his saliva drooled on her right hand, she lost all composure and whacked his jaw with her right arm, like a baseball bat hitting a pumpkin face.

The local crowd around Jane silenced. The heckling man touched his finger to his bleeding mouth and looked at it.

"That's assault," he said, but his voice shook.

His friends sitting behind Jane went silent for a moment before breaking out into drunken laughter. They teased and picked on the heckler unmercifully.

"He's got no guts," jeered one, referring to the beaten heckler.

"Whipped by a woman," said another.

"It's not a woman!" he cried in agony.

The heckler left Jane's row and returned to his seat. But his jaw pain grew, and tears of pain rolled down his bleeding face. His friends teased him further about crying like a sissy, and he left the game never to return.

Trudy sat down.

"Jane—you have to be careful," Trudy whispered. "This is a family outing. People are looking at us like we're crazy. I'm fearful someone will remove us from the game."

"Why?" Jane said. "I wasn't doing anything."

"You were staring at that outfielder, Jane. You were staring! A woman doesn't stare at another woman the way you were! Are you sick?"

"You're imagining things," Jane said defensively.

"They put people on the funny farm for things like that. It's against the law!" Trudy warned.

"We're here to watch the girls play ball. I don't know what you're talking about," Jane said.

"You know exactly what I'm talking about," Trudy said to Jane in a hushed voice. "And if you act like that again, I'll be forced to distance myself from you. I'm not going to an institution for something you do."

"You're kidding," said Jane.

"And it doesn't help that you're wearing slacks," Trudy said.

"I like slacks," said Jane.

"You should look ladylike in public, not like you're lounging around at home," said Trudy.

"These aren't pajamas. I paid good money for this outfit. And it's comfortable. So don't tell me what to wear," Jane grinned.

The outfielder finished signing autographs and ran off to rejoin her teammates. The players stood in a patriotic "V" formation—the "V" standing for "Victory"—in preparation for the National Anthem.

"Look—they're almost ready to start the game," said Trudy. "Now for the National Anthem."

The announcer praised the troops overseas on this Memorial Day Sunday. The crowd joined in with the players and sang the Star-Spangled Banner.

"Play ball!" yelled the umpire after the people finished singing.

"I can understand why that outfielder has so many fans—the way she looks and walks and all," said Jane.

"Hush! She has fans because she's from Kenosha," Trudy said.

"So? The Comets are from Kenosha. What's the big deal?" Jane asked.

"The big deal about that outfielder is that she's the only Comet from Kenosha," said Trudy. "She grew up here. Everyone loves her."

"Huh? The only Comet from Kenosha? That doesn't make sense," Jane said.

"Most Kenosha Comets are from out of state—Illinois, Canada—" Trudy said.

"Canada!"

"Didn't you know?"

"No," Jane said.

"It was all in the Kenosha Evening News," said Trudy.

"Kenowhere," Jane said sarcastically.

"All players had tryouts at Wrigley Field, and the players were assigned to different teams based on ability—to even things out. Jeez Louise, Jane! You don't read much, do you?"

"Sure I do!" Jane said.

"Yeah?"

"Yeah!"

"Like what?" Trudy asked.

"All kinds of things."

"Name one."

"At work the other day...I read the Machinists' Handbook," Jane said.

"You call that reading?"

"Yeah, I do."

"That isn't reading," said Trudy. "Besides, that's not even the right title. We use the Machinery's Handbook at Daschwirk."

"No one calls it that," said Jane.

"Because no one can read," said Trudy.

"They read the handbook," said Jane.

"They pretend to read it and ask someone what it means," said Trudy.

"No way! I never ask for help. Never. And I take it home to read, too," boasted Jane.

"What about reading for knowledge, for fun?"

"I like reading for knowledge—the Machinists' Handbook has all kinds of knowledge."

"Knowledge of the world? Of current events? Did you see yesterday's *Saturday Evening Post*?" Trudy asked.

"No, I was busy working overtime at the plant," said Jane. "It was late when I got home, and I didn't have a dime for the *Post*."

"Well I did. I brought it with me. Look at the cover art," Trudy said before being interrupted by the game.

"Foul ball!" called the loudspeaker.

"Look out!" Trudy warned Jane.

Jane turned but too late. The softball landed squarely on Jane's forehead. Stunned, she tried standing up as if to do something, but she didn't seem to know where she was or where to go.

"Hey you! Sit down. You're being a door again," said a male voice from behind.

"Ah shut up!" Trudy yelled back. "Janie, Janie, sit down dear. Are you all right?"

"What? What?" Jane said with her eyes darting.

"Arbie! Over here!" Trudy called and waved.

"Trudy!" said Arbie.

Arbutus "Arbie" was selling beer at the game and darted into Trudy's row from the aisle with a tray full of beer-filled cups.

"Janie—this is my sister, Arbutus Hansen," said Trudy.

"Arbutus Hansen," Jane replied in a trance.

"She's my sister," Trudy continued while massaging Jane's head.

"My sister," repeated Jane.

"No—my sister, not your sister," Trudy said.

"Not your sister," Jane repeated.

"Better give her this," Arbie said, handing a cup of beer to Trudy.

"How much, Arbie?" Trudy asked.

"Shhh," Arbie whispered. "It's on the house."

"Hold this to your head," said Trudy.

"No," said Arbie. "Have her drink it. Medicinal treatment."

"Here, Janie, drink it," Trudy said.

Jane took a sip of beer. Her eyes straightened out, she sat resolutely, and she drained half the cup.

"Mmmm. Nice head of beer. What happened?" Jane asked as she returned to her senses.

"You were struck by a foul ball," said Arbie.

"Arbie, this is my friend, Jane O'Leary. We work at Daschwirk together. Jane—my sister," Trudy said.

"Hi, my sister!" Jane grinned.

"You!" Trudy laughed as she playfully slapped Jane on the shoulder. "You were pretending!"

"Beer lady!" called a patron, and Arbie departed after a, "Nice to meet you," with Jane and a, "See you at Sheepshead," with Trudy.

"Your sister—is she married?" Jane asked.

"Yeah."

"What's her husband's name?"

"Arnold Knoxberger."

"Then why do you call her Arbutus Hansen? Is she using her maiden name?" Jane asked.

"Yeah. She says that with her husband off to war, she feels like a single woman, so she's using her maiden name," said Trudy.

"What about you? Do you go by Sheppe or Hansen?" Jane asked.

"I go by my husband's name—Sheppe. I never use my maiden name," Trudy said. "I think Wilton would flip out if I didn't use his name on everything. What about you?"

"O'Leary," Jane said. "I gave up MacNessi when I married Jack."

"Grandma Sheppe!" said Calico with a few tears.

"I thought your last name was Shepherd," said Jonara.

"No—that's the name they gave me in the Elrod 402. My real last name is Sheppe—just like Grandma Sheppe," said Calico. "But don't you tell anyone in the Elrod 402, you hear?"

"I hear," said Jonara. "But how can you threaten a voice like me?"

"I brought you here, didn't I? I can do it again."

Calico had a point, and Jonara realized it. She wasn't sure if Calico's use of the stone was good or bad, but whatever the case, the two were there, and Jonara decided this encounter might be part of whatever she was meant to do.

"So what's this cover art you're talking about? On the *Post?*" Jane asked.

"Look! It's you. And the red hair, too!" Trudy said.

Jane stared at the cover art of The *Saturday Evening Post* for May 29, 1943.

"Rosie the Riveter," Jane said. "I'm not a riveter. I'm a machinist."

"But that's you—red hair, strong build, and eating a sandwich on lunch break. You work in a factory," Trudy said. "Don't you see? This is the age of women! We're getting our recognition! After all these years. Susan B. Anthony started it, and we're finishing it."

"Oh Grandma, if only you knew!" Calico cried. "You're just a ray of sunshine in the storm!"

"I'm surprised to hear you talk like that," Jonara said to Calico. "I thought you were the tough one."

"I have feelings like any woman," said Calico. "And don't you tell that to the others, either."

"What's the other magazine you have with you?" Jane asked.

"It's nothing," said Trudy.

"Don't hide it from me. You have the latest *Life* magazine. Well?" Jane asked.

"There's an article on Penicillin," Trudy said while quickly flipping the *Life* magazine to page fifty-three. "It kills bacteria, and it's produced by bread mold. Isn't that wonderful? No more sulfa drugs. And look—here's a history of air training in the army. And in theater—"

"Let's see the cover art," Jane said as she grabbed the magazine from Trudy. "Peggy Lloyd. Hmmm. She doesn't look like a factory worker. In fact, she looks like a model. Oh look, what do we have here on page ninety-four? 'LIFE Calls on 16 Cover Girls'. Jean Colleran. Look again, here's Peggy Lloyd. Betty Jane Hess. Karen Gaylord and Susan Shaw. And more girls. Cover girls. This is the real state of women's 'progress'—the right to look cute for the boys overseas!"

"Now come on, Jane. You know some folk are still old-fashioned. They'll come around. Just another year or two and this cover-girl stuff will be in the past," Trudy said to comfort Jane.

"Hah!" Calico blurted.

Jane rolled up the magazine and pitched it down the bleachers.

"Hey you!" said a male voice from below. "Watch what you're throwing!"

"That was mine!" said Trudy. "I paid a good ten cents for that magazine. Money doesn't come easy, Jane MacNessi O'Leary!"

"I don't want to be pumped up with fake promises that women are allowed the same rights as men."

"You're watching one of those promises now on the ball field! And I bet you're too chicken to pick up a bat and ball to those women down there on the field," Trudy said.

"I could hold my own against them. Better, in fact," Jane bragged.

"Oh yeah?" Trudy asked.

"Yeah!"

"Then I dare you to try out with one of the teams."

"We work and live in Kenosha," said Jane. "Besides, the teams have been chosen. And even if I made it, who knows how much I'd be on the road."

"Chicken."

"I could take on any of them. It's nothing. Like easy street," Jane said.

"Then you do the tryouts next year, if you're so hot! But you're full of air," Trudy said.

"Who's full of air but you? I dare *you* to try out with the league next year," Jane said.

"Me?" Trudy asked.

"Yeah, you!" Jane answered. "You're the one preaching progress and equal rights. I dare you to try out."

"It's a deal!" Trudy said. "We'll try out together!"

"Kenosha's cutie belts out a bingle," said the announcer. "She's rounding first...looking to stretch it into a double...out at second!"

Fog rolled in from Lake Michigan into the stadium. Calico and Jonara's vision of the ball diamond faded followed by the bleachers. When the fog cleared, the two had returned to Calico's dorm room in Redjet.

"What happened? It ended," said Calico.

"The stone works on vibrations," said Jonara.

"Little Voice—you're still here?" Calico asked.

"Yes. The stone brought me here," said Jonara.

"So it did. Now how did I make it work like before? All I did," said Calico as she retrieved the Moissan Ruby from the wall, "was toss the stone in the air like this, and whack it with rolled-up newspaper like this."

Whack! The stone lodged into another part of the wall.

1943 Sep 3, Fri. Daschwirk Factory. Kenosha, Wisconsin.

Calico and Jonara appeared inside the Daschwirk factory in Kenosha. Next to them was Jane O'Leary, and not far from her was Trudy Sheppe. Jane was grinding and polishing aluminum propellers. Trudy was welding together 1.5 ton utility trailers. Jane's manager, Mr. Henrock, walked up to check on her work.

"Good morning, Jane."

"Good morning, Mr. Henrock," Jane replied while grinding a propeller.

"Please—can you stop grinding for a moment? Thank you. I'm very impressed with your work," he started.

"Yes sir. I take pride in helping out the war effort," Jane said.

"Mr. Daschwirk is also impressed. He says he's never seen such smooth propellers. And you've caught every defective propeller. Not a one of your polished props has failed prematurely in the field," said Henrock.

"Thank you, sir. May I return to work?"

"Just one more thing," said Henrock.

Mr. Henrock reached for something in his vest pocket and pulled out an envelope.

"What's that?" Jane asked.

"This is for you," said Henrock.

Mr. Henrock passed the envelope to Jane. She held it in her hand, puzzled.

"Open it," he said.

"It's a twenty-dollar bonus! And a raise! I'm now making...eighty cents an hour! Oh how can I thank you!" Jane said.

She hugged Mr. Henrock and immediately realized she had soiled his white shirt with her dirty blue-colored outfit.

"Oh I'm sorry, I shouldn't have done that. It'll come out. I can wash it for you," Jane fretted.

"Don't worry about the shirt. My wife will take care of it. Look in the envelope again—there's something else in there," Mr. Henrock grinned.

"A pair of tickets to every Kenosha Comets playoff game!" Jane said.

"They're doing well. They won the second round championship Wednesday night. Tonight they start the final series against the Racine Belles at Lake‑Front Stadium—for the championship. Best three out of five wins it all. Tickets just went up for sale today. Have you been watching the games?" Henrock asked.

"Just the first day—back in May—when they split the double-header with the Racine Belles," said Jane.

"Helen Nicol is leading the league in wins. Everyone expects her to pitch the Comets into the championship," Mr. Henrock said. "Wagner and Jameson are cleaning up with homers and hits. The other girls are great too. The Comets are just a good team altogether. And again, on behalf of Mr. Daschwirk and the Daschwirk factory, congratulations, and enjoy the playoffs!"

"Wow! Thank you, Mr. Henrock. Thank you again!" Jane exclaimed.

Jane ran over to Trudy to share the good news. The two jumped up and down in celebration.

"This is my true calling," said Jane. "I'm the best machinist in the world! Long live Daschwirk! And my friend Trudy Sheppe!"

"You did it, Jane, you did it!" Trudy said.

"And now that I'm making thirty-two dollars a week—"

Trudy's smile slipped into a half-smile.

"What's wrong? That's a good salary!" Jane said.

"Not as good as the girls pro-ball team," said Trudy.

"Huh?"

"You remember—when we promised to try out next spring?" Trudy said.

"Oh, that was just talk."

"Talk nothing. We should do it," said Trudy.

"I'm happy here. I make good money—" Jane said.

"You can make more as a ballplayer. Those girls start at forty-five dollars a week," said Trudy.

"Forty-five?" Jane asked with interest.

"And that's starting pay. They make all the way up to eighty-five a week. We could play all summer and go on vacation the rest of the year. That's the life, Jane. We could do whatever we want in the off season," Trudy dreamed.

"Aren't you forgetting those two dogs at home?" Jane asked.

"Yeah, well, I'd hire a sitter," said Trudy, "or leave them with Arbie."

"Those are your pets!" Jane said.

"I trust my sister," Trudy said.

"Won't you miss them?"

"They're a couple of animals. With all the trouble they get into, who would miss that?" Trudy asked.

Jane laughed and said, "Maybe you're right. But I still like being a machinist. Playing ball—I'll have to think about it."

"You do that—and by spring we'll be done thinking and on to the tryouts!"

1944 Spring. Wrigley Field. Chicago, Illinois.

"I hear singing," Trudy said. "Do you hear singing?"

Jane O'Leary and Trudy Sheppe arrived in Wrigley Field for tryouts—each hoping to qualify for the All-American Girls Baseball League. Women were grouped together doing various things—some were batting, others pitching, and still others fielding. Jane and Trudy joined a line of women waiting to be processed—it was this line of women from where the singing came:

American people, hear our call,
All-American girls, let's play ball!
No bat is too big, no game is too small,
We'll play every day through summer and fall.

From Canada, North, South, and West,
We'll play to the end, we'll play our best.
We love our teams, we love our league,
We love our towns, we're full of intrigue.

Batter, batter, we'll swing our bats,
We'll take to the fields, we'll tip our hats.
Americans all, we're here to say,
All-American Girls are here to play.

"You there," said one of the organizers. "What's your name?"

"Jane O'Leary."

"Position?"

"Huh?"

"What position do you play? Pitcher, first base, outfield?"

"I've never played—" Jane started to say.

"She's a pitcher, one of the best. She can strike out Babe Ruth," Trudy interrupted.

The organizer seemed puzzled and said, "Go over there to the pitching coach and show him your stuff."

Jane turned to Trudy and started to say, "I can't—" but Trudy pushed her along toward the pitching coaches.

"And you, what's your name?"

"Trudy Sheppe."

"You're a little small for this game. Have you ever played before?" he asked.

"Oh yes, all the time. I'm the best short-field player in all of—"

"We don't have short-field players. You want to try out for an infield position?"

"Oh yeah, I—"

"It doesn't matter. We'll find out if you're qualified. Take this over to the fielding coach. Next!"

"Jane, Jane, I'm in!" Trudy said, running up to Jane and patting her on the back.

"I have a strange feeling we didn't come through the right entrance," said Jane. "Look—there's a larger crowd of women over there."

"Those are returning from last year," said a coach. "I'm Joe Henrock. And you're—"

"Trudy Sheppe," Trudy interrupted as she fawned all over Joe. "I'm so grateful to meet you."

"Are you here for pitching?" Joe asked Trudy.

"Yes," she replied as she stared at his eyes.

Joe looked distrustfully at Trudy. She seemed too short to pitch a ball competently.

"What about you, Miss?" Joe asked.

"Jane O'Leary."

"You have a good softball frame," he said.

"Excuse me, isn't this the baseball league?" Jane asked. "And are you related to—"

"Yes, it is," Trudy continued while in a trance.

"It's girls professional ball. Something between softball and baseball. The regulation ball is larger than a baseball but smaller than a softball. You have a good point, Jane. Where have you pitched before?" Joe asked.

"Everywhere," Trudy said dreamily.

Joe's face showed amazement at Trudy's statements.

"I've never played ball—no baseball, no softball. I couldn't tell you the difference between a bat and a glove," Jane said.

"Well at least you're honest," Joe laughed. "Tell you what—take this ball and throw it to Mum over there."

Mum, the Racine Belle player who returned for another season, fielded Jane's one-hopper. "Mum" was her nickname—after a flower she liked.

"You threw that like a football," Joe said. "You ever played quarterback? I'm sorry, that was a stupid question."

"It's a wonderful question," Trudy gleamed.

"Trudy," Jane said. "Why don't you go on to your fielding coach?"

Trudy ignored Jane.

"Look at your slip of paper," Jane said.

"I'll take a look. Yes, Miss Trudy—you should go over to Bill. He'll help you," Joe said.

"You can help me," Trudy continued.

"I know, doll. Go over there," Joe urged.

Trudy walked away but kept her eyes fixed on Joe. She didn't see where she walked, and a wild grounder clipped her legs and sent her into a somersault.

"Oh, I'm sorry," said Petunia—a nickname for the Wisconsin native who would end up on the Racine Belles that season. "I didn't see you there. Did you get hurt?"

"No, I'm fine," Trudy said.

"You should be more careful. This isn't a fashion show," Petunia said.

"She didn't mean anything, Petunia," Joe said.

Trudy waved a last time and headed off.

"What's wrong with Grandma?" Calico asked.

"What do you think?" Jonara said. "She's going gaga over that Joe guy."

"Grandma? Never. She's Grandma. She can't flirt with men. What would Grandpa do if he found out?" Calico added.

"Let's try it again, Jane. Only this time, hold the ball like this," Joe said, "with your index and middle fingers extended, your thumb down, and your other two fingers to the side. Now throw it."

Jane held the ball as instructed and threw it to Mum. Mum jumped up to field the ball, but it sailed over her head.

"Whoa!" Mum said as she ran after the ball.

"You have a strong arm," said Joe. "All you need is a little control. Think about distance, trajectory, and speed."

"Distance, trajectory, speed. Speeds and feeds. Drilling through the air. Rough cuts. Calculate the cutting tool through the air," Jane thought aloud.

"What's that?" Joe asked, but before he could get an answer, Mum returned the ball to Joe.

"Here—try it again," Joe said.

Jane threw the ball again with more thought—thoughts of machining that she translated into pitching. The ball seared through the air and landed squarely in Mum's glove. Mum caught the ball but immediately removed the glove and shook her hand to relieve the slapping pain.

"That's a zinger," Mum said.

Mum threw the ball back to Joe who again handed it to Jane.

"Now try that underhanded."

Jane threw the ball side-armed, and it hooked to the left. Mum stretched and barely caught it.

"That was side-armed. I mean under-armed. Like this," Joe said as he demonstrated an underarm pitching motion.

"That's pitching?" Jane asked. "That's like a toss."

"Just think of your arm as a windmill and let go."

Joe caught the ball from Mum and returned it to Jane. Jane whipped her arm in a circle and released the ball underhanded. It burned along the ground. Mum fielded it and returned it to Joe.

"Again," he said.

Jane repeated and landed the ball squarely in Mum's mitt.

"Good. Not as fast as the overhand pitch, but promising. Can you catch a ball?" Joe asked.

"I've never tried," Jane said.

"Mum," Joe said as he tossed the ball to Mum. "Toss a few to Jane O'Leary here."

Mum threw a quick one to Jane who attempted to catch it with her bare right hand.

"That hurts!" Jane said.

"You're supposed to catch it with the glove on your left hand," Joe said.

"But I'm right-handed. I catch and throw with my right."

"You'll have to adjust. Catch it with your left. You'll need your right for throwing," Joe said. "Toss it to Mum, and she'll throw it again."

Mum threw the ball with the same intensity to Jane. It tipped off the top of her glove and bounced off her scalp. Jane's eyes opened wide when she realized she could have been seriously hurt.

"A girl can lose her head in this game!" Jane said.

"You just need some practice. You'll be fine," Joe said.

"My question—the one I was going to ask," said Jane.

"Yes?"

"Are you related to George Henrock?" Jane asked.

"You're from Kenosha, aren't you?" Joe asked.

"Yes, I am."

"You know George?"

"He's my boss at—"

"Daschwirk. You're the one—the machinist he always talks about," Joe said.

"Me?"

"Tall, determined, red-head. Works long hours. He's always talking big of you. And you're trying out for the league. Boy, do I have bragging rights over him now."

"Please, don't say anything yet," Jane said.

"You mean you didn't tell him? Doll, if you want to be in the league, you'll have to give up your Daschwirk job," Joe said.

"I know, but if things don't work out, well, I don't want to look like I failed," Jane said.

"Ah c'mon," Joe said, and he gave Jane a hug, but Jane didn't hug Joe back—it didn't seem right somehow. "No girl out here is a failure. Here—you practice with Mum a little more. I'll check back with you in a bit."

"All right, Joe."

Later, at the Belmont Hotel.

"I bombed," Trudy said while she ate dinner with Jane in the hotel restaurant. "Every coach said I have the right feminine qualities, but no ball-playing talent."

"So what does that mean?" Jane asked.

"It means I'm done with tryouts," Trudy said. "I can go home tomorrow. Oh well, it was a silly dream. To think I could play ball as well as these other girls here. They're all very good."

"Yeah, they are," Jane said.

"I've played softball. Lots of times. But the girls are aggressive here. I thought it would be like the softball games I used to play during summer picnics on Sundays. It's not like that at all."

"Yeah," said Jane.

"I made a fool of us—me with my cute looks but no talent, and you with your not-so...your...you know, you've never played," Trudy stumbled.

"Grandma!" Calico said. "You quit? No way! I can't believe it."

"I didn't look like a fool," said Jane.

"What!?"

"They want me to report tomorrow. Joe says I have a good arm. I had no trouble batting the ball—comes natural. All I have to do is think about that pumpkin-headed guy from last year—"

"What guy?" Trudy asked.

"The one at the first Comets game—remember? I smacked him with my arm. I just think of smacking his skull, and the bat connects with the ball. You'd be surprised."

"I am surprised," said Trudy.

"Why would this stone...why are you showing this to me, Little Voice?" Calico asked.

"It's not me...well, it is me...but not really...it's the diary. But I don't understand how it knows about your grandma. My great-grandma wrote it—how could she know?" Jonara said to Calico.

"I don't know, but I'm getting tired of seeing my grandma being shown up by this Jane woman. Who is she?"

"I don't know," said Jonara.

"Little Voice, if you don't tell me," Calico started.

Calico stopped short to hear Trudy and Jane finish their conversation, but the Belmont Hotel went dark, and Calico returned to her dorm room.

"Oh, what a day!" Evanita said as she entered the room. "I can barely move."

"Good gobs of tobacco," exclaimed Calico. "I didn't realize it's so late. Lockdown is at nine in the evening. What are you doing out until eleven? You gotta be careful—you'll get us both in trouble."

"I couldn't help it," said Evanita.

"Yes you could. You better tell me why you've been out past lockdown or else," Calico ordered.

Evanita plopped into her desk chair and broke into tears.

"What are you bawling about? You get in a fight?" Calico said without sympathy, but Evanita kept her back toward Calico.

"Turn around and look at me when I'm talking to you," Calico said.

Calico grabbed Evanita by the shoulders and twisted her around so Calico could speak eye-to-eye with Evanita, but Evanita let out a yelp of pain.

"Hey, I didn't hurt you or anything yet. But I'm going to give you a reason to yelp if you don't stop that crying," Calico ordered.

Calico shoved Evanita lightly in the shoulder, and Evanita let out another yelp. Puzzled, Calico shoved Evanita in the other shoulder, but Evanita didn't react.

"What happened, you fall down and dislocate your precious shoulder?" Calico asked.

She ripped open Evanita's shirt and backed up a step when she saw the black swelling on Evanita's shoulder.

"Whoa, ho, hum!" Calico remarked. "Who beat you up to-night? Lemme guess—Ox-Two caught you out late and disciplined you."

Evanita shook her head no.

"Ox-Three? Those are the only ones patrolling Redjet at this hour," Calico said.

Again, Evanita shook her head no.

Calico stepped out of the room for a moment, flagged down Ox-Two, chatted, and returned to the room as Ox-Two resumed her patrols.

"You should be proud," said Calico, "that Oxia chose you. It's a special privilege most girls don't get."

"I don't want to be her privilege. I have a boyfriend. He's special to me. I'm not the girl Oxia wants me to be."

"But that's how this place works," said Calico. "You have to catch the ball. See? They play ball no matter what. If you don't play back, they'll use your shoulder or leg or something for a baseball. They're all too happy to swing their bats however they please. So you better please them before they 'please' you with their sticks."

"I don't play baseball," said Evanita.

"You gotta. It's required. I admit, it took me a long time, but I worked my way up to Ox-Two. You're better off having an Oxian for a sponsor than a Barian, Dazian, or the others. The only one more important is O Grammeni, but she never picks up one of the girls...at least not that I've heard. Still, there was a rumor last month about—"

"Oh stop it! Just stop it!" Evanita begged.

"You cut that out. I'm talking to you," Calico ordered.

"I can't stand it here. I wanna go home," Evanita whined.

"You are home—until your sentence is up. Twelve months, right?"

"I can't survive twelve months. I wanna die," Evanita cried.

"Uh oh, don't say that too loud. They'll put you on suicide watch. That means isolation. You don't want that. Besides, who will clean up after me?" Calico grinned.

Evanita stopped crying and looked up at Calico. Calico gave Evanita a warm smile—the first one Evanita had seen. Evanita managed a small smile of her own.

"There, it's not so bad, is it? Here's a box of tissue," Calico offered. "Clean up your face and go to bed. You'll feel better in the morning. But think about what I've said. And play ball with Oxia. If she pitches, you catch!"

Evanita crawled into bed, leaving her crutches on the floor. It was enough of a struggle with her legs in casts, but now she had a bad shoulder, leaving just one working limb on her body.

"I'll run out of limbs," she whispered to herself, "before Thanksgiving. What's to be thankful for?"

Evanita's spirits sank, and her blood pressure dropped. A crushing feeling descended on her heart, and she felt her life force descending into Hell. The best she could do was whisper herself to sleep. She repeated the following:

"Jesus—lead me away from this misery. You're all I have. My heart aches, my shoulder is in pain, and my legs are broken. Take me away and leave my tortured body behind. Please, Jesus, help me. Help me."

CHAPTER 8

Butcher The Donkey

2023 Oct 5, Thu Early am. Corpus Christi, Texas.
2006 Nov 21, Tue. Elrod 402.

Evanita coughed and gagged on thick mucus in her throat. She rolled over to early-morning sunrays cutting through the window. Evanita coughed again. Smoke irritated her eyes and the lining in her respiratory tract.

"You're smoking," Evanita grumbled.

"Come down and have a smoke yourself," Calico offered, who was in her usual pose of smoking her pipe and drinking coffee by the window.

"No thanks," Evanita said, "but I'll crawl down to get some air. I can't breathe in this haze."

"You'll feel better if you have some coffee. No, you like mocha coffee, don't you?" Calico asked. "I have a chocolate bar right here. You can dip as much chocolate in your coffee as you want."

Evanita crawled down from the bunk and sat close to Calico. Calico handed a cup of regular coffee to Evanita, and Evanita dropped the entire chocolate bar in the coffee. She sipped it down—not as quickly as the day before—but enough to savor the taste and derive immediate caffeine benefit.

"That's quite a stone you have," said Calico. "Makes you hallucinate all kinds of things, doesn't it?"

"You tried it?"

"Yeah. Smacked it into the wall over there," Calico said while pointing to divots in the wall.

"My boyfriend gave it to me. I don't want it mistreated like that," said Evanita.

"Well take it back, then," Calico said, and she handed the stone and unattached necklace chain to Evanita.

"It's meant to be worn around the neck," Evanita said as she struggled to attach the chain to the stone.

"Give it here—you'll never get it back together," said Calico.

Calico took the stone and chain from Evanita, reattached the two into a single necklace, and returned it to Evanita.

"There," Calico said. "Put it around your neck."

"Calico?"

"Yeah?"

"What did you see? With the stone?"

"Nothing," Calico said.

"But you did see something. You said it makes a person hallucinate," Evanita said.

"Yeah, what of it?"

"I saw my Great-Grandmother Margene give birth to my Grandmother Geneva," said Evanita. "But the stone is supposed to just scan people and things in the present. It doesn't—"

"Who cares about your measly stone!" Calico said.

Calico took a deep puff of her pipe, held the puff for several seconds, and exhaled. She dipped some tobacco in her coffee and smeared the wet leaves onto her arms.

"Why do you do that?"

"Calms my nerves," said Calico. "Wakes me up in the morning, too."

"Did I upset you?" Evanita asked.

"You? No way! Nothing upsets me."

"There is a little voice. Sometimes two, but mostly one. It was with me when I saw my baby grandma. It was 1939 in Spain, and—" Evanita started.

"Okay, already," Calico said, getting anxious. "I saw my grandma too. Happy? I saw her back in '43. Watching a softball game in Wisconsin. And working."

"Was she alone? My grandma was alone after my great-grandma and great-grandpa died. It was sad," Evanita explained.

"No, she wasn't alone," an irritated Calico said. "Why all the questions? It was a stupid hallucination. Maybe it was a dream. Yeah, I napped through it."

"Did she have a friend? What was her name?"

"Yeah, she had a friend. Jane O'Leary. Strong gal. But my grandma...she...I was disappointed. I thought she'd be a stronger person. She was flirting all the time. Disgusting. I hope you keep your stone away from everyone."

"You shouldn't hate your grandmother. We're only people doing the best we can," said Evanita.

"You're one to talk. You can't even take care of yourself. Why are you so up-beat this morning?" Calico asked.

"I don't know...the words...they just came out. I love my grandma."

"Calico loves her grandma too!" Jonara shouted.

"Did you say something?" Evanita asked Calico.

"Me? Why are you up-beat?"

"No, after that," Evanita said.

"You're still asleep. Go shower and dress. You've got school this morning, and after that plenty more chores I'd imagine," Calico ordered.

Evanita heard Jonara's voice. Jonara repeated that Calico loved her grandmother, and Evanita smiled in agreement without alerting Calico that Evanita was hearing Jonara's voice.

Evanita attended school as was required at the Elrod 402. Classes were held in Patriojet—the same jet where church services were held. For school, the seats were rearranged with small tables to form desks. The Dazians returned to instruct all the usual classes—English, math, science, social studies, and exploratory classes of music, art, craftwork, business, and gym. Evanita participated in all classes except for gym, where she stood outside watching the other girls run, play soccer, and play basketball.

"Eve Carson?" called a voice.

Evanita turned her head to see a security guard approach her. Calico also noticed Evanita's name being called and walked over to attend the ensuing conversation.

"Yes?" Evanita replied as the guard arrived.

"I'm Ox-One. We haven't met, but I've heard about you through Ox-Two, and my boss—Oxia."

"I'm sorry. I can't do gym. My legs won't let me—"

"Never mind that," Ox-One said.

"What's this about?" Calico asked, now arriving.

"Never you mind, Fiori Sheppe," said Ox-One.

"Watch it, Ox-One, you know the rules about using real names," Calico replied.

"Who will you tell? Ox-Two? She's my inferior. Or Oxia? O Grammeni? You don't hold water with them."

Calico held her tongue and said nothing. She turned red in the face, and Evanita realized Calico wanted desperately to speak.

"That's better. Eve, you are to come with me."

"Have I done something wrong? I'm still in school," said Evanita.

"You must learn that when we say to do something, you comply without questioning," Ox-One said. "School is out for the day, at least for you. Come now at once. And you, Sheppe— you're still in school."

Calico shot Ox-One a sassy glance. Meanwhile, Jonara followed along as Ox-One removed Evanita from the main Elrod 402 grounds and transported her to Whalejet's intake section.

"You have a visitor," Ox-One said. "I'll be outside if you need me."

Evanita entered the room while Ox-One closed the door behind. A person sat with his back to the door and his face toward the window. Evanita wasn't sure at first who the visitor was until he spoke.

"A strange arrangement—jumbo jets in a circle surrounded by layers of barbed-wire fencing."

Evanita hobbled as quickly as she could over to the person. He stood up. Evanita threw her good arm around him and hugged him as best she could.

"Johnny Pindus! My Johnny. My sweet, adorable, loving-dear Johnny."

"Wow, what a welcome!" he said placing both arms around her.

Evanita kissed Johnny on each cheek, shoulders, and cheeks again.

"I should visit more often," he said.

"No talking—just for a moment," she said.

Evanita kissed Johnny fully on the lips, closed her eyes, and daydreamed she was with Johnny in the Portland Rose Garden—walking, talking, laughing, holding hands, healthy, and happy with no problems and no cares. After a minute, Evanita pulled away slowly from the kiss, kept her eyes closed, and nudged her head into his shoulder.

"There, there," he said. "You're with me. You're safe."

"Oh Johnny, please take me away. I'm terribly alone and miserable here. I'm in so much pain, but everyone expects too much of me," Evanita said.

"Shhh, Johnny is here. Forget about all that. Shhh."

"Johnny...I...the pain...it..." Evanita stumbled.

Johnny placed his hand over the Moissan Ruby just under Evanita's neck. Evanita shivered from the cold anxieties of the Elrod 402 and soaked in Johnny's warmth and love. The Moissan Ruby glowed and connected Johnny with Evanita. He closed his eyes tightly as the details of Evanita's suffering crossed through his arm up his neck into his mind. Several times he twitched his head as if fighting off a demon. Evanita held her eyes closed and envisioned herself as she was during the coma—being pursued by a demon as she flew on Blue Jane. Only Johnny was there to rescue her.

"Johnny," Evanita said with a calm yet soft voice as she opened her eyes.

"Yes, Evanita. I scanned you. I know what you've been through."

"What will I do?" she asked. "Where's Mama? And Grandma? I tried the Y-O-U at the Portland Detention Center, Johnny. I did—they wouldn't let me attend. There's no Y-O-U here. I let Ms. Zyla down. I'm sorry."

"I know, Evanita, I know."

"They won't call me by my name here. They make everyone call me Eve Carson. Please, Johnny, don't ever call me by that name," Evanita begged.

"I won't. Not ever, not even in jest," he reassured her. "You are and always will be Evanita from the proud family of Carreña, who dwell and hail from the Peaks of Europe and settled in a town just outside the Peaks, in Carreña, in the country of Spain. The Iberian Peninsula. Conquered many times by many people. But never have the hearts of Spain been conquered, and especially not the hearts of Family Carreña. I'll never forget who you are."

Evanita cried in both joy and sadness. She hugged Johnny even tighter than before. In that moment, when the two hugged and shared their love and affection for each other, the Moissan Ruby responded by forming a connection. Johnny's metabolism reached out to Evanita's and assisted in repairing tissue. Evanita wasn't sure what was happening at first. She only knew that a warm, loving feeling was coating over her points of pain and melting through her body like hot marshmallows over crispy squares. The swelling in her shoulder shrank, and she recovered feeling and strength. The breaks in her leg bones calcified over and healed with strength anew. It seemed impossible—Evanita thought she imagined these good feelings. She worried that releasing Johnny from her hug would return the stains of River Wood and Battery factory to her legs and Elrod 402 to her shoulder.

Evanita didn't want the moment to end, but common sense told her it was time. She released Johnny from her tight hug and sat down. Johnny reached inside his shirt through the neck hole, pulled out the Aromani candleholder, looked at it briefly, and returned it inside his shirt.

"I wish I could take your love with me everywhere," she said, "But I know as soon as I return to the main compound, everything good about you will fade from me and leave me to rot. And I'll suffer."

"Stand up," Johnny commanded.

Evanita's eyes opened wide in shock, as if he'd said the impossible.

"Stand up! No, leave your crutches there—don't touch them. Stand up and walk on your own!" he commanded again.

Evanita released her grip from Johnny and stood—not believing she would—but stood she could. It was good.

"I'm standing!" she said.

Evanita felt her shoulder, and there was no pain. She lifted it up as if flapping a wing. No pain.

"My shoulder is healed too!" she said.

"Remove your casts!" he said.

Evanita took a crutch and whacked it across the cast on her right leg. Smack. The cast cracked into several pieces and fell to the floor. Then she took the crutch to her left cast and smashed it. Rails of cast material flew off leaving powdered trails. Evanita kicked the plaster and mesh material aside and walked—first one step and then another—but walk she did and did very well.

"How!?" Jonara shouted, but no one heard her. "The Water Ruby only receives information. It doesn't heal, does it? I don't understand! Wait—was it the candleholder? Does that have power?"

Ox-One opened the door.

"What's this all over the floor?" Ox-One asked.

"I can walk!" Evanita bragged.

"I can see! You heal quickly then," Ox-One said. "But this mess will have to be cleaned up."

"I'll be happy to clean it up," said Evanita.

"I just came in to tell you that your visiting time is up. Time to return to the main campus. Your guest will have to leave," Ox-One said.

"Thank you for allowing me to visit," said Johnny.

"You're welcome. It's good to see our detainees benefiting from a good influence," Ox-One said.

Evanita didn't say anything at the time, but she thought Ox-One was rather unusually nice considering the people she'd met at the Elrod 402. Was there some ulterior motive? Evanita didn't know, but for the moment she was going to take advantage of the situation and enjoy what consideration and respect she could get.

Ox-One radioed. Ox-Four arrived and escorted Johnny to the exit while Ox-One supervised Evanita's clean-up effort. Evanita tossed cast shards into a plastic-bag-covered wastebasket. She took a broom and swept the plaster powder into a dustpan, and when the last of the powder was swept up, Evanita dumped the dustpan into the wastebasket. The dust fell through the air and appeared to settle, but to Jonara the dust plumed up and blurred her view of the room. Jonara drifted out of the Elrod 402 and landed somewhere else—a house in Racine County, Wisconsin, circa World War II.

1944 May, Sat Eve. Arbie Knoxberger's Apartment. Racine, Wisconsin.

"Trudy, Jane—come on in! You're just in time for the game!" Arbie said.

Trudy and Jane entered Arbie's apartment. It was clean, tidy, and smelled of spring-fresh flowers. Trudy was plenty familiar with her sister's home, but for Jane this was the first visit. She looked around—not many books, but lots of magazines, framed pictures from magazines, and plants. Living plants— vines, flowers, and broadleafs.

"I made up lots of snacks for the party. And there's plenty of beer in the fridge. Help yourselves—don't wait to ask!" Arbie said.

"Would you like a beer?" Trudy asked Jane.

"Yes please."

"I'll get you one," Trudy said.

"Oh come, come!" said Arbie. "None of that courtesy stuff. Let's just kick back and relax. Jane—help yourself! Don't ask, just take whatever you need!"

"Thank you," Jane answered.

She followed Trudy to the fridge where each took a beer. Trudy struggled to open her beer with a bottle opener while Jane simply used her own hand to remove the top. Trudy looked at Jane in amazement.

"Doesn't that hurt?" Trudy asked.

"Nope."

"Come on over, you two, and have a seat at the card table," said Arbie. "I'd like to introduce you to my friends. This is Mum, and this is Petunia. Well, 'Mum' and 'Petunia' are their nicknames."

"Hi, have we met before?" Trudy said. "I've seen you both somewhere."

"Jane O'Leary," said Mum. "How's your arm?"

"Not as sore as I thought," said Jane.

"Ice the first day and heat the following day," said Petunia.

"You know each other?" Arbie asked. "Oh, the surprise is ruined!"

"Wait a minute—now I know!" Trudy said. "You were at the tryouts."

"That's right," said Mum. "We play for the Racine Belles."

"I live here in Racine," said Petunia.

"And I used to live in Milwaukee, but now I in Racine, too," said Mum.

"Arbie brags about how good a Sheepshead player she is," said Petunia.

"Oh did she tell you who taught her everything she knows about the game?" Trudy asked.

"You play?" Mum laughed.

"Arbie!" Trudy said.

"I did embellish a little," shrugged Arbie.

Mum and Petunia laughed uncontrollably.

"Don't get bent out of shape," said Petunia. "Arbie put us up to the joke. She told us about your skills."

"Says you're the Sheepshead Shark of Sheridan Road," said Mum.

"We just want to know if it's true," said Petunia. "We're good Sheepshead players too."

Mum held a straight face with Petunia and burst into laughter.

"Hey, I think we're good. I know I am, especially after I warm up," said Petunia.

"What about you, Jane, how good are you?" Mum asked.

"Uh, what's Sheepshead?" Jane asked.

Arbie gave a stare of disappointment to Trudy.

"Oh, uh, that," said Trudy.

"Yes, that!" Arbie returned.

"What's she talking about?" Jane asked Trudy.

"I was supposed to teach Jane how to play...before we came over...actually while we were at the Belmont Hotel," said Trudy.

"A-hem!" Arbie coughed to correct Trudy.

"All right! I was supposed to teach Jane sometime over the winter," said Trudy.

"And why didn't you?" Arbie asked.

"I never had time...never got around to it...those dogs... they're such a handful...and work...welding...you know...shoveling snow...Thanksgiving, Christmas, New Year's...where did the time go?" Trudy dragged.

"You should have brought Jane over here earlier. We could have done a three-player game," Arbie offered.

"I know," lamented Trudy.

"Heck, you could have played two-player Sheepshead with her," said Arbie.

"I know," said Trudy.

"Wilton was home over Christmas, wasn't he?" Arbie asked.

"Come to think of it, I think Jack said something about going over to Wilton's for Sheepshead back in December," said Jane.

"You could have played a four-handed game," said Arbie.

"Enough! Why do I get blamed for everything? And why is everyone ganging up on me?" Trudy asked.

Everyone but Trudy laughed.

"We're not ganging up on you," said Mum.

"We're just having some fun," added Petunia.

"We'll teach you how to play," Mum offered.

"That is, if Trudy isn't too busy," jabbed Arbie.

"Oh brother!" said Trudy.

"Oh sister!" Arbie added.

"I need a drink," said Trudy.

"You have a drink," said Mum.

"I mean a real drink!" said Trudy.

"There's wine in the fridge," said Arbie. "I was going to save it for the announcement, but you can have some early."

"What announcement?" Jane asked.

"Something stronger," Trudy interrupted.

"Stronger than wine?" Petunia asked.

"I know my sister," said Arbie. "The vodka is in the cupboard above the stove."

"When did you move it there? Is that safe?" Trudy asked.

"It won't catch fire," Arbie explained. "And I knew you'd never think to look there when you're snitchin' in the kitchen. That's why I put it there. Shot glasses are up there too."

Trudy poured her shots of vodka while Jane sat down with beer and snacks.

"It's not that hard a game once you start playing," said Mum.

"And it's a lot of fun," Petunia added.

"We have a magazine clipping here that shows the order of strength," said Mum.

"And the point values," added Petunia.

"I have a magazine that explains how to play," Trudy called from the kitchen.

"Had a magazine," Arbie said under her breath.

Mum and Petunia mouthed the words for, "Oops," under their breaths.

"You said that was your magazine," Mum whispered.

"I consider any magazine left in this apartment as mine," Arbie whispered back.

"I can hear you whispering in there," Trudy called. "I know you swiped my magazine and clipped out the article, Arbie."

"Serves you right for leaving your things here and not taking them back home. Might as well get some use out of them," Arbie called back.

"That was my favorite magazine, Arbie," Trudy said as she consumed two shots of vodka and joined them at the table. "I loaned it to you so you'd have something to read."

"Look around you, Trudes," Arbie said as she waved her arm around at the magazine piles. "Do I look like I'm short of literature?"

"But there was a good article on housekeeping—'How to Keep a Superior Home'," Trudy said. "It was my favorite article. You didn't have to turn around and *butcher the donkey.*"

"You haven't seen that magazine in years," Arbie said. "It was getting all yellow and ratty. Its usefulness was over and done with."

"Butcher the donkey? Where's the donkey?" Jane asked.

"It's a Chinese saying," said Mum. "The idea is that you use a donkey to work hard, and when you have no more work for the donkey, you butcher it for the meat."

"It's not meant to be kind," said Petunia.

"But it's what people do sometimes," said Mum.

"Corporations more than anyone," said Petunia.

"That poor donkey—it worked so hard," said Mum.

"And got slaughtered as a thank you," said Petunia.

"I hope that never happens to any of us," said Jane.

"I'll drink to that," said Mum.

"Cheers!" Petunia said.

Everyone held up beverages and clinked glasses as a toast to one another.

"May we succeed in whatever we do!" Arbie added.

The girls enjoyed their drinks and their company. Arbie sifted through a 52-card deck and removed cards, leaving a 32-card deck ready for Sheepshead play.

"If you forget, just look at the clipping," Mum said to Jane. "This is a game of taking tricks. Cards have a power ranking as well as a point value—power is not the same as points. Let's start with trump suit. The four queens are the most powerful—clubs, spades, hearts, and diamonds in that order from strongest on down. Next are jacks in the same suit order. The rest of trump goes ace, ten, king, nine, eight, and seven of diamonds. That's it for trump. All the other cards are part of the fail suit. Trump always takes fail."

"Wait," said Jane. "Something doesn't sound right."

"You're wondering about the kings, right?" Petunia asked.

"Yes—how did you know?" Jane asked.

"Everyone wonders. Most card games place kings high in power and always over queens. Not in Sheepshead. Kings don't have much power," said Petunia.

"As it should be," said Arbie.

"I like a game where queens are worth more than kings," Jane admitted.

"Here are the point values," said Mum. "Aces and tens are worth the most, followed by kings, queens, and jacks. The other cards have no points."

"Enough already," said Trudy. "Let's play a game."

"This will be a practice game for Jane," said Arbie. "We'll deal all cards up so we can explain what's going on."

Arbie dealt out six cards to each player and set aside two.

"That's the blind," said Arbie. "Whoever takes the blind is the picker."

"The picker has one partner—these two play against the other three," said Mum. "Or the picker can play alone—without a partner."

"You should only pick if your hand is strong enough," said Petunia.

The girls continued in this way, explaining the rules and completing the practice game. Petunia became the picker and had Trudy for a partner. The girls played out their cards, and by the end, everyone was ready for another game.

"Are you ready for a real game, Jane?" Arbie asked.

"I think so. If I can keep the clipping next to me," Jane said.

"Of course," said Mum who passed the clipping to Petunia who passed it to Jane.

Arbie dealt the cards one at a time around the table to Mum, Petunia, Jane, Trudy, and herself until each player had six cards. Like in practice, two cards were set aside for the blind. Mum started—she passed. Petunia passed. Jane, not sure of how good she could do also passed. Trudy held her cards over her mouth and also passed. Arbie looked around the room at each girl—searching for signs of deceit.

"Someone is mauering," Arbie said.

"What does that mean?" Jane asked.

"Mauering is when someone has a strong hand but doesn't pick the blind," Mum explained.

"It's considered rude," Petunia added.

"And I'm annoyed," said Arbie, "but I don't want our first real game to be a leaster."

Jane looked again to the Belles for help.

"Leaster," Petunia said. "Yes, that's when no one picks the blind, and we play to get rid of points."

"It tends to punish a mauerer," said Mum.

"Well I don't want hard feelings," said Jane. "I'll be a good sport and pick the blind."

"It's too late," said Arbie. "You already passed. So did Trudy."

Arbie gave Trudy a knowing stare.

"What?" Trudy replied.

"*What* yourself," said Arbie. "I'm going to pick—just to keep the game going—and there better be something good."

Arbie picked the two cards, rolled her eyes, and tossed them back on the table face up.

"Worthless! Nothing but fail!" she said as she showed the women two black sevens. "Someone mauered!"

"I guess I should confess," said Jane as she started to tilt her cards forward to expose them.

"No," said Petunia. "Don't show your cards. Play out the game."

"My partner has ace of hearts," said Arbie.

Mum led round one with the ten of hearts. Petunia threw the king, Jane the ace, Trudy the jack, and Arbie threw the nine—all hearts.

"So I win?" Jane asked.

"No," said Mum. "Look at the power ranking."

"I know it's not the king. But ace is higher than the other hearts," said Jane.

"Except for trump," said Petunia. "Do you see a trump card here?"

"Yes, Trudy," Arbie said with irritation in her voice. "Is there trump on the table?!"

Trudy grinned.

"Oh, the jack is trump. The jack wins," Jane explained.

"The jack wins," said Arbie to Trudy. "Did you notice Mum's strategy? She led the suit I called."

"I did so in hopes someone had a trump to take the trick," Mum said. "When on defense, it's best to get the partner suit out as soon as possible."

"So I'm partner?" Jane asked.

"Yes," Arbie said. "You're my partner, but the Jack won the trick, which means the Jack will now lead the next play. Go ahead, Jack—throw the next card."

Trudy led round two by playing the queen of diamonds.

"You had one of the queens," Arbie said.

"Aggressive move leading off with a queen," said Mum.

"It's like she's forcing the issue immediately," said Petunia.

"This better not be a trick," said Arbie.

Arbie threw the eight of diamonds, Mum the jack of clubs, and Petunia the seven of diamonds. Jane hesitated.

"You have to throw a trump card," said Mum.

"If you have trump," said Petunia.

"Yes, all right, I have trump," Jane said.

She threw the jack of spades.

"I win the trick," said Trudy.

"You are a trick," said Arbie.

"Trudy wins," said Mum, "so she leads the next round."

Trudy threw the queen of hearts to lead round three.

"I don't believe it," said Arbie. "You're going to do it—in reverse order."

Arbie threw the nine of diamonds, Mum the eight of hearts, Petunia the king of diamonds, and Jane paused again.

"Mum's out of trump," said Petunia.

"Play trump if you have it," said Mum to Jane.

"I do, but I don't want to," said Jane.

"You must," said Arbie. "But try to beat Trudy's card. Can you beat her card?"

"No, I can't," Jane said.

Jane threw the ten of diamonds. Gasps from the girls except from Trudy.

"I won't even make schneider," said Arbie.

"It's your turn, Trudy," Petunia said.

Trudy threw the queen of spades to lead round four. The other girls groaned. Arbie threw the jack of diamonds in disgust, Mum the ten of spades, Petunia the ace of spades, and Jane tossed the ace of diamonds.

"I'm sorry," Jane said. "I tried."

"You did fine," said Arbie.

Trudy led round five with the king of spades.

"What?" Arbie said.

Arbie threw the king of clubs, Mum the eight of spades, Petunia the nine of spades, and Jane paused.

"You have to throw a spade if you have one," said Mum.

"I don't have a spade," said Jane. "But if I had trump, I could take it."

"We know you don't have trump," said Mum.

"You do? How?" Jane asked.

"For the same reason my sister led with a fail," said Arbie, "because she knows all trump has been played except for one—and it's in her hand!"

"Play a card, Jane," said Petunia.

Jane threw the eight of clubs. Each player had but one card left to play for the final round, and Trudy was to lead.

"What's that card in your hand, Trudy?" Arbie asked.

Trudy held the card, but the others didn't wait for her to play. They threw their cards on the table (in order from Arbie to Jane)—ace of clubs, seven of hearts, nine of clubs, and ten of clubs.

"Give me that card!" Arbie said, and she ripped it from Trudy's hand.

Arbie faced the card toward the girls. It was the queen of clubs.

"Look girls, it's the top bitch!" Arbie said as she first pointed to the card and next pointed the card at Trudy.

"There's the mauerer," said Mum.

"We won!" Trudy proclaimed as she held out one arm to Mum and the other to Petunia.

"You had a grandma hand! You were supposed to pick!" Arbie said.

"I won anyway," said Trudy.

"I'll show you a win with my fist!" Arbie said.

"Girls, girls," said Petunia. "Try acting like women."

"Why did you do it?" Arbie said.

"Because I knew it would irritate you," grinned Trudy.

"Well it didn't," Arbie lied, though her face was red. "You know, you're setting a bad example for Jane."

"It's just a game, Arbie. Get over it," Trudy said.

"Forget it," said Arbie.

Arbie left the table and straightened magazines in the living room.

"All right. It's four-player Sheepshead," bragged Trudy.

Trudy gathered the cards and shuffled them.

"I don't feel like playing anymore," said Jane.

"C'mon, Jane, I'll explain it to you," Trudy said.

"I need another beer," said Mum who left the table for the refrigerator.

"I'll just freshen up a bit," said Petunia who headed to the ladies' room.

"Oh well. There's always two-player Sheepshead," Trudy said to Jane, but Jane stood up and walked over to Arbie.

"What are you doing?" Jane asked Arbie.

"Just straightening up a little. I never can keep my magazines organized. They take over after only a little while," Arbie explained.

Jane looked around and saw many issues of *Life*, *Time*, *Newsweek*, and *The Saturday Evening Post*. On an end table next to the couch sat a clear jar filled with dimes. The jar rested atop a magazine.

"What's this?" Jane asked, pulling the magazine out from under the jar.

Jane looked at the cover of a woman in uniform on Time magazine's January 17, 1944 edition.

"The last woman to appear on an issue of *Time*," said Arbie.

Jane opened the magazine and began reading the article on the cover woman—Colonel Oveta Culp Hobby of the Women's Army Corps.

"Anyone want to bet on whether the next issue of *Time* will feature a woman on the cover? Ten cents a bet. Winners split the pot," Arbie announced.

"I'll put in a dime," said Mum.

"Forget it," said Trudy. "*Time* almost always features men. If you put a bet on *Life* magazine, I'm in."

"No, just *Time* magazine," said Arbie.

"Well then forget it! Who will they get on the cover? We're at war. There's always some General or dictator in the wings," Trudy said.

"You never know. Eleanor Roosevelt might be on it," Arbie said.

Trudy laughed.

"She might," Arbie said defensively.

"I'll bet a dime," Jane said.

"Good for you," Arbie said. "Hopefully we'll win soon."

Arbie deposited her dime after Jane's.

"There's a shortage of women in the army," said Jane. "Maybe staying at home isn't—"

"Oh don't you start reading that stuff," said Trudy. "We women are already doing enough for the war effort. Working in the factories, entertaining with ball games—we're doing plenty."

Mum had returned with her beer and smiled to the ball-game reference.

"You would make a good G.I. Jane," Arbie said. "You have the right build for it."

"Really?"

"Front line, yup," Arbie said. "That would only be at first. I'm sure you'd be promoted quickly. My sister, on the other hand, would only be good for radio duty behind a desk."

"I can do anything a man can do," Trudy answered.

Trudy started a three-player game of Sheepshead as Petunia returned and joined the table along with Mum.

"Desk duty," Arbie repeated.

"Front line!" Trudy said.

"Then sign up," Arbie taunted.

"Why should I?" Trudy replied. "It's not like the war is on our soil. Besides, Wilton doesn't like the idea. He'd rather fight the war and keep me safe at home."

"You see, Jane, that's why she goes by Sheppe—she is her husband's property. Now take me—I married a Knoxberger, but while he's at war, I'm a Hansen," Arbie said, and she raised her voice and directed it to Trudy, "while my sister over there is always a Sheppe and never returns to being a Hansen like I do."

Jane skimmed through the article and read about the Colonel's difficulties in raising the number of women needed for the war.

"What last name do you go by?" Arbie asked Jane.

"O'Leary—my husband's last name," Jane said.

"Hah!" Trudy blasted.

"Ick. Jane—don't give in completely. Have a little freedom. What's your maiden name?" Arbie asked.

"MacNessi."

"Yeah," said Arbie. "I'll call you Miss MacNessi—you don't mind, do you?"

"No, it's all right," Jane smiled.

"Good!" Arbie replied.

Arbie gave Jane a hug, and Jane hugged back. Jane had a weird feeling. Hugging Arbie was a pleasant experience. Jane wasn't used to hugging people—most people didn't hug her, and she wasn't sure if it was a safe experience. Jack never hugged her—he would shake hands, pat her on the shoulder, or engage in quick sexual activity with the lights off and no foreplay.

Then Jane felt terrible, like she'd betrayed the Kenosha outfielder. It was a foolish feeling, and she knew it.

"Umph, you have a strong hug," Arbie said.

Jane flipped the magazine to another article.

"Anything interesting?" Arbie asked.

"Here's a strange one—Francisco Franco is congratulating the Japanese puppet government."

"Politics is very strange," Arbie said. "I've been reading the news for years, and there's always something shocking to read. Like the one about the Pope not caring about democracy."

"What?!" Trudy said. "You're making that up."

"No I'm not," Arbie said. "I read it somewhere."

"You just said that to sound important," Trudy said with a chuckle.

"No I didn't. And it's pathetic," Arbie replied. She turned to Jane and said, "Help me find the article—it's in one of these *Time* magazines somewhere...wait, here it is in the February 14th edition of this year—1944."

"Valentine's Day," Jane said.

"Oh, you're not talking about that Kremlin article, are you?" Trudy asked. "Jane—don't bother. It's just Russian propaganda to drive a wedge between Catholics."

"It can't all be propaganda," said Arbie. "There's always some truth behind what people say."

"Not always," Trudy said back.

"Read the article, Jane. Tell me what you think," Arbie urged.

"'Impartial love for all nations'," Jane read.

"Read the democracy part," Arbie said.

"It's talking about the Pope," Jane continued. "It says, 'He is not a supporter of democracy but is just what he claims to be—indifferent to political forms, accepting any Government which will meet the minimum demands of the Church.'"

"See?" Arbie said to Trudy.

"Hogwash," said Trudy.

"It really says that," Jane said to Trudy. "The article is 'Devious Diplomacy'. Do you want to read it?"

"I've read it already," Trudy said. "Arbie knows I have. We've argued that one for hours. People can say anything about anyone and make it sound believable."

"Keep your eyes open in this world," Arbie said to Jane. "Institutions only care about their own agenda. As long as you support that agenda, they'll ignore other evils—like dictatorships or fascist governments. It could be an exaggeration that

Franco is a Vatican pet, but if Franco supports the Vatican, wouldn't it be easier for the Pope to look the other way when Franco commits his atrocities?"

"I don't know anything about Franco," Jane said.

"Generalissimo Francisco Franco, His Excellency Benito Mussolini, Herr Fuehrer Adolf Hitler, Hirohito a.k.a. Emperor Shōwa, and General Joseph Vissar Stalin," Trudy said. "Mention any of those names, Jane, and Arbie will talk your ears off for hours."

"Vissarionovich," Arbie corrected. "Stalin's middle name—it's 'Vissarionovich' not 'Vissar'."

"Who can remember?" Trudy asked. "But all those dictators are somewhere else and not here, so who cares?"

"Oh, the horror of them all," said Arbie. "Which one is the worst? And we should care, Trudy! The people suffer so much. I can tell you—"

"See what I mean?" Trudy said. "Come back over here, Jane. Let's play four-player Sheepshead."

"See, Jane? Trudy represents American isolationism. 'Let someone else worry about it. Not in my backyard.' Because of that, this country waited until the Japanese bombed Pearl Harbor before entering the war."

"Uh oh," Trudy said. "Here comes the war mongering."

"It's not war mongering!" Arbie retorted. "Jane—that article on Colonel Hobby and the WACs—I read it. It says women are needed in the army, but American women are slow to join. Some don't because it's 'over there'—that's the isolationist attitude. Others don't because their husbands pressure them to stay at home and do housekeeping. We're better than that, Jane, we are."

"Of course we are," said Trudy. "But we don't have to meddle in other countries' affairs to prove it. Besides, it's more fun flirting with the boys at home."

"We're all human beings!" Arbie said.

The tension in Arbie's home increased, leaving Jane, Mum, and Petunia uncomfortable. No one spoke for a moment—the only sound being cards slapping on the table.

"I win," Trudy said, referring to the Sheepshead game.

Arbie let out a sigh of disappointment.

"I think it's time for the surprise," Mum announced to break the angst between sisters.

"What surprise?" Jane asked.

"It's a wonderful surprise," replied Petunia. "And it's for you."

"You mean?" Trudy asked. "She is going to be—"

"Jane, you did it! Congratulations!" Arbie said.

"You deserve it. You have a natural talent. I knew you'd make it," said Trudy.

"Deserve what?" Jane asked. "What am I going to be?"

"I'm so jealous of you," Trudy said. "I wish I could go."

"Someone tell me what's going on!" Jane said, a little frustrated she had not figured out what the surprise was about.

"Now this is unofficial—the formal announcement will be made the day after tomorrow, but Mum and I learned—" Petunia started.

"Yes," Mum continued. "Petunia and I learned that you, Jane O'Leary, will be selected to join the league. Congratulations!"

"Me?! I'm going to be a professional ballplayer?" Jane asked.

"Yes you are!" Petunia said. "You'll have to tell your boss at Daschwirk."

"Yes, you'll have to give up your day job," Mum grinned.

"I can do that," Jane said with glee. "I'll do that tonight!"

The girls laughed.

"Well, maybe not tonight," Jane added.

"Of course not," Trudy said.

"There's just one thing we need to do," Mum said.

"What's that?" Jane asked.

"We need to give you a crash course on charm school," Petunia said.

"And we need to start with makeup," Mum said.

"And clothing," Petunia said.

"Clothing?" Jane asked in astartlement.

"I gave them your size," Trudy said. "I hope you don't mind."

"Come along, Jane," Mum said.

"We'll doll you up and teach you everything you need to know," Petunia added.

"It's all right, Jane," Arbie said. "I told the girls they could use the guest bedroom for your conversion."

"Conversion?" Jane said.

"Yes—we're going to convert you into an attractive, eye-catching woman," said Mum.

Mum and Petunia led a bewildered Jane to the guestroom while Arbie and Trudy remained behind. Trudy put away the cards and sat in the living room with a magazine.

"Do you think it will work?" Trudy asked.

"Of course!" Arbie replied. "Mum and Petunia are the best."

"Arbie, there's something I need to tell you about Jane," said Trudy.

"Oh?"

"Something she did...something she shouldn't have done," Trudy said.

"Did she rob a bank?" Arbie asked.

"No."

"Did she kill a man?"

"No!"

"Too bad," Arbie grinned.

"Nothing criminal," Trudy said.

"Then why are you upset?" Arbie asked.

"I'm not upset. She was...looking...she was looking at another woman," Trudy said.

"Oh, get a life, Trudy," Arbie said.

"No, really," Trudy continued.

"Really what? You're too vain."

"No, listen—we were at the Kenosha Comets and Racine Belles opening game last year. She was staring at one of the players," Trudy continued.

"Trudy, please! This is absurd. She wasn't staring—she was watching the game like anyone else," Arbie said.

"No, not like anyone else, and it was before the game. She stared at one of the players, and she got a funny look on her face like she does when she sees her husband," Trudy explained.

"Funny look of disgust?" Arbie said. "Like when a husband walks through snow and salt and tracks it through the house?"

"No, no, no!" Trudy said. "There was another time, too. Remember early September last year, when the Comets played the Belles for the championship?"

"How can I forget? The Belles swept the Comets for the championship. Mum and Petunia have talked my ears off about it for the last nine months," Arbie said.

"Jane was so incredibly happy during those three games. She was in a daze Friday evening, Saturday, and Sunday," Trudy said.

"That's perfectly normal. Everyone loved those three games. The Racine Belles winning the first championship?! Absolute jubilation!" Arbie said.

"Not if you're from Kenosha!" Trudy said.

"Oh get over it," Arbie said.

"No, you don't understand," Trudy said. "The Kenosha Comets—the City of Kenosha—the fans—we fought so hard to get that second round championship that we were exhausted. Burned out. We had no pep left for the final championship. It was all a great burden. It shouldn't have been, but it was."

"What burden?" Arbie said. "The Belles were well rested. In fact I remember—the second round championship ended on a Wednesday night, and the final series started on the following Friday night. Plenty of rest."

"Easy for you to say. The Racine Belles had already won the first championship a couple of months back. They didn't have to do much of anything. They coasted into the final series," Trudy said.

"So what's your point, Trudy? Are you complaining?" Arbie asked.

"Not complaining, no. Just describing the general mood in Kenosha. But Jane didn't have the same mood. She was ecstatic the entire three games. And she kept her eye focused on one particular person."

"Who?" Arbie asked.

"A Kenosha outfielder. The same one she watched during the first game of the season," Trudy said.

"Let me ask you, Trudy," Arbie said. "Were you drinking at those last three games?"

"Well yes, but that doesn't—"

"Then I'd say you had a little too much. Now quit ragging on Jane and leave her be. We've got to build up her image for the ball league. And she's your friend, for Peterina's sake! Where's your support?"

"All right, all right! I'll support her!" Trudy promised.

The two sat for an hour or so in the living room while Jane's conversion was in progress. Trudy seemed anxious, but Arbie was relaxed and cheerful.

"How can you be so relaxed at a time like this?" Trudy asked.

"A time like what? If you're so jittery, have a beer or another shot of vodka. There's plenty," Arbie offered.

"No, I better sober up for this," said Trudy. "I don't want extra surprises."

"You surprise me," said Arbie. "But don't you worry—Mum and Petunia aren't auditioning Jane for the circus."

It wasn't long before Mum and Petunia appeared in the living room.

"Ladies and gent...er...ladies, may I present to you, the next All-American Girls Baseball player, Mrs. Jane MacNessi O'Leary."

Jane walked in slowly.

"Who's this?" Trudy asked. "Why isn't Jane coming out?"

"This is Jane!" Mum said.

"Egad!" Arbie said. "You girls are geniuses!"

"I don't believe it," Trudy said.

"Take a closer look," Petunia said to Trudy.

Trudy walked up to Jane and took a closer look. Jane wore a tight dress with a low-cut back. Her legs were smooth and elegant, her arms graceful, and her chest was well shaped and prominent. Her hair was styled up, and her face was more charming than a magazine model's face.

"Jane?" Trudy asked.

"It's me," Jane's familiar voice answered.

"It is you!" Trudy said. "Wow! You look better than me!"

"Walk for us, Jane," Arbie said.

Jane walked a few paces into the living room, turned, and walked back.

"You taught her to walk, too!" Trudy said.

"Anything is possible," said Mum.

"Now what we need is a charming nickname for Jane," said Petunia.

"Hmmm, Jane O'Leary," said Mum. "Jo Leary—it could work."

"What about Nessi?" Arbie offered.

"Nessi? As in the Loch Ness monster?" Trudy asked.

"No. Her maiden name is MacNessi," Arbie said.

"We could call her Mac," Trudy said, but Arbie shot down that suggestion with a curdled expression of disapproval. "Sorry, just kidding. How about doing something off her last name?"

"Like what?" Petunia asked.

"Well," Trudy continued, "if instead of O'Leary we say 'O-lee' or 'Ollie'—"

"No Ollie," said Arbie. "And no Lee."

"What about Janna?" Petunia said.

"I like Janna," said Trudy.

"I still want Nessi," Arbie said.

"Jane," Mum said, "What do you think?"

"I don't want people to think I'm a monster from Scotland," she said. "I like Janna."

"Then Janna it is!" Mum proclaimed.

The Next Monday at Daschwirk.

It was early morning at Jane's home, and she dressed for the day. Instead of wearing her usual drabbish clothes, she threw on an attractive business-office outfit with proper hosiery. She put up her hair, applied makeup, and touched up her fingernails. She slipped on high-heeled shoes and finished her attire with a cute hat and matching purse.

"I wonder what kind of reaction I'll get," Jane chuckled. "If I can turn a few heads, I'll know I can pass charm school."

Jane walked to Daschwirk as she usually did.

"Ugh. High-heeled shoes hurt my feet," she said to herself.

Jane suffered through the foot pain and arrived at the security gate. Not thinking, she walked past the gate as she normally did. The guard stepped out of the booth and approached her.

"I'm sorry, Miss. We're not hiring any office staff. Try the factory across the street. They might be hiring."

"Jeff," Jane said. "It's me—Jane O'Leary. Don't you recognize me?"

"Huh?" Jeff asked. "It can't be."

"It is," Jane said. "Look closely."

Jeff inspected Jane closely.

"Well bust my buttons, what on Earth are you doing in that getup?"

"It's the new me. Do you like it?"

"Like it? Oh boy...wait...oh girl!" Jeff said.

"See you after work!" Jane said, and she headed into the factory building leaving Jeff scratching his head.

Jane entered the locker to change into her machinist clothes. The other girls stopped their carefree chatter for a moment—mistaking Jane for a manager. One of the girls recognized Jane after a moment and spoke.

"Oh, it's just Jane," she said.

"We thought you were a manager," said another.

"Why are you dressed up?" said the first.

"I'm working on my look," said Jane.

"Honey, who needs a look here? This is a factory!" said the first.

"I might be playing in the All-American Girls Baseball League," Jane said, "and I'm practicing for charm school."

"Did you have to practice here?" said the second. "We don't want to be shown up."

"Yeah," said the first. "What's the big idea? Do you think you're better than us?"

"No," said Jane. "I...just..."

"I bet she's doing it for extra privileges," said the second.

The other girls in the locker room clamored in agreement.

"Well don't expect any privileges from us," said the first.

"I'm not doing it—" Jane started to say.

"You can't fool us, honey," said the second. "We know how it works. The men will start doing things for you, and they'll expect things back. Just what are you trying to prove?"

"She's a big star now," said the first. "Gonna be on a ball team and everything."

"She wants to alienate herself from us, that's what," said the second.

"Well let her, I say," said the first.

"No, no, no! You're making a mountain out of a molehill," said Jane. "Listen, I—"

"We can't stand around and look pretty all day," said the first. "We've got work to do. Come on, girls."

As the girls left the locker room, Trudy entered.

"What's up?" Trudy asked. "Why the big rush?"

"Ask your prima donna there," said the first girl.

The locker room emptied leaving Jane and Trudy to themselves.

"Jane?" Trudy asked. "What happened? And why are you dolled up?"

"I...wanted to...ugh!" Jane stumbled, and her eyes moistened up with tears.

"Don't cry, it'll make your mascara run," Trudy said. "Here—dab your eyes with this tissue. Don't talk. Take a deep breath and finish changing. Let's get you doing something so you won't mope around. Think—what's the first thing you need to do on the floor?"

"I have that hub to machine," Jane said.

"There—think about machining your hub. Do you have the right cutting bits?"

"No, I need some slot drills and reamers from the crib," Jane said with a sniff.

"There, you see?"

"I feel better," Jane said, and she stopped sobbing. "Thank you, Trudy."

"You're welcome. Now let's get to work and forget about those other girls."

Jane and Trudy exited the locker room. Trudy proceeded to her welding station while Jane stopped by the crib for her cutting bits.

"Oh hello, Jane!" Jim, the crib manager said with extra enthusiasm. "What can I get for you?"

"I need these cutting tools," she said, handing him a list on a paper.

"You're so organized," he said, passing the paper to one of his helpers. "The other guys tell me what they need and come back a few minutes later to get something they forgot or something a little different in size. I never have that with you—you get things right the first time."

"Well, I try," she said.

"If there's anything I can do for you—anything you need—just ask," Jim offered.

"I will," Jane said.

"Do you have any plans for lunch? I'd like to take you to lunch," Jim offered.

"That's kind, but I don't need—"

"What about dinner? Or the pub down the street? I have a friend—he's the bartender—and it's half-price on drinks. What do you say?"

"Jim, I'm married!" Jane said. "What's gotten into you? You're never like this."

"Oh, well, I'm just being friendly. If you get lonely, let me know."

"All right," Jane said.

Jim's assistant handed the tools over to Jim, who handed them to Jane. In doing so, he touched his hand on Jane's and held contact for several seconds with a devious smile. Uncomfortable, Jane pulled away. She carried the tools to her milling station, attached the slot drill to the machine head, and proceeded to cut her work.

"Hello," said another machinist as he walked up to Jane, a young man named Bill.

"Hello, Bill," Jane said without interrupting her work.

"You're looking fine today," he said while staring at her.

"Thank you," she replied without looking back.

"I have an extra bottle of detergent coolant you can borrow," he offered.

"No thank you, I have plenty here," she said.

"Need some clean rags? I have some in my toolbox," he said.

"No, Bill, I have enough," Jane replied.

Jane was trying to focus on the work, but her attention slipped, and she broke the slot drill.

"Oh that's too bad. Your feed was too fast for the speed," he said.

"I know, Bill," she said, a bit irritated with her mistake and Bill's loitering.

"I can get you another slot drill," he said.

"No, I can manage," she said, but Bill had already headed over to the tool crib.

"How are things going?" another voice asked—a voice belonging to Hank the floor cleaner.

"Hank, can you help me?" Jane asked.

"Sure, anything for you, doll," Hank said.

Hank had never called Jane "doll" before, and her eyes jumped when he called her by that name.

"Divert Bill," she said.

"Huh?"

"Tell him he is needed somewhere. Tell him the sweeper is broken," Jane said. "I can't work with him bugging me."

"For you, anything," Hank said.

Hank intercepted Bill on the way back from the tool crib and motioned over to his sweeper. Jane changed in a reamer and reamed out a different part of the work until she could get a new slot drill.

"Here you are," Hank said. "This is the slot drill Bill got for you."

"Thank you, Hank," Jane said.

Hank stood over Jane's shoulder and did not move. Jane continued reaming the hole but felt disturbed by Hank's breath rolling down her neck. He smelled as if he hadn't brushed his teeth in three weeks.

"Hank?" Jane asked.

"Yeah."

"Why are you standing behind me?" she asked while continuing to ream the hole.

"You smell nice today," he said. "I was trying to figure out what kind of perfume you're wearing."

"I'm not wearing perfume," she said.

"But you smell nice," he said.

"Hank, when did you last take a shower and brush your teeth?" she asked.

"What kind of question is that?" he asked, becoming defensive.

"I can't breathe when you get that close," she said. "It makes me sick."

"What makes you sick?" he asked, becoming more irritated.

Hank grabbed her by the shoulders and turned her around. The reamer kept descending into the hole but without white coolant applied from Jane's detergent bottle.

"Your breath, your body odor. Now let me go," she said.

Jane turned back around to apply coolant on the reamer. It smoked excessively from the coolant, indicating it had built up more heat than it should have.

"Kiss me!" he said again.

Hank spun her around again by the shoulders. The detergent coolant bottle fell from Jane's hand onto the floor. Hank forced his body around hers and held her lips to his in the most unpleasant, brutish kiss one could imagine. Hank was large and strong, even despite Jane's own strength. She beat him on the back to get him to stop, but he didn't.

The reamer descended without coolant until the workpiece heated into colors of dark red, bright red, and orange. The metal became heat-treated, and it hardened beyond the strength of the reamer. The reamer made a horribly low grinding sound as it was caught between the descending force of the mill and the resistance of the work. It was an all too-familiar sound to a machinist that something big is about to break.

"Let go!" she yelled, and she kneed him in the groin.

Hank backed off. Jane spun around as quickly as she could and launched her fist at the red emergency stop button. The reamer broke with a factory-echoing crack just before her fist hit the button. Hank stole away as if he had nothing to do with the incident. The other workers stopped their machines briefly and stared at Jane and her mill. Jane ignored them and resumed work. With the excitement over, the other workers resumed working as well. Jane repositioned the mill to give her access to the work, and she removed the broken reamer. She attached a grinder to a line of compressed air and started grinding out the hardened metal.

"Jane," said another voice while she was grinding.

Jane looked up and saw Mr. Henrock.

"Yes, Mr. Henrock?"

"May I see you for a minute in my office?"

Jane knew what that phrase meant—Trudy had told her it was the equivalent of, "You're fired," or, "Your husband is dead." Jane didn't want bad news, but what could she do?

"Have a seat please," he said once the two entered his office.

Mr. Henrock sat in his chair with Jane on the opposing side of his desk.

"You look different today," he said. "Haircut or something?"

"Or something," she replied, shocked that he didn't respond to her new look like the other guys had.

"A telegram just arrived for you," he said. "I don't normally interrupt a workday for this, but you're our best machinist, and I want you to know that whatever family crisis you have, the company is behind you. Take whatever time you need."

"What does the telegram say?" she asked.

"I haven't read it, of course," he said as he handed it to Jane.

Jane opened the envelope with a grim expression, fearing she'd learn her husband was killed.

"You have been accepted into the All-American Girls Baseball League!" Jane screamed.

Jane jumped for joy and danced all about Mr. Henrock's office. Mr. Henrock was quite stunned and wasn't sure what to say.

"What's this?" he asked once Jane semi-calmed down.

Trudy entered his office on seeing Jane through the office window dancing.

"Trudy!" Jane said as the two embraced. "It's official! I'm in the league!"

Both girls hooted and hollered in Mr. Henrock's office and danced a jig of joy.

"Does this mean you're leaving Daschwirk?" Mr. Henrock asked.

Jane shook her head, "Yes," while continuing her whoops and hollers with Trudy.

"Well, we'll miss you here," he said, though he had to speak up a bit to get his voice through the girls' cheering. "There's always a job for you here if things don't work out."

"Thank you, Mr. Henrock," Jane said while jumping.

"Which team?" Trudy asked.

"Kenosha, I guess," Jane said without really thinking.

"You guess?" Trudy said as she broke off the jumping and dancing.

Trudy's tone grew serious.

"Why not? That's where I live," Jane said.

"No, no, no. Don't you remember what I told you last year?" Trudy said. "They assign your team based on league balancing. Read the telegram. Does it say what team?"

Jane read the second half of the telegram and looked down in disgust.

"What's wrong?" Trudy asked.

Jane handed the telegram back to Mr. Henrock.

"What did you do that for?" Trudy asked.

"I'm giving the telegram back," Jane replied.

"That's silly," Trudy said. "You can't give a telegram back."

"I am," Jane said.

"Trudy's right," Mr. Henrock said. "Whatever you do, you must let the league know. Giving this to me won't help. I can't send it back."

"Will you tell the league for me, Mr. Henrock? Will you?" Jane asked.

"It's not my place to do that," he said.

"You can tell your brother. You can tell Joe," Jane said.

"Janie," Trudy said, "Why are you acting like this? Being on the league is the best thing that has happened to you. And you'll get more money! What team?"

Jane did not answer.

"What team, Mr. Henrock?" Trudy asked.

Mr. Henrock put on his reading glasses, opened the telegram, and scanned through the message to the end.

"'Team: Minneapolis Millerettes'," Mr. Henrock read. "'Position: pitcher'."

"They had to put you somewhere," Trudy said.

"But why Minnesota? Why can't I play here?" Jane asked.

"You must be a good pitcher," said Mr. Henrock, "to be sent there. Kenosha has the best pitcher with Helen Nicole, and Racine has Mary Nesbitt. They'd never put all the good pitchers on one team."

"He's right," Trudy said. "They put you on the Millerettes because you're too good to put on the Comets or the Belles. But you'll get to play games in Racine and Kenosha. We'll watch your games."

"I don't want to move to Minnesota. I like it here in Kenosha!" Jane said.

"Jane—why don't you think about it? Take the day off with pay. Just give me your timesheet, and I'll sign today's entry," Mr. Henrock offered.

"Thank you, sir, but I can't accept gratuity like this. I would like the rest of the morning off, but I'll come back after lunch. Unpaid leave," Jane insisted.

"As you wish," Mr. Henrock said.

Trudy left Mr. Henrock's office with Jane in tow.

"Aren't you forgetting something?" Mr. Henrock asked Jane while she was in the doorway to his office.

Mr. Henrock stood from his desk and walked over to Jane with the telegram.

"You'll have to tell them."

"All right," Jane said.

"Jane—we like you here, and you'll always have a job. But—" he started to say.

"But what?"

"Sometimes you have to look after yourself first," he said.

Jane kissed Mr. Henrock on the cheek and left his office. Mr. Henrock returned to his desk, wiped the lipstick off on a tissue, and threw the tissue away. Jane went home, removed her makeup, changed into her old clothes, and returned to work. She finished the day as Jane O'Leary the machinist instead of Janna the Baseball Beauty. She arrived home from a long workday, telephoned the league office (reversing charges as instructed by the league), and informed the league of her decision. The league was disappointed and offered her a chance for the following season. Jane no-thank-you'ed the league, and her ball-playing career ended for the time being.

Jonara's environment swirled and eddied with the fire and smoke of war. Days passed quickly, bombs fell, and soldiers died. Jonara felt suspended above the world—tugged in this direction, blown in that direction. But above all, she held an eye on Jane, who decided to help the war effort as best she could. Jane worked harder than ever before at Daschwirk, churning out milled works as quickly as she could, taking shorter breaks, and working longer hours. The little time she had off from work was spent buying groceries and sleeping. She had no time for friends—including Trudy and Arbie. Trudy urged Jane to work less and enjoy more. Invitations to pubs, movies, beach volleyball in Racine, and swimming in Lake Michigan went unanswered. Jane was highly motivated to help the American war effort. She remembered reading the *Time* magazine article about Colonel Hobby—that American women didn't feel a need to contribute as much to the war effort since it wasn't on their soil. Jane didn't want her portion to be short, nor did she want anyone saying she didn't put enough into helping her country win.

In mid-December of 1944, Jane's husband—Jack O'Leary—was granted Christmas leave. He returned by express airline passage over the Atlantic. Jane welcomed Jack at Milwaukee's airport—General Mitchell Field (later General Mitchell International Airport).

"I'm so happy to be home," Jack said to Jane as the two boarded a bus to Kenosha. "One thing I'm going to do after the war is buy a car. I'm so tired of walking, marching, running, and hiding. Officials drive Jeeps, soldiers drive tanks—it's much better than being forced to use one's legs and getting stuck in a wet stinking trench."

"Don't think about the war," Jane said. "I'm just glad to see you. Let's get you home and into a hot shower. I'll make you some lunch. You'll feel better soon!"

Jane did the best she could to be cheerful for Jack. But Jack complained about everything and wouldn't stop—even after the two arrived home. He complained while in the shower. He complained during lunch. He even complained about Trudy when she visited with some fresh flowers—something Jane was pleasantly surprised to see considering the time of year. At Jane's quiet request, Trudy agreed to leave and return at a better time.

"Jack, you seem different somehow," Jane said.

"Me? I'm the same man you met a few years ago. I think you've changed, Jane. You used to look to me for everything. But I see you've been getting along very well here," he said.

"I'm doing the best I can," Jane said.

"Guess you don't need me," he said.

"Oh that's not true. I miss you, Jack."

"It doesn't feel that way, Jane. Something is different. Something is wrong. Everything's rotten," he continued.

Jack repeated these phrases the rest of the day. Jane had never seen him get stuck in his speech. She urged him to read a magazine or two, but after a few minutes, he tossed the magazine aside and went back to how everything was different and how bad things were.

"I've been working long hours at Daschwirk," Jane said. "Mr. Henrock says I do the work of three men. He's raised my pay several times. Do you want to know what I'm making now?"

"No. The war is bad. People are bad," he said.

Jane continued her good news in hopes of breaking Jack's funk.

"I'm now making eighty cents an hour!" Jane bragged. "That's thirty-two dollars a week, not counting overtime."

"Whoop-dee-doo. Any man will make fifty-five a week—easy," Jack said.

"That can't be true. Mr. Henrock would—" Jane said.

"Mr. Henrock pays you what you're worth. A man is worth more. Quit bragging about nothing," Jack said.

Jane's eyes flared with rage. She took a step toward Jack with a fist but paused to restrain herself.

"What are you doing? Think you can take me on? I beat up Nazis for fun. Don't try anything stupid," he said.

"Jack, I think you need to talk to someone," she said. "I really do. You sound sick."

"I'm as healthy as an ox," he said. "Stronger than a bull. Smarter than a hog. Go on. Get me a beer and make dinner before you start bawling."

Jane left Jack in the living room and walked to the kitchen where she opened the refrigerator for a beer. She paused, and her anger inverted into sadness. She took a beer, closed the door, and set the beer on the countertop while she took a tissue to her eyes and nose. Tossing the used tissue in the wastebasket, she delivered the beer to Jack and returned to the kitchen to prepare dinner. Jack rummaged through some newspapers and magazines but was discontent. He turned on the radio and waited for it to warm up. He adjusted the volume and fiddled with the tuning, but the radio never produced sound.

"When was the last time you had this radio on?" he yelled across the home.

"I haven't used the radio," Jane said. "No time."

"Well it's got a burned-out tube. You should have had the tube replaced while I was gone. What's wrong with you, can't you keep up house for a man?" he ranted.

Jane held her tongue. She pulled out a package of ground beef, tossed the wrapper in the wastebasket, and placed the beef on the chopping board. Washing her hands clean, she planned on taking bits of the beef and fashioning simple hamburgers for the two. But she was tense and needed a way to vent her frustrations from Jack's foul mood. She lifted a skillet in the air and held it. She stared at the ground beef, and for a moment she envisioned it as Jack's head. She developed a real need to knock sense into the ground beef.

Jane slammed the skillet's mass into the beef glob. Repeatedly. Before she could issue the fourth blow, Jack intercepted her arm in mid-motion. He squeezed her forearm—forcing her release of the skillet (which fell to the floor with a clang).

"What are you doing?" she asked him.

Jack appeared possessed. His eyes stared through her, his face turned pale, and sweat peppered his skin. He forced Jane against the wall as if he'd caught the enemy. He held his hand over her mouth to muffle her screams.

"Caught you, didn't I, you sneaking Fascist!" he gargled.

"Mmmph, mmph," Jane mustered.

She writhed and squirmed to evade Jack's steel grip, but she could not escape. Jack crushed his weight against her body. Jane gagged.

"That's right, little Fascist. Grunt like a pig. Here, little piggy!" Jack continued in his mad delirium.

Jane tried freeing her arms. She could not. She tried maneuvering her legs to knee Jack. She could not.

"Mmmmmphh!" she screamed through his hand.

"You can't call for help," Jack said in his continued gurgly voice. "No one can hear you in the trench."

Jonara felt horrible. She had no idea who this woman was, but she was in a terrible situation. How could Jonara help? She knew that interfering was impossible. Yet she tried anyway. She swung her arms through Jack and tried stamping on his feet, but her limbs passed through his.

Jack choked Jane. She flapped madly for want of oxygen and release of carbon dioxide. Then Jack said something strange. Jane wasn't sure, but it sounded like German. With what little German she knew, it sounded like Jack was saying, "God save our country."

A car backfired outside the window. The sound resembled gunshot, and Jack stood erect as if waking from a bad dream. He released his grip on Jane, and she fell to the floor in a daze. Slowly, she regained her breath. As color returned to her face, Jack looked at her in apuzzlement.

"What are you doing on the floor?" he asked in his pre-delirium voice.

Jane could not talk—she gagged every time she tried. Jack looked at her again and seemed to remember something.

"It happened again," he mumbled to himself.

Jack raced for his coat and walked briskly to the door.

"Jack," Jane gagged.

"To my own wife," he mumbled without turning to her.

He was gone. As Jane regained her strength, she realized the full horror of what had happened. Unsure of what to do, she walked around her home for ten minutes before deciding to clean up, consume a few shots of Irish whiskey, and sit on the couch to a magazine. This was how Trudy found Jane an hour later, when Trudy decided to bring dessert.

"What happened?" Trudy asked. "You look like you've been in an accident. Your face is all beat up."

"I...he..." Jane started, but she was exhausted.

Trudy sat next to Jane, and Jane buried her head into Trudy's shoulder and cheek.

"You go ahead and have a good cry," said Trudy. "Everything will be all right."

Jane looked up at Trudy and realized Jane had scuffed a bit of makeup off Trudy's face, revealing a dark bruise.

"Your face," Jane said. "A bruise...you...did Wilton..."

Trudy withdrew, turned her back on Jane, pulled a mirror from her purse, and applied foundation on her cheek to cover the bruise.

"It's nothing," Trudy said. "It was just an accident. Wilton is tired...and...well...accidents will happen."

"Your husband...he...hit you too?" Jane asked.

"Don't talk like that," said Trudy. "It only makes things worse. Our men have been through a lot. This is how we help them. Now cover your face up with makeup, and brush your hair—you'll feel much better."

Jane tried to say something about how it was wrong, Jack shouldn't have attacked her like that, but Trudy shushed her by explaining the role of women in America during war.

"Let's get something to eat at the diner," Trudy said.

"I'm not hungry. And I don't want to go out," Jane said.

"You have to keep up your strength. Besides, you need to get out and get your mind off this place," said Trudy.

"This place is my home!" Jane said.

"Yeah, yeah, yeah. Come on, let's go," Trudy insisted.

Jane managed to forget about Jack and the war after she filled her stomach with a chicken sandwich at the local diner. The makeup covered her scrapes and bruises, and she laughed along with Trudy—especially after the two had a couple of drinks.

"I should be getting back," said Jane.

"Are you going to be all right?" Trudy asked. "Do you want to stay at my house?"

Jane shot Trudy a funny look as if to say, "Your house is no better."

"Yeah, that was a stupid question," Trudy said.

On arriving home, Jane changed into nightclothes and climbed into bed. She dozed lightly on and off during the evening until loud garbage-can-kicking sounds broke through the night air. Jane buried her head into a pillow, but the sounds grew louder and closer. She could now hear a loud, obnoxious, male voice stirring the nighttime calm. Jane walked to the window and opened it only a little to prevent the winter blast from chilling her body.

"Ladies, ladies, I can't stay with you all night."

"Awe, c'mon, Jackie-pooh," said a woman. "Stay with us to-night."

"Now Cookie, you know I'm married," said the drunk who Jane recognized as Jack.

"You don't need her to keep you warm," said another woman.

"Muffin, I know I'm the finest hunk on the block, but I have to go," he said.

"Can we come in?" Cookie asked.

"The wife won't mind," Muffin said.

"I do mind!" Jane yelled out the window.

"Oh," Muffin said. "The hag is home."

"Let's find another chump," said Cookie, and the two women left.

"Hiya, darling," Jack said with a drunk accent.

"Jack, come inside before you catch cold," Jane said, trying to start over.

"All right then," he said.

Jane threw on a night robe and helped Jack into their home. He stumbled and drooled so badly that Jane wondered how he found his way back. Jack couldn't manage to remove his coat or shoes—leaving Jane to take care of him like a pre-school child. Despite stinking of cigars and alcohol, Jane put him to bed and crawled in with him.

"Maybe I should sleep on the couch," she whispered.

"Sleep where?" Jack said, not aware of his surroundings.

"Go to sleep, Jack," Jane said.

Jonara drifted above the home and hovered high over the city of Kenosha. Streetlights dotted the ground like strings of Christmas lights. The night was cold, and snow swirled around in the air. Parts of the sky opened to the stars above, but the stars raced by as if avoiding Kenosha and the O'Leary home. Hours passed. The clouds closed up leaving no gaps for star viewing. Jonara descended back to Kenosha and into the O'Leary home. Jane and Jack's bedroom was dark, and Jonara couldn't see anything.

For which she was thankful.

"Give me some loving," Jack said to Jane.

"Jack, go back to sleep," Jane said.

"Is this how you greet your husband? The lonely soldier?" he asked.

"Jack—you're still drunk. Sleep it off," Jane urged. "I have a headache."

"No," he said in anger. "No headache!"

And he forced himself on her.

It was at this point in Jonara's life that she realized she would never marry a man nor have children by a man. The savage, barbaric beast within the male chromosome as demonstrated by Jack was more than any human should bear, Jonara decided. She would never risk placing herself in the same position as Jane. More than ever, Jonara felt the adult world was a lie. How many men had appeared cheerful and polite to her on the street only to spend the night ravaging their wives as Jack had done?

"It's all a lie!" she kept repeating to herself.

The Tooth Fairy, the Easter Bunny, Santa Claus—all of the mythical figures she questioned her father on the flight down to Corpus Christi came flooding back to her mind.

"Is there a God?" she asked herself. "Is God the final lie?"

She wasn't sure. Evanita prayed to Jesus before falling asleep in the Elrod 402. Geneva was a devout Catholic. Johnny was a Baptist. Eva seemed to believe in God though in a looser fashion. Jonara couldn't think—it was too much for her—and the last events of 1944 made her forget her questions.

It was Christmas Eve. Jane and Jack had largely been quiet since his first night of heavy drinking and assault. He continued going out to drink but slept on the couch each night, leaving Jane a little peace during the nocturnal hours. But he set aside his drinking that Christmas Eve and suggested he turn over a new leaf.

"Let's go to confession and clear the air," he said. "And we'll go to Midnight Mass afterward. What do you say? We'll have a new start. Isn't that the best Christmas gift a man can have?"

Jane had mixed feelings about his tone. Jack seemed sincere, but only for himself and not for the marriage as a whole. Still, it was the best she could do at the time, so she agreed. The two walked several blocks down the street to the local Catholic Church—the very one in which they were married. As luck would have it, there were two priests performing confession, and even luckier—the flood of parishioners were following instead of preceding them in line. Jane and Jack led each of their lines, and the two nearly entered their respective confessionals at the same time.

"In the name of the Father and of the Son and of the Holy Ghost," the priest led.

"Amen," Jane and the priest said together.

Jane knelt by the screen separating her from the priest and began.

"Bless me Father, for I have sinned. It has been one month since my last confession. I slept in late three times, I bragged about being taller than my friend Trudy twice, I cursed at work too many times to remember, I said rude things to my husband, I—"

"Your husband?" the priest asked.

"Yes," Jane said.

"What kind of rude things?" the priest asked.

"When he came home the first day...well...when we went to sleep...I...I refused him," she said.

"And how did he react?" the priest said.

"He didn't care. He exercised his marital right anyway," she said.

"Yes. Do you have any other sins to confess?"

"I was going to talk about forgetting to water the plants," she said.

"Don't worry about that," he said. "That is but a small thing. But God is concerned about your failure to live up to His Sacrament of Matrimony. When you refuse your husband, you are refusing the sacrament, and Christ himself who binds your marriage together. Do not refuse Christ. Welcome him into your heart as you would your husband. For the way to Heaven is through Christ our Lord. For your penance, you will say ten Our Fathers, twenty Hail Marys, and you will offer yourself to your husband and to Christ each night throughout the Christmas season. Say now the Act of Contrition while I give you Absolution."

Jane recited the Act of Contrition as instructed, and as she did so, the priest recited a prayer that absolved Jane of her sins. He concluded the prayer (and thus Jane's confession) with:

"...In the name of the Father, and of the Son, and of the Holy Ghost, Amen. Go now and sin no more."

Jane left the confessional and entered a pew to say her Our Fathers and Hail Marys. By the time she finished, Jack exited his confessional, but he did not stop in a pew to say prayers. Instead, he grabbed Jane and led her out of church.

"Let's grab a bite at the pub. We don't want to be hungry before Midnight Mass," he said.

"As long as we finish an hour before Communion. You know the rule on fasting," she said.

"The what?" he asked, not seeming to remember. "An hour, oh yeah, of course, we'll have that hour of fasting, sure thing."

It was this way, then. Jane offered herself up to Jack each night so as not to go against her religious beliefs. Jack accepted and took advantage of her willingness. It was unfortunate for Jane. She wasn't relaxed and suffered greatly—both physically and mentally. More than once Jack referred to Jane as his pack mule to carry his burden. Jane's only happy moment was the day she bade farewell to him as he boarded the military plane at General Mitchell Field—a plane departing for the European war theater.

Jonara ascended high above the earth into the stratosphere where cold and ice dominated. Below, the world engaged in its final throes of World War Two—General Eisenhower advanced the Allies and defeated the Nazis in Germany while American soldiers grueled through the unsurrendering Empire of Japan.

In one small sliver of light, Jonara saw Jane in Kenosha with her friend, Trudy. They watched the Kenosha Comets playing ball in Lakefront Stadium by Lake Michigan. It was early August, and Jane was very pregnant. She had felt some mild contractions, but on Monday, August 6, 1945, she went into labor. Trudy took her to the Kenosha hospital, but after twelve hours of painful contractions, Jane's uterus stopped.

In the following couple of days, Jane learned of a horrible new bomb created by the Americans and its use on the Japanese city of Hiroshima. The thought of thousands of innocent people dying overwhelmed her, and by August 9th she was in the hospital again going through contractions. She delivered a healthy, baby girl—6 lbs. 5 oz. and 19 inches long. Jane worried that her baby was smaller than most. Had she done something wrong? Did she give birth to a premie? As it was, the baby girl passed all initial tests, and Jane took her new baby—Roberta MacNessi—home. Jane had dropped the O'Leary name from Roberta. Was it a whim? Subconscious rebellion? A way to avoid tarnishing her little girl with the name of a man who didn't seem to love her anymore or deserve a child? Jane didn't know or care. Jack wasn't there, and by the time he returned, it would be too late. He could yell all he wanted—it would be no worse than how he acted during his Christmas break.

Jane nursed her baby and thanked the Almighty for a gift of life. She especially treasured Roberta's healthy, innocent cooing once she learned of the second atomic bomb dropped on the Japanese city of Nagasaki—the very same day Roberta was born. Baby Roberta's ignorance of the world's horrors was Jane's bliss.

Jane had worked at Daschwirk up until late July. Her feet had swollen too much for her to stand for long hours, and Mr. Henrock granted her unpaid leave. He promised she would have a job once her six-week post-birth checkup was complete. Much to Jane's relief, Japan surrendered to the Allies on August 12th, and with that a massive wave of soldiers returned home. Jane had a slim but wishful hope that Jack would return overjoyed with both the war's conclusion and a new person in the home to love.

This was only partly true. Jack was happy the war was over, but Roberta's normal crying annoyed him to no end. He shouted at Jane to shut Roberta up for good, which only made Roberta cry more. Jane was convinced Jack's yelling set Roberta against men from this early age and regretted not realizing it at the time.

Jane returned to the factory in early October, but unfortunately, Mr. Henrock suffered a coronary and died two days after she resumed her machining job. Jane felt sick to her stomach. Attending Mr. Henrock's funeral didn't help, and she had a horrible feeling that something good was gone forever. It was more than just his death. Jane had read Margaret Mitchell's book, *Gone With The Wind*, and she had the feeling her life was suddenly very much like the Old South—disposed of and tossed aside for the wind to carry away.

A new manager replaced Mr. Henrock. His name was Mr. Grundle, and he barked at everyone and everything. When he wasn't barking, he was chain-smoking cigarettes. Jane thought nothing of the man until he stopped by her station not even a week after Mr. Henrock's funeral and said, "Ms. O'Leary, may I see you in my office for a minute?"

She had a bad feeling again, a feeling she would be fired. And she was right. Mr. Grundle stated that while Jane may have been good enough to machine airplane parts, she wasn't good enough to machine die sets for automotive parts. He declined to continue her job. She mentioned that she was able to machine die sets—she had started doing that already in the short time she'd returned, but Mr. Grundle was set in his ways. No matter what Jane said, he repeated that she wasn't good enough for the job.

Jeff, the security guard, escorted Jane from Daschwirk.

Jane searched the entire county for work as a machinist, but the story was the same—the war was over, she was a woman, why couldn't she stay at home with her child like the rest of the "normal" American women?

Meanwhile, Jack was hired at Daschwirk—the same factory where Jane worked during the war. He obtained his machinist's license while on the job, and made a dollar-fifty an hour (sixty dollars a week)—almost double what she made without overtime. Jane felt suddenly dependent on Jack for food, clothing, and shelter, and she didn't like it. Jack became more hostile and ordered her into household servitude. By December she was fed up, and by Christmas she had moved out and into Arbie's home. Arbie was now a widow—her husband died in the last efforts of war, and she was in mourning. Yet Arbie welcomed Jane and little Roberta as one opens curtains to let sunshine into the home. Jane and Roberta became a new spring day for Arbie, and Arbie became Aunt Arbie for Roberta.

Jane sought a divorce, but the Catholic Church did not allow it. She sought an annulment—that too was disallowed. In the end, she settled for a separation from Jack.

"I was the donkey," Jane said to Arbie one evening while the two were playing with Roberta.

"That's silly," Arbie said to reassure her.

"No, it's true. I worked my skin off at the factory during the war. Now I'm thrown away and sent to be butchered by my husband."

"Maybe that's not so silly," Arbie said with a smile.

Jane looked up at Arbie, and for the first time in a year, she smiled too. She gave Arbie a big hug (without crushing her) and said, "I love you, Arbie."

CHAPTER 9

Boiling, Skiing, Meeting

2023 Oct 5, Thu Early am. Corpus Christi, Texas.
2006 Nov 22, Wed. Elrod 402.

The world shifted back and forth. Jonara became disoriented for a moment as the sun and moon danced in the heavens. Clear sky gave way to fog and haze, and Jonara wondered where she would go next. She worried about Jane—what would become of her? And baby Roberta? Then the thought occurred to Jonara—was this the same Roberta as in the photo, the photo on Grandma Eva's desk? Jonara thought about it—there *was* a resemblance between the photo of Roberta and Jane—red hair, Irish-like face, and strong character lines.

Jonara swam through the haze and heard a familiar gagging sound. It was Evanita, and she was waking up for the day.

"Can you open the window when you smoke?" Evanita asked Calico.

Evanita rolled out of bed and jumped to the floor. It was a good feeling—being able to jump out of bed instead of crawling down the ladder.

"As I said last night," Calico said while smoking her pipe and drinking coffee, "you've made a miraculous recovery in the last twenty-four hours."

"Except for gagging on your smoking," Evanita said while accepting dark mocha coffee from Calico.

"All in good time," Calico said. "But tell me, Eve, how did you recover so quickly? Casts on both legs and a black shoulder bruise—those things don't heal by magic. Or do they?"

"What do you mean?" Evanita asked.

"I think you know what I mean, Eve Carson," Calico replied. "Where did Ox-One take you yesterday after gym?"

"I told you last night—she took me to the Whalejet Intake," Evanita replied. "I had a visitor."

"But when you came back, you were walking. No one gets healed from a visitor—unless the visitor slips 'em something," Calico said. "What did she slip you?"

"It was a *he* and he didn't slip me anything," Evanita said.

"You can't keep a secret for long around here," Calico said between puffs. "But you have to ask yourself—who do you want to find out first? A lot depends on that. You'll see."

Evanita showered, dressed, and ate breakfast. Ox-Two and Ox-Three escorted her along with the Redjet girls to Patriojet for morning classes. Some of the girls whistled at Evanita, others made comments expressing their attraction for her. Evanita blocked it out as best she could by thinking of Johnny.

"What's wrong, sweetie?" called one of the girls. "Can't you take a compliment?"

"Yeah, sugar, stop by my room tonight for a good time," said another.

"Knock it off," Ox-Two yelled.

Evanita attended her classes that morning in Patriojet. She was on Shift A—a schedule for half the Elrod girls such that morning was spent in class and afternoon doing work. Class ended for Evanita at noon—lunchtime—and Calico made sure she sat with Evanita while the two ate. Halfway through lunch, Oxia located Evanita and asked Evanita to sit with her.

"May I come with you?" Calico asked in a tone of courtesy Evanita had never heard before. "I am her mentor and big sister."

"No, Calico, you stay here," Oxia said.

"I—" Calico started.

"You can be a big sister to her later. I will take care of her mentoring for the afternoon," Oxia said.

"Yes ma'am," Calico said.

"Where are we going, Miss Oxia?" Evanita asked while the two exited Cafederijet.

"That all depends on you, Eve Carson," Oxia said.

"On me? How?" Evanita asked.

Oxia led Evanita into the center of the compound—the point where all airplane noses faced a triple H-shaped structure, an unusual collection of metal poles welded together and painted brown—the same color as dried blood. Four metal posts had been driven into the ground at equal lengths apart to form a square. The square of poles was square with the cardinal directions of north, south, east, and west. A horizontal bar at waist level connected the two southern poles together, another horizontal bar connected the northern poles together at the same height, and a third horizontal pole connected the first two horizontal poles together. In this way, the structure when viewed at a right angle appeared as an "H" from all three dimensions— from east-to-west, from north-to-south, and when looked down-upon from above. At other angles, one could see the letters "E" and

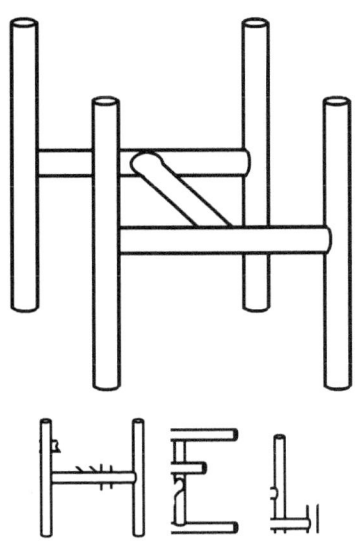

"L" through pole intersections. These then formed the first three letters of the H-E-L rod structure.

"This is the Helrod," Oxia said. "Do you know why it's here, Eve Carson?"

"No, I don't," Evanita replied.

"It's here as a reminder to every girl at the Elrod 402 that obedience and discipline are to be maintained by all," Oxia said.

"I don't understand," Evanita said.

"I'll show you," Oxia said. "I'll tie you to the Helrod and show you how one wields a whip."

"No, wait, can you show me without tying me up?" Evanita asked.

"You learn quickly, Eve Carson," said Oxia.

Oxia pulled three empty paper cups from her jacket. She placed one on the ground next to a pole, another on top of a pole, and one straddling atop two horizontal poles.

"You'll notice there are four squares—like bases on a ball diamond—around the Helrod?"

"Yes," Evanita said.

"I'll stand on one of them," Oxia said, and she led Evanita to the plate. "Watch!"

Oxia took a whip from her belt and whipped one of the lower cups from its spot without touching the Helrod pole.

"That's a girl's foot," Oxia said.

Oxia whipped the other cup from the top of the pole with similar precision.

"That's a hand," she said.

Oxia lashed at the straddling cup and sent it flying as well.

"That's her lower back or her head, depending on how she's tied up and how I feel," said Oxia.

"Are...are you going...to...to punish me now?" Evanita stumbled.

"Oh no. We never perform private Helrod punishments. If you should be punished on the Helrod, you'll have a full Elrod 402 audience—the staff and the detainees are all welcome to attend," Oxia explained.

"I understand now," Evanita said.

"Good. I have a special job for you, Eve Carson, and it simply cannot be fouled up," Oxia explained.

"I'll do my best," Evanita said.

"It must be better than your best," Oxia said. "It must be perfect. Tomorrow is Thanksgiving, and Macron needs volunteers to help prepare the extra food—turkey, stuffing, potatoes, beans, bread—you get the idea. She needs reliable help—girls who won't slack off and who won't tire easily. Seeing how your health has improved, you're a perfect candidate."

"I don't know how to cook," said Evanita.

Oxia took her whip and cracked it at the Helrod approximately where Evanita's head would be if tied up.

"I just taught you how to cook," Oxia said. "You are to report to Macron immediately. I'll escort you to Cafederijet now."

They proceeded from the Helrod to Cafederijet. Evanita had been inside the jet before, but only to eat. Oxia led Evanita toward the back beyond the eating area but before reaching the infirmary. Here Evanita met Macron—the cafeteria chief.

"She's yours for the afternoon," Oxia said to Macron. "I'll be back for her this evening."

"So you're Eve Carson?" Macron asked.

"No...I..." Evanita started.

Oxia gave Evanita a sharp look followed by a finger gesture. Oxia held up the index and middle fingers on her left hand and formed an "H" by crossing those fingers with the index of her right. She repeatedly tapped the right index finger against the left fingers. Evanita caught this to mean, "Answer correctly or the Helrod awaits you."

"Yes, I'm Eve Carson," Evanita said immediately.

Oxia smiled and left.

"Have you ever cooked before, Eve?" Macron asked.

"No," Evanita replied.

"Hmmm," Macron said. "Before we have you start on the turkey dinner, you'll need a trial run. I'm assigning you to Mac-Two. Mac-One and I are arranging the Thanksgiving dinner. Once Mac-Two says you're good enough, you'll be assigned to us."

Evanita opened her mouth to say something, but Macron held a right finger against two left fingers. This formed the letter "H" and reminded Evanita of the Helrod. Evanita fell silent.

"Mac-Two," Macron called.

"Yes, ma'am?" Mac-Two replied after running up to the two.

"See that Eve Carson here gets an education in cooking dinner," Macron ordered.

"Yes ma'am," Mac-Two replied.

Mac-Two led Evanita to the storeroom where large, institutional-sized canisters sat on shelves. Each canister was labeled—flour, sugar, tomatoes, beef, chicken, cheese, potatoes—the list went on and on.

"Everything is dry," said Mac-Two, "and must be reconstituted with water. We do that by boiling."

"This is cooking?" Evanita asked.

"Eve—I didn't say you could talk. Raise your hand if you need something," Mac-Two said.

Mac-Two led Evanita out of the storeroom and into the kitchen.

"Pots and pans are stored in these cupboards," Mac-Two said. "Pots are measured in quart size, and we start everything in a pot by boiling the dried food in water until ready. I know, when is it ready? Every canister has the boiling time listed, but in case you forget, there's a big poster on the wall behind you. Turn around, Eve. See? Potatoes are five minutes, chicken is ten, and...well, you can read the rest for yourself. Each day we have a master list of food we must prepare—see it on the other wall? Those numbers next to the food item are the number of quarts to be prepared. When you finish boiling a batch, dump it into the master vat over here."

Mac-Two walked Evanita over to several vats of reconstituted food.

"Check off the tally here on how much you've reboiled. Usually one of us Macs will draw a line on the vat—that's the fill line—when the food reaches that line, go boil something else that needs filling. The easy way to do it is to look for a vat where the food hasn't reached the fill line yet. See these vats for potatoes and cake? Not filled yet, are they? Well, what are you waiting for? Grab some dried food, a pot, and get boiling!"

Evanita looked at the master list. Then she looked at the vats.

"Lasagna," Evanita said. "The lasagna vat needs filling."

Evanita went to the storeroom, climbed a ladder, and retrieved a large container of dried lasagna mix. She nearly lost her balance twice while descending the ladder—the container's mass was greater than she anticipated. Once safely on the floor, she breathed a sigh of relief. Temporarily setting the container aside, she put the ladder away. It was time to boil the lasagna mix, and she knew it. She carried the container to the kitchen and placed it on a preparation table. Evanita next searched for a pot. She opened up a cupboard—no, just pans. Another cupboard—cookie trays. Where were the pots?

"Well? Where do you think the pots are kept?" a new voice said.

"I—" Evanita started.

Mac-Three was the new voice. She walked over and read Evanita's identification tag.

"Eve Carson. Heard about you. The sexy one from Redjet. Good to see you're walking. That was a nice dress you wore on Sunday to church. Do you like dessert? I can get you extra pie and chocolate if you like," Mac-Three said.

"I love chocolate," Evanita said. "But I'm supposed to make dinner."

"Oh yeah, that's right. Boil up a few pots, and we can talk in a bit about how much chocolate I can get for you. You wanna eat dinner together?" Mac-Three asked.

"I, uh, don't know if I'll get a dinner," Evanita said.

"Nonsense. We all get dinner. We just have to wait 'till the regulars—the detainees—eat first. We'll get our chance. Now about dinner—is it a date?"

"Is it a date?" Evanita asked. "Like going out on a date?"

"I hope so!" Mac-Three laughed with a wink. "Oh yeah, the pots are under the stove. See you around!"

Evanita filled the pot with water and placed it on the burner. She set the flame to HIGH and waited for it to boil. The flame was powerful, and the pot heated the water rapidly. Evanita leaned over the pot, peered down, and saw bubbles at the bottom. As she did, the Moissan Ruby slipped out of her shirt, plopped into the water, and dangled part way down. The necklace chain around Evanita's neck prevented the Moissan Ruby from completely falling into the pot.

The water suddenly boiled madly, and the excess heat forced Evanita back from the pot. In doing so, the Moissan Ruby was lifted out of the pot. It rested against her chest, yet it was not hot. Strangely, it was cold. However, the water vibrations from the boiling water activated it.

Evanita touched the countertop and sensed its molecular structure as she'd never done before. She closed her eyes and envisioned the entire airplane—its fuselage, its cargo bay, the cafeteria, and the infirmary. She was aware of who was in Cafederijet, what they were doing, saying, and feeling.

"Mommy, can you see me?" Jonara asked.

"The voice," Evanita said. "It's here."

"Look over here," Jonara said. "To your right—do you see me?"

"I see you, Little Voice. I see a bright shape, like a glowing pleated white robe. It's almost too bright for my eyes. Are you an angel? Has God sent you?"

"I'm not an angel," Jonara said. "I'm your daughter from the future."

"Did God send you?" Evanita asked.

Jonara was about to say, "No," but could she know for sure? Jonara always believed in free will, but if that were the case, how was it she was traveling back in time? No, it was the diary, that had to be it, or so Jonara thought. A magic diary. She questioned herself. Nanna Geneva wrote it, but Nanna Geneva was dead. Jonara's mind raced for an answer, and the slim thought that there could be a connection with Geneva, God, and seeing Evanita in the past might be related.

"I don't know," said Jonara. "I didn't think so, but it could be true. I only know I love you and don't like seeing you suffer—now or in the future."

Evanita stopped in place and shook.

"What happens to me in the future? How will I suffer?"

"You...it...just like..." Jonara stumbled.

Evanita walked to the bright shape and embraced it.

"Help me out of here, if you can," Evanita said.

Jonara hummed a song—something she thought Cerafina played on the piano or that she played on the viol—she wasn't sure which—but as she hummed, the vibrations in her vocal cords carried across to Evanita and the Moissan Ruby. Jonara led Evanita back to the boiling pot. Both stared in the pot and watched the bubbles percolate. Bubble-ie, bubble-ie, bubble-ie, pow! Something pulled the two inside the boiling pot and up through another boiling pot.

"Where are we?" Evanita asked Jonara.

"I don't know," Jonara replied.

1947 Mar 21, Fri. Kefer Toothe Co. Racine, Wisconsin.

"You got more coffee brewing?" Arbie asked.

"Yes—four pots," said Jane.

"That should do," Arbie said. "The lunch crowd will be in soon, and we've got to get that fish cooked. Friday fish—you should know the rules being a Catholic."

Arbie and Jane cooked lunch for the workers at Kefer Toothe Company—a manufacturer of industrial transmissions and transmission supplies.

"Strange thing," Jane said. "Ever since I moved in with you, I don't feel like a Catholic."

"What do you feel like?" Arbie asked.

"Liberated."

Both women laughed.

"Who are these women?" Evanita asked. "Do you know where we are?"

"I know the women—Arbie and Jane. But I don't know where we are. Jane was working at a place called Daschwirk in Kenosha," Jonara said.

"Where's Kenosha?" Evanita asked.

"It's next to Lake Michigan. In Wisconsin," Jonara answered.

"Holy Moses! Wisconsin! And Lake Michigan! What on Earth could be going on there?"

"Maybe if we walk outside this building, we can see where we are," Jonara said.

Holding her hand, Jonara led Evanita through the cafeteria wall, across the greased-black wooden floor where many-a-part had fallen without being damaged, and through the factory wall to the outside where it was sunny and clear.

"Look at the funny cars!" Evanita said. "And the clothes!"

"This looks a lot like the other time," Jonara said.

"What other time?"

"I was just here—and it was 1943, then 1944, and then 1945," Jonara said.

The two walked up to a newspaper stand. It read, "*Racine Journal Times*. Friday, March 21, 1947."

"Racine," Jonara said. "That's where Arbie lives. Jane and baby Roberta moved in with Arbie at the end of 1945."

"Roberta? Where have I heard that name before? I saw it...where?" Evanita asked.

"Grandma Eva...she has...oh, I don't know if I should tell you," Jonara said.

"Is it important? Does my mother know something about this baby Roberta?" Evanita asked.

"Maybe—it might be the same one," Jonara said.

"What same one? Tell me," Evanita said.

"The photo in your mother's...my grandma's exercise room...it says 'Roberta' on the back. And the photo looks like Jane," Jonara explained.

"Well let's not stand out here in the cold, though I'm not chilled. Let's find out what Jane and Arbie are doing inside," Evanita said.

The two returned to the Kefer Toothe Co. kitchen where Jane and Arbie were preparing lunch.

"Today is the first day of spring," Arbie said.

"And the last day of the old moon," Jane said.

"Soon it will be baseball season," Arbie said. "I'm going for tryouts."

"Really?" Jane said.

"I'm sure I can do better than my sister," Arbie said.

"Anyone can do better than Trudy," Jane said.

"Including you," Arbie said.

"Roberta is only nineteen months old," Jane said. "How can I play ball and take care of a toddler?"

"Do you want to spend the rest of your life brewing coffee and beating eggs?" Arbie asked. "It's time we did something with our lives. Time we get a college education."

Jane laughed.

"What's so funny?"

"College, yeah, that's right. We need money to pay for college. But if we had a college degree, we would have high-paying jobs and could afford college in the first place. People like us are blocked from college," Jane said.

"What are you making now?" Arbie asked.

"Same as you. Forty cents an hour," Jane said.

"That's sixteen dollars a week," Arbie said.

"Don't remind me. I made double that two years ago," Jane said.

"You can make from three to five times that amount playing baseball," Arbie said. "And they give out scholarships to boot. This is the chance of a lifetime! Of a generation!"

"I went through all this before, and—" Jane started.

"That was back in '44," Arbie said. "And you scared yourself out of doing it."

"I didn't want to move to Minnesota," Jane said.

"Well that team doesn't exist anymore. And it won't," Arbie said.

"There's still the glamour thing," Jane said.

"You scared yourself out of that, too—you dolled yourself up for work—that was a mistake!"

"I wanted to know how people would react," Jane said. "And now I know. Men look at you differently."

"Let them look—but from a distance only," Arbie said with a knowing grin.

"You might be right," Jane said.

"I know I am. And there's something else. I've already contacted the league and told them you're interested," Arbie said.

"You did what?!" Jane said.

"Don't get upset. I did it for your own good—and the league's. They're disappointed you haven't played the last few years," Arbie said.

"Yeah, but I—" Jane started.

"And I told them you'd only come back if they assign you to the Racine Belles," Arbie continued.

"But the Kenosha Comets—" Jane objected.

"Do you want to play baseball for the same city as where your husband lives?" Arbie asked.

"I love Kenosha," Jane said.

"Which is why you've been living in Racine for over a year? Hmmm," Arbie grinned.

"I...you...now you know that isn't...you're playing games!" Jane said.

Arbie let out a good laugh.

"You know I'm right," Arbie said.

"But the glamour thing. I mean, Trudy could flirt with any guy she wanted. She's a natural charm. I could never be like her," Jane said.

"And you don't want to be. Look at her—terrible, just terrible," Arbie said.

"Trudy's last name is Sheppe," Jonara said.

"Is she related to—" Evanita asked.

"I think so," Jonara replied. "Calico came with me on one of my trips back in time—when Jane and Trudy were at the try-outs in 1943. It was called softball then, but now it's called baseball. Calico recognized Trudy as her grandmother."

"That's weird!" Evanita said. "This is all so strange. I don't know what to think of it."

"Me neither," Jonara said. "Let's listen some more."

"I don't know if I should feel sorry for her or..." Arbie said.

"Or what?" Jane asked.

"Or knock some sense into her. And how can you stand there and not react? When Trudy left Wilton and moved in with Jack—that's Jack your husband—I thought you'd go over there and kill one or both of them."

"Why should I? I want nothing to do with Jack. And Trudy was my good friend, but we had a falling out," Jane said.

"I noticed. But you never said why," Arbie said.

"After Jack first attacked me, she came over and made me feel like I had no right to be mad at Jack, that I should accept abuse—the same way she does," Jane said.

"Now I understand things better," Arbie said. "And it makes sense. Jane—Trudy believes in abuse as a normal-day form of love. Now Wilton used to beat her, just like old man Hansen did to us all. But Wilton reformed after the war ended. Got a house under the G.I. Bill. Worked as a printer for the Racine Journal Times. Made good. Became respectable."

"And that's why Trudy left him?" Jane asked.

"Yes. Because Trudy felt neglected. For Trudy, love means attention—any attention. And getting a bruise now and then is much better than the loneliness of neglect," Arbie explained. "And they divorced. No, they're not Catholic—they just had a civil marriage to break."

"But Jack is still married—to me!"

"And he will be unless one of you dies," Arbie said.

"I hope it's him," Jane said.

"Don't keep that hope alive," said Arbie. "The bad ones have a way of hanging on for years on end."

"Tell me about it," Jane said.

"But I'd be worried about you," Arbie said.

"What do you mean?" Jane asked.

"I mean this—I know my sister—and when there's a man involved, she gets a little goofy in the head. As in—obsessed. If she decides—if he decides—to marry each other...well...the idea may come to one of them that making Jack a widower is the easy way of doing it."

"That's illegal!"

"Yes, it is. But the law won't bring you back from the dead," said Arbie. "All the more reason to make yourself less available. And what better way than a tour with the Racine Belles as a pitcher? I plan to try out as catcher, or even a utility player. What do you say, Jane?"

Jane paused for a moment, but lunch was a-brewing, and in Jane's divided attention, one of the pots overcooked and the lid blew off with a sudden bang!

Bang!

Evanita was back in Cafederijet. Her pot had stayed on the burner too long, and the lid blew off to the ceiling. She rushed to salvage what rehydrated lasagna had not flown to the floor, wall, or ceiling. Bits of the food shrapnel landed in other burners, and burnt-food smoke filled the kitchen.

"What happened here?" Mac-Two asked as she rushed in. "You're supposed to rehydrate, not redecorate. And only one pot at a time? That will never do! You need to boil at least six pots at the same time. I myself do eight without even thinking. You'd better hop to it, dearie, if we're to get those vats filled for dinner. And clean up this mess!"

Mac-Two exited the kitchen through a doorway. Waiting around another doorway was Mac-Three.

"Pssst!" Mac-Three called.

Evanita looked up and watched Mac-Three enter the room.

"I couldn't help but overhear," Mac-Three said while helping Evanita clean up.

"I don't understand why I'm the only one in here cooking," Evanita said. "It's too much work."

"You know why they do this, don't you?" Mac-Three asked.

"No, I don't. It's unfair," Evanita replied.

"That's what it's supposed to be—unfair. And you're supposed to go begging Mac-Two for help, that you'll do anything in exchange for help," Mac-Three explained.

"Why didn't she tell me that? I would have asked for help at the start," Evanita said.

"It doesn't work that way," Mac-Three said. "You have to want it—badly—through frustration and deep desire. Then you'll beg. And that's when they have you."

"They? Aren't you one of 'they'?" Evanita asked. "But what am I to do?"

"I'm not one of 'them'. I can help you. A pretty girl like you," Mac-Three said while she drew her finger across Evanita's face, shoulder, and waist, "deserves better than them. I'll be very gentle, I promise. A girl can't find many comforts in a place like this."

Evanita backed away.

"You and Oxia," said Evanita. "But I have a boyfriend. And I don't like making dishonest deals."

"What's dishonest about sharing a little love?" Mac-Three asked while reapproaching Evanita.

Evanita backed up slowly until a wall blocked her egress.

"And as for Oxia, she's not like me. She's rough with her girls. She likes whips," Mac-Three said.

"I know, I saw a demonstration on the Helrod," said Evanita.

"That's not the only place she uses a whip," said Mac-Three as she ran her fingers through Evanita's hair. "But I would never do that to you, Eve Carson. I wouldn't harm a strand of your beautiful hair."

"Please, I must—" Evanita squirmed, but Mac-Three prevented her from escaping.

"You have the most interesting hair," Mac-Three continued. "Strong dark strands with highlights of glistening red. And yet, your red highlights have no roots. It looks natural."

"It is," Evanita said as she slouched down to avoid Mac-Three.

Mac-Three pulled Evanita back to her feet and set her away from the wall.

"I could call in a few favors, have some girls in here, and help you finish making dinner," said Mac-Three.

"What about Mac-Two? Doesn't she want me to beg? And Oxia is going to pick me up after I'm done here," Evanita said.

"Mac-Two only hunts the weak ones. If you show any sign of initiative—like getting the dinner cooked with the help of my friends—she'll back off. In fact, she won't want you back," said Mac-Three.

"And Oxia? You're only a Mac-Three. What kind of power can you have?" Evanita asked.

"I was Mac-Four last month, Ox-Seven the month before, and Diali-Six before that. Oh yes, you haven't met a Diali yet, have you Eve Carson? I know about you—I have friends. The Dialis are in charge of sanitation, landscaping, and renovation. But they don't do any sanitation—the Oxians make sure independent-minded girls like you do all the dirty work. I'm working my way up in this organization. And I can deal with Oxia. I can put the word out that you're helping late with Thanksgiving dinner—if you're willing. Yes, I'm helping Mac-One with Thanksgiving."

"You'll do that? You'll keep me from having to stay with Oxia?" Evanita asked.

"Of course! But remember my price," Mac-Three said as she stroked her finger along Evanita's arm.

Evanita jumped back with fear and anxiety.

"No, I won't," she said. "If I have to boil every canister of dried food, I won't ask for your help. I'll just have to figure out something with Oxia."

"They all say the same thing," Mac-Three said. "You'll be back after you learn. And I'll be waiting—the offer is always good," and Mac-Three leaned over and whispered into Evanita's ear, "because I know how you could be a really, good girl for me!"

Evanita finished cleaning up. She placed six pots of water on burners and filled them with lasagna. Carefully, she turned on all burners such that they would not heat the pots uncontrollably fast.

"Of all the unfair things," Evanita muttered. "Caught in the layers between Oxia and Macron, Mac-Two and Mac-Three."

Evanita moved too quickly and knocked over a lid, stepped on it, lost her footing, and fell on the floor. She grimaced in pain and nearly shouted, "It isn't fair. Where's justice? Where does democracy start?"

"With my metal spatula on your hinny, if you don't stop chattering," yelled Mac-Two from another room. "Now stop that racket and get that dinner hydrated, before I hydrate you!"

"Little Voice, Little Voice!" Evanita said. "Can you help me? Little Voice?"

"I'm here, Mommy," Jonara said, but Evanita could not see or hear Jonara.

"Little Voice? Why don't you answer me?" Evanita asked again.

"I'm here, I'm here! Activate the Water Ruby!" Jonara urged.

"I'm alone," Evanita whispered to herself. "I've painted myself between two walls. How do I get the little voice back? Think, Evanita, think! How did you do it before? Yes, I dipped the stone in boiling water."

Evanita dipped the Moissan Ruby in boiling water as before. Again, Jonara appeared as an angel.

"Mommy," Jonara said. "Can you hear me?"

"I can hear you, I can see you!" Evanita said.

"Mommy—the stone—it works on vibrations. Don't boil it in water again. Bad things can—" Jonara started to say.

1940 Oct 28. Pindus Mountains, Greece.

Evanita and Jonara found themselves caught between layers—two mountain slopes, two opposing armies, the sky and ground, and the rain and mud. Men fought on foot and horseback with rifles and swords. Cannons blasted the air, and the girls quickly acquired headaches from the shock waves.

"Where are we?" Evanita shouted so Jonara could hear her over the noise.

"I don't know," Jonara shouted back. "I was trying to say—"

"What? Speak louder!" Evanita shouted.

Bombs and gunfire continued around them with soldiers fighting and dying.

"The Water Ruby around your neck works on vibrations. Like singing. Sing a song," Jonara said.

"What song?"

"Any song," Jonara shouted. "But you might have to sing loudly to drown out the explosions around here!"

Evanita sang a song. The Moissan Ruby reacted, but the two girls remained in the mountain pass.

"Nothing happened," Jonara shouted.

"Something did happen," Evanita shouted back. "The stone told me where we are."

"Where are we?" Jonara shouted back.

"In northern Greece. October 28, 1940. This is the Pindus Mountain range, and we're in the Battle of Pindus," Evanita said.

"No wonder it's so noisy," said Jonara. "Hey! Pindus is my last name!"

"And we're next to the Greek soldiers. They're fighting off Italians. No wait, now it says they aren't Greek. Now it says they are," Jonara said.

"Are they or aren't they?" Jonara asked.

"They are...are not...are...Aromanian—at least some are," Evanita said. "What a crazy place! In Greece! The birthplace of democracy!"

"You asked where democracy starts," Jonara said.

"You heard that? I didn't expect this fighting!" Evanita said.

"Is this where Daddy is from?" Jonara asked.

"You mean Johnny? I don't know. He doesn't have a foreign accent. Little Voice, we have to get out of here," Evanita said.

"The Water Ruby works on vibrations—like I said before. Humming or singing. If we sing a song together, maybe," Jonara said.

"Okay. What song?" Evanita asked.

"How about Row-Row-Row Your Boat?"

"You've got to be kidding! Here? In this?!" Evanita said.

"We can sing in a round. You start," Jonara said.

"There must be something better to sing," Evanita said.

"Then sing it, and quick!" Jonara said.

Evanita paused for a moment.

"Well?" Jonara asked.

"I can't think of anything better," Evanita said.

Evanita started singing, "Row-Row-Row Your Boat," and partway through, Jonara started singing such that the two sang in a round.

The shooting stopped. Evanita and Jonara appeared briefly in the Cafederijet's kitchen before whisking away to another gunfight.

"We're back in Greece," Evanita shouted over gunfire. "The Pindus Mountain range again."

"Something is pulling us here. Funny, I feel like I know this place," Jonara said.

"Have you been to Greece?" Evanita asked.

"No—you and Daddy never took me," Jonara said.

Evanita and Jonara dove under an overhanging rock for cover to avoid gunfire.

"What does the Water Ruby say?" Jonara asked.

"We're in the Battle of Pindus, but now it's December 16, 1940," Evanita said.

"The rain and mud are gone," Jonara said.

"Yeah, the ground is frozen, and there's snow everywhere," Evanita replied.

"I hear voices," Jonara said.

"Shh," Evanita said.

"It's okay. They can't hear us," Jonara said.

"I know. I want to hear what they're saying. Look—it's a Greek company on skis!" Evanita said.

"Are they speaking English?" Jonara asked.

"It sounds like a strange kind of English," said Evanita.

"The Water Ruby could be translating," Jonara suggested.

"Axon," said one of the men just outside the overhang where Evanita and Jonara hid. "Take your group of men and ski to that ledge. I'll take the rest to the other side. On my word, we'll attack the Italians from two angles."

"Yes, sir," Axon said.

The two groups skied to their points. Jonara glanced at Axon and gasped.

"Did you see Axon, Mommy? Look!" Jonara said.

"Too late," Evanita replied. "His back is to us."

"He looked like...I'm not sure...like Daddy!" Jonara said.

"Johnny? Here? How?!" Evanita said. "Are you sure?"

"I'm almost...maybe...I only saw him for a moment," Jonara said.

"I'll get a better look. You wait here," Evanita said.

"No, wait—" Jonara cried, but Evanita had already dashed ahead.

Evanita ran toward Axon's skiing group, but they sped off practically out of sight. Jonara ran after Evanita as best she could, but Evanita's longer legs and strength as a runner increased her lead on Jonara. The slope steepened, and Jonara was surprised to find herself panting hard.

"I can't be out of breath! This is a dream!" Jonara said to herself.

But Jonara was out of breath. Overdrawn on energy, her legs could no longer support her. She fell forward into the snow and rolled uncontrollably and unable to stop. The snow clung to her, and before she could yelp for help, she became a human snowball, rolling down the hill while picking up speed and mass. She caught up to Evanita and engulfed her into the snowball. The two rolled down together in a hodge-podge mass of crystallized frozen water sending thunder across their wake.

"Axon, look!" said one of Axon's men.

Axon turned to see the snowball leading an avalanche down the mountainside.

"Avalanche sir—headed our way," Axon radioed to the other leader.

"Take cover," the leader said.

"No, we must out-ski it," Axon said.

"Axon—stay at your perch—that's an order," the other leader said, but by then Axon had abandoned his radio and led his men down the slope.

"We have the wrong skis for this," said one of the men. "We should have downhill skis. These cross-country skis will never do."

"No time to change equipment. Now make for the valley!" Axon commanded.

Axon led the charge. He turned his back for a moment to see his fellow leader and his group buried under the snow. Jonara and Evanita's snowball continued down the mountainside pursuing Axon. But things changed when Italian troops fired on Axon and his men. Axon's men now swerved to avoid the avalanche and Italian bullets. One of Axon's men took a fatal hit. Italian bullets chipped away at Jonara and Evanita's snowball, reducing its size a little—but not much. Axon became enraged and returned fire. He skied his company directly into the Italian company—firing his rifle with precision and yelling, "Greece forever, Greece forever!"

The frontline Italians fell dead. Some fled. Others repositioned themselves and took fire at Axon's company as they skied past. Axon did not let those off so easily. Having gained considerable speed, he looped his company back up the slope and around—catching the Italians from the rear. None escaped alive. Axon paused at the place where the Italians had been perched while his company chased the last of the fleeing Italians. Axon realized the avalanche was still a threat. He looked at his company and calculated they had sufficiently skied to the side to avoid a snow burial, but he was yet at risk.

With no time to spare (and realizing he could not get up enough speed to ski off to the side), Axon lunged down the slope like mad—barely keeping ahead of Jonara's and Evanita's snow-ball. Axon figured he could ski just past a cabin at the slope's bottom and clip around the back side to escape the avalanche.

"I think we should try getting out of this snowball," Evanita said.

"What?!" Jonara shouted as she strained to hear Evanita over the thundering avalanche just behind them.

"I SAID...I...THINK...WE...SHOULD—" she started but never finished.

The snowball and avalanche closed in on the cabin and Axon quickly. Axon attempted to veer to the right to avoid the cabin, but his skis hit an ice patch and lost traction. His legs went out from under him, his feet came free from the skis, and he belly-flopped down the last bit of the slope toward the cabin's front door.

Axon smacked the front door. Bang! The snowball and avalanche hit the cabin. SMASH! Evanita and Jonara slipped out of 1940 and into 2006 where Evanita fell from the air into a somersault and rolled into the oven door. CRASH! Jonara slipped out of 2006 back to 2023, rolled out of her bed and landed into the bookcase where a large container of marbles shook free and fell atop her and the floor. Chakity-chak-chak-chak!

"Miss Jonara, Miss Jonara," Anna said as she ran into the bedroom. "Are you hurt?"

"No, just a bump on the head," Jonara said.

"Oh, what a mess. I clean it in the morning. You should return to bed. I help you," Anna said.

Anna fluffed Jonara's pillow, and as she did so, she noticed the diary.

"Oh—that should not be there—Miss Jonara," Anna said as she reached for the diary.

Jonara dove onto the bed and snatched the diary from Anna.

"It's dark magic it is," Anna said with fear in her eyes.

"I'm keeping it safe," Jonara said as she hopped off the bed and stood with the book behind her back.

"Miss Geneva wrote in that...oh, I dare not think what terror it possesses. It will possess you, Jonara. Give it to me," Anna insisted.

"No, Anna, no!" Jonara said while shaking her head to say, "No."

"Jonara—you give me that diary, or else I'll go down to the hospital and wheel your grandmother down the street into this house. And she'll know what to do with the diary!"

"No, Anna, no!" Jonara said, but her refusals became shouts, and her loud voice awoke Johnny and caught his attention.

Johnny walked into Jonara's bedroom and winked at Jonara.

"Mr. Johnny sir, Miss Jonara has taken Miss Geneva's diary. A girl should not play with dark magic, Mr. Johnny. She—"

"I know, Anna," Johnny said as he reassured her and took her by the shoulder out of the bedroom.

"But she should not have it, Mr. Johnny," she continued.

"Of course," he said while escorting her through the doorway.

"Wait—she has it—I must take it," Anna said, turning back for the bedroom.

"We'll take care of it first thing in the morning," he said, turning her back around and closing the bedroom door behind him.

"Whew!" Jonara said, pulling the diary out from behind her back.

The bedroom door reopened without warning. Jonara gasped and rehid the diary behind her back. The door remained ajar for a few tense seconds, and through the opening appeared a head.

"Goodnight, Jonara," Johnny said, and he re-closed the door.

"Double whew!" Jonara said.

Jonara placed the diary between the pillow and the bed and climbed into bed between the blanket and the mattress. With both the diary and herself between the bedding layers, Jonara fell fast asleep.

"I told you I'd take the metal spatula to you," Mac-Two said.

Jonara reappeared in the Cafederijet kitchen just moments after Evanita bowled into the oven door. Mac-Two held a metal spatula in hand and was in the motion of swatting Evanita on her rear-end—repeatedly.

"Stop hitting my mommy!" Jonara yelled, but Mac-Two did not hear.

Evanita heard Jonara, but barely, like a distant echo from atop a mountain.

"This is for over-boiling the food," Mac-Two said with a swipe at Evanita.

Evanita jumped with a yelp.

"This is for banging into the oven and leaving a dent where your head hit it," Mac-Two said with another.

"Yowp!" Evanita yelled.

"You could have kept me informed of your slacking off," Mac-Two continued.

"Yawp!" Evanita said from another swat.

"And I could have given you help. But you didn't!" Mac-Two said.

"Yeep!" Evanita cried.

"Now dinner will be late!"

"Yipe!" Evanita exclaimed.

"Use the Water Ruby, Mommy, use it!" Jonara urged.

"I should send you back to Oxia. She'll tan your hide plenty!" Mac-Two said with another swat of the spatula.

"Aik!" Evanita said, and she muttered, "The stone, the stone."

"Are you back-talking me? Are you calling me 'stoned'?" Mac-Two asked.

With that, Mac-Two gave Evanita an especially large swat but landed her blow on Evanita's lower back. The vibration carried through Evanita's body and activated the Moissan Ruby. Evanita's mind raced, and in it she visualized every cellular construction of Mac-Two's body.

"Your right forearm was broken twice—once last year, and once when you were a child. You have a large bruise on your back from Macron beating you—just this morning! I'm sorry. Your left big toe has an ingrown nail. You never sleep well at night—that's why you've been ornery all your life. You—"

"What is this? Are you telling me what I am? How dare you! Who's been ratting on me? Better tell me, or I'll...I'll..." Mac-Two stumbled.

"Who knew about your broken arm when you were a child?" Evanita asked. "And your father always ordered you around."

"Stop it!" Mac-Two yelled and swatted Evanita.

"He's the one who broke your arm. You didn't get him beer and pretzels quick enough. That was the first time," Evanita continued.

"I told you to stop!" Mac-Two yelled and changed from swatting Evanita to punching her in the upper arm.

"The second time he sexually assaulted you," Evanita said.

Mac-Two slapped Evanita in the face, but the Moissan Ruby gave Evanita the strength to continue.

"He controlled you. Your biggest fear—your nightmare—is losing control over yourself, because that's how you grew up."

Mac-Two punched Evanita in the face. Evanita fell to her knees.

"You've been beaten all your life," Evanita continued. "Now you figure it's your turn to beat back. That's why you're beating me."

"Lies! All lies!" Mac-Two shouted.

"All you know is how to beat, because that's the only thing you were taught! But there's no control in beating!" Evanita said.

Mac-Two's psyche snapped. She smacked the spatula against everything in the room—pots, countertops, sinks—and smacked things onto the floor. She stopped talking and kept smacking, making a horrible ruckus. Macron, Mac-One, and Mac-Three entered the kitchen and realized Mac-Two had lost control.

"Ox-Cafederi to the kitchen," Macron radioed.

Two Oxians entered the kitchen, lunged at Mac-Two, and forced her to the floor. An Oxian held Mac-Two's arms behind her and placed a knee in her back. Mac-Two writhed and growled random phrases like, "I'm in command. I'm in control. Democracy is a metal spatula."

"Take her to isolation in Whalejet," Macron said while ripping Mac-Two's nametag from her shirt. "I'll file a report with O Grammeni."

The two Oxians removed Mac-Two from the room.

"Well, things could be worse," Macron said. "Still, dinner preparations have fallen behind. Mac-Three—you are in charge of driving the rehydration to completion. Use whatever resources you need."

"Yes, ma'am," Mac-Three said.

"Oh yes, Mac-Three. You're now promoted to Mac-Two. Return your Mac-Three name tag and kneel before me," Macron said.

Mac-Three knelt before Macron.

"Stand beside her as a witness, Eve Carson," Macron ordered.

Evanita complied.

"I, Macron, chief of cafeteria services in Cafederijet, with powers fully vested by O Grammeni, of the Elrod 402 facility, do hereby grant you, Tara Tushenne, the status of Mac-Two and revoke your position of Mac-Three. Rise now."

Old Mac-Three stood up. Macron attached the new nametag and said, "I now proclaim you Mac-Two. Accept your position as required by the code."

"I, Tara Tushenne, accept whole-heartedly the position of Mac-Two, with all powers and responsibilities hereto set upon me. I promise to accept and execute all orders to the utmost. O Macron, O Grammeni, O Elrod!"

"Congratulations, Mac-Two," Macron said.

"Macron, if I may," Mac-Two said.

"Yes, Mac-Two?" Macron asked.

"I wish to add Eve Carson as one of my non-commissioned resources," Mac-Two requested.

"Your first request in your new role is granted," said Macron. "Now back to work—everyone."

Macron left the room. Mac-Two radioed for help, and four detainee girls along with Mac-Four entered the room. Mac-Two gave instructions on what remained for preparing dinner and set the girls to work. Mac-Two led Evanita from the kitchen to the back portion of Cafederijet.

"Thank you for the promotion, Eve Carson," Mac-Two said.

"I didn't mean to get you promoted," Evanita said.

"Are you saying you're against my promotion?" Mac-Two grinned.

"No, it's not that. I—" Evanita said.

Mac-Two turned to Evanita, hugged her, and kissed her on the forehead.

"You're one of my resources now," Mac-Two said.

"I never asked to be one of your resources—and what does that mean? Fuel and raw materials are resources. Am I a raw material?" Evanita asked.

"Yes you are—you're raw fuel for my little group," Mac-Two said.

"But Oxia—" Evanita said.

"—will not pick you up tonight if I'm right about your physical condition."

"Am I hurt?" Evanita asked. "Well, I have a headache, but I haven't looked at myself in the mirror."

"We'll soon find out. This is the infirmary," Mac-Two said. "You need treatment for those injuries the old Mac-Two gave you."

"Tara," Evanita said.

"Ah, ah, ah! Role name only," Mac-Two said.

"But it's too confusing. I mean, you were Mac-Three a moment ago, and Mac-Two beat me. Now you're Mac-Two, and it was the 'old Mac-Two' who beat me," Evanita said.

"Yes, Eve Carson, that's right," Mac-Two said.

"But how do you keep things straight with everyone else? If someone says, 'Mac-Two,' they might confuse you with the old Mac-Two," Evanita said.

"We have datetime stamps too," Mac-Two said. "It's all on the staff record. Don't worry about it, Eve Carson. In fact, I would take it easy for the rest of the day, if I were you. You may have a concussion."

"Let's see if she does," said Baria, the chief of Elrod 402 health services. "I'll check her vitals myself. Come over here, Eve Carson."

"Mac-Two, are you—" Evanita started.

"Mac-Two?" Baria asked as she turned her head toward Mac-Two's nametag.

"I was promoted," Mac-Two said.

"Well so you have. I would have read about it in the morning report, of course. Congratulations!" Baria said.

"Thank you," Mac-Two said.

"You may leave her with me if you have other more pressing duties," Baria said.

"I will stay with Eve Carson," Mac-Two said. "I have some other things for her after we're done here."

"As you wish," Baria said. "Sit here for a moment, Eve Carson. I've been meaning to see you—especially since your legs healed miraculously. I want to learn more about you."

Evanita sat on a padded bench while Baria applied finger pressure to Evanita's injuries.

"Ow!" Evanita said to each one.

"They hurt, don't they?" Baria asked.

"She has a black welt on her temple," Mac-Two said. "Did she sustain a concussion?"

"Follow my finger with your eyes," Baria said. "Wait, don't bother."

"What is it?" Mac-Two asked.

"Eve Carson's left pupil is dilated, but her right is not," Baria said. "Eve Carson—how does your left arm feel? Your right arm? Your leg?"

"Cold in my right arm and leg. And tingly," Evanita said.

"Quick—we must get you into the MRI (Magnetic Resonance Imaging) chamber," Baria said.

Baria radioed ahead. Mac-Two and Baria lifted Evanita upright to the floor, but Evanita protested.

"I can walk," Evanita said.

"We can't take the chance. Sit in this wheelchair," Baria instructed.

Evanita looked to Mac-Two for approval, and Mac-Two nodded in agreement. Mac-Two held Evanita's hand as Evanita sat in the wheelchair. Mac-Two pushed the wheelchair along a hallway while Baria cleared the way. Arriving in the MRI room, Baria, Mac-Two, and two Barians lifted Evanita to the MRI bed and strapped her down. Baria operated the MRI controls— sending Evanita into the MRI chamber. Electromagnetic waves penetrated her body, and the Moissan Ruby activated— connecting Evanita with Jonara and sending the two back in time.

1947 Mar 21, Fri Eve. Racine County, Wisconsin.

Jane played with Roberta and her toys in Arbie's apartment when Arbie arrived through the main door.

"I have something to show you," Arbie said.

"What is it?" Jane asked.

"It's a surprise. But I'll have to blindfold you and lead you outside. Roberta too," Arbie said.

"What? Are you kidding?" Jane asked.

"No, I'm not," Arbie said as she held out blindfolds in her hand. "First there's the blindfold around Roberta."

"No, Aunty Arbie," Roberta said while hiding behind Jane's leg. "Mommie do it. Mommie do it."

"All right," Arbie said, and she handed the blindfolds to Jane.

"It's just a game," Jane said to Roberta. "Aunty Arbie is playing a game with us, isn't she Aunty Arbie?"

"Yes," Arbie said. "It's a game—with a surprise."

Jane first blindfolded Roberta and next blindfolded herself.

"I can carry Roberta," Arbie said.

"No," Roberta said. "Mommie. Mommie."

"I'll have to carry her," Jane said. "But you'll have to lead me, Arbie."

"That I'll do," Arbie said. "Here—let's get your coats on."

Arbie put a coat on Roberta and one on Jane and led the two into the apartment's hallway, locked the apartment, and led them outside.

"There's a bench behind you," Arbie said while guiding Jane's free hand to the side of the bench. "There—see?"

"I don't 'see'," Jane replied. "But I do feel the bench, and I understand. Is this the surprise?"

"No, this isn't. But I'd like you to sit. You'll need to sit so you won't injure yourself or Roberta once you see the surprise," Arbie explained.

Jane sat with Roberta sitting in her lap.

"You'd better have Roberta sit next to you. I wouldn't want you to throw her over the sidewalk," Arbie warned.

"Dear me!" Jane said. "This must be some kind of surprise if you think I'll do something silly like that."

"Just making sure everyone is safe," Arbie said.

"Can you hurry up?" Jane said. "It's cold out here."

"Are you ready for the surprise?" Arbie asked.

"Yes!" Roberta said.

"Yes, please! It's cold! It must be around freezing!" Jane said.

"All right. At the count of three—remove your blindfolds," Arbie said. "One...two...three!"

Jane and Roberta removed their blindfolds.

"Fiyetwuck!" Roberta yelled. "Fiyetwuck!"

"No, it's not a fire truck," Arbie laughed.

"It's a car!" Jane exclaimed. "A new, red, car! I've never seen one like that before. It's small, and it's a convertible! Why is the top down in this cold weather?"

"It's down because it's my brand-spanking new car, and I can do what I want!" Arbie said. "It's a 1947 Studebaker Champion—the first new car after the war. Even the Big Three don't have brand new cars—they just remade their pre-war models. What do you think of my new car?"

"Fiyetwuck!" Roberta said.

"It's wonderful!" Jane said.

"I have an idea—let's go for a ride!" Arbie said. "We'll keep the top down!"

"Are you crazy?!" Jane said. "We'll freeze!"

"We're Wisconsinites! We're young, and we're tough!" Arbie said. "It'll be liberating. Besides, it's not as bad as the Polar Plunge."

"Yay!" Roberta said.

"Roberta will catch her chill of death!" Jane said.

"We'll bundle her up well," Arbie said. "She'll be fine."

"Yay! Fiyetwuck!" Roberta yelled.

"I guess Roberta's decided," Jane said. "We'll ride with the top down. But I'm going back in to get blankets. And lots of them!"

Arbie accompanied Jane and Roberta back to the apartment. Jane and Arbie took extra blankets, relocked the apartment, and went back outside where they jumped into the front seat bench with Arbie in the driver's seat, Roberta in the middle, and Jane to the right. Arbie and Jane positioned the blankets over legs and torsos to keep warm.

"I have to be careful I don't get the blankets caught under the clutch pedal," Arbie said.

"Or the gas pedal," Jane said. "We don't want to be screaming down the highway because we're going too fast."

Evanita and Jonara sat in the back seat. Arbie depressed the clutch, started the engine, placed the shifter into first gear, released the clutch, and sped away from the sidewalk.

"We're going!" Arbie said.

"Yay! Fiyetwuck. Wooh, wooh!" Roberta cheered.

"Where are we going?" Jane asked. "You're driving west—we just left Racine."

"This is Sturtevant, but we're just passing through that too," Arbie said while driving the car.

"I think you're going somewhere," Jane said.

"Of course we're going somewhere," Arbie said. "We're driving west along Durand Avenue."

"No, I mean there's some specific place you're driving us to. We're not just out for a drive in the country, are we?" Jane asked.

Arbie smiled.

"You have something up your sleeve, don't you?" Jane asked.

"Are you hungry? It's dinnertime you know," Arbie said.

"Yum, yum," Roberta said.

"Yes, Roberta, we're going to yum-yum—a surprise dinner yum-yum," Arbie said.

The Studebaker proceeded west on Durand Avenue, but to Arbie's disappointment, a slow-moving cabbage truck blocked their path.

"A cabbage truck! What on Earth is it doing here?" Jane asked. "It's March! And where did the cabbage come from?"

"Old leftover cabbage from last year—cabbage that didn't sell or couldn't be used," Arbie said.

"Pee-yoo," Roberta said.

"Yes, Roberta, it stinks. We'll fix that!"

Arbie mashed the accelerator to the floor, and the Champion whizzed around the cabbage with Arbie, Roberta, Jane, Evanita, and Jonara screaming in the thrilling moment. The cabbage truck driver looked out his window in astonishment at two women and a child passing him in a small convertible with the top down. In his diverted attention, he drifted off the road's right side and ran over a rural mailbox. Jolted back into reality, he wrenched the steering wheel back to the left and regained directional control. Several rotten cabbages loosened from the back of the truck, rolled down Durand Avenue, and later were beaten flat into the pavement by passing cars.

Arbie drove farther west in Racine County. The sun was setting, and the women could see nothing but farm after farm in all directions.

"There's nothing out here," Jane said. "No restaurants—nothing."

"Oh but there is, if you know where to look," Arbie said.

"Mommy," Jonara said.

"I can't get used to that," Evanita said. "Being called, 'Mommy'. Maybe you should call me 'Evanita'."

"Okay, Evanita," Jonara said. "Huh, that feels funny too. Anyway, look at Arbie's steering wheel."

"What about it?" Evanita asked. "There were no airbags on steering wheels in the olden days."

"Yeah, but the shape, the design," Jonara said. "It looks familiar."

"How? There's the wheel— the circle—for the hands. The horn—well, that's an inner circle," Evanita explained.

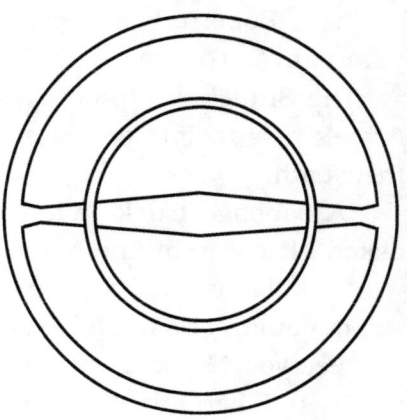

"And there are two spokes," Jonara said.

"Yes—the spokes connect the wheel to the steering column," Evanita said.

"The spokes divide the circles into exactly two halves," Jonara said.

"Yes, they do. I don't understand—what's so interesting about it?" Evanita asked.

"Do you remember the Cerossi Café?" Jonara asked.

"Yeah. When were you there?" Evanita asked.

"I was there when you were there—back in your October of 2006," Jonara said.

"Yeah, that was last month," Evanita said. "I still don't understand. What does a steering wheel from a Studebaker have to do with a restaurant?"

"The flames in Cerossi—do you remember the flames? They moved—they made a pattern—like a canoe in a circle," Jonara said.

"Yeah, I do remember now that you mention it. But I never learned why those flames were like that," Evanita said.

"It means something, I know it does," Jonara said. "There were two spheres in the middle of the flames—do you remember?"

"Yeah, I remember," Evanita said.

"And they were perched on little rock holders," Jonara said.

"And? There are no rocks on Arbie's steering wheel," Evanita said.

"I know, but what if the spheres moved around each other in a circle. That would be like the circle for honking the horn, and the flames are like both the spokes and the outer wheel," Jonara said. "Don't you see how they're similar?"

"It's probably a coincidence," said Evanita. "You do see things I've never thought of. And you did pull me out of the El-rod 402. Those airplanes are in a circle. Does that mean something too?"

"I'm not sure yet," Jonara said. "But the airplanes form a circle, and the barbed wire forms a circle."

"What would represent the spoke? There's nothing dividing the campus into two halves," Evanita pointed out.

"I know, I know. The Elrod 402 is not following the same pattern. It has an extra airplane outside the circle. And then there's the Helrod in the very center."

"Don't remind me," Evanita said. "I don't want to think about the Helrod."

"Those poles—going in all directions—it just doesn't fit—it's like the poles are all doing their own thing once and that's it. There are no circles—no traveling on and on. The Helrod...it's so..."

"So final," Evanita said. "Like death. It's evil, I know it is."

"Yeah, that's it," Jonara said.

Arbie directed the Studebaker off Durand Avenue and onto a gravel side road.

"Arbie, you're scaring me. What are we doing on this dirt road?" Jane asked.

"It goes to a special place," Arbie said.

"Into an old corn field?" Jane asked. "Turn around—the joke has gone on long enough."

"Mommie," Roberta said, and she hugged Jane. "I scared."

"Relax," Arbie said. "We're almost there."

The convertible drove up to an old, apparently abandoned barn. The sun had now set, and dusk turned into night. The barn's double-doors were tied open with ropes on each side, creating a hole large enough for a car to drive through—which Arbie did.

"We're driving into an old barn!" Jane said. "And we don't even have the roof of the car to protect us. Arbie—have you lost your mind?"

"Not yet," Arbie said.

With only the car's headlights for illumination, Arbie drove through the L-shaped barn, turned a corner, and parked next to several other recent-model cars.

"We're here," Arbie said.

"There are other cars here!" Jane said. "What on Earth is this all about?"

"You'll find out. Come—follow me!" Arbie said as she lit a kerosene lantern and waved Jane her way.

Arbie led Jane and Roberta through the barn to a small door leading to a silo.

"That's a silo—for grain!" Jane said.

"It's a passage leading to our destination," Arbie said.

"I hope our destination is a happy one. I want to see tomorrow!" Jane said.

"Don't fret, Jane. Trust me!" Arbie said. "Come—there is a ladder here. Climb up with me."

Arbie led the way up the ladder with the kerosene lantern. Jane held Roberta against her hip with one arm and used the other for climbing the ladder. Evanita and Jonara followed without the first three's awareness of the young girls' presence. Arbie climbed to what would be the hayloft level and disappeared through an opening.

"Hey there," Jane said. "Where did you go?"

"I'm in the other silo," Arbie said while peering through the opening.

"Another silo! Is this some strange sort of exercise?" Jane asked—still in the first silo and unable to see into the second.

"You're in the roughest part," Arbie said. "Just climb up and through the opening. It gets better. You'll see."

Jane managed the last few ladder rungs with Roberta on her side. Arbie offered a hand, and the two women lifted Roberta to the opening. Jane got her first look and saw a landing on the other side of the opening. Jane climbed through the opening herself. Her eyes opened sharply. While there were no entrances directly from the silo to the barn or the outside, there was an opening at the very bottom of the silo—a bottom that was below ground level, and leading to this opening was a circular staircase spiraling down along the silo's inside wall. But Jane could not see this opening quite yet. With the limited light from the lantern, darkness obscured the bottom, giving Jane the sense that there was no bottom.

"Does this go to China? I'm carrying Roberta down these steps—I don't want her falling to the center of the earth!"

"She'll be fine," Arbie said. "Come—the stairs are easy. We're nearly there!"

The five descended the steps for what seemed a chilly eternity (and were becoming disoriented) until without warning the steps reached a bottom.

"Ah, the ground!" Jane said. "No more worries about falling! But there's nothing down here! Wait, what's that sound?"

"We are actually below the ground," Arbie said. "That sound is a sump pump. Not only are we below ground level, we're below the water table."

"We're not going to drown, are we?" Jane asked.

"No, we're not. Now look—there's a door. Be patient and polite. I'll introduce you and do most of the talking until the others are convinced you're not spies."

"Spies? Here? There's nothing here but earthworms," Jane said.

"Shh!" Arbie said.

Arbie knocked on the door with a special rhythm, as if providing a code word. The door opened slowly, and a stream of golden light seeped from the cracked door and filled the lower silo with warmth.

"Arbie!" said a female with a Russian accent. She opened the door fully and said, "Please, come in!"

"Dr. Alina Zavuski," Arbie said as she followed the doctor inside. "This is my roommate, Jane, and her daughter, Roberta."

"Nice to meet you," Jane said.

Alina led the group through a short entryway into a large room with high, stone walls, wood furnishings, and a wooden floor. Lining the walls were bookcases stretching to the ceiling, bookcases that were jam-packed full of books. Several rolling ladders adorned the walls, allowing one to move the ladder quickly to a desired shelf, climb the ladder, and retrieve a book from a high shelf. The room was furnished with electricity and was lit by lamps placed on end tables next to couches, lamps on the center of four-chair tables, and lamps in a few open places in the bookcases.

Already seated on couches and at tables were the two players from the Racine Belles—Mum and Petunia—along with several other women and their daughters. They were all eating dinner of some sort.

"Oh, we're interrupting," Jane said.

"Nonsense," Alina said. "You are in time for dinner. Help yourself—food is just around corner in kitchen."

"Arbie and Jane," Mum said. "Nice to see you again. And this is little Roberta?"

"Thank you," Jane said, "Yes—Roberta is my little girl."

"Come here, sweetie!" Mum said with her arms out, but Roberta hid behind Jane's leg.

"She's just a little shy," Jane said.

"Help yourself to some dinner," Petunia said. "Maybe we can get some Sheepshead in later."

Arbie led Jane and Roberta around the corner where a variety of foods rested on platters and in bowls on a countertop—meats, Wisconsin cheese, legumes, fresh-baked bread, and several already-opened wine bottles.

"There's also cream soda and root beer, or even milk," Arbie said.

"Is this really the place for children?" Jane asked.

"Of course! Dr. Zavuski doesn't erect barriers to knowledge based on age. Girls of any age are welcome here—to learn whatever they wish," Arbie said.

"What's this about knowledge? And the girls-only thing—I see there are no men," Jane said.

Arbie slapped her hand over Jane's mouth.

"Shh," Arbie said. "Don't say that word or anything similar in this place. This is a safe harbor for women who wish to enrich themselves."

Arbie removed her hand from Jane's mouth just as Alina walked in.

"Oh, I not mean to intrude," Alina said with a wink. "I wish to tell you we begin meeting soon. It is informal—bring your dinner to table or whatever and enjoy it while we hold meeting. Do not worry about rudeness or anything—we are friends here. Get up if you need more food or whatever—we do not mind. Also, you may call me Alina."

"All right," Jane said.

Arbie and Jane carried their dinner (Jane carried Roberta's as well) from the kitchen into the main gathering area and sat comfortably on a small couch.

"Is this a settee?" Jane asked.

"Actually, we call it a 'cuddle chair'," Arbie said. "It's wide enough for two big people. But we can sit here and have space for Roberta too."

Roberta sat between Jane and Arbie while Evanita and Jonara stood to Jane's side of the cuddle chair. Alina stood at the front of the gathering area next to a large fireplace. She reached for a small bundle of sticks and held them in her right hand.

"Before I start," she said, "I would like to cheer up our gathering by flogging the fire."

"What?!" Jane blurted while standing up in shock.

Alina removed the screen, tossed the sticks into the fireplace, and replaced the screen to catch popping embers.

"You do not wish to be warmed up by a flogging, Miss Jane?" Alina asked.

"That's inappropriate!" Jane said.

"Jane," Arbie said, "Please—sit down."

"Did I say something wrong? My English not always best," Alina said.

"Jane misunderstood you, Alina," Arbie said. "She doesn't realize you meant 'stoking the fire'."

"Yes—stoking the fire. Flogging. Is this not right word?" Alina asked. "I study English at Oxford in London, England."

"The word means something else," Arbie said.

"Oh? What does it mean?" Alina asked.

Petunia stood up, walked over to Alina, and whispered something into her ear.

"Oh!" Alina said. "I sorry. I never wish to offend anyone, especially not those already persecuted. I will say 'stoking the fire' or 'add firewood' in future. Is this acceptable?"

Jane nodded, "Yes," and sat down next to Roberta.

"We welcome Jane and little Roberta to International Sapphonic Illumination Society (ISIS), Racine Chapter. I am Alina, I emigrated from Russia many years ago, and I host this session. Our goal is to help women learn about their world and themselves. No knowledge is off limits. We like to focus on issues and events that affect women's rights, their wrongfully assigned roles and how to break out of them, women's education and careers, family, and future. We have many chapters throughout world, but unfortunately for now, we must remain underground to protect our rights others wish to take away."

"I see many familiar faces, and I see new ones," Alina continued. "So we start by going around room, and each person say name and little bit about herself. Mum, you start please?"

Each woman in turn provided an introduction. There were women of all ages and backgrounds—white, black, Hispanic, Asian, rich, middle-class, poor, single, married, and lesbian. Mothers, daughters, and grandmothers attended. A side room with a large window held a nursery for very young girls—babies and noisy toddlers—which had an audio feed from the main room, but it was little used and only really necessary for young babies who would not stop crying. Roberta was not out of place in her setting as there were other girls her age and older in attendance.

Jane finished up the introductions with her name and description of her work at Daschwirk and Kefer Toothe.

"And soon she'll be a Racine Belle," Arbie bragged.

"Whoo, hoo!" Mum and Petunia hollered.

"Well, I'm thinking about it," Jane said in modesty.

"I'll drag her to tryouts—don't worry Mum and Petunia," Arbie said.

"*Khorosho*," Alina said. "Thank you everyone. I start by reading something from Truman Doctrine."

General boos at the mention of a male name. Alina placed her hand out to subdue the boos.

"Now I know what you think. However, he is President of United States. And he issue statement to Congress. Some of you read this doctrine in newspapers. I not bore you with entire speech—"

Applause from the women.

"But there are little sentences to repeat," Alina said. "President Truman speaks to provide support to Greece and Turkey in response to threat of totalitarianism. There are universal concepts in his speech, and I reread portions and substitute words as necessary so you see how universal truths for democracy apply to us."

"The world is not static, and the status quo is not sacred. But we cannot allow changes in the status quo in violation of equal rights by such methods as coercion, or by such subterfuges as misogynist infiltration."

"At the present moment in world history, nearly every woman must choose between alternative ways of life. The choice is too often not a free one. One way of life is based upon equal rights for women, and is distinguished by free institutions, representative government, free elections, guarantees of individual liberty, freedom of speech and religion, and freedom from political oppression. The second way of life is based upon the will of misogynists forcibly imposed upon women. It relies upon terror and oppression, a controlled press and radio; fixed elections, and the suppression of personal freedoms."

"Lack of sufficient equal rights has always forced women to work hard to make both ends meet."

"As a result of these tragic conditions, the misogynist—exploiting female want and misery—is able to create political chaos which, until now, has made equal-rights recovery impossible."

"The seeds of totalitarian regimes are nurtured by misery and want. They spread and grow in the evil soil of poverty and strife. They reach their full growth when the hope of women for a better life has died. We must keep that hope alive."

"One of the primary objectives of women is the creation of conditions in which we and other women will be able to work out a way of life free from coercion. This is a fundamental issue in the war for women's rights. Our victory will be won over those who seek to impose their will, and their way of life, upon women."

"I believe that it must be the policy of all people to support women who are resisting attempted subjugation by misogynists or by outside pressures. I believe that we must assist women to work out their own destinies in their own way."

"We shall not realize our objectives, however, unless we are willing to help women to maintain their free institutions and their national integrity against aggressive movements that seek to impose upon them totalitarian regimes. This is no more than a frank recognition that totalitarian regimes imposed on free women, by direct or indirect aggression, undermine the foundations of international equal rights and hence the security of women everywhere."

"This is a serious course upon which we embark."

"We must take immediate and resolute action."

Alina placed her notes aside and nodded her head, indicating she had completed her recitation. The women in attendance clapped. And clapped. And the clapping broke into a rhythm followed by a chant with the women saying, "Zavuski Doctrine, Zavuski Doctrine!"

"Thank you, thank you," Alina said. "Time is now for us to act. Think critically about everything you see, everything you read, and everything others say and ask yourself—does this represent equal rights? Do not confuse 'equal rights' with 'identical'. No one is identical to another, but all deserve equal rights."

"Not all," shouted one woman referring to men. "Not the *feks*."

The women erupted in multiple heated discussions.

"What's a *fek*?" Jane asked.

"One who affects us badly and is male," Arbie said. "*Fek* is short for *affect*."

Alina held out her hands to silence the women.

"*Equal rights* means equal rights for all people. Anything else is regime—no matter who is on side of power. How can you ask to become regime where women have all power?"

"Why not?" yelled one.

"It's only fair," said another.

"It's our turn!" yelled Arbie, to which Jane looked at her in surprise.

Arbie returned a wink to Jane.

"No. Regime sets itself up for failure. Coup always hides in shadows awaiting opportunity to overthrow regime, only to become regime itself. How can we live in world of repeating regimes?" Alina asked.

"There's no other way," said another.

"There is," Alina said. "There are many ways—and all peaceful. Our society for one—International Sapphonic Illumination Society."

"ISIS rules, ISIS rules," the women chanted.

"Purpose of Illumination Society not to rule," Alina said.

The crowd booed.

"We are not militant group. We are peaceable women. And that should be our goal," Alina said. "This Society is to provide illumination—that means information and knowledge on world around us. From there we grow and develop into independent people, and in time become force where we peacefully protest our rights."

"We want action now," said one woman. "I've been suffering for years with substandard pay and discrimination."

"Yeah," said another. "What good are books and knowledge when the *feks* are the ones causing problems and taking the wealth?"

"We need to protest now! There's time for knowledge later," said a third.

"Demanding is one thing, but we must have power to back our position," said Alina.

"Give 'em a bloody nose," Arbie said. "That'll give us power."

"Bloody nose, bloody nose!" the group chanted.

"It is trap—the same trap totalitarian regimes play out over and over. There is no long-term stability in coercion," Alina said.

"But we have to start somewhere," said a woman.

"Yeah," others agreed, and the group talked and yelled in random means such that the stone-encased room thundered in deep echo.

"Quiet," Alina tried to say, but the crowd drowned her out. "Please, listen," she said.

Jane walked to the kitchen, brought out a pan and metal serving spoon, and struck the spoon against the pan. The group quieted down.

"We must learn how world works—current events, law, government, and politics, not to mention math, science, engineering, and literature," Alina said.

"Math and science?" one woman laughed.

"*Eee* equals *em cee* squared," another laughed.

"It took credit for that equation from its first wife, Mileva Marić," laughed a third.

"But what good is learning math and science?" Arbie asked.

"The good is that it shows other women who are less confident that they can succeed—all they have to do is work at it and learn," Alina said. "ISIS is one way to help women find out how to learn, what avenues to explore and conquer. Why? Because regime controls information lines, and those lines are polluted with false hopes and dead ends for women. We must find working lines and share that knowledge with others. We are like explorers—discovering ways that are hidden from us. We will find these ways and share them—this is democracy for women—open to all women for scrutiny and adjustment. We will make mistakes along way—there is no question there. But as long as we reveal our successes and failures to all women around world—we will win. It is that simple. We will win!"

The group broke into varied arguments with one another. Alina urged them to keep things civil but to discuss what she'd said. Spontaneously, small discussion groups formed. Alina visited each group and urged them to continue discussing what she'd said—the pros, the cons, and anything else they could think of. In this way, the initial reaction to go running out of the room and break any man's nose they could find was redirected into thoughtful and productive discussion. After a half hour, the women settled into less heated exchanges and into more orderly exchanges of ideas. Jane stood up and browsed various books in the bookcases. Roberta walked with her, and Jane came across one plainly marked book near the corner of the room, *The Well of Loneliness* by Radclyffe Hall. Jane opened the book and skimmed through the pages until she stopped at one passage. She read it silently several times before speaking it aloud, "Give us also the right to our existence."

"You found book," Alina said.

"Oh, I'm sorry," Jane said. "I was just—"

"Do not be," said Alina. "Do not ever apologize for reading. Even with this book—which people either love or hate—deserves right to be read."

"Why do people hate this book? Is it poorly written? Is it boring?" Jane asked.

"Oh heavens no!" Alina said.

"Then why?" Jane asked.

"For some, it is bigotry," Alina explained. "Bigotry is ugliest of human crimes—worse than murder, because bigotry leads to mass murder of worst kind. Hitler hated Jews, and now we learn by how much."

"Is this book about Jews?" Jane asked.

"No," Alina said. "It is about two women in love. In love, Jane. Can you believe it? Most precious gift in world—most important element of life—act of love between two people—and some cannot deal with that reality."

"There's another controversy with the book," Arbie said after overhearing the conversation from a distance.

She walked over to Alina and Jane with a slim book opened in her hand.

"What's that in your hand?" Jane asked, referring to the paper.

"This? Why it's just a paper, it's called: 'Studies in Spermatogenesis' by N.M. Stevens, published by the Carnegie Institution of Washington in September 1905," Arbie said.

Jane shot Arbie and Alina a puzzled look.

"Arbie did not explain 'N.M.' stands for 'Nettie Maria'," Alina said.

"Yeah, good old Nettie. Some say she discovered the role of X- and Y-chromosomes in determining sex, others say Edmund Wilson or even Clarence McClung did. Wilson's paper was published in August of 1905, and well here you see Nettie's was published in September," Arbie said.

"McClung stated in 1901 that sex is determined by chromosomes, and Nettie Stevens added research about X and Y, though if you look in her paper you not see it written as 'X' and 'Y'. Wilson did its own independent research and reached same conclusion as Nettie—it even incorporated Nettie's work into its work, if I remember," Alina said. "The XX/XY system began with them."

"But people forget about her. They remember Wilson, or if they forget Wilson, they remember Thomas Morgan because it owned the lab," Arbie said.

"Do not speak that name so loudly here," Alina said. "It said uncomplimentary things about Miss Stevens after she died in 1912. It demeaned her work."

"How did she die?" Jane asked.

"Breast cancer," Alina said.

"Oh, that's terrible," Jane said, and the three fell into an uncomfortable silence for several seconds.

"The other book, then," Arbie said to break the silence. "*The Well of Loneliness*—some don't like themes of self-hatred and exhibitions of the other gender traits."

"Yes, that is true," Alina said. "But single most important thing *The Well of Loneliness* did was to get people to talk. Whether book's themes are good or bad, it got them to talk— and that was its greatest gift to world. All we have to do is open door of knowledge, and universe is limitless."

Alina waved her arm to the groups in the room—groups who were discussing all sorts of topics from social progress to sexual savviness.

"What about the Tree of Knowledge?" Jane asked. "Genesis says knowledge is evil. Eve gave the fruit to Adam, and—"

"That should explain everything," Alina said. "Regimes preach ignorance is virtue to protect their stranglehold on knowledge."

"In other words, that passage was written by the *feks* to oppress us," Arbie said.

"You see how Eve was blamed for everything," Alina added.

"Eve should have kept the apple for herself and let Adam stumble along in his own stupidity," Arbie added.

"Or she should have left Adam and sought out Lilith," Alina said.

The three women laughed, but Jane soon fell into sadness and shed two tears.

"Why sad, Jane?" Alina asked.

"I wish Trudy were here. She would benefit more than I," Jane said. "But how could I get her to see how badly she's trapped under Jack's thumb? She's so blind."

"It's my fault," said Arbie. "I should have tried harder to show her how the *fek* world works when old-*fek* Hansen used to beat us."

"You cannot go beating yourselves up forever," said Alina. "It is waste of time and does no good."

"Then what can we do?" Jane asked. "How can I convince Trudy to attend one of these Sapphic sessions?"

"Sapphonic," Alina said.

"Shouldn't it be 'Sapphic'?" Arbie asked.

"No," Alina said. "I know what you thinking—there no such word as 'Sapphonic'. But our society not limited to Sapphics. It is for all women. And what better name than 'Sapphonic'? It is like 'symphony'—orchestra of musical voices from all backgrounds and faiths. But to your concern, Jane, I say—greatest challenge we have today is not what we discuss—although others might disagree and say content quality is critical. No, greatest challenge is bringing women from shadows of oppression to discussion table—to reach out to them and shed our illumination into their dread of darkness. But it is difficult. There are many layers and walls blocking light—most created by *feks*, but some created by women too. I think most walls created by women are coerced walls—not of their own free will. And they are scared, Jane—scared they will have no place to go if they admit they receive light. That is why we must stick together and support each other no matter what regime we in. It is tough road ahead, but if women like Radclyffe Hall can risk their necks on chopping block to further our cause, we can."

"I think—" Jane started to say before being interrupted.

A loud pounding on the front door echoed through the main room.

"Open up in there!" yelled a voice. "This is the Racine County Sheriff."

The women fell as silent and cold as the surrounding stone walls. Alina walked deliberately to the door. She turned off all lights leaving just fireplace light for illumination. She opened a small slot in the door where she could see who was on the outside.

"Open up! What are you doing in there?" shouted the voice.

"Yes?" Alina said through the door.

"Racine Sheriff," the man said. "Open up!"

"I am owner of this property," Alina said through the opening. "May I see your badge?"

"You open up or else!" he said.

"Your badge," Alina said. "You must identify yourself. Or I report you as trespassing on my property."

"You? The owner of this farm?" the voice laughed in a deep, gargly manner. "What are you doing at the bottom of a silo? Get out of there."

"I warn you, I call the police," Alina said. "You best leave now."

"You're bluffing. Women have no power, and you know it," he said. "You got no telephone in there. What are you doing, sleeping with goats?"

Alina could see this was no police officer but instead a drunken vagabond who'd wandered onto her property. She debated what to do—she did have a telephone inside the chamber, but should she risk revealing the location of the Racine Chapter of ISIS? She didn't have long to think. The drunk shouldered his body weight into the door and broke it down. The door fell on Alina and trapped her.

"Get off, get off!" she yelled, but the drunk stepped on the door and held his weight firmly upon Alina's body—pinning her lower body effectively between the layers of door and floor.

"You're gonna give me a good time," he growled, "and no one's gonna hear about it, see?"

He pulled out a knife and pressed it against her throat. The women held silent inside. Jane motioned to stand up, but Arbie held her back with an extended arm. Roberta shook in fear and clung to Jane. Jane tried consoling Roberta, but Roberta could not be comforted. She didn't like the sound of the male voice, and she couldn't stop from speaking.

"Mommie. Stop the *fek*. Stop the *fek*!" Roberta said.

"What was that?" the drunk asked.

An image of *Gone With The Wind*'s Scarlet O'Hara killing a northern soldier flashed through Jane's mind, followed by a fear that the drunk would find Roberta and kill her. Jane's Celtic blood boiled and would not abate. Jane harried her long legs to the door where she dove into the drunk and sent him back into the silo. The two fell to the silo's bottom, but Jane stood first and pulled the dazed drunk to his feet. The women turned on all lights. Some helped Alina from under the door while others cheered Jane on. Jane didn't wait for the drunk to respond to her blows. She threw punch after punch after punch into the drunk—first the gut, then the temple, and an uppercut to the jaw. Jane's adrenaline prevented her from feeling the pain in her fist from colliding with the drunk's skeletal frame. The universe consisted of a single thought—beat this man until there was nothing left to beat, and then beat some more.

The women went wild, but Alina cautioned them to control their shouting as she didn't want their location revealed. Recovering her senses, Alina pleaded with Jane to stop beating the *fek*, that going to jail for murder wasn't worth it, but Jane did not hear these words. She tossed Alina back into the chamber and continued systematically breaking every bone in the drunk's body. The man stopped breathing and stopped reacting to her assaults.

"Get up," she commanded to the drunk. "Get up!" she commanded again as she lifted him to his feet, but it was no use. Blood poured out of multiple orifices, and his limbs moved in unnatural shapes as if he were made of rubber.

"It's over, Jane," Arbie said. "It's over."

"No," Jane said. "It's not."

"Mommie stop!" Roberta pleaded. "Stop!"

Jane paused for a moment for the only voice that could touch her soul so deeply. Her own daughter—she was there—and she watched her mother kill a man.

"My God, what have I done?" Jane asked the cold air.

"Quickly, ladies, let's clean up here," Alina beckoned.

Arbie took Jane and Roberta to a cuddle chair as far from the main door as possible. Arbie gave several shots of whiskey to Jane, who downed them quickly.

"Irish," Jane said.

"What?" Arbie asked.

"The drink—it's Irish whiskey. Good spirits," Jane said.

Roberta clung to Jane and felt safe. Arbie stared at Jane with new admiration, while the other women eliminated the corpse and all evidence of its existence at the chamber.

"Jane," Alina said an hour later as Jane, Arbie, and Roberta were ready to leave. "I want you to know I not condone violence, and ISIS is about peaceful establishment of equal rights."

"I'm sorry for everything," Jane said. "This is the worst night of my life."

"I am glad you came," Alina said with a loving smile. "You saved my life and those of everyone here. The women found vagabond's possessions in hayloft. No doubt he hid in barn for several days. We check barn and property more often for such derelicts."

"But...I...killed..." Jane stumbled.

"Shhh. Don't think about that now. You defended these women and your daughter from harm. That is most important thing. You are always welcome here. Arbie—bring Jane to house for tea sometime. We must have tea and long talk," Alina said.

"You mean...you don't hate me?" Jane asked with anxiety in her voice.

"Of course not," Alina said as she broke into tears.

Alina hugged Jane and kissed her several times on the lips—kisses of friendship, gratitude, and sisterly love.

"I speak for all women here when I say we love you," Alina said.

Jane looked inside the chamber at the remaining women. They smiled, nodded in affirmation, and blew kisses and friendly waves to Jane. Jane's anxiety melted away, and she smiled.

"That's better," Alina said. "Go now and be at peace with yourself. Our world is better place with you."

"I have a headache," Evanita said to Jonara. "I can't stay here. Ow, I feel like my head is going to explode!"

CHAPTER 10:

Fantina di Pindos

2023 Oct 5, Thu Early am. Corpus Christi, Texas.
2006 Nov 22, Wed. Elrod 402.

Evanita and Jonara reappeared in Cafederijet's MRI room. Evanita tried to speak and move, but her entire left side was paralyzed.

"We must get her into surgery immediately," Baria said to Mac-Two. "She has a massive brain clot developing. Help me lift her onto the gurney."

Mac-Two and two other Barians helped Baria transfer Evanita to a gurney. Evanita was awake but in pain, and she writhed in agony.

"I have the worst sinus headache!" she moaned.

"We must hurry!" Baria said.

The Barians and Mac-Two raced the gurney down the hallway to an operating room. Mac-Two helped the Barians transfer Evanita to the operating table, and Mac-Two wheeled the gurney out of the way.

"You should leave now," said Bar-One to Mac-Two. "You can wait outside if you like."

Mac-Two left as instructed. The Barians strapped Evanita down but gave her nothing for the pain.

"Little Voice!" Evanita cried.

"She's delirious, doctor," Bar-One said to Barian.

"We must relieve the pressure now!" Baria said.

Bar-Two prepared a medical drill and handed it to Baria. Baria jogged the drill's on/off switch several times with the drill in the air to test its function. The drill's sound scared Evanita.

"No, no, no! Don't hurt me!" Evanita begged, and she did her best to writhe free from the restraints.

"Clamp her head tightly!" Baria ordered. "Give her a mouth guard so she doesn't bite her tongue."

"Shouldn't we wait for the anesthesiologist?" Bar-One asked.

"No time," Baria replied.

Baria activated the drill and bored a hole through Evanita's skull. Evanita screamed as best she could through the mouth guard, and Jonara endured a horrible sinking feeling in her gut. Jonara ran to comfort her mother, and as she embraced Evanita, the drill's vibrations carried frequency waves through Evanita's skull, down her spine, into her rib cage, and into the Moissan Ruby. The Moissan Ruby activated.

1940 Dec 19. Pindus Mountains, Samarina, Greece.

Evanita and Jonara appeared in a cabin. A man rested in a bed with many blankets atop him, a young woman with white hair and fair skin cooked something in an iron pot over the fireplace, and an old man with white hair sat in a chair reading a book. The sun was setting. Much of the cabin was made of old wood, but the front door, frame, and surrounding wall were newly constructed from fresh timbers.

"Are we in Greece again?" Jonara asked.

"Let me check the stone. Yes. We're in the village of Samarina, in the Pindus Mountains. It's December 19, 1940," Evanita said.

"Has the soldier regained consciousness yet, Fantina?" the old man asked.

"Fantina," Jonara said. "I've heard that name before."

"You have?" Evanita asked. "Where?"

"I don't remember," Jonara said.

"No, Father," said the woman. "He has been asleep since the avalanche three days ago."

"He must wake soon," the old man said. "He must eat to regain his strength. His wound—"

"I have cleaned it every day," said Fantina.

"His leg will go gangrene soon," said the father. "The infection in his foot is spreading."

"I am a failure for not healing him," said Fantina.

She walked over to the soldier. Evanita and Jonara took a closer look at him.

"It's Axon," Evanita said.

"The Greek skiing soldier," Jonara said.

"Our snowball trapped him," Evanita said.

"We hurt him?" Jonara asked. "That's bad."

"It is, but there's nothing we can do," Evanita said.

"There must be something I can do for him, Father," Fantina said.

"Sing him the song," the father said. "The one I sang you every night when you were a child."

"*The Children of Samarina?*" Fantina asked.

"Yes. Do you know the words?" he asked.

"I think so," Fantina said.

A peculiar thing happened in the cabin. At first, Evanita and Jonara weren't aware of the difference, but after a few seconds, it became clear the two were experiencing multiple days simultaneously. The father sat at his chair reading books with four gray shapes overlapping his own but reading different books. Axon had four gray shapes overlapping his own—all in the same position. Fantina also had four shapes, but these were standing in different positions next to Axon's bed.

Fantina sang the first verse:

And oh you young Greek freedom fighters
Children of Samarina
Oh you poor children
Children of Samarina
And though you may be grimy.

The other four Fantinas also sang the verse, but they appeared to be singing on different days. After Fantina said, "grimy," her color changed to gray, and another gray Fantina became colorful.

"The day is now December 20th," Evanita said to Jonara.

As you, oh you, go up into the mountains
Toward Samarina
Oh you poor children
Toward Samarina
And though you may be grimy.

All four Fantinas sang the second verse. As before, the colorful Fantina became gray, but now another gray Fantina (not the first) became colorful and led the singing of the third verse.

"It's December 21st," Evanita said.

May you, oh you, not throw rifles
Songs may you not sing
Oh you poor children
Songs may you not sing
And though you may be grimy.

The cycle continued. Another gray Fantina became colorful. Jonara had been watching the old man and noticed his gray and colorful selves would shift at the same time that Fantina's selves shifted.

"December 22nd," Evanita said.

And if my mother should ask, oh you
My deceitful sister
Oh you poor children
My deceitful sister
And though you may be grimy.

The last gray shapes became colorful.
"The 23rd," Evanita said.

Do not say, oh you, that I've been killed
That I am wounded
Oh you poor children
That I am wounded
And though you may be grimy.

The cabin darkened. Evanita and Jonara saw nothing followed by a blinding light.

"Is it the sun?" Evanita asked, but before Jonara could answer, the two understood.

2006 Nov 22. In Cafederijet's Operating Room.

"The left eye is still dilated," said Baria while shining a light in Evanita's eyes. "I had hoped drilling in the first spot would relieve the pressure, but it hasn't. We'll drill at the second spot now."

Baria drilled into Evanita's skull at a second location. The Moissan Ruby reactivated and sent Evanita and Jonara back to 1940.

1940 Dec 24. Samarina, Pindus Mountains, Greece.

Evanita and Jonara stood atop a peak on the Pindus Mountain range with sunlight blinding their eyes. The two watched as the sun sank below the horizon, and as the world changed from orange to blue, Evanita and Jonara drifted through a double-walled barn filled with cattle. Steam rose from cracks in the floor and kept the barn unusually warm. The two drifted through the barn, along a short passage, and into a smaller building.

"We're back in the cabin," Jonara said.

"It's Christmas Eve," Evanita said. "But I don't see a Christmas tree in here."

"That's weird. Where are the decorations?" Jonara asked.

"There aren't any," Evanita replied.

"The woman called 'Fantina'," Jonara said. "Do you see her?"

"Yes," Evanita said. "She looks so young—like she's in her twenties, but her hair is white as snow."

Though darkness shrouded the outside air, Fantina and her father's cabin filled with warm light from a fireplace and kerosene lanterns.

"Ugh, grugg, garoff," coughed Axon. "Where am I?"

"Fantina!" the father called. "He's awake!"

Fantina entered the living room from a side room with a *menorah* in hand. She placed the *menorah* on a table close to Axon's living-room bed but away from the window.

Axon looked at Fantina's white face, white hair, white clothing, and loving smile.

"Are you an angel?" he asked.

"No," Fantina giggled.

"Then I am dead and you are God," he said. "But what is that? Is it for Advent?"

"No to both. I am not God, and this is not for Advent," Fantina said. "The sun has set and so Hanukkah begins now. This is a *menorah*. There are eight places for candles, and an extra place for the *shamash*. Over here is a box of candles. Watch—I will place the candles in like this—there—all nine candles are ready. Would you like to light the *shamash*?"

"The what?" Axon asked. "What's the date?"

"Fantina—he does not know our ways. Better not to involve him," the old man said.

"Nonsense," Fantina said. "God is for everyone."

"I believe in God," Axon said. "And the saints and the Holy Trin—"

"He is not one of us," the old man said. "He does not understand."

"Oh Father!" Fantina said, rolling her eyes. "But you, sir," she said, now speaking to Axon. "Today is the 24th of December, 1940. Do you remember your name?"

"Axon," he said. "Axon Deh...Axon Deh...that's strange. I can't remember my last name."

"You hit your head," Fantina said. "And you broke your ankle. And an arm. And your ribs. But your papers say you are Axon Dendritous."

"Yes," Axon said as he started to get up. "Ow!"

"Rest here!" Fantina said. "You have an infection. I cleaned it while you slept, but the infection is spreading."

"We can't get you to a doctor—all roads are closed," the old man said.

"I can't stay here," Axon said. "My men, the battle."

"The Greek Army overpowered the Italians," Fantina said. "Greece is safe."

The old man laughed.

"Well it is," she said.

"Oh Fantina! The Italians have been beaten for now, but how long will it be before Hitler takes over where Mussolini failed?"

"Never! The radio says we're the first European country to defeat Hitler's alliance. And I say we keep it that way," Fantina bragged.

"I hope you are right, Fantina," Axon said. "But I fear he may be right. Say, I don't think we had a proper introduction. I shouldn't be saying *he* in a man's house. I should pay my proper respects."

"This is the woman's house," Fantina said. "And I am a woman."

Axon looked at Fantina's attractive body and said, "You are a woman. I thought you were God or an angel, but you are definitely a woman. I wouldn't say otherwise without getting my eyes checked."

The old man stood from his chair and walked over to Axon and Fantina.

"You'll have to forgive my daughter, Mr. Dendritous," the old man said.

"Please, call me Axon," Axon said.

"Yes, Axon. My name is Samouel Karrano. And this is my daughter, Fantina. We live in this cabin all year round. Fantina was born in this cabin, I was born in this cabin, and so was my father. My grandfather fought in the Greek War of Independence back in 1821 and kicked those Turks out of our country. When the war ended, he married and built this cabin and barn on top of a small thermal vent. That's how we can stay here. We keep the cattle inside our barn all winter, and they do not freeze."

"I hate Turks," Axon said.

"You must learn to forgive your enemies," Samouel said. "Hate serves no good."

"That sounds like something I learned in religion class when I was a lad," Axon said. "Are you Christian? I see no Christmas decorations. Don't you celebrate Christmas?"

Samouel locked a stare with Fantina as if to say, "Tell him nothing."

"We're Jewish," Fantina said to Samouel's dismay.

"There, now you did it," Samouel said.

"Why must we hide our faith, Father? We should be proud of who we are," Fantina said.

"I am proud, and I'm especially proud of you. But the rest of the world doesn't need to know. I've lived a long life because of our secrecy—and you will too. Our people have been and continue to be tortured and killed for our beliefs," Samouel said.

"He's right, Fantina. It's dangerous—especially now—to let people know you're Jewish. Hitler doesn't like Jews, and there is a story going around that thousands of Jews have been forced into a ghetto in Warsaw. That's in Poland, Fantina, and it started two months ago. Last month, a wall was built around the ghetto to keep Jews from leaving. No Jews can leave, and many are already starving. Yet more go in. I would hate to think of such a beautiful creature as you being forced into such a horrible place."

Fantina blushed and turned away briefly.

"You speak wisely, Axon. Fantina and I will remain in these mountains as we have our entire lives—tending our cattle and worshiping God—free of intervention from men of vice. Are you a man of vice or a man of God?"

"Oh Father!" Fantina said. "I'm sure Axon is a man of God. Someday I wish to marry and have a large family. But I should think I must leave this place for my dream to come true. There are no men up here in the winter, and the summer only brings visitors. How I wish to see the city, like Athens!"

Samouel walked over and slapped Fantina across the face.

"You'll not soil this house with such blasphemy against your family," Samouel said.

"Whoa, Samouel, let up a little bit. Fantina meant nothing against you," Axon said.

"She should know to respect her father in his house," Samouel said.

"It's my house!" she said, and she stormed off to her bedroom in tears.

Meanwhile, the *menorah* remained on the table unlit.

"The *menorah*," Samouel said, realizing the neglect. "I will light it."

"No, wait," Axon said.

"You certainly don't think you can light it, Axon Dendritous!" Samouel said. "I only allow my family and Jewish neighbors to participate in Hanukkah."

"That's your right, and I respect it, sir," Axon said. "But I'm betting Fantina should be here for this too. She offered the *shamash* to me for lighting—"

"Which I would not allow," Samouel interrupted.

"And I respect that too. But sir, what I'm trying to say...heck, I'll just have to show you," Axon said.

"Show me what?" Samouel asked.

Axon sat up in bed with his feet landing on the floor. He grimaced in pain and muffled a yell. He placed a hand on the headboard and pulled himself up as more pain entered his leg.

"What are you doing? You should not walk on that foot," Samouel said.

"I'm going to get your daughter," Axon said.

"Don't be a fool, lad. If she wants to be an overgrown girl, let her. She's only a woman," Samouel said.

"But she's your daughter. And she's a nice woman too," Axon said.

Axon pushed himself along into a hobbling sort of walk. He limped from his bed to the doorway of Fantina's bedroom. She held her face in her pillow and cried without being aware of his presence. Axon attempted to cross her doorway, but his foot gave out, and he slumped.

"What are you doing?" she said, pulling herself out of her pillow.

"Your father wants to light the candles," he said.

Fantina jumped up and helped Axon to his feet.

"But you're in pain," she said.

"I know. So are you. But I told him to wait for you to light the candles. It's Hanukkah," Axon said.

Fantina helped Axon walk from her bedroom doorway to the eating table where she helped him sit.

"I have an idea," Fantina said.

"Oh?" Samouel asked.

Fantina took the *menorah* and placed it on the eating table. She took the *shamash* candle in her right hand and lit it by the fireplace. Returning to the eating table, she asked Axon to hold her right hand as she lit the first menorah candle with the *shamash.* Axon did so, and the two lit the candle without offending Samouel.

"My daughter is very clever," Samouel said.

Fantina eeked out a half-smile. She said a prayer for the Hanukkah occasion, and it went like this:

We kindle these lights to remember the miracles, wonders, and saving acts in battle You made for our forbearers, in those days and that time, and about Your glory and Your wonders through Your Holy Kohanim.

During the eight days of Hanukkah these lights are sacred, and we are not permitted to make ordinary use of them, but only to look at them in order to offer thanks and praise to Your great Name for Your miracles, Your salvations, and Your wonders.

Fantina finished the prayer and darted into the kitchen. She returned with three bowls, a pitcher of fresh water, three cups, and three small towels. She gave a cup to each person at the table—including Axon.

"Fantina," Samouel said. "Three of everything? The hand washing is only for—"

"Father, I respect your words. Axon is our guest, and we cannot deny him food," Fantina said.

"But he is not kosher," Samouel said.

"Would you have him eat with unclean hands? As our guest, we should offer every hospitality of a loving Jewish home to Axon," Fantina said.

"I would be honored to participate," Axon said.

"He is not kosher!" Samouel repeated.

"Father, please! Does not God love all his children? Even Gentiles?" Fantina asked.

Samouel let out a sigh of light frustration.

"Lord forgive me and my daughter for eating in this fashion," Samouel said.

"Oh yes, Father, yes!" Fantina cheered. "The Lord welcomes us—all of us!"

Fantina jumped over to her father, kissed him on the cheek in gratitude, and returned to her chair.

"Do as we do, Axon," Fantina instructed.

Fantina filled her cup with water and passed the pitcher to her father, who performed the same maneuver. Samouel hesitated in passing the pitcher to Axon. He looked at Axon with disapproval, but Fantina grabbed her father's arm and shook it. He looked at her, and she nodded in affirmation and motioned with her free hand for him to pass the pitcher to Axon. Samouel darted his eyes between Fantina and Axon with indecision. Fantina took the pitcher from him and handed it to Axon. She smiled at Axon. Axon filled his cup and returned the pitcher to Fantina.

Fantina poured her cup over the top and bottom of her right hand, allowing her bowl to catch the drippings while Samouel did the same. Axon, on seeing this motion, repeated it with a time delay of a few seconds. Axon moved to dry his right hand, but Fantina reached out and blocked him. She poured her cup over the top and bottom of her left hand much as she did with her right. Again Samouel synchronized his motion with Fantina, and Axon performed his hand washing with less delay after Fantina's. Fantina prayed:

Blessed are You, Lord our God, King of the Universe, who has blessed us with His commandments and commanded us in washing of hands.

Fantina dried her hands, and she nodded to Axon that he could now dry his, which he did. Samouel hesitated but wiped his to complete the hand-washing prayer. Fantina smiled. She gathered the hand-washing items, disappeared into the kitchen, and emerged with plates, eating utensils, cloth napkins, and mugs. Back to the kitchen, and she delivered a large platter of potato pancakes, meats fried in olive oil, and cheese. She placed them on the table. Another trip to the kitchen, and she reappeared with bread, wine, and custard-filled sufganiyot—or sugar-powdered doughnuts. Fantina sat and prayed:

Blessed are You, Lord our God, King of the Universe, who creates bread of the earth, fruit of the vine, fruit of the tree, variety of sustenance, and by whose word everything comes to be. Amen.

"We may eat now," Samouel said.

Fantina started by taking bread and passing the breadbasket to her father, who took a piece and passed the basket to Axon.

"It smells good," Axon said. "Everything smells good. I'm in Heaven."

Fantina laughed, and Samouel smiled.

"Fantina makes the best food—kosher or no—in all the Pindus Mountains," Samouel said.

"I'm growing quite fond of your daughter," Axon said.

Fantina blushed, but Samouel held a grave expression. The three continued passing around food dishes.

"I have hopes my daughter will marry a good Jewish boy," Samouel said.

"There's not much time for that," Fantina said

"Why do you say that?" Axon asked. "You hardly look twenty-five."

Fantina giggled.

"That must have been a bad blow to your head, Mr. Dendritous," Samouel said. "Your eyes do not see very well."

"Shut up, Father!" Fantina said between giggles.

"You're older?" Axon asked.

"Of course she's older!" Samouel said. "Can't you tell?"

"I apologize then. I don't like to overestimate a woman's age. Thirty, and that's my top guess."

Fantina broke into a big laugh, leaned back in her chair, and nearly fell backward.

"Ooops!" she said, regaining her balance. Samouel was about to say something, but Fantina said, "Don't say anything, Father. Just shush!"

"Thirty-two?" Axon asked.

"By the time he guesses, Hanukkah will be over and done with," Samouel said. "Tell him, Fantina."

"I'm forty," she said.

"Forty!?" Evanita asked.

"Forty!?" Jonara asked.

"Ah, you're fooling me," Axon said.

"No, truthfully I tell you—I am forty years old. I was born in 1900. My father is eighty—he was born in 1860," Fantina said.

"She speaks the truth, Axon," Samouel said. "But we are Jews. We believe in keeping things kosher. That means Fantina should marry a Jew to remain faithful to God."

Fantina looked down with some reservation and said, "God works in strange ways. He has a plan for me, and I will follow His Will."

"As long as it's Jewish," Samouel added, but Fantina did not return his gaze.

"Hanukkah is very special for us this year," Fantina said, changing subjects and brightening her tone. "God has helped the Jewish people in battle before, and today my father and I celebrate His favor on our people in these northern parts of Greece. He has lent his strong arm to our Greek soldiers and pushed back the Fascist Italians. Oh forgive my manners—you two must be terribly thirsty. I forgot to pour the wine."

Fantina opened a bottle of wine and filled glasses for her father, Axon, and herself.

"Let's drink a toast to Greek freedom!" Fantina said.

The three clinked their wine glasses together and drank.

"The wine, it's—" Axon started.

"Do you like it? I pressed the grapes myself," Fantina said.

"Fantina makes all of our wine," Samouel said.

"It's like...food...not just spirits...the wine has a soul. I swirl the red fluid in my mouth, and I can feel the trees, vines, and mountains that have labored to create such a drink. I can feel something else too—something of you in the wine," Axon said.

"Dear me, are all Greek soldiers so colorful? We may not hold the battle lines at all should Fantina's wine get loose among the troops," Samouel said.

"I should say not! We must keep Fantina's wine to ourselves, for Greece's sake!" Axon laughed. "But tell me—are you Greek, or are you Romanian?"

Fantina and Samouel exchanged looks of indecision.

"We...uh...well..." Fantina stumbled.

"It's a question with a complex answer," Samouel said at length.

"I know you are Jewish—that much is clear," Axon said.

"Yes," Fantina said. "We are and always will be Jewish—that is most important of all."

"And? Who else do you pay allegiance?" Axon asked with a little anxiety.

Fantina looked down, and up, and at her father.

"We are Aromanian," Samouel said. "But that is more of a question than an answer."

"I should say so," Axon said.

"At times we are Greek, and at others more Romanian," Samouel said. "My grandfather grew up with the Aromanians, and my family has kept ties with them ever since. But it has been difficult—to be called Greeks by Romanians and Romanians by Greeks. And we are Jewish above all that! You can see how forces come at us from different directions. We are caught between the layers, and that has meant remaining somewhat secluded in Samarina where we deal less with politics and more with living and praising God."

"Father tells me our family is not from Greece, not even Romania or Albania," Fantina said.

"I'm guessing your family is from old Israel," Axon said.

"Going back a thousand or two thousand years—most likely. Unfortunately, we have no records going back that far. But I do have records going back to the 15th century, when Karla Karrano left Spain and settled in Greece," Samouel said.

"The 15th century," Axon mused. "That was after the Byzantium Empire fell. But how can you be Aromanian and Spanish?"

"Again, it's complex. Aromanian culture is part of our heritage. As I said, my grandfather grew up with Aromanians, even if his ancestors came from Spain," Samouel said. "But Spain, yes, the 15th century. Karla Karrano left Spain in 1492 and arrived in Greece the same year. By then, the Turks had been ruling Greece for almost forty years."

"That makes no sense—why would she move into Greece when the Turks were ruling?" Axon asked.

"And Karla was a Sephardic Jew," Samouel added.

"The Turks were Muslim, and they spread their faith throughout Greece. Karla would have been better to stay behind in Spain," Axon said.

"You don't know Spanish history, do you?" Samouel asked.

"It was the Spanish Expulsion," Fantina said. "Spain became Roman Catholic, and Jews were forced out. The Queen of Spain said it was God's will—can you believe such nonsense?"

"It wasn't nonsense for those who had to leave. Their homes and lives as they knew them were gone," Samouel said.

"Only God stayed with them," Fantina said.

"Some went to Portugal—that was not so good," Samouel said. "And some stayed in Spain and pretended to convert to Christianity."

"Some went to Turkey," Fantina said. "And those who weren't drowned where welcomed as skilled tradesmen."

"Drowned?!" Axon asked.

"Karla never made it to Turkey, because she met a Greek Jew in Athens," Samouel said.

"Didn't you tell me, Father, that Karla got along well with Greek Orthodox Christians?" Fantina asked.

"Yes, I did. And with those Christians, Karla and her new husband—"

"What was his name?" Fantina asked.

"No one remembers, unfortunately," Samouel said, "but they used her last name, moved to the mountains, and lived with a Christian group. Over the generations, the Karrano family moved from one mountain village to another, until—as I already told you—my grandfather Kailos helped defeat the Turks in the Greek War of Independence and built this cabin and barn."

"Your last name—Karrano—you'll forgive me, but it...I've never heard of it as a Jewish—" Axon said.

"It's not a common Jewish name," Fantina said. "Father says Karla took the name from the village in Spain where she lived."

"Mommy," Jonara said. "Their name—Karrano. It sounds a lot like—"

"Carreña," Evanita said.

"Mommy—where does your last name come from?" Jonara asked.

"From my mother, and her mother, and Margene," Evanita replied.

"But before that?" Jonara asked.

"I don't know," Evanita said.

"Daddy, I mean Johnny, said there's a city in Spain called Carreña. What did he say? It's in the province of Asturias, close to Picos de Europa National Park," Jonara said.

"When did he tell you that?" Evanita said.

"He never told me. He told Grandma Eva—at his sister's funeral when you and Grandma and Nanna Geneva went into the church. He was greeting people with a girl named Denise, and—" Jonara said.

"You were there? And you remember all that? I remember him talking about Spain or something, but I never made the connection between my last name and a Spanish city," Evanita said.

"What if our family is from Carreña? And what if the Karrano family is from Carreña? That means—" Jonara started.

"It means this Karrano family may have known ours," Evanita said.

"Is it important?" Jonara asked.

"I don't know," Evanita said.

The three finished eating dinner, and Fantina cleaned up. Axon stood to help, but she insisted he remain at the table.

"Keep him company while I do dishes," Fantina said to her father from the kitchen doorway.

Samouel continued to view Axon with suspicion, but the meal helped put him in a better mood. Axon was uncomfortable with the silence and spoke.

"So you have a radio," Axon said.

"What of it?" Samouel asked.

"I meant nothing by it. Does it work?" Axon asked.

"Why?"

"I...perhaps there's news...things in the world," Axon said.

"Perhaps there is," Samouel said with indifference.

"Oh Father!" Fantina said as she poked her head in from the kitchen doorway. "Don't be so obstinate."

"You want to hear the news, is that it?" Samouel asked. "Be my guest. Listen to what you like."

Axon stood from the table and hobbled over to the radio despite the pain in his foot. He flipped the switch on, adjusted the volume and tuner, but there was no sound.

"I don't understand, it should have warmed up by now," Axon said.

He looked for a power cord for plugging into the wall but instead found two sets of cables for connecting batteries.

"There is no conventional power cord," Samouel said. "And if there were, there is no power outlet."

"Oh," Axon said. "These look like battery cables."

"They are," Samouel said.

"Do you have batteries?" Axon asked.

"Yes, in the barn. They should be fully charged by now," Samouel said.

"You have a generator?" Axon asked.

"Of sorts. A windmill pumps water and drives a small electric generator. In the barn to your right, there is a tack room. The batteries are on a shelf. Be careful when you disconnect the cables. If they touch each other, you'll short out the generator," Samouel said.

Axon opened his mouth but stopped himself. He wanted to ask Samouel for help due to his injured foot.

"Are you a man who can take care of himself?" Samouel asked, seeming to read his mind.

"Yes, I am," Axon said with a heavy breath.

Axon hobbled over for his coat, threw it on, and exited the cabin with an oil lamp. Going out through the back door, he met a biting cold with a sting worse than a thousand wasps. His foot initially felt worse, but after a few moments, it went numb with the cold, and he felt relieved. He reached the barn, lifted a latch, and allowed himself in.

"The old man was right—the cabin and barn *are* built on a thermal vent," Axon said as he allowed the hot, rising steam to warm his body.

He basked in the warmth and panned the barn with his eyes. The cattle rustled a little as if being awaken from a comfortable sleep. The barn had an unusually fresh smell, as if instead of holding animals it held a floral nursery. Axon peered down one side of the barn, and next to the windows were tables of small-flowering plants growing in little containers. Above the table was a sign:

—Flowers—
Fantina Karrano from Pindos

Axon's feet thawed, and the pain in his foot gnawed. Axon grimaced from the pain and said:

"Back to reality."

He hobbled his way to the tack room where he limped past several well-oiled bridles and saddles.

"On the shelf," Axon reminded himself. "Which shelf? There."

Axon disconnected the battery cables carefully and reached for the batteries.

"These are too big to carry in my condition," he said.

Axon looked about for something to support his bad foot—a stick or crutch. He left the tack room and searched a bit more. At Fantina's flower station, he found a nicely lathed pole with a tee formation at the end. Axon looked around and saw items hanging from nails high above the flower tables.

"She hangs things up high and retrieves them with this pole. She won't mind if I break it in half to use as a crutch—she's just a woman," Axon said.

Axon set his lamp on the table and took the pole in hand.

"I can't believe he's going to break Fantina's reaching pole," Jonara said to Evanita.

"Wait," Evanita said.

Axon lifted a thigh, held the pole horizontally with both hands, and pulled the pole down toward his knee, but at the last possible moment, he checked up.

"He didn't do it," Evanita said.

"It's just a stick," Axon mumbled. "Break it."

He attempted the motion again, but twice he stopped himself short of breaking the pole across his thigh.

"Why did he stop?" Jonara asked Evanita.

"I think I know...but let's see," she replied.

"Flowers," Axon said. "I haven't seen flowers like this since...since I was a child. Since I saw my mother...before she died...before everything died. My soul...I thought it was dead too...but I see these flowers...Fantina's flowers...and I remember what it was like...when I was a child...when I could see colors...when I could smell flowers. This pole...she reaches with it...her extension...her beacon...to break it...to break it...the last light goes out."

Axon returned the pole to the table with the utmost care.

"I will make my own beacon!" he said.

Returning the lamp to his hand, Axon borrowed a hatchet from the barn, walked outside to the death of blustery winter, and descended a short ways into the forest. The wind picked up and blew snow everywhere. Axon could no longer see the cabin or barn and had only a vague idea as to the correct direction for a safe return.

He didn't panic. Finding a crutch that would help him without causing loss to others drove him farther into the woods. He had an idea he would have to chop down a small tree and felt he would know the tree when he saw it. He passed pines, oaks, beeches, poplars, and willows, but none seemed right. His foot was now numb again. This relieved his pain, but he was growing frustrated at not finding the "perfect" sapling to sacrifice as an aid to his locomotion.

"Axon!" a faint voice called.

Axon recognized it as Fantina's. She seemed miles away in some isolated ravine.

"I must find something—anything—to use as a crutch," he said in desperation.

Axon hacked at a pine tree. The tree was larger than he would have liked, and it dumped snow all over him, turning him into a living snowman. Fortunately, the oil lamp did not go out. He stopped chopping and worked at brushing the snow off him when something stung the sides and back of his neck.

"Wharga, wharg!" a vicious predator growled as it tore into Axon's neck.

Evanita and Jonara screamed in fear from the wolf now attacking Axon. Neither could help the unfortunate man and remained paralyzed in suspense of who the victor would be.

"Get off, get off!" Axon yelled.

He swung the ax around toward his back, but he couldn't reach the wolf. Its grip tightened, and he felt tingling in his lower limbs—like the pins and needles one feels when sitting on a leg too long and it has "fallen asleep".

Axon took another swing, but the ax flew out of his hand in the tussle. Where it landed, he did not know.

"Axon!" Fantina's voice yelled. "Are you out there?!"

Axon tried to yell, but by now the wolf's jaw had pinched his throat shut, and he could no longer breathe. Axon tried swinging the oil lamp onto the wolf, but it bounced off the wolf, landed on the ground, and went out.

"I'm dead, I'm dead!" he mouthed.

Axon's last hope was to dislodge the wolf by any means possible. He ran backward in wild directions as quickly as he could—hoping he would collide with something. The snow was deep, visibility was nil, and his last hopes were fading. Fantina's calls were all but gone, and in one last attempt to dislodge the wolf, he jumped backward and downhill.

CRASH!

Axon landed backward onto a tree with the wolf being crushed between layers of man and bark. The wolf yelped twice, squirmed out of entrapment, and limped away on its newly injured legs.

The wind whirled around Axon. He thought he was alone and abandoned, but Evanita and Jonara were there. Evanita stepped over to Axon and tried pulling him to his feet, but her hand passed through his.

"Hum something," Jonara said. "Or speak. You need to make the Water Ruby work so you can touch his hand."

"But what?" Evanita asked.

"Anything. Try anything until you feel something back," Jonara said.

"Let me touch his hand," Evanita said to the stone. "Let me touch his hand."

Evanita reached for Axon's hand, but her hand slipped through his.

"It doesn't work," Evanita said. "Maybe we're not supposed to help him. Maybe he's supposed to stay here and die."

"We can't leave him here to die in the cold," Jonara said.

"What else can we do? Talking to the stone doesn't work," Evanita said.

"You must...whoa...I'm dizzy," Jonara said.

"The aura around you is fading, Little Voice," Evanita said. "Little Voice—don't leave me here in these mountains."

"Must think...can't see straight...dizzy," Jonara said.

"What's wrong, what's wrong? Little Voice, what's wrong?" Evanita pleaded.

"I feel like...like...fading," Jonara said.

"Oh my gosh! He's tied to you. If we let him die, you won't exist! He's your ancestor!" Evanita said.

"I remember now," Jonara said. "I remember where I heard Fantina's name. It was on a medal Daddy showed me. The medal said, 'Aromani, son of Fantina di Pindos'."

"That clinches it," Evanita said. "Aromani was Johnny's father. That makes Fantina his grandmother, and Axon must be his grandfather. But Axon is dying! Oh this is terrible! We can't let this happen! Think, Little Voice—how can I control the stone?"

"Daddy...he spoke strangely...strange words...when you were in a coma...being chased on a horse," Jonara said.

"I don't know the words," Evanita cried. "I don't know how to speak like Johnny."

"Hold onto me tightly," Jonara said, "and I'll speak like Johnny. We'll see if we can lift Axon."

Jonara's Words	Translation
Reigino di nau,	Look to me,
Barafa opeifu oshelefa.	Stone of awareness.
Tiugo nui zhuala	Lock my spirit
Di shai Moishiana.	To the Water Ruby.
Shorifo shai aula,	Sense the air,
Shai thelina, dhaku shetoga.	The wind, and snow.
Geleko shai delaifi	Know the trees
Dhaku Elesha.	And Earth.
Pelosho rau di muipa-yufida,	Bridge us to nineteen-forty,
Di teshunu kelifikiou nosha, Akson,	To this discarded man, Axon,
Dhaku di teshunu delaifa.	And to this tree.
Rauko Akson e di felausha.	Lift Axon to life.
Paumubo rau di shai delaifa,	Bind us to the tree,
Shai delaifa yoshu heme,	The tree as one,
Shai delaifa di rauko Akson	The tree to lift Axon
Di felausha.	To life.

Evanita and Jonara reached out to Axon and held his hand fast. The tree fractured a branch and lifted Axon as the two girls pulled. Slowly, Axon elevated to his feet, but his daze prevented his full awareness as to how he'd regained his stance.

"The wolf," he said. "It bit me."

Axon reached back around his coat, touched something slushy-wet, and placed his hand to his tongue.

"Blood," he said. "I'm bleeding."

Jonara spoke again:

Jonara's Words	Translation
Nago dho geliata	Make a crutch
Veletu delaifa mahilu pelikiou.	From tree now broken.
Teshamela til e giro tileshfal.	Juniper it calls itself.
Teshamela til e hautho kail.	Juniper it heals you.

Axon reached toward the ground and pulled the broken branch from the tree. He smelled the freshly broken end and recognized the tree.

"Juniper," he said. "And it's broken in just the right place and height for a crutch. What luck! Or should I thank God? In ancient Greece I would thank the Gods!"

"You can thank the Little Voice!" Evanita said, but Axon could not hear her.

"We must lead him back to the cabin," Jonara said.

Jonara's Words	Translation
Vauriko nuish e botesha,	Follow our path,
Vauriko rau mahilu.	Follow us now.
Vauriko rau	Follow us
Di thauna dhaku zhuda,	To warmth and safety,
Teshanu kail	Though you
Oi lorifa kodi geleko hialu.	Might not know how.

Axon followed Evanita and Jonara, though he did not realize he was following them.

"I'm in shock," Evanita grinned. "I didn't understand a word you said. But it worked. How did you learn all that?"

"I...don't know," Jonara said. "I didn't really learn it. I felt it...from your Water Ruby. I felt like everything was in slow motion. I just started moving my lips, tongue, and jaw, and your Water Ruby gave me incredibly quick feedback. It kept responding 'yes' or 'no' to every little micro-movement I made with my speech. It's hard to explain."

"What did you call your language? What's the name?" Evanita said.

"It's not my language, it's Daddy's...it's Johnny's language. But I'm wondering if he really invented it," Jonara said.

"Maybe he did the same as you and learned it from the stone. Ask the stone what language you were speaking," Evanita said.

"Miramish," Jonara replied.

"Miramish?" Evanita repeated.

"Miramish, Miramish, Miramish," Jonara repeated out of fun, but she fell to the ground immediately and held her hands over her ears.

"What's wrong? What's happening?" Evanita asked.

"I hear...everywhere...a billion voices...thousands of languages...everywhere, Mommy, everywhere!" Jonara cried. "Shh, shhhh!"

"Can't you stop it?" Evanita said. "Stop it, Little Voice!"

"They won't stop!" Jonara said.

Progress to the cabin halted. Axon seemed confused—he didn't realize he had stopped because of the two girls. He circled around and tripped over his oil lamp, picked it up, felt around for his ax, and retrieved it.

"Miramish, Miramish, Miramish," Evanita yelled in desperation to mimic Jonara.

Now Evanita heard the billion voices. She fell to the ground with hands over her ears to subdue the pain.

"Now we're together," Evanita said.

"But it didn't stop the voices," Jonara said.

"Maybe if you say something else," Evanita said.

"I can't think with all these voices in my head!" Jonara said. "How can people think with such a racket!"

"Axon!" Fantina called from the cabin. "Can you hear me?"

"I hear you!" Axon said.

"Can you walk?" she asked. "Can you walk to the cabin?"

"Yes, yes!" Axon yelled with glee.

"Follow my voice," Fantina said. "Follow my voice to the cabin."

Axon left the two girls at the site where the wolf first attacked.

"He's going back. We have to follow him," Evanita said.

Jonara spoke:

Jonara's Words	Translation
Vauriko Fantinanga thaipa	Follow Fantina's voice
Dhaku mau mishei.	And no other.
Vauriko Fantinanga thaipa	Follow Fantina's voice
Dhaku zhoifo mishi.	And silence others!

The voices stopped. Evanita and Jonara stood up and re-moved their hands from their ears—relieved they could think again.

"Let's get back in the cabin!" Evanita said.

While Evanita and Jonara walked back to the cabin, they realized something about Johnny.

"I still can't believe these are Daddy's grandparents," Jonara said.

"It means our Carreña ancestors are from the same city as Johnny's—they may have even known each other," Evanita said. "Oh my god, I can't believe what I just said. Suddenly the world seems much smaller. Johnny is a Jew? And yet he's a Baptist. But he's smart, and he has strong facial features. He does look Jewish. And here I can't decide what religion to be—I thought I was confused. Johnny is a Christian-Jew. Is that pos-sible?"

"It's like he's caught between two religions," Jonara said.

"He's in a religious sandwich, that's for sure," Evanita said. "But it's like Samouel and Fantina—they're caught between Greeks and Romanians."

"Wow, I never thought of that," Jonara said.

"Or like my life in the Elrod 402," Evanita said. "Caught be-tween Oxia and Macron, between old Mac-Two and old Mac-Three. Is this what life is all about? It's a horrible trap."

Evanita and Jonara left the cold winter to their backs and entered the warm cabin where they rejoined Fantina, Axon, and Samouel.

"Where did you go?" Fantina asked as Axon returned inside the cabin.

"I went to get the batteries," he said while Fantina helped him with the lamp, the hatchet, and his coat.

"O dear!" Fantina said. "You have been attacked!"

"Let me see," Samouel said as he walked over. "Yes—a wolf."

"That I know," Axon said.

"Those are deep wounds," Samouel said. "And we don't have any sulfa."

"I must clean those," said Fantina, "and bandage them as best I can. Father, you should have told him where to find the radio batteries."

"I did," Samouel protested. "I told him where to find the batteries—in the tack room."

"Did you tell him the tack room is in the forest?" Fantina asked without expecting an answer.

Fantina started cleaning Axon's wolf wounds.

"I told him to go in the barn and to the right is the tack room where he will find the batteries. I never told him to go into the forest," Samouel said.

"Don't blame Samouel," Axon said. "I did go into the tack room, but I couldn't carry the batteries with my bad foot. I looked for a crutch, or something I could make into a crutch. Ow, that stings!"

"Good. I'm glad Father's alcohol is cleaning your soul. But you should have come right back in and had Father build you a crutch," Fantina explained.

Axon fell silent.

"He's a man and a soldier. He doesn't ask for that kind of help," Samouel said. "It's the code."

"Well it's the silliest code I've ever heard," Fantina said.

"I did find a crutch," Axon said. "It's made of juniper."

"Impressive," Samouel said. "There isn't a juniper tree anywhere close by. You must have hiked quite a ways."

"Stupid," Fantina said.

"Actually, I was running to get the wolf off my back," Axon grinned. "Ow! Don't pour so much in the wound."

"You need more than that to clean yourself up, and I'm not talking about your wound. You should be dead—if not from the wolf then from the cold. You would be frozen until spring—with my fresh cooking still in your stomach. What a waste! And I mean my cooking!"

"Ow!" Axon said.

"Don't be such a baby!" Fantina said.

"Your bedside manners, Miss Karrano, make me wonder if I should make friends with the wolf again," Axon grinned.

"Oh, you shouldn't joke with Fantina about death," Samouel said. "She takes death seriously."

"As a soldier, I have to joke about it. People die every day. How else is a man supposed to carry on?" Axon said. "Ow!"

"Well I'm proud to say I'm not an unfeeling man," Fantina said. "I am a woman and in touch with my feelings. Death is a horrible tragedy, and we should be more careful with life. It's a gift from God."

"Ow!" Axon said again. "Aren't you done yet?"

"Yes, I'm done," Fantina said, and she put the cleaning tools away.

"I better get those batteries now," Axon said.

"Don't bother. I carried them in and attached them to the radio," Fantina said.

Fantina walked over to the radio and turned it on.

"See?"

The tuning indicator lit up, and music filled the room.

"Oh, what about news?" Axon asked.

"You've had enough excitement for one day," Fantina said.

"Be careful, Axon," Samouel said. "She'll order you to bed early if you don't behave."

"I'm a proud soldier. I won't have a woman order me around," Axon said.

"You will in my house!" Fantina said, who turned to Samouel and said, "The one who works the house is in charge of the house."

Samouel's eyes opened widely. He opened his mouth to say something, but she shot him a gaze, and he fell silent with a smirk.

"Now if you're done making a fool of yourself, Mr. Dendritous, see if you can stand up and walk over here," Fantina said.

"Why?" Axon asked.

"Because if you're strong enough to go running around the woods, you're strong enough to do as I say and walk over here," Fantina said.

"I'm beginning to like her," Evanita said.

"She sure does have Axon hopping. Look at him now," Jonara said.

Axon stood and crutched his way over to Fantina, who stood in the middle of an open area near the fireplace's hearth.

"Stop right there," Fantina said.

Fantina walked over to Axon and faced him.

"How is your foot? Does it hurt?" she asked.

"It's better. Strange, it hurt quite a bit before," he said.

"Now how does it feel?" she asked, and she stamped her heel toward Axon's bad foot, but he pulled back before she could land the heel.

"What was that for?" Axon asked.

"I'm checking your reflexes," she said.

"They work very well, thank you," Axon said.

"You're welcome," she said. "Do you like the music?"

"It's a little slow," he said. "I like marching music."

"You would, wouldn't you?" she asked.

"Yes, I would. Now can you please explain why you have me standing here?" Axon asked.

"I want you to think about this music. Slow your mind down to this music. It's good for you. Think about—" Fantina said.

"I can't. I'm still thinking about the wolf. I can't relax," Axon said.

"You need to learn how to relax," she said. "Think about the music."

"No," Axon said.

"That's an order, soldier," Fantina said.

Fantina forced Axon's hand to her waist and took his other hand into her hand. The crutch fell to the floor, and Fantina kicked it to the side.

"I need that crutch," he said.

"Learn to work with me," Fantina said. "Work with me. Dance."

Axon attempted a quick dance.

"No, no, no!" she said. "This isn't a beehive. Slow dance."

"What?" Axon asked.

"Slow dance! Haven't you ever slow danced a woman?" Fantina asked.

"Yes, but in a tavern. Not after dealing with a wolf," he said.

"Forget the wolf. Hold me close, close your eyes, and concentrate on the music. Lead me in a slow dance," Fantina ordered.

Axon complied, but he was stiff and shaky from the wolf-induced adrenaline in his system.

"I'm not a wolf, and I won't bite you," she said.

"Why don't you leave the lad be?" Samouel said.

"Go to bed, Father," Fantina ordered.

"See what I mean? She orders you to bed when the evening grows on and you don't behave for her. I'll never understand why she suddenly lights up in the evening when the day is over," Samouel said.

"Go to bed, Father. You know where your room is," Fantina ordered.

"I'm going, I'm going," Samouel said as he entered his room. Before he closed the door, he said, "But remember—Axon isn't kosher!"

Samouel shut his bedroom door quickly but only just in time to avoid being hit by a small couch pillow Fantina threw in his direction.

"You should show more respect to your father," Axon said.

"You should listen to me and respect the woman of the house," she said.

"But I—" Axon started.

"Shhh. Respect the music. Respect the dance. Respect me," Fantina said.

The two danced throughout the song. As the song finished, Axon's leg grew fatigued and would no longer support his weight. He limped and dragged the last few dance steps, and Fantina realized he had danced enough.

"Don't fall down," she said as Axon started to lose his balance. "Sit here at the table. There, that's better. Would you like some more wine, Axon?"

"Yes, please," Axon said.

Fantina disappeared into the kitchen and reappeared with a picnic basket.

"What is this?" Axon asked.

"I have a special treat for you," Fantina said. "First, let me get the essentials."

From the basket, Fantina removed two wine glasses, two plates, a small platter of crackers, and cheese. She set one glass and plate for Axon and another for herself.

"This is wine?" Axon asked.

"No, silly. These are snacks to eat with your wine," Fantina said. "Now pay attention. When my grandfather dug the cellar for this house, he found an ancient catacomb."

"You mean this cabin is built on a grave?" Axon asked.

"We're not sure," Fantina said. "No one found remains in the catacomb. But we did find other things—ancient armor, swords, and pottery. And we found something else—this!"

"It's an ancient wine bottle. But it's covered with something crusty," Axon said.

"This bottle is at least two thousand years old," Fantina said. "And it's from the island of Lesbos."

"Lesbian wine," Axon said.

"And not just any kind of Lesbian wine. This is Pramnian," Fantina said.

"It is said that Pramnian wine was the sweetest and most delicious wine of the ancient world, like nectar or honey," Axon said.

"We saved this for years," Fantina said, "and since I am the owner of the house, the wine is mine. I waited for a special occasion, but now with war all around us, there's no telling what day will be our last."

"Do not speak like that," Axon said. "We Greeks are very passionate about our country."

"Passion may not be enough," Fantina said.

"We are beating the Italians," said Axon. "We are driving them back. This battle in Pindus is the turning point. I feel victory."

Fantina opened the bottle. Immediately, the room filled with a wholesome country freshness of new life.

"I haven't smelled that aroma since...since...I can't remember. When I still believed in the world," Axon said. "It's like—"

"Like returning to the ancient days when the world was Greek. Alexander the Great. Zeus and Mount Olympus. Ambrosia," Fantina said.

Fantina poured the Pramnian wine into Axon's glass and then hers.

"Taste it," Fantina said.

"We will taste at the same time," Axon said.

Fantina and Axon sipped their Pramnian wine at the same time.

"Is this wine?" Axon said. "It truly is like nectar. Better than honey. It sustains a man, like meat or bread. This is a drink for the Gods."

"Does this wine surprise you?" Fantina asked.

"I knew that Greece has harvested grapes for thousands of years. But never did I know such excellent grapes existed on these shores to produce such wine nectar. I could taste the country and land with your wine, but with this wine I can taste the ancient philosophers, the Athenian Navy, and the Spartans. Such greatness."

"It saddens me," Fantina said.

"Oh but why? How can one be sad with such great Pramnian wine?"

"It is like tasting the death of a great people. Oh how would it be to live in ancient Greece, rulers of the Mediterranean world? Now we are trapped between two armies, ready to crush us."

"Two armies? The Italians are but one," Axon said.

"I have heard a rumor," Fantina said, "that Hitler is upset with the Italians, that he had planned to invade Greece at his convenience, but Mussolini had his own ego to defend and invaded Greece to show up Hitler."

"Mussolini is a fool!" Axon said. "His army is being defeated as we speak."

"But you know what Hitler's response will be, don't you?" Fantina asked.

"Invade Italy?" Axon joked.

"It's no joke. Hitler will invade Greece and do what Italy could not. And that will be the final end for Greece, won't it?" Fantina asked.

"I don't like that kind of talk," Axon said. "Are you a patriot or not? Your family is from Spain. What Greek roots can you possibly have?"

"Did you not pay attention earlier? My great-grandfather fought for Greece in the Greek War of Independence. I and my family are as much Greek patriots as you," Fantina said. "But reality is harsh. The Pindus Mountains are a layer of protection from main Greece in this battle, but what about the next? Hitler may decide to attack from a different direction."

The two drank their Pramnian wine and ate snacks.

"I worry too much," Fantina said. "But I have a layer of protection that has helped me over the years. And I would like you to have it. It is this."

Fantina produced a codex book from the picnic basket.

"What is it?" Axon asked.

"This is a Tanakh—a collection of Jewish books that resemble many of your Old Testament books in your Bible. Do not confuse it with the Torah—the Books of Moses. It is not. But it contains many stories of people in the ancient world who had struggles just as we do today. When you're tired, the day is bad, and you need something to help you sleep, open this Tanakh. It is translated into our native Greek language, so you do not need to learn Hebrew. Read, Axon, and you will sleep at night."

"I accept your gift," Axon said. "And I thank you."

"You are welcome," Fantina said.

"You realize I must return to battle soon," Axon said.

"But not tonight!" Fantina said.

"No, not tonight. But I should leave in a day or two. Tomorrow is Christmas, and begging your hospitality I will stay here," Axon explained.

"Of course you are welcome here," Fantina said. "But I will miss you, Axon. You will remember me, won't you?"

"Yes, of course," Axon said. "Tell me about your name."

"My name?" Fantina asked.

"Yes. It's beautiful, and I want to know how you came by it."

"My mother named me after *Fantina Likiraou*," Fantina said.

"Spring of the Lady," Axon said.

"It's a spring in the forest of Kioyrista, just above Samarina," Fantina said.

"I've heard of this spring. Some of my men say anyone who drinks the water will fall in love with a beautiful fairy with a pure heart," Axon said.

"I've never heard that one!" Fantina said. "One of your men must tell wild stories of the most untruthful nature."

"After meeting you," Axon said, "I think he might be right."

Axon stood up, walked around the table, and sat next to Fantina.

"You are a Greek goddess," he said quietly, and he kissed her.

Fantina returned the kiss. The two wrapped their arms around each other. The room dimmed into gray and darkness. Suddenly, the room went awash in bright light such that nothing else could be seen.

2006 Nov 22, Wed Eve. In the Cafederijet's Recovery Room.

"Your pupils are both normal," Baria said. "You may go now. Ox-Two and Mac-Two will escort you back to Redjet. You are to rest in your room for the day's remainder. Call for help if you have a headache, nausea, or dizziness. Ox-Two—tell Calico to check Eve Carson's pupils periodically. If either one dilates, bring Eve back here immediately. Those are the orders of Dr. Baria, Chief Medical Officer of Elrod 402."

"Yes, ma'am," Evanita and Ox-Two said simultaneously.

Evanita exited Cafederijet with a bandage over her head, and she walked along the grounds toward Redjet. A crowd of inmates gathered around the Helrod in the center of the campus. The sun had set, but campus lights illuminated the activity.

"Something's happening," Ox-Two said. "Mac-Two—take Eve Carson back to her room. I need to assist."

Ox-Two raced toward the crowd of women.

"C'mon," Mac-Two said as she pointed toward the crowd of women. "Let's go see."

The two walked to the crowd of women and managed to squirm through an opening where they saw the German and Russian girls attacking Calico.

"You girls ain't no match for the Calico," Calico said.

The German girl swung at Calico's face. Calico allowed the girl's fist to land. Calico's jaw held firm and reverberated the impact back into the German girl's fist. The German girl whipped her hand in the free air as if she were ridding something from the fingers. Calico grabbed the German girl by the arms and shoved her into one corner of the Helrod.

"Okay, Ruskie, you're next!" Calico said.

"Why aren't the security guards stopping it?" Evanita asked Mac-Two.

"Shh," Mac-Two replied.

As Evanita observed, the four Oxians in attendance did nothing to stop the fight. They did, however, maintain crowd control.

"I know Systema," said the Russian girl as she jumped in place, preparing to attack.

"I don't care what you know," Calico said, preparing to defend herself.

"It is Russian martial arts," the Russian girl said. "I show you."

The Russian moved in toward Calico and kicked in the side of Calico's knee. Calico fell on that knee, but she caught the Russian as the Russian went for Calico's neck. Calico vaulted the Russian over her head and onto the middle section of the Helrod. The Russian dangled on the pole for a few seconds before falling to the ground. The German girl came back at Calico with a shovel.

"Oh you want more, do you?" Calico asked.

The German swung the shovel at Calico's head, but Calico grabbed the end of the shovel, yanked it from the German, and poked her in the abdomen. The German fell backward.

"That'll teach you," Calico said. "Anyone else want to shirk off their work duties? 'Cause today I'm the complaint department! Who has a complaint?"

"I do," the Russian girl said again.

She used Systema against Calico's wrist, arm, and shoulder, and in this way twisted the arm behind Calico such that Calico fell to the ground. Calico lost grip of the shovel and turned her attention to the Russian.

"You're pissing me off now," said Calico. "And you'd better let go if you want mercy from me."

"Not until you apologize," the Russian said.

"Calico ain't apologizing to nobody no way," Calico said.

Calico spun around and whipped the Russian girl against a Helrod corner post while the German girl picked up the shovel. The German came at Calico from behind with the shovel and used it to choke Calico.

"That's no good," gagged Calico. "If you can't kill me, I'll come back the stronger."

But Calico didn't react quickly enough. Temporarily immobilized by the German girl, the Russian employed her Systema training and kicked Calico at strategic weak points—the elbows, knees, kidneys, and groin. Calico fell to the ground in a prone position. The German and Russian systematically kicked Calico. Calico waved her arms around to catch one of the legs, but just as she reached for a kicking leg, another diverted her attention.

"Come on, Calico, pick yourself up," yelled one of the girls.

"Calico, come on!" yelled another.

The girls watching the event chanted and stomped, "Cal-i-co, Cal-i-co."

The vibrations triggered the Moissan Ruby around Evanita's neck, and Evanita sensed pain and internal bleeding with Calico.

"They'll kill Calico!" Evanita blurted.

"Don't interfere," Mac-Two said. "It would be worse than grousing on someone."

"Grousing?"

"C'mon, Eve," Mac-Two said. "Complaining, ratting, squealing, tattle-telling."

"I don't like seeing anyone getting hurt!" Evanita said.

The girls' chanting increased, and along with it so did Evanita's perception of Calico's internal injuries being sustained. Then the girls' chanting broke up into millions upon billions of voices. Evanita clasped her hands against her ears. She went hoarse and struggled to say something as simple as, "Stop chanting."

"Help," Evanita gasped, but only Jonara heard.

"I'm here, Mommy," Jonara said.

Jonara hugged her mother from behind. The Moissan Ruby around Evanita's neck reacted to the chanting and the diary in Jonara's possession, forcing the two back in time yet again.

1941 Mar 21, Fri. Samarina, Pindus Mountains, Greece.

"The sun will set soon, Father," Fantina said as she and her father stared out the living room window.

"And *Shabbat* will begin," Samouel said.

"We're back in that cabin," Jonara said.

"Yes," Evanita said. "Johnny's Grandma Fantina and Great-Grandpa Samouel are here, but Axon isn't."

"Where did he go?" Jonara asked.

"Probably back to war like he said," Evanita said.

"He better not die!" Jonara said. "Daddy hasn't been born yet!"

"Maybe your Great-Grandma Fantina knows," Evanita said. "She might say something. Let's listen."

"Twenty minutes before the sun sets," Fantina said.

"You have two minutes to prepare," Samouel said.

Fantina left the living room for the kitchen. Samouel knew the routine. He sat down to the dining room table and awaited the preparations. Fantina reappeared quickly with a tray. She placed the tray on the table and began setting the table.

"Two candles for two commandments to remember and observe Shabbat," Fantina said as she placed items on the table. "A bottle of wine for Kiddush, two Kiddush cups with saucers, bowls for washing to make us clean, clean water for a clean wash, and two loaves of Challah for the two portions of manna God gave our people in the desert. Oh yes, plates for the Challah."

Fantina kept the Challah covered with a cloth. She returned the empty tray to the kitchen and reappeared with matches.

"It is time," Samouel said.

Fantina placed two candles on the dining table. She lit both and said the following prayer:

With these candles
We pray to God
The God of our fathers
Abraham, Isaac, and Jacob
To grant us good life and health
To all my dear ones
And the whole world.
With these candles
We pray to God
The God of our mothers
Sarah, Rebecca, Leah, and Rachel
To grant us good life and health
To all my dear ones
And the whole world.

Fantina opened the bottle and poured wine in her father's Kiddush cup until it overflowed slightly. They laughed. She filled her Kiddush cup in the same manner such that the wine overflowed. They laughed again, but their laughter fell into a brief silence followed by prayer.

There was evening and there was morning.

The sixth day. Heaven and Earth and all their host were completed. On the seventh day, God completed the work He had been doing, and He rested on the seventh day from all the work He had done. God blessed the seventh day and called it holy, because on it God rested from all the work of creating He had done.

Attention, father!

Blessed are You, Lord our God, King of the Universe, who creates the fruit of the vine.

Blessed are You, Lord our God, King of the Universe, who made us holy through His commandments. In His love and favor He has given us His holy Shabbat, as a memorial of creation. For it is the first name of sacred days, a reminder of the Exodus from Egypt. For You have chosen us apart from all nations and in loving favor have begifted us Your holy Shabbat. Blessed are You, Lord our God, who makes Shabbat holy.

(Fantina and Samouel washed their hands in small bowls.)

Blessed are You, Lord our God, who begifted us holiness through His commandments and the commandment for washing of hands.

(Fantina removed the cloth and cut a slice of Challah bread for each of them.)

Blessed are You, Lord our God, who begifts us bread of this earth.

"Shabbat Shalom!" Fantina and Samouel said at the same time, and they laughed.

Fantina and Samouel ate the Challah and drank their wine. Fantina left the dining room and returned with different foods on the tray—apricot chicken, boiled carrots, fruit salad with beans, potatoes, olives, and stuffed vine leaves.

"It amazes me how much food you cook for Shabbat," Samouel said.

"God has blessed this cabin and our farm. He feeds us well," Fantina said.

"My daughter feeds me well too!" Samouel said.

The two helped themselves to dinner.

"Mmmm, looks good," Jonara said.

"Just looking at the food makes me hungry," Evanita said to Jonara.

"Can you smell the chicken?" Jonara said. "What makes it smell so good?"

"Yes, I can smell the chicken, and I think the apricot gives it that wonderful aroma," Evanita said. "I wish Mama had told me about Sabbath dinners—I would have insisted we visit every Jewish household in the neighborhood for a bite to eat."

"Do you think she knows?" Jonara asked.

"Probably not. She grew up part Baptist and part Catholic before she fled to the Unitarians," Evanita said.

"What do Catholics eat on Fridays?" Jonara asked.

"Grandma Geneva told me once. During Lent, it's fish only— no regular meat. Otherwise, there's no special menu. In the old days before Vatican II, it was fish every Friday," Evanita said. "Catholics were supposed to make a sacrifice."

"I like the Jewish way better," Jonara said. "I can practically taste the chicken."

"The Challah smells good too. I wonder if these visions of the past will let me sneak a peek at the recipe," Evanita wondered.

Jonara and Evanita giggled.

"I must savor every bite," Samouel said. "I want to remember what your good cooking tastes like."

"What strange talk!" Fantina said. "You sound like someone who is preparing for a journey."

Samouel said nothing.

"Are you leaving me, Father?" Fantina asked.

Samouel nodded with a small, "Yes."

"Whatever for? Are you ill? You should tell me if you need anything. You know I'll make the journey down the mountain for you—food, medicine, anything," Fantina offered.

"It's not that," Samouel said.

"Then what?" Fantina asked.

"It's the world we live in, or what it has become," Samouel said.

"You mean the war?" Fantina said.

"Yes, the war," Samouel said.

"Greece is holding off the Italians," Fantina said. "We've heard this news on the radio—"

"The last Greek victory was on January 10th of this year. That was over two month ago," Samouel said. "The situation is a stalemate."

"I still don't understand. Why must you leave? Our home is safer than most places. We can hide in the catacomb if we must," Fantina said.

"Fantina, let me explain something to you. Our Jewish brothers and sisters have been persecuted ever since the days of Pharaoh in Egypt," Samouel said. "And the question always remains—what as a diaspora do we do about it?"

"We flee and hide, just as our family did during the Spanish Expulsion of 1492," Fantina said. "We do not need to announce our faith to other people. Only God need know."

"But if we hide, Fantina, what becomes of our Jewish neighbors? Do we let them die at the hands of Gentiles? What would Moses do?" Samouel asked.

"Moses led our people out of Egypt. He fled," Fantina said.

"He led, not fled. Anything else is distortion, and I won't hear of it in this house," Samouel said. "Or have you forgotten your Torah?"

"No Father, I have not forgotten," Fantina said.

"Moses didn't run or hide—you know that. I'm surprised you are saying such a thing. He made his demands known to Pharaoh to release our people. And each time the Pharaoh denied Moses, God sent forth a plague—ten plagues in all," Samouel said.

"But Moses did flee, Father. Before the Ten Commandments and before the plagues, he fled after killing an Egyptian slave," Fantina said.

"Just as our family fled in 1492," Samouel said.

"But our family did nothing wrong," Fantina said.

"Except live in a country when Jews were no longer welcome," Samouel said. "Jews are welcome in Greece—for the moment. But Hitler is moving his eye this way. He is sending troops to Greece—I know he is. He will rip this country apart of our Jewish neighbors as he did with Poland."

"Father, what are you saying?" Fantina asked.

"I have prayed to God about this for many months," Samouel said. "And the answer is always the same—I must do what I can to send ten plagues on the enemy—for the sake of Jews and Greeks. I'm leaving for the army tomorrow."

"What?! You can't leave tomorrow! It's Shabbat! And you're eighty years old! Father, what good can you do?"

Samouel stood up, walked over to Fantina, and hugged her.

"My dear child, I have had a full and peaceful life. What more can a man ask? Our ancestors paid for our freedom, our neighbors are paying for our freedom, and look at me—I pay nothing! I must go and do what I can."

"But Father, you could die!" Fantina said.

"I am at the end of my life," Samouel said. "I cannot sit in this cabin and waste away any longer. I must give back to God."

"But the farm—I can't run it alone—what will I do? I will be lonely," Fantina said.

"You already run the farm," Samouel said. "I do nothing but eat, drink, and sleep. Your animals will keep you company, as will your flowers."

"Father!" Fantina protested.

"Do you continue to receive letters from Axon?" Samouel asked.

"You know I do," Fantina said.

"Yes. He is fighting on the Albanian border," Samouel said. "Soon I will join him in combat. And soon, I wish you to join him in marriage."

"What!? I can't believe what you're saying! You protested against Axon, that he's not kosher!" Fantina said.

"Yes, he is not kosher, but he is a righteous Gentile. It is permitted—provided he honors our ways," Samouel said.

"And the way you are leaving, Father, on Shabbat! That's not kosher either!" Fantina said.

"I'm afraid there will be nothing left that is kosher if we do not send our ten plagues against the evil of Hitler and Mussolini," Samouel said. "General Francisco Franco is no better. Rumor is he met with Hitler in October last year to negotiate for Gibraltar and North Africa. Even Hitler backed away from Franco. No, Fantina, my kosher life is ending—either as I fight to defend our faith, or through old age. Your ability to create new kosher life is also fading—either because I have isolated you in these mountains, or again because evil armies wish to destroy us. We cannot flee any longer, Fantina. It will only delay the inevitable. Disease flourishes in the hearts of greedy men."

"Then I want to come with you. I want to help fight," Fantina said.

"But if you die now, who will make the nursery of tomorrow? Who will renew what is kosher once the German swine have sown their stench? No. Let Axon know I have given my blessing, and marry him. Start a family. If things go ill, find a way to survive. Leave Greece if you must. I know, I know, I said this is not the time to flee. It is not the time to flee for me, but it is the time for you to build a new life. Your future will have its ten plagues. Mine is now."

"I don't know if I can let go of you, Father," Fantina said. "I love you so much."

"You must move on with your life, Fantina. You are the lady of the spring. You will bring clear, kosher water from the mountain and feed God's crops," Samouel said. "Marry Axon, Fantina. Marry Axon."

Fantina paused. Samouel returned to his seat at the table, ate some Challah, and drank wine. The two ate in silence for ten minutes. Finally, Fantina spoke.

"I will marry Axon," Fantina said.

"Good, my child," Samouel said.

"And you better be alive to accompany me to the *chuppah* (wedding canopy)!" Fantina said.

"I wouldn't think otherwise," Samouel said.

The light faded. Evanita and Jonara floated in the air above northern Greece. The world turned to gray, and the sun circled around the earth quickly. Time passed. While the Greek Army held off the Italians along the Albanian border, Germans invaded Yugoslavia on April 6, 1941 and plowed through into northern Greece on April 13. The Greek Army—being outflanked by Italian troops from Albania and German troops from Yugoslavia—withdrew to the Pindus Mountains. Evanita and Jonara fell back to Earth on top of Fantina's cabin.

1941 Apr 13, Sun. Samarina, Pindus Mountains, Greece.

Alerted by artillery fire, Fantina watched many soldiers from the Greek Army retreat along a path a stone's throw from her cabin. The soldiers looked tired and defeated. Fantina, in a risky move, hurried from her cabin to the path with a large basket of food. She offered this food and water from a nearby well to any who would take it. The men took her provisions and ordered her back to her cabin, citing the impending arrival of Italians and Germans.

Fantina lingered by the path. She felt her stomach fall to her feet, and she did not want to go back. The thought of Italians and Germans overtaking her Greece depressed her. She looked desperately for Axon and her father, but she saw neither. The day grew late.

Without warning, the line of soldiers stopped retreating. They pitched camp for the night where they stood. Fantina begged to help the wounded. A commander, after much badgering from Fantina, gave in to her risky request and ordered five of the wounded be taken to Fantina's cabin for treatment and rest. Fantina led the way up the hill to her cabin. No truck could drive up the hill, meaning the wounded would have to be walked or carried up the hill. Attempts to move two of the wounded up the hill nearly ended in disaster as unsteady earth caused the helper soldiers to lose footing and fall, dropping the wounded onto the ground. The commanding officer was ready to recall all wounded from Fantina's care, but she badgered him again. After seeing two of the wounded fall on rocks, the third of the five wounded refused to go up, leaving just two wounded men to visit Fantina's cabin. These two could not refuse, as they were unconscious. They lay on stretchers with blankets atop them to keep them warm and out of shock.

Fantina advised the helper men as to which rocks to avoid and what steps to take. They followed her to her cabin. Fantina opened the front door. She instructed one of the wounded be placed on the couch, and the other be placed on the very bed in the dining room where Axon once stayed. The helpers left the cabin and returned to their company.

Fantina stoked the fire and filled several pots with water to get them aboiling. She pulled the blanket up from one of the soldiers and cleaned the filth and blood from the man's face. As she cleaned the face, a horror filled her eyes—the soldier's face became that of Axon!

"Axon, Axon!" Fantina cried, but Axon remained motionless.

Fantina ran into the barn and grabbed a jar of pungent herbs. She returned to the cabin, opened the jar, and smeared the herbs between Axon's upper lip and nose. Axon's eyes opened quickly, and his face grimaced from the fumes.

"Fantina!" he said. "Here I am as before."

"Almost!" she said. "Last time you crashed into my home from the mountain slope above. Today you were carried to my home from a path below by your own men."

"Your father," Axon said. "He..."

"Where is my father?" Fantina asked. "Is he safe? Is he well?"

"He is deeply wounded," Axon said. "He took a mortar for me and saved my life. I have a few wounds that need stitching, and I lost some blood, but my wounds are clean. He has mortar fragments in his wounds, Fantina. He may not survive the night."

"I ask again, Axon. Where is he?" Fantina asked.

Then Fantina understood.

"Is it, is it?" she asked.

"He was with us on one of the stretchers," Axon said.

Fantina ran to the other covered soldier, whipped up the blanket, and saw another filthy, blood-encrusted face. She wiped away the dirt and blood and to her horror (again) she revealed Samouel's face.

"Father, Father, Father!" she said.

She began hugging him in excitement, but something shifted in his form that shouldn't have, and she felt horrible as if she'd just stepped on him.

"Be very careful," Axon warned. "Your father has broken ribs and legs."

The water boiled over in the pots. Fantina didn't notice. She was too obsessed with her father's condition to notice.

"Fantina," Axon said. "The pots are boiling over. I would get them, but I'll bleed. Fantina!"

Axon's voice broke Fantina from her spell.

"He will need stitches too. And he will need a splint," Axon said. "Fantina, if you sew me up first, maybe I can help."

"You're in no condition to do anything," Fantina said. "You're pale from lack of blood. Stay there and rest."

Fantina lifted the blanket fully from her father and saw several large bloodstained bandages. Fantina started to shriek, but she bit her hand to soothe her nerves.

"Can we help them?" Evanita asked Jonara.

"How?" Jonara asked.

"That language you spoke when the wolf attacked. Can you say something again?"

"Yeah, but...the voices...the billion voices...they might come back," Jonara said.

"If we could just give Fantina the knowledge of what to do," Evanita said.

"But we don't know what to do," Jonara said.

"The stone knows," Evanita said. "It always knows. We have to get the stone to contact Fantina. Can you use that language, Little Voice, and help Fantina?"

"I'll hug you from behind," Jonara said, "and you hug Fantina."

"Okay," Evanita said.

Jonara did as she said—she hugged Evanita from behind, and Evanita in turn hugged Fantina as Jonara said the following:

Jonara's Words	Translation
Moishiana boshu rau mahilu,	Water Ruby with us now,
Paumubo di Fantina,	Bind to Fantina,
Feifo shan e hialu	Show her how
Di liapo shash e votetanga inoina,	To read her father's injury,
Zhau sha ferepa kodi zhuveto	So she can succeed
Ishu mofita.	In surgery.

As Jonara spoke the words, Evanita felt a solid connection form between her arms and Fantina's abdomen. Warm energy flowed from the Moissan Ruby through Evanita's arms and around Fantina's waist. Fantina did not realize she was being hugged, but she felt this warmth and gained the strength and resolve to care for her father's injuries.

"I will tend to my father," Fantina said.

She returned to the pots and removed them from the fire. Evanita and Jonara continued the hug chain around Fantina, but each time Fantina walked or ran somewhere in the cabin, she dragged Evanita and Jonara with her.

"The water is too hot," Axon said. "It will scald your father if you use it like that."

"I know," Fantina said. "I must cool it. And it needs salt."

Fantina threw a pinch of salt into one of the pots. She then took an empty pot in one hand, the full pot in the other, and poured from the full to the empty. She poured the water back and forth like this to cool the water in the air without adding cold, unsterilized water to the mix. Once Fantina felt the water was just right, she took the full and empty pots and placed them on a short stool next to her father. She went to the kitchen and found a baster bulb. She brought that and the other boiled pot, threw a pinch of salt in that pot, and took these items to the stool next to her father. She went back to the kitchen where she found a sewing kit and back to her father's side where she placed the sewing kit on the floor.

"What will you use to sew him up?" Axon asked. "You can't use sewing thread. It will cause infection. You need catgut."

"I know," Fantina said. "And this is the hardest part. We don't have prepared sheep or goat intestine I can use to make catgut."

"What will you do, Fantina?" Axon asked.

Fantina froze in thought.

"We must help her again, Little Voice," Evanita said. "We're still hugging her, but she can't think. Give her encouragement!"

Jonara's Words	Translation
Giaula, giaula, berugao feliniu,	Fire, fire, burning bright,
Gailo Fantina thulo shai feluana.	Help Fantina see the light.
Shupo dho dolita	Find a thread
Sha ferepa kodi beriako,	She can use,
Di gereto dho gerulika	To close a wound
Zhau til e faboteio.	So it will fuse.

"I know what I must do," Fantina said to Axon.

Fantina walked to a tall cabinet, opened a door, and pulled out a case.

"Not again!" Jonara said.

"I wonder what's inside?" Evanita asked.

"I'm guessing another musical instrument," Jonara said.

But Jonara was wrong. Fantina placed the case on the table, opened it, and pulled out a heavy scroll.

"This is the family Torah," Fantina said. "Our most prized possession. It has been with us for hundreds of years. We only open it on very special occasions."

"Spells and prayers can't help now," Axon said.

"You have such little faith, Axon," Fantina said. "One's devotion to God is all encompassing. He is more than prayer and song. This Torah will save my father's life and yours too. Now rest there and be quiet. I'm going to begin treatment."

Axon opened his mouth to say something, but Fantina pointed a finger at him, and he backed down.

"I'm going to read selected passages from Judges 5. The actual passage is much longer, but I abbreviate it for your benefit,

Axon. I find Judges inspirational in these times. It's about the renewed devotion of two women—Deborah and Jael—and their people to God as they defeat the enemy."

Deborah and Barak son of Abinoam sang on that day, saying:

Praise the Lord for the avenging of Israel,
When the people offer themselves willingly,
Praise the Lord!

In the days of Shamgar son of Anath,
In the days of Jael,
The roads were abandoned;
Travelers took to winding paths.
Village life in Israel ceased,
Ceased until I, Deborah, arose,
I arose a mother in Israel.

Awake, awake, Deborah!
Awake, awake, sing a song!
Arise, Barak!
Take captive your captives,
O son of Abinoam.

The stars fought from the heavens,
They fought against Sisera from their paths.

O my soul, march on in strength!
Then the horses' hooves pounded,
The galloping, galloping of his steeds.

Blessed above women be Jael,
The wife of Heber the Kenite,
Most blessed of tent-dwelling women.
He (Sisera) asked for water,
And she gave him milk;
And brought butter in a noble bowl.
Her hand reached for the tent peg,
Her right hand for the workman's hammer.
She crushed his head with the hammer,
And pierced his temples with the peg.
At her feet he sank, he fell;

He lay still.
At her feet he sank, he fell;
Where he sank, there he fell dead.

So let all your enemies perish, O Lord!
Let them who love you be like the sun
When it rises in its power.
And the land had peace forty years.

"Is this what you will do to us?" Axon asked. "Will you drive a stake through our foreheads?"

"Of course not!" Fantina said. "Now do you see what I have in my hand?"

"Catgut?" Axon asked.

"Yes, catgut. This scroll is sewn with catgut. As I spoke the words, I unfastened a little bit. It's quite strong, and I will replace it when times are better," Fantina said.

Fantina returned the Torah to its case and the case to the cabinet. She walked over to her father with the string and dipped it in the boiling pot.

"There," she said. "Now I have sterilized catgut."

Fantina poured warm saline water into her father's wounds and used the baster to suction out the old blood and filth. She deposited the filth in the empty pot. The Moissan Ruby gave her knowledge on where the mortar fragments lay in her father's body. She took a tool much like needle-nose pliers, dipped it in the boiled water, and one-by-one plunged it into her father's wounds, grasped the mortar fragments, and removed them. She poured more warm saline water into the wounds and suctioned them dry.

Jonara let go of Evanita, and Evanita let go of Fantina. Fantina dipped a curved sewing needle in the hot water and threaded it with the catgut.

"And now, Father," Fantina said, "the very country that injured you will save your life, for this is Roman catgut—the finest catgut string one can buy for a musical instrument. This catgut was part of our Torah musical instrument, an instrument that plays the songs of God. I will play the last song on this string, and it will save your life."

Fantina sewed the wounds, making suture after suture. She completed knotting the sutures and wiped her father's flesh clean.

"Now for your bones," she said. "There's nothing I can do about your rib fracture. But your left leg needs a splint, and I will make one."

Fantina started for the barn leaving Jonara and Evanita behind. Fantina felt light on her feet and increased her gait from a walk to a light run. Moments later, she returned with flat boards, padding material, and straps. She felt for the bone break. It was his shin, she was sure, but how to set it back? Fantina hesitated.

"What's wrong?" Axon asked.

"I'm not sure how to reset the bone," Fantina said.

"We let go too soon," Jonara said.

"You're right. We have to hug her again," Evanita said.

"I'll give her more encouragement," Jonara said.

Jonara's Words	Translation
Kapi kulo tiopu	Hands be nimble
Kapi kulo bereifu,	Hands be light,
Shupo heish e delishi	Find his fractures
Dhaku fepo tiren e dieku.	And set them right.

Fantina felt encouraged. She touched her father's leg. Knowledge of the bone break's nature carried through from the Moissan Ruby to Fantina, and Fantina understood how to reset the bone. She held onto the shin at its ends, and in one quick motion pulled the shin apart slightly and realigned it back together.

The pain must have been incredible for her father, because just as she completed the realignment, her father awoke from unconsciousness in a howling state.

"Shh," Fantina said. "You're home with me, your Fantina. Everything will be fine."

"My leg!" Samouel said. "The pain! I cannot stand it! Give me something for the pain!"

"Do you have any morphine?" Axon asked.

"We don't keep such things in this house," Fantina replied. "This is a righteous house of God, not one of vice."

"Then he's going to suffer," Axon said. "Give him something to bite on."

Fantina removed a short strip of leather from her sewing kit and placed it in Samouel's mouth. He bit, but the pain in his leg was too strong.

"He will stress himself out with the pain," Axon said. "A man can handle stress for only so long before it kills him."

"I must stop his pain!" Fantina said.

"We need another spell," Evanita said. "Something so Fantina can stop the pain."

"This isn't witchcraft," Jonara said. "What do I say?"

"Anything," Evanita said. "Give her the knowledge to relieve her father's pain. Fantina needs help now."

"Okay," Jonara said, and she spoke:

Jonara's Words	Translation
Loivi kiro razhu	Nerves are long
Loivi kiro dinalu	Nerves are thin
Gerutho Fantina shai geleka	Give Fantina the knowledge
Di beliro zhiago ishu shai loikana.	To block pain in the shin.

Again, the Moissan Ruby carried knowledge through Evanita into Fantina. Fantina reached for her thinnest sewing needle, dipped it in boiling water, and inserted it carefully in the back of Samouel's injured leg high on the thigh just below the buttocks. Immediately, Samouel stopped howling, and a serene look took hold of his face. He relaxed.

"Fantina, my daughter! Axon is right—you are both an angel and a goddess!" Samouel said.

"Is the pain gone? I did the best I could," Fantina said.

"You did well, my child. If you could give me something to drink, I would be thankful," Samouel said.

"Yes, of course, of course!" Fantina said.

Fantina secured padding and boards around her father's leg and secured them with straps.

"There, the splint is complete," she said.

Fantina scurried off to the kitchen with Evanita and Jonara dragging around her waist.

"Now can we let go?" Jonara asked.

"What if she needs us again?" Evanita said.

"Then we'll hug her again. But I don't like getting dragged around like this," Jonara said.

"Okay, okay!" Evanita said.

The two let go and fell on the floor again. Fantina returned from the kitchen with goat's milk, cheese, leftover Challah from the day before, and honey. Samouel ate and drank as if he had not been at home for years.

"Mmm, thank you my child," Samouel said.

"What about me?" Axon said. "Do I get my wounds attended to, or do I have to get up and sew myself up?"

"Don't move a muscle," Fantina said. "I will take care of you next."

There was little effort in sewing up Axon. Despite Axon wincing every time Fantina stuck the needle through his flesh, she managed to suture up his open wounds. At one point, she told him to hush up and take it like a man instead of a big, old baby.

"Didn't I warn you she'll order you around if you're not careful?" Samouel said to Axon.

"She seems to think she runs things here," Axon said. "Ouch!"

"You deserve it!" Fantina said after pushing the needle a little deeper than it needed to go.

Soon, Fantina finished suturing up Axon's wounds. She cleaned and put her sewing kit away, washed, and put away the baster and pots.

"I'm hungry!" Axon said. "When do I get something to eat?"

"You just hush up and be patient. I can't do everything at once. Let me finish cleaning up here, and I'll find something. Who do you think I am, your wife?" Fantina asked.

"If you were my wife, you wouldn't let me go hungry for so long," Axon said.

"If I were your wife, I'd make you get your own food," Fantina said. "And if you were my husband, I'd...I'd..."

Fantina stopped. She couldn't finish her sentence.

"Do we need to give her encouragement again?" Jonara asked Evanita.

"No, not this time. Something more powerful than the stone is at work here," Evanita said. "Watch."

Fantina walked over to Axon slowly, knelt by his prone body, and whispered, "If you were my husband, I would do this."

Fantina kissed him softly on the lips. Axon responded by kissing back. He combed his fingers through her beautiful hair, and it felt good. Fantina held her eyes closed, backed away slowly with her head bowed down, turned around, and walked to the kitchen. She emerged with more goats' milk, Challah, cheese, and honey.

"This Challah I dedicated to Shabbat. By our Lord's hands you are now fed," she said.

Axon stared into her eyes as he ate bits and pieces of bread and cheese. He reached for the cup of milk from Fantina's out-stretched hand, but the two locked gazes and didn't realize Axon had no grip on the cup. Fantina released the cup, and it fell to the floor with a splash!

"Oh dear me!" Fantina said.

She cleaned up the mess and returned from the kitchen with more milk.

"I will leave you in peace to eat your fill," she said, and she disappeared into the kitchen.

Evanita and Jonara drifted above the cabin into the grays of the world. War did not wait for the weary. While Axon and Samouel rested in the comfort of Fantina's cabin, the Axis war machine plowed downward from the north, pinching the Greek Army into further retreat. The stars and sun circled around quickly, and when they slowed to a normal pace, two days had passed.

1941 Apr 15, Tue. Fifth Day of Passover. Samarina, Pindus Mountains, Greece.

War did not wait for the weary, but a small part of the Greek Army gathered around Fantina's cabin for a Jewish wedding ceremony. Yes, a Jewish wedding. Fantina and Samouel argued for two days about a Jewish marriage during Passover.

"It's illegal. Definitely not kosher," Samouel said.

"Nor is joining the Greek Army on Shabbat," Fantina replied.

"You must wait until after *Shavuot*," Samouel said.

"That's in June," Fantina replied. "There won't be a Greece in June. Axon could be dead—we could all be dead! There won't be a *kosher* person alive!"

"You'll never find a rabbi to perform the wedding," Samouel said.

"Then Axon and I will elope. We'll run away and get married in his Christian church," Fantina threatened.

"How dare you blaspheme our Jewish heritage!" Samouel said.

"It isn't fair!" Fantina said. "Why must our faith bind our hands when the enemy walks all over us?"

"You must wait," Samouel said.

"You said it earlier, Father. We are trapped in layers. Italy and Germany have trapped us, and now I am trapped between faiths. Is there no means to freedom? Did you wait before joining the Greek Army? And what was your reason? The Ten Plagues, wasn't that it? And you said it was my duty to create that which is *kosher*. Well, I want to create! And respectably. I won't raise a child out of wedlock!"

"You still won't find a rabbi to perform the ceremony. And don't fall into Christian hands. The three demons of Europe— Hitler, Mussolini, and Franco—have or had some sort of Christian affiliation. And how can you forget our family's expulsion from Spain because of a Christian mandate?!" Samouel said.

"I won't become a Christian if I can have a Jewish wedding," Fantina said.

"No rabbi will perform it!" Samouel said.

"But he will if you pay him well enough," Fantina said. "Isn't there one in your unit?"

"Fantina!" Samouel said.

"Father!" Fantina replied.

Samouel shook his head in disbelief and let out a long sigh. He stood eye-to-eye with Fantina for those two days, but she didn't back down. Instead, she tapped her feet nervously and crossed her arms. Fantina let Samouel know time was running out, and she would act if he did not.

Samouel's resolve disintegrated. He brought up the subject to his company's rabbi—Rabbi Evenstein. The rabbi reacted in disgust. Samouel offered money, food, whatever. The rabbi still refused. Finally, Samouel described Fantina's plans to elope and marry in a Christian church. The rabbi reacted in disgust again, but he agreed to perform Fantina's wedding during Passover.

"These are evil times indeed," Rabbi Evenstein said, "but I cannot allow one of our own to stray into dark waters. I will perform the wedding. Moses must be turning in his grave. May the Lord our God have mercy on us all."

The wedding ceremony began. Fantina sat in a chair with no family or friends to accompany her (outside of her father), but two women from the Greek Army stood with her for companionship. Axon stood several yards away with his army friends. Axon's officer stood in as Axon's father figure and toasted to Axon's good health (which was becoming better every minute). Samouel beckoned the officer to come over, and he did. The officer and Samouel stood together (with Samouel on crutches) and broke a plate.

"Marriage is a serious commitment. A broken marriage and a broken plate cannot be repaired," Samouel said.

The officer returned to Axon and his army friends. Rabbi Evenstein stood under the *chuppah* (canopy) and beckoned the *kallah* (bride) and *chatan* (groom) along their paths to the *chuppah*.

"Did I not promise to accompany you on your wedding day?" Samouel said to Fantina as he limped along on crutches.

"Yes you did," Fantina said. "And I am glad."

The bride and groom reached the canopy. Axon entered while Fantina stopped just outside.

"This is goodbye, Father," Fantina said.

"I am losing my little girl," Samouel said with a tear.

Fantina kissed Samouel on the cheek, and he returned to his seat. Axon came out from the *chuppah* and escorted Fantina in. Rabbi Evenstein looked sternly at Axon and glanced at Fantina.

"Axon," Fantina whispered. "Remove your watch."

"What?" Axon asked.

"Jewelry is looked down-upon," Fantina whispered. "Remove your watch and your dog tag. Give them to your army officer."

Axon did as he was told. The officer took Axon's jewelry and gave Axon a new *tallit* (prayer shawl). Axon shrugged his shoulders at Fantina. She rolled her eyes and placed the *tallit* over Axon's head and shoulders.

"Say the blessing like I told you," Fantina whispered into Axon's ear.

"But I'm not a—" Axon said.

"Say it!" Fantina repeated.

"Blessed are you, Lord our God, King of the Universe, who has given us life, sustained us, and brought us to this occasion of joy," Axon said.

Four men removed the *tallit* from Axon and held it above the couple.

Rabbi Evenstein proceeded with the betrothal blessings. After Axon and Fantina recited the blessings, they drank from a cup of wine.

Axon produced a golden ring from his pocket and held it before her.

"Behold!" Axon said. "With this ring, you are betrothed to me, according to the law of Moses and Israel."

Axon slipped the ring onto Fantina's right index finger. Axon and Fantina smiled, as they knew this meant they were officially married.

"Now is the best part," Fantina said. "The *ketubah*—the marriage contract."

"Marriage contract?" Axon said. "What marriage contract?"

"You did not tell him?" the rabbi asked Fantina.

"I did not wish to scare him," Fantina said.

Axon's eyes lit open. In the following *ketubah*, Rabbi Evenstein narrated, Axon read his promise to Fantina, and Fantina read her promise to Axon:

This ketubah witnesses before God, the Jewish community, family and friends, that on the 3rd day of the week, the 18th day of the month of Nisan in the year five thousand seven hundred and one since the creation of the world according to the reckoning which we are accustomed to use here in the city of Samarina in Greece, corresponding to April 15, 1941.

That Axon son of Barton of the family Dendritous said to this maiden Fantina daughter of Samouel of the family Karrano,

"Be my wife according to the law of Moses and Israel, and I will cherish, honor, support, and maintain you in accordance with the custom of Jewish husbands, who cherish, honor, support, and maintain their wives faithfully. I will give you your food, clothing, and necessities according to the law of Moses and Israel, and live with you as husband and wife according to the universal custom."

"Be my husband according to the law of Moses and Israel, and I will cherish and honor you with faithfulness in accordance with the custom of Jewish wives."

The groom and bride have also promised to build a home on openness, trust, respect and integrity, to be sensitive to each other's needs so that they may attain warmth, peace, love, and spiritual fulfillment, guided by Torah values and our Jewish community. May their home and family be bestowed with blessing and peace.

All is valid and binding.

Bride _____   *Groom* _____
Witness _____   *Witness* _____
Rabbi _____

Fantina and Axon signed the *ketubah*. Samouel and Axon's army officers signed as witnesses. Rabbi Evenstein also signed. Fantina held up the *ketubah* with great pride as if she'd won a trophy.

Rabbi Evenstein proceeded with the *Sheva Brachot* (Seven Blessings). Fantina and Axon took more sips of wine from the cup as the rabbi read the blessings. At this point, Fantina felt unsettled. She couldn't place a finger on it, but she had a strange feeling her wedding ceremony wasn't properly Sephardic.

The rabbi completed the *Sheva Brachot* and placed a glass on the floor for Axon. The rabbi pointed at Axon and pointed at the glass.

"Huh?" Axon asked.

"Step on the glass," Fantina whispered.

"What?" Axon asked.

"Step on the glass!" Fantina said much louder.

Axon stepped on the glass and broke it. Those in attendance cheered. The official wedding ceremony was over, and it was time to eat. The women accompanying Fantina brought out all kinds of food for the men—food that all but depleted the Karrano farm of its stores.

"Father," Fantina asked Samouel.

"Yes, my child! Congratulations! You are a beautiful bride. And you got your wish! You are married in the Jewish faith! I didn't lose my little girl, I gained a son."

"Father!" Fantina demanded with a slight frown.

"What's the matter?" Samouel asked.

"Is Rabbi Evenstein Sephardic?" Fantina asked.

"He's a Jewish rabbi," Samouel said. "Jewish rabbi—that's redundant."

"Father!" Fantina protested.

"What?"

"You didn't answer my question. Let me rephrase. Is Rabbi Evenstein Ashkenazi?" Fantina demanded.

Samouel loosened the collar around his neck.

"I need fresh air," Samouel said.

"You're outside, Father. You have plenty of fresh air. He's Ashkenazi—not Sephardic. Isn't that right, Father?"

"What difference does it make in these evil days? We're lucky to have a rabbi at all!"

"I don't believe it. I was married by an Ashkenazi rabbi. Me, Fantina, a lowly Sephardic woman married to a Christian by an Ashkenazi rabbi. This is the most mixed up wedding ever!"

"This is what you get when you marry at the last minute during Passover with the Angel of Death flying over us and whatnot. Even God himself needed six days to make the earth. Yet you demanded a wedding in two. It wasn't until last night that Rabbi Evenstein agreed."

"But the wedding ceremony—was it Sephardic or Ashkenazi?" Fantina asked.

"I instructed him on our Sephardic ways. I think he hit most points correctly," Samouel said.

"Hit most points? Is my wedding target practice? How terrible," Fantina said, and she started to cry.

"Don't cry, Fantina, don't cry. God loves us all. There are worse things—much worse—and I've seen them too recently. Men getting their brains spread across battlefields and spurting their lifeblood all over you. And the rotten stench of death. Nothing can compare. This is your day, Fantina. Enjoy it. Come, here's Axon. Axon—help your wife to some dinner."

Axon took Fantina in his arms and kissed her. The two helped themselves to food and sat at a head table. But they didn't have long to eat. War doesn't wait for wedding celebrations. The Germans and Italians pressed too close for the Greek Army to hold them further, and they resumed their retreat. Axon was permitted two days furlough as was Samouel, but Samouel left immediately with the Greek Army—leaving Axon and Fantina alone for those two days.

For Evanita and Jonara, the world fell gray again.

1941 May 3, Sat. Samarina, Pindus Mountains, Greece.

Fantina sat on her front doorstep. It was *Shabbat* (the Sabbath), she had two candles lit in her home, and the radio played music with periodic news bulletins. She had kept up with the war. All of Greece and Crete were now under Axis rule. To add more injury to Fantina's soul, a German-Italian parade marched in Athens to celebrate the victory. It was an odd feeling for Fantina—the sour news of the Axis celebration intermixed with the loveliness of classical music. Fantina was alive physically, but in her heart she worried about Axon and Samouel. There had been no news from either of them since she last saw them—her father on her wedding day, and Axon two days later when he rejoined the Greek Army.

"God. I know it is your day of rest, and you command that I rest as well," Fantina said. "Help me find the strength to enjoy what you gave us and not work my worry to exhaustion."

Fantina looked across the Pindus Mountain range. It was a stretch between the West Macedonia periphery—where she lived—and the Epirus periphery. Majestic mountains graced Samarina—the highest village in Greece. Did that make her closer to God? She liked to think so. Such beauty in the landscape, but could she enjoy it? Fir trees and wildlife adorned it. Snow melted off it. Life around her said it was spring, but Fantina did not feel the same joy as the chirping birds.

Fantina gazed in the distance and saw a small speck heading her way. Could it be Axon? Hope filled her heart, and with great anticipation, she awaited. The spec was in fact a small truck. It was an army truck.

"Axon!" she said. "My love is returning home."

She ran toward the truck. But it wasn't Axon. The truck parked. The driver remained inside, and from the passenger seat emerged Samouel.

"Father!" Fantina said.

She ran to him and hugged him. He was dressed in his army uniform and continued using crutches to move about, although his splint had long ago been replaced with a proper cast.

"The doctors removed that needle and gave me painkillers," he said. "Sometimes I think the needle was better—it let me keep my senses about me."

"Where's Axon, where's Axon?" Fantina begged.

"That's why I'm here," Samouel said.

"Oh no. Don't say it. It isn't true. He can't be dead," Fantina begged.

"He isn't," Samouel said.

Fantina's face filled with mixed relief and grief, much like the way the radio intermixed bad news with delightful music.

"He's alive? Then why isn't he here?" Fantina asked.

Samouel struggled for words.

"He's not here because he couldn't travel, isn't that right, Father?" Fantina asked.

"Yes," Samouel sighed.

"And he can't travel because he's either a prisoner or critically wounded," Fantina said.

"Right again," Samouel sighed.

"But the radio says the Greek Army has been released. So he's not a prisoner, is he Father?" Fantina asked with a new horror welling up in her face.

"He's not a prisoner," Samouel admitted.

"Oh Father!" Fantina cried, and she hugged him quite hard.

"Careful," Samouel said. "My ribs are still healing."

"I'm sorry," Fantina said as she abruptly released her father.

"I'm not just a messenger," Samouel said, "or a visitor. I am here to bring you to Athens."

"Athens?" Fantina asked.

"To see Axon. The brave man. He put up a brilliant fight in one of the last stands in Greece. It did not go well for him or many others. But he is alive."

"Will he survive?" Fantina asked.

"It's touch and go. Hour by hour. He asks for you. Repeatedly. The doctors think if you're there, he might relax and pull through."

"Yes I will go!" Fantina said. "Just wait right there. I'll pack a few things and be right back."

"Fantina," Samouel called as she started rushing to the house.

"Yes, Father?"

"Bring the Torah," he said.

"Why?" she asked. "We never take the Torah from the house, unless we are moving. Are we moving, Father?"

Samouel paused in thought. Fantina rushed back to him.

"What's happening? Why do I need to bring the Torah?" Fantina asked.

"This house is no longer safe," he said. "The enemy has conquered Greece and soon will be scouring these hills. You had better bring the special Shabbat candlestick too. And candles. And the menorah. Some extra Challah wouldn't hurt. And Kiddush cups. And—"

"Am I to bring all of Israel on my back?" Fantina asked.

"We should bring what we need to celebrate Shabbat—definitely. Oh, and wine too—the ancient bottles from the catacomb," Samouel said.

"I'll bring it, I'll bring it already," Fantina said.

Fantina turned and walked back toward the house.

"Fantina," Samouel called while her back was turned.

"What?" Fantina replied, turning to meet his call.

"Don't you think it's rather unkosher to run off like this on Shabbat?" Samouel asked.

"Oh my father is the sarcastic one today!" she replied, and she disappeared into the cabin for perhaps ten minutes. She reappeared with traveling clothes, a suitcase, and the Torah case.

"Do you have everything?" Samouel asked.

"If you want anything else, I suggest you get it yourself!" Fantina said.

Samouel started for the cabin. He reached the front door when Fantina felt sorry for him and rushed to help. The two brought out a large trunk filled with his things and other common things.

"What about our livestock?" Fantina asked.

"I'll send word to have them given away, that is, if the Germans or Italians haven't taken over our cabin yet," Samouel said.

"Oh, I do hate leaving them behind," Fantina said. "I love them all so much."

"There's nothing we can do. We best get going now. We won't arrive until late," Samouel said. "It's nine to ten hours from here to Athens."

"Very well," Fantina said. "Let's go."

The truck drove down the mountain range with the driver, Samouel, and Fantina in front with Evanita and Jonara in back. The road was bumpy, and after ten minutes of driving, Fantina felt queasy.

"Pull over, pull over!" she said.

The truck stopped. Fantina jumped out and vomited along the side of the road.

"Are you well? Should we take you back home?" Samouel asked.

"My home is where my husband is," Fantina said. "Drive on."

The truck drove for another ten minutes. Fantina sniffed the truck and crunched her face up like a prune.

"What's the matter?" Samouel asked.

"This truck stinks," she said.

"Stinks?" Samouel said. "That's silly. We just cleaned this truck before we drove up—inside and out. It's in tip-top shape."

"What did you do, take a shortcut through a manure patch?" Fantina asked.

"I don't smell anything," Samouel said. "You're imagining things."

"Pull over," she said.

The truck pulled over, and she vomited again. She got back in the truck, and it continued down the road.

"Here, drink this," Samouel said. "It's my canteen of water. You'll dehydrate if you keep emptying your stomach."

Fantina took several sips and spat the water out the window.

"The water is safe," Samouel said. "It's clean."

"It tastes foul. The air smells foul," Fantina said. "And my chest hurts. Slow down, will you?"

"We're going twenty kilometers per hour as it is," Samouel said. "It will take three days to reach Athens at this rate. What is it with you? I haven't seen a woman act like this since your mother was expecting...Fantina! I know why you are sick!"

"Why?" Fantina said.

"You are with child!" he said. "My grandchild. Oh, this is a glorious day."

"If it's such a glorious day, why do I feel so rotten? And how can you be sure I am with child?" Fantina said.

"My dear child, I *did* raise you in a secluded home. You have morning sickness, smells are stronger, and your chest is tender because it is changing," Samouel said.

"And here I thought it was the bumpy ride," Fantina said.

The truck proceeded for another ten minutes, and Fantina made a request.

"I'm hungry," she said.

"I have some bread for you in my knapsack," Samouel said.

"No, I mean *hungry*. I could go for some lamb kebabs, a gyro, grilled octopus, cabbage rolls, and some strong Greek coffee," Fantina requested.

"Jumping Jehoshaphat!" Samouel said. "You really are eating for two!"

"Maybe it's the excitement," she said.

"Is that why your hair is flatter than a pancake?" Samouel asked.

"I don't know what's wrong with my hair. I can't do a thing with it," Fantina said.

"Because you are with child!" Samouel said. "You have all the symptoms."

"You make it sound like a disease," Fantina said. "But if I am with child, I am happy. And I want Axon to be with me during my pregnancy and birth. I want my baby to know its father."

"Then we came in time," Samouel said. "Axon will be glad to see you."

After another twenty minutes or more, the truck pulled over to a Greek restaurant. Fantina ordered everything she had mentioned and ate it all! Samouel and the driver had no trouble watching her eat everything except, strangely, the cabbage rolls. Fantina refused the first set of cabbage rolls brought out to her and insisted she be allowed into the kitchen to choose her own cabbage leaves. What she chose even the cook recommended against—the smelliest cabbage leaves she could find. The cook tied a mask around his face to deal with the smell, and when the cabbage rolls were delivered to her table, nearby customers got up and moved to more distant tables.

"These are the best tasting cabbage rolls I've ever had!" she said.

"I'm going to be sick!" Samouel said. "Driver, pull over the truck and let me out!"

"Silly Father," Fantina said. "We're not in the truck!"

The driver and Samouel tied their napkins over their mouths and noses to suppress the smell. This did not help much, but it did allow them to sit with Fantina as she finished her meal. Samouel paid the bill and left a generous tip.

"Now I am ready," Fantina said.

"Good," Samouel said.

The three returned to the truck and proceeded to Athens. Fantina fell fast asleep and remained that way for the entire trip down the peninsula except for each time the truck stopped for fuel. The three arrived in Athens late that night, and the driver dropped Samouel and Fantina off at the army hospital.

"The army has prepared a room for you," Samouel said. "I will show you to your room, and you can see Axon tomorrow."

"I want to see him tonight," Fantina said.

"Are you sure? He's most likely asleep."

"Please," Fantina begged. "It's important."

"Yes, it is, isn't it?" Samouel answered. "Very well. I'll show you to your room where you can drop off your things and freshen up if you like, and then we'll see Axon."

"Thank you, Father," Fantina said.

Fantina freshened up, and her father accompanied her to the hospital wing with Axon. Many men moaned in pain and agony, and the smell left Fantina feeling sick to her stomach. She pulled away from Samouel and rushed into a bathroom to vomit. She rinsed out her mouth with water at the sink and returned to her father, who was now accompanied by Rabbi Evenstein.

"Doctor's orders," the rabbi said.

"But this is his wife, Fantina. She must be allowed to see him."

"The disease is contagious. One stray flea or louse bite, and she'll contract the disease too," the rabbi said.

"I must see him," Fantina said.

"Fantina," the rabbi said. "Your father told me you carry a child. I'm happy for you. But think of the danger you pose to yourself and your child. Once contracted, there is no cure."

"What is the disease? What is its name?" Fantina asked.

Rabbi Evenstein and Samouel paused—each afraid to answer Fantina. Finally, Samouel spoke up.

"It's typhus, Fantina. Axon has typhus."

"NO!" Fantina screeched as she held her hands over her mouth. "How, Father, how?"

Samouel looked at the rabbi, and the rabbi shook his head, "No."

"I will tell you," Samouel said. "The Italians and Germans forced the Greek Army into a massive retreat. We fought as best we could, but we were exhausted, and the Germans were too strong. Axon was determined to preserve Greek sovereignty. He led a special-forced group to ambush the Germans at night. Many Germans paid with their lives, but Axon and his group were captured and confined to filthy prison camps. He was imprisoned for just a couple of weeks and was released on May 2nd."

"I knew something was wrong when I first saw him," Samouel continued. "His mind was in a daze, like it was filled with smoke. He was delusional, thinking he could take back Greece all by himself. I took him to this hospital, and the diagnosis was clear—typhus."

"There must be a treatment, there must!" Fantina said.

"There isn't," Samouel said.

"Little Voice," Evanita said. "Can we help them? How do we cure Axon's typhus?"

"The stone doesn't act, it gives knowledge," Jonara said. "If only they had access to drugs."

"I'm trying to remember what my mother told me about typhus. I think there are three drugs used—tetracycline, doxycycline, and something like Clara Muff Nicol," Evanita said. "What does the stone say? Hug me and ask it, Little Voice."

Jonara hugged Evanita and asked the Moissan Ruby on a nonverbal level.

"This is what the Water Ruby says," Jonara said. "Tetracycline is a treatment, but it won't be discovered until 1948. Doxycycline is also a treatment, but it won't be created until the 1960s."

"And Clara Muff?" Evanita asked.

"There's nothing called 'Clara Muff'," Jonara said. "But there is something called Chloramphenicol."

"Yes, that's it. Maybe we can show Fantina where to find it," Evanita said.

"She can find it in 1949," Jonara replied.

"Another dead end. Then this is it. This is the passing of Axon," Evanita said.

"Have you visited him, Rabbi?" Fantina asked.

"Yes," Rabbi Evenstein replied.

"Why did they let you? Are you immune?" Fantina asked.

The rabbi held silent.

"He is not immune," Samouel said. "He had to wear a heavy, protective suit with antiseptic sprayed over it."

"Then that's what I want. I want a suit," Fantina said.

"It's hardly worth it," the rabbi said. "Your entire body is covered. You won't be able to touch him or hold his hand."

"I don't care," Fantina said. "I want that suit!"

Fantina stared at the rabbi. The rabbi looked at Samouel, and he nodded, "Yes."

"All right," the rabbi said. "But we will go with you."

The three walked into a small room. Hospital staff placed body-length hoods over the three with two openings to see. Next, the staff placed goggles over each of the three's eyes and finished by spraying antiseptic on their hoods.

"Follow me," Rabbi Evenstein said.

Fantina followed. The three walked down the hallway and into Axon's room. The room smelled of rotting flesh. Fantina felt the need to vomit, but she placed her hand (still under her hood) over her mouth and prevented it.

"Rabbi, is that you?" Axon asked.

"Yes," Rabbi Evenstein said. "I am here with your father and Fantina."

"Oh Axon!" Fantina cried.

Fantina rushed to hug him, but the rabbi and Samouel blocked her advance.

"I am visited by three ghosts," Axon said, referring to the three's full-length hooded appearance which made them look like Halloween ghosts.

Axon was covered with gangrenous sores and red spots. His face was covered in sweat, and he rolled his head back and forth in agony.

"It's so hot," he gasped. "Fantina, did I hear my Fantina?"

"Yes, Axon my love, you did! I am here!" Fantina said. "And I have good news. I am with child! You are going to be a father!"

"A father," Axon gasped. "Oh how I missed you, Fantina."

"I missed you too," Fantina said.

"Did I ever thank you for lending me your Tanakh?" Axon asked.

"It was a gift. You keep it," Fantina said.

"Those few times when the fighting stopped, I read it. Before we got married, I read it. And when I was imprisoned by the Germans, I read it. And do you know what I thought as I read it?" Axon asked.

"No, what?" Fantina sobbed.

"I thought of my proud Fantina, daughter of the Karrano line, exiled from Egypt, most likely exiled from Israel, and exiled from Spain. Yet her family survives—and this book was one piece of the puzzle that made it happen."

Fantina could only respond with a muffled sob.

"It's strange," Axon said. "I was brought up Eastern Orthodox Christian. I think I told you. Our Old Testament has these stories. But we ignored them. Why, I don't know. They're good stories."

"Yes," Fantina sobbed. "They are."

"When we get home, I want to read these stories with you," Axon said. "Is it a bargain?"

"Of course, Axon my love," Fantina sobbed.

"Hey, why the crying? Are you crying about me?" Axon asked.

"No," Fantina lied. "I'm just a silly woman who loves her husband."

"My wife. Fantina Karrano. Fantina di Pindos. I've thought of a name for our baby," Axon said. "You'll laugh at me, I know, but I was thinking if it's a girl, you could name her Aromina, and if it's a boy, Aromani, after the Aromanians."

Fantina cried. For the first time, Axon spoke as if he wouldn't be around for the childbirth.

"I'm fooling myself, aren't I Rabbi?" Axon said.

Rabbi Evenstein replied by saying the following prayer:

Hear, O Israel, the Lord is our God, the Lord is One.

Blessed is the name of His glorious Kingdom forever and ever.

Love the Lord your God with all your heart, with all your soul, and with all your might. Let these words which I command you today be upon your heart. Teach them thoroughly to your children, and speak of them when you sit in your house, when you walk on the road, when you retire, and when you arise. Bind them as a sign upon your arm, and let them be for a reminder between your eyes. Write them on the doorposts of your house and on your gates.

Fantina and Samouel recognized the *Shema* all too well. It was a prayer they said many times for many happy occasions. But this was not one of them.

"It's stuffy in here," Axon said. "Could someone open the window?"

Fantina did the best she could to open the window through her hood. Outside down below, Italians and Germans continued celebrating in the streets. Many carried beer in their hands and behaved in obnoxious fashion.

"The walking dead," Fantina whispered out the window, "are those who are trapped between the celebration of the enemy, and the death of a loved one. And as the walking dead, I hide under layers to avoid disease."

Fantina turned around and walked over to Axon. Rabbi Evenstein and Samouel thought nothing of it, but without warning, Fantina slipped her hand under her body-length hood and lifted the garment up a bit so she could hold Axon's hand with her own bare hand. With her touch, Axon relaxed, gave out a final gasp, and expired.

"No, no!" the rabbi and Samouel said.

The men forced Fantina away from Axon and scuttled her to a decontamination room. They removed their hoods and sprayed Fantina's hand with antiseptic.

"Axon!" Fantina cried. "Axon!"

"He's gone," Samouel said.

The three returned to the hallway in time to see a large body bag being rolled by.

"Is that him?" Fantina said.

"Yes, Fantina," Samouel said.

"Where are they taking him?"

"To Palestine," Rabbi Evenstein said.

"What?!" Fantina said. "He's my husband. He's Greek! He should be buried in Samarina."

"It's too late for that," the rabbi said.

"What is he talking about, Father?" Fantina asked. "What's too late? Father? Speak to me!"

"We must go, Samouel," Rabbi Evenstein said. "The ship to Palestine leaves soon, and we must be aboard."

"Father!"

"We can't go back to our home, Fantina," Samouel said. "Come—I will explain on the ship."

"I'm not going anywhere until you tell me everything," Fantina said.

"It's begun," Samouel said. "The Germans have started rounding up Jews for deportation to concentration camps. Isn't that enough? The Greek Army is regrouping in Palestine with the help of the New Zealand Army. One of their ships leaves to-night. We must be aboard it. Every minute we stay in Greece increases the chances we will be discovered and sent to a con-centration camp. My friend, Pierce Wilkinson, will see to our comforts on the ship. He's our New Zealand Army liaison."

"But Palestine—is it kosher?" Fantina asked.

"We have Jewish friends ready to help us," Rabbi Evenstein said. "Come—you and your child will be well taken care of."

Fantina, Samouel, and the rabbi disappeared into restrooms and reappeared wearing merchant-sailing uniforms. Evanita and Jonara followed the three to the docks of the Mediterranean where Evanita and Jonara watched the three board a cargo ship. Evanita and Jonara attempted to board with them but could not. Some force or wall prevented them from leaving mainland Greece. The two watched Fantina appear on the other side of a porthole where she lit two candles in the special Shab-bat candlestick.

Suddenly, Evanita and Jonara acquired tunnel vision. The tunnel bored directly to the porthole, and the effect of a power-ful vacuum pulled the two through the tunnel and up to the porthole and through it, where they faced the candle-stick holder at point-blank range. The candles burned brightly and nearly blinded Evanita and Jonara, but they had enough stamina to comprehend the shape of the special candleholder.

"It's the wooden thing from Daddy's keychain! And it looks like the symbol from the viol, the Water Ruby, and the diary!" Jonara yelled.

"The candleholder has a turtle-like shape," Evanita said.

"Or one egg over another," Jonara said.

"If you look carefully, it looks like a young fetus—the smaller ellipse is the head with an eye, the larger ellipse is its tail with a heart," Evanita said.

"Or a face with two eyes, and the middle ridge for a nose," Jonara said. "I wonder what that little ramp between the upper ellipse and lower ellipse is all about?"

"I don't know," Evanita replied. "But the wood grains look different."

"The lower wood is white," Jonara said.

"And the upper is crimson," Evanita said.

"The little ramp is dark brown," Jonara said.

Then just as suddenly as the two were thrust toward the candleholder, the two were shot away from it, out through the porthole, and into the water, where the two seemed to choke and drown.

"Give her some air," Evanita and Jonara heard from a far-off place.

The world faded to gray, and blackness overtook them.

CHAPTER 11:

Jane Goes South

2023 Oct 5, Thu Early am. Corpus Christi, Texas.
2006 Nov 22, Wed Eve. The Ground Near Helrod.

"Hey Eve?" Calico asked. "What are you doing down there? Give her some air, girls."

Calico helped Evanita to her feet. She looked at Calico, and Calico—though bruised—was all smiles. Evanita looked at the Helrod and saw the Russian and German girls tied to the Helrod such that each Helrod lower corner had a foot tied to it, and an upper corner had a wrist tied to it. Calico pointed back to them with her thumb.

"They were getting on my nerves, so I tied 'em up," Calico said.

"Why were they attacking you?" Evanita asked.

"They were supposed to clean litter off the campground. Instead, they'll get punishment," Calico explained. "You fainted there for a bit. I heard you just came back from surgery. A head injury, is that right?"

"Yeah. I just need to sit down," Evanita said.

"Just sit in one of the stands," Calico said.

"What stands?" Evanita asked.

Suddenly, four sets of stands wheeled into positions around the Helrod. These stands had built-in motors and wheels. They were remote-controlled by Oxians. Evanita and the other girls took seats in the stands. Calico ensured Evanita had a first-row seat so she wouldn't have to climb steps, and Calico sat next to her. Jonara sat on Evanita's other side and watched. Four Oxians took their positions on the "bases"—what resembled bases of a baseball diamond—around the Helrod. Each "base" had an assigned corner of the Helrod. A fifth Oxian took her place behind a large drum, and she began beating in a steady rhythm—hard, soft, soft, soft. On each hard beat, the Oxians on bases lashed their whips at the Helrod corners—catching a foot or hand in the process. The girls in the stands cheered when there was a hit—resulting in the German or Russian girl flinching, and booed at misses. One of the lashes went astray and knocked off a lock of the German girl's hair. Another stray lashing ripped a line through the back of the Russian girl's blouse.

This beating of the drum and lashing of the whip went on for nearly nine minutes. The drum halted. Friends of the Russian and German (but not Calico) ran up and released the ropes. The Russian and German girls collapsed and had to be carried back to their rooms.

"Well, what did you think of that, Eve Carson?" Calico asked Evanita. "Ain't that great entertainment?"

Evanita was horrified, but she didn't want to let on.

"It was...uh...my first time watching," Evanita said.

"You'll get a thirst and a trained eye for this sort of thing. Soon you'll know a good hit from a bad," Calico said. "C'mon. It's time to return to our rooms. I've got some laundry for you to do."

"I just got out of surgery," Evanita said. "My head hurts."

"Oh, so you want to go on the Helrod next?" Calico asked.

"No, I don't. I'm just saying—"

"Well quit saying and get ready for some laundry. I don't ask much, but when I do, I expect it to be done," Calico said. "Is that clear?"

"Yes," Evanita replied.

The two returned to Redjet. Calico had a large hamper, and it was heavy.

"You need wheels for this," Evanita said.

"You're the wheels. Now start rolling," Calico said.

Evanita could not pick up the hamper. And she could not drag it. She didn't like the idea of placing dirty clothes in a laundry basket, but what choice did she have? She pulled out piece after piece of Calico's laundry and did just that.

"You do know about separating whites from colors. And delicates get their own cycle," Calico said.

"You have delicates?" Evanita asked

It was a mistake to ask that question. Calico slapped Evanita across the face, and Evanita fell to the ground. For a brief moment, she felt she was not in her jail room, but in a stadium somewhere watching a baseball game. The vision faded, and she stood up to retrieve more of Calico's clothing.

"I'll separate them," Evanita said.

"Good. And use fabric softener. I can't stand static cling," Calico ordered.

Evanita carried the laundry basket to the laundry room on Redjet. It was empty—the other girls were too busy either discussing the fight Calico had with the Russian and German, or preparing for Thanksgiving in some strange form of gift giving. Evanita sifted through the clothes for whites and threw them in.

"Calico's clothes look clean already. Good. I won't have to use bleach," Evanita said to herself.

She finished throwing the white clothes in, started the washer on the hot cycle, and poured in liquid detergent as the tub filled with water. Jonara accompanied her mother during this chore but could not communicate with her. Evanita started a second washer for colors. This nearly emptied the laundry basket with only a few delicates remaining. Evanita returned to her room and placed more clothes in the laundry basket. She sorted through the laundry basket and found a few more whites. She quickly threw them in the washer, but as she did, the vibrations of the washer carried through her body and activated the Moissan Ruby. Jonara recognized this event and hugged her mother. The two traveled back in time again.

1948 Aug 17, Tue. Simmons Athletic Field. Kenosha, Wisconsin.

Jonara and Evanita hovered over the city of Kenosha, Wisconsin. They descended gently onto a baseball diamond where the Kenosha Comets were preparing to play the Springfield Sallies. The two landed in the Comets' dugout just as the Comets' manager, Chet Grant, gave a pep talk to his team.

"Ladies," Mr. Grant said. "You may or may not have heard the news, but the baseball world has lost a great legend. Babe Ruth died of cancer last night at Memorial Hospital in New York City. All baseball leagues around the country have been asked to keep our flags at half-staff until after the funeral. Simmons Field is no exception. People like Babe Ruth made baseball popular. Without him, there might not have been a women's baseball league."

Jane stood up.

"Mr. Grant, I respect Mr. Ruth, but do you really think we should be thanking him for the women's league? It was really us who made it popular."

Some of the women chimed in agreement. Others kept quiet.

"MacNessi, I won't have you talk out of turn like that. This is a day of remembrance, not a day for promoting women."

"I'm sorry, sir, but I am a woman, and I'm playing in a woman's league. The fans come to see us. I'm sorry Mr. Ruth died, but we shouldn't have to thank him for our hard work."

"That's it, MacNessi," Mr. Grant said. "Keep your trap shut or hit the locker room. Now the rest of you, pay attention. Back in 1920, I was the backup quarterback at Notre Dame. Our coach was the legendary Knute Rockne, and our quarterback the great George Gipp. George died that year, but before he did, he told something to Knute. He told Knute that when things are wrong and breaks are beating the boys, ask them to win one for the Gipper. Gipp inspired us all. In 1921, the year after George Gipp passed away, I led our team to a 10-1 season."

"Our baseball season has had its ups and downs," Mr. Grant continued. "We've fought hard but we struggle to get the wins we need to lead our division. The Racine Belles are dominating, and I want that to stop. We must dominate. Only the Springfield Sallies are worse than us in the Western Division, and we play them tonight as the visiting team. We can't afford to lose to them."

"Isn't that strange that we're playing at home as the visiting team?" Jane asked.

Mr. Grant stared her into silence.

"Sorry," Jane said.

"So I'm telling you now," Mr. Grant said. "Think about people like Babe Ruth who made baseball into what it is today. Think of Ruthville, the House that Babe built. Think of the cancer that took his life away, and think about how precious life is. Every minute counts. Remember that. And no matter what happens on that field tonight, no matter how the ball is pitched or how the Sallies bat, I want you to think baseball and win one for the Babe!"

Most of the girls cheered. Some kept quiet. Jane grumbled something, but she did so while the others cheered so as not to be singled out by Mr. Grant.

"That was the weirdest speech I've ever heard," Jonara said.

"A girls baseball team being inspired by Babe Ruth," Evanita said. "That is an odd one. But maybe these are odd times."

Evanita and Jonara watched the game as if in fast-forward. Baseballs went back and forth, bats swung, and women circled bases. When the game finished, the Kenosha Comets had defeated the Springfield Sallies six to nothing.

1948 Aug 27, Fri. Simmons Athletic Field. Kenosha, Wisconsin.

Jonara and Evanita drifted on Lake Michigan a hundred feet from the shores of Kenosha, Wisconsin. Ten days passed, and they floated onto the shores of Simmons Island. They walked through the park and leaned over a bridge on 50th Street at the water below. Boats trolled by from their docks toward Lake Michigan. The girls' peaceful view was disturbed by a pickup truck backfiring on the bridge. The truck's engine died, and the driver restarted it. Evanita and Jonara hopped on the truck. It drove west on 50th a few blocks until it reached Sheridan Road. It turned south onto Sheridan and drove approximately seventeen blocks until it reached Simmons Athletic Field where the Comets and Sallies were already playing. Evanita and Jonara jumped from the truck onto the sidewalk, crossed Sheridan

Road, and entered the stadium. The two entered the Comets' dugout and watched as Jane awaited her turn to bat. Evanita and Jonara looked around and saw Trudy with Roberta in the stands just behind the dugout.

"Dottie Naum is at bat for the Comets," the Kenosha announcer said over the loudspeaker. "Marlow in the windup. The pitch is high and inside—ooo! Naum is hit by the ball."

Several boos from Kenosha fans.

"Naum takes a step toward Marlow," the announcer continued, "but the umpire blocks her and points to first base. Naum shaking it off. She's trotting to first. Naum is okay."

Kenosha fans cheered.

"Marge Villa up to bat for the Comets. Villa is the tying run. Naum at first. Marlow with the pitch. High and inside. Villa ducks in time."

More boos from Kenosha fans.

"Villa points a finger at Marlow," the announcer said. "Marlow in the stretch. Villa swings. And a hit way high to center field. Stoll can't reach it in time. Fair ball. Villa on the way to second, and Naum reaches home. Villa runs past second...the relay to third...Villa runs back to second...the throw to second...safe!"

"MacNessi," Mr. Grant (the Comets' manager) said to Jane. "Get up there in the warmup circle. Score Wagner for the win."

"Audrey Wagner up to bat for the Comets. She's the winning run unless Marlow can cool things off for the Sallies. Marlow with the pitch. In the dirt. Wagner jumped to avoid that pitch. Villa thinking about stealing third. Hansen slings it to Wenzel covering second base. Villa gets back in time. Hansen with a big save catching that pitch in the dirt."

"This is exciting," Jonara said.

"If only this were family," Evanita said. "Then it would be even more exciting."

"Where is our family in 1948?" Jonara asked.

"Grandma Geneva was still in Spain," Evanita said. "And Johnny's family just left Greece."

"Marlow's in the stretch. Here's the pitch. Wagner...swing and a miss!"

"What about Grandpa?" Jonara asked.

"Grandma Geneva didn't meet Grandpa until the 1960s," Evanita said.

"No, not your grandpa, my grandpa," Jonara said.

Evanita paused for a moment.

"Villa gets another big lead. Marlow looks her back to second base," the announcer said.

"Ooops, I forgot. Your mother didn't tell you. I'm sorry," Jonara said.

"Don't be. She keeps insisting I never had a father, which is medically impossible," Evanita said.

"I wonder if Roberta will grow up and meet your father/my grandpa," Jonara said.

"Marlow's in the stretch," the announcer said. "Here's the pitch. High foul ball. Can Hansen reach it? No, it lands in the third row."

"Roberta must be important somehow for my mother to have her photo in the exercise room," Evanita said.

"Marlow in the stretch," the announcer called. "Villa taking a big lead. Here's the pitch. Wagner swings...It's a long single to right. Villa rounds third and heads for home. Wagner rounds first. She's going for a double. The throw to second...safe! The game is tied four-all with MacNessi up to bat."

Evanita and Jonara followed Jane as she entered the batter's box.

"Pitch 'em low and away for this one," Arbie yelled to her pitcher.

The first pitch was low and away.

"Ball!" the umpire called.

"You'll have to do better than that with me," Jane grinned.

Arbie signaled to Marlow. Marlow pitched one a little high and a little inside. Jane thought it would be called a "ball" and let it slide by.

"Strike!" the umpire called.

"What?" Jane said. "That was inside."

"Baseball is a game of psychology," Arbie chuckled.

Arbie signaled her pitcher again. Marlow threw a curve ball, but it hung, and Jane in her eagerness swung a bit early. The ball sailed high into left field but hooked left of the foul pole.

"Foul ball. Strike two!" the umpire called.

"You had me scared for a moment there," Arbie said.

"I was too eager," Jane said. "But I dare you to try that again."

Arbie gave the signal, Marlow pitched the ball, but the ball slipped out of the Marlow's hand and shot directly for Jane's head. Jane angled her body back and down as if she were doing the limbo and barely avoided getting beaned in the head. The ball flew beyond Arbie's reach and thudded against the backstop. Wagner started running for third but slipped and fell. Arbie ran like mad to the backstop, grabbed the ball, and zung it back to second base where the shortstop covered. Wagner barely got back in time.

"Ball two!" the umpire called.

"Trying to kill me?" Jane said to Arbie.

"That was a little wild," Arbie said.

"Lucky for you Wagner fell," Jane said. "That would have been an easy steal."

The umpire called time and signaled for the ball. Marlow threw the ball to Arbie, and Arbie handed the ball to the umpire. He didn't like the scuffmarks on the ball. He placed it in his pocket and dropped a fresh baseball into Arbie's glove. Arbie tossed the ball to Marlow.

"Marlow's in the stretch," the announcer called. "Wagner with another big lead. Here's the pitch. The runner is going!"

Arbie called for a pitchout. Marlow tossed the ball quickly to Arbie who stood up and caught the ball well beyond the strike zone. Arbie slung the ball to third base where Schofield awaited the play. Wagner went in for the slide. Arbie's throw was high and sailed over Schofield's head. Wagner slid into third standing up, saw the ball flying off, and made the turn for home. The shortstop ran for the ball and threw it home. Arbie caught the ball and attempted the tag.

"Safe!" the umpire called.

"Wagner scores. The Comets win!" the announcer called.

The Comets' bench ran onto the field and congratulated Wagner and Jane. The Sallies left the field while the Comets continued celebrating.

"I just remembered something," Jonara said. "Wasn't Jane going to play for the Racine Belles?"

"Yeah, she was. And wasn't Arbie going to play for the Racine Belles too?" Evanita asked Jonara.

"Yeah, that's right. But Jane is a Kenosha Comet, and Arbie is a Springfield Sallie," Jonara said.

"I wonder what happened?" Evanita asked.

"Let's find out," Jonara said.

"How?" Evanita asked.

"Maybe we can scan Arbie or Jane with the Water Ruby. Maybe then we'll know," Jonara said.

"Okay, let's try with Arbie," Evanita said.

Evanita and Jonara walked over to Jane and attempted to touch her, but she wouldn't stay still. Jane continued to dance, run, hop, and celebrate with any and every Kenosha teammate.

"Let's try with Arbie," Jonara said.

"Okay," Evanita said.

The two left the playing field and looked for the locker room.

"Um," Jonara said. "This doesn't look like a locker room."

"It's a utility room," Evanita said. "I know. Let's go this other way."

Again, the two ended up in a utility room and not the locker room.

"It can't be that hard to find," Evanita said.

"Look—let's follow that Springfield Sallie there. She must know the way," Jonara suggested.

"Okay," Evanita said.

The two followed the Springfield Sallie, but when the Sallie entered a room, the world flashed with a brilliant white light for several seconds.

"What happened?" Evanita asked.

"I don't know," Jonara said. "But I can't see anything with this bright light."

The light faded after several more seconds, and the two found themselves in a restaurant next to the bridge on 50th Street—the same bridge where they had leaned over and watched the boats go by. They sat at a table with Jane and Arbie. Jane and Arbie were cleaned up and dressed for going out.

"What can I get for you two ladies?" the waitress asked Jane and Arbie.

"I'll have the chicken cacciatore," Arbie said. "And make sure the chicken is well cooked. With sweet onions. No red peppers. Extra olives. And I want to see your wine list."

"Okay, I'll bring the wine list in a jiffy," the waitress said. She turned to Jane and asked, "What can I get for you?"

"I'll have the meatloaf dinner, with baked potato, rice, and a beer," Jane said.

"Thank you," the waitress said. "I'll get this order in and bring a wine list."

The waitress walked away.

"Don't do her job," Arbie said to Jane.

"Huh?" Jane asked. "What are you talking about?"

"You told her exactly what you wanted," Arbie said.

"Yes. What's wrong with that?" Jane asked.

"You have to make them work. Be picky. Give them a hard time," Arbie said.

"What's gotten into you?" Jane asked. "These waitresses don't have an easy job."

"They get tips, don't they?" Arbie asked. "They should earn them."

"I'm surprised to hear you talk like that," Jane said.

"You're just sore that you didn't drive in the winning run today," Arbie jested.

"Hogwash," Jane said. "And you know it is, too."

"Here you are ladies, our wine list," the waitress said as she started to leave.

"Oh wait a moment," Arbie said to the waitress.

The waitress returned.

"Is this all you have for wine?" Arbie asked.

"We carry the very best," the waitress said.

"Yeah, but this is all California wine. What about a good Chablis?" Arbie asked.

"I'm sorry, but we don't have any French wines at the moment," the waitress said. "But any of the California wines—"

"I don't want a California wine. I want a Chablis! Is that so hard to ask? Chablis!"

"Forget it, Arbie," Jane said.

"No! You won today, and I want a good wine to celebrate!" Arbie stated.

"We have excellent champagne if you are looking for something special," the waitress said.

"Do you have a list?" Arbie asked.

"It is on the back of the wine list," the waitress said.

Arbie flipped the list over.

"Oh," Arbie said. "Wait a moment—these are Italian champagnes. Where's the French stuff?"

"Our Italian champagne is the best," the waitress said.

"Not good enough," Arbie said. "I want to see the manager."

"Arbie, no!" Jane said. "Don't make a scene."

"I'm not making a scene. I just want an explanation," Arbie said.

"Order a beer and be done with it," Jane said.

"No," Arbie said.

"Yes!" Jane said, and she squeezed Arbie's wrist.

Arbie shot Jane a mean look. Jane let go, and Arbie's frown changed into a look of disappointment.

"Give me a beer, too," Arbie said.

The waitress forced a smile, took the wine list, and disappeared.

"I've never known you to be like this," Jane said. "What happened? Is there something wrong?"

"There's nothing wrong!" Arbie shouted.

Nearby patrons stopped talking and stared at Arbie.

"Then why are you shouting?" Jane asked.

Arbie gave no answer.

"Well, I'll tell you something, Arbie. Things haven't been the same since we played for the Racine Belles last year," Jane said.

"For one thing, the Kenosha Comets aren't as good. For another, I miss hanging out with you. I'm up in Kenosha, and you're way down in Springfield. I don't like how the league reassigns us to different teams each season."

"They felt the Racine Belles had too much talent," Arbie said. "Last year the Comets were dead last. And the Sallies were just an idea. So the league had to rearrange and even things out. You know that."

"Yeah, I know that. But they could have moved other people around. Me—I'm at least in the same area, but they shipped you way down there. It's unfair," Jane said.

"Actually, while I live in Springfield, the Sallies don't have a home field. You know that," Arbie said.

"I know. You're always on the road. The girls call you the Springfield Orphans," Jane said.

"And people get us confused with other teams," Arbie said. "Remember that game back on June 21st?"

"We scored four runs late to win seven-to-five," Jane said. "How could I forget?"

"Did you read the next day's Kenosha Evening News?" Arbie asked.

"Probably," Jane said.

"You would have remembered this. The sports editor referred to us as the 'Sallies' in the headline—which is correct—but as the 'Lassies' in the article. Now tell me—how can the Springfield Sallies be confused with the Muskegon Lassies?"

"Maybe the editor mixed the words up," Jane said.

"That's exactly what he did. He could have dyslexia," Arbie said.

"I don't even know what that word means," Jane said.

"It's a medical term. I've been learning a lot of them," Arbie said.

The waitress returned with their beer. Jane and Arbie took several gulps before returning their mugs to the table.

"The beer is good," Arbie said.

"Then why all the fuss with the waitress?" Jane asked.

"It's our job as women to give other women a hard time about food," Arbie said.

"There you go again," Jane said. "Ever since you moved to Springfield, you've been acting like this. Is it the weather? The people? Is it true what they say about people from Illinois? Are they 'ill-annoying'?"

"Oh what does it matter?" Arbie said. "Besides, Springfield can't support a good team anyway. So what do I care?"

"What do you mean? The Sallies just started this year," Jane said.

"I heard they're going to be dropped from main competition. Oh they'll stick around, but only as a touring team. They're already touring this year, so that's nothing new. But it won't count toward a championship. Ah, yes. Nothing to fight for. Nothing to win for," Arbie said.

"That's too bad," Jane said. "But don't take it out on everyone."

"Why not? I need to let off steam. And a waitress makes a good target," Arbie said.

"They've really soured you down there. I'm sorry to hear that," Jane said.

"Well, at least I put away my money from playing ball. I know this team won't last forever. I'm moving on," Arbie said.

"Moving on to what?" Jane asked.

"Do you remember what I said about a year and a half ago?" Arbie asked.

"You said many things," Jane said. "Can you be more specific?"

"When we worked in the cafeteria at Kefer Toothe Company in Racine. I said it's time we get a college education," Arbie said.

"Yeah, now I remember. So you're going back to college? Where?" Jane asked.

"In Springfield, Illinois!" Arbie said.

"Down there?" Jane asked.

"Yes. Springfield Junior College," Arbie said.

"What will you study?" Jane asked.

"I was thinking prenursing studies," Arbie said.

"So that's how you know what 'dyslexia' means. But Arbie, I can't believe it. You, a nurse? A slave to some male doctor?" Jane said.

"What else can I do? I'm not smart enough to be a doctor," Arbie said. "And if it doesn't work out, I'll try something else."

"Yeah, but a nurse...it just seems...I don't know. What can I say, I don't have any kind of college degree," Jane said.

"You could apply too," Arbie said.

"What?" Jane said.

The waitress arrived with their food. Arbie was so engrossed with her conversation with Jane that she forgot to make petty complaints to the waitress. The waitress wisely did not ask if Arbie needed anything else.

"Yeah. Be my roommate in my apartment. Bring Roberta with you. Apply for admission. We'll become nurses together," Arbie said.

"I don't know. I wouldn't mind being something like a doctor or dentist, but I can't see myself moving down there to Springfield. I'm still playing for the Comets," Jane said.

"And you're still living with Jack, aren't you?" Arbie asked. "You didn't have to move back in with him after we split up last year."

"What was I supposed to do?" Jane asked. "I'm still married to him. The Catholic Church doesn't give out divorces. And your sister, Trudy, moved back in with Wilton. Now they're expecting a baby."

"You could have gotten a little apartment for you and Roberta," Arbie said.

"It's not that easy. Jack insists on seeing Roberta frequently. And I'm on the road a lot with the Comets. Jack watches Roberta. That means I don't have to pay for a sitter."

"Does he still hit you?" Arbie asked.

Jane didn't respond.

"I take that as a 'yes'. Don't let him get away with it, Jane," Arbie said.

"He's always hanging something over my head," Jane said. "Says I'm a bad mother because I'm not around for Roberta all the time, that I'm a bad role model because I play baseball—a male sport. I'm caught between my career and being a good mother to Roberta."

"That's abuse too," Arbie said. "Mental abuse. And what does he do for you and Roberta?"

"He doesn't. He used to take us to Chicago Cubs baseball games, but this year WGN started broadcasting the games out of Chicago. Jack spent $400 on a television set and installation," Jane said.

"A television? Whatever for?" Arbie asked.

"So he can watch the Cubs without having to drive to Wrigley Field. Sometimes he takes off early on Friday to catch the game on afternoon television. And he always watches the weekend television games. He wasn't satisfied with getting the two Chicago stations—WGN Channel 9 and WBKB Channel 4. He had to get the Milwaukee station too—WTMJ Channel 3."

"How did he manage that?" Arbie asked.

"He put up two antennas—one facing Chicago, and one facing Milwaukee. At first, he joined the antenna wires together, but the reception wasn't good. So he made a switching post for the television. Three antenna cables go to that box—one to the Milwaukee antenna, one to the Chicago antenna, and one to the television. He switches between antennas depending on what station he's watching."

"That's crazy!" Arbie said.

"He seems pleased with himself that he's living between two television markets and taking advantage of both. He drinks beer, eats pretzels, and watches television," Jane said.

"Television!" Arbie said. "It's the new curse. Is it true what they say about a person becoming a zombie? What does Jack look like when he's watching the television?"

"He doesn't move at all. It's like he's frozen. His eyes are wide open, and they don't move," Jane explained. "The only time he moves is when he yells at me for more beer, yells at the Cubs for being in last place, or gets up to go to the bathroom."

"He is a zombie," Arbie said. "This television is a one-way trip to Hell. Don't you see what this means?"

"No, what does it mean?" Jane asked.

"People won't go out and do things like they used to. They'll stay home and zombie-out with the television," Arbie explained.

"And if they're not going out, they're not watching our games either."

"I didn't think of that," Jane said.

"It's just a matter of time before this television spreads around to everyone. It's the new plague," Arbie explained. "Do you sit down and worship the television god too?"

"No, I don't," Jane said.

"Well don't you start. I've heard it's like opium—once you start, you're hooked," Arbie said. "And it rots your brain."

"Jack has Roberta watch with him. Mostly she likes *Howdy Doody*, and *Kukla, Fran, and Ollie*," Jane said.

"It'll stunt her mental growth," Arbie said. "Don't let her watch."

"What else can I do? I'm on the road with baseball, and television waves are constantly beamed into our house. Television has taken over."

Arbie tapped her fingers on the table nervously.

"Television has taken over, has it? You need to get out of that trap," Arbie said. "C'mon, Jane. Move down here in Springfield with Roberta."

"And quit the Comets? You were pushing me into baseball a year and a half ago," Jane said.

"I know, I know. But the league won't be around forever," Arbie said.

"What do you mean?" Jane said. "It's doing fine."

"Look around you, Jane. It's still a man's world. You lost your factory job when men came back from the war. The women's league started in a vacuum during the war. Now men are back, and they're displacing us again. That's another reason I'm going into nursing. Do you think they can displace us in nursing? They never had control of that profession."

"Going into nursing sounds reasonable. But it's hard to believe the league will just disappear," Jane said.

"It's already started. I told you the Sallies won't be around next year," Arbie said. "And with television keeping people at home, no one will pay to watch us play."

"Is that gossip?" Jane asked.

"More like rumor. But rumors are often true, and I think this one is," Arbie said.

Jane took several bites of meatloaf and chased them down with beer. Arbie savored her chicken, but periodically she looked at Jane as if expecting an answer.

"What?" Jane finally said.

"So is that a 'yes'?" Arbie asked.

"I'll think about it," Jane said.

"Don't think too long. We're still young, but we won't be young forever," Arbie said.

1948 Oct 8, Fri 11:30 am. Kenosha, Wisconsin.

"I want to thank you for inviting us over for the baseball game," Bill the Daschwirk machinist said to Jack.

"I'm honored," Jack said.

"Can we turn it on?" Hank the Daschwirk floor cleaner asked. "I read in the paper there's a World Series Preview show at 11:30."

"It's already 11:35," Jack said. "I better turn on the set. The game starts in ten minutes, and the set takes a few minutes to warm up. Look—I'll show you how it works."

Jack had taken off work early and invited his co-workers from Daschwirk. Besides Jack, there was Bill, Hank, Jim the crib manager, Jeff the security guard, and Mr. Grundle—Jack's boss. Jack turned on the television and adjusted it.

"That's excellent reception," Mr. Grundle said.

"Look—the game is on four Chicago stations—4, 5, 7, and 9!" Jack boasted. "And if I flip the antenna switch in back to Milwaukee—"

"No!" the men said in unison. "Leave it be!"

"Oh, all right," Jack said as he sat back down. "Jane—you got those snacks ready yet?"

Jane busily prepared cheese, crackers, chips, pretzels, and dip.

"And more beer. Lots of beer," Jack added.

Jane juggled several platters of snacks and struggled to set them on the coffee table. None of the men helped. Jane went back to the kitchen and brought beer for each of the men. None said, "Thank you." In fact, none of the men noticed Jane's presence—unless she happened to walk in front of the television.

"Jane!" Jack yelled. "Don't walk in front of the Tee-Vee! Can't you see there's a World Series starting?"

"Sorry!" Jane apologized.

But Jane wasn't sorry. Jack and the men were getting on her nerves.

"Shh!" Jack said to Jane. "They're throwing the first pitch!"

The game proceeded quietly with no runs in the first or second inning. The men called for more beer and snacks. Jane ran back and forth between the kitchen and living room to feed the men as the game transitioned into the top of the third inning.

"Grounder to the pitcher," said Jack.

"Stanky's running to third," Mr. Grundle said.

"That's it," Jeff said. "He has to hold."

"Two outs for the Braves," Jack said. "Dark is up to bat."

"Come on, Dark, get a base hit and bring in Stanky," Mr. Grundle said.

"What about a sacrifice fly?" Jane asked, though she was hardly paying attention to the game.

"That will not work. There are two outs already," Jack said. "Why don't you do what's best and dummy up!"

"Yeah," the men resounded.

"I don't like that tone, I don't like it!" Jane muttered.

"Fly ball to right field!" Jeff called.

"He's out!" Mr. Grundle said. "Damn!"

As Mr. Grundle cursed, he mishandled his beer and launched it onto the floor. "Dammit! Dropped my beer. Sorry, Jack! I'll make it up to you!"

"Forget it! Slave girl here will clean it up. Here, slave girl, come clean up this beer!" Jack taunted.

Jane quietly cleaned up the beer.

"Hurry up!" Jack complained. "You're blocking the set, and the bottom of the third is about to start!"

"I'll start your bottom third," Jane wanted to say, but she bit her lip.

"And don't make any more stupid comments about the game. You just cursed the Braves—you made them fly out!" Jack said.

"That's superstition!" Jane said.

"Quiet!!!" Jack yelled.

"The bottom of the third is starting," Jeff said.

Jane gave Mr. Grundle another beer. He barely noticed and certainly didn't thank her.

"The Indians are up to bat," Jeff said.

"Hegan is at the plate," Jack said.

"Swing," Mr. Grundle said. "It's another fly ball."

"It's foul," Jack said. "The catcher has it. Out. Another fly ball, and Jane is in the room. She cursed it again."

"That's crazy!" Jane said.

"Jane—go in the kitchen until this inning is over," Mr. Grundle said. "We'll call you if we need you."

"What!?" Jane said.

"You heard him," Jack said. "Get out of the living room!"

Jane went into the kitchen.

"I hate Jack," Evanita said. "And I hate Mr. Grundle."

"They're all obnoxious," Jonara said. "The men, that is."

"What does Jane see in him?" Evanita said. "She should take Arbie's advice and leave Jack!"

"Amen!" Jonara said.

Jane entertained Roberta in the kitchen with bits of bread and drink while the men continued watching the game.

"One out, and Bearden's up to bat," Jack said.

"Big base hit!" Mr. Grundle said.

"He's rounding first," Jeff said.

"It's a double. It's a double!" Jack said. "That proves it. The first time Jane leaves the living room, and Bearden gets a double!"

"She's a jinx, Jack," Mr. Grundle said. "Good thing I fired her from Daschwirk. She would have messed things up but good at the factory."

"Mitchell's up to bat," Jeff said.

"Ball one," Jack said.

"Ball two," Jeff said.

"Ball three," Hank said.

"He walked!" Mr. Grundle said.

"Men on first and second," Jeff said.

"With only one out," Jack said. "Gentlemen, this could be the first score of the game, the first World Series run on this here television screen. I want to propose a toast."

"*Prost!*" the men said as they toasted one another.

"Doby is up to bat," Jeff said.

Jane walked in.

"Did someone want something?" Jane asked.

"No!" the men yelled.

And it happened. Doby grounded to the second baseman.

"Double play!" Mr. Grundle predicted.

"He's out at second!" Jack said.

"And he's...son-of-a bitch!" Mr. Grundle said.

The men watched the shortstop throw the ball toward first base in an attempted double play to end the inning and prevent the run, but as Mr. Grundle spoke, the picture tube went black, and the audio went silent.

"God dammit, Jane!" Jack yelled, "You jinxed the entire television set! You killed it!"

"Turn it on and off, Jack," Mr. Grundle said. "Maybe a tube is loose!"

"Someone's tube is loose, and it ain't mine!" Jack said while staring at Jane.

"I didn't do anything!" Jane replied. "I was just standing here."

"You're a jinx if I ever saw one," Jack yelled.

Mr. Grundle got up and turned the television off and on, but the television did not respond. Jack beat and kicked the television set a few times, but again nothing happened. A vacuum tube had burned out, and nothing short of a new tube would get the television working again.

"Show's over, folks," Mr. Grundle said. "A tube is burned out."

"The real show is about to start," Jack said to Jane. "I ought to beat you like I did that set."

"Time to go," Mr. Grundle said. "Come on over to my house, gents. We'll listen to the game on my radio. It ought to be safe—there are no women in my house."

The men except for Jack grumblingly agreed. They filed out of Jack's front door with Jeff in the rear.

"Coming, Jack?" Jeff asked.

"I'll be over in a little bit," Jack said. "This shouldn't take long."

"Okie-dokie," Jeff said as he closed the door behind him.

Jack sank a left hook into Jane's jaw. Jane let out a yelp and fell to the floor.

"Mommie!" Roberta called from the other room.

"Jack—not in front of Roberta," Jane pleaded. "For her sake, don't!"

"You've been asking for it, and now you're gonna get it. That set cost me $400 including taxes and installation. Now it's only good for kicking. And so are you!" he said.

Jack kicked her and kicked her.

"Get up!" he yelled.

"Mommie!" Roberta cried from the kitchen. "Mommie has an owie."

Jane started to sob.

"Don't come out here, Roberta," Jane said. "Stay in the kitchen!"

"Mommie need help!" Roberta cried. "Roberta coming to help Mommie!"

"No, honey, stay in the kitchen!" Jane pleaded.

Jack pulled Jane to her feet. He punched her in the gut. She doubled over, and as she did, he popped her in the lower back. Jane fell to the ground again. Roberta got out of her chair in the kitchen and ran into the living room in time to see her mother writhing on the floor in pain. Jane moaned and rolled. She held one hand to her gut and another to her back.

"Mommie hurt!" Roberta said.

"Mommie is being bad," Jack said to Roberta. "She's getting punishment."

"No, Daddie is baddy!" Roberta said.

Roberta walked up to Jack and punched her little fist into his groin. Jack buckled over a little. He swatted Roberta in the face. She backed up and cried. Jack picked her up and tossed her across the room. She landed on the couch and cried harder.

"You shouldn't throw her on the couch!" Jane said.

"I meant to throw her at the Tee-Vee," Jack said. "You've been corrupting my daughter again."

"How do you expect her to react?" Jane said.

Jack kicked his boot across Jane's face and ripped her cheek open. Blood poured onto the floor.

"Now look at the mess you made," Jack said. "Clean it up! And clean up this house while I'm gone. I'm going over to Grundle's! Oh yeah. Call the department store where I bought the TV. Tell them you have the owner's policy. They'll fix the TV free of charge. And get it done before I return!"

Jack left.

Jane looked at the television and heard Arbie's words echo in her mind, "It's a curse. This television is a one-way trip to Hell."

"Mommie, I'm scared," Roberta said.

"I need a walk," Jane said. "But what a mess with the snacks! And I'm too tired to clean up right now. This situation is for the birds."

"Birdies? Can we feed birdies?" Roberta asked.

Jane looked at the snacks and looked at Roberta.

"Yeah. Let's feed the birds," Jane said.

Jane tossed the snacks in a paper bag and walked Roberta from their house to a park along the shores of Lake Michigan on the south side of Kenosha.

"Do you see the white and gray birds?" Jane asked Roberta.

"Birdies!"

"Those are gulls!" Jane said. "But most people call them seagulls. Here—take this cracker and throw it in the air."

Roberta took the cracker and threw it up. A gull dove down and caught the cracker in its beak. Several other gulls chased the first gull out into the lake. The cracker fell from the gull's beak, and a swarm of gulls gobbled up the cracker.

"Throw this one in the water," Jane said.

Roberta threw it. A gull dove down, landed on the water, and gobbled it up. Other birds landed too, but the first gull ate the cracker too quickly. In this way, Jane disposed of the left-over snacks. Jane and Roberta walked from the shore up the bank to the park where they bumped into Trudy and Trudy's dog.

"Jane, what happened?" Trudy asked.

"I fell and hit my—" Jane started.

"Baddy Daddie hit Mommie," Roberta said.

"You must have done something wrong," Trudy said.

"How can you say that?" Jane asked. "You weren't even there."

"Well," Trudy said, "you answered my question with a lie. So you're covering up something."

"I was covering for Jack. But maybe I shouldn't," Jane said.

"We should always support our husbands," Trudy said.

"Like the way you left Wilt and slept with Jack?" Jane asked.

"I admit to my sin. But I made a mistake. Wilt and I reconciled. Now we have a little baby. You should reconcile with Jack, too," Trudy said.

"What?"

"Find out what you're doing wrong, and correct it," Trudy said.

"I told you. I wasn't doing anything wrong. Jack blames me for everything. Now the television is broken, and he wants me to call in for repairs," Jane said. "Why can't he do it? He bought the blasted television and watches it."

"Did you call the repair man?" Trudy asked.

"No. I needed to get out of the house. I came down here with Roberta," Jane said.

"You won't help your husband in time of need, and you want sympathy from me? Who do you take me for?" Trudy asked.

"I thought I took you for a friend," Jane said. "At least a few years ago you were."

"You turned your back on that when you moved in with my sister," Trudy said. "Jack was heart-broken when you moved out. I only tried to comfort him."

"You did more than comfort him," Jane said.

"Things went a little too far. I know that. My feelings were all confused. But I'm better now. I saw a psychiatrist. I did a lot of talking. Cleared things from my chest. Got a fresh start," Trudy said. "You should do the same."

"You know what, Trudy? The people who want to give me the most advice are the ones who know the least about anything," Jane said.

"Well I never!" Trudy said. "That's the thanks I get for helping a friend. I guess we really aren't friends anymore. So long, Jane. Tell Jack if he ever needs a real woman's comfort, he can call me anytime. I should have known that he could never be happy with a half-woman, Jane the former machinist who secretly wants to be a man!"

Jane slapped Trudy across the face. Trudy's dog barked at Jane and bit Jane in the leg. Jane kicked the dog off. Trudy sneered at Jane and walked her dog away with the dog barking back at Jane until Trudy and the dog were beyond visual range of Jane and Roberta.

"Bad doggie!" Roberta said.

"There are many bad things in this world," Jane said. "And the evil increases. Who can stop it?"

"I wish we could help her," Evanita said to Jonara.

"I wish we could too," Jonara replied.

The world faded into gray. Evanita and Jonara hovered above Kenosha briefly as day became night. The stars circled above, and when the two landed, it was late Saturday afternoon.

1948 Oct 9, Sat. Racine, Wisconsin.

"The market is closing soon, Dr. Zavuski," said a groundskeeper at the Racine Farmer's Market. "You need any help packing up?"

"Oh no," Alina said. "My apples sold first, and I sold most pumpkins."

"I'm not surprised. The great apple-pie bakeoff is tomorrow at the apple harvest festival," said the groundskeeper. "Then the festival closes."

"It is good year for apples," Alina said.

"They say your apples make the best pies," the groundskeeper said. "It's no wonder you sold out so soon."

"If only cabbage would sell like apples," Alina said.

"Everyone in Racine County grows cabbage," the groundskeeper said.

"I should grow more apples?" Alina asked.

"I would if I were you," the groundskeeper said.

"And here I try for diversity," Alina said.

"That only goes so far. Well, good luck to you on the cabbage. Maybe it'll sell tomorrow," the groundskeeper said.

"I hope so. They not keep much longer," Alina said.

Alina turned to her pumpkins and cabbage. She loaded the pumpkins into crates and wheeled the crates onto her Studebaker box truck with a hand truck. She returned with the hand truck to her market stand when a hand tapped her on the shoulder.

"Yes?" Alina asked as she turned around.

Jane and Roberta stood before her.

"Well Jane, this is pleasant surprise. You brought your lovely daughter Roberta," Alina said.

"You remember me?" Jane asked.

"Of course I do! I remember you both. I much in debt to you for your courage and quick thinking. But what is awful injury on your face?" Alina asked.

"I slipped and fell—"

"Onto husband's boot. Oldest lie in human history," Alina said.

"I...was wondering...do you...I don't mean to impose...those meetings," Jane stumbled.

Alina held a finger to Jane's lips to shush Jane.

"Help me pack," Alina said.

Jane packed pumpkins into crates and wheeled them onto the truck as Alina walked with her.

"You drive here?" Alina asked.

"No. I don't have a car, and I don't know how to drive. We took the train from Kenosha—the North Shore Line," Jane said.

"Hmm," Alina said.

Roberta tagged along the two women, and when the three entered the inside of the truck's box, Alina spoke.

"We meet tonight. I go there very soon. I need to make stop on way," Alina said. "You welcome to come, of course, but I must make special request. You must ride here with cabbage."

Jane looked at Alina funny.

"But you have room in the front seat," Jane said. "Roberta and I could sit—"

"I know. I not have time to explain. You must trust me. You find out soon why I ask. Not worry about ride. There is fresh air and light. See? Roof has opening."

"We get to ride in back?" Roberta asked.

"Yes you do," Alina said.

"Yay! Let's go, Mommie!" Roberta said.

"All right. We'll ride back here. You'll let me know when we can come out, right?" Jane asked.

"I have little sliding window I open to talk to you. I let you know everything," Alina said.

Jane agreed. She sat with Roberta on a crate. Alina closed the back door and drove the truck from the farmer's market.

"This is fun, Mommie," Roberta said.

"I'm glad you're enjoying it," Jane said. "But I wish this seat were more comfortable."

Roberta looked through a small peephole in the side of the truck and watched the scenery go by.

"I spy, Mommie. I spy," Roberta said.

"What do you see?"

"Trees. Brick walls," Roberta said.

The truck traveled for ten minutes with Roberta watching in this fashion. Without warning, Roberta said, "Oo, oo! Going in! Going in!"

"We arrive at pickup place," Alina said. "Be ready for guests."

To Jane's surprise, the back of the truck opened to a crowd of women. They quickly moved the crates from the truck into a small storage room. By the time Jane offered to help, the crates were completely removed. The women removed Jane's crate and replaced it with a chair. Roberta sat on Jane's lap. Each woman in turn brought her own chair and sat in the back of the truck with Jane. One woman closed the back door behind her, and another signaled Alina to begin driving.

"Would you like a beer?" one of the women with a hat and sunglasses asked Jane.

Jane accepted.

"Can your girl have a bottle of soda?" the woman asked Jane.

"Soda! Soda!" Roberta begged.

"Yes, she can. Thank you," Jane said.

The woman smiled. She pulled two bottles from a wooden chest—a beer and a cream soda. The woman removed the tops from the bottles and handed them to Jane. Jane passed the cream soda to Roberta.

"What do you say?" Jane asked Roberta.

"Thank you!" Roberta said.

"You're welcome!" the woman said. "You're the one, aren't you? Jane the Emancipator."

"Me?" Jane asked. "No, you must be mistaken."

"Ladies!" the woman said. "It's Jane the Emancipator with her daughter Roberta!"

The women said, "Welcome!" and nodded their heads in reverence.

"I'm not an emancipator," Jane said. "Why do you call me that?"

"Everyone knows the story," the woman said, "about how you stopped the *fek* during an ISIS meeting at Dr. Zavuski's farm."

"I hope not too many people know about that. I could go to prison for that," Jane said.

"Don't talk like that," the woman said. "Everyone knows the circumstances. You saved Dr. Zavuski's and our lives."

"I guess I did," Jane said.

"Of course you did! It's certainly a better thing than winning at Sheepshead, isn't it?" the woman asked.

"Huh?" Jane asked. "Who are you?"

"Don't you recognize me?" the woman asked.

The woman removed her dark glasses and hat.

"Petunia!" Jane said.

"I wondered how long it would take you to recognize me."

"I didn't know...but this is so strange with the truck and all," Jane said.

"Dr. Zavuski's new idea. You remember how everyone drove to the farm on their own in the before time?" Petunia said.

"Yes. Arbie parked in the barn with the other cars," Jane said.

"Well not anymore," Petunia said. "We don't take chances with people seeing lots of cars driving onto the farm. So we meet at the warehouse and hide in Dr. Zavuski's truck. She drives out to the farm and makes sure no one follows us. The only bad thing is we all have to leave at the same time. No one leaves early or late."

"It sounds inconvenient," Jane said.

"It is. But that's how things go. Women can't meet freely without interference from *feks*. We now have to take steps to protect our rights," Petunia said.

The truck picked up speed.

"We're on the county road," Petunia said. "It won't be long now. Oh yes, I meant to congratulate you, Jane."

"On what?" Jane asked.

"On your fine work as a pitcher for the Kenosha Comets," Petunia said.

"I'd rather be playing for the Racine Belles again," Jane said.

"I know. We miss you, too," Petunia said. "And Arbie."

"Arbie says I should go back to school and get a college degree," Jane said.

"That's a great idea. I've been thinking about it myself," Petunia said.

"You have?" Jane asked.

"Yeah. At Marquette University. I was thinking of becoming a doctor of medicine. I have $2000 put away—that should pay for the first four years and some med school," Petunia said.

"That's how much I have saved, too," Jane said.

"We could study together!" Petunia said. "We could become doctors!"

"Actually," Jane said, "I was thinking of dentistry."

"Yes, of course! You were always good with tools and small tolerances at Daschwirk, weren't you? At least that's what Trudy told me. You'd be a natural."

"But it's too late. The fall semester has started," Jane said.

"We could apply for admission and start in the spring," Petunia said.

"It's funny—Arbie was saying almost the same thing—that I should move down to Springfield with her and go to one of those schools."

"It's not a bad idea, but your home is up here with Jack, isn't it?" Petunia asked.

"If you can call it that," Jane said.

Petunia hugged Jane.

"Listen, if you ever need an evening away from him, you can come over to my place. I'll find space for you and Roberta. Mum lives with me now, but she's clean. No *feks* allowed. Deal?"

"Deal," Jane agreed. She paused for a moment then said, "Petunia—do you think...it's about Trudy...we used to be good friends...lately she's...she says I need to be more supportive of Jack."

Petunia rolled her eyes.

"Trudy hasn't been the same since she had a baby with Wilt," Petunia said. "She has this gung-ho-be-a-slave-to-the-husband attitude now. I blame it on baby hormones. Some women lose their sense of right and wrong after giving birth. Trudy is one of them. Don't pay her much attention. You're one of the good ones. Look—the truck stopped. We're here."

The truck parked inside Alina's barn. The women opened the back of the truck and entered the silos as Arbie and Jane had done before.

"The door looks different," Jane said to Petunia as they entered the meeting room with Roberta.

"It's reinforced," Petunia said. "To prevent unwanted *feks* from breaking in."

Two women were already in the meeting room and had prepared a buffet dinner spread on a line of tables when Alina ushered the women in. The women formed two lines—one on each side of the tables. They filled their plates with meats, cheese, vegetables, fruit, bread, rice, potatoes, and desserts. On another table stood a punch bowl with punch, a coffeepot, a teapot, bottles of beer, soda, and a pitcher of ice water. Jane and Roberta held onto their drinks from the truck, as they were not quite empty.

"I can't fit any more on my plate!" Petunia confessed.

"Does Mum come to these meetings?" Jane asked as she helped Roberta with her plate.

"Almost every Saturday," Petunia said. "But tonight she had to work overtime at the department store. There's a run on television sets, and the store is staying open late. She can't keep up with the buyers. They're actually waiting for her in the store when she brings in each load from storage. There's no chance to put them on display—the customers buy the sets immediately. And she's getting up early tomorrow morning to help with installation."

"On a Sunday?" Jane asked.

"Can you believe it? This World Series baseball is to blame. For the first time, people in this area can watch some of the games on television," Petunia said. "But the prices for these sets are high. Our best model goes for $2100."

"That's too expensive. No one would pay that kind of money for a television set," Jane said.

"But they do, Janie, they do!" Petunia said.

"Where do they get the money?" Jane asked. "A person could buy—"

"A car with that kind of dough, yeah, I know," Petunia said. "But they find the money somewhere. There will be a lot of empty savings accounts after this weekend."

Petunia, Jane, and Roberta enjoyed their dinner at a table.

"Mmm, good!" Roberta said.

"Your daughter is cute," Petunia said.

"Do you have any children?" Jane asked.

"No. I'd like to have a daughter, but I doubt it will happen."

"Why not?" Jane asked.

"I don't want to settle down with a *fek*," Petunia said. "But if I could find a *fek* who would marry me, help me conceive, and let me live apart from him without having to be a slave to oppressive marriage ideals, then I'd do it."

"Wow!" Jane said. "But why bother to marry?"

"I believe in marriage," Petunia said, "just not the kind most *feks* believe in."

Alina took a position behind a podium.

"Good evening, ladies," Alina said, "and warm greeting for young ladies too," she continued, referring to daughters like Roberta. "Welcome to Saturday ISIS meeting. My name Dr. Alina Zavuski. I hope you find plenty food."

Many nods of approval from the women.

"Good. Tonight I talk about First Woman of Radio—Mary Margaret McBride. How many listen to her radio show?"

Many hands went up, including Petunia's. Jane's did not.

"Who would like to tell little bit about Miss McBride?" Alina asked.

Petunia raised her hand.

"Petunia?"

"Mary Margaret McBride was born in 1899 in Paris, Missouri. She received her journalism degree in 1919 from the University of Missouri. She was a reporter at the *Cleveland Press* and *New York Evening Mail* and wrote freelance articles for several magazines like the *Post* and *Cosmo*. She has a daily radio show out of New York where she interviews people. WBBM 780 AM out of Chicago has carried her, but now she has her own television show on NBC at eight on Tuesday evening—right after *Texaco Star Theater*."

"Thank you, Petunia," Alina said.

"That sounds like an easy job," Jane said. "Interviewing people every day."

The women laughed.

"Did I say something funny?" Jane asked.

"Petunia, would you like to respond?" Alina said.

"It's a lot of work," Petunia said. "Miss McBride prepares for each interview the night before by reading the guest's books or other things about the guest. That's how she gets good interviews. Anyone can ask questions, but asking the best questions requires research."

"Wow," Jane said. "I never knew."

"Maybe we listen to little bit of show," Alina said. "I have phonograph record of broadcast from last year."

Alina placed the disc on a record player. The women listened. It was an interview with Eleanor Roosevelt. After five minutes, Alina removed the needle from the record.

"What you think?" Alina asked.

"She sounds like a normal woman," Jane said.

The women laughed again.

"Did I say something funny again?" Jane asked.

"The beauty of Miss McBride is just that," Alina said. "She sound like ordinary woman, like one of us. Maybe not your Dr. Zavuski. I from Soviet Union. But she sound like working American woman, like one of you, no? Any one of you can become like Miss McBride. Find dream and work hard like McBride."

"But how do we make time for family and work?" one of the women asked, "when we can't count on our husbands to raise our children properly?"

Alina hesitated. Other women chimed in with the same question and affirmation.

"Does Miss McBride have children?" Jane asked Petunia while the commotion continued.

"No," Petunia replied. "And she's not married either. But you could say she's married to her job, and her interviews are her children. Jane—did you ever consider that maybe the barefoot and pregnant stereotype is not for all women? Life can give fulfillment in other ways. We don't have to be restricted to a narrow definition handed down by the *feks*."

"Yeah, but it seems we have to hide for this fulfillment," Jane said.

"Miss McBride doesn't hide. She's on the air every day. Listen to her," Petunia said. "She's not a flashy sales artist. She has simple, straight values, and she believes in working hard. You and I are hard workers, too. That's something to be proud of. But we can't rest on our laurels. Otherwise, we become barefoot and pregnant. Having a baby is one thing, but depending solely on a *fek* with no means of supporting ourselves is entrapment. That's what I mean by 'barefoot'."

"I have another surprise for you," Alina said.

The women continued discussing without allowing Alina a chance to speak.

"Please! I know this is difficult topic," Alina continued. "Following dream and raising family is difficult. Better to work it day by day than let dream slip away. Results not always quick and plentiful. But I want to show you something else."

Alina motioned to one of the women who had helped prepare dinner. The woman left the room and returned wheeling a cart with a movie projector. Alina remained at the podium with the record player.

"I have movie projector and silent movie of Miss McBride's television show," Alina said.

"You have a movie of her Tee-Vee show?" Petunia asked. "How?"

The other women expressed amazement and wonder.

"I keep it secret until now. I want big surprise," Alina said. "Miss McBride have television show. You know that already. But show not seen here. No NBC station to carry it. WNBQ in Chicago not doing regular NBC broadcasting yet. So I go to New York with 8mm movie camera and stay with ISIS friend. ISIS friend have television. I record show with safety film. I bring back here to share. I also make phonograph record."

Alina pulled out another record and placed it on the record player.

"Watch film and think about format," Alina said.

The lights dimmed. The movie projector was set in motion. Alina started the record player to provide the audio portion of the broadcast. The projection was as clear as one could expect from an 8mm film, however, the images of the television screen strobed, and the audio broke synchronization with the film. Alina often pushed the record a little quicker to catch up with the film, but nothing could be done about the strobing. The broadcast continued for only twenty minutes. There were several breaks in the film where commercials were cut out, and Alina made quick corrections to the record to get the audio back in sync with the film. At the end, the film stopped, Alina removed the needle from the record, and the lights were turned fully on.

"What you think?" Alina asked.

There was a brief silence followed by one woman saying, "It was wonderful."

"Okay. Now tell Zavuski what you really think," Alina said.

"It was hard to watch," Jane said.

Several women groaned as if Jane were being rude.

"It okay. Jane say something important. Go on," Alina said.

"The picture kept flashing," Jane continued. "I know you tried hard, doctor, but the lips didn't match the voice. And it just seemed strange to see Miss McBride like that after hearing her on the first interview. I never would have imagined she looked like that."

"Anything else?" Alina asked.

"Yeah. With all the distractions, I couldn't pay attention to the interview," Jane said.

"Jane!" Petunia said.

"No, Petunia, do not scold Jane. I ask for honest answer," Alina said. "Honesty very important, especially to self. I do not judge you here, I ask you look for honesty. How many others agree with Jane?"

Petunia did not raise her hand. Roberta was the first to raise hers. Alina smiled at Roberta. Two other women raised their hands. Then two more. Then much of the group raised their hands, including the woman running the movie projector. Finally, Alina raised her hand, and Petunia was the last. All women had their hands raised.

"It is difficult to pay attention to quality of interview, no?" Alina asked. "Quality of film very important or interview become distraction. Now I play interview on phonograph record again, but with no film."

Alina played the record. The women listened with intensity, and after twenty minutes, Alina took the needle off the record again.

"How many followed interview?" Zavuski asked.

All women raised their hands.

"It was much easier to pay attention," Jane said. "I concentrated on what was said. I didn't have to worry about watching anything. And I can think back to different parts of the interview and hear them in my mind again. But when I think about the film, I get this headache from the flashing like someone's beating my head."

"Yes," Alina said. "Miss McBride have nothing to beat her in audio format. Think about this in your life. You have dream. You have voice. Voice tell you how to reach dream. But film get in way. Film can be like vanity. Looking good takes away dream. Or film can be like flashing problem, like drum beating, but is someone's drum, not your drum. Someone's drum make you do things against dream. Fracture dream, break fluidity. Distract you from dream. Drum break dream. Sometimes you must turn film off. Listen to voice only. Work with voice. Make dream work for you."

"The *feks* beat the drum!" Petunia exclaimed, and the women erupted in agreement.

"Down with *feks*, down with *feks*," the women chanted.

"Wait!" Alina said. "I ask you. Hear me!"

The women continued chanting and mixing sayings, such as, "*Feks* are film," "No more *feks*," "Mary Queen McBride," "Long live Alina," and "Justice Jane."

"Please, ladies!" Alina said. "Be careful!"

"We're just letting off some steam," Petunia said. "We know what the flashing and film symbolize. And I'll say the forbidden word, because it's very important. Men are beating us like drums and killing our dreams!"

The women erupted again. More chanting followed, "End the men," "Petunia and Alina," "Justice Jane," and "Alive like McBride."

"Hear me, please!" Alina said.

"It's all true," Petunia said. "You asked us for honesty. Well? Here it is!"

The women cheered again.

"But you must be careful!" Alina said. "The evil here is not men!"

"What?!" some women said. Others said, "What's wrong with her?" "She can't say that," "She's off her rocker."

"I not off rocker!" Alina said. "You make big mistake just now. No, two mistake! First you make mistake of bundling."

Many confused responses.

"Huh?" Jane asked. "Who's bundling?"

"Real evil is regime! Do not forget! I tell you before, I tell you again. Regime is real evil. Regime beat drum, drum kill dream," Alina said.

"But the *feks* are the regime. They are beating us like drums!" Petunia said.

"That may be true," Alina said.

"There's no 'maybe' about it," Petunia said. "They are the regime. They are the evil!"

The women applauded and congratulated Petunia by shaking her hand.

"And here's Jane the Emancipator," Petunia said. "She saved our lives when the intruder beat on our door and beat on our doctor."

More applause. Chanting resumed with "Justice Jane," and "We want Petunia."

"I warn you about dangers of regime," Alina said.

"We've been hearing you preach about regime in every meeting. But you never say what to do about it," Petunia said.

Several women agreed vocally.

"I think it's time we take these ISIS meetings and make them more active, more aggressive," Petunia said.

"Careful," Alina said. "I warn you."

"Warn me of what? Of replacing you as leader of these meetings?" Petunia said.

"Petunia, no!" Jane urged.

"Look at us," Petunia said. "We come here every Saturday in secret, and what do we do? We eat dinner. We talk about things. We listen to things or watch a film. And we talk again. But that's it. How can we make a real difference down here in this underground tomb?"

"Petunia!" Jane said. "Stop!"

"No, Jane," Alina said. "I ask for honest expression. Let her finish. And I will show her dark path she take."

"There's no dark path that I can see," Petunia said. "But I do see a dead end if we continue these meetings down here. We need to actively protest on the streets, in the stores, and at home. Slogans, banners, the works!"

The women chanted again. Alina held up her hands to silence the chanting.

"But this is not ISIS way. ISIS is for illumination, to learn. Not for destruction."

"Who's talking about destruction? But I think it's time we redefine *illumination*. We need to illuminate the men around us. Show them what they are, and show them what they should be."

"Show the men, show the men!" the women chanted.

"So," Alina said. "A new drum beats. But it does not come from men."

"What are you talking about?" Jane asked.

"Only this. I warn you of bundling flaw. You bundle when you mix regime with men. So you hate men. But you ignore regime in other forms. And other form is here, in this meeting room, right now!"

The women broke into confused conversation. Many could not believe what they heard.

"Are you serious?" Jane asked.

"Very. You chant like drumbeat. You obsess about action against men. Where is dream? Dream gone. You beat dream away when you chant like regime," Alina said.

"We'll act first and dream later," a woman said.

"Too late by then. Dream gone. Forgotten. Replaced with new regime, new obsession," Alina said. "Mary McBride work every day, keep dream alive. You must too."

Some of the women grumbled.

"Are you saying we must put up with men and let them do whatever they want?" Jane asked.

"No, of course not!" Alina said. "Do what you must do, but do not let drumbeat trap you like most men do. Anything else is regime."

Petunia looked down. Then with a strange resolve, she stood up and walked around the room.

"You know, Alina," Petunia said.

"Are we on first-name basis now?" Alina said.

"I think so. You are very quick to dismiss things as being part of a regime when they do not fit your beliefs. I submit that this in itself is a type of regime," Petunia said.

"I ask for open opinion, and I ask for honesty. Is this regime?" Alina asked.

"No, but you lure us into thinking we're free, then you play your trump card: you cry 'regime', and this is supposed to silence us. I think it's time we change that," Petunia said. "In fact, I propose that Jane should be our new leader."

"What!?" Jane demanded.

"I'll help, of course," Petunia said. "I'll be your spokesperson. And don't cry 'regime' about it, Alina."

"No? You claim Jane as your new deity, so none may challenge. But you take the power. When you are challenged, you deflect to Jane. Jane say nothing, so she cannot be challenged. This is different kind of regime—cult," Alina explained.

"We'll see about that. All in favor of following Jane the Emancipator, raise your hands," Petunia said.

Petunia raised her hand. Two women raised theirs. And two more. Then most of the women raised their hands.

"Good. All in favor of following Alina, raise your hand," Petunia said.

The women who helped make dinner raised their hands. Jane started to raise hers, but Petunia shot Jane a stare. Alina didn't raise her hand.

"Aren't you going to vote for yourself?" Petunia asked.

"No. I not participate in vote. Like old Soviet Union. *Coup d'état* always hold one-party vote to authenticate power," Alina said.

"See, ladies? There's the regime thing again," Petunia said.

"Petunia," Jane said. "Don't you think we should—"

"Attention everyone, Jane the Emancipator wishes to speak," Petunia said.

Petunia walked back to Jane and whispered into her ear before sitting down.

"And it better support the new movement," Petunia replied.

"I think it's been a long week and a long day. Why don't we finish the meeting with some songs? Do we have any music?" Jane asked.

Petunia frowned, but Alina smiled.

"A good idea," Alina said. "Of course we have music. I put on phonograph record."

Alina placed the needle on a record by the Andrew Sisters. The woman sang, drank, and sang some more. By the end of the meeting, they had largely forgotten about Petunia's request, but Petunia was determined to make a change, and she was determined to get support.

1948 Oct 10, Sun 10:30 am. Kenosha, Wisconsin.

Evanita and Jonara had witnessed the last of the ISIS meeting as the women entered the box truck and headed back to the warehouse. The end of Saturday had turned gray, and the two found themselves sitting on Jane's and Jack's front porch Sunday morning. Jane and Jack walked home from church with Roberta and entered their house through the front door, unaware of Evanita and Jonara. Ten minutes after Jane and Jack arrived home, a delivery truck backed into the O'Leary driveway. A woman dressed in a dark-blue laborer's outfit knocked on the door. Jane opened the door.

"Mum!" Jane said. "Come in! What a surprise visit. And you're dressed up! Petunia told me about your overtime work this weekend. Are you on break?"

"Actually, I'm not," Mum said. "I have a delivery for Jack."

"You do? What kind of delivery?" Jane asked.

Mum pointed to her co-worker who was wheeling a crate off the truck.

"That? It's huge! What's in the crate, an icebox?" Jane asked. "Wait—don't tell me."

"A television, of course. It's all the rage with the World Series," Mum said.

"I don't understand. Jack already has a—"

"Television?" Jack said as he entered the doorway in front of Jane. "Grand. Just put it in the living room. The antenna cable is ready to go. Just hook it up."

"In the living room, Pete!" Mum yelled.

Mum held the door for Pete. Pete wheeled the crate through the door with a hand truck. Mum, Jane, and Jack followed behind.

"Are you familiar with our one-year service policy, Jack?" Mum asked.

"One year onsite free repair service including tubes and labor," Jack said.

"You got it! If you'll just sign here saying you accept delivery, please?" Mum asked.

Jack signed the document. Mum gave him copies of the paperwork.

"There you are," Mum said. "Pete is setting up your General Electric Model 901 right now. You have purchased the top-of-the-line television encased in genuine mahogany. It has original FM radio, new FM radio, standard AM radio, shortwave radio, and an automatic phonograph. And of course, there's the television tuner with channels one through thirteen."

Mum helped Pete with uncrating and setup.

"That looks heavy," Jane said.

"It's 400 pounds," Mum said.

"Where's the screen?" Jane asked.

"You're going to like the screen," Jack said. "Just watch them set it up."

Mum opened the front cabinet doors, and Pete raised the screen.

"It's a projection screen!" Jack yelled.

"A 432 square inch projection screen," Mum said. "One of the biggest screens money can buy."

Pete reached to turn on the television, but Jack stopped him.

"Wait, I want to turn it on first," Jack said.

Jack flipped the power switch. A few minutes later, the screen warmed up, and an image of WTMJ-TV Channel 3 Milwaukee appeared.

"It's like a dream come true!" Jack said.

"Your account is all paid up," Mum said. "Enjoy your purchase!"

"Wait," Jane asked Mum. "What do you mean, 'all paid up'?"

"There's no payment plan," Mum said. "It was paid in full on Saturday with cash."

"There must be a mistake," Jane said. "Jack doesn't have that kind of money."

"It's what my document says. 'Paid in full.' If you'll excuse me, I have a delivery at Mr. Grundle's house—a General Electric Model 810. It's much smaller, only 52 square inches, so it'll be a snap to set up. His television is paid in full, too."

"Excuse me, Mum, but how much was Mr. Grundle's Model 810?" Jane asked.

"$325," Mum replied. "Funny, isn't it? The 810 is only 52 square inches, but the 901 is 432 square inches. Like a thimble versus a mountain. Well, gotta go. See you around, Jane."

Mum and Pete drove off. Jack fiddled with knobs and dials on the new television like a boy with a new toy. Jane didn't like the comparison of $325 for a thimble versus a mountain. How much did the mountain cost? She worried—for good reason—but she wasn't sure of the specifics.

"Jack," Jane said.

"Don't you see I'm busy?" Jack said.

"I don't understand why we have two televisions," Jane said.

"Because I can't afford to have a Tee-Vee burn out in the middle of a ball game. I need a backup Tee-Vee. And I might as well get a bigger screen in the process. Look at this," Jack said.

Jack powered on the smaller television and tuned it to Channel 3.

"Both Tee-Vees are on the same station," Jack said. "If one burns out, the other one will cover the game. I'm guaranteed to see the entire game!"

"But Jack, can we afford—"

"Oh look at the time!" Jack said. "It's 11:30! The preview is starting. The boys will be here any second. Quick! Fix up some snacks for us."

"I just want to know where you got the money—" Jane started.

"No time for twenty questions," Jack said. "Get hopping with the snacks."

Jack clapped his hands three times.

"Like a drumbeat," Jane muttered to herself.

Jane ran to the kitchen and prepared snacks. She was in such a rush—with Jack's friends coming over and his incessant hand clapping—that she quite forgot to ask the price of the new television. Jack's friends watched the World Series Preview show, the World Series, and the Green Bay Packers football team lose to the Chicago Cardinals. By the end of the football game, Jane was exhausted from servicing the men. The men were disappointed with the Packers' loss and left soon after the game ended. Jack grumbled about something but found another television program to watch. Jane took Roberta for a walk to the beach and forgot all about Jack and his new television.

1948 Oct 11, Mon. Marquette University. Milwaukee, Wisconsin.

Jane took the North Shore Line train from Kenosha to Milwaukee and a short bus trip on Wisconsin Avenue from downtown Milwaukee to Marquette University. She brought Roberta along with her, and the two entered the Office of the Registrar. She met with a counselor, Father O'Riley, to discuss her plans for attending the university.

"Full name," Father O'Riley asked.

"Jane MacNessi O'Leary," Jane said.

"Birthdate?"

"November 3, 1923."

"Religion?"

"Roman Catholic."

"Very good. Education?"

"Graduated from Kenosha Central High School in 1942," Jane said. "No wait, that was the old name. It changed while I was there to Mary D. Bradford High School."

"Any university courses to transfer?"

"None. I have a copy of my high school transcript here," Jane said.

Jane handed her transcript to the counselor, and he looked at it.

"We will have to request an official transcript of course," he said. "But based on this unofficial transcript, your grades appear to be good enough to admit you. To what school do you wish to apply?"

"The College of Dentistry," Jane said.

The counselor's eyes widened.

"If you'd said 'nursing,' I would have admitted you without hesitation. But the College of Dentistry is a stringent program. And you must have a Bachelor's degree first before entering. What other things have you done in your life to demonstrate your commitment to the program?" Father O'Riley asked.

"I was a machinist during the war at Daschwirk factory. Here—I have a letter of recommendation. It's signed by my former boss, Mr. Henrock, and the owner, Mr. Daschwirk."

The counselor looked at the document.

"This is dated three years ago," Father O'Riley said. "Are you still employed at Daschwirk?"

"No."

"Why did you leave?"

"I didn't leave. I was let go."

"Due to poor performance?"

"No. Things changed. The war ended. They said they didn't need me, but then they hired many men. I asked for my job back, but they said I wasn't qualified," Jane said.

"Wasn't qualified," Father O'Riley wrote down and mumbled aloud.

"That's not why I was let go. I'm qualified—better than many of them. I think it was because I'm a woman," Jane said.

"Gives verbose answers," the counselor wrote but did not mumble.

"What would Mr. Henrock say about you if I call him up? You do have his telephone number, don't you?" Father O'Riley asked.

"You can't call him," Jane said.

"Oh? What's the problem? Did you have a falling out with him?"

"No. He died in '45."

"I see. So what have you done since then?" Father O'Riley asked.

"I worked at Kefer Toothe Company in Racine," Jane said.

"As a machinist?" Father O'Riley asked.

"No, as a cook," Jane said.

"Why?"

"They said I wasn't qualified as a machinist, but I know I am. It's because I'm a woman," Jane said.

"Did they tell you that?"

"Of course not."

"Are you still employed at Kefer Toothe Company?"

"Only in the off season," Jane said.

"Off season of what?" Father O'Riley asked.

"I play baseball."

"You do? How?"

"This year I played for the Kenosha Comets. Last year I played for the Racine Belles," Jane explained.

The counselor didn't seem to understand.

"The All-American Girls Baseball League," Jane said. "Milwaukee had a team—the Chicks. Back in '44? You must remember."

"Back in 1944. Oh yes, something about girls playing softball while the boys went to war. Never heard of them after that summer. And the war ended three years ago."

"Well, the league is still playing, even if the Milwaukee Chicks aren't, but we play baseball now, not softball," Jane said.

"Did you serve overseas in the war?" Father O'Riley asked.

"No. But my husband did. He was in the European theater," Jane explained.

"So he's a G.I. but you are not, is that right?" Father O'Riley asked.

"I'm the wife of a G.I. Doesn't that count?" Jane asked.

"Mrs. O'Leary," the counselor said. "I'm afraid that based on your background, I cannot offer you a scholarship. Nor can I assist you under the G.I. Bill. Cooking by day and playing softball by night—"

"Baseball. And it's professional," Jane said.

"Yes, um-hum. Well. I'm afraid you will have to come up with the full tuition amount for school here. You do know that eight years of school are necessary to become a dentist. Four years as an undergraduate majoring in biology or chemistry, and another four years in dental school. Can you afford all that?"

"I have $2000 in a savings account," Jane said. "That should count for something."

"$2000? A girl like you? Really? Seems hard to believe," Father O'Riley said.

"Believe it! I saved every penny from professional baseball, and a little extra from Kefer," Jane boasted.

"Well, that's a horse of a different hue," Father O'Riley said. "I'll tell you what. We can admit you under a predentistry curriculum plan majoring in biology or chemistry. You can choose which major, but you have plenty of time. You may start courses in the spring semester. See if you like school. If you do well, you may continue classes until you receive a Bachelor's degree. But there are no loans. For the beginning of each semester, you must pay the full tuition amount in cash. Now we do have limited enrollment for spring. If you bring, say, $400, I can hold you a place."

"Oh, I have more than $400. I have $2000," Jane bragged.

"Yes, you said that already," Father O'Riley said.

"I can get that to you today—in an hour or less. I keep my savings up here in Milwaukee so no one can get to it. I could almost walk to the bank. I could run!" Jane said with excitement.

"Please, don't overexert yourself. I will be here all day. You may drop by anytime, except from 12:00 to 1:00 when I take my lunch. If you are back during that hour and do not wish to wait, our clerk will take your tuition amount and credit it to your account."

"Oh thank you, Father O'Riley! Thank you very much," Jane said. "Come along, Roberta, your Mommie is going to the bank so she can enroll in school to become a dentist!"

"You're welcome. And if you ever have the need for confession, do not hesitate to call. I hear confessions from six to six-thirty every morning at the Gesu Church," Father O'Riley said.

Jane rushed out of the registrar's office (with Roberta riding piggy back) and jogged east on Wisconsin Avenue past 11th Street, 10th Street, 9th, 8th, and so on until she passed 2nd Street and Plankinton Ave.

"River, Mommie, river!" Roberta said.

"Yes, Roberta. We're crossing the Milwaukee River to my bank. Isn't the water pretty?" Jane asked.

The two started across the bridge and paused to look over the edge.

"I'm crossing the river of change, Roberta. I'm leaving my old life behind and starting a new one."

With high hopes of a great future as a dentist, Jane crossed the Milwaukee River with Roberta riding piggyback. The two turned north onto Water Street and walked almost a block until they reached the First Wisconsin National Bank. Jane walked up to the next available clerk, placed Roberta on the ground, and asked for a withdrawal.

"I would like $400, please," Jane said.

Jane handed the clerk her identification and bank book. The clerk looked at the identification, at the bank book, and at her records. The delay was longer than expected.

"Is there a problem?" Jane asked.

The clerk returned a fake smile, said, "One moment please," and walked to a back desk where she spoke with a manager.

"Mommie, hurry! You have to go to school!" Roberta said.

"Mommie will start school soon, but she must get tuition money from her savings account first."

"What is 'savings account'?" Roberta asked.

"It's a safe place where I keep money and no one else can steal it," Jane said, but as soon as she spoke the words, a sinking feeling filled her stomach.

The clerk returned with her manager.

"Mrs. O'Leary," the manager said. "There seems to be a problem with your request."

"There can't be," Jane said. "I have $2000 in my account. I'm only requesting $400. Do I have to wait for my money?"

"Mrs. O'Leary, I'm afraid your account is overdrawn," the manager said.

"There's a mistake," Jane said. "There must be. I know the money is there."

"It's overdrawn by $100," the manager said. "I need you to cover the shortfall immediately."

"No! My money is supposed to be safe in this bank. How can it disappear just like that? Look at my bank book. See? It shows a balance of $2000!" Jane said.

"I'm afraid this bank book was not updated properly," the manager said.

"Updated from what?" Jane asked.

"There was a special charge against this account on October 8th. Unfortunately, there was an error and $2100 was withdrawn. Only $2000 should have been permitted. I apologize for the mistake, but you must replace the funds."

"The money disappeared on Friday? How? Who took it?" Jane asked.

Jane didn't need them to answer. The withdrawal of $2100 matched what Petunia had told her earlier about expensive television sets going for $2100, and Jane realized where Jack had obtained his money for the projection television.

"No! Don't say it was Jack," Jane said.

"Jack O'Leary. Your husband withdrew the money," the manager said.

"But this is Wisconsin, the progressive state. You're not supposed to let this happen!" Jane said.

"I'm sorry, but you must cover the shortfall. Otherwise, you are in breach of contract, and this bank will be forced to file a lawsuit for recovery. You don't want that, do you Mrs. O'Leary? Lawyers can be quite expensive."

"My money, my money!" Jane screamed.

Jane fell into hysterics. Nearby bank patrons watched as two security guards ushered Jane out of the bank. Roberta beat on the guards, telling them to give back her Mommie's money. The guards forced Jane out of the building and blocked the doorway. Jane beat on the door and demanded her money. The manager opened the door and spoke.

"If you do not leave the premises immediately, I'll call the police!" he said.

He slammed the door behind him. Jane stared through the bank windows with a wet face and dejected spirit. Roberta beat on the door for her mother's money. Jane was now hoarse and could barely speak.

"Come along, Roberta," Jane barely managed.

"Bank has Mommie's money!" Roberta protested.

"I know," Jane said. "I know."

"Bank is safe," Roberta said.

"I know. Come along," Jane said.

Jane retraced her steps down Water Street onto Wisconsin Avenue. She stood with Roberta overlooking the Milwaukee River and allowed teardrops to fall from her face to the river below.

"What can Jane do?" Jonara asked. "Her money is gone. She can't go to school."

"I know what I'd do—I'd kill Jack!" Evanita said to Jonara. "That bastard stole her money!"

"Jack is beating me like a drum," Jane said to herself. "I must stop his drumbeat. Stop his heartbeat? No. I can't kill Jack. I would go to prison, and his drum would beat out the years of my prison sentence. The state would take away Roberta."

Jane knelt down and gave Roberta a big squeeze.

"You're the only thing he hasn't taken away—yet," Jane said to Roberta. "He must never take you away. You're all I have left."

Jane carried Roberta piggyback to the North Shore Line station where she hopped on the next train to Kenosha. Evanita and Jonara accompanied her. Jane arrived in Kenosha and took a bus home. She looked at the new television's bill of sale—$2100 for the television, another $100 for installation, taxes, and one-year free service.

"He stole it right under my nose," Jane said to herself. "Even during installation, he didn't say anything. How did he think he could get away with this?"

Jack arrived home from work.

"What's for supper?" he asked. "I've had a hard day."

"You've had a hard day?" Jane asked with surprise.

"Yeah!" Jack yelled. "Now get me my supper!"

"You don't get anything!" Jane said.

"You better get my supper, or else!" Jack warned.

"You stole my money!" Jane yelled.

"What are you talking about?" Jack pretended. "Gimme my supper and stop babbling!"

"You stole my $2000 from my First Wisconsin National Bank account. And you overdrew it by $100. I owe the bank $100!" Jane said.

"Oh that? You owed it to me for breaking my first set," Jack said.

"That's a lie!" Jane said.

"It ain't!" Jack retorted. "Matter of fact, you haven't been pulling your share around here. Not even a little. I asked you to have the old set repaired. An easy task! Just call up the department store, and they send a guy out to repair it—free of charge! Is that so hard? But no! You just ignored it and went to the beach. Heck, I wish I could lounge around the beach all day."

"That's not the way it was!" Jane said.

"Shut up! Don't interrupt while I'm lecturing you!" Jack said.

"Of all the nerve!" Jane yelled, but Jack slapped her, and she held her tongue.

"What am I going to do with you, woman?" Jack said. "You go running around with that baseball team or whatever you call it, and I'm always watching Roberta. That's for starters. Then there's the way you treat the boys when they're over. Okay? You're supposed to be like a rosebush, see? You're only worthy when you're producing roses. But you won't produce roses unless you're trimmed way back to the stump. And that's what I'm doing—I'm trimming you to the stump to make you more productive again."

"You're crazy!" Jane said.

"You just don't know how the world works," Jack explained. "Look at today's *Kenosha Evening News*. The sports section. Look at what Curly Lambeau said."

"The Cardinals won 17-7," Jane said. "Curly was upset. Jack—this has nothing to do with—"

"It has everything to do with us. I'm like Curly Lambeau, and you're like the Green Bay Packers. I have to mold you and shape you to make you a winner. When you win, I win."

"Jack, this is crazy talk," Jane said.

"Shut up already!" he yelled. "Now read the paper. Look right there. See? Lambeau says he can't remember the Packers looking as unspirited in the last ten years. I see the same thing in you, Jane. You're unspirited. You know why?"

"Yes, I do know why!" Jane said.

"I'm glad you've figured it out. You've obviously read the article. Look. Lambeau says, 'We're going to correct this situation this week, or else. There'll be salary adjustments and changes made until it is corrected—one of the big reasons it (meaning the low spirit) exists is that the boys are getting good salaries and they're content. For that reason, there's got to be a penalty for losing.'"

"That's stupid," Jane said.

Jack slapped Jane across the face.

"You don't call the great Curly Lambeau stupid. When you coach a team into an NFL Championship, you understand psychology," Jack explained.

"Curly hasn't won the championship since '44," Jane said. "That was four years ago. Did you ever consider that maybe the problem is with him?"

Jack punched her across the jaw.

"That's for blasphemy. Lambeau can't do everything. It's about time he took serious action. Things have deteriorated with the Packers, as it has with our marriage. And it's because you're earning too much money. First, it was at Daschwirk, now it's with baseball. You're too comfortable, Jane. You're dropping the ball. You gotta learn to catch the ball when it's thrown to you—every time. I gotta take you down a peg or two, wake you up, and help you smell the coffee again. You'll be productive again soon enough."

"Well you're right about one thing, Jack. Our marriage has deteriorated," Jane said. "But I'm not the one with the problem!"

Jack swung at Jane, but Jane jumped back out of the way. He came at her, but she fought back. Physically she was as strong as ever, and she bravely stood up to Jack. Every punch or slap he threw, she blocked. She tried to think—should she attack him? She thought of Petunia and Alina at the ISIS meeting—Petunia would tell her to punch Jack, while Alina would tell her to block Jack long enough for Jane to get out of there.

"Take your medicine like a good girl!" Jack yelled. "Don't block me. It'll only take longer!"

Roberta screamed. Jane knew that she couldn't block Jack forever, but she needed him to stop long enough so she could get together a few things and get out without his interference. She gave in to Petunia's advice and kicked Jack in the groin. Jack bowled over and fell to his knees in pain.

"Now look what you've done!" he said. "You've ruined everything, you bitch!"

Jane packed a bag of things for herself and Roberta.

"I'm leaving," she announced.

"Don't you take my daughter from me," Jack said. "It's kidnapping, and you know it. You'll go to jail for kidnapping and for assaulting me."

Jane hesitated for a moment. Jack's words almost convinced her to stay. She did assault him, and she was taking his daughter away. Then she remembered what Alina said during the ISIS meeting, and she spoke to Jack again:

"I'm no slave to your drumbeat!"

Jane walked to the train station and took the North Shore Line back up to Racine. She walked to the department store where Mum worked. Mum was getting off work and saying goodbye to her friends.

"Janie!" Mum said. "What happened to your face! And why all the luggage?"

"I fell on...no, I won't lie anymore. Jack and I had a fight," Jane said. "I need help."

Mum hugged Jane and Roberta.

"Come with me. I'm on my way home. Petunia always makes extra for dinner; there will be plenty for the four of us."

Mum unlocked a 1947 Studebaker very similar to Arbie's, but it was not a convertible.

"There's that steering wheel again," Jonara said to Evanita.

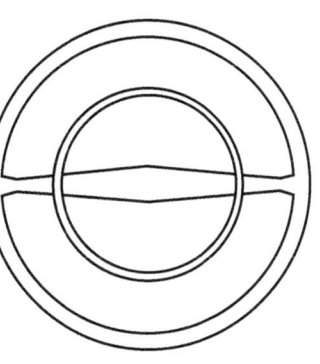

"There's something about concentric circles in all of this, Little Voice," Evanita said. "I wish I knew the answer."

"Me too," Jonara said.

Mum pulled into the driveway of Petunia's and her house. As predicted, Petunia had dinner waiting.

"Petunia, we have guests tonight," Mum said.

"Well come in, come in!" Petunia said. "I have a surprise for you too, Mum."

From the hallway emerged Alina.

"Dr. Zavuski, this is an honor," Mum said.

"Thank you," Alina said. "Nice to see you, Jane and Roberta. But Jane, what become of face? You fall on husband's boot again?"

"We got into a fight over money," Jane said. "My money."

The women and Roberta sat down to dinner. Jane explained what had happened with her trip to Marquette University, the bank, and the confrontation with Jack. At the end, she wiped her face with a napkin. The retelling drained her emotionally.

"Sad tale," Alina said. "But I not surprised. This evil happen everywhere."

"What are you going to do?" Mum said.

"I don't want to go back," Jane said. "But I have nowhere to go."

"Hmm," Alina said. "I have story too. I moving to Alabama."

"What!?" Mum said.

"You're kidding," Jane said.

"Did you know, Petunia?" Mum said.

"I knew," Petunia replied. "I'll be taking over ISIS meetings for the Racine chapter. I'm in the process of buying Alina's farm as we speak."

"You didn't tell me," Mum said.

"I thought you liked farms," Petunia said.

"I do, but this is a big surprise," Mum said.

"Very big," Dr. Zavuski said.

"Dr. Zavuski, please don't go. We need you here," Jane said. "I need you now more than ever."

"My child," Alina said as she leaned over and kissed Jane on the cheek. "My time complete in Racine. I from Soviet Union. I had nothing there. I start with nothing here and make something. Petunia carry on. Petunia strong. And Mum. You too, and little Roberta."

"But I have nothing now," Jane said. "I'm leaving Jack. He's ruined me."

"He ruined life you had before tonight. Rest of life yours," Alina said. "But I make offer, Jane MacNessi O'Leary."

"Please," Jane said. "Call me Jane MacNessi. I never want to hear 'O'Leary' again."

The women clapped.

"Very well, Jane MacNessi. I make offer. You come with Dr. Zavuski to Alabama, no? We start new ISIS chapter. No drumbeat to ruin dream. Only dream. What you say?"

"And leave my friends here?" Jane asked. "And the Kenosha Comets?"

"Janie," Petunia said. "We love you very much, of course. We'll help you no matter what you choose. But don't let us hold you back. If you want to start a new ISIS chapter with Dr. Zavuski, go for it! The baseball league won't be here forever. You heard about the Springfield Sallies and Chicago Colleens being dropped from main competition next year? Well there's more. Rumor is more teams will be forced to drop as the years go on. The Kenosha Comets will probably be next. One or two years are all we figure they'll have left. Men and television have ended the league. Don't let your hopes be crushed again. Mum and I will be fine here in Racine, and I imagine Arbie will want to move back up here after a bit. But your time here has ended. It's time to move on."

"What you say, Jane?" Alina asked.

"Would you like to move down to Alabama?" Jane asked Roberta.

"What is Alabama?" Roberta asked.

"It's a place in the South. It's warmer than here, and you can play outside all year round," Jane explained.

"Yay!" Roberta said. "I want to go Al-bama. I want to go, Mommie!"

"Then it's settled," Jane said. "Roberta and I are going south."

1948 Dec 31, Fri 11:50 pm. Montgomery, Alabama.

"Hour is late," Alina said. "You stay up for New Year, no?"

Jane and Roberta huddled around the radio sipping hot chocolate and eating cheese crackers.

"Times Square celebrated the new year an hour ago," Jane said. "Now I'm listening to the Montgomery New Year countdown."

"New Year start soon. You make resolution?" Alina asked.

"I resolve to put the past in the past," Jane said, "and put my feet in the future. Do you see this newspaper?"

Jane pointed to the December 20th, 1948 edition of the *Montgomery Advertiser.*

"Sports section," Alina said. "American football."

"It shows the result of the final game of the season. The Philadelphia Eagles beat the Chicago Cardinals in the championship game. But the paper also shows the win-loss records for all teams. Look at where the Packers finished."

"I not know much about football. You have thoughts?" Alina asked.

"I sure do. If I had stayed with Jack even a week, he would have bragged about Curly Lambeau's effective new policy of salary cuts," Jane explained. "After the Packers lost to the Cardinals on October 10th, the Packers shut out the Los Angeles Rams 16-0. But after that, the Packers lost the rest of their games in the season—all seven of them. So much for Curly's method. The Packers finished with three wins and nine losses— only Detroit did worse in the division and only by a game."

"Twisting tail work for short time only," Alina said. "Is this your meaning?"

"I think so," Jane said.

"Countdown, Mommie! Countdown!" Roberta cheered.

Jane, Roberta, and Alina counted down the final seconds of 1948.

"Three, two, one. Happy New Year! Happy 1949!"

Jane and Roberta blew horns and threw bits of paper in the air. Alina joined them in celebration, and 1948 faded into gray.

2110 Dec 28, Sun Noon. 376 Grey Road, Hamilton, New Zealand.

"And that was 1948," the elder Jonara said. "Would you like some lunch? No, now just a moment, I remember from yesterday. You brought sack lunches."

"Actually, in our haste to get out the door this morning, we forgot," Kristi said.

"Well that won't do, now will it? I will whip something up quickly for the two of you—no, the three of you," Jonara said. "Do you have names picked out yet?"

"If it's a girl," Kristi said, "we want to call her 'Marci Fernandez'."

"And if she's a girl?" Jonara asked.

Kristi and Margaret laughed.

"That's the nice thing about female parents—the children are always female," Kristi said.

"Yes, they are, aren't they?" Jonara said. "I had meant to go through my notes and see if there was a way for two women to have a boy. But I swear I'd lose my head in these papers if it weren't attached. Now then, follow me into the dining room. I make a great egg sandwich."

CHAPTER 12

Aitch, Eitch, Haitch

2110 Dec 28, Sun 1 pm. 376 Grey Road, Hamilton, New Zealand.

"This is the attic," the elderly Jonara said.

"What was that?" Kristi asked.

A bat flew toward the women, and all three ducked.

"It's a bat," Jonara said. "I've been meaning to get rid of it, but I think about all the mail I need to open, and I never get around to it."

"A broom will solve your problems," Margaret said. "One quick swat while the bat is sleeping, and no more bat."

"That's a good idea," Jonara said. "And I can use the broom to sweep up the old bat droppings."

"You have a lot of them to clean up," Kristi said as she stepped carefully on the attic floor.

"I've always liked full-height attics," Jonara said. "I can walk around all I want without bumping my head, unless I get too close to the sides."

Kristi and Margaret noticed lots of cardboard boxes piled everywhere and several tables with partially completed jigsaw puzzles.

"I love jigsaw puzzles," Jonara said. "I do them whenever I get the chance. This one celebrates America's tricentennial. I bought it in 2076 and started on it immediately."

"How many times have you completed the tricentennial puzzle?" Kristi asked.

"I'm almost finished with my first try," Jonara said.

Margaret and Kristi rolled their eyes at each other as they had for every other thing that needed doing at Jonara's home.

"Just kidding! I've completed the puzzle at least eighty times," Jonara said.

"Whew!" Kristi said. "We thought this was another thing you started years ago and didn't finish."

"There are some things I haven't finished, but many things I have. The means for women to have children with women, for example—that was completed years ago," Jonara said. "Now there was something else I wanted to do today—what was it? Don't tell me, I'll get it in a moment. Yes, I remember—the interview! Why can't you girls remember anything? Come along! We must go to the living room now."

The three returned to the living room.

"The next part is what I call, 'Aitch, Eitch, Haitch'," Jonara said.

"What does that mean?" Kristi asked. "Is that German?"

"Oh heavens no," Jonara said. "It's just a way of saying the letter 'H' three times. Would you like to guess what 'H' stands for?"

"The H-bomb?" Margaret asked.

"Yes. Exactly!" Jonara said. "Let me tell you about it."

Jonara told the story, and Kristi narrated it here:

2023 Oct 5, Thu Dawn. Corpus Christi, Texas.
2006 Nov 22, Wed Eve. Redjet Laundry Room.

Evanita and Jonara returned to the Redjet laundry room. The washer had long ago stopped running, and Calico tapped Evanita on the shoulder.

"What are you doing, daydreaming? Hop to the laundry!" Calico said.

Without warning, a flash through the windows caught Evanita and Calico by surprise. Jonara turned in time to see a bright-orange fireball ascend from the place where the Helrod once stood. Pole remnants of the Helrod shot laterally in all directions.

"Explosives," Calico said. "Someone blew up the Helrod."

The explosion jolted Jonara out of 2006 and into another time and place.

1962 Jul 10. Kiritimati Island, Pacific Ocean.

Jonara had no time to adjust to her new environment. The explosion from the Elrod 402 transferred her to a nuclear explosion from Operation Dominic Sunset. Jonara watched as a bright fireball floated upward creating layers of expanding yellow, orange, and red concentric rings. She could not break her eyes away from the brilliant light, not even for a blink. She stared and stared. She stood on the ground next to military personnel.

"You'll burn your eyes out if you look too long," said a voice.

"I must look into the fusion reaction until it ends," Jonara replied.

"It won't burn out—not in your lifetime. It will undergo fusion for another four and a half billion years," said a familiar voice.

"It's so beautiful, and so deadly," Jonara said.

"Blink, Jonara. Your eyes are drying up. Look at me, Jonara. Look!"

Jonara turned from the fireball and looked at the military person next to her. The man's uniform was dark and blurry. Jonara's vision had been temporarily diminished from staring at the light, but in a few seconds, her vision returned to normal, and the man with the military uniform was now dressed in a night robe and had white hair.

"Daddy!" Jonara said.

Jonara was now fully awake and in her guestroom of Geneva's house, the day being Thursday, October 5, 2023.

"You're staring at the sunrise again," Johnny said. "Did you dream about the past?"

"Yeah. I did," Jonara said.

Johnny hugged Jonara.

"Relax, honey," he said. "Your heart is racing like crazy. Come downstairs and have some breakfast."

The two descended the stairs and entered the dining room.

"Breakfast is ready," Anna said. "Help yourself to scrambled eggs, bacon, toast, hash browns, and orange juice. There's cereal in the cupboard and milk in the fridge if you like."

Jonara took a plate and filled it with scrambled eggs, bacon, and toast. She grabbed a glass of orange juice, eating utensils, and sat at the dining table. Johnny and Anna followed her to the table with their own plates of food. Anna brought forth the coffeepot and filled both Johnny's and her mugs with coffee.

"You sleep well?" Anna asked, but she saw the dark circles under Jonara's eyes and realized the answer. "No, you did not sleep well. You worry about your Mamma?"

"I worry about lots of things," Jonara said.

"Well eat up," Anna said. "Breakfast make you feel better."

Jonara took two bites of eggs and washed them down with orange juice.

"It's good," Jonara said.

At that moment, a door knock disturbed the silence. Anna opened the door, and Cerafina appeared.

"Come in, Cerafina," Anna said. "Sit down and have breakfast with us."

"Thank you," Cerafina said.

Cerafina helped herself to eggs, toast, and coffee.

"You're young for coffee," Anna said.

"My mother serves me coffee all the time. And I love it," Cerafina said.

"I can't believe you like coffee," Jonara said. "I tried it yesterday, but it's bitter."

"One acquires a taste for it," Cerafina said. "Jonara—you look so tired. Did you read the—"

"Shhh," Jonara said.

"What you going to say, Cerafina?" Anna said. "Did Jonara do what?"

"Nothing, Miss Anna," Cerafina said.

"Not nice to play games with Anna," Anna said. "Jonara—why you tired this morning? You read that diary again? You were told not to."

"It's okay, Anna," Johnny said. "Jonara is my daughter, and I will take care of her health."

"Men not so good at watching over young people's health. Mr. Johnny prevent broken bones but not broken spirit," Anna said. "Jonara—stay away from the diary. It brings misfortune."

"So you did read it?" Cerafina said.

"A little," Jonara said.

Cerafina gave Jonara a questioning gaze.

"Okay, maybe a lot," Jonara said.

"Without me? I wanted to travel back in time too! Who did you go back in time with?" Cerafina demanded.

"No one!" Jonara said.

"Was it that Almarita on the telephone?" Cerafina asked.

"You know that's impossible. And Almarita is jealous of you anyway," Jonara said.

"How do you know that?" Cerafina asked.

"I talked with her last night," Jonara said.

"While you were reading the diary?" Cerafina asked.

"No. Before," Jonara said.

"Honest?" Cerafina asked.

"Yes, honest! But I feel like I'm trapped between friends," Jonara said.

"Not good to be trapped," Anna said.

"I know, I know!" Jonara said.

Johnny laughed.

"It's not funny!" Jonara said.

"I'm not laughing at you, Jonara. I'm just happy you have more friends than you know what to do with," Johnny said.

"Huh? You're not making sense," Jonara said.

"When you're older, you'll understand. People grow apart as they age," Johnny said. "Then we hold onto keepsakes to remember the good old days."

"Like the candleholder?" Jonara asked.

Johnny removed the Aromani candleholder from the inside of his shirt.

"I didn't know about that," Cerafina said. "May I see it?"

"Mr. Johnny," Anna said. "Eva said these relics are not good thing. Mr. Johnny!"

"Yes, Anna, I know. But she's not here now. Everything will be fine. Why don't you start cleaning up from breakfast?"

"I will do that, Mr. Johnny, but I still not happy about relics," Anna said, and she disappeared into the kitchen.

Johnny passed the candleholder to Cerafina.

"This candlestick holder," Cerafina said, "is made of the same wood as the viol—Norway white spruce, Norway Crimson King maple, and lignum vitae. And the shape of the candleholder—it looks like the half-face symbol on the viol."

Cerafina passed the candleholder back to Johnny.

"It was Fantina's. She used it to celebrate the Sabbath on the boat to Palestine," Jonara said.

"Who's Fantina?" Cerafina asked.

"Fantina was my grandmother," Johnny said. "She gave the candleholder to Aromani—my father—when he was a little boy. When Father died, I found the candleholder hidden in a little box."

"Who's Aromani?" Cerafina asked.

"Funny thing, Jane MacNessi didn't have a relic," Jonara said.

"Who's Jane MacNessi?" Cerafina asked.

"You met her too? I'm surprised you didn't see her oboe," Johnny said. "It's also made of Norway maple, Norway spruce, and lignum vitae."

"You mean she had one of these things too?" Jonara asked.

"What oboe?" Cerafina asked.

"Yes. She gave it to Roberta. But I'm afraid it was lost in the early 1990s."

"Would someone tell me what's going on?" Cerafina asked.

"Last night I went back in time with the diary," Jonara said.

"I know that part," Cerafina said.

"Well...there's too much to tell," Jonara said after pausing in thought.

"Wait," Johnny said. "There's another way to let Cerafina know everything you learned from last night."

"How?" Jonara asked.

"With the Moissan Ruby," Johnny said.

"But I thought that only works in reading things," Jonara said.

"By itself, yes," Johnny said. "But when used with something like the candleholder—something with layers of Norway maple, Norway spruce, and lignum vitae, you can communicate. Here."

Johnny handed the Moissan Ruby to Jonara, and she hung it around her neck just below her neckline atop the upper part of her sternum.

"Now you will also wear the candleholder," Johnny said, and he passed the candleholder to her.

"Like a necklace?" Jonara asked.

"No, like a belt," Johnny said. "The candleholder must be placed over your belly button."

"How can I wear it like a belt? It's not a belt," Jonara said.

"Maybe more like a belt buckle," Johnny said.

"I still need a belt attached to it. How did you do it back at the Elrod 402?" Jonara asked.

"Do what?"

"Mommy had broken legs. You visited her in Whalejet. You hugged her, and somehow you healed her legs," Jonara said.

"I had the Aromani candleholder on a long necklace chain," Johnny said. "I hung it around my neck, and it rested just above my belly button. I kept it under my shirt so no one would see. For now, just hold the candleholder over your belly button with one hand and hold your other hand to Cerafina's forehead. Then think about what you dreamed last night."

Jonara did as Johnny told her.

"Nothing," Cerafina said. "I don't feel anything."

"Because the Water Ruby needs activating, doesn't it Daddy?" Jonara asked.

"You're right—it does," Johnny said. "Hmm. Stand by the refrigerator when the compressor is running."

Jonara and Cerafina walked into the kitchen and both leaned against the fridge. Jonara did as before—she held the Aromani candleholder over her belly button and held her other hand to Cerafina's forehead.

"Nothing," Cerafina said.

"The compressor isn't running," Jonara said.

Jonara opened the fridge door and adjusted the temperature to the lowest setting. The compressor kicked on. She closed the door and repeated the procedure.

"I'm getting something," Cerafina said. "Good god! Too much, Jonara. Too much! Slow down! I can't handle it all at once!"

Jonara pulled the Aromani candleholder away from her abdomen a little bit. Cerafina's grief mellowed into a low strain.

"Much better. Whew!" Cerafina said.

After a minute, Cerafina removed Jonara's hand from her (Cerafina's) forehead.

"Wow!" Cerafina said. "Wow."

"Is that all you can say?" Jonara said.

"Yeah. Wow," Cerafina continued. "Wow that you saw all that. Wow that you told it to me so quickly. Wow that this kind of power runs in your family."

"Except Jane MacNessi isn't in my family," Jonara said.

Johnny coughed from the dining room as if choking on something.

"Or is she, Daddy?" Jonara asked. "Is she one of your relatives?"

"No," Johnny said.

"Is she one of mine?" Jonara asked.

"This goes back to what I was trying to explain before," Johnny said. "You need time to absorb the facts. Otherwise, they will seem distorted."

"Father!" Jonara said.

"That's the best I can do," Johnny said.

"I could probe you for the information," Jonara said.

"Have you mastered that skill yet?" Johnny asked. "It's one thing to read whatever happens to be the strongest pulses in the environment, it's another to focus in on a specific thing and extract precise and accurate information. Be careful. If you don't focus correctly, you'll receive a distortion."

Jonara stood up and walked over to her father. She kept the Aromani candleholder against her abdomen and placed a hand on his forehead. Johnny shivered a little as if cold.

"I don't read anything," Jonara said.

"That's because you're using the device backward," Johnny said.

"Huh?"

"When you use a laminated Norway piece with the Moissan Ruby, you send—not receive," Johnny explained. "Without realizing what you've done, you just told me everything in your dream during the night. And I can say that everything you dreamed happened. It's true. But there's something that concerns me, Jonara. You've started using Miramish."

"Strange," Jonara said. "I can't think of a single Miramish word to say right now. But when I was dreaming, I could construct entire sentences."

"The Moissan Ruby gives you that skill," Johnny said. "And you used the one in the past. But past or present, be careful. This use of power has a price. It tires you, wears you out, and ages you. It does not age you as much when you receive, but it ages you significantly when you send."

"Daddy—in my dream, you healed Mommy's legs. Why can't you heal her now, like you did at the Elrod 402? Daddy, you must!" Jonara said.

"I can't," he said.

"Well if you won't, I will!" Jonara said.

"Jonara—do not be impulsive!" Johnny warned. "The stone and Norway laminates have powers beyond our comprehension. You may do more damage than good. But I will tell you this. The power to heal is nothing more than giving cells precise information on the most efficient way to heal."

"That makes no sense. Cells can't think," Jonara said.

"Cells have no brains, true. But they are directed. Normally, they receive general commands from various systems and gradually accumulate a healing, but there's much inefficiency. Cells don't always know how to proceed along one line and ignore another. Much energy is spent in a sort of exploration and resource balancing," Johnny said.

"I still don't understand," Jonara said.

"In the Elrod 402, your mother had simple injuries. I gave her cells the information they lacked to expedite the healing process," Johnny explained. "But it wasn't a purge. She still has heavy metals from the River Wood and Battery factory. Your mother is suffering because of those heavy metals. The Norway woods give, they do not take away. I cannot remove the metals from her body. And there's no new information I can give her cells to work around the metals. I already gave her as much leg-healing information I could when I healed her at the Elrod. The best I can now do is block her endorphin system for a little while to build up a reservoir and release the block. When that happens, she'll be pain-free for a few hours. But that's something I'll only consider if she's ready to die. And I don't plan on her dying!"

"What about Grandma Eva?" Jonara asked. "Can we help her cells?"

Johnny looked down.

"It's so hard, so hard," he muttered. "When I was younger, I understood. But everything is confusing."

"What are you saying?" Jonara asked.

"It's possible," Johnny said. "But it's difficult. She has cancer. You have to find a way to tell the bad cells to die, and tell the good cells to repair the damage. One message, but interpreted in exactly two opposite ways."

"Why does Mommy have to have preeclampsia? And why does Grandma have to have cancer?" Jonara asked.

"I'm surprised she has cancer at all, the way she drinks red wine. But maybe it was all a myth anyway," Johnny said.

"What do you mean, Daddy?" Jonara asked.

"It's called the French Paradox," Cerafina said. "Supposedly, the French people who drink red wine in France live longer and have lower rates of heart disease than the world population."

"What does that have to do with cancer?" Jonara asked.

"Some theories suggest resveratrol plays a role in cancer prevention," Johnny said. "Others say phenols play a role. But Cerafina is right. The French Paradox has nothing to do with lower cancer rates—it's about lower coronary disease."

"Can't we give her some red wine to get rid of her cancer?" Jonara asked.

Johnny laughed.

"I wish it were that easy," Johnny said. "But even if it were, she's been drinking red wine every night after dinner for as long as I've known her. That should have accounted for something. It doesn't. I think the French Paradox is a myth. Research says there isn't enough resveratrol in red wine to make a difference, and most of it is destroyed in the stomach anyway."

"Daddy, in all my dreams of the past, I see lots of misery. Sometimes I can help, and when I do, things are much better," Jonara said.

"Things are good for a little while longer, but misery comes soon enough," Johnny said.

"What a terrible thing to say," Cerafina said. "Why would someone want to live thinking like that?"

"I'm only talking about the people Jonara has seen in the past," Johnny said.

"Yeah, but these people are her family," Cerafina said. "How can you talk like that about them? It's rude. Good god, I sound like my mother!"

"He's right," Jonara said. "There's always some misery waiting around the corner for the people I've seen. I wish I could help them all. I wish I could help everyone. But we can try to help Grandma Eva, can't we Daddy?"

"What's to do? The cancer is spreading," Johnny said.

"There's something I've learned, Daddy," Jonara said. "No matter what time or place I visit, I figure out something when I'm in the middle of things, not before when I don't know what's going on. We need to visit the hospital, Daddy. We need to go today. Right now!"

"I don't know, Jonara. I think it's best we let the doctors—"

"The doctors won't do anything, Daddy. They'll charge us thousands of dollars to watch her die," Jonara said. "Is that fair? Is that right?"

"No, it's not," Johnny said. "Very well. Let's go to the hospital."

"May I go too?" Cerafina asked.

"Cerafina," Johnny said. "Don't you have school today?"

"No. The teachers are still on strike. I doubt they'll reach an agreement until next week or later," Cerafina explained.

"All right," Johnny said. "You may go along with us. Anna? Anna!"

Anna entered the dining room from the kitchen.

"We're going to the hospital for a visit," Johnny said.

"Not me, Mr. Johnny. Anna stay here and keep house nice and clean for Carreña family. Anna stay."

"As you wish," Johnny said.

Johnny drove Geneva's car to the hospital with Jonara in the front passenger seat and Cerafina in back. It marked the first family-sanctioned visit for Jonara, and she felt some satisfaction in her house-restriction being lifted.

"Does this mean I'm no longer grounded?" Jonara asked Johnny as Johnny wheeled the car into the hospital parking lot.

"Interesting question," Johnny said. "Since your Grandma Eva grounded you, it depends on her. While she's in the hospital, you're not grounded. If she gets well and comes home, you're grounded again."

"It's almost better that she doesn't get well," Jonara said. "She'll restrict me again, and I don't want that."

"Don't talk like that," Cerafina said. "This is family. You don't want to wish harm on family."

The three opened their doors and exited Geneva's car. They closed their doors, and Johnny locked them.

"Wait!" Jonara said. "We're forgetting something."

"What?" Johnny asked.

"Grandma Eva's red wine," Jonara said.

"Jonara—we've been through this," Johnny said.

"We need to conduct an experiment," Jonara said. "And I'm sure Grandma Eva will approve. We need to monitor her cells while she drinks red wine."

"It won't cure her cancer," Johnny said.

"I know it won't," Jonara said. "But maybe we'll learn something—anything—that we can use. A step in the right direction. We have to try."

The three returned to the car. Johnny wheeled the car off the parking lot and toward the nearest liquor store.

"What's her favorite wine?" Cerafina asked.

"Pinot noir," Johnny and Jonara said in unison.

"That's a wine?" Cerafina asked.

"It's a grape," Johnny said, "mainly grown in Burgundy, France for many, many years. But a few other places in the world are cultivating it. The Willamette Valley in Oregon grows this grape and makes wine almost as good as the Burgundy brand. Some say better."

"I didn't know that," Jonara said.

"It's one reason your Grandma Eva moved to Portland," Johnny said.

"And I thought it was for dentistry," Jonara said.

"That too. She claims the Willamette Valley makes the best Pinot noir wine in America, and second best in the world behind Burgundy. She often alternates between the Willamette and the Burgundy wines from day to day," Johnny explained. "It's strange how she'll drink a wine from Oregon but not California."

Johnny drove Geneva's car and parked it at the liquor store.

"You girls have to stay in the car," he said.

Johnny returned shortly thereafter with two bottles of red wine.

"Pinot noir wine," he said. "One from Burgundy, one from Oregon."

"Daddy," Jonara said.

"Yes, honey?"

"To make this a proper experiment, we need a control wine," Jonara said.

Johnny laughed.

"You're very smart," Johnny said. "And you're taking this very seriously."

"Wouldn't a white wine make a good control wine?" Jonara asked.

"Wait, wait!" Cerafina said. "You're going to control the experiment with white wine?"

"No," Johnny said. "Jonara uses the word 'control' in the experimental sense. When doing experiments, one tries different things expecting different results. The 'control' item is not supposed to produce any results. It validates the experiment itself. If the 'control' produces unexpected results, then something is wrong with the experiment. I haven't taken this 'experiment' seriously, so I didn't think much of having a control item. But shouldn't we use water as a control, Jonara?"

"That's too neutral," Jonara said. "Doesn't Grandma Eva drink white wine from time to time?"

"Rarely," Johnny said. "Usually she drinks it at social occasions when the red has run out, or if she's switching between reds."

"Switching between reds?" Cerafina asked. "What is that supposed to mean?"

"She gets loyal to certain red wines," Johnny explained. "But sometimes she feels a need for change. Instead of jumping to another red wine on the rebound, she goes cold turkey for a week or so with white wine."

"You make red-wine drinking sound like a romantic relationship," Cerafina said.

"Oh it is for my Grandma Eva," Jonara said. "And that's also why I think we need a bottle of white wine for the control group. It's what Grandma Eva uses to neutralize herself between her red-wine relationships."

"This is almost as strange as the Water Ruby, the diary, and the *viola de gamba*," Cerafina said. "But one thing is for sure— I'm never bored when I'm around the Carreña family!"

"There's only one white wine even worth considering," Jonara said.

"One based on Pinot gris," Johnny said. "It's almost identical to Pinot noir except for the color. I'll be back in a few minutes."

Again, Johnny returned very quickly from the liquor store.

"I only got one bottle of Pinot gris-based wine," Johnny said. "This is also from the Willamette Valley. Eva will never admit it, but this is her favorite Pinot gris wine. She says it tastes fruity—something between apples and pears."

"Why won't she admit it?" Cerafina asked.

"Because she likes to brag about how the best wines are from France," Jonara said.

Johnny drove the car from the liquor store back toward the hospital.

"What's funny is that Spain produces wine too," Johnny said. "You'd think your Grandma Eva would brag about those."

"Why doesn't she?" Jonara asked.

"I think it's because your Nanna Geneva drank Spanish wine," Johnny said.

"So?" Jonara said.

"I get it," Cerafina said. "She wanted to be different from her mother."

"Yes," Johnny said. "Nanna Geneva told many stories about the Franco regime. One of those stories was how the booming Spanish wine industry contributed to the fall of Franco."

"You're kidding," Jonara said.

"No, I'm not. Nanna Geneva believed Spanish wine single-handedly brought about the end of Franco's regime. Some argue Franco's death had something to do with it. Anyway, I won't go into it any more than that. And don't mention anything about Franco in front of your Grandma Eva. She's guaranteed to go into spasms, and you won't make friends with her."

The three arrived at the hospital.

"Help me with these, will you?" Johnny asked the girls.

Jonara took the Burgundy red wine while Cerafina took the Oregon red wine. Johnny carried the white wine. The three entered the hospital unnoticed and entered Eva's room. Johnny placed his bottle on the nightstand next to the bed on Eva's left side and in turn took the bottles from the girls and placed the bottles on the nightstand.

"I forgot to bring a wine glass!" Johnny said.

The girls looked around, and it was Jonara who brought several disposable cups from the bathroom.

"Wine in disposable cups. Not elegant. But it will have to do," Johnny said.

Johnny sat on the side of the bed with the nightstand. The girls sat on the other side with Jonara closest to Eva's head. Johnny sat for a moment, lost in thought. He tapped his forehead a few times, stuck his hand in his pocket, and nodded his head once as if remembering something he meant to do.

"Here," Johnny said as he pulled a cell phone from his pocket. "This is an old cell phone. It has no service. But if you press this button, it vibrates as if someone is calling. Put this in your pocket and use it to activate the Moissan Ruby."

Johnny handed the old cell phone to Jonara. She took it and placed it in her pocket.

"Now, we are ready," Johnny whispered. "Jonara. Read your grandmother for a baseline."

Jonara held her left hand on Eva's shoulder and with her right pressed the button on the cell phone. It vibrated intermittently in her pocket. Each time it did, Jonara felt waves coming from Eva's body, waves that translated into three-dimensional internal structures of her body. She saw Eva's heart pumping in her chest. At first, the sight was beautiful—her grandmother's heart pumping with such strong beats. But Jonara saw other tissues—the lungs, the liver, the stomach, spleen, and kidneys. She saw blood and fluids flowing. Jonara trembled in fear, but her trembling strengthened the Moissan Ruby, and the images of Eva became more graphic. Jonara wanted to stop the Moissan Ruby, but she couldn't. Her left hand gripped harder on Eva's shoulder, and her right froze in place—unable to move.

"Jonara," Cerafina said, noticing distress in Jonara's eyes. "Are you okay?"

Jonara did not answer Cerafina. Instead, Jonara's eyes gazed at a particular bit of tissue in Eva's lower neck—the cancerous thyroid with two nodules—one on each side of the left half of her thyroid gland.

"Stop!" Jonara said.

Jonara broke her grip from Eva's shoulder and turned off the cell phone. Eva stirred from sleep.

"Who's here?" Eva asked.

Eva blinked her eyes several times and looked at Johnny, straining to recognize him in her groggy state.

"Johnny," Eva said.

Eva turned from her left to right side and struggled to recognize the girls.

"Jonara," Eva said, "and her friend...her friend."

"Cerafina," Cerafina helped.

"Yes. Cerafina. What a surprise. But Jonara is grounded. What is she doing here?" Eva asked.

"I want her to be here," Johnny said.

"Is it Thursday yet?" Eva asked.

"Yes," Johnny said. "It's Thursday."

"The doctors will perform surgery on me today," Eva said. "I don't want them to. Not yet. I want to be conscious for Evanita, and I want to bury my mother. But they won't hear otherwise, Johnny."

"I know," Johnny said. "We're here to help."

"How?" Eva asked. "Not with black magic, I hope. Not with that Moissan Ruby of yours."

"Mummy Eva—Jonara wants to help you. I'm helping her along the way. She loves you and wants nothing ill of you," Johnny explained. "Permit her this moment with the Moissan Ruby."

"It could scar her psychologically," Eva said.

"Watching her grandma die would be worse, don't you think?" Johnny asked.

Eva turned to Jonara. Jonara shed a few tears at the thought of losing her grandma.

"You can't die, Grandma, you can't!" Jonara said, and she hugged Eva.

"Oh child," Eva said. "The surgery will probably clean me up."

"Probably?" Jonara cried. "No. No 'probably'. You must live."

"Then it's settled," Johnny said. "Let's begin with the first test."

"What test?" Eva asked. "Johnny, shouldn't you get permission from me first? It's my body, and I have a right—"

"To choose how to die," Johnny said. "Yes, but we've found a test that we think you'll approve."

"What's that?" Eva asked.

"We bought some wine," Jonara said, now sitting up after hugging Eva. "We want to see how it affects the cancer."

Eva laughed.

"Please, Grandma! It's not funny!" Jonara said.

"No, it's okay. I haven't had a good laugh in a long time. So what do you plan to do—perform some exorcism and celebrate the Holy Eucharist or something?" Eva asked. "That's the superstition my mother would have recommended."

"It's a little more scientific than that," Johnny said. "We want to see how red and white wines affect your cancer. You'll drink a small glass of each, and Jonara will measure the response."

Eva laughed again.

"Is this the French Paradox mythology?" Eva chuckled. "Well, I could use a good glass of wine—even if it won't cure the cancer. And fortunately, I haven't taken naltrexone in a while. What did you bring?"

Johnny produced the two bottles of red wine for Eva.

"A Pinot noir wine from Burgundy," Eva said. "And another Pinot noir wine but from the Willamette Valley. I know the producer. These are excellent choices. At least I'll enjoy myself before going under the knife. What else is in your bag?"

"Part of the experiment requires a control group," Johnny said.

"So you brought a bottle of water?" Eva asked.

"No, this," Johnny said as he produced the white wine and gave it to Eva.

Eva laughed.

"Well at least you have a sense of humor. A light Pinot gris wine from the Willamette Valley," Eva said.

"I suggested it," Jonara said.

"And again it's a good choice," Eva said. "Fortunately, these bottles are chilled. But you better get some ice to keep them that way."

Johnny exited the room and returned shortly thereafter with a bucket of ice. He placed the bottles in the ice bucket, and Eva smiled with approval.

"That's better," Eva said.

"Let's start," Johnny said. "Jonara, turn on your cell phone and touch your grandmother's shoulder. Mummy Eva, drink this small glass of Burgundy red wine."

Jonara activated the cell phone and touched Eva's shoulder. Jonara sensed the metabolic activities of Eva's fluids and tissues.

"All right, bottoms up!" Eva said.

Eva gulped the wine quickly. Jonara sensed a small amount of phenols and resveratrol absorbed through Eva's cheeks and throat while the bulk entered her stomach and quickly disintegrated. The resveratrol and phenols from her cheeks seeped into Eva's tissues and attacked the cancer, but the amount was small, and the cancer was powerful. At best, the resveratrol and phenols tickled the cancer's outer wall.

"Almost no benefit," Jonara said.

Eva laughed.

"I could have told you that, Jonara," Eva said. "I've been drinking red wine for years. I know about the French Paradox. If it were true, I wouldn't have the cancer. Also, the French Paradox only applies to heart disease, which I don't have."

"But there was something," Jonara said.

"Yes?" Johnny asked. "What was it?"

"A little bit of the red wine was absorbed through Grandma Eva's cheeks. It traveled through her tissues and attacked the cancer, but the amount absorbed was too small," Jonara explained.

"Interesting," Johnny said. "Mummy Eva, is this how you always drink wine?"

"Lately it is," Eva said. "With the stress of everything, I hurry my glasses of wine."

"You used to swirl the wine in a wineglass before drinking, if I remember," Johnny said.

"And I used to swirl it in my mouth and enjoy the wine's character. Those were the days. Sometimes I wish I could be young and enjoy those days again," Eva said.

"That's it!" Jonara said. "That's the next part of the experiment."

"What is?" Cerafina asked.

"Grandma needs to swirl the red wine in her mouth for as long as possible," Jonara said. "Maybe more of the good stuff will be absorbed through her cheeks. But first, we have to use the white wine as a rinse."

Eva laughed again.

"I told her how you would drink white wine between reds as a way of avoiding wine rebound," Johnny said.

Eva laughed again and said:

"I can't believe how crazy this is! And yet you two have reasoned out everything, haven't you—Johnny and Jonara? Someone could write a dissertation paper on this. And if anyone is crazy enough to believe it, the author could receive a Ph.D!"

Johnny prepared a small glass of white wine.

"No, make it smaller," Jonara said. "I have a two-part control I want to try."

Johnny poured half of the wine into another glass—yielding two glasses of very little white wine.

"Wine rationing?" Eva asked.

"No," Jonara said. "You'll see. I'm ready for the first glass. Drink it quickly, like the glass of red wine."

Johnny handed the first glass of white wine to Eva. She drank it quickly. The wine pulled a bit of red-wine residue from Eva's mouth and carried it to Eva's stomach. Jonara suspected as much, and the Moissan Ruby confirmed it.

"Yeah, I was right," Jonara said.

"About what?" Cerafina asked.

"The white wine carried what was left of the red wine from Grandma Eva's mouth into her stomach," Jonara explained.

"You didn't need an experiment for that. I could have told you that would happen," Eva said.

"Are you ready for the second glass?" Johnny asked Jonara.

"Yes. But Grandma—please swirl it in your mouth for at least ten seconds," Jonara said.

"Dear child, white wine doesn't have the same character as red. Swirling in my mouth won't add much to the experience," Eva said.

"I know, but I have an idea, and I want to test it. I'll explain in a minute," Jonara said.

"Very well," Eva said.

Eva swirled the white wine in her mouth. Jonara sensed the white wine did not penetrate Eva's cheeks as the red did. But Jonara noticed the bits of red-wine stuff that had previously been absorbed through Eva's cheeks now exited from her cheeks into the white wine being swirled around. Eva swallowed, taking the little bit of extracted red wine with it.

"Swirling the white wine pulled some of the red wine out of your cheeks," Jonara said.

"I've heard of using white wine to remove a red-wine stain from carpeting, but this beats everything," Eva said.

"Hold on," Johnny said. "We might have something here. Could the white wine pull out the cancerous cells?"

"I didn't see it doing that. It only pulled out the red wine. The cancer stayed put," Jonara said. "Now I'm ready for the next test—swirling red wine in Grandma's mouth."

Johnny poured another small glass of Burgundy wine and handed it to Eva. Eva swirled the wine in her mouth, and Jonara felt for reaction. Cerafina and Johnny touched Eva to connect with Jonara's experience. At first, the effect was similar to before—bits of red wine passed into Eva's cheek tissues. With each swish in Eva's mouth, the resveratrol and phenols continued in waves through her cheek tissues. They migrated down Eva's neck and attached to the outer walls of the cancer tissue.

A bright light blinded Jonara, Johnny, and Cerafina, but not Eva. The three regained their vision after a few seconds and realized they were no longer in the hospital but rather in a military plane above Kiritimati (Christmas) Island—where Jonara was before.

1962 Jul 10. Kiritimati Island, Pacific Ocean.

The three witnessed a nuclear explosion—Operation Dominic Sunset—much like Jonara had seen before. But strangely, the explosion appeared in reverse. The fireball slowly descended and shrank as large circular disks from above contracted around the fireball until they merged with the fireball. The disks were not colors of yellow, orange, and red like before but were instead colors of violet, cerise, and pink. The lower half remained red.

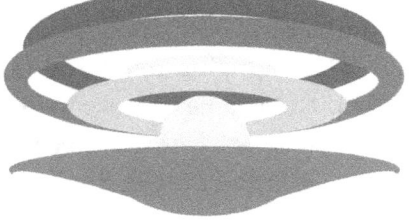

"It's beautiful," Cerafina said.

"It's Operation Dominic Sunset," Johnny said, "but it's going backward, and the colors are strange."

"Are we really watching a nuclear explosion?" Jonara asked.

"What do you mean?" Johnny asked.

"Some of those hoops are similar in color to red wine," Jonara said. "Could the hoops be attacking the fireball like the red wine is attacking the thyroid cancer?"

"An interesting analogy," Johnny said. "What's even more interesting is how we are seeing the past without help from the diary."

"We are connected differently," Cerafina said. "It's not just history this time."

"Cerafina's right. Grandma Eva must be tied to a nuclear explosion somehow. But how?" Jonara asked.

"Thyroid cancer is often common after a radiation burst," Johnny said. "But your Grandma Eva never witnessed these explosions. Her cancer must have come from Marcus Cracbern's X-ray machine. She worked in his office, and she wasn't diligent about protecting herself when she took X-rays of patients."

"Then we should be seeing an X-ray machine in action," Cerafina said.

"But we're not. There's something to this nuclear explosion. And finding out could cure Grandma Eva of cancer."

The explosion faded, and the three returned to the hospital room with Eva. Jonara watched the bits of red-wine friendlies attack the cancerous tissue. An outer layer of the cancer tissue softened, but after a few seconds, the unaffected part of the cancer refortified the softer part and held strong against the red wine.

"The red wine can weaken the cancer for a little bit, but the cancer seems to rebuild what the red wine has weakened," Jonara said.

"The red wine needs a boost," Johnny said. "I say we mix a little bit of the Oregon red wine with the Burgundy."

"Now wait! I never mix red wines. It's a matter of principle. You don't go on two dates with different people at the same time," Eva said.

"Grandma, please, for me! This is important. It's science," Jonara said.

"Are you sure? Are you recording clinical data? Are you testing a hypothesis?" Eva asked.

"Not as stringently as could be hoped," Johnny said. "But we must try this. Mummy Eva, please! Swish this mixed red wine in your mouth as long as you can."

Eva took the glass to her mouth. She tasted it and withdrew. She tasted it again, shrugged her shoulders, and slurped the entire red-wine mixture into her mouth. She swished and swirled it around in her mouth, and Jonara sensed the red-wine mixture being absorbed through her cheeks and traveling down her neck.

1954 Mar 1. Bikini Atoll, Pacific Ocean.

"This is Rainbow Vortex, we are in position," called the pilot.

Jonara, Cerafina, and Johnny found themselves cramped in the back two seats of an American bomber jet.

"Where are we?" Cerafina asked.

Johnny peered at the instruments and papers of the airmen in front.

"We're near the Bikini Atoll, Marshall Islands. It's March 1st, 1954," Johnny said. "And close to sunrise."

"What kind of airplane is this?" Jonara asked. "And where are the propellers? All those old-fashioned planes had propellers."

"This looks like a B-47," Johnny said. "Or a B-47E, or maybe an RB-47. There are four seats instead of three. And there's no rear gun turret."

"Keep sharp, Cracbern," the pilot said to the copilot. "We couldn't spare a navigator, so you'll have to do double duty."

"Cracbern?!" Johnny said. "That's impossible. Marcus Cracbern wasn't even born yet."

"Yes sir," the copilot said.

"Activate the reconnaissance and air-sampling equipment. Make sure we have clean coverage of the blast. We don't want out-of-focus or jittery images," the pilot said.

"We'll have the best manned footage of the Bravo shot, or my name isn't Theodore Cracbern," the copilot said.

"The Bravo shot?" Jonara asked.

"Of course!" Johnny said. "They're filming Castle Bravo."

"What's that?" Jonara asked.

"The largest thermonuclear test by the United States," Johnny said. "It registered a 15 megaton blast."

"But why are we here?" Cerafina asked.

"Theodore Cracbern," Jonara said. "Is he related?"

"To Marcus? I think Theodore is his father," Johnny said.

"You never told me who Marcus is," Jonara said.

"And now is not the time. We're about to witness one really, big, dirty nuke," Johnny said.

"Thirty seconds," the pilot said. "Put your goggles on, Cracbern."

"Yes, sir."

"Five, four, three, two, one," the pilot said.

The pre-dawn sky lit up with a brilliant, blinding light. After a few seconds, the light diminished enough so the five could witness the mushroom cloud.

"My god, it's horrific!" Cerafina said.

"It's like life and death mixed into a ball of fire," Jonara said.

"We're not as far away as we should be," Johnny said. "We'll be dangerously close to the radiation if we don't change course."

"Will it hurt us?" Jonara asked.

"I don't know," Johnny replied.

"Cracbern, isn't that the most beautiful thing you've ever seen?" the pilot asked, but Cracbern simply stared at the consumptive fireball. "Something's wrong. The fireball is still growing. The shot went big. Navigator, plot us a course away from the shot. Navigator!"

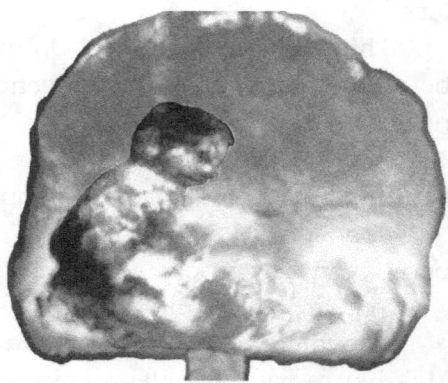

Cracbern stared at the blast. Mesmerized by the display, he choked out the following words:

"I see my son. My unborn son! Oh the horror and beauty of it."

"Navigator!" the pilot ordered, but Cracbern was singularly focused on the fireball.

"I must meet my son," he said with a psychotic voice.

Cracbern fired the eighteen jet-assisted take-off (JATO) rockets and pointed the B-47 directly at the fireball. The aircraft roared and strained under the rocket load. The pilot fought for control of the aircraft, but Cracbern fought back. The aircraft pitched and rolled.

"Cracbern's gone mad. He's on a suicide flight into the nuclear fireball," Johnny said.

"Shockwave!" Cracbern boasted.

The aircraft shook violently. Indicator lights flashed randomly as the electromagnetic radiation disrupted electronic operation.

"We're losing control," the pilot said. "Cracbern, break off!"

"Daddy, we have to do something," Jonara said.

"Should we?" he asked.

"What?!?" Jonara asked. "We must act! We'll be killed."

"We're safe. But if Cracbern dies, things might be better," Johnny said.

"Grandma Eva is tied to this somehow. We have to save the plane to save Grandma," Jonara said.

The instrument panel went blank. The booster rockets and regular jets halted operation. Only the wind from the nuclear blast could be heard. Thermal radiation heated up the plane, and the five sweated profusely.

"We're burning up," the pilot said.

Without thinking, Jonara held the candleholder to her belly button and spoke:

Miramish	Translation
Thoana kulo fieshu	Wine be red
Thoana kulo yuanu,	Wine be white,
Gurapo shai fieshu	Gulp the red
Tinato shai yuanu.	Taste the white.
Gerutho rau mahilu	Give us now
Nuish e hauthu peliola,	Our healthy way,
Lukiroko shai yaiya	Reduce the wow
Dhaku gereiaga diviuliu.	And mania today.

The pilot ripped the oxygen mask from Cracbern. Cracbern gasped twice before passing out from hypoxia. The pilot steered the aircraft away from the mushroom cloud. After several desperate attempts, he restarted the jet engines. As the aircraft turned, the mushroom cloud's light changed from blinding them head-on to creeping over their left shoulders from behind. The sudden change in light created a brief flashing effect. Jonara, Cerafina, and Johnny blinked their eyes and saw themselves back in the hospital, then back in the plane, back in the hospital, and so on. This effect continued, like an automobile sputtering from lack of gasoline.

"Grandma," Jonara said through the flashing. "Swallow the red wine. Daddy, give her a glass of white wine. Hurry! Grandma—swish but don't swallow!"

Eva and Johnny did just that. As Eva swished the white wine in her mouth, the flashing period increased as the fre-

quency decreased. Then something odd happened. Jonara, Cerafina, and Johnny flashed between the B-47 in the Pacific as it
was outracing the nuclear blast, and a landing approach in
Montgomery, Alabama. The B-47 approached the runway.
Flash! The B-47 in the Pacific reached the safety zone. The pilot
restored the air to Cracbern's mask. Flash! The B-47 landed on
the runway. The flashing changed again, and the three flashed
into a remote hangar deck with the B-47 under maintenance.
The pilot and copilot had long ago departed the B-47.

1954 Mar 2. Outskirts of Montgomery, Alabama.

"This craft has scorch marks," said Jane MacNessi, who was
dressed in an aircraft mechanic's uniform. "And there's ash all
over it. Where's it been flying, over a volcano or something?"

"That's classified," said her supervisor. "Here's the inspection report."

Jane thumbed through the many pages.

"Wow, this craft has a lot of damage," Jane said.

"Get your scrubbing crew together and clean the exterior
first. Then get to work on overhauling the turbines. They
sucked in a lot of debris," the supervisor said.

"I don't have enough electronic replacement parts for this
bird," Jane said while thumbing through the list.

"By the time you finish with mechanical, your electronic
parts will arrive. I have them on order."

"I don't understand why I'm lugging my tools and crew to
this abandoned hangar in the middle of nowhere. Why aren't we
servicing this bird in the main hangar with the other birds? The
main hangar has much better facilities for—"

"Are you questioning orders, MacNessi?" the supervisor
asked.

"No, sir," Jane said.

"Then carry on. And when you're done for the day, leave
your mechanics clothes in the locker room here. Do not remove
them from these grounds."

"That's a strange request," Jane said.

"Those are the orders. Carry on," the supervisor said, and he left.

"That's Roberta's mother," Johnny said.

"So this is the one who played baseball?" Cerafina asked.

"Yeah. But she's a little older now," Jonara said. "Daddy—that ash on the airplane. What is it?"

"It's from the nuclear explosion," Johnny said. "It's fallout, and it's radioactive. Why did they bring the plane so far inland with this stuff?"

"And why didn't they tell Jane it was radioactive?" Cerafina asked.

"Would you want to clean an airplane if you knew it was radioactive?" Johnny asked.

"No," Cerafina said.

"I wouldn't either," Jonara said.

A man walked over with a nine-year-old girl. She had red hair.

"Jack!" Jane said. "What are you doing down here in Alabama? I thought—"

"You thought I was as drunk as a skunk in Wisconsin, didn't you Janie? Not true! I'm still Roberta's father, and I decided to come down for a visit."

"Jack, this isn't a good time for a visit. I'm up to my ears in service work," Jane said. "How did you take Roberta from the sitter? And how did you get clearance on this military site?"

"I have clearance. I fought in Europe, remember? I've reactivated my military status in the Reserves. But don't worry. I came down to visit Roberta, not you. Look at your poor daughter's shoes. They're full of holes, and the soles are coming apart. See?"

Jack tugged at Roberta's shoes.

"I'm taking her into town to get some good shoes," Jack said.

"Jack, I can take care of Roberta. Don't go running around town and spoiling my daughter," Jane said.

"Like I keep saying, she's my daughter too. And keeping one's daughter well fed and clothed is hardly spoiling. Look at these rags she's wearing. And look how thin she is," Jack said.

"Don't feed her fatty foods. She'll be a woman someday, and she'll regret what she ate as a child," Jane said.

"Don't worry about us. I'll take good care of her," Jack said. "Well, see you around!"

Jack left with Roberta.

"I can't believe I let Jack take Roberta from me. He might not come back," Jane said.

Flash! Jonara, Cerafina, and Johnny appeared in a diner. Roberta ate a large burger and fries. Flash! Jonara, Cerafina, and Johnny appeared in a department store. Roberta took several dresses and hats to a dressing room. Flash! Roberta stood in front of a shoe store wearing a dress and hat she chose in the department store.

"This is the finest shoe store in Montgomery," Jack said

"Daddie," Roberta said. "Can you afford all these things for me?"

"Nothing but the best for my daughter," Jack said.

"But they're so expensive. Mommie can't afford these things," Roberta said.

"I know," Jack said. "That's why I'm buying them. Come now. This shoe store has the most advanced technology for determining the right shoes for your feet. They have a pedoscope. It shows an image of your foot inside your shoes. You'll see."

Jack opened the door and ushered Roberta into the shoe store. An attractive saleslady with a rash on her right hand and permanent red scorch marks on her legs welcomed them inside.

"What a beautiful girl in a beautiful dress!" the saleslady said.

"I'm Jack O'Leary, and this is my daughter, Roberta," Jack said. "She needs two pairs of shoes."

"I thought I only needed one pair," Roberta said.

"Oh no. You need shoes to match your dress, and another pair for everyday use," Jack said.

"Your father is right," the saleslady said. "Here, I'll show you our selection. We have a nice assortment of green shoes to match your green dress."

Roberta followed the saleslady to a selection of green shoes. Roberta looked at one pair, then another, and another.

"What's the matter?" Jack asked.

"I can't make up my mind which shoes I like best. These three are my favorite," Roberta said.

"That's not a problem. We'll try all three pairs," the saleslady said.

The saleslady grabbed the three boxes and led Roberta and Jack to a shoe-fitting station with a pedoscope.

"Try these on first," the saleslady said.

Roberta slipped on the shoes.

"Now step into the pedoscope. It will measure the fit," the saleslady said.

Roberta looked up at her father and asked, "Is it safe?"

"Of course it's safe," Jack said. "They wouldn't have it in the store if it weren't safe. Besides, they're made in Milwaukee by the Adrian X-Ray Company. I've been to their plant. Totally safe. I'll take you there on a plant tour sometime."

Roberta stepped onto the pedoscope and positioned her feet inside the device. The saleslady set the timer for twenty seconds.

"Look inside, Mr. O'Leary, and you'll see your daughter's feet. You too, Roberta."

Jack and Roberta peered into the device. The saleslady turned the device on.

"Amazing," Jack said. "I can see my daughter's bones."

"It's scary," Roberta said, and she started to shake.

"Do your shoes fit?" the saleslady asked.

"I don't know," Roberta said.

Fright seized Roberta, and she couldn't concentrate on how well her shoes fit. She could only think about how she was seeing the inside of her feet—the bones—and it reminded her of scary skeletons from Halloween.

"I don't want to die!" Roberta said.

"Here, let me adjust your feet," the saleslady said.

The saleslady stuck her hand into the pedoscope and squished Roberta's feet.

"Is that better?" the saleslady asked.

Roberta did not answer. The timer ran out, and the image went dark.

"Well?" Jack asked Roberta, but Roberta did not answer.

"The shoes are tight," the saleslady said. "She'll outgrow them in a few months. She needs a slightly larger shoe. Here, let's try the next pair."

"Daddy," Jonara asked. "How does the pedoscope work?"

"It's an X-ray machine," Johnny said. "An X-ray tube is positioned just under the feet and fires X-rays upward through the feet to a screen, creating an image of the feet and shoe outline. Mirrors reflect the image to portholes—you see there are three—one for the salesperson, one for a parent, and one for the person trying on the shoes."

"How safe is it?" Cerafina asked.

"Not very. X-rays leak everywhere, and store workers take the biggest dosages since they work close to the machine all day long. Those scorch marks and rash on the saleslady's legs and hand are from the X-rays," Johnny explained.

Roberta changed to the new pair of shoes and stood in the pedoscope again. The saleslady set the timer for another twenty seconds and activated the device. The saleslady and Jack looked inside.

"The fit looks good. Let me squish them to be sure," the saleslady said.

"You see," Johnny said. "She squishes Roberta's feet while the machine is on. Doing that every day with every customer exposes her hand to high accumulated levels of X-ray radiation."

"If the machine is so great, why does she squish Roberta's shoes?" Jonara asked. "She could squish them without using the machine."

"Yes, you're right, Jonara," Johnny said. "That's exactly the point."

"Look at your feet, Roberta," Jack urged.

Roberta shook her head "no".

"It's not dangerous. It won't hurt you," Jack said.

Roberta shook her head "no" again.

"Fortunately, we have science to tell us that the shoes fit, don't we Miss?" Jack asked.

"Yes, they fit," the saleslady said.

Jack held onto the green pair of shoes, and Roberta selected a pair of everyday shoes.

"Daddie," Roberta said. "Can we just buy these? I don't need to try them on."

"Nonsense!" Jack said. "I won't have you damaging your feet from ill-fitting shoes. The pedoscope will protect your feet from harm."

"There is a saying," Johnny said to Jonara and Cerafina. "The road to Hell is paved with good intentions."

"What does that mean?" Jonara asked.

"It means Jack thinks he's doing good by making Roberta step in the pedoscope, but really he's causing harm by exposing her to unnecessary X-ray radiation," Cerafina said.

"Well spoken, Cerafina!" Johnny said.

Jack led Roberta back to the pedoscope with the everyday shoes. The saleslady repeated the procedure as before—twenty-second exposure, a squish of the feet, and an analysis.

"These are a little tight," the saleslady said. "She needs room to grow."

"I like tight-fitting shoes," Roberta said.

"Nonsense," Jack said. "We'll get the next size up, and we'll try them on to be absolutely sure they're medically right for you."

The saleslady brought the next larger size, and Roberta tried them on as before. The pedoscope, the twenty seconds, but Roberta in her nervousness moved her feet restlessly inside the device.

"Hold still!" Jack said. "We can't see your X-ray image with your feet moving."

"I want to go home," Roberta said. "Take me home!"

"Mr. O'Leary, if you could hold your daughter's feet so I can get a steady image, I would appreciate it," the saleslady requested.

Jack stuck his hands through the machine to Roberta's feet and pressed them down. The feet remained motionless. The screen revealed a superimposed image of Jack's hands over Roberta's feet.

"I'm sorry, Mr. O'Leary, but your hands are blocking the exposure. Could you hold her feet from the sides? I'll reset the device for another twenty seconds," the saleslady said.

Jack struggled to hold Roberta's feet down. Roberta stamped, squirmed, and pushed against the top of the device. With one last effort, Jack pushed Roberta's feet down against the floor of the device—a one millimeter-thick aluminum plate—and broke through it. Startled, he jerked his arms up and cracked the pedoscope's outer case. Unimpeded by the aluminum plate, the X-ray tube blasted upward and exposed Jack, the saleslady, and Roberta to excessive X-ray radiation. The twenty-second timer ran out, and the device shut down.

"I'm sorry," Jack said. "Did you get the image? Do the shoes fit?"

"Yes," the saleslady said. "The shoes fit."

"I'm very sorry I broke your pedoscope," Jack said. "I'll compensate you for the repair bill."

"There won't be a repair bill," the saleslady said. "We are instructed that once these break down, they are to be returned to Milwaukee for decommissioning. We'll be reimbursed for expenses."

"I don't understand," Jack said. "How will you get another?"

"We won't," the saleslady said.

Two men with blue overalls appeared from the back of the store.

"It's broken at last," the saleslady said in relief. "Take it away and dismantle it."

The men unplugged the device and took it out back. The saleslady waited for a moment, and then she heard with great satisfaction a loud Smash! as the men destroyed the pedoscope.

"You act as if you wanted the pedoscope broken. You should be fired!" Jack said. "We don't want shoes from this store. We'll do business elsewhere."

Jack stormed out of the shoe store with Roberta in tow. He led her to another shoe store where Roberta repeated the experience of trying on shoes in a pedoscope. Roberta did not fight, however, and the shoes were purchased rather quickly.

"Now I know why Roberta couldn't conceive," Johnny said. "This accident with the pedoscope damaged her reproductive system."

1954 Dec 1. Montgomery, Alabama.

"Push harder, Ms. Cracbern," said the doctor.

"My name is Alice," said the pregnant woman. "Call me Alice. What's yours?"

"Dr. Jelana Margo," the doctor said. "Push, Alice, push!"

"I am pushing!" she replied.

"The baby is crowning," the doctor said. "Just a little more...there!"

Alice Cracbern delivered her baby into the hands of Dr. Jelana Margo. The doctor smacked the baby, the baby started breathing, and the doctor tied and cut the umbilical cord. Kaila, one of the nurses, cleaned up the baby and placed him next to Alice.

"Do you have a name for your baby boy?" Kaila asked Alice.

"Yes," Alice said. "His name is Marcus Theodore Cracbern. 'Marcus' after his grandfather, and 'Theodore' after his father."

"I heard about your husband," Kaila said. "I'm sorry about his death. Do you have any other children?"

"The cancer took him so quickly," Alice said. "He was as healthy as an ox on Valentine's Day. But after he came back from that mission in early March, he wasn't the same. I thought he had a sunburn, but it was worse. He never told me what gave him the sunburn, and no one in the military explained it either. No, Marcus is the only child. But I'm thankful I have a baby boy as a little gift from my late husband. I'll cherish and spoil my baby to the ends of the earth. Ow!"

"Another contraction," said another nurse. "Dr. Jelana—it's not the afterbirth. It's something else."

Alice pushed out a small, black, and bloody clump.

"An undeveloped twin," Dr. Jelana said. "It's necrotic. Take it to pathology, immediately."

"What was it, doctor?" Alice asked. "Did I have another baby?"

"No," she said. "Just some leftover material. We'll keep you here an extra few days for tests and observation to make sure you're fine."

"The afterbirth, doctor," said a nurse.

"Hmm. Strange lumps in the placenta. Take this to pathology too," she said.

"What's wrong with my body?" Alice asked.

"Now don't worry, Mrs. Cracbern," Dr. Jelana said.

"I'm Alice!" she said.

"Yes. We'll make sure you're all cleaned up and fit as a fiddle before you go home. We'll have to perform some tests on your baby—just to make sure he's healthy," the doctor said.

"Can't he stay here a little longer?" Alice asked.

"No. You can see him later," Dr. Jelana said.

Alice wrapped her arms around Marcus and heavily protected him.

"Now Mrs. Cracbern, don't be childish. Release your baby," Dr. Jelana said. "You don't know the risk you're taking by keeping him here. There's a strong chance he has a bacterial infection. You don't want to be responsible for your baby's death, do you?"

"There's nothing wrong with my baby. There was nothing wrong with my husband, either. He was healthy, I am healthy, and my baby is healthy. That's all there is to it," Alice stated.

Dr. Jelana grabbed for the baby, but Alice struggled.

"Nurse, I need help," Dr. Jelana said to Kaila.

Kaila pulled and pulled at Alice's arms. Alice groaned and growled, and as Kaila peeled Alice's arms from the baby's body, Dr. Jelana took the baby away from Alice. Alice screamed at the loss of her baby. Dr. Jelana handed the baby off to a nurse, the nurse took the baby from the room, and Kaila held Alice steady while the doctor administered a sedative. Alice continued to scream, and she thrashed about in bed.

"Doctor, she's bleeding heavily!" Kaila said.

"Strap her down," Dr. Jelana ordered.

Kaila and another nurse strapped Alice to the bed. Dr. Jelana administered another sedative and worked on stopping the bleeding. Alice calmed a little as the sedative kicked in. Kaila removed towel after towel of soaked blood. The doctor worked frantically to stop the bleeding, tying suture after suture, but Alice's tissues were soft and ripped from the stress of her struggling. Alice fell unconscious, but her eyes darted under her eyelids frantically. Her blood pressure skyrocketed. As Dr. Jelana sutured up a bleeder, a new one sprouted.

"We've got to get her blood pressure down," the doctor said. "Administer a standard nitroglycerin injection, 400 mcg/mL strength."

"Yes, doctor," Kaila said.

Dr. Jelana could not stop the bleeding. Though Alice was unconscious, her muscles writhed and squirmed. Blood from Alice poured everywhere—the delivery table, towels, and the floor. Finally, Alice gave out a brief scream, and her body went limp.

"Asystole!" Kaila yelled.

Alice's heart had stopped.

"Begin ventilation," Dr. Jelana said to a nurse while the doctor began chest compressions. "Kaila—administer one milligram atropine and six milligrams epinephrine."

A nurse pumped air into Alice's lungs. Kaila injected the atropine and ephinephrine into Alice, and Dr. Jelana continued compressing Alice's heart. No response from Alice. Dr. Jelana pounded on Alice's sternum several times, but Alice's heart remained asystolic.

"Kaila—another milligram of atropine and six milligrams of epinephrine," the doctor said.

Kaila injected Alice again while the other nurse pumped air into Alice's lungs and Dr. Jelana continued chest compressions. No effect. More pounding on Alice's chest. Nothing.

There was no defibrillator available to Dr. Jelana on that day of December 1, 1954, and its use in Alice's case was questionable at best. After twenty minutes of no heart activity, Dr. Jelana stopped working on her patient. Alice never returned to life.

"I'm calling it," Dr. Jelana said. "Time of death...4:31 pm."

Dr. Jelana and the nurses cleaned up. Alice was wheeled away to the morgue, and the other nurses except one were called to other duties, leaving one nurse and the doctor alone.

"There is no next of kin," Kaila said. "Shall I make arrangements at the orphanage for little Marcus, Dr. Jelana?"

"No. This is my responsibility. I will look after Marcus," Dr. Jelana said.

"Doctor," Kaila said quietly. "No disrespect, but is that wise? You're not married. The baby is white. America is white and Christian. We're black and Muslim."

"I appreciate your concern, Kaila. And I understand the risks. But I took the Hippocratic Oath to become a physician. Simplified, it says, 'Above all, do no harm.' Somehow, harm is done, there is a patient, and I must not add to the harm. I will raise Marcus as my own."

1962 Jul 10. Kiritimati Island, Pacific Ocean.

Jonara, Cerafina, and Johnny appeared on Kiritimati Island like before, but Operation Dominic Sunset ran forward, and the halos were green and black.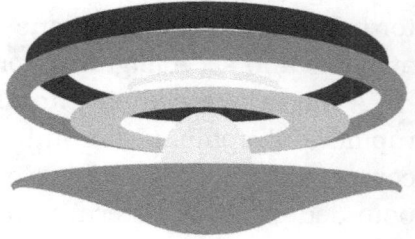

CHAPTER 13

The Margos Embark

2023 Oct 5, Thu 9 am. Corpus Christi Hospital, Texas.

Jonara, Cerafina, and Johnny returned to the hospital room with Eva. Eva choked and gagged. She spit out the white wine, but instead of it being clear or slightly amber, it was a mixture of green and black. Johnny placed a kidney-shaped catch-pan under her chin in time to catch the ejecta.

"What's happening?" Eva asked. "Where did this come from?"

Jonara handed Eva a paper napkin, and Eva wiped her lips clean.

"This should go to pathology," Eva said. "It has a foul taste, but it doesn't taste like bacteria. I should rinse my mouth again. I need to get up."

"Wait!" Johnny said. "You have an IV attached to your arm."

"It's attached to a portable stand," Eva said. "I can wheel it with me."

Eva stood up and wheeled the IV stand to the bathroom. She gargled mouthwash and spat into the sink out of view.

"What progress did you sense?" Johnny asked Jonara.

"Uh, what?" Jonara asked.

"Her thyroid gland," Johnny said. "What did you sense? Are the tumor nodules destroyed? Are they still there? Jonara?"

"I'm sorry, Daddy. I'm still thinking about the nuclear bombs, the pedoscope, and Alice dying in childbirth," Jonara said.

"Those are all disturbing things," Johnny said.

"And you know, those cancer thingies look a lot like ugly nuclear mushroom clouds. And the halos, Daddy, the purple and pink halos over that one bomb—those looked a lot like the halos the red wine made when it attacked the cancer. And the green and black spit from Grandma—that was the same color as the other halos—"

"Over Dominic Sunset," Johnny said. "I know."

"What does it mean?" Jonara asked.

"The Moissan Ruby is strange. Sometimes it mixes things together, like a badly tuned old-fashioned radio picking up two different stations. The halos were the wine, and the Dominic fireball was the cancer."

"I knew the cancer looked like a nuclear mushroom cloud," Jonara said. "But I still don't understand—the Water Ruby can't see into the past, can it?"

"No, it can't," Johnny said.

"Then how can it be tuned to two different stations, as you said? How is it seeing both the present and the past?" Jonara asked.

"Because the past is in the present," Johnny said.

"Huh?" Jonara asked.

"Is it the cancer?" Cerafina asked. "Does the cancer hold the past?"

Johnny looked at Cerafina, smiled, and said, "Very astute, Cerafina. Yes, the cancer is providing a link from the past to the Moissan Ruby."

"That's impossible," Jonara said. "Only the diary can see into the past."

"But how does the diary let you see into the past, hmm? Haven't you wondered?" Johnny asked. "Think about it—the diary is external, the cancer is internal."

"I don't know," Jonara said. "It doesn't make sense. The diary has those special woods and special paper."

"But so does the *viola de gamba*," Cerafina said, "and that sees into the future."

"Shh," Johnny said. "Not so loud. I don't think Grandma Eva knows it still exists."

"I bet I know," Cerafina said.

"I bet you don't," Jonara said.

"I bet I do," Cerafina continued. "Your Nanna Geneva wrote everything down."

"Like duh, we know that," Jonara said.

"So whenever she had a problem or grief, she poured it into the diary. The diary absorbed it. Your Nanna Geneva relieved herself of the burden," Cerafina said.

"So what's so special about that?" Jonara asked.

"I bet your Grandma Eva doesn't have a diary. And from what I've heard, she keeps her problems to herself most of the time. Too much it seems, because she carries her burden with her, and it gets channeled into her thyroid," Cerafina said.

"But why her thyroid?" Jonara asked. "Explain that part of your theory."

"I'm not sure," Cerafina said. "People are supposed to get ulcers from worry, aren't they?"

"You're very close," Johnny said to Cerafina. "People get ulcers because their immune system is weakened by stress. Eva's thyroid was damaged by X-rays—that started the cancer, but the immune system was weakened by worry, so the cancer spread. The engrams of her worry were written into the cancer. When you probe her cancer with the Moissan Ruby, you're reading both its current pathological state, and the engrams of worry from the past."

"But how could she know those things?" Jonara asked.

"That puzzles me too," Cerafina said. "How could she worry about Theodore Cracbern or Alice when they died before Eva was born?"

"The cancer engrams have a three- or four-degree of separation," Johnny said.

"What's a degree of separation?" Jonara asked.

"Is that like we're all connected to each other by six degrees of separation?" Cerafina asked.

"Very much like that. Anyone Eva has worried about or come in contact with spreads their worries to her through a chemical reaction," Johnny said.

"What do you mean? Do they share blood or something?" Jonara asked.

"More subtle than that," Johnny said. "It's in the air—the shedding of skin cells, respiration, and perspiration—there's a plume of human chemicals wafting around. Normally, we aren't conscious of it, but there are chemical messages sent between people. For example, when two or more women live together, they tend to synchronize their menstrual cycles. Do they share blood? No. Airborne chemical messengers exchange information between bodies. So it is with memory engrams."

"That sounds like science fiction," Jonara said.

"Perhaps it is. Now, did you get a look at the cancer as she spat out the dirty white wine?" Johnny asked.

Jonara closed her eyes and thought.

"Yes," Jonara said. "I did get a look. The cancer is shrinking. But Daddy, I had hoped it would be ripped away from the good tissue."

"Was it?" Johnny asked.

"Yes, but something else ripped too," Jonara said. "Grandma's thyroid ripped in half. Her right half is still attached to her throat, but her left half is not. It's floating, and so are the two cancer nodules."

"Is she bleeding internally? Is that where the black and green ejecta came from?" Johnny asked.

"She is not bleeding internally. The black and green stuff came from the cancer," Jonara explained.

"Her thyroid is split," Johnny said. "It must be reintegrated."

"I guess we broke the Hippocratic Oath," Jonara said. "The part that says, 'Above all, do no harm.'"

"Yes, we did break it," Johnny said.

"I'm so sorry, Daddy," Jonara said.

"Don't get stuck on what happened," Johnny said. "Concentrate on the remedy. Think about what you saw and what we should do differently."

"I think she swished the white wine in her mouth too long," Jonara said. "It made too much pulling power."

"What about focus?" Johnny asked.

"Focus?" Jonara asked.

"Yes. We want to remove the cancer from her body without removing the thyroid gland. And we must get the thyroid gland back into one piece," Johnny said.

"We might try a different angle," Jonara suggested. "She could gargle white wine instead of swishing it in her mouth. But do we put the thyroid back together first, or do we attack the cancer?"

"We should put the thyroid back together first," Johnny said. "The longer the thyroid is ripped apart, the more it suffers—even if we do nothing. No, being split apart is worse than leaving cancer floating in her body. We have to put them together again."

"The red wine," Jonara said. "We'll have Grandma start with that again."

"It may have been a mistake using both Burgundy and Oregon red wine simultaneously," Johnny said.

"But we needed the extra power," Jonara said.

"I know, I know," Johnny said.

"Jonara, can't you use that Miramish language like you did before?" Cerafina asked.

"I...I did?" Jonara said. "Strange, I hardly remember it."

"Yes, Jonara, you did. Cerafina has a good idea. Use Miramish with the Moissan Ruby and the candleholder. It's more work for you, I know, but we can't risk mixing red wines again. When your grandmother comes back, we'll start with just the Burgundy red wine. Okay?"

"Okay," Jonara said.

Eva returned to bed with her IV stand.

"I feel much better now," Eva said. "That stuff in my mouth was nasty. So what about the cancer, did the voodoo work?"

"Not yet," Johnny said.

"Not yet," Eva repeated. "I might have known. Still, I gather Jonara and Cerafina are getting some fun out of this hocus-pocus. But remember, girls, there's no substitute for hard evidence and medical training."

"Let's start," Johnny said. "Mummy Eva, here's another spot of Burgundy wine. Please swish in your mouth but do not swallow."

"I hope you girls appreciate the entertainment I'm giving you," Eva said. "Although I must admit I haven't swished as much as I used to. I enjoyed the character of wine when I was younger. Did I say that already?"

"Yes," Jonara, Cerafina, and Johnny said in unison.

"Oh," Eva said. "All right. More wine and less talk."

Eva took the red Burgundy wine into her mouth. She closed her eyes and thought of the vineyard that grew the Pinot noir grapes. Jonara reactivated the cell phone, and the three touched Eva as before. With her free hand, Jonara touched the candleholder to her belly button, and the three traveled back in time again.

1954 Dec 19, Sun. Montgomery Outskirts, Alabama.

"Thank you for inviting me to dinner," Kaila said.

Dr. Jelana drove her yellow 1950 Studebaker Champion coupe toward her parents' house with her nurse and friend, Kaila, riding in the passenger seat. Kaila held baby Marcus in her lap.

"Another Studebaker!" Jonara said. "Daddy, look at the steering wheel. Do you see the two circles with the spoke through the middle?"

"Yes. Do you believe it means something?" Johnny asked.

"It must," Jonara said.

"But how could an automaker hide a message in a steering wheel? The design is simple—there is a wheel for steering, a smaller circle for the horn, a spoke to divide the circles in half, and a steering column," Johnny said.

"I know, Daddy, but I see two circles in so many things—the candleholder, the half-face symbol on the musical instruments, and everything. It's gotta be there for a reason," Jonara said. "But how can I find out the reason?"

"Give it time," Johnny said.

The Studebaker left the paved highway and traveled down a dirt road.

"Your parents are down here? There's nothing but farm-land," Kaila said.

"True. My parents live on a farm," Dr. Jelana said.

"Where's the corn? Where are the peanuts, peaches, and cotton? Did you say your parents are farmers?" Kaila asked.

"They are farmers, but not that kind. They raise sheep, goats, cattle, and *Equus africanus*," Dr. Jelana said.

"Equus what? They raise African horses?" Kaila asked.

"The common name is African Wild Ass," Dr. Jelana said. "Very similar to the donkey but with zebra stripes on the legs. They are highly prized animals. They can survive in arid climates on grass and leaves while only needing to drink once every three days. The pure line is an endangered species. They are either hunted or bred with the common donkey. My parents use only registered African Wild Asses for breeding and sell to several zoos and preserves. In fact, they are planning to leave for Africa in a few days to buy fresh stock. They still have friends over in the country of Eritrea."

"Is that where they're from?" Kaila asked.

"Yes."

Dr. Jelana wheeled the Studebaker around a grove of trees, revealing a grandiose plantation-style house.

"It's huge!" Kaila said. "Who keeps it clean?"

"My mother hires help," Dr. Jelana laughed.

Dr. Jelana parked the car by the back door. Her mother rushed out the door to hug her daughter, while her father walked out more casually.

"Mamma, Pappa, this is my co-worker, Nurse Kaila Baker," Dr. Jelana said. "This is my mother, Isha Jelanaka Margo, and my father, Amiri Margo."

"Nice to meet you," the three said.

Isha hugged Kaila while Amiri shook her hand.

"And what do we have here?" Isha asked, referring to baby Marcus.

"Mamma," Dr. Jelana said. "This is a small patient of mine— Marcus Cracbern."

Isha gave Dr. Jelana a funny look.

"Is there something you're not telling me, Jelana? Do you have a white boyfriend?"

"Oh no, no, no," Dr. Jelana said. "It's nothing like that. I'm adopting this baby. His mother died during childbirth, and his father died several months ago."

"Jelana, I know you're an adult, but...how will you explain this? People will think badly of you," Isha said.

"Mamma, I've decided if there's one thing this country needs, it's unity. I'm simply doing my share," Dr. Jelana said.

"Nothing simple about it," Isha said. "Oh dear, look at the time. It's six o'clock."

"Prayer is in eleven minutes," Kaila said.

"Kaila is a Sunni Muslim like us," Dr. Jelana said.

"Oh how wonderful!" Isha proclaimed with excitement. "Come in, come in! We have extra prayer rugs and everything."

Jonara, Cerafina, and Johnny followed Isha, Amiri, Dr. Jelana, and Kaila into the Margo house.

"First, you'll want to wash up. The bathrooms are over here," Isha said. "Or if you prefer, we have little ablution jugs with water and small towels we keep with the prayer rugs."

Dr. Jelana offered Kaila the bathroom, and Kaila washed up. Dr. Jelana washed her hands and Marcus's. Kaila followed Dr. Jelana into the living room where Isha had set out four adult prayer rugs. The five gathered together with Dr. Jelana holding Marcus, and they began the *salat*—the Muslim prayer ritual. Jonara, Cerafina, and Johnny watched.

"They must do this five times a day," Johnny said.

"I've never seen this kind of prayer," Jonara said.

"It's more than just saying words," Johnny said. "The ritual is driven by intent for cleanliness, thankfulness of God—who Muslims call Allah—praise, and remembrance. This is expressed in motions and words. True believers often feel strengthened after the experience."

A few minutes later, the five completed the *salat*.

"Please," Isha said. "Have a seat at the dinner table."

"I'll help you, Mamma," Dr. Jelana said. "Kaila, would you be so good as to hold Marcus?"

"Be happy to," Kaila said.

Isha and Dr. Jelana disappeared into the kitchen. When they returned, Dr. Jelana carried a large covered pot and placed it at one end of the table where Amiri sat. Isha carried in several other dishes—rolls, vegetables, and a small rack of condiments. The two disappeared into the kitchen and reappeared with several beverage containers—water, tea, apple juice, and goat's milk. Isha and Dr. Jelana sat, and the four said grace. After grace, Amiri spoke:

"Let's see what surprise we have for tonight."

Amiri opened the cover and revealed a stew.

"It's beef stew with apples and white grape juice," Isha said.

Kaila laughed.

"Is this funny to you?" Amiri asked.

"I meant nothing by it. It's perfect, better than perfect. Other folk use white wine instead of grape juice. I'm glad you didn't. It would be *haram.*"

"Yes," Dr. Jelana said. "Some argue that the alcohol evaporates. Others argue a little alcohol remains in the meat—not to mention having to buy the wine in the first place. No, my parents taught me not to take chances with alcohol."

"Grape juice!" Jonara said. "Why didn't I think of that? Daddy! We didn't need to use red and white wine with Grandma Eva. We could have used grape juice!"

"Can you imagine what your Grandma Eva would say if we asked her to drink grape juice?" Johnny asked. "We might as well ask her to eat baby food."

"He's right," Cerafina said. "We had to start with wine."

"Start," Jonara said. "That's the key word, isn't it? Maybe we can finish with grape juice."

"Possibly," Johnny said. "If you can convince your grandmother to drink it."

"Somehow we have to convince her to drink it, so we can pull the cancer out without tearing up the thyroid," Jonara said.

"We still have to integrate the thyroid before we can think about getting rid of the cancer," Johnny said. "Let's continue with the Margo dinner."

Each person in turn passed a plate around the table to Amiri. Amiri placed two or three ladlefuls of stew onto each plate—more if requested. Marcus received a little stew on his plate. Vegetables and rolls were passed around, and within a short time, the five were eating and enjoying dinner.

"Jelana tells me you're planning a trip to Africa," Kaila said. "I've never been to Africa. What's it like?"

"Well," Isha said. "It's hard to explain. The continent varies considerably—from desert to lush vegetation. Mountains, valleys, savannahs—Africa has it all. Even the little country we're going to—Eritrea—has different climates."

"Huh? How?" Kaila asked.

"Mountains and valleys," Dr. Jelana said.

"Yes," Isha said. "Eritrea is divided by the Great Rift Valley— a very long chain of mountains running from Syria in the north to Mozambique in the south."

"Syria's not in Africa," Kaila said.

"True," Dr. Jelana said. "That shows you how long the mountain range is. It extends out of Africa into the Middle East."

"We're from a town in that mountain range, Amiri and I are," Isha continued.

"What's the name of the town?" Kaila asked.

"Asmara," Dr. Jelana said. "And that's where we're going in a few months."

"So you've changed your mind?" Isha asked Dr. Jelana.

"Yes," Dr. Jelana said. "It's time I see where my family came from."

"You didn't feel that way a month ago at Thanksgiving dinner," Isha said.

"That was different," Dr. Jelana said.

"Because of Marcus?" Isha asked.

"Yes. I want him to go, too," Dr. Jelana said.

Amiri shook his head.

"Out of the question," he said. "What will you say to customs?"

"That I adopted him," Dr. Jelana said.

"But he has white skin," Amiri said. "Jelana—you've never been to Eritrea. The sun is brutal. We are from there—our bodies and those of our ancestors adapted to the climate. But this white boy with his pale skin—he'll break into burns and blisters."

"I'll keep him covered," Dr. Jelana said.

"It might be all right, Amiri," Isha said. "It's only Asmara. The climate is more like Italy than Africa. But I was hoping to visit my old village in Dallol."

"There, you see?" Amiri said to Dr. Jelana. "Dallol. Your mother is one of the proud Afar people. Sturdy, able to survive on little water, and able to withstand incredible heat. And you want to take a fragile, white baby to Dallol? Are you trying to murder this child?"

"We'll be careful," Dr. Jelana said.

"You're spoiled by this American climate. It is nothing compared to Dallol," Amiri said. "Even I had difficulty when I first traveled down from Asmara to the Afar people in Dallol to purchase your mother."

"What?!" Dr. Jelana asked. "I never heard this story."

"He didn't really buy me," Isha said. "We fell in love, and I moved to Asmara for a few years."

"But I paid a month's wages to your father first. And your family insisted the wedding be conducted there in Dallol. I almost died of dehydration. And your daughter thinks a white baby can tolerate the conditions. I warn you, Jelana, bad things may come of this."

"You almost died because you wouldn't drink our water," Isha said. "Why? I don't know. It was safe to drink."

"I heard otherwise," Amiri said.

"And I didn't know you paid my father," Isha said. "He never said anything at the time."

"Yes, I did. I didn't want another man to marry you," Amiri said.

"There was no worry of that. Father was a radical. He insisted my body be untouched by female circumcision. My mother and grandmother said I would never find a husband if there were no proof of my virginity. But Father didn't want his little girl cut up."

"For which I am glad. Your father may be considered a radical, but he had a good heart," Amiri said.

"I'm glad he protected me," Isha said. "It's a horrible thing having your baby factory cut up and sewn closed. Too many women die that way. But there's great pressure to have the procedure performed. Some of my friends died from complications after the procedure—from excessive bleeding or infection."

"That would upset me terribly to lose a sister to that procedure," Amiri said. "You see, Jelana, I care about people. I do not wish to see them harmed. That is why I forbid you to bring Marcus along. He should not be endangered by the sun."

"I'm willing to take that chance. And I want Kaila to come with us."

"Me? I don't know anything about Eritrea or Afar people," Kaila said.

"Kaila may go. Her skin will tolerate the sun well. But Jelana, the baby."

"I'm a doctor, Pappa! I know how the human body works. I know its needs and limits," Dr. Jelana said.

"No, I forbid it," Amiri said.

"You know I can afford my own plane ticket," Dr. Jelana said. "Whether you forbid it or not, I'm going. The only question is this—do you want my companionship or not?"

"Isha, the kitchen," Amiri said.

Isha and Amiri departed for the kitchen.

"Jelana!" Kaila said. "I don't want to be mixed up in trouble with your parents."

"Nonsense. Pappa is a little old-fashioned, that's all," Dr. Jelana said.

"Is it really that bad over there?" Kaila asked.

"Bad?"

"Yeah. Scorching heat, like a desert."

"Asmara is in the mountains," Dr. Jelana explained. "It's moderate—more moderate than here. You'll love it. It's like going to Italy. In fact, it used to be called *Little Rome.* You'll see lots of Italian influence there. Even my father, who is full-blooded African, has an Italian last name. My parents left Asmara for the United States while the Italians were still in control. That was in 1923. A year later, I was born. We learned through the news that in 1943, the British took over Eritrea and kicked the Italians out, but then the British left several years later. Now Ethiopia has some sort of claim. I'm not sure if that's good or bad for Eritrea. Anyway, Asmara is nice, but Dallol is in the valley, and it is one of the hottest places on Earth with almost no water. We don't have to go there. We'll see. No, you're fine. Pappa just has to warm up to Marcus going over there. See? I'm helping to integrate the races already."

"Yeah, but the sun doesn't favor white people. Marcus's skin will get badly burned," Kaila said. "You and I will be fine."

"I can put Gletscher Creme on his skin and cover him up. And there are other medicines to help his skin. Come on, Kaila, we're medical professionals. We know what we're doing," Dr. Jelana said.

"I know what I'm doing. I hope you know what you're doing," Kaila said.

Without warning, the distant echo of gunshot carried through the house. Isha and Amiri returned to the dining room.

"What was that?" Kaila asked.

"Sounded like gunshot," Amiri said.

Amiri and Isha looked out the window.

"Something's happening on the Madison farm," Amiri said. "Looks like a gathering of torch lights."

"It's the Ku Klux Klan," Amiri said. "I didn't think they would come out this far from the main city."

"We have to call the police," Kaila said. "If they're from Montgomery, then maybe the Montgomery police can help."

Amiri shook his head.

"The Bombingham Police?" Amiri asked. "They're in league with the Klan, I'll warrant. You've seen what the Klan did to College Hills. They call it Dynamite Hill now."

"This is what I was talking about yesterday," Isha said to Amiri. "The dry desert in Dallol is nothing compared to this white hatemongering group. We must leave Montgomery, Amiri. We must move north or west."

"We can't just sit here and do nothing," Kaila said. "Our brothers and sisters are under attack."

"And they could be killed," Dr. Jelana said.

"We must go over there and help them," Kaila said.

"How?" Amiri asked. "They have rifles and torches. There are hundreds of them. What would we do?"

"Yell, scream, anything," Kaila said.

"And get ourselves killed, too," Amiri said. "No, we stay here."

"How will you live with yourself after tonight?" Kaila asked. "Well, I can't sit here. I'm going over there. Give me a weapon, anything. I'm a nurse, and I'm going to mend my sisters' injuries. Jelana, what do you think? You're always speaking of peace and integration."

"I think we—" she started, but her father interrupted.

"Uh, oh," Amiri said.

"Uh oh what?" Dr. Jelana asked.

"We don't have to worry about going over to the Madison farm to see the Klan. The Klan is coming over here," Amiri said.

"I have an idea," Dr. Jelana said. "Kaila, watch Marcus for me. I'll be back in a moment."

Dr. Jelana disappeared upstairs for a few minutes and returned. She had changed into a simple, white dress with flower patterns. She wore a blond wig, and her face, hands, arms, and legs were covered with light-colored makeup.

"You look like the white devil herself," Isha grinned.

"Jelana?" Kaila asked. "Is that you?"

"Give me Marcus," Dr. Jelana said. "Pappa—how much time?"

"Another minute, and they'll be on the doorstep."

"All of you—go into the cellar and wait until I call for you," Dr. Jelana said.

The three did as Dr. Jelana asked.

"This is horrible, Daddy," Jonara said.

"This was the South in the 1950s," Johnny said. "Self-centered, insecure, irrational, and deluded white men terrorized Blacks, Jews, Catholics, and immigrants."

The door thudded with heavy knocking. Dr. Jelana held Marcus in her arms, a peaceful baby sucking on a pacifier. Dr. Jelana walked slowly to the door. The door thudded again with the echo traveling through the house.

"In the name of God's chosen Klan, open up this door!" a man on the outside yelled.

"Open up!" another man yelled. "We hear tell there are Negroes in this house!"

With a split-second thought, Dr. Jelana ripped the pacifier from Marcus's mouth and tossed it across the room. Marcus cried and would not stop. Dr. Jelana opened the door.

"Yes?" Dr. Jelana asked.

Men in white robes with rope belts, red crosses affixed to their chests, white conical hats, rifles, and torches greeted Dr. Jelana. The Ku Klux Klan. They backed up a step in surprise when they saw what looked like a white woman with a white baby. Dr. Jelana with her strong education spoke with the clarity and enunciation of a New York sophisticate. To the men, she sounded like a white professor.

"Oh," said one of the Klansmen. "We thought—"

"My baby needs settling. Would you like to hold him for a moment?" Dr. Jelana asked.

"It's a white woman," a Klansman said.

"With a white baby!" said another.

Marcus cried and cried. The lead Klansman handed his rifle and torch to another and held Marcus. He tickled Marcus, and Marcus stopped crying and cooed.

"Cute little bugger," the Klansman said. "I got one at home just like him."

The sound and smell of flatulence emanated from Marcus. Marcus smiled. Two other Klansmen peered over the lead Klansman's shoulder to see the baby, but the smell told them it was time to back off.

"Ugh," the lead Klansman said as he peeked into Marcus's diaper. "Yup. Your baby needs a diaper change."

The other Klansmen groaned and backed off. One said, "I ain't never changed a diaper, and I ain't never gonna." Another said, "That's women's work." A third said, "Quit wasting time with the baby, we got black-hacking work to do."

The lead Klansman handed Marcus back to Dr. Jelana.

"Thank you for settling him down," Dr. Jelana said.

"My pleasure. Better get him changed soon so he doesn't get diaper rash. Cute little bugger. He'll grow up strong and be one of us one day."

Dr. Jelana returned a plastic smile, and the Klansmen left.

"I hope not," she said to herself.

Dr. Jelana walked down to the cellar and called for her parents and Kaila to come out.

"It's safe," Dr. Jelana said. "They're gone."

The four returned to the dining room. Amiri looked out the window.

"The good news is this—the Klan is gone," Dr. Jelana said. "The bad news is—the Madison barn is on fire. We must go over and help put it out."

"I'll go," Isha said.

"Me too," Kaila said.

"Jelana should stay here with the baby, in case the Klan returns," Amiri said.

"She's old enough to make her own decisions," Isha said. "Let our daughter speak her mind."

"It's all right, Mamma," Dr. Jelana said. "Pappa has a good idea. I'll stay here and watch the baby and the farm."

Jonara, Cerafina, and Johnny followed Isha, Amiri, and Kaila into Amiri's car and rode over to the Madison farm. The Madison barn was on fire, a shed had collapsed, and the windows to the house were smashed in with rocks. Amiri knocked on the front door.

"Go away, go away!" a frightened woman yelled from inside.

"Lashanda, it's us—the Margos," Isha yelled. "Are you all right in there?"

Lashanda opened the front door slowly. Her dress was ripped and covered with blood. Isha hugged the shaking woman, and Lashanda led the party inside.

"Do I look all right?! Does anything look all right?!" Lashanda said.

"Where's Larry?" Amiri asked.

Lashanda pointed outside.

"Is he all right?" Amiri asked.

Lashanda buried her face in her hands.

"We have to help him!" Amiri said.

"They hung him from a tree by the barn!" she screamed, and she collapsed.

Isha and Kaila took Lashanda to the couch. Amiri went outside by the burning barn. A makeshift man-high wooden crucifix had been erected and burned brightly. Amiri looked up and saw a tree, a rope, a noose, and Larry's limp body dangling from the noose.

"Thugs! Cowards! Demons from white hell!" he yelled.

Amiri ran inside and begged for Kaila's help. Kaila followed Amiri to the tree. Amiri asked Kaila to catch Larry's body while he cut the noose, but Kaila just screamed and screamed.

"Go back inside," Amiri finally said.

Kaila did so. Amiri did the best he could to cut the rope and lower Larry gently, but it was difficult. Amiri had to use a ladder to reach the rope, and Larry was a big man. Amiri cut the rope. Larry's body swung, caught the ladder, and felled it, taking Amiri with him. Amiri fell to the ground and sprained his ankle.

"Why did we need to see this?" Jonara asked.

"I don't know, honey," Johnny said. "Life is tough at times."

"It's terrible," Cerafina said. "To think this kind of thing happened in the United States. So much for liberty and freedom. What did Larry do that deserved this?"

"Look at this farm," Johnny said.

"What about it? It's a normal farm," Jonara said.

"Is it because it's a normal farm and not a poor farm?" Cerafina asked.

"Yes, it is. The Madisons were successful farmers, and they're black. That breaks the ignorant stereotype the attackers wish to believe. When a belief is challenged like this, the evil response is to attack and destroy, to maintain a grip of power over those who challenge the belief."

"But farming isn't evil," Jonara said. "And it's not like the Madisons are making nuclear weapons or something powerful like that. It doesn't make sense."

"You're right, Jonara," Johnny said. "Bigotry doesn't make sense. It's the ugliest vice known to humankind."

"Larry my brother," Amiri said into Larry's ear. "Can you hear me? Larry, wake up."

Larry did not respond. Amiri took his pulse. Nothing. Amiri, despite being in pain from his sprained and swelling ankle, straightened Larry's body and performed cardiopulmonary resuscitation (CPR). Larry did not respond. Amiri continued performing CPR—pushing on the heart with his hands and pushing air into Larry's lungs with his mouth. Amiri took a brief rest to catch his breath. He breathed heavily. Then back to work at CPR on Larry's unresponsive body.

"He's dead, isn't he Daddy?" Jonara asked.

"Yes," Johnny said.

"Can I bring him back to life with the Water Ruby and candleholder?" Jonara asked.

Johnny paused as if lost in thought. Finally, he answered.

"No. History will not allow it," Johnny said. "What bigotry hath destroyed one cannot bring back to the living. To do so would require a rebirth of those who have bigotry in their hearts, and that cannot come about using the same methods bigotry itself employs—coercion and force."

"Then how?" Jonara asked.

"In this situation, we cannot help," Johnny said. "Respect, openness, dialog, knowledge, understanding, and compromise are better tools. Enforcing equal rights for all is the goal, but there's that word again—force. But I wonder—we're in the time period when demonstrations start. We may yet see the beginnings of the solution."

The world turned dark. Jonara, Cerafina, and Johnny left the Margo farm and traveled forty miles into the upper atmosphere. The three saw a black sky above and a blue glow along the curved horizon. Inner peace consumed them. The serenity did not last long. The world had more violence than the atmosphere could accommodate, and with stray fingers of violence nudging them from below, the three descended back to Earth.

1955 Feb 25, Fri. Montgomery, Alabama.

Airline fare was not cheap, and the Margos knew it, but the Margos felt it was necessary to spend the money to visit Eritrea for a number of reasons. For Isha and Amiri, the primary goal was to arrange for more African Wild Asses, yet the two also saw the trip as an opportunity to flush out old "ghosts"—compare memories of the past against their wisdom of the present and the changes in Eritrea since the Italians left. For Dr. Jelana, it was an opportunity to see where her parents came from. For Kaila, it was a once-in-a-lifetime chance to fly overseas. Dr. Jelana insisted on paying for her own ticket, for Marcus's, and for Kaila's. Nonstop flights were almost unheard of in 1955, and so it was the group took several connecting flights to reach their destination.

Dr. Jelana drove her Studebaker to Kaila's home and picked her up along with luggage.

"Are you ready to go?" Dr. Jelana asked Kaila as she jumped in the Studebaker.

"Yeah! I'm so excited," Kaila said.

The two drove down the highway to rendezvous with Isha and Amiri at Dannelly Field. Kaila was so excited that initially she didn't notice the baby in the back seat until he cooed.

"I forgot to say, 'Hello,' to Marcus," Kaila said.

Kaila turned around in her seat and was shocked to see a dark-skinned baby.

"What happened? Where's Marcus? Whose baby is this?" Kaila asked.

"This is my baby," Dr. Jelana said. "It's Marcus in the back seat."

"Huh? I don't understand. Marcus is a white baby, but this one is black."

"This baby is Marcus with dark skin," Dr. Jelana said. "I decided to minimize confusion and conflict on this flight by darkening his skin."

"How?" Kaila asked.

"The same way I treat patients with vitiligo," Dr. Jelana said. "I give him xanthotoxin."

"You're treating Marcus for vitiligo?" Kaila asked.

"That's right," Dr. Jelana said. "Funny, isn't it? Having white skin can be classified as a disease, and there's medicine to treat it! But of course white skin is considered the standard race in America by whites, isn't it? Using that illogic, the standard race is diseased. Ick. Let's forget about that political insanity. Marcus is safe. Don't worry about him. I'm monitoring his blood. If his liver levels are off, I'll stop treatment."

The three arrived at the airport and met with Isha and Amiri, who were also surprised by Marcus's appearance. Dr. Jelana gave them the same explanation as she gave Kaila. Isha seemed concerned, but Amiri laughed.

"There's some use in being a doctor after all," Amiri said. "You can change your skin color at will with a pill."

"It's a little harder going the other way," Dr. Jelana said. "And I'd never recommend it. The risk of skin cancer jumps considerably when skin loses its protective melanocytes."

The trip began. The party boarded an Eastern Air Lines plane from Montgomery to Birmingham, waited a short time, and left Birmingham for Atlanta, Georgia where they landed and had a scant forty minutes to board their next flight, a Delta C&S Air Lines flight to Cincinatti, Ohio. In Cincinatti, the group caught a Trans World Airlines (TWA) flight to New York and boarded a Pan American flight to Boston followed by another Pan Am flight to Santa Maria Island in the Azores archipelago. The flight over the Atlantic was long—jet planes had not entered commercial service yet, and propeller planes were approximately half as fast as a jet. As the party crossed the Atlantic, they crossed from one day to the next.

1955 Feb 26. Over the Atlantic Ocean.

About thirty minutes before the plane landed on Santa Maria Island, Amiri warned the younger women.

"We won't be flying all the way to Asmara like this," he said.

"What do you mean?" Dr. Jelana asked. "Are we to swim the rest of the way?"

"No, nothing like that," he said. "We will fly to Asmara, of course. What I mean is this—instead of flying to an airport and waiting for the next flight, I thought we'd spend a day of sightseeing in each overseas city."

"We both agreed to it," Isha said. "Since we're in the area, why not? We don't do this all the time, and it's a good way to rest after these long flights."

"We will be going on tour rides," Amiri said. "Now pay attention. It's very important you stay with the tour group. Do not deviate from the group for one moment. These countries are not like the United States. The Azores are part of Portugal, and Portugal is run by the dictator António Salazar. I might add he's on good terms with his Spanish neighbor, the dictator Francisco Franco. After we spend a day in the Azores, we catch our next flight on TWA to Lisbon in Portugal. Same warning applies— stay with the tour group. We don't want to draw the attention of Salazar's gaze. From Lisbon, we will stop in Madrid in Spain, and that is under the watchful eye of Franco."

"From Madrid we proceed on to Rome, Italy," Amiri continued. "Fortunately, Italy is now a democracy and ally of the United States, so we shouldn't have any trouble. From Italy we fly to Cairo, Egypt. I considered the leg from Rome to Athens to Cairo, but I don't want to take chances in Athens. Greece ended a bitter civil war five years ago, and the people are still deeply divided politically. The country is suffering economically. We'll skip Greece."

"We won't have to worry about things stolen if we skip Greece, right?" Kaila asked.

"Wrong," Amiri countered. "Watch your things—people may try to distract and steal things from you no matter what country you are in. We probably won't see this in the Azores, but it could happen anywhere. Be careful of your things. I think Spain is also suffering economically under Franco, and I'm still debating whether we should stay there a day or not."

"Our last leg on TWA takes us to Cairo, Egypt. Now Egypt just underwent a revolution two years ago. A year ago, the new Egyptian Republic was declared, but just this past year, the first president, General Muhammad Naguib, was forced to resign by Gamal Nasser. Is this a dictatorship? It doesn't appear to be, but it's early, and things may go one way or another. Like other places, stay together and avoid conflict."

"Cairo ends our trip with TWA. From Cairo, we fly on Ethiopian Airlines to Port Sudan," Amiri said.

"Port Sudan, Port Sudan!" Kaila exclaimed.

"What's so special about Port Sudan?" Jonara asked.

"It's on the Red Sea," Cerafina said. "Is that why it's special?"

"Close," Johnny said. "Port Sudan is a crossing point for Muslims on a pilgrimage to Mecca. On the other side of the Red Sea is Jeddah, and Mecca is closeby."

"Pappa," Dr. Jelana said. "Are you holding out on us?"

"What do you mean?" he faked.

Isha smiled and said, "You can't keep it from them any longer. You might as well tell them."

"Very well," he said. "As you know, it's strongly urged that all Muslims make a *Hajj* to Mecca at least once in their lifetimes. Your mother and I made one shortly before we moved from Asmara to the United States. Wonderful place. Crowded, but wonderful. We've decided that since we're in the area, we're going to take the both of you and little Marcus to Mecca."

Kaila jumped out of her seat and nearly started to scream, but Dr. Jelana jumped up, restrained Kaila, put a hand over Kaila's mouth, and pulled Kaila back to her seat.

"We're on an airplane," Dr. Jelana said. "You don't want to cause a scene."

"Mecca, Mecca, Mecca!" Kaila repeated.

"Yes. We'll take a ferry across the Red Sea from Port Sudan to Jeddah, and from Jeddah we'll take a bus to Mecca," Amiri said.

Kaila hugged Dr. Jelana, hugged Isha, and hugged Amiri.

"I will be considered your guardians," Amiri said, "since I am the only male to accompany you two. You know the rules—women must be accompanied by a guardian male."

"I know," Dr. Jelana said. "It seems like a throwback. But it's not as bad as the segregation laws in Alabama. At least we're not prevented from making the *Hajj* to Mecca."

"Non-Muslims, however, are prevented. How will you explain Marcus?" Amiri asked.

"How does any woman explain an infant who can't understand anything? I'll raise him as Sunni Muslim, of course," Dr. Jelana said.

"Good," Amiri said. "When our *Hajj* is complete, we'll fly on Ethiopian Airlines from Jeddah to Asmara. I have booked reservations at a nice hotel in Asmara, and from there our adventure begins."

"I think our adventure has already begun," Dr. Jelana chuckled.

Isha and Kaila laughed.

"I guess you're right at that," Amiri said. "I'm still uneasy about you girls and Marcus going anywhere outside of Asmara. Asmara has running water and toilets, but the rural parts of Eritrea do not. Rural lifestyle is very basic, very simple."

"We'll manage, Pappa," Dr. Jelana said. "Look, the plane is ready for touchdown."

The Pan Am propeller plane landed on Santa Maria Island. The party exited the plane, picked up their baggage, and headed for a hotel where they rested a bit before joining a tour boat. The tour boat motored around the Azores islands. Dr. Jelana and Kaila took many photographs of the scenic mountains, terraced hills, gentle shorelines, classy orange-roofed and white-walled buildings, and lush vegetation.

"This is the best vacation I've ever had!" Kaila said. "I can hardly wait to see how the other cities turn out. Things can only get better. There's so much to do. I want to go hiking, I want to climb the mountains, and I want to go swimming."

"The terrain might be too tough for mountain climbing. But you're right—there are plenty of things to do," Amiri said. "Perhaps we can stay an extra day or two. The Azores are very beautiful. They also help with easing jet lag."

"And the best part of the Azores," Kaila said, "is that people don't stare at us like the do in Montgomery."

"Yes," Amiri said. "The more money we spend here, the happier they are with us."

"I could live here forever," Kaila said.

"Marcus is doing well," Isha said to Dr. Jelana. "I can't believe you darkened his skin so much. What magic do doctors have these days?"

"It's called *xanthotoxin*. I give him a dose and expose him to sunlight or a black light," Dr. Jelana said. "Not only does he look more like me now, but the darker skin should help protect him when we're in Africa."

Isha, Amiri, Dr. Jelena, Kaila, and Marcus enjoyed their two-and-a-half days at the Azores. Dr. Jelana and Kaila wanted to stay longer, but Amiri reminded them that their primary goal was to visit Asmara to negotiate more African Wild Asses for his farm in Montgomery. With much disappointment that the Azores vacation had ended so quickly, the party packed up their things, checked out of the hotel, headed for the Santa Maria airport, and boarded a Trans World Airlines flight to Lisbon, Portugal.

1955 Feb 28, Mon. East of Azores, Atlantic Ocean.

The flight to Lisbon took approximately six hours. The party arrived in the early evening with enough time to check into a hotel, eat dinner, and relax before falling asleep. The party had high expectations of Lisbon after having a delightful Azores holiday.

1955 Mar 1, Tue. Lisbon, Portugal.

The party awoke afresh, ate breakfast, and toured the area. To their delight, there was plenty to see in Lisbon. The party started with a tour boat in the bay where the Tagus flowed into the Atlantic Ocean.

"I would have expected the buildings to be much older," Kaila said to a tour guide on the boat.

"A great earthquake in 1755 destroyed many buildings," Amiri said. "Many lost their lives. But Lisbon recovered and prospered. Did you know that at one time, these lands in Portugal and Spain were ruled by the Moors? Those were Arabs from the Middle East. And they brought Islam with them. They built mosques and planted the Arabic language here. Unfortunately, many mosques were lost in the 1755 earthquake. Some areas were unaffected, such as Alfama, which is named after Al Hamma."

The party completed their tour boat, ate a late lunch, and explored the city on a tour bus.

"Hi, I'm your tour guide. If you have any question, just ask. I'm a student at the University of Lisbon and work these tours in my spare time. To help support my education, I'm selling a brochure that explains the sights we'll see today," a tour guide said.

The tour guide was male and tall with black, straight hair. He was well built and had olive skin. The bus passed from sight to sight, and the tour guide explained each of them.

"This is the Lisbon Cathedral," the tour guide said. "It was built in 1147 over the remains of a mosque."

"What happened to the mosque?" Kaila asked, who by now was showing an interest in the tour guide.

"It was destroyed during the *Reconquista*," the tour guide said. "Christian crusader knights attacked and reconquered Lisbon. After this mosque was destroyed, the cathedral was built."

"And that was it? All Muslims were forcibly removed in 1147?" Kaila asked.

Kaila reacted with disappointment after hearing about mosques being destroyed and Muslims being expelled. The tour guide lowered his voice so only Kaila and her party could hear, to assuage her feelings.

"No. The *Reconquista* in Portugal did not end until many years later—some say as early as 1238. After the forcible removal of Muslims in 1147, there were many Muslim raids against Iberian Christian kingdoms. A single Lisbon raid in 1189 captured 3,000 women and children, taken by caliph Yagub al-Mansur," the tour guide said. "There are many more stories. Portugal and Spain hosted tensions between Christians and Muslims for hundreds of years. But this started to end in 1492 when all Jews were expelled from Spain. Muslims grouped in the Kingdom of Granada where they were given tolerance. But even those Muslims were expelled in 1502. Contrary to popular belief, Jews and Muslims have not always hated each other. They were practically brothers in Iberia before the great expulsions. As it was, many Jews and some Muslims fled to Portugal from the Kingdom of Spain in 1492, but their safe haven ended in 1496 or 1497 when both groups were expelled. After that, Portugal and Spain began sailing the world, colonizing new places, and growing in wealth. It all started when the Portugese and Spanish looked for new routes to India and China to avoid heavy tariffs paid to Middle Eastern countries for overland passage. Both countries started by sailing farther and farther around Africa. Of course, Christopher Columbus had his journey to the New World—he was really looking for and thought he found India, but that is another story."

"Wow, you know everything about Portugese history," Kaila said, who now felt much better.

"It's my job," the tour guide said.

"But I can't believe Portugal and Spain had a set-to against Muslims. We're not so bad, really," Kaila said.

Amiri and Dr. Jelana attempted to hush Kaila with their facial expressions. They felt Kaila was conversing along a dangerous line.

"The silent majority are always the nice ones," the tour guide said. "But it seems there are a few loud ones who become very demanding. And so wars begin. Peace and love as taught by religions are ignored in favor of greed and glory."

"You're a philosopher too," Kaila said.

"Sometimes," the tour guide said. "Much of Portugal is still Christian, but some of us are Muslim," he grinned and winked. "What is your name?"

"Kaila. What's yours?"

"Justino. If you're not too busy, I can take you to a movie. I know the right movie for you. It's playing just down the road a bit with English subtitles."

"What's the name of this movie?" Kaila asked.

"*Les amants du Tage*," Justino said. "Or in your language, *The Lovers of Lisbon*."

"I'd like that," Kaila said. "Jelana, do you want to—"

"Oh no. I have little Marcus, and four would be a crowd," Dr. Jelana said.

"Kaila," Amiri said. "Remember what I said about staying together."

"He's right," Justino said. "You can't be too careful. Is this your brother?"

"No," Amiri laughed. "Kaila is a friend of our family. I'm Amiri. This is my wife, Isha, my daughter, Dr. Jelana, and her boy, Marcus."

"Mr. Amiri—if you would like to chaperone, or if you could recommend a chaperone, I would be honored," Justino said.

"No!" Kaila said. "That would spoil the movie."

"What kind of movie is it?" Amiri asked.

"Oh come on, Amiri," Isha said. "*Lovers of Lisbon*? It's obviously a romance movie. You'll be bored out of your mind."

"Then perhaps Mrs. Isha would like to chaperone?" Justino said.

"I won't let my wife out of my sight," Amiri said.

"And I won't have a chaperone. I'm an adult, not a little girl. I can take care of myself," Kaila said.

Another tourist held up money, and the tour guide rushed over to sell his brochure. The tour ride was ending, and others purchased his brochure before departing the bus.

"When do you get off work?" Kaila asked Justino quietly.

"In about ninety minutes," Justino said. "Where are you staying?"

"At the Hotel Lisboa Plaza," Kaila said. "Please—I really want to go. But I don't want a chaperone."

"Are you sure?" Justino asked.

"Yes. How soon can you pick me up?" Kaila asked.

"I can pick you up in two hours," Justino said.

"Meet me in front of the hotel in two hours then," Kaila said as she gave him a light kiss on the cheek.

The tour ended, and the party returned to the hotel to freshen up before dinner. The party then walked along the street in front of the hotel and found a nice Portuguese restaurant with plenty of fresh ocean fish. The party enjoyed food, drink, music, and a friendly environment.

"You were striking up a good conversation with that tour bus guide," Dr. Jelana said.

"I was interested in learning about Lisbon and Portugal," Kaila said.

"I think you were more interested in the tour guide than the tour," Dr. Jelana said.

"No!" Kaila giggled.

"Yes!" Dr. Jelana giggled back and nudged Kaila.

Kaila nudged Dr. Jelana back.

"Kaila," Amiri said. "I must warn you about your tongue."

"Nothing's wrong with my tongue," Kaila said.

"He means be careful what you say," Dr. Jelana said.

"Yes. Not all countries view Muslims in a good light," Amiri said. "You heard the tour guide talk about the Muslims being expelled from Spain. Muslims ruled in Iberia for a time, and some of the local people did not like it. Many know the history and some harbor ill will toward us. Do not let them know you are Muslim unless you are sure they are comfortable with our faith. Fortunately, it seems our tour guide is a Muslim himself, but we cannot always count on such luck. Once we reach Africa and the Kingdom of Saudi Arabia, we'll be safe."

The party returned to the hotel room.

"I'm going downstairs for some fresh air," Kaila said.

"Don't be gone long," Amiri said.

Dr. Jelana had her suspicions. She looked out the hotel window in time to see Justino drive up in a car and Kaila enter the passenger seat. Before Dr. Jelana could say anything, Kaila closed her door and Justino drove away.

1955 Mar 2, Tue. Lisbon, Portugal.

The party awoke and ate a late breakfast. Kaila was with them, but she said nothing about sneaking out with Justino. The party checked out of their hotel and boarded a Trans World Airlines plane to Madrid, Spain.

"After the incident with the tour guide, I've decided we won't be spending a day in Spain," Amiri said. "I don't want to risk being found out we're Muslim. No telling what Franco's regime would do to us. We will wait in Madrid only long enough for the plane to leave again. We will, however, spend a day in Rome, Italy. That should be safe enough."

Kaila started to protest, but when Dr. Jelana supported her father, Kaila backed down. The TWA plane took off from the Lisbon airport.

"Did you have a good time?" Dr. Jelana asked Kaila.

"What?" Kaila pretended.

"That must be the record for getting a breath of fresh air. And I saw Justino pick you up in his car," Dr. Jelana continued. "But I can't say when you got in. It must have been late. We were all asleep."

"It was a great movie," Kaila said. "I'm glad I went."

Kaila proceeded to describe the movie in detail to Dr. Jelana. Amiri, Isha, and Marcus fell asleep, and Dr. Jelana started to doze near the end of Kaila's monologue.

"Jelana, aren't you paying attention?" Kaila asked.

"I'm a little tired," Dr. Jelana said. "And I don't know how you can be so perky. You must have been up half the night."

"Most of the night," Kaila said. "But I can't stop thinking about Justino."

"Well you'll have to," Dr. Jelana said. "Portugal is behind us, and we have to think about our next destination—Spain or Italy depending on if you count a short stay in Madrid or not."

"Justino, Justino, Justino!" Kaila repeated.

Kaila stared out the airplane window and placed her hand against the pane, as if reaching out for the young man. The remaining party kept mostly quiet—napping when possible—until the plane landed in Madrid. As the propeller plane landed on the runway, lights flashed from outside the window.

2006 Nov 22, Wed Eve. Redjet Laundry Room. Portland, Oregon.

A second explosion lit up the Helrod structure, flashing light through the windows.

"Another explosion!" Calico said. "It's sabotage."

A siren sounded throughout Redjet and the Elrod campus.

"What happened?" Jonara asked Johnny.

"We're not in Spain anymore," Cerafina said.

"Eva isn't with us," Johnny said. "But we must still be linked with her in the hospital back in Corpus Christi."

"I don't understand," Jonara said. "We were following the Cracberns, the Margos, and now we jump into the future?"

"The Elrod is the past," Cerafina said.

"I mean the Margos' future," Jonara said.

"We were traveling into the Margos' future," Cerafina giggled, "at a rate of one second per second."

"Cerafina!" Jonara said.

"I'm joking with you, Jonara," Cerafina grinned.

"The jolt from landing in Madrid must have shifted your focus onto another stress point in Eva's past," Johnny explained.

"Is the washer done, Eve?" Calico asked Evanita.

"Yes. The clothes need drying, and I have another two loads to wash," Evanita said.

"Don't wash any more clothes, and don't run the dryer either. Take everything—wet and dry—and haul it back to our room. We're going into lockdown, and you can't stay in the laundry room," Calico explained.

"But your clothes—they're wet," Evanita said.

"Hang 'em up to dry. Now get crackin'. I'm on the fire team, and I got a complaint to put out," Calico said. "Move, Carson!"

Evanita gathered up Calico's laundry and hauled it back to her room. Ox-Three slammed Evanita's door closed with a boom and locked it with a clank. The Russian and German girls' room was next—boom and clank. Each door in turn received a boom and clank from Ox-Three, and as Ox-Three continued down the corridor, booms and clanks echoed from farther away until the very last dorm room resounded with the distant echo of boom and clank.

Evanita threw a rope up across the room several times and hung up Calico's wet laundry. Periodically as she hung the laundry, she peered out the window to see what was happening. Ox-Two, Ox-Three, and Calico wore red fire hats and directed the firefighting. Prison girls dragged large hoses to the fire and sprayed water onto the flames. The fire roared, and the wind whipped the flames back and forth like an inverted tornado. The prison girls made gains only to be driven back by fiery flames. Several women from the sanitation team (Diali-One, Two, and Three) waited for the flames to dispel before hauling the damaged remains away.

The main core of the fire did not last long. After forty-five minutes, the flames were reduced to a smolder. By this time, Evanita had finished hanging up Calico's wet clothes and folding away her dry. As she finished the last bit of clothing, the door unlocked.

"Lockdown is over?" Evanita asked.

"Naw, it ain't," Calico said. "But I let myself in all the same."

Calico was covered in sweat and grime from the fire.

"I need a shower and a good smoke," Calico said.

"I thought you only smoke in the morning," Evanita said.

Calico whumped Evanita on the head.

"No one questions when the Calico smokes," Calico said. "I'm too dirty to touch things. Get me a sweatshirt and sweatpants, and put them on the bathroom sink."

Evanita did as she was told, though she didn't like it.

"Good," Calico said.

As Calico took her shower, she sang. Her voice was loud, low, and it shook the walls. Evanita put her fingers in her ears to block the low singing, but she could not stop the room from shaking. The room went gray, and the three travelers—Jonara, Cerafina, and Johnny—found themselves in a rumbling propeller airplane as it was about to take off.

1955 Mar 2, Tue. Madrid, Spain.

The wait was only forty-five minutes, and the plane departed for Italy. The Margo party arrived in the evening, checked into their hotel, and had only enough time for a quick bite to eat before retiring for the night.

1955 Mar 3, Wed. Rome, Italy.

The party awoke as they did on other mornings—fresh and ready for breakfast. They hopped on a tour bus and rode around Rome, seeing such sights as the Colosseum, the Baths of Agrippa, the Gardens of Lucullus, and the Stadium of Domitian. The party noticed lots of construction wherever they went.

The tour bus stopped for lunch before proceeding to Vatican City where the group spent extensive time visiting the museum, the Sistine Chapel, St. Peter's Basilica, the Papal Tombs, and the Vatican Gardens.

"So much opulence and extravagance for the Roman Catholic Church," Dr. Jelana said.

"Vatican City is to Catholics what Mecca is to Muslims," Amiri said, "although there aren't nearly the crowds here in Vatican City."

"That's because there is no requirement to make a pilgrimage here," Isha said.

The tour at Vatican City used up much of the afternoon. The party grew hungry, and Amiri arranged for a late afternoon boat tour with dinner. The party boarded the boat, the boat pulled away from port, and it picked up speed. Music flowed through the boat's audio system with an Italian folksong, *Eh Cumpari*, sung by a young woman. The sun set in the west, and as the last flickering light danced across the boat, Cerafina felt a sharp pain in her temple. She gasped and screamed briefly.

"What is it?" Jonara asked. "Are you hurt?"

"For a moment I thought I was somewhere else," Cerafina said. "I thought I was on my grandmother's yacht in the Gulf of Mexico—in my future."

"Strange," Johnny said. "But I wonder what caused it? Does your grandmother know Eva Carreña?"

"No," Cerafina said. "Not at all. But she's from Italy."

"That may be the connection," Johnny said.

"But why the future? Why my future? I thought the diary and tumor only recorded the past," Cerafina said.

"Music seems to trigger the future," Johnny said.

The sunlight danced again, the verse in *Eh Cumpari* grew longer, and the three travelers found themselves on the Verona Ancona, a megayacht with amas and hydrofoils owned by Cerafina's grandmother, Elina Ancona. Jonara, Cerafina, and Johnny were in the yacht's brig, where an older Cerafina (by four years) was in conversation with three boys her age.

2027 Dec 24. The Verona Ancona, Gulf of Mexico.

"Thanks Frenchie," Hank said. "Let's set the record straight, your highness!"

"What?!" older Cerafina said.

"Yeah. You're a spoiled kid. You don't have to work at all. Everything is given to you," Hank said.

"How dare you! You don't know me at all," older Cerafina said.

"Oh I know your type. Pretty girl. Expects guys to wait on her hand and foot, just because she can sit and look nice."

"That's not true," older Cerafina said.

"Oh, *tais-toi* (shut up)!" Jean-Jacque said. "Let Hank speak without interruption."

"Go on then," older Cerafina said. "Say what's on your mind."

"We guys here, and our fathers, have busted our butts for your grandmother and her yacht. Business deals, construction, and shipping. She didn't make her money on her own. I know, I know, she sells cargo ships. Fast cargo ships. But she couldn't do it without Bernardi's ship design or Montaine's ship controls. And oil! Do you know how expensive oil is today? The Ghawar Field is running low. So is Burgan. Those are the largest two oil fields. Countries pay top money for oil that's shipped quickly. And your grandmother's cargo ships do that," Hank said.

"My grandmother is a good woman," older Cerafina said. "Don't you say anything bad about her."

"She was in the right place at the right time," Hank said. "That's all. She bought the rights to Bernardi's technology in the last recession when he was about to go bankrupt and when the major cargo carriers were going bankrupt."

"Greedy men caused the cargo lines to suffer," older Cerafina said.

"Greedy countries caused banks to issue bad loans that forced honest cargo lines into bankruptcy," Hank said. "Your grandmother—"

"MY GRANDMOTHER SAVED THE INDUSTRY!" older Cerafina shouted.

"*Ta gueule* (Shut up)," Jean-Jacque said.

"GET IN THE BRIG!" older Cerafina ordered Jean-Jacque. "YOU TOO, HORACE THURGOOD."

Jonara, younger Cerafina, and Johnny felt the lights go gray, and they were back with the Margo party. The Margos and Kaila ordered dinner, and as the waiter finished with the order, the same woman who had sung *Eh Cumpari* took to the stage with her band. She wore a dark robe and hood that all but obscured her face and body. She sang *El Negro Zumbon*. The world went gray, and the three travelers were back on the Verona Ancona.

2027 Dec 25. The Verona Ancona, Gulf of Mexico.

Jonara, Cerafina, and Johnny appeared in a breakfast galley. The older Cerafina was there at one table along with Cerafina's mother, grandmother, and grandmother's friend. Cerafina's father and her older brother, Leo, sat at another table.

"Who hijacked my daughter's body?" Cerafina's mother said about the older Cerafina.

Cerafina's father told a story and waved his hands wildly. He pointed to the older Cerafina. Leo made faces at older Cerafina.

"Ignore him," Cerafina's mother said to older Cerafina.

Leo pantomimed swimming, turned his head, and held his hands to his throat as he pretended to drown. Older Cerafina slapped her fork to her plate.

"Cerafina," Cerafina's mother said to older Cerafina. "Let it slide."

Leo pointed at older Cerafina, stood up, and turned around in place as if being turned in a Salsa. He fell to the ground clumsily, on purpose.

"Mother," older Cerafina said. "He's making fun of my dancing."

"Look the other way," Cerafina's mother said to older Cerafina. "Look...the...other...way."

Leo made a lewd hand signal by inserting his thumb on one hand into his open mouth. With his other hand, he made an L-shaped hand signal to his forehead.

Older Cerafina stood up abruptly and caught her arms on the table. All plates on her table jumped a foot in the air. Eating utensils leapt off the table. Coffee cups spilled coffee into laps. Leo stood up next to his table, slowly, but he maintained the L hand sign on his forehead. Older Cerafina placed the back of her right palm against her forehead and made the following hand signals:

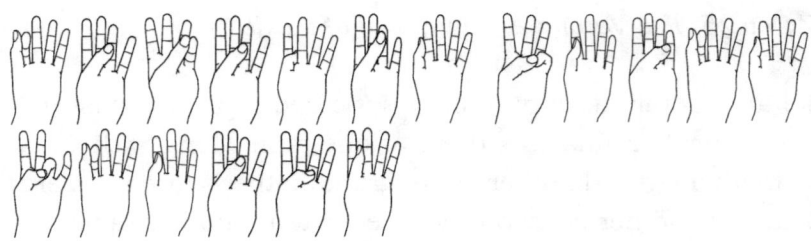

"Ravage your throat."

Leo thrust his fist into his mouth and blocked his throat. He choked. He gagged. He pulled and beat with his right hand, but his left continued to violate his throat.

"Leo!" Cerafina's mother yelled, and she ran to him.

1955 Mar 3, Wed. Rome, Italy. Dinner Boat.

Jonara, Cerafina, and Johnny returned from the year 2027 and sat with the Margo party for dinner. The Margos and Kaila had just finished eating and were sipping the last of their drinks.

"You know what I like?" Kaila said. "We can sit here and enjoy dinner with all different kinds of people. No black section, no white section, just people. Italy is so advanced."

"Or America is more backward," Dr. Jelana said. "But Italy is growing, that's for sure. Did you notice how much construction there is?"

"Italy is going through an economic boom," Amiri said.

"I never would have guessed it," Kaila said. "Weren't they the enemy?"

"They were," Isha said. "And run by Benito Mussolini, too. But that ended with the war."

"Yes," Amiri said. "Italy became a republic in 1946."

"Isn't it strange how some countries like Italy became a republic, while other countries like Spain remain a regime?" Dr. Jelana asked.

"Spain was never conquered by the Allies," Amiri said. "That's the main difference. Italy benefited from America's Marshall Plan."

"You want to know something else that's strange?" Isha asked.

"I think I can guess. It's about where America spends its money," Dr. Jelana said.

"You know your mother well," Isha said. "As you know, the Marshall Plan was set up to aid reconstruction in Europe after the war and to repel communism. You could say a benefit of the plan was to encourage and protect democracy. So why can't the feds spend money in the South to repel discrimination and protect American democracy?"

"Because America is white, male, and Christian," Kaila said. "I've said it before, and I'll say it again."

"That's not true," Isha said. "There are many Americans who aren't white, male, or Christian."

"But white America would have us believe the standard is white, male, and Christian," Kaila said. "Look at the white man—he makes his wife stay cooped up at home while he earns the money. When does she get to go out and be a success? Never. Do you see our black sisters forced to stay at home? No. Our sisters are out mopping floors and cleaning toilets for the white man. A few of us like Jelana and me have done better, but we've had to fight for it."

"It's a double standard," Amiri said. "There's the aid offered to Europe in the name of democracy, yet at home, nothing is done to liberate all Americans."

"More like hypocrisy, if you ask me," Dr. Jelana said. "But do you think anyone in Europe knows about this hypocrisy? I doubt it."

"Sometimes it's easier to clean out your neighbor's closet than to purge skeletons from your own," Amiri said.

"That's a horrible thing to say," Isha said.

"I don't like it any more than you. But that's the attitude we have in Alabama," Amiri said. "Sometimes I wonder if we should have remained in Asmara and never immigrated to America. At least in Asmara, we are treated as equals."

"I'll go back to the Azores any day," Kaila said.

"What about that guy in Portugal?" Dr. Jelana giggled.

"I wonder if Justino would like to live in the Azores too," Kaila mused.

Kaila and Dr. Jelana giggled.

Several waiters moved tables out of the way, clearing room for a dancing area. The band started playing another song, *Papa Loves Mambo*. The dark-robed woman sang again.

"Come on," Isha said to Amiri. "Let's do the mambo."

Isha and Amiri walked over to the dance floor and danced.

"What was that?" Kaila asked. "The mambo?"

"Yeah," Dr. Jelana said. "Come on, I'll show you."

Dr. Jelana led Kaila to the dance floor and showed Kaila a simple form of the mambo. The brass instruments kicked in, and the three travelers shifted from 1955 to 2027.

2027 Dec 25. Early Morning. Aboard the Velita Spaceship.

Jonara, Cerafina, and Johnny found themselves in a conference room with the older Cerafina, two young muscular women, and an older muscular woman. On a display screen were other women in strange attire. Older Cerafina stood at the end of a table. The older woman, Vadafa, and a younger woman, Tioma, stood next to Cerafina. The other young woman, Biorna, brought two tissue scanners and placed them on the table near older Cerafina.

"Tioma," Vadafa said. "Biorna is helping me and will not be able to operate the data recorder and analyzer. I need you to take over that function for Biorna."

"Yes," Tioma said, and she whispered something into older Cerafina's ear.

Vadafa held her right hand against older Cerafina's abdomen and made hand signals. Biorna did the same with her right hand. After their hand signals, the two placed their thumbs on older Cerafina's navel. Vadafa's and Biorna's free hands reached for the scanners. Another display screen swirled with clouds, and the image of a beautiful princess appeared with outstretched arms.

"Boost the isolation gain," Vadafa said to Tioma. "We are ready to extract the other half."

The princess faded from the screen, and another image appeared dressed in red and black with a shield in one hand and a sword in the other.

"Her tissues are disintegrating," Vadafa said about older Cerafina. "We must hurry. Tioma—do you have a confirmation lock on the second half?"

"One moment," Tioma said.

Tioma pressed several buttons.

"Hurry, Tioma," Biorna said. "We cannot hold this scan much longer."

"Almost...there, I have it," Tioma said.

"Do we have a full confirmation read?" Vadafa asked.

"Yes," Tioma said. "Full read."

"Are there any moishan remnants or artifacts?" Vadafa asked. "Make the reading, quickly."

"None. Two root owners, no artifacts," Tioma said.

Vadafa and Biorna released their hands from the scanners, performed a few more hand signals with their hands that were touching older Cerafina's belly button, and they released. Older Cerafina sat in a chair with the help of Vadafa and Biorna.

"There, there," Vadafa said. "The scan is over. You can sit here and rest."

Tioma and older Cerafina chatted for a bit. The people on the display screen chatted. Vadafa said something. Then all facial expressions went grim, except for older Cerafina's.

"This is bad news indeed," Vadafa said.

"Admiral," the woman on the display screen said. "The girl must be destroyed by casting her into Seris. It will unfortunately destroy Princess Felifia's half of the moisharn, but this is the only way to ensure total disintegration of Nekara the Red's half."

"I don't want to die!" older Cerafina said.

The world flashed back to March 3, 1955 on the tour boat with the Margos. Jonara, Cerafina, and Johnny stood by the Margos while Nekara the Red continued singing.

"I'm going to lock us into this time," Jonara said.

"How?" Johnny asked.

"By speaking in that foreign language," Jonara said.

"Wait, you shouldn't—" Johnny started to say, but Jonara had already started speaking.

Miramish	Translation
Biorita opeifu shai Moishiana,	Power of the Water Ruby,
Biorita opeifu shai Lanudaka.	Power of the half-face symbol.
Tauko shai zhaba ishu dauna,	Stop the jump in time,
Di Serafina shai Arovwela.	To Cerafina the Older.

The robed woman finished the song abruptly. She removed her hood, exposing her face. She stared at Jonara and spoke the following in a raw, caustic tone. While she spoke, a variegated crimson/cerise light shone from her abdomen, caught the top of Marcus's hair, and hit squarely upon Jonara, Cerafina, and Johnny.

Non-Miramish Language	Translation
Nia vikel shair deirzhwan!	I *am* the pitcher!
Kair vil shair karftwaik.	You are the catchers.
Paunirsf ishte kiursh!	Bounce into chaos!

The beam from the robed woman pushed the three travelers out of time. Flash! The three landed in Redjet where Calico and Evanita prepared to sleep despite dripping wet clothes, then another flash and the three were onboard the Verona Ancona where older Cerafina was in a swimming pool racing against a boy her age, then back to Saint Stellan Catholic Church with the flying pew followed by the River Wood and Battery fire as Evanita crawled out. Other flashbacks continued.

"What's happening?" Jonara asked.

"We're stuck between moments in time," Johnny said. "We're like a steel ball in a pinball machine."

"Why is this happening? And why am I going to die?" Cerafina asked.

"That woman in the robe has a power," Johnny said, "a power much like ours. The Moissan Ruby must have reacted with something she has. She spoke a different language. It wasn't Miramish."

"She's the woman in conference room," Jonara said.

"No she's not. She doesn't look like any of those women with my older self," Cerafina said.

"Not with you. The woman on the screen—remember?" Jonara asked.

"You mean Nekara the Red?" Johnny asked.

"Yeah," Jonara said. "But I thought only musical instruments could send us into the future."

"The instrument only takes you in the future when it's played, or perhaps when it's heard," Johnny said.

"That's the same thing," Jonara said.

"Not quite," Cerafina said. "People get a reaction when hearing music."

"Yes," Johnny said. "That's the answer. Music is music because it evokes reactions—thoughtful, emotional, or whatever. This Nekara the Red must also evoke a reaction. She may have a strong influence on people. She certainly has one on us."

"The people on the spaceship didn't like Nekara the Red," Cerafina said.

"No, they didn't. She must have had a powerful influence on other people, a power that those women in the conference room and screen did not like," Johnny said. "Jonara—we're going to remain stuck between times unless we break off our link with the Margos—at least the Margos in Italy. It's time we changed Eva's wine anyway. Break the link."

"How?" Jonara said. "The last time I spoke in the foreign language, we got hit with the beam."

"But we're not with Nekara the Red anymore. Speak again to break the link," Johnny said.

Miramish	Translation
Peliko shai roisha boshu Iva.	Break the link with Eva.
Peliko shai roisha teshunu binota.	Break the link this moment.

The three appeared in the hospital with Eva for a few seconds but regressed back in a pinball cycle to Redjet, the Verona Ancona, the Velita, and back to Redjet.

"*Peliko, peliko, peliko* (Break, break, break)!" Jonara yelled.

She squeezed the candleholder against her abdomen and shook in frustration. The cycle faded into a small dot. The three returned to Eva in the hospital room.

"Grandma," Jonara said. "You're not swishing the wine."

"You trembled like a wet leaf in the rain," Eva said. "I thought something was wrong, so I swallowed the wine."

"You helped us a lot, Mummy Eva," Johnny said.

"Why did you tremble, Jonara?" Eva asked.

"We were trapped between times," Jonara said.

"What a strange thing to say," Eva said. "It's the kind of thing someone on LSD would say. Johnny, what are you pushing on my granddaughter? Did you give her a hallucinogenic?"

"No," Johnny said. "The Moissan Ruby is creating strange things."

"It never did this," Eva said. "You only used it to read things, like an MRI or X-ray. What's this talk about being stuck between times?"

"We encountered some problems," Johnny said. "Jonara, did you get a reading of your grandmother's thyroid?"

"No," Jonara said. "It was hard enough breaking the link."

"Do you think you could read it now?" he asked. "Jonara— set the candleholder aside. Cerafina—keep clear of Jonara and Eva. I'll do the same. We don't want to cause a misread. Okay, Jonara, take a reading."

Jonara tapped the cell phone. It vibrated. She placed her hand onto Eva's shoulder and closed her (Jonara's) eyes.

"It's the same as before," Jonara said.

"Hmm. We must find a way to make progress without interference," Johnny said. "Jonara—we can't resume at the same point in time where we left off. We must skip ahead."

"How far ahead?" Jonara asked.

"Hmm," Johnny mused. "That is the great question."

"The Margos were traveling to Cairo next," Cerafina said. "Then Port Sudan. And crossing the Red Sea to Jeddah. Then Mecca. And lastly, Asmara."

"You have a good memory, Cerafina," Johnny said. "Yes. They're in Rome on March 3rd. So if they go to Cairo on the 4th then to Port Sudan and take a boat across to Jeddah plus time in Mecca—that's a lot for one day."

"If they do it all in one day," Cerafina said.

"Yes, *if,*" Johnny said. "Then back to Jeddah—they'll probably stay at a hotel in Jeddah. That means they fly to Asmara on the 5th—no earlier. Or will they take a boat? Hmm."

"So how do we do this, Daddy?" Jonara asked. "Are we going to jump to March 5th of 1955 and wait for the Margos in Asmara? That could be a long time."

"Or we could jump to the Margos wherever they are on the 5th," Cerafina suggested.

"Jumping to the Margos wherever they are is the most efficient," Johnny said. "But it's also the most dangerous."

"They'll be long out of Italy by then," Cerafina said.

"Yes," Johnny said. "But they could be in Saudi Arabia."

"What's wrong with that?" Jonara asked.

"Nothing's wrong with the country. But there could be reactions between things in the country and the Moissan Ruby," Johnny said.

"What are you talking about?" Jonara asked. "What things?"

"Like a genie?" Eva laughed. "Honestly, Johnny, you get carried away with things."

"Don't underestimate the Arab world," Johnny said. "Arabs were the ones preserving ancient Greek and Roman writings when the Christian world was busy burning libraries. While Europe fell into the dark ages, Arabs made engineering gains. And there may be some connection between genies and the Moissan Ruby."

"Johnny!" Eva said. "Listen to yourself. Tell me you're sane."

"That Nekara the Red looked like some sort of genie," Cerafina said.

"She did look like an Arab woman," Jonara said. "Maybe she is a genie."

"But what language was she speaking? It sounded a lot like the language you spoke," Cerafina said.

"Similar, but different. It didn't sound like Arabic, did it?" Jonara asked.

"No, it didn't," Cerafina replied. "What are we going to do?"

"We'll have to choose some sort of starting point. Let's go back in time to March 5, 1955, but we'll go to the Asmara airport in Eritrea," Johnny said. "Agreed?"

"Agreed," Jonara and Cerafina said.

"Good. Eva, we need you to—" Johnny started.

"I know. You need me to swish red wine in my mouth," Eva said. "Gimme a glass."

"Which wine should we give her?" Jonara asked.

"Let's see—we gave her Burgundy last time, we should give her Oregon now," he said.

"But won't they mix a little?" Cerafina asked.

"Good point," Johnny said. "Everyone—stand clear. Eva—swish a little white wine to clear out the red."

"May I swallow it?" Eva laughed.

"Um. Yes, it should work out. Swish and swallow," Johnny said.

"That sounds like something I would say," Eva said. "There was a poster I used to see as a child with a girl holding a glass of water. The poster said, 'If you can't brush, swish and swallow.' Now I'm the poster child, is that it?"

Johnny did not answer. Instead, he poured Eva a bit of white wine. She swished it in her mouth, some bits of leftover Burgundy red wine was pulled into the white, and she swallowed.

"Good. We're ready," Johnny said.

1955 Mar 5, Sat. Asmara, Eritrea, Africa.

Johnny prepared a small glass of Oregon red wine and handed it to Eva. She swished the wine in her mouth, the three travelers touched Eva, Jonara activated the cell phone, and the three travelers landed outside an Italian-styled café in Asmara.

"What happened to the airport?" Cerafina asked.

"Hmm," Johnny mused. "Jonara's focus is a bit off."

"I'm thirsty," Jonara said. "I wish we could go in and get some hot chocolate."

"What about coffee?" Cerafina asked.

"I tried that back in Texas. Too bitter," Jonara said.

"Unfortunately," Johnny said, "we can't consume food or drink in the past."

Jonara and Cerafina peered inside the window at the assorted coffeecakes, cinnamon rolls, tiramisu, brioche, panini, and frittata.

"Look at all the sweets!" Jonara said.

"Mr. Pindus," Cerafina said. "Look at the containers on the shelf."

"Those containers hold coffee beans," Johnny said, "of all different kinds. I would imagine Ethiopian coffee is the most common here given how close Ethiopia is the Eritrea."

"I thought coffee came from Colombia," Jonara said.

"Some does, but other beans come from other countries. Story goes that Ethiopia first recognized and harvested the coffee bean for use in coffee. Ethiopia grows lots of coffee," Johnny explained.

"Oh how I wish I could try Ethiopian coffee," Cerafina said. "I love coffee. I'm biased toward Italian coffee, of course, but I have an open mind."

"That's very interesting," Johnny said, "considering Italy imports their coffee beans."

"You know what I mean. Italian-made coffee," Cerafina laughed.

"Daddy," Jonara said. "What's that on the wall?"

Jonara pointed to something on the wall—a pair of padded objects wrapped with cord.

"That's an early form of boxing glove," Johnny said. "The competitor holds onto padding and wraps his hand up with flax cord. Some African villages continue using this sort of glove. Look—below is a pair of modern boxing gloves."

Cerafina noticed the gloves, paused in thought, turned her head, and saw a sign down the street.

"Look!" she said while pointing to the sign.

"There's a boxing match tomorrow night," Johnny said as he and Jonara looked in the direction of Cerafina's finger.

"Boxing tomorrow. Aman Kwen vs. Quadri Dakari. The fight of the year," a sign said in English and Italian.

"Boxing! How barbaric!" Jonara said. "Where the goal is to hurt the opponent in the head."

"There's a bit more than that," Johnny said. "But the short response is, yes."

"Stupid," Jonara said.

"It's a macho sport," Cerafina said. "Italian men like to box."

"Italy may have introduced Asmara to the modern form of boxing with skills and strategy," Johnny said.

"I hate macho sports," Jonara said.

"Why should we care if men want to beat their brains out?" Cerafina said.

"Because some women go for that sort of thing. They drool all over fighting men," Jonara said.

"You're thinking of Almarita, aren't you?" Johnny asked.

"Yeah."

"Do you miss her?" Johnny asked.

"Not as much as I miss the old Almarita before she started talking about hooking a powerful man," Jonara said. "She'd be the first in line for one of these boxers."

"She's a little young for dating a boxer," Johnny said.

"Maybe now. But I can see her dating boxers in the future," Jonara said. "And what happens when he starts boxing on her?"

"That doesn't always happen," Cerafina said.

"But sometimes it does. I've read it in the news," Jonara said.

"Yes, it's a sad thing," Johnny said.

Cerafina looked up and pointed to an airplane flying overhead. A few seconds later, the sound waves of propellers tickled their ears.

"That could be the Margo family," Johnny said.

Johnny looked down and saw only Cerafina.

"Jonara? Where are you?" Johnny asked while looking around frantically.

"There!" Cerafina said, pointing to the boxing arena. "She's running to that boxing building."

"Jonara! Come back!" Johnny yelled, but she did not reply.

"Now what's she doing?" Cerafina asked. "She's saying something and pointing at the building."

"She means to destroy the building," Johnny said. "Come, we must stop her."

Cerafina and Johnny ran down the sidewalk to stop Jonara. As Cerafina stated, Jonara pointed the candleholder at the building, and as she did so, she chanted the following:

Miramish	**Translation**
Vuko teshunu voritaola	Push this building
Liemu tilesh e shoita,	On its side,
Boshu leshi opeifu heidona	With waves of water
Veletu luishaolu gelita.	From rising tide.

"Stop!" Johnny shouted.

The air in front of Jonara's hand distorted as if distant heat waves on desert sands were creating a mirage of water. But the mirage became water and bellowed out from the candleholder onto the building. The building rocked back and forth a bit. The water circled around the building as if catching it in a whirlpool, but without warning, it came back at Jonara with a boomerang effect, picked her up, and tossed her across the road with a great splash!

The three returned to Eva's hospital room. Jonara had fallen backward onto the floor. Johnny and Cerafina went to her aid and uprighted her.

"What happened?" Jonara asked.

"You fell on the floor!" Eva said, who by now was a little inebriated.

Eva had also gulped the wine down when Jonara broke the connection.

"You must be very, very careful when launching an attack," Johnny said. "The outcomes are unpredictable more often than not."

"But it was a simple command," Jonara said.

"It's the simple command that often goes astray. You did not take into account the variables," Johnny said.

"What variables?" Jonara asked.

"There, you see? You're not even aware of them. Did you learn nothing from the Castle Bravo shot?" Johnny asked.

"Huh?" Jonara asked while in a daze from hitting the floor.

"I missed that too," Cerafina said. "The bomb was bigger than expected, is that right?"

"Yes. It was two-and-a-half times bigger than expected," Johnny said.

"You never told us why," Jonara said.

"I didn't explain that?" Johnny asked.

"No, you didn't," Jonara said as she rubbed the welt on the back of her head.

"The lithium? I didn't explain the lithium?" Johnny continued.

"No, Daddy, you didn't. I didn't know there was a lesson about Castle Bravo," Jonara said.

"So what does lithium have to do with the boxing arena that Jonara tried to destroy?" Cerafina asked.

"I'll explain," Johnny said. "But let me finish before you ask more questions."

"Okay," Jonara said.

"Okay," Cerafina added.

"The Castle Bravo shot was the first dry thermonuclear device detonated by the United States. It was also the largest. It used lithium deuteride as the fusion fuel. Seems simple so far, right?"

"Yeah," Jonara said. "Ooops, I didn't mean to interrupt."

"It's okay," Johnny said. "Now the designers of the Castle Bravo shot used the isotopes lithium-6 and lithium-7. Lithium-6 was rare at the time, so lithium-7 was added as an inert fuel."

"What does 'inert' mean?" Jonara asked.

"It means it wasn't supposed to react to anything," Johnny said. "But it did. The designers decided it wouldn't react, but it reacted and added the extra yield to the blast. And that's the point I'm trying to make. You may think that things won't react, that they are inert and unchanging. But they aren't. You may not always see the results, but they react. The building reacted.

Something in its walls maybe, or something else. That part isn't always known. What is known is that whenever you launch an attack, most often there are side effects, and these side effects can be worse than the original attack. The Castle Bravo shot, for example, contaminated over seven thousand square miles of the Pacific Ocean with radioactive fallout. Parts of the fallout reached the United States, Japan, India, Australia, and Europe."

"How big is seven thousand square miles?" Jonara asked.

"Larger than Connecticut, smaller than New Jersey," Johnny said.

"A small state becoming barren," Cerafina said. "How terrible."

"What is barren?" Jonara said.

"We must improve your vocabulary," Johnny said.

"It means unable to support life. Like a desert," Cerafina said.

"Now Jonara, you must be very careful when using the candleholder and Moissan Ruby, especially in the past or future. Sometimes they are helpful for reading things, sometimes you can risk helping someone, but never use them for attack—the attack always bounces back at you. You were lucky you didn't chant something about destruction or death."

"You mean I could have been killed?" Jonara asked.

"Or badly injured," Johnny said. "These things are like power tools. A slip of the hand in the table saw, and your fingers are gone. Used with care, you can accomplish something. How's the bump on your head?"

"Hurts. And it's swollen," Jonara said.

"You were lucky. Now, can we resume the connection?" Johnny asked.

Jonara nodded her head in affirmation.

"I need more wine," Eva said, who was warming up to the idea of "helping" by drinking wine.

"Good. Here's another glass of Oregon red wine," Johnny said.

Johnny refilled the small glass and returned it to her. Eva sipped the wine and swished it in her mouth. As before, the three travelers touched Eva, and Jonara activated the cell phone while holding the candleholder to her abdomen.

1955 Mar 6, Sun. Asmara, Eritrea, Africa.

"Boxing Tonight!" a new sign said.

"We're back in front of the boxing arena!" Jonara said.

"Strange," Johnny said.

"Where are the Margos?" Cerafina asked.

"Jonara—do a scan. Are the Margos in Asmara yet?" Johnny asked.

"Is it safe to do a scan in front of the boxing arena?" Jonara asked.

"Just don't point the Moissan Ruby at the arena for too long. Turn around in a circle and scan," Johnny said.

Jonara did just that.

"No, they're not here. They're on an airplane over the Red Sea. But they'll be here soon," Jonara said.

"We should go to the airport," Cerafina said, "and meet them."

"Good idea," Johnny said.

The three attempted to walk away from the arena, but a flash of light and what felt like a wall of bees stopped them.

"What's that?" Jonara asked.

"A time wall," Johnny said.

"What?" Jonara asked. "You mean we can't go wherever we want?"

"We're at the mercy of whatever we're reading. We can't work solely off our whims. Eva's thyroid cancer doesn't extend to the airport at this time. It's restricted to this boxing arena."

"Why, why, why?!" Jonara asked. "Grandma Eva hates boxing as much as I do. It makes no sense."

"Not now, but it may," Johnny said. "It's an unknown variable."

"Confound the unknown variable and everything!" Jonara said.

Cerafina wanted to ask Jonara how Jonara knew about the word "confound" and not other words, but Jonara did not stand still. Jonara ran at the wall and bounced back. She held the candleholder against her abdomen with one hand and pointed at the wall with the other. She opened her mouth to speak, but Cerafina put one hand on the back of Jonara's head and the other over Jonara's mouth to prevent speech.

"Not another disaster!" Cerafina said.

Jonara rolled her eyes and signaled Cerafina to let go.

"Only if you promise not to launch an attack," Cerafina said.

Jonara nodded her head in agreement and removed the candleholder from her abdomen. Cerafina let go. Without warning, Jonara ran several steps away from Cerafina into a patch of overgrown, brown grass leftover from the prior summer. She pressed the candleholder against her abdomen and opened her mouth to chant.

"Oh no you don't!" Cerafina said.

Cerafina ran after Jonara. Jonara ran and tried to chant, but she couldn't keep her focus while being pursued. She ran in circles, but Cerafina continued the chase. Cerafina had the greater speed and eventually caught up to Jonara. Cerafina dove onto Jonara and tackled Jonara into the tall, brown grass and out of Johnny's sight.

"Stop!" Cerafina said as she put a hand over Jonara's mouth.

Jonara attempted to place the candleholder against her abdomen with her right hand.

"No!" Cerafina said as she used her other hand to pin Jonara's right hand to the grass.

Jonara took the candleholder into her left hand and attempted to press it again. Cerafina, without a free hand, was forced to remove her hand from Jonara's mouth to pin Jonara's left.

"You can't hold me here forever, Cerafina Vagatti," Jonara said. "I can say whatever I want now. I'm going to blast a hole through that time wall, and you can't stop me."

"There's only one way to stop that mouth of yours from speaking," Cerafina said.

Cerafina stared into Jonara's eyes. Jonara looked left and right to avoid her gaze, but the more Jonara darted her eyes, the closer Cerafina drew her face to Jonara's. Jonara could no longer avoid Cerafina's gaze or her close proximity. Jonara looked into Cerafina's eyes. Cerafina maintained her gaze on Jonara's eyes as she pressed her lips to Jonara's. Jonara struggled a little, but Cerafina advanced her pressing to a full kiss, a deep kiss, and Jonara settled down and stopped struggling. She kissed back. After a time, Cerafina withdrew her lips from Jonara's and stood up.

"Now what were you saying?" Cerafina asked.

Jonara looked up at Cerafina. The city and sky behind her changed. They were no longer in Asmara, nor were they on Earth. Two suns filled the sky—one yellow, the other cerise. Trees behind Cerafina were crimson and white. Jonara sat up and looked on the ground. The grass was crimson, and small rocks moved along a little green path as if they were snails. Cerafina looked much older—perhaps ten years older. She wore a cherry-red flowing dress with ruffles and white trim. Jonara wore a slim, white dress with flower patterns and cherry-red trim.

"You fell down," the older Cerafina said. "We'll have to clean you up before our wedding starts. Are you hurt? Can you stand up?"

"What?" Jonara asked.

The world changed back into Asmara of March 6, 1955.

"Can you stand up?" Cerafina asked.

"Oh," Jonara said.

Jonara stood up.

"I must have sucked the air out of you. You were dazed for a few minutes," Cerafina said. "Something else happened. The sun moved in the sky, as if we jumped ahead several hours."

"Jonara? Cerafina?" Johnny called as he walked over. "There you two are. I've spent the last five hours looking for you. Follow me. The Margos have arrived and are heading this way."

Jonara and Cerafina followed Johnny from the grass to the sidewalk. The Margos walked toward Jonara-Cerafina-Johnny—Isha, Amiri, Dr. Jelana, Marcus, and Kaila. The women carried their purses over their right shoulders as usual. Another person walked with them—a tall, strong man with a dark complexion but not of full African descent.

"This is where I'll entertain tonight," the man said to Kaila.

"*Boxing Tonight. Aman Kwen vs. Quadri Dakari. The fight of the year,*" Dr. Jelana read from an English/Italian sign.

"You said you were an entertainer, Quadri!" Kaila said. "Not a fighter."

"A fighter is an entertainer," Quadri said.

"I went to Mecca to be enlightened," Kaila said. "And I thought I was when I met you. But I was wrong."

"Don't say that," Quadri said. "Come see me entertain tonight. Here are tickets to the bout. Little Marcus can watch for free."

"I don't think Marcus should go to a fight," Dr. Jelana said.

"My mother lives two blocks away. She would be happy to watch Marcus for you," Quadri said to Dr. Jelana. "I wouldn't want Kaila's best friend to miss the fight."

"And I don't want to be a part of your fight," Kaila said. "Men are supposed to grow up from such childish things like fighting."

"Mr. Dakari," Dr. Jelana said. "How is it your mother has time to watch Marcus? Doesn't she attend your boxing matches?"

Quadri threw on a grimace.

"She, uh, has other plans," he said.

"She doesn't like your fighting either," Kaila said. "Is that what you mean by 'other plans'?"

"I earn a good living boxing," Quadri said. "And I support her. But I would like a wife to care for. I would support you too, Kaila."

"And live here?" Kaila asked.

"Is it worse than living in Alabama?" Quadri grinned.

"He has you there," Dr. Jelana said.

"I won't go," Kaila said.

"I'll go," Amiri said. "I could use a diversion. Isha, if you would—"

"Absolutely not!" Isha said. "But I wouldn't mind going to a play or ballet."

"There is a play tonight," Quadri said, "on the other side of Asmara."

"What kind of play? What's it about?" Kaila asked.

"The play tells the life story of Michelangelo," Quadri said. "Today is his birthday. There's also a little restaurant next door where you will find good food and drink."

"Oh that sounds great. Why don't you take me to the play?" Kaila asked Quadri.

"I cannot. I must box tonight!" Quadri said.

"Mrs. Margo?" Kaila asked.

"We'll go together," Isha said to Kaila. "What about you, Jelana?"

"I hate to leave Pappa alone with his heart condition," Dr. Jelana said. "And Pappa, I'm surprised at you. You wouldn't let Mamma out of your sight in Portugal."

"Ah, yes, that was, uh, different. Jelana, go with your mother," Amiri said.

"No. I won't let you out of my sight," Dr. Jelana said. "Even if your obvious love for boxing is allowing Mamma out of yours. I'll take you up on your offer, Quadri, and leave Marcus with your mother. But I must meet her first. I can't just leave Marcus with a complete stranger."

"I understand completely," Quadri said. "And I appreciate your attendance at my bout."

Quadri suddenly lost interest in Kaila and took a new interest in Dr. Jelana. Dr. Jelana felt his probing eyes and averted her own eyes.

"I must prepare for the fight soon," Quadri said. "Doctor, we should visit my mother now so you may get to know her."

Quadri hailed a taxi for Isha and Kaila. The taxi stopped, and the two women sat in back.

"Driver, take these two to the Asmara Theater," Quadri said.

Isha and Kaila bade farewell to Amiri and Dr. Jelana.

"And now, we must go to my home where we will find my mother," Quadri said.

The group walked down the street a few blocks until they reached Quadri's home. Quadri introduced his mother to Dr. Jelana, Marcus, and Amiri. Dr. Jelana chatted with Quadri's mother for a bit and found her quite personable.

"We must leave now for the fight," Quadri said.

The world turned gray for a moment, and the three travelers found themselves inside the boxing arena. Amiri sat in the second row close to Quadri's corner, and Dr. Jelana sat next to her father.

"I didn't know you liked boxing," Amiri said.

"I don't. I told you I came to watch after you," Dr. Jelana said.

"Are you sure it was me you wanted to watch?" Amiri grinned.

"I'm not thrilled with boxing or watching people box," Dr. Jelana said. "I've treated too many boxing injuries during my internship."

"And if Quadri needs aid, will you treat him?" Amiri laughed.

"Hmph!" Dr. Jelana said.

The champion, Aman Kwen, entered the arena with his people. He wore his boxing robe and gloves. The host announced Kwen, and the crowd cheered.

"Quadri is the underdog," Amiri said.

"How do you know?" Dr. Jelana asked.

"I asked him," Amiri said.

The challenger, Quadri Dakari, entered the arena from the other side with his people while wearing a robe and boxing gloves. Amiri and Dr. Jelana waved to Quadri, and he nodded in affirmation. Quadri took to his corner, and the two fighters prepared for the first round. After a brief moment, the referee beckoned the two fighters to the middle of the ring. The boxers met each other in full boxing gear—high trunks, boxing boots, gloves, and mouth guards.

"I want a good, clean fight," the referee said. "Touch gloves."

The fighters touched gloves. They returned to their corners momentarily, and the bell chimed. Aman and Quadri began. Aman kept a stance in the middle while Quadri danced around him. Each traded jabs, combo jab-crosses, hooks, and under-cuts.

"Both boxers are in the traditional stance," Amiri explained to Dr. Jelana.

"What does that mean?"

"They are both right-handed. So they lead with the left hand for a jab or hook, and power through with the right for a cross or uppercut. See how they lead with their left feet and trail with their right?" Amiri asked.

"Yes, I do," Dr. Jelana said.

Aman closed in on Quadri and pinned him against the ropes, but each time Aman did so, Quadri clinched with Aman, and the referee broke them up.

"Why does Quadri hug Aman?" Dr. Jelana asked.

"He's not hugging. It's a clinch. It keeps Aman from punching him. Boxers do that when they are caught in a bad situation or are tired. It's too early for Quadri to be tired, so he must not like Aman boxing that close."

Aman landed several powerful right crosses on Quadri. Quadri's head snapped backward, and he stumbled away with his back to Aman.

"That's not a good sign," Amiri said. "Showing your back to your opponent says you're losing balance. Quadri won't get through many rounds like this."

"Fight, Quadri, fight!" Dr. Jelana urged.

"Are you cheering?" Amiri joked.

"No," Dr. Jelana tried to cover, "I'm just urging him to be safe."

"Uh, huh," Amiri said. "I understand."

The first round came to a close with the bell, and Quadri staggered to his corner.

"His face is bleeding," Dr. Jelana said.

"Yeah," Amiri said. "Aman opened a cut above Quadri's eye. The trainer will clean that up."

The bell signaled the start of the second round. Aman's trainer must have said something to Aman, because Aman came out much more aggressively. He chased Quadri against the ropes and pummeled away at Quadri's head and body. Quadri tried to clinch, but Aman fought off the clinches with little punches. Quadri protected his head with his gloves, but Aman punched onto Quadri's chest each time, forcing Quadri to lower his gloves to block.

"He's going for a knockout," Amiri said. "Quadri must get off those ropes."

Dr. Jelana stood up and yelled, "Get off the ropes!"

Amiri pulled her down to her seat.

"Sorry, I don't know what came over me," Dr. Jelana said.

"I do," Amiri grinned. "You don't like seeing Quadri lose."

Quadri received more pummeling and tried to fight his way out, but Aman ripped an uppercut to Quadri's jaw. Quadri lost his balance and sat on the lower rope briefly before falling to the canvas. He stood up immediately, but by then the referee had sent Aman to a neutral corner and had begun a standing eight count on Quadri.

"Are you all right?" the referee asked Quadri.

"Yeah," Quadri replied.

The referee resumed the round. Quadri danced around, but his sense was skewed, and he let his gloves down.

"He's vulnerable," Amiri said. "He's supposed to keep his gloves up to guard his face, but he's dropped them low."

Dr. Jelana stood up again and yelled, "Keep your gloves up!"

Quadri raised his gloves and kept fighting. Amiri pulled his daughter back to her seat.

"He heard me, Father!" Dr. Jelana said. "He heard me!"

"Never have I seen my daughter so excited over a boxing match," Amiri said.

The second round ended, and Quadri returned to his corner. His trainer cleaned up his cut a bit more and sprinkled water on his head. Quadri took a sip of water and spat it out. Round three started with the bell, and Quadri went out. He successfully clinched when forced against the ropes but could not land anything better than standard jabs on Aman. Aman ripped into Quadri's face and opened the cut. Blood covered much of Quadri's left face, and he repeatedly wiped his left eye with his glove. He punched back at Aman but often missed. Quadri spent most of the round clinching and dancing to avoid Aman.

"Quadri will lose this round for sure," Amiri said. "Aman is racking up lots of points with his punches, but Amiri has only a few."

"He can't see—that's the problem," Dr. Jelana said.

"I think you're right," Amiri said. "His left eye is swollen shut and covered in blood. It's just a matter of time before Aman knocks him out or the referee stops the fight and awards Aman a technical knockout."

"We can't let Quadri lose this way," Dr. Jelana said.

"That's boxing. Nothing will save him now. A traditional boxer needs his left eye to see, and Quadri's left eye can't."

"But his right is okay," Dr. Jelana said.

"Sure, but his stance blocks his left peripheral vision. That's where Aman will throw his crosses," Amiri said.

"Well then he needs to change stance," Dr. Jelana said.

"Only a southpaw boxes leading with the right," Amiri said.

"Then Quadri better become a southpaw and fast," Dr. Jelana said.

"That's shooting two cannons at each other at point-blank range," Amiri said. "He could be knocked out with a hook."

"He will certainly be knocked out if he doesn't do something," Dr. Jelana said. "There must be some way to box southpaw effectively."

"He must box to his right a little bit and counter Aman's hook with a hook," Amiri said.

Dr. Jelana ran up to the trainer.

"You have to make Quadri switch to southpaw," Dr. Jelana said. "It's the only way he can compete."

"Young lady, go sit down," the trainer said.

"You have to. He can't see out of his eye well enough to box," Dr. Jelana said.

"I know he can't see out of his left eye," the trainer said.

"When he switches to southpaw, he must box a little to the right and block Aman's hook with his own hook," Dr. Jelana said.

"Young lady, I know all about southpaw boxing. Now go sit down," the trainer said.

A security guard returned Dr. Jelana to her seat. Round three ended, and Quadri returned to his corner. The trainer cleaned up the wound and said something in Quadri's ear. Quadri turned around in surprise and started to argue, but the trainer turned him back around and became forceful in his speech with Quadri. Quadri rolled his one remaining good eye. The bell rang, and the fourth round started. Quadri stood up and walked toward Aman, but he changed his stance and led with his right glove.

"He switched to southpaw!" Dr. Jelana exclaimed.

"I don't believe it! This could get ugly," Amiri said.

Quadri could see much better with his right eye leading. Aman seemed confused, and Quadri was able to land several right hooks into Aman. Stunned, Aman lowered his gloves a little, and Quadri threw in a jab-cross combination. Aman threw punches, but Quadri ducked and continued his combinations on Aman. Aman stumbled and fell to the canvas. The referee counted over Aman. Aman tried to stand but could only get up to his knees. The referee reached, "Ten," and awarded the match to Quadri.

"Yes! Yes! Yes!" Dr. Jelana screamed.

Dr. Jelana jumped for joy. Amiri stood up with her, and she hugged him. Quadri's trainer and friends jumped in the ring with him and congratulated him. They took him out of the ring, lifted him on their shoulders, and paraded him around. Aman's team worked on him and brought him back to full consciousness. He walked under his own power from the ring and into the locker room.

"That was a great fight," Amiri said.

"Excuse me," said Quadri's trainer. "My name is Hakim. I am Quadri's trainer. Quadri would like for you two to join him in a victory celebration at the *Pasticceria moderna.*"

Jonara, Cerafina, and Johnny followed Dr. Jelana and Amiri to the *Pasticceria moderna* where they found live music, food, and drink. Quadri's people kept the party strictly nonalcoholic in proper Sunni Muslim fashion. Dr. Jelana and Amiri met Quadri inside, and Dr. Jelana gave Quadri a big hug and kiss. Onlookers clapped.

"If I knew I'd get this kind of welcome, I'd fight much harder," Quadri said.

"Oh, your poor eye," Dr. Jelana said. "It's still swollen."

"Bartender, ice for the champion," said Hakim.

The bartender prepared a bag of ice and handed it to Hakim. Hakim handed it to Dr. Jelana who in turn applied it to Quadri's tissues around his eye.

"There, there," Dr. Jelana said. "The swelling's going down already. Hmm, what's this? Quadri—stare into the light."

"What's wrong?" Hakim asked.

"Nothing," Quadri said. "She's just mothering me."

General chuckling from the guys.

"No, wait," Dr. Jelana said. "Your left eye was dilated, but now it's fine. Follow my finger."

Dr. Jelana moved her finger from side to side.

"You pass. Your eyes followed my finger. For a moment, I thought you had nystagmus in your left eye," Dr. Jelana said. "But you should get that cut sewn up."

"I feel fine. Let's celebrate," Quadri said.

The party resumed. Dr. Jelana went to her father and begged him to reason with Quadri.

"Tell him to go to a hospital," Dr. Jelana said. "His cut could open up again."

"What power do I have?" Amiri asked. "Look around you. Everyone sees Quadri as a hero. What would they say if I asked Quadri to go to the hospital? That would be an insult."

"Father, please!" Dr. Jelana said.

"He is a man, and he has pride," Amiri said. "There is nothing I can do."

Without warning, a woman burst into the *Pasticceria moderna* yelling and screaming.

"They took them hostage! Save them!" she yelled.

Dr. Jelana ran to the woman's aid.

"Calm down," Dr. Jelana said. "What happened?"

"Barbarians with white skin raided Asmara," she said. "They broke into the theater. They took...they left."

"What did the barbarians take? Where did they go?" Dr. Jelana asked.

The woman sobbed and stuttered.

"Relax," Dr. Jelana said. "You're with friends. Try to speak clearly."

"The women tourists were watching the play. They took the women. They are gone!"

The woman buried her head in her hands. The horror of the event sank in with Dr. Jelana. She looked at her father, and he returned her gaze.

"Isha!" he said.

"Kaila!" Dr. Jelana said.

"We must go," Dr. Jelana said to her father. "We must find Mother and Kaila."

"I will tell Quadri," Amiri said.

"No, let me," Dr. Jelana said.

Dr. Jelana pushed her way through to Quadri.

"What is happening?" Quadri said.

"White people attacked the theater and kidnapped many women," Dr. Jelana said.

"The criminals," Quadri said. "They must be caught."

"I must go to the theater to find my mother and friend," Dr. Jelana said.

"Yes. I will go with you. I know the theater layout very well. They may be hiding," Quadri said.

"You should be going to the hospital. But I welcome your company," Dr. Jelana said.

Quadri, Dr. Jelana, and Amiri rode with Hakim in Hakim's truck to the theater. Asmara police circled the theater and prevented anyone from going inside.

"You cannot go in," said a policeman. "This is a crime scene."

"Please," Quadri said. "We are looking for friends who were here."

"Dakari?" the policeman said. "Is that you?"

"Yes. I'm Quadri Dakari."

"Who are you looking for?"

"My mother—her name is Isha, and my friend—her name is Kaila," Dr. Jelana said.

"Come this way," the policeman said.

The policeman led the group to a building adjoining the theater. Inside, police took statements from people who were in the theater but not kidnapped.

"Isha!" Amiri exclaimed.

"Amiri!" Isha said.

The two rushed to each other and embraced.

"Mamma!" Dr. Jelana said, and she hugged her mother.

"Where's Kaila?" Dr. Jelana asked. "Is she safe?"

"She...was...kidnapped!" Isha blurted.

She broke into tears. Dr. Jelana and Amiri exchanged despondent looks.

"This is terrible news," Quadri said. "I take full responsibility."

"It wasn't your fault," Amiri said. "You had nothing to do with it."

"It is my fault. You are guests in my city and my country. I am responsible for your well being," Quadri explained.

"They fled east into the mountains toward Nefasit," the policeman said. "We have all the roads watched. We think they'll head for Massawa."

"Why Massawa?" Dr. Jelana said.

"Massawa is a port on the Red Sea," the policeman said. "We think they'll smuggle the hostages on a boat and ship them to another country where they will be sold as slaves. But it's too dark to pursue them now. We must wait until morning."

"By then it will be too late," Quadri said. "They will slip away under your noses."

"All police forces in Asmara, Massawa, and Nefasit are alerted," the policeman said. "There are checkpoints along the road."

"That's if they use the road," Quadri said.

Quadri turned to Dr. Jelana, Isha, and Amiri.

"You will stay at my home tonight with my mother. There you will be safe. I will go after the barbarians," Quadri said.

"I want to go along," Amiri said.

"No, Father," Dr. Jelana said. "Your heart is too weak. You should stay with Mamma, Marcus, and Quadri's mother."

"You're certainly not going," Amiri said.

"Yes, I am," Dr. Jelana said.

"You cannot. The pursuit must be carried out by strong men," Quadri said.

"And you're a strong man?" Dr. Jelana said. "You have a deep cut above your left eye. It could open up any moment and cause severe bleeding. No, you need a doctor to observe and treat you, Quadri. And I'm that doctor."

"I will not have a woman hinder me," Quadri said.

"And I will not let your ego get in my way," Dr. Jelana said. "I'm going with you, and that's final."

Hakim looked at Quadri and said, "Yes, she should go. Your cut looks bad. If only I had some medical supplies with me."

"I have some in my purse," Dr. Jelana said.

The group piled into the trainer's truck. They drove past several police checkpoints, announced who they were, and asked for information. The police had no solid leads other than the kidnappers had fled into the mountains toward Nefasit. Hakim stopped the truck at the very point where the kidnappers left the main road.

"We must make a decision," Hakim said. "Do we follow the kidnappers into the mountains, or do we go to Nefasit and hope we meet them there?"

"I know Nefasit very well," Quadri said. "There are many secret hideouts leftover from the old slave trade. If they hide in Nefasit, we will find them."

"And if they don't?" Dr. Jelana asked. "Then what? Hakim— are there police in Nefasit to catch the kidnappers?"

Hakim asked the same question to one of the police on the road, and Hakim relayed the answer.

"Yes, there are," Hakim said. "They will spot the kidnappers should they make a move into the village."

"Then we must go off road and follow them into the mountains," Dr. Jelana said. "It is the only way."

"Quadri?" Hakim asked.

"Yes. Go off road, Hakim."

Hakim drove the truck off road and continued the pursuit as far as the path would carry the truck, but as the group headed into the mountains, the path dwindled into more pronounced bumps and jagged rocks until the truck could proceed no farther. Hakim parked the truck, and the three exited with Quadri's forehead starting to bleed.

"The bumpy ride must have done this," he said.

"Your cut has reopened," Dr. Jelana said to Quadri.

"Where are we?" Quadri asked. "I can't see."

"The blood is running in his eyes," Hakim said.

"The bleeding must be stopped," Dr. Jelana said. "But we have no time to get him to a hospital. I feared this might happen. Hakim—do you an astringent and disinfectant?"

"I have some in a storage box," Hakim said.

"Good. Please retrieve it," Dr. Jelana said.

"Disinfectant? For what?" Hakim asked.

"I'm going to suture your cut closed," Dr. Jelana said.

"Nobody is sticking a needle in my head!" Quadri said.

"I have a solution for that too," Dr. Jelana said.

She reached into her purse, fumbled around with something, then pulled out a small, wet cloth and placed it over Quadri's nose and mouth. He fell unconscious.

"That was chloroform. Now for the surgery," she said.

Dr. Jelana applied the astringent to Quadri's cut. The tissues contracted, and the bleeding slowed. Next, she applied the disinfectant and cleaned the wound.

"Hold his head steady," Dr. Jelana said to Hakim.

Hakim steadied Quadri's head next to a pillar in the truck. Dr. Jelana disinfected her suturing materials and inserted the needle into Quadri's cut with a precise angle and depth. She pulled the needle through, pushed it through a second time, pulled it through, and tied off a suture in an X pattern. A little blood flowed out of the remaining unsewn cut, and she applied a clean boxing towel to absorb the blood.

"Hold this towel, Hakim, while I finish sewing the cut closed," Dr. Jelana said.

Hakim held the towel while Dr. Jelana finished the remaining sutures.

"That should keep the cut closed," Dr. Jelana said. "Hold these towels for a moment while I prepare a proper head dressing."

Dr. Jelana fashioned additional boxing towels into a head dressing. Hakim removed the first towels, and Dr. Jelana wrapped the dressing around Quadri's head while Hakim steadied the head. Dr. Jelana completed wrapping Quadri's head, and she pulled smelling salts out of her purse. She held them under Quadri's nose, and he awoke immediately.

"Wake up," she said. "Can you speak?"

"Yes, I am awake. I can speak," Quadri said clearly and with no stuttering.

"Look into my eyes," she said.

Quadri looked into Dr. Jelana's eyes.

Dr. Jelana removed a flashlight from her purse and shined it into Quadri's eyes. His eyes contracted as expected.

"Follow my finger," she said.

Quadri's eyes followed her finger.

"Good. He's normal," Dr. Jelana said.

"We must hurry," Quadri said. "Hakim—break out the electric torches. We will track the kidnappers on foot."

"I have a flashlight already," Dr. Jelana said.

"Save your power," Hakim said. "I have three *knijpkats*—hand-powered dyno torches from the war. They need no batteries. Squeeze for a minute, and the light lasts fifteen minutes. See?"

Hakim squeezed a dyno torch for a minute, and it emitted light.

"These are special *knijpkats*," Hakim said. "The flywheels were replaced with capacitors so you don't have to squeeze constantly."

Quadri led the way with Dr. Jelana at his side. Hakim watched the rear in case of a surprise attack. Jonara, Cerafina, and Johnny followed behind Hakim. Hakim seemed to look directly at them, but he never saw them. The group proceeded into a valley and up a mountain, following a fresh path made by the kidnappers.

"The path narrows," Quadri said. "We must walk single-file."

Dr. Jelana walked behind Quadri, and Hakim walked behind her. Even Jonara, Cerafina, and Johnny walked single-file. After twenty minutes, Quadri stopped.

"Why are you stopping?" Dr. Jelana asked.

"The tracks stop here," he said.

"Where do they go?" Dr. Jelana asked.

"They don't. It doesn't make sense. It's as if they were suddenly lifted into the air," Quadri said.

"Let me see," Hakim said.

Hakim knelt and looked carefully at the footprints.

"These prints have been stepped in twice," Hakim said. "They played an old trick. They stopped here and walked backward to fool anyone who might follow them."

"And that anyone is us, isn't it?" Dr. Jelana asked.

"Yes," Quadri said. "We must go back and find where they left the path. They will have brushed their tracks to avoid detection. Look for branches or anything that could be used to brush the ground."

The three backtracked and found a broken branch tossed aside.

"There," Quadri said. "We'll go that way. We must be careful now. We don't want to be seen or heard."

"We'll certainly be heard with these *knijpkats*," Dr. Jelana said. "I feel like I'm squeezing a cat!"

"She's right," Quadri said.

"Here," Hakim said. "I have some battery-powered flashlights. We may use them for a few minutes to be quiet. But only a few minutes. We may need their power later."

The three did not go far when the path stopped.

"We can go no farther," Quadri said.

"There should be an entrance somewhere," Hakim said. "I'm sure of it. But it's hidden."

"I don't know about an entrance," Dr. Jelana said. "But something stinks—like rotten eggs."

"Yes, it should stink," Hakim said.

"Why should it stink?" Dr. Jelana asked.

"Rumor is the caves are full of minerals from volcanic vents, including sulfur," Hakim replied.

"Sulfur fumes can be poisonous," Dr. Jelana said.

"If they are, the kidnappers would not have chosen this route. Likely the fumes are tolerable enough for quick passage," Hakim said. "Unfortunately, my nose doesn't work like it used to. Test the side of the mountain for weakness—maybe the entrance will reveal itself."

"How can we?" Dr. Jelana asked. "There are shrubs everywhere."

"Follow your nose," Quadri said.

"You're one to talk," Dr. Jelana said. "I don't know how you can smell. Your nose is beat up almost as much as your eye."

"Then you must lend us your nose," Quadri said.

Dr. Jelana sniffed and sniffed and sniffed.

"The stench is strongest here," she said. "Wait—these plants are strange."

"They're fake," Quadri said. "I ripped a leaf, but it remains dry."

"The entrance must be here," Hakim said. "Push, Quadri, push!"

Hakim and Quadri pushed against the side of the mountain by the fake shrubs.

"It won't move," Quadri said. "Jelana—help us push."

"Pushing isn't working," she said. "I'm resting on this rock until you two decide on another plan."

Dr. Jelana sat on the rock and leaned against the side of the mountain. Her hand slipped into a little alcove, and without much thought, her fingers pushed a lever. Something released its hold. Quadri and Hakim made another thrust against the mountain, and to their surprise, a door gave way and allowed them to over-push into the entranceway where they fell over each other. A plume of stench poured out of the cave entrance.

"Pee-yoo," Dr. Jelana said. "We've found the entrance."

"Shh," Hakim said.

Hakim and Quadri rose to their feet and stepped back outside where Dr. Jelana waited.

"Do you know this cave?" Dr. Jelana asked.

"No, I don't," Quadri said.

"It must be an old slave-trade passage to Nefasit," Hakim said. "But I thought these caves were a myth."

"Listen," Dr. Jelana said. "Do you hear talking? People are inside."

"It sounds like English," Quadri said. "But not British English."

"It's American English," Dr. Jelana said. "Sounds like a New York accent. How strange to find people from New York in Eritrea."

"There will be guards posted," Quadri said. "If we go inside, the guards will surely catch us."

"We must disable them," Dr. Jelana said.

"Why didn't I have you bring your gun from the truck?" Quadri asked.

"My gun isn't in the truck," Hakim said. "This is bad—we have no weapons. We can't go in naked."

"Even if we had a gun, the entire group would be alerted after the first shot. We must pick them off one-by-one," Quadri said.

"*If* these are the kidnappers," Hakim said.

"I wish I could switch into a southpaw to defeat this enemy," Quadri said.

"Maybe you can," Dr. Jelana said. "I can be your southpaw."

"How?"

"With the chloroform," Dr. Jelana said. "I'll lure a guard out here, and you cover his face with a rag of chloroform."

Dr. Jelana ripped a piece of material from her blouse and pulled a bottle of chloroform from her purse.

"Here's the rag, and here's the chloroform," Dr. Jelana said. "And here, don't lose my purse."

"You can't do this," Quadri said. "You're a woman. They'll overpower you. No, it's too dangerous. I'll go inside and lure them out."

"If you go in, they'll think they're being attacked," Dr. Jelana said. "It's because I'm a woman that I should go in. I'll convince them I escaped from the captives."

"And they'll make you a captive," Quadri said. "You won't be able to lure them out here."

"Give me fifteen minutes," Dr. Jelana said. "If I don't come back, then come in after me."

"I don't like this idea. It's dangerous. You don't have to do this," Quadri said.

"There's no better way," Dr. Jelana said. "And we have no time to tell the police. The kidnappers could be gone by then. No. We do the 'southpaw' method. Keep your flashlights out of the entrance. And don't use the *knijpkats*—they make too much noise."

Dr. Jelana disappeared into the entrance. Quadri and Hakim waited a minute, two minutes, five. Ten minutes, and no word from Dr. Jelana. Voices continued to carry from the caves, but none were Dr. Jelana's, and the voices did not grow louder.

"We've waited long enough," Quadri said. "We must go in."

"Another five minutes," Hakim said. "That was the doctor's order."

"I don't like waiting," Quadri said. "We must go now."

As the two men debated whether to go in or not, a loud splash! echoed through the caves followed by the sounds of someone yelping briefly from under a liquid. The original distant voices continued without interruption.

"She's fallen in water," Quadri said.

"The voices have not changed," Hakim said. "They must be very far into the caves. Let's hope she only fell in water."

"What do you mean?" Quadri asked.

"The sulfur fumes could be from sulfuric acid," Hakim explained. "If she fell into a pool of acid..."

"Then we go in and find Jelana right now," Quadri said.

"Wait," Hakim said. "Charge up your *knijpkat* out here so no one will hear. Let's turn off the battery-powered flashlights and save power."

"There's no time," Quadri said. "She could be dissolving as we speak."

Quadri and Hakim entered the cave using the battery-powered flashlights.

"Watch the first step," Quadri said.

"Whoa!" Hakim said.

The two walked onto a narrow ledge with a rock face on the left side and a steep dropoff with a wide expanse on the right.

"Do you think she fell down there?" Quadri asked.

"She couldn't have spent ten minutes falling off a ledge next to the entrance," Hakim said.

"Or maybe she was on the way back and fell over," Quadri said.

Quadri pointed his flashlight down the side of the cliff.

"Jelana?" Quadri called with a hand by his mouth to keep his voice from traveling down the cave toward the kidnappers. "Can you hear me?"

No response. Hakim took a loose stone and dropped it over the edge. Thirty seconds later, Quadri and Hakim saw a light flickering from far below.

"That's her electric torch," Quadri said. "We must climb down there."

"Wait," Hakim said. "The light is strange, and the air is rising from below."

A distant rumbling sound thundered from below.

"Quick—against the wall," Hakim said as he shoved Quadri against the rock face.

Moments later, a blast of hot air followed by a fireball shot from below into a venting shaft above the gorge. Had the two been peering over the cliff's edge, the blast would have carried them into the shaft above.

"Something down there is extremely explosive," Hakim said. "Simply dropping a stone will detonate it."

"And the light?" Quadri asked.

"Was a chemical ignition," Hakim said. "It was not the doctor. She must be elsewhere. Also, I doubt there are any guards. That air blast would have alerted them to intruders, and we've seen no one. Come—we can use our *knijpkats* again and save battery power. We'll charge them as we walk, but we must move on. This air is hot, and the sulfur is burning our lungs."

The two turned off their battery-powered flashlights and resumed using their dyno torches. They continued along the ledge until they heard a liquid gurgling over the right edge of the path.

"Let's look," Quadri said. "She could have fallen here."

The two pointed their dyno torches over the edge and saw the distant trickling of a fluid along a steep incline down below.

"Jelana, are you down there?" Quadri called, but there was no reply.

Quadri's head wavered, and he nearly toppled over the edge. Hakim caught him in time, pulled him away from the edge, and pushed him against the rock face.

"The sulfur fumes are thick," Hakim said. "We must be careful not to take deep breaths when we look over the edge."

The two marched only a little farther when the path next to the rock face narrowed. A natural bridge to the right crossed over the sulfuric liquid.

"Look," Hakim said. "We cannot continue along this rock face. It narrows to a point just beyond this bridge."

"There's a pool of water at the end of the path," Quadri said. "And the pool drains into a waterfall that begins just before and underneath the bridge. We may not have a chance to get water deeper in the cave. Let's refill our canteens here."

"No! You must be out of your wits from boxing," Hakim said. "The pool could be poisonous. Do you see the yellow crystals all around the pool? Test it by throwing a bit of leather strap into it."

Quadri walked to the end of the path and stood next to the pool of liquid. He cut a strip of leather from his belt and dropped it into the pool. The leather boiled and dissolved into the pool rather violently, leaving no traces ten seconds after it had first made contact.

"Sulfuric acid," Hakim said. "Extremely deadly. Don't touch it. Now I understand the explosion. The sulfuric acid mixes with other chemicals at the bottom of the gorge creating an explosive ready to detonate. Quadri—if she fell here, she's gone."

"Then all is lost," Quadri said.

"We can't stop and mourn her. She may have fallen somewhere else and survived," Hakim said.

"In another pool of sulfuric acid?" Quadri asked. "Who can survive that?"

"What about the kidnappers? We can't leave Kaila to their vices," Hakim said. "Quadri—we must keep moving. We'll have time for mourning later."

The two crossed the natural bridge over the sulfuric acid waterfall. Upon reaching the other side, Quadri looked back.

"What are you doing?" Hakim said.

"I'm looking for traces of Jelana," Quadri said. "But I see nothing."

"Charge your *knijpkat*," Hakim said. "That will help keep your mind occupied."

Quadri squeezed his dyno torch for fifteen seconds. He nodded his head toward the sulfur pool as if saying, "Goodbye," turned back around, and led Hakim from the end of the natural bridge into a tunnel to the next part of the cave. The two traveled for about a minute when the ceiling opened up, the left side was against a rock face, and the right opened into another gorge.

"The air is much better and cooler here," Hakim said.

"It smells like gunpowder," Quadri said.

"That's potassium nitrate," Hakim said. "Come—let's look over the edge."

The two shined their dyno torches over the right edge.

"I can see the bottom," Quadri said.

"This is not nearly as steep as the sulfuric acid gorge," Hakim said. "This fluid is much less corrosive if at all."

"I can see water, but it is cerise," Quadri said.

"Most likely the fluid, if water, contains chemicals giving it the cerise color," Hakim said. "Based on where it appears to be going, I'd said this stream eventually mixes with the sulfuric acid a mile underground."

"These crystals—they are white, black, clear, and cerise, but none are yellow," Quadri said.

"Interesting," Hakim said. "There's no sulfur in this part of the cave."

Hakim sniffed the crystals and touched one to his tongue.

"These are all potassium compounds," Hakim said. "I would say we're looking at mixtures of potassium carbonate, potassium perchlorate, potassium nitrate, and potassium permanganate. It's the potassium permanganate that mixes with sulfuric acid to create the highly explosive manganese oxide, although potassium nitrate and potassium perchlorate are also explosive."

"This cave is Hell itself," Quadri said. "If fumes and acid don't kill a person, an explosion will. And how do you know so much about chemicals? You're my boxing trainer!"

"I did not grow up in the isolation of Asmara," Hakim said. "My family comes from these rugged mountain areas, remember? I learned about chemicals while mining. But I saw too many mining deaths and felt boxing would be safer. Come along—we must follow the path farther. Still there are no guards, yet we hear the voices as we did at the cave's entrance."

"The tunnels play tricks with echoes," Quadri said. "But I will continue forward."

"You still have hopes of finding the doctor?" Hakim asked.

"Yes. She is too smart to jump into a pool of acid," Quadri said.

The two continued along the path until they reached another natural bridge.

"We have a decision to make," Hakim said. "We can continue along the rock face next to this cerise stream, or cross this natural bridge and go down that side tunnel."

"The voices come from the path along the rock face," Quadri said. "But there's a sound coming from the tunnel across the bridge. It sounds like water dripping."

"Which way would the doctor go?" Hakim asked. "It's a difficult question."

"I would think our doctor would have also paused here to think. Should she now go back and let us know there is no guard? It has taken us nine minutes to reach this point—this means the doctor reached this point and spent another minute traveling before we heard the splash."

"Which we're assuming was her falling into a liquid," Hakim said.

"I would say she would want to investigate the dripping sound first. And then she planned to return to us," Quadri said.

"Then she fell into whatever is down that tunnel over the bridge," Hakim said. "We must be extremely careful if we go that way. Here."

Hakim unraveled a rope from his belt.

"What are you doing with that?" Quadri asked.

"I'm going to put this around my chest," Hakim said. "You tie the other end around your waist. I'll go first, and if something happens to me—"

"No, I will go first," Quadri said. "I want to take the risk. If things go badly, cut the rope and get help. I'll stay with Jelana."

"If she's here," Hakim said.

"Yes. If she's here," Quadri said.

"Very well. Tie the rope around your chest and under your arms. I'll tie my end around my waist. Good. Give me the doctor's purse for safekeeping. Thank you. Now charge up your *knijpkat*," Hakim said.

The two spent a minute fully recharging their dyno torches.

"I'm ready," Quadri said.

"Proceed very slowly," Hakim said. "Don't force a path. If you're stuck, come back."

"I will, I will," Quadri said impatiently, but Hakim knew better.

Hakim let out the full length of rope. Quadri proceeded across the bridge, and as he disappeared through the tunnel opening, the rope went taunt. Hakim followed slowly behind. He heard nothing except for the distant voices from the kidnappers down the main passage. Quadri said nothing and gave no information regarding his progress. Hakim crossed the bridge over the cerise stream. Suddenly, the rope yanked Hakim to the ground, like a tug-of-war game gone bad. Hakim slid sideways until he reached the tunnel opening where his right shoulder and right-side hip caught against the tunnel opening. He came to an abrupt stop. The impact felt worse than any boxing injury he had sustained in the years before he switched from boxing to training. He cried out in pain, and his shoulder and hip swelled.

"Quadri," he called as carefully as he could without letting his voice carry toward the kidnappers.

Quadri did not answer, but Hakim felt strong tugs on his waist as if someone were trying to yank him through the opening. After lying on the ground like this for five minutes, the yanking stopped, and the rope went slack. Quadri appeared after a minute.

"What are you doing there?" he laughed.

"That's not funny," Hakim said. "I'm hurt."

"Here," Quadri said. "I'll help you stand up."

Quadri helped Hakim stand up.

"What happened?" Hakim said. "Did you fall?"

"Yes," Quadri said. "The tunnel opens up into a chamber to the right with crystals, pools, stalactites, and stalagmites. There is also a loose stone covered in a slippery substance on the path. I stepped on it and fell. Fortunately, I did not fall to the bottom. But while I was hanging there, I saw Jelana. She is in one of the pools and holding onto the edge. She is conscious but cannot pull herself up. I told her I'd come back with help. I pulled myself up, and here I am. Lucky for me you held the rope firm."

"Lucky for you my shoulder and hip held firm," Hakim said. "I told you to be careful."

"Come," Quadri said. "I'll show you the loose stone."

The two proceeded through the tunnel, and as Quadri predicted, the tunnel opened up into a chamber.

"Jelana," Quadri said. "I'm back. Hakim is with me. It's all right now. We'll help you. Just hold on a little longer."

"Hurry," Dr. Jelana said. "There's an undertow pulling my legs, and I don't know how much longer I can hold on."

"Stop," Quadri said to Hakim. "This is the loose stone. See?"

Quadri pushed it lightly with his foot and nearly lost his balance. Hakim caught him in time and pulled him back to solid ground.

"Lower me down," Quadri said.

Hakim looked for and found a small crevice in the wall. He produced a hook from his pocket with a pin, took his hammer, and beat the pin into the crevice. He tested the hook for strength, and when he was confident, he placed the rope in the hook. He untied the rope from his body for extra length, put on leather gloves, and held onto the rope tightly.

"We will do this slowly," Hakim said. "Use whatever ledges you can to reduce the load on the rope. I am strong, but I do not have infinite endurance."

"Good," Quadri said.

Hakim lowered Quadri down the side of the ledge. Quadri grabbed protrusions and eased his journey down.

"Are you at the bottom yet," Hakim called.

"No," Quadri said. "I need another ten feet."

"I'm at the end of the rope," Hakim said. "I can't let you down any more."

"I'll cut the rope," Quadri said.

"No. We need to rethink this. I'll pull you up," Hakim said.

"No time," Quadri said. "Jelana can't wait."

"I won't be able to pull you up if you cut the rope. It will be too short," Hakim warned.

"Then I'll untie it," Quadri said.

"You can't. Your weight is holding the knot tight," Hakim said. "I'm pulling you up."

"No," Quadri said.

Quadri yanked at the rope in desperation while trying to undo the knot. The hook's grip in the rock face loosened.

"Don't yank. You're pulling out the hook," Hakim said.

"What?" Quadri called. "I can't hear you."

Quadri increased his yanking, and Hakim fought to keep the hook in the wall, but he couldn't hold it and the rope at the same time. The hook let loose, and the full weight of the rope tugged on Hakim. Hakim, still holding onto the rope, was pulled into a protruding rock formation. He hit his head, released the rope, and fell unconscious on the ledge. Quadri fell the ten feet into the pool, and the rope fell atop him.

"Hakim?" Quadri called, but Hakim could not answer.

"Quadri," Dr. Jelana called. "Help me, please!"

Quadri swam to the edge where Dr. Jelana held on. He pulled himself onto it and pulled Dr. Jelana onto it too.

"The water is cold," Quadri said. "Your arms and legs are frozen. You're shivering."

"I'm...so...cold," Dr. Jelana stuttered. "You...must...massage my limbs...to...to restore circulation."

Dr. Jelana sat next to Quadri, who held her in his arms. He rubbed her arms and legs to warm them and move the blood around.

"Hakim!" Quadri called again, but still no response.

Quadri pointed his dyno torch up toward Hakim and saw him unconscious.

"He's unconscious," Quadri said. "And there's no way up without the rope."

"We have to do something," Jonara said.

"Can we wake Hakim?" Cerafina asked.

"Try it," Johnny said.

Miramish	**Translation**
Hakim e, Hakim	Hakim, Hakim
Ishu paugili bushipu,	In caverns deep,
Ominopo veletu belorifa	Awake from slumber
Ominopo veletu perusha!	Awake from sleep!

Hakim did not wake up.

"Something's wrong," Jonara said. "*Ominopo!* (Awake!)"

Again, no response from Hakim.

"What does the Moissan Ruby tell you?" Johnny asked.

"Nothing. I can't read anyone. It's like something's jamming it."

"There are chemicals and crystals everywhere in this cave," Johnny said. "They may be interfering with the stone and the candleholder."

Something stirred in the pool below.

"What's that?" Cerafina asked.

"I don't know," Johnny said. "Jonara?"

"I didn't do it," Jonara said.

"I think you did," Cerafina said. "You awoke something from sleep."

Seeing the disturbance, Quadri pulled Dr. Jelana away from the pool.

"They can see it," Jonara said.

"Because it's real," Cerafina said. "You awoke something from the deep."

The bubbling grew like a broad fountain rising from the depths. The water took on a shape—the upper half of a woman's body. She had a symbol 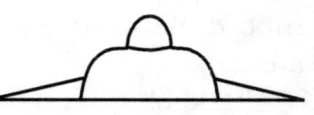 on her forehead, and with her arms she reached for Jonara.

"It's Nekara the Red!" Johnny said.

"This is her cave," Jonara said.

"Look out!" shouted Cerafina to Jonara.

Jonara spoke:

Miramish	Translation
Viuka opeifu heidona	Force of water
Ishu paugili bushipu,	In caverns deep,
Lukaimo di belorifa	Return to slumber
Vifo vaka di perusha!	Go back to sleep!

Nekara the water woman shot a burst of cerise light at Jonara. Jonara ducked. The light bounced around the cave, setting off microexplosions the size of acorns.

"*Geravugo* (Dissolve)!" Jonara shouted.

The water froze in place for a moment, and suddenly it lost all cohesion and slapped into the pool below. A wave rippled in all directions and slapped over the ledge onto Quadri and Dr. Jelana. Both coughed and gagged for several minutes to regain their breath.

"Hakim is still asleep!" Jonara said.

"Jonara!" Cerafina said. "Is that all you can think about?"

"What?!" Jonara said.

"*What* yourself. You could have gotten us killed with your chant," Cerafina said.

"Sorry! But I got rid of her, didn't I?" Jonara said.

"Did you? I wonder. I think you stirred up something by mistake," Johnny said.

"Did I hear you right?" Cerafina asked Jonara. "Did you say this is Nekara's cave?"

"Did I say that?" Jonara asked.

"Yes, you did," Johnny replied. "And it concerns me."

"Wow, I didn't realize I said that," Jonara said.

"Because it wasn't you saying it. The Water Ruby must have told you," Cerafina said.

"This is bad," Johnny said.

"But we saw her before," Jonara said.

"It's not good to stir up evil," Johnny said. "It's like feeding a monster with an infinite appetite."

"What about Hakim?" Jonara said.

"Is that all you can think about, Jonara?" Cerafina said. "Didn't you hear your father? You've stirred up a monster."

"I heard him, Cera. But I got rid of the monster," Jonara replied.

"Yes, you did," Johnny replied. "For now. She'll be back, I'm afraid. She's been after us since Italy."

"Maybe a little before that," Jonara said.

"Oh?" Johnny asked.

"Did you see the symbol on her forehead? I've seen it before," Jonara said.

"Where?" Johnny asked with a concerned tone.

"On the forehead of Christine, the Vice of Christ," Jonara said. "And the cat at Page Clinic. Oh yeah, the oak tree's trunk at Barnseed Baptist Church."

"Now I understand," Johnny said. "That's Nekara's symbol. She's been appearing to you in various forms. Jonara—you must be extremely careful to avoid this Nekara the Red. I've warned you before, I know, but something about her is quite evil."

Jonara jumped as if being hit by an electric shock.

"What happened?" Cerafina asked. "Why did you jump?"

"The Water Ruby shocked me. It was like...it...it bit me!"

"Hmm," Johnny said. "Could there be another Moissan Ruby nearby? Make a conservative scan of the chamber. And don't chant any Miramish commands. You've done enough for the moment."

"I'll try," Jonara said. "Hey, Hakim is right. Lots of potassium compounds in this cave. Oh look, there's an unusual crystalline thingy next to Dr. Jelana. It's smooth and looks a lot like the candleholder. It's smaller, and it's not made of wood."

"What is it made of?" Cerafina asked.

"Monopotassium phosphate. Potassium niobate. Lithium iodate. More potassium perchlorate and potassium permanganate. And other chemicals I can't read. Macromolecules too," Jonara said. "What does it mean?"

"I wonder. If this *is* her cave, could this be her device? The *duavisha*?" Johnny pondered.

"What are you talking about?" Jonara asked. "And what is a *duavisha*?"

"Search your feelings," Johnny said. "It's a Miramish word."

"Yes, it is," Jonara said. "It means *fertility stone*."

"This could be the one she used," Johnny said. "When Roberta and Marcus—"

"Did what? Roberta? And Marcus? Daddy, what are you talking about?"

"Dr. Jelana had it first," Johnny said. "Then Marcus. Now if we could stop Dr. Jelana from taking the duavisha...maybe we could make her leave it here...no, that would change what must be...if there were some other way...one follows another...oh this is too much thinking for my poor brain."

"Daddy, explain!" Jonara said. "You're babbling, for all I know."

"It's too complicated to explain. And it hurts just thinking about it," Johnny said. "But I hope things will make sense soon. Look, Jelana is reaching for the duavisha now."

"I found something very interesting," Dr. Jelana said to Quadri. "It's a fossil or something. See how it glows?"

"It almost looks man-made," Quadri said. "It is shaped so perfectly and beautifully."

"Or woman-made," Dr. Jelana said. "Could a man put such harmonious colors and curves into a piece like this? I'm keeping it as a souvenir. If we get out of here, I'll wear it as a necklace."

"That's a big *if*," Quadri said. "Hakim is our only way out, unless a rescue party comes after us."

"Or the kidnappers come back this way," Dr. Jelana said.

"Let's hope that never happens," Quadri said.

"Look," Dr. Jelana said playfully. "This fossil fits in my navel."

The duavisha glowed in shades of green, cerise, and blue.

"The fossil glows," Quadri said.

"I feel strange," Dr. Jelana said. "Like I'm smoking something I shouldn't."

Dr. Jelana looked around the chamber.

"I see colors," Dr. Jelana said. "So many colors pulsing back and forth. Hakim is up on the ledge. I see his breath displacing the air. And you. Quadri, I see you differently too."

"What do you see?" he asked as he suddenly worried she could read his mind.

"You were never interested in Kaila at all. You only pretended to like her. You appreciate intelligent women, assertive women, women who throw the first punch. You've never met a woman like that until you met me," Dr. Jelana said. "You have a crush on me. How absolutely adorable!"

"I don't like that fossil," Quadri said. "It gives you too much power!"

"It's wonderful. And it makes no scientific sense at all. The illnesses I could cure—it amazes me. Do you know that the most difficult problem with practicing medicine is in determining the root cause of a condition or disease? I could see the problem clearly and quickly. I wouldn't have to waste time testing and eliminating improbabilities."

"This sounds like the occult," Quadri said. "But I will test you. How many fingers am I holding up behind my back?"

"One thumb up, four fingers pointed to the side, and the other hand is a closed fist," Dr. Jelana said. "Well?"

"Impossible," Quadri said. "Correct, but impossible."

"Daddy!" Jonara called. "She has some sort of power like the Water Ruby!"

"It really is a duavisha," Johnny said.

"What is it? What is it really?" Jonara asked.

"Some sort of hybrid Moissan Ruby and candleholder," Johnny said.

"What?!" Jonara asked. "What is a Jewish candleholder ruby thingy doing in a cave in Eritrea?"

"Relax, Jonara," Cerafina said. "It's not at all like that. The duavisha has a shape similar to the candleholder. That doesn't make it a candleholder or Jewish. Do we know where it came from, Mr. Pindus?"

"I want to say, 'outer space'," Johnny said, "because that's where I think the Moissan Ruby came from. But then how did it get inside here? Is it Nekara's? I asked that already, I know. How can I be sure?"

"There's something else too," Dr. Jelana said. "I have this great urge to have a baby. And I want you to be the other mother."

"Don't you mean the father?" Quadri asked.

"I know it doesn't make sense," Dr. Jelana said. "But I see the mothering part of you. This fossil is a strange thing!"

"There is one thing I know," Quadri said. "When we get out of here, I want to marry you. Marry me, Jelana Margo."

Dr. Jelana laughed.

"And you'll be a good mother to our children? Including Marcus?" Dr. Jelana asked.

"I'll be a good mother, father, and friend. Anything. Marry me, Jelana," Quadri said.

"I do want to marry you, but the fossil might be doing that to me. I never thought I'd settle down for a man. I don't want to lose my independence," Dr. Jelana said.

"Then take the fossil out," Quadri said.

Dr. Jelana removed the duavisha from her navel and placed it in her pocket.

"I no longer see you as a woman," Dr. Jelana said.

"That's a good start," Quadri said.

"And now I'm not so sure if I should marry you," Dr. Jelana said. "You are a boxer, a fighter. I'm a healer. I can't condone violence."

"Don't think of it as violence," Quadri said. "Violence is like an explosion, an uncontrolled burst of destruction. Think of it like combustion in an automobile engine—a controlled burst of energy for performing work. My boxing is controlled work. It provides entertainment for my audience. They watch, they learn what works and what doesn't, and they appreciate success. My work earns a wage so I can support my family."

"You sound so convincing," Dr. Jelana said. "But it's still a dangerous sport."

"Look at Hakim up there," Quadri said.

"I'm looking. He's unconscious!" Dr. Jelana replied.

"Besides that," Quadri continued. "He comes from a mining family. Now you know what that's like, or you should know. People losing limbs if they're lucky or dying if they're not. But no one questions that occupation. Hakim switched to boxing when he was younger, and as he grew older, he trained boxers. It's safer than mining. Yet there is this great push against boxing because it's considered violent. Violent? Boxing is combustion, mining is the explosion. But there's a difference. The public sees and talks about boxing. They never see mining. It's a secret, dirty job. Look at us now, Jelana. We're in a cave. We're trapped. We may not get out alive. Ask yourself—is this safer than boxing? When I box, I can quit at any time, the match ends, and everything goes back to normal. I have people looking after me—my trainer, the referee—if they see something wrong, they can stop the match. Now look at us here. There's no safety net, no backup, no help. We are truly alone. Is boxing really worse than this? I don't ask others to box. I don't whip up an agenda and preach it to the world. Boxing is a personal sport. No one else gets hurt, except the other boxer, but his philosophy is the same as mine. And when the match is over, it's over. The engine shuts off. No dieseling. We don't go into the streets and fight people. Boxing is combustion."

"You have a silver tongue," Dr. Jelana said.

"Let's see if I have a silver arm," Quadri said.

"What are you going to do?"

"Throw rocks at Hakim," Quadri said.

"Don't aim for the head," Dr. Jelana said. "He's already knocked out. Hitting him in the head could make things worse."

"You are giving advice to the last person on Earth who should receive it. I know all about blows to the head. I've given and received many. I'll aim for the extremities—a hand or leg should do," Quadri said.

Quadri threw a rock.

"You missed," Dr. Jelana said.

"It's a long way up," Quadri said. "And the target is very small. His right hand and right ankle are all I can see."

"Try again," Dr. Jelana said.

Quadri threw another rock. It also missed.

"Let me try," Dr. Jelana said.

Dr. Jelana picked up a black stone and threw it high in the air toward Hakim. It didn't reach Hakim, and it hit the cliff face below Hakim's ledge. It exploded on impact.

"Get down!" Quadri said.

The two fell to their knees with their hands over their heads. Falling debris peppered them and the ground around them for several seconds. Dust filled the air. The two looked up but couldn't see anything. A breath of air for each threw them into new coughing fits.

"Breathe through your shirt," she said.

The two pulled their shirts up over their faces. Someone coughed.

"I said pull your shirt up," Dr. Jelana said.

"I did," Quadri said. "Why aren't you breathing through your shirt?"

"I am, of course," Dr. Jelana said.

Another cough.

"Then why are you coughing?" Quadri said.

"I'm not coughing," Dr. Jelana said. "I thought you were coughing."

"No, I'm not," Quadri said.

"Hakim?" they asked at the same time.

"Hakim!" Quadri yelled. "Hakim!"

"Don't shout so loudly," Hakim replied.

"You're alive!" Dr. Jelana called.

"Yes, I am," Hakim said between coughs. "What happened?"

"You hit your head against the rocks and fell unconscious," Quadri said.

"Yeah," Hakim said. "And after that? What caused the explosion?"

"I threw a rock up to wake you," Dr. Jelana said. "It hit the rock face below you and exploded."

"Well it changed things up here," Hakim said. "The loose stone is gone, and there is another passageway a little lower than this one. I can climb down to it I think...yes, I can."

Hakim climbed down to the lower passage.

"I can't pull you up—I lost the rope," Hakim said.

"It's down here," Quadri said.

"Bundle it up and throw it to me," Hakim said. "And make your throw good. If we lose the rope—"

"I know," Quadri said.

Quadri bundled the rope into a coil and wrapped the end around the coil to hold it fast. He got as close as he could to Hakim and threw the rope up underhanded. The rope stopped its upward trajectory just in front of Hakim's face. Hakim plucked the bundled rope out of the air as if it were floating.

"I have it," Hakim said. "Get ready. I'll secure the hook."

Hakim secured a hook and pin into a crevice in the wall. He unbundled the rope and threaded it over the hook.

"Here," Hakim said, and he tossed the free rope down. "Send the doctor up first."

Quadri tied the rope under Dr. Jelana's arms.

"You go up first," Quadri said. "If I can't make it..."

"You'll make it," Dr. Jelana said, and she kissed him on the lips. "That's to motivate you."

"I will make it, if it means I can receive more kisses like that," Quadri said.

Hakim pulled the rope and hauled Dr. Jelana up to the lower ledge. Dr. Jelana climbed on all fours until she had her balance, and she stood on her feet.

"See?" Hakim said between huffs and puffs. "There's another cave. Listen—the voices sound much closer."

"What are you waiting for?" Quadri called. "Throw the rope down."

"Hakim, you're breathing hard," Dr. Jelana said. "Look at my eyes."

Hakim looked at her.

"Your eyes look good," Dr. Jelana said. "But you're exhausted."

"That Quadri wore me out," Hakim said.

"Come on!" Quadri called.

"You just wait a moment," Dr. Jelana called back. "Hakim is catching his breath."

"When he first fell," Hakim continued, "I anchored him. But I hurt my right shoulder and hip."

Dr. Jelana looked at his shoulder and hip.

"They're swollen. You should rest in bed," she said.

"I know," Hakim continued, "and when I lowered him, I think I pulled something in my shoulder. It hurts like hell."

Dr. Jelana inspected his shoulder.

"Does this hurt?" she asked.

"Ow! Yes!" Hakim screamed.

"Your shoulder is dislocated," Dr. Jelana said.

"What's the delay?" Quadri yelled from below.

"Hakim's shoulder is dislocated," Dr. Jelana called back.

"Pull me up, and we'll fix it," Quadri said.

"Hakim can't pull you up with this shoulder," Dr. Jelana said. "Now be patient so I can treat him."

"Can you give me something for the pain?" Hakim asked.

"I can, but you'll be out of your senses. Wait a moment—I don't have my purse," Dr. Jelana said.

"You gave it to Quadri," Hakim said, "and he gave it to me. But I don't have it with me. When did I last have it? Yes, just before I knocked my head against the rock. Your purse must be on the upper ledge. I should get it."

"No," Dr. Jelana said. "You stay here and rest. I'll get it."

Dr. Jelana climbed from the lower ledge to the upper. Resting next to the rock face was her purse. She had a strange feeling, like seeing a child abandoned.

"I won't abandon you," she said to her purse.

She placed the purse over her shoulder and prepared to descend to the lower ledge, but she paused for a moment.

"Let's see what the fossil shows me from up here," she said.

Dr. Jelana removed the duavisha from her pocket and placed it in her navel. She looked around the chamber and saw the colors as she did before.

"Dry my clothes," she said as if giving a command.

Her clothes did not dry.

"Dry, dry, dry, dry, *norst*," she said.

Dr. Jelana did not know where the word came from. It simply popped into her head. Steam rose from her clothing, leaving the fabric dry.

"She spoke Miramish," Jonara said.

"No, she didn't," Johnny said. "It was something else."

"How can you tell, Mr. Pindus?" Cerafina asked.

"Most Miramish words consist of consonants separated by vowels. And they do not use the letter *s*," Johnny explained. "But *norst* slaps consonants together and uses an *s*. Very odd. Not Miramish. Something else. This bothers me. But one thing is for sure—the fossil is definitely a duavisha. And it came from the same place as the Moissan Ruby. She learned the foreign word for *dry* from the duavisha."

"This fossil has power to affect," Dr. Jelana said to herself. "I must not reveal this power to the others. It would create jealously and crime beyond belief."

Dr. Jelana descended from the upper ledge to the lower.

"I found my purse," she said. "I will give you something for the pain. Then I must reset your shoulder."

Dr. Jelana removed a syringe from her purse, but she did not fill it with medication. It remained empty.

"You might feel a small but sharp pain," she said.

"All right. Give me the painkiller," Hakim said.

Dr. Jelana pressed the syringe next to Hakim's arm to give him the sensation of being stuck with a needle. With the dua-visha still in her navel, she whispered, "Block pain, block pain, *birasle zhiarge.*"

The duavisha activated a pain-blocking mechanism in Ha-kim's shoulder.

"She spoke that language again," Jonara said.

"The duavisha taught her, just as the Moissan Ruby taught me and later you," Johnny said. "But what language is she speaking? I wish I knew."

"Let's find out," Jonara said.

"Be careful," Johnny said. "This could be dangerous."

"Don't worry," Jonara replied, and she chanted:

Miramish	Translation
Moishiana, Lanudaku Thorithua,	Water Ruby, Candleholder,
Kairsh e bioriti kiloito.	Your powers beseech.
Haku duavishu varitha	What duavisha language
Gerutho Dzhelana shash e talisha?	Gives Jelana her speech?

A robed woman's image appeared in midair—the same woman who sang on the Italian restaurant boat.

"Not her again," Cerafina said.

Non-Miramish Language	Translation
Nia vikel shair deirzhwan!	I *am* the pitcher!
Kair karfsteit nui viersh!	You will catch my fury!

A cerise fireball emanated from her abdomen. It expanded and prepared to engulf Jonara, Cerafina, and Johnny.

"*Tipeliaroko* (Disintegrate)!" Jonara yelled.

The fireball dissipated, the image of Nekara the Red faded, and the three returned to the cave as if nothing had happened.

"That was Nekara the Red," Johnny said. "We were lucky this time, but it's clear this duavisha does not mix well with the Moissan Ruby and candleholder. Jonara—you must not per-form a Miramish chant against the duavisha again. Somehow, your chant invoked Nekara the Red."

"I think she's connecting to the duavisha, not Jonara's chant," Cerafina said.

"But how?" Jonara asked. "Nekara hit us in the boat while we were in Italy. That was before the Margos arrived in Eritrea. She couldn't have a link with the duavisha."

"Hmm," Johnny said. "Maybe, maybe. Still, Cerafina might be onto something. Nekara used a non-Miramish language, just as Dr. Jelana did. They sounded similar. They could be the same. If so, there could be a connection between the duavisha and Nekara. But, she did appear immediately after Jonara's chants. I should say Nekara has links to the duavisha and Jonara. On the other hand...hmm...too much. There are many things I don't understand."

"Being in the dark about the duavisha and Nekara is the worst of all," Cerafina said. "How are we to know what to do, what is good, and what evil to avoid?"

"I don't know, Cerafina," Johnny said. "But I hope we learn the answer before we make a big mistake. Let's not worry about it. We need to follow what Dr. Jelana is doing."

"If only Dr. Jelana could keep the fossil in her belly button without it falling out," Cerafina said.

"Yes, she must be careful," Johnny said.

"Do you feel any pain?" Dr. Jelana asked Hakim.

"No," he said. "The injection worked."

"The fossil works," she whispered to herself.

"What did you say?" Hakim asked.

"I said, 'The shoulder needs work'," Dr. Jelana lied. "It needs to be reset."

"Then do it quickly," Hakim said.

Dr. Jelana stared intently at Hakim's shoulder. The duavisha gave her an improved perspective of his dislocated shoulder, as if she were looking at an exotic X-ray. With this precise knowledge in mind, Dr. Jelana quickly yanked on Hakim's arm and reset the shoulder perfectly. Hakim gasped as if expecting it to hurt, but it didn't. A sense of relief crossed his face, and he smiled. But his smile looked normal—no special colors that the duavisha should have given her. She reached for her navel and realized the duavisha was no longer there.

"Wait!" she said. "I dropped something!"

Dr. Jelana looked about the ledge and did not see the duavisha. She slipped into a light panic, almost a frenzy.

"The fossil! The fossil!" she blurted.

"Calm down," Hakim said. "Relax."

"I can't, I can't! I must find it! I must! I'll go crazy without it!"

Hakim stared at her in shock.

"I saw something fall from your blouse," he said. "It rolled over there. Yes, it's at the edge of the ledge. If I strafe my leg, I'll kick it off."

"DON'T MOVE!" she yelled.

Hakim froze in shock and surprise. He'd never seen the calm Dr. Jelana act like this. She crept to the ledge's edge and with the utmost care retrieved the duavisha. She clasped her fist tightly over the duavisha, kissed her fist, and whispered:

"I will not be so careless with you again."

Dr. Jelana placed the duavisha securely in her pocket and returned to her medical care of Hakim—completely relaxed as if nothing had happened.

"How do you feel? Is your arm better?" she said with the softest, most caring voice.

"Yes, my arm is wonderful. Thank you doctor," he said as he moved his arms about. "I feel much better now. If you will help me, we'll pull Quadri up together."

Dr. Jelana threw the free end of the rope down to Quadri. Quadri tied it under his arms, and the two above pulled on the rope until Quadri reached the lower ledge.

"I must rest again," Hakim said.

"The voices from the tunnel are strong," Quadri said.

"Yes," Dr. Jelana said. "We were just talking about that. This could be a shortcut to the kidnappers."

"Let's go!" Quadri said.

"Wait a moment," Hakim said. "Give me a moment to regain my strength and my rope."

Hakim wound up the rope and attached it to his belt. He removed the hook and pin from the rock crevice and returned it to a pouch.

"Let's charge up our *knijpkats*," Hakim said. "We'll want to approach quietly."

"I lost mine in the fall," Dr. Jelana said. "I'll have to use my battery-powered flashlight."

"Save your power and follow behind me," Quadri said. "I'll lead the way."

"And I'll follow from the back again," Hakim said.

"All right," Dr. Jelana said. "Hakim, are you ready?"

"Yes," he said.

"I'm ready too," Dr. Jelana said. "Let's go."

Quadri led the way. The three traveled through the tunnel, which was narrow and not very high. They ducked a bit to get through. There were no side chambers or openings—just a single tunnel. In perhaps five minutes, the three reached an opening partially blocked by fallen rocks. Fresh air and light poured in from the hole, and the voices were very strong. Quadri made a signal to Hakim, and the two placed their dyno torches in their pockets to conceal the light. They gathered close enough to the opening to hear and see but far enough back to avoid detection. They saw a wide expanse with buildings, machines, tables, and chairs. In an area close to them, rows of benches were laid out before a small stage. Young black women sat on benches with their hands tied behind their backs and their mouths gagged. White men guarded the women and the main tunnel openings. No guards stood by the three's opening, which was in fact elevated over the expanse. A white man with two companions stood at a podium and spoke into a microphone.

"You are the selected ones," said the white man with a New York accent. "And we have selected you for a growing list of elite jobs in the United States. We will provide passports and immigration papers. You will start in a variety of service sectors— cooking, cleaning, and waitressing—until you work your way up. There will be a small fee for your passage to the United States that you can work off."

"Do you see Kaila?" Dr. Jelana asked.

Hakim and Quadri panned the group of women.

"She is not there," said Quadri.

"This may be a different group of women," Hakim said.

"Or she may be somewhere else," Dr. Jelana said. "How do you plan to rescue her?"

Hakim and Quadri looked at each other and shrugged their shoulders.

"You mean you don't know?" Dr. Jelana asked. "I should have known. It's up to me to get things started."

"If we only knew where Kaila is," Quadri said.

Dr. Jelana placed the duavisha in her navel and whispered quietly, "Show me Kaila, show me Kaila, *feirsf nau Kaila.*"

The world became whites and grays, and from a small white building close to the benches, an aura of cerise and crimson radiated through the walls.

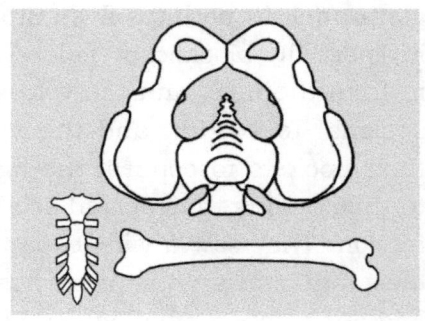

"She's in that building with the gray flag," Dr. Jelana said. "They're saying something to her, that they know she's an American, and that she'll be shipped to Lebanon instead of the United States. She wants to protest, but she's gagged. They're saying her travel party died, her family back home was murdered, and her only hope of returning to the United States is to work in Lebanon to pay her travel passage. All lies, of course."

"How do you know?" Hakim asked.

"You're using the fossil?" Quadri asked.

"Yes, I am," Dr. Jelana said.

"What fossil?" Hakim asked.

"No time to explain," Quadri said. "The building with the gray flag, you say? The flag with the face, beetle, and bone?"

"Face?" Dr. Jelana asked. "That's not a face, and that's not a beetle. The 'face' is an upside-down pelvis of a woman. And the 'beetle' is a sternum, or breast bone. The long bone is a femur, or thighbone."

"What does it mean?" Quadri asked.

"It's the flag of human traffickers," Hakim said.

"Yes, we know they're kidnappers," Quadri said.

"But the flag—the parts—these girls are to be sold into prostitution," Hakim said.

"Of course," Dr. Jelana said. "Each bone represents a point of sexual attraction on a woman—the hips, the chest, and the legs. I should have realized that immediately. We have to stop these traffickers here and now!"

"I have an idea," Hakim said.

"Finally!" Dr. Jelana said.

"We'll make bombs and throw them," Hakim said.

"And kill everyone—kidnappers and women," Quadri said. "That's a terrible plan."

"No wait," Dr Jelana said. "If we think of this as surgery..."

"What?" Quadri said. "There's no patient, and there's no knife."

"Just a moment, Quadri. The doctor has an interesting idea," Hakim said. "Go ahead, doctor. Explain."

"This group of women is our patient," Dr. Jelana said. "The kidnappers are the disease. We must kill the disease without killing the patient. Throwing bombs blindly is like poisoning the patient. But if we target the kidnappers specifically at very close range..."

"At point-blank range," Hakim said. "That would be ideal. I could make small deflagrants."

"De-what?" Quadri asked. "Are they bombs?"

"No," Dr. Jelana said. "Bombs put out a supersonic compression wave. Deflagrants are subsonic combustions—like fire, only I imagine you're not planning on building little torches."

"No. Fireworks," Hakim said.

"Combustion. You're going to box with the enemy!" Quadri said. "Now I understand."

"There are plenty of chemicals back in the chamber where you fell," Hakim said. "But there's one part that's tricky. I can make little rockets for our fireworks, but how will we get the correct aim? Rifle shooting would be easier."

"I'll handle the aim," Dr. Jelana said. "You make the fireworks. We'll need two very large fireworks on small rockets to get everyone's attention, and then we'll need maybe twenty little fireworks on rockets."

"I can't do it alone," Hakim said. "I'll need help. We need sulfur, charcoal, potassium nitrate, potassium perchlorate, and powdered aluminum."

"Most of those are in the chamber where I fell," Dr. Jelana said. "And the sulfur is in the prior chamber."

"Well what are we standing here for?" Quadri asked. "Let's go back to the chamber."

Dr. Jelana removed the duavisha and placed it in her pocket so she wouldn't lose it during the walk. The three journeyed back to the chamber where Dr. Jelana first fell. She stopped walking and placed the duavisha in her navel. With Dr. Jelana identifying raw chemicals, the three found most of what they were looking for. Quadri ventured farther back to the sulfur chamber, scraped some yellow sulfur from the walls, and returned.

"I have most of what I need," Hakim said. "But I still need aluminum and charcoal. And we have no paper! How can we roll up black powder if we have no paper?"

"What is the charcoal for?" Quadri asked.

"We need a propellant for the rockets," Hakim said. "Common black powder is made of two parts sulfur, three parts charcoal, and fifteen parts Salt of Petra or potassium nitrate."

"Salt of Petra?" Dr. Jelana said. "A chemical named after a woman?"

"And an explosive one at that," Hakim said.

"Are you saying women are explosive?" Dr. Jelana asked.

"I didn't give the name, someone else did," Hakim said.

Dr. Jelana laughed.

"I'm only pulling your leg," Dr. Jelana said.

"Can we use something in place of charcoal?" Quadri asked.

"What else do we have?" Hakim said.

"I have a few things in my purse," Dr. Jelana said. "But I don't have charcoal. I should—it's useful for treating poison ingestion. But I have other things—syringes, morphine, anesthesia, cotton swabs, sugar pills, and—"

"Sugar pills!" Hakim exclaimed.

"Why do you carry candy?" Quadri asked.

"It's not candy. It's glucose, for a diabetic who's taken too much insulin," Dr. Jelana said.

"Glucose! It's perfect! We can make sugar rockets out of your glucose pills and Salt of Petra," Hakim said. "And let me think—yes! Show me those cotton swabs."

Dr. Jelana passed a cotton swab to Hakim.

"Those are very long," Quadri said. "What kind of ears do you clean with those?"

"They aren't for ears; they're for taking throat cultures. Would you like me to demonstrate on you?" Dr. Jelana asked. "I guarantee the swab will make you gag."

"No thank you," Quadri said.

"Yes! It's hollow!" Hakim exclaimed. "How many swabs do you have?"

"About twenty, maybe more," Dr. Jelana said.

"Perfect! The cotton will be the fuse, the hollow stick will hold the rocket propellant, and the top of the stick will hold the payload. But we still need aluminum. I doubt we'll find any here. There's not a trace of aluminum or bauxite in these mountains," Hakim said.

"Is there a substitute for aluminum?" Quadri asked.

"If we had another metal," Hakim said.

"What about magnesium?" Dr. Jelana said. "There are pockets of magnesium all around us."

"There are?!" Hakim asked. "Magnesium is an excellent substitute. Show me!"

Dr. Jelana dug a little bit into a rock face and revealed a pocket of brittle magnesium.

"This needs grinding," Hakim said.

"I'll do that," Quadri replied.

"Be careful. Grind it—don't strike it," Hakim warned. "Doctor—if you would be so good as to grind up those sugar pills, I would appreciate it."

"I'll do that," Dr. Jelana said.

"Excellent," Hakim said.

"Here's the first batch of ground sugar," Dr. Jelana said.

"And the first batch of ground magnesium," Quadri said.

"Set it down there," Hakim said. "Good. Now the formula for the sugar propellant is three parts potassium nitrate to one part sugar."

Hakim mixed up the potassium nitrate into the sugar, created a funnel, removed the cotton from one end of a swab stick, and poured the mixture into the stick.

"We need something to hold the payload," Hakim said. "Do you have anything else in your purse? Little containers? Small pouches?"

"Just these rubber gloves," Dr. Jelana said.

"Excellent. We'll cut the fingers off those gloves and use them for the payload. Good. Now for the payload. I need three parts sulfur to six parts magnesium to sixteen parts potassium perchlorate," Hakim said.

Dr. Jelana found some floss and handed that to Hakim, who used it to tie the snipped glove to the swab stick. In this manner, the three produced twenty small rockets, each with a firework payload.

"We have extra magnesium," Quadri said.

"And I have extra sugar pills," Dr. Jelana said.

"Good. We can make your larger rockets," Hakim said. "But the swab sticks will be too small. Do you have any syringes left?"

"Yes," Dr. Jelana said. "I have two."

"I think we should make one rocket then," Hakim said. "Save the other syringe in case you need to treat a patient."

"I also have the metal container for the sugar pills," Dr. Jelana said.

"I'll take that," Hakim said. "I can make an emergency bomb with it."

"Emergency?" Quadri asked. "What kind of emergency?"

"If we are being attacked by the white men, I can use this to stop them," Hakim said. "Now—I'll pour the last of the sugar propellant into the syringe and place the last payload on top of it. Good. We'll use a swab stick as a tail."

Hakim completed assembling the syringe-based rocket. He tied the payload to the top of the syringe and a swab stick to the side.

"And for the bomb," Hakim continued, "I think three parts potassium perchlorate to one part magnesium should be enough."

Hakim mixed the ingredients into the sugar-pill bottle and closed the lid with a fuse trailing out.

"We now have twenty little rocket fireworks, one big one, and my emergency bomb," Hakim said.

"I want to name these," Dr. Jelana said. "The little ones I wish to name, 'Petra candy sticks', and the large firework I will call 'Petra lollipop'."

"What about the bomb?" Quadri asked.

"That can be a Petra jawbreaker," Dr. Jelana laughed.

"Very well," Hakim said. "We have twenty Petra candy sticks, one Petra lollipop, and a Petra jawbreaker. I understand how we will aim the Petra lollipop at the ceiling, but I don't understand how we will aim each Petra candy stick at the white men."

"I'll light the Petra lollipop to start things off. When I give the signal, we'll light the Petra candy sticks," Dr. Jelana said.

"And how will we aim them?" Quadri asked.

"Aim for the center of the opening," Dr. Jelana said. "I'll take care of the rest."

"The fossil?" Quadri asked.

"The fossil," Dr. Jelana said.

"I hope this works," Quadri said. "Things will turn ugly if it doesn't."

"I hope so too," Hakim said. "But we should be able to run back here without being caught. It will take them too long to reach us by the other tunnel. We can escape outside and return to my truck."

"I won't be returning to the truck unless Kaila is with me," Dr. Jelana said. "If you two want to bail out, so be it. I will carry on alone."

"Don't talk like that," Hakim said. "These are trained killers."

"Jelana is a stubborn woman," Quadri said.

"No, just determined," Dr. Jelana said.

"Then I also agree to return outside only if Kaila is with us," Quadri said.

"I can't let you two stay in here alone. I'm staying too," Hakim said.

"Good. It's settled then," Dr. Jelana said.

Dr. Jelana again removed the duavisha from her navel and placed it in her pocket for the walk back. The three carried their Petra sticks from the chamber to the opening where the kidnappers remained. The white man continued his long speech to the women prisoners.

"The United States is a great believer in equality and human rights. You will be treated with the utmost respect," the white kidnapper lied.

"I need to speak to my little Petras," Dr. Jelana said.

"A prayer?" Hakim asked.

"Not exactly," Dr. Jelana said. She placed her hands on the Petra sticks and whispered, "Petra lollipop to ceiling top, Petra lollipop to ceiling top, *Petra lolipop dir galnafautu daurp.* Petra candy sticks to white men's faces, Petra candy sticks to white men's faces, *Petra gutmorlu shneftyek dir yuarnu noshkingek thoirshyek.*"

Dr. Jelana looked at Hakim and Quadri. Hakim stared intently at the targets and appeared the same as ever. Quadri looked like a woman to Dr. Jelana, and she thought about what sort of evening gown would look best on him.

"Why are you looking at me like that?" Quadri asked.

"I was just thinking," Dr. Jelana said.

"About what?" Quadri asked.

"About what sort of evening gown and other women's clothes would look good on you," Dr. Jelana said.

"Can we do the transgender talk later?" Hakim asked. "Every minute we delay increases our chances of being discovered."

"Of course," Dr. Jelana said.

Dr. Jelana removed the duavisha from her navel and placed it in her pocket. She aimed the Petra lollipop rocket toward the ceiling above the kidnappers. She lit the fuse. The three waited. The rocket launched through the opening, went into the chamber, lifted up to the ceiling, and exploded with a loud bang! and fiery shower. The kidnappers appeared stunned for a moment but quickly grabbed their semi-automatic weapons. Some fired shots in the air to intimidate whatever enemy they could not see. Others looked around and prepared to fire at any suspicious movement.

"Get into the buildings," another group of kidnappers said to the women on the benches.

The women scurried from the benches toward the buildings.

"Now!" Dr. Jelana called.

Dr. Jelana, Quadri, and Hakim lit the Petra candy sticks. They zung through the air and chose individual white men for targets, exploding just as they reached each white man's face. The men cried out in pain. Each blast rendered them temporarily blind and deaf.

"It's working," Dr. Jelana said. "Launch them all!"

The three continued lighting Petra candy sticks. Those white men who had yet to be immobilized fired randomly about the chamber, sending bullets high into the rock face with a few landing through the opening where the three launched their candy sticks.

"Keep your head down," Hakim said. "They're throwing a counterpunch."

The three ducked. Several bullets whizzed by Cerafina and Johnny. One hit Jonara in the arm.

"Ow!" she called.

Another bullet hit her in the arm. She dropped the candleholder, and the three returned to Eva's hospital room. Eva swallowed the wine.

"How long was that?" Johnny asked Eva.

"You mean how long have I been swishing? About a minute," Eva said.

"It seemed like hours," Jonara said.

"Take a scan of your grandmother's thyroid," Johnny said to Jonara. "See if there's any change. Do not use the candleholder."

Jonara scanned Eva's thyroid.

"The left half has reattached itself to the right," Jonara said. "And the tumors are dissolving. It's like...like..."

"Like little Petra candy sticks are attacking them?" Johnny asked.

"Yeah! That's exactly what it's like. How did you know?" Jonara asked.

"Potassium perchlorate. It's used—" Johnny started.

"For treating hyperthyroidism," Eva said. "But there's no potassium perchlorate here."

"No, not here," Johnny said. "But back in the cave, yes. This is how the past works with these relics. The past influences the present. The fight against the kidnappers affects our fight with Mummy Eva's cancer."

"Then they must win for us to win," Cerafina said.

"Their victory would help us win," Johnny said. "Their loss would only make our road tougher, but their loss doesn't guarantee ours. The past influences the present, but it does not control it completely."

A nurse stepped into Eva's room with a wheelchair.

"Oh, you have visitors, Ms. Carreña," the nurse said. "I'm afraid the visit will be interrupted. You're due for a T-Ray exam, and I'm here to wheel you to radiology."

"What's a T-Ray?" Jonara asked.

"Cute child," the nurse said. "You must be Jonara, the inquisitive one. Your grandmother is very sick, but we'll treat her soon, and she'll be all right."

"We're treating her," Jonara said. "We're making her better. We do it with—"

Cerafina elbowed Jonara in the side.

"Ow!" Jonara cried.

"It's good to see you giving your grandmother emotional support," the nurse said. "But she needs more than that. We'll take good care of her. Come along, Eva."

Eva stepped out of bed and sat in the wheelchair. She waved goodbye as the nurse wheeled her and the IV bags away. Before the nurse exited Eva's room, he noticed the wine bottles.

"Is that wine?" the nurse asked.

"No," Johnny lied. "It's grape juice."

"I don't want a drunken patient," the nurse said. "This is a serious illness."

The nurse left.

"What's a T-Ray?" Jonara asked again.

"A T-Ray is a terahertz radiation image," Johnny said. "It's like an X-ray, but uses nonionizing radio waves below the visible spectrum—between infrared and microwave. It's a safe alternative to X-rays, and it's cheaper than an MRI. 'MRI' stands for—"

"Magnetic Resonance Imaging," Jonara said.

"Yes. How is it you know about MRIs but not T-Rays?" Johnny asked.

"I learned about X-rays and MRIs in history class, but the books must be too old for T-Rays," Jonara said.

"Hmm. I'm disappointed in your school," Johnny said.

"What about your grandmother?" Cerafina asked. "And the Margos? We can't just stay here and argue about T-Rays."

"We can't go back in time without Grandma Eva," Jonara said. "Isn't that right, Daddy?"

"We'll have to wait," Johnny said. "A T-Ray doesn't take long to process. Mummy Eva will be back soon."

And she was. The nurse wheeled Eva back to her room, repositioned the IV bags, and helped her into bed.

"Sorry for the delay, folks," the nurse said to Jonara, Cerafina, and Johnny. "The T-Ray machine gave us some strange results. We'll schedule you for an MRI soon."

The nurse left.

"What were the results?" Jonara asked Eva.

"The machine says I have almost no cancer," Eva said. "The nurse seems to think the machine is broken. How else does one explain the magical disappearance of cancer?"

"I can think of a zillion ways!" Jonara boasted.

"But will the cancer disappear completely?" Cerafina asked.

"I don't know," Eva said. "I don't know what to think any-more. I still hate these relics, Johnny Pindus, but if I am cured of cancer, maybe I can look the other way just this once."

"That's the Mummy Eva I know," Johnny bragged.

"How do we get rid of the last bit of cancer?" Jonara asked.

"We have to go back in time, don't we Mr. Pindus? To make sure the doctor and her friends finish the job," Cerafina said.

"Yes. The job must be completed," Johnny said. "Jonara—pick up your candleholder from the floor. Let's join together as we did before. Jonara—begin."

"Do I get more wine?" Eva asked with a grin.

"I'm surprised the nurse didn't smell your breath," Johnny said. "You best not have any more wine. You're loaded."

"That's the only reason I'm helping out," Eva said.

"We'll finish this without the wine," Johnny said to Eva. "Jonara—take us back with a Miramish chant."

Miramish	Translation
Moishiana, Lanudaku Thorithua,	Water Ruby, Candleholder,
Giaukioki opeifu fuifa	Fireworks of flight
Dhaku shetobiufa.	And smolder.
Goko rau mahilu	Take us now
Di Dzhelananga pauga,	To Jelana's cave,
Tolu Kaila Bakera	Where Kaila Baker
Dhai thoritho dho sheraipua.	Is held a slave.

The three travelers appeared in the chamber where the kid-nappers had been instructing the women. The kidnappers rolled on the floor in pain as they struggled to see and hear. Quadri launched the last Petra candy stick; it flew out a dozen yards and returned straight for Quadri. Quadri ducked, and the rocket landed below the opening, exploded, and opened up a coarse set of ledges usable as a stairway.

"Why did it come back?" Quadri asked.

"There were no more white men to attack," Dr. Jelana said. "But you have some white blood in you. The Petra stick decided you were the next best target."

"How is it the rest of the world says I'm black, but the Petra candy stick says I'm white?"

"Things look at what they want to see," Dr. Jelana said. "I'm sorry, Quadri. I forgot about your Italian father. Next time I'll—"

"There won't be a next time," Quadri said, "because we're getting out of here right now."

Dr. Jelana, Quadri, and Hakim descended from their opening, untied the women, and beckoned them to follow. Dr. Jelana ran straight for the building with the gray flag and released Kaila from her bindings.

"Jelana! Jelana!" Kaila cried as the two hugged. "What's happening? How did you get here? I'm so glad to see you."

"No time for small talk," Dr. Jelana said. "We have to leave here at once."

Dr. Jelana and Kaila joined up with Quadri and Hakim as the group ascended the newly created stair ledge up to the opening where the three had launched their Petra sticks. Dr. Jelana helped them from the bottom, Hakim from the middle, and Quadri at the top. In this way, the three were able to rescue about two hundred women or more. As the last women made their way up, a few of the kidnappers regained their sight, saw what was happening, and fired their semi-automatic guns toward the escapees.

"We must hurry!" Dr. Jelana yelled. She placed the duavisha in her navel and said, "Bullets must stray, bullets must stray, *deifatyek nirshke kodi floshsk.*"

Bullets from the kidnappers' weapons curved away from the escapees thus sparing them from harm. Dr. Jelana placed the duavisha back in her pocket and helped the last woman up to Hakim who in turn helped her up to Quadri.

"You next, doctor," Hakim said.

The kidnappers who had regained their vision realized the bullets were ineffective. They threw their weapons to the ground and charged the escape route.

"Hurry!" Hakim said. "They're running this way!"

Dr. Jelana climbed up to Quadri, who helped her to the tunnel. Hakim struggled next, Quadri pulled him up, but Quadri lost his footing on the ledge and began to fall with Hakim. Dr.

Jelana pulled at Quadri, but she too was being drawn over the edge—all while the kidnappers approached the stair ledge.

"Help me!" Dr. Jelana called.

Kaila rallied the women to help, and they all formed a human chain to pull Dr. Jelana, Quadri, and Hakim up the ledge and into the tunnel.

"We made it!" Quadri said as he and Hakim reached the tunnel.

"Not yet!" Dr. Jelana called. "The kidnappers are climbing the ledge!"

"Down the tunnel," Hakim yelled. "FAST!"

The escapees ran down the tunnel. Hakim lit the fuse to his emergency bomb and threw it at the opening, just as a kidnapper raised his head above the opening. The bomb exploded, the kidnapper fell down, and he in turn took the other kidnappers down with him. The blast sealed off the opening, shot air down the tunnel, and pushed the escapees along rather quickly. In fact, some slid along as the blast pushed them. The force dissipated just as the first group of women reached the lower ledge where Hakim had pulled up Quadri and Dr. Jelana from the pool.

"Stop!" yelled one of the women. "We can't go any farther."

Dr. Jelana squeezed past the line of women and made her way to the front.

"This way," she said, and she led them up to the main ledge out of the chamber (where she had previously fallen into the pool), through the short tunnel, across the natural bridge of potassium permanganate, down the path, back through the tunnel to the sulfuric acid chamber and across that natural bridge, and down the ledge to the cave's opening. It was dark outside, but Dr. Jelana had her battery-powered flashlight from her purse. She turned it on and led the party through the mountain paths until she reached Hakim's truck, which by now was surrounded by police cars.

"These women are in need of assistance!" she stated.

Several busses arrived and began loading the women. Hakim and Quadri ran up to her and stood for a moment, completely out of breath.

"I'll show you where the kidnappers are," Hakim said. "Quadri, this could take a while. Take the doctor and Kaila to your home. Use my truck. I'll get a ride back with the police."

"Thank you," Quadri said.

"And I thank you too," Dr. Jelana said.

Kaila walked up to Hakim and kissed him on the cheek.

"I thank you too," Kaila said.

"Say nothing to my wife about this, all right?" Hakim said, and he disappeared with one of the policemen.

The police continued loading the women onto the busses and prepared to take them to the hospital for examination.

"You too," a policeman said to Kaila.

"Please, sir," Dr. Jelana said. "Kaila is with us. She's been through a lot, and we'd like to go home."

"She must be checked out," the policeman said. "And her safety is at risk. There could be retaliation."

"I am a doctor and will tend to her medical needs," Dr. Jelana said.

"And I will vouch for her safety," Quadri said.

"Very well. We will visit you tomorrow morning," the policeman said.

"Why?" Dr. Jelana asked.

"To ensure your safe passage back home to America," the policeman said. "A consulate from the U.S. embassy will explain your options. Goodnight, folks."

"Our options?" Dr. Jelana asked Quadri.

"Something strange is going on," Quadri said. "We'll go back to my home now and get a good night's rest."

"And tomorrow?" Kaila asked.

"Tomorrow we'll find out what the consulate has to say," Dr. Jelana said.

1955 Mar 7, Mon. Asmara, Eritrea, Africa.

Early Monday morning, Quadri answered a knock at his front door. He welcomed a policeman and consulate from the U.S. Embassy.

"Come in, come in," Quadri said. "This is my mother, and this is Amiri Margo, Isha Margo, Jelana Margo, Kaila Baker, and baby Marcus Margo. Would you like something to drink?"

"No thank you," the two replied.

"Mr. Margo," the consulate said. "I'm afraid that in the interest of your party's safety and American security, we must insist you return to the United States immediately."

"But we're not finished here," Amiri said. "I came here on business to purchase African Wild Asses for my farm in Alabama."

"I'm sorry, Mr. Margo, but that's no longer possible. As long as you remain here in Eritrea, your life and those of your party are in grave danger. There are those who would avenge their compatriots' capture with the loss of your own lives. We cannot allow this. Try to understand. You must leave Eritrea today and return to the United States. And you cannot use your airline tickets. You must return on a military cargo plane."

"What? I paid thousands of dollars for those tickets," Amiri said.

"You will be reimbursed," the consulate said. "We'll work with you regarding your donkey purchase."

"It's not a donkey, it's the African Wild Ass," Amiri said.

"Consulate," Quadri asked. "Could you make room for one more person?"

"Is this a proposal?" Dr. Jelana asked.

"We could marry on the cargo plane by the ship's captain," Quadri said. "Jelana—will you marry me?"

"Oh!" Kaila said in excitement. "Quadri proposed to you! Say yes, say yes!"

"I thought *you* liked him," Dr. Jelana said.

"I thought I did. But I like Justino better," Kaila said.

"Then you better tell him when we land in Lisbon," Dr. Jelana said.

"There will be no landing in Lisbon," the consulate said, "and no room for non-Americans on the cargo plane."

"But once Jelana and I marry, you must take me along to America," Quadri said.

"No marriage can be performed by a ship's captain—that's an old legend. I'm sorry, Mr. Dakari, but you can't go on the cargo plane."

"We could marry here in Asmara," Quadri said. "I know a nice Sunni Mosque just down the road where we can marry. Bring your family. Kaila can be your maid of honor; Hakim can be my best man."

"Nothing like pressure to excite the occasion," Dr. Jelana said. "Pappa?"

"You're a grown woman," Amiri said. "You must make your own decision."

"Mamma?" Dr. Jelana asked.

"It is short notice. Do you love Quadri?" Isha asked.

Dr. Jelana looked at Quadri and thought about that young boxer who spoke of his profession as combustion, who risked his life for Kaila's and the other women, and how the duavisha gave her a feeling of affection for him and no one else.

"Yes, I do," she said as she hugged and kissed Quadri.

"The cargo plane leaves at one o'clock this afternoon," the consulate said. "You must be married by then for Quadri to be allowed on the cargo plane."

"We will," Quadri said. "We will."

Later, at Noon.

Dr. Jelana and Quadri ran out of the mosque while onlookers cheered them on. They were married—in the Sunni faith, under the civil authority of the U.S. consulate, and under Eritrea law.

"We are now married under Allah, Eritrea, and America," Quadri asked. "How does it feel to be Mrs. Quadri Dakari?"

"I think I'd much rather be called Dr. Jelana Margo Dakari," she said.

The two kissed and hugged.

"It's time you get going," Hakim said. "I'll take you to the airport."

Quadri said farewell to his mother. He hugged her again and again, but she didn't want to let go.

"I will write often," he said. "Once we are settled, I will send for you."

"I will take good care of her," Hakim said. "I *am* sorry about one thing—I'm losing a great boxer."

"Then you must come to America and watch me fight," Quadri said. "You're always welcome in our home."

"Goodbye!" Dr. Jelana called to the people.

"Goodbye!" Amiri and Isha also called to the people.

"Bye, y'all!" Kaila said.

Hakim took the Margo party to the airport.

"Did the consulate say where to go?" Hakim asked.

"Yes. There's a Boeing C-97 Stratofreighter at the military terminal," Quadri said. "That's our flight."

Hakim said goodbye as Amiri, Isha, Dr. Jelana, Kaila, and Marcus boarded the C-97 with Quadri delaying his boarding shortly.

"Write when you can," Hakim said. "I'll keep you updated on things here and your mother's health."

"Thank you, Hakim. You are an excellent trainer and friend. Goodbye, then," Quadri said.

The two exchanged handshakes followed by hugs. Quadri ascended the steps to the C-97, and he gave one last wave of his hand to Hakim before disappearing into the plane.

"Hurry, Daddy!" Jonara said. "We gotta catch that plane!"

Jonara, Cerafina, and Johnny ran up the steps to the C-97 and entered. They sat behind the Margo party. After a brief wait, the C-97 taxied on the runway, accelerated, and flew into the sky. It flew a nonstop route to Aviano Air Base in Italy, flying 2600 miles in eight hours and forty minutes. It landed late in the evening, giving the Margo party a short time to eat dinner before retiring in a military hotel under the watch of the U.S. Air Force. Dr. Jelana had terrible dreams—that another woman had killed her husband and stolen Marcus. She awoke in a cold sweat, but she felt Quadri sleeping next to her and fell asleep in comfort.

"The woman in Dr. Jelana's dream," Jonara said.

"It was Nekara the Red," Cerafina said.

"Will we see her again?" Jonara asked.

"I hope not," Johnny said. "My heart says we will, or at least some of us will."

1955 Mar 8, Tue. Aviano Air Field, Italy.

The Margo party arose at 5 am, cleaned up, ate breakfast, and boarded another C-97 cargo plane. The C-97 took off at 7 am, traveled 2060 miles for nearly seven hours, and landed at Lajes Field in the Azores. It stopped long enough to refuel, exchange some cargo, and pick up new passengers. It took off from Lajes Field and flew nonstop over the Atlantic Ocean for 3240 miles in eleven hours. The plane landed at Maxwell Air Force Base Tuesday evening in Montgomery, Alabama, but the party felt they had landed early Wednesday morning.

"Jet lag," Amiri said. "We came back too fast. It will take a few days to adjust."

The Margo party exited the C-97 and descended the steps to the runway.

"MacNessi," a military person called. "Escort the Margo party to the military hotel tonight. Tomorrow morning, take them wherever they wish to go."

"Yes, sir," Jane said. She turned to the Margo family and said, "My name is Miss Jane MacNessi. You may call me Jane. I've been informed of your situation and am at your service to make you as comfortable as possible for your stay with us tonight."

"If you could just drive us to the hotel," Isha said, "we'd be grateful. We're very tired from jet lag."

"I understand," Jane said. "If you'll all hop aboard the van, I'll take you to your rooms."

Jane assisted the Margo party with their luggage, and once all were aboard, she drove them toward the military hotel.

"You have an accent," Kaila said to Jane. "Where are you from?"

"Kenosha, Wisconsin," Jane said.

"I knew you were a Yankee," Kaila said. "What do you think of Alabama?"

"It's nice in the winter," Jane said. "There's almost no snow. But it's hot in the summer. How can you stand the heat?"

"Iced tea," Kaila said. "Lots of iced tea."

"Are you military?" Dr. Jelana asked.

"Yes," Jane said. "I'm part of the Air Force, but I can't fly. I keep applying for admission to Air University, but I get rejected because I'm a woman. I hope to be a pilot someday. Who knows if I'll get through? I thought I would be a dentist when I lived in Wisconsin, but that fell through."

"My name is Jelana Margo Dakari. I just married my husband, Quadri, and I'm a doctor of obstetrics and gynecology. I'm here to say you should never give up on a dream. If you want to be a dentist, pursue it. If you want to be a pilot, soar for the stars. Don't let anyone stop you. There's more than one way to skin a cat. Learning to fly comes in many forms. Civilian flying schools, for example."

"Thank you," Jane said. "That's good advice."

"Is it true what they say about airmen switching places on the Montgomery city buses?" Isha asked.

"Switching places?" Jane asked.

"Yeah. The white airmen sit in back while the black airmen sit in front," Isha said.

"Yes, I heard that rumor. It's true. They did it more than once, too. Created quite a stir with the City of Montgomery and the State of Alabama. It's like the airmen are poking fun at segregation," Jane said.

"I do not understand," Quadri said. "The way we were treated on the cargo plane—there was no special segregation."

"Yeah," Kaila said. "Some parts of the world are backward, some are not. Montgomery happens to be one of the backward places."

"It's so hard to believe," Quadri said. "People struggle just to survive in Eritrea, especially in the desert. But here in the United States, there is opportunity everywhere for a happy life."

"Only if you're white, Christian, and male," Kaila joked.

"That's enough, Kaila," Dr. Jelana said. "The days of black slavery are over."

"But segregation is alive and well," Kaila said. "It's been how many years since Abraham Lincoln liberated the South?"

"Too many," Isha said. "And there's no excuse for it."

"We should protest," Quadri said. "We should sit on different parts of the bus, just like the airmen."

"And get yourself lynched," Amiri said. "That's what happened to our next-door neighbors."

"It doesn't have to be an explosion," Quadri said. "We can throw punches here and there, wearing down the opponent until he can no longer punch back."

"That's been the strategy since Lincoln," Amiri said. "It only works so well, like sanctions or an embargo. But it builds up tension, like water backing up behind a dam. We need to put a crack in that dam and make it burst. Then things will change, and fast."

"Combustion?" Quadri asked Dr. Jelana.

"Sometimes combustion is not enough," Dr. Jelana said.

Jane finished the drive to the military hotel.

"Here we are," Jane said. "If you need anything, ring the operator for room service. For other emergencies, ask for Ms. MacNessi—that's me. I can be over in five minutes. Let me help you with your luggage."

Jane helped unload the Margo party's bags.

"Thank you very much for helping us," Isha said.

"It's nothing," Jane said.

"Oh but it is," Isha said. "To you this is ordinary service, but once we leave this military hotel and return to the ways of Montgomery, it's back to the out-of-balance southern culture. You're from Wisconsin you say?"

"Yes," Jane said.

"You don't wear white-colored glasses like the southern white folk around here," Isha said. "You're a good person. Remember that."

"Thank you," Jane said. "Goodnight, friends."

"Goodnight," the Margo party called back.

1955 Dec 1, Thu. Montgomery, Alabama.

"Thank you for coming over to my home, Jane," Dr. Jelana said. "My ankles are terribly swollen. Did you get the papers from the hospital?"

"Yes," Jane said. "Here's the package of papers. And I'm happy to deliver it. You saved my life when you removed my ovarian cancer in August."

"Regular checkups," Dr. Jelana said. "That's the key. And avoid any further exposure to radiation."

"You look like you've dropped," Jane said, "But you aren't due for another two weeks."

"This baby is in a hurry to enter the world," Dr. Jelana said. "And I'll be happy when it does. Now I can appreciate the endurance my patients go through when carrying a baby to term. I have stretch marks, and my back is killing me."

"Maybe you should rest more. The papers can wait," Jane said.

"Doctors make the worst patients," Dr. Jelana said. "You're right, I should rest. But these lab reports won't wait, and each day of delay means a greater chance my patients could develop untreatable cancer. I'm a slave to my profession. Well, I suppose there are worse vices."

"Well, while I'm here," Jane said, "I think you should take a break."

"All right. Would you like something to drink?" Dr. Jelana asked. "I have coffee, juice, and biscuits."

"That would be great," Jane said. "No, don't get up. I'll get them."

"What made you think I'd get them?" Dr. Jelana asked.

"You're obsessed with work," Jane said. "I've learned that much about you in the short eight-and-a-half months I've known you."

Jane left Dr. Jelana and Quadri's living room for the kitchen where she prepared coffee, juice, and biscuits. She returned to the living room to find Dr. Jelana standing by the radio.

"I thought a little music would brighten up the day," Dr. Jelana said. "There's something stirring in the air in Montgomery today, I can feel it."

Dr. Jelana turned on the radio and tuned it to a Montgomery station playing swing jazz music.

"This is one of my favorites," Dr. Jelana said. "It's called, 'Southland.' This particular version is performed by Hod Williams and his orchestra. What do you think?"

"It's very dramatic," Jane said.

The two sat down to their coffee, juice, and biscuits.

"So how is Quadri feeling today?" Jane said. "He didn't look too good after being knocked out last night."

"He'll recover," Dr. Jelana said. "I think his ego is hurt more than anything. Ow!"

"What happened?"

"A sharp pain. It was a contraction," Dr. Jelana said. "What time is it?"

"It's 5:30 pm," Jane said.

"Half an hour," Dr. Jelana said. "Same as the last. I'm in labor, but I'm not ready to go to the hospital. Quadri should be home in time to take me."

"Is he up to it? I mean with the concussion and all," Jane asked.

"He was out of it last night after the fight. Today, he went in for training. He's a little groggy but otherwise feeling much better. Boxing in America is more rigorous than he imagined. He doesn't win as easily as he did in Asmara," Dr. Jelana said. "But he gets tired of riding in the back of the bus so white folk can sit in the front. A proud boxing champ like Quadri being forced to get up and move every time the driver moves the 'Colored' sign another two rows back—it's just killing him."

"Have you two picked a name for the baby?" Jane asked.

"Not quite. We've discussed it. Argued about it. If a boy, Quadri wants to name him Benito Dakari," Dr. Jelana said.

"That's horrible," Jane said.

"I joked that we might as well call him Adolph," Dr. Jelana said, "or Dixiecrat Dakari. Quadri actually liked the name, 'Dixiecrat,' until I explained what it stood for. He said he still likes it, and that made me angry, so I said we're not having a boy."

"But you can't choose whether you have a boy or girl," Jane said.

"We'll see," Dr. Jelana said.

"What about a girl's name? Have you picked any?"

"Quadri wants to call her, 'Asmara,' after his hometown. That's not bad," Dr. Jelana said.

"And you?" Jane asked.

"I was thinking of, 'Shalana,' a combination of my mother's name—Isha—and my name—Jelana," Dr. Jelana said. "Ow!"

"Another contraction?" Jane asked.

"What else?" Dr. Jelana said. "But it came too quickly. It's only 5:45 pm. That's fifteen minutes since the last one. I should get my hospital bag. I'll just—"

"Don't get up," Jane said. "I'll get it for you."

"It's in the bedroom," Dr. Jelana said. "Thank you, Jane."

Jane walked into Dr. Jelana's bedroom and found the hospital bag neatly packed on the bed. Curious, she opened the bag and looked at the contents: undergarments, maternity clothes, pads, towels, ear plugs, a wash bag, and sponges. Seeing the contents of Dr. Jelana's bag reminded her of when she packed her own bag before having Roberta. Jane cried a little bit out of sadness, but she muffled her cry so Dr. Jelana wouldn't hear. It was a bittersweet moment—the magic of bringing Roberta into the world and the realization that her little girl of ten years old was growing up fast and would soon leave her.

"Here's your bag," Jane said as she carried it into the living room.

"Jane? Have you been crying?" Dr. Jelana asked.

"I tried to cover it," Jane said.

"Give me a hug," Dr. Jelana said.

"Just a little one," Jane said, and she gave a little hug to Dr. Jelana.

"Having a baby is an emotional moment," Dr. Jelana said. "You were thinking about your daughter, weren't you?"

"Yes, I was," Jane said.

Several songs had played on the radio. The radio personality announced the next song as, "Oh Lady Be Good," sung by Kay Margo and performed by the Frankie Reynolds band.

"Quadri should be home by now," Dr. Jelana said. "I told him to come home early today. What's taking him so long? Ow! This contraction isn't letting go. It's a big one!"

"It's five of six," Jane said. "We have to go now!"

The two left the Dakari apartment and walked the short distance to the bus stop. Bus number 2857 stopped and picked them up. The women entered and paid their fare.

"Nuh, uh. Colored must enter through the back door," the driver said, referring to Dr. Jelana. "You can move along," he said, referring to Jane.

"I'll be fine," Dr. Jelana said.

She exited the bus through the front door and made for the back. The driver grew a wicked smile on his face, closed the front door abruptly, and rolled the bus along without opening the back.

"What are you doing?" Jane said.

"Go sit down," the driver ordered.

Jane pretended to trip and fall. As she did so, she opened the front and back door, rolled down the steps, and landed hanging partway out of the door. The driver stopped and pulled her to her feet.

"I said sit down!" he said. "This is no place for a woman!"

Jane pretended to thank the driver, and as she walked down the aisle, she noticed Dr. Jelana had boarded and sat down near the back of the bus.

"There's something familiar about what just happened," Johnny said.

"What?" Jonara asked.

"Something about having to exit the front of the bus and getting left behind," Johnny said.

"Who was it? When did it happen?" Jonara asked.

"I can't remember," Johnny said. "I'll think of it in a moment."

"Let's sit up front," Jane said as she reunited with Dr. Jelana.

"I can't sit with you in the white section," Dr. Jelana said. "These buses are segregated. And I'm in a bad position to protest."

"Then I'll sit with you back here," Jane said. "We can still move up to that damn 'Colored' sign."

"We shouldn't sit in the first few rows of the colored section," Dr. Jelana said. "They're poisoned. Could be converted into white seats. Let's stay back here. Besides, with you being white and sitting in the colored section, we want to attract as little attention as possible. I don't want my baby born in a jail cell."

The two sat far back in the bus. The first rows of the colored section remained empty for only a few more seconds. Dr. Jelana and Jane watched as a young woman of forty-two years old wearing glasses sat in the first row of the colored section. Other black people filled the first rows. The bus made several more stops, and the bus continued to fill normally.

"Daddy!" Jonara said. "The woman with the glasses in the first row of the colored section!"

"Yes," Johnny said. "That's Rosa Parks."

"Is this the bus? Is this the day?" Jonara asked.

"Yes it is," Johnny said.

"Most of the white people on this bus are men," Jane said. "But there are men and women in the colored section."

"That's because white women are expected to stay confined at home all day," Dr. Jelana said. "But black women are expected to go out and work in menial jobs."

"That sounds familiar. Someone else said the same thing," Jonara said.

"Kaila did on the riverboat in Italy," Cerafina said.

"You have a good memory, Cerafina," Johnny said.

"It's crazy," Jonara said. "What a whacked-out world!"

"It's hard to understand, yes," Johnny said.

More white people entered the bus, and the white section filled. On seeing this, the bus driver walked to the "Colored" sign and moved it back several rows.

"Y'all better make it light on yourselves and let me have those seats," the driver said to the occupants, including Rosa Parks.

The occupants initially refused, but they eventually stood up and moved, with the exception of Rosa.

"This is it," Johnny said. "This is the Genesis."

"She's not getting up," Jane said.

"Good for her," Dr. Jelana said. "Ow! Another contraction."

The driver contacted police. The bus remained stopped while he waited for the police to arrive.

"We can't wait on the bus," Dr. Jelana said. "This will end our bus ride. We must get up and walk the rest of the way. It's only two more blocks. Come on, Jane, let's walk."

Dr. Jelana and Jane exited the bus through the back door. The police arrested Rosa and took her to the police station.

"Now I remember," Johnny said. "In 1943, Rosa entered this driver's bus through the front door. He told her to exit and enter through the back. She exited, and he drove off then too. Rosa missed the bus and walked home in the rain."

"Bastard," Jonara said.

Dr. Jelana and Jane entered the hospital. A nurse placed Dr. Jelana in a wheelchair and took her to a prep room. But there wasn't much time. Dr. Jelana was prepped quickly and wheeled to the delivery room. Jane was not allowed to accompany her but was instead restricted to a waiting room.

"I'm being segregated from Dr. Jelana," Jane said.

Dr. Jelana's labor was fairly quick but quite painful. She refused any sort of pain medication, vowing to keep her baby drug-free from the start. But the pain took a toll on Dr. Jelana. She became slightly delirious, thinking she was back in the caves in Eritrea fighting white kidnappers. But in all of this, a song kept running through her head over and over. It was the last song she heard on the radio before leaving for the hospital,

"Oh Lady Be Good." Dr. Jelana sang the song over and over in between screams of pain. When her daughter was finally born, the doctor asked what the baby's name should be. Dr. Jelana could only think of the song and the vocalist, and in her delirium, she shouted, "Kay Margo."

"Kay Margo Dakari?" the doctor asked.

"Kay Margo Dakari," Dr. Jelana repeated without thought.

Then Dr. Jelana fell asleep and did not wake until the next day. In the following days, Dr. Jelana made a healthy recovery. Quadri was initially angry that his daughter was not named after Asmara, but his new daughter's smile filled him with warmth, and he forgot his name preference and proudly called his daughter Kay Margo Dakari.

The months passed by. Rosa Park's refusal to give up her seat triggered the Montgomery Bus Boycott—an avalanche in the Civil Rights Movement. Dr. Jelana, Quadri, Kaila, and Jane joined together and walked, carpooled, and took taxis of boycott supporters throughout the end of 1955 and most of 1956. Jane visited the Dakaris frequently, bringing ten-year-old Roberta along. Roberta enjoyed playing with baby Kay and toddler Marcus, although Marcus started an unfortunate bad habit of biting people when he didn't get his way. By now, Dr. Jelana had stopped giving him xanthotoxin, and his dark skin vanished in favor of his natural white skin. The Dakaris and Jane often went out on picnics. Sometimes when people asked who was Marcus's parents, Jane would lie and say she was the mother to minimize ugly stares from white strangers. Jane brought Dr. Jelana and Kaila to Montgomery ISIS meetings that Alina hosted, and Dr. Jelana found a psychiatry job for Alina at the hospital.

The Montgomery Bus Boycott ended December 20, 1956. The U.S. Supreme Court declared Montgomery's and Alabama's segregation bus laws unconstitutional. Rosa Parks became the "Mother of the Civil Rights Movement." And for the first time, Dr. Jelana and her family felt real hope for the recognition of equal rights to all Americans. Dr. Jelana had a few more nightmares of Nekara the Red, but she stopped using the duavisha, and her nightmares faded.

Jonara, Cerafina, and Johnny returned to Eva's room. Eva was no longer there.

"Where's Grandma?" Jonara asked.

"They must have taken her away while we were traveling back in time," Johnny said.

"I think I heard something about being time for an MRI," Cerafina said. "But I'm not sure when that was."

"Is that the end?" Jonara said. "Of the Margos, I mean."

"For the moment," Johnny said. "No story is ever completely finished. But I will say this—Kay Margo Dakari worked with your grandmother at the Page Street Clinic."

"What about Jane and Roberta?" Cerafina asked.

"I'm not sure about Jane, but Roberta has an interesting life ahead of her. I'm sure we'll hear more of her," Johnny said.

"Good news!" Eva said as she walked in.

"You're not in a wheelchair!" Jonara said. "Can I hug you?"

"You can hug me forever and ever!" Eva smiled. "I'm free of cancer!"

"Hooray!" Cerafina cheered.

"That's wonderful news!" Johnny said.

"The radiologist took my MRI, and no cancer, a healthy thyroid, and...well...I'm free to go home."

"The MRI didn't tell the last part," Johnny said.

"No, but the doctor did," Eva said. "Let's go. I'm starved! I could eat a horse!"

CHAPTER 14:

Spiritual Divide

2023 Oct 5, Thu Noon. Geneva's House. Corpus Christi, Texas.

"Anna," Eva said. "Come with us. We're going out to eat."

"I prepare little lunch if you like," Anna said. "I have sandwich meat and bread in refrigerator."

"No sandwiches," Eva said. "We're celebrating. I beat the big C."

"Oh bless you, Miss Eva, bless you!" Anna said.

Eva, Johnny, Jonara, Cerafina, and Anna went out to a barbeque restaurant.

"I'll have a full rack of barbeque pork ribs," Eva said, "with coffee. And a bottle of red wine, let's see, it should be a fruity Grenache."

The others ordered soup and sandwiches of a sort. No one had near the amount of food Eva ordered.

"That's huge!" Jonara said. "Can you eat it all!?"

"Yes, and you can't have any!" Eva laughed.

Eva finished eating before anyone else in the party. A live musician with a guitar performed while customers ate.

"Listen!" Eva said. "Do you hear that song?"

"It sounds like a Spanish song," Johnny said. "From Andalusia, if I'm not mistaken."

"It's *Asturias Leyenda*," Eva said. "I used to dance to this as a child. I'm so happy, I could dance now."

"Please don't embarrass us," Jonara said.

"Oh hush, child!" Eva said.

Eva stood up in the restaurant and began a flamenco dance to the song. Excited by Eva's initiative, Anna also stood up and joined Eva in dance. Neither had castanets, so to improvise, they tapped their feet for every moment they would have clicked with castanets. This resulted in much tapping, but Eva and Anna worked it into leg movements, side steps, and twirls. They clapped their hands to the rhythm at times and at other times stretched and lifted their arms as if carving the air for dancing. The restaurant patrons noticed them, appreciated their dance, and clapped in rhythm. The vibrations from Eva's and Anna's heels carried through the floor and triggered the Moissan Ruby and candleholder into action, sending Jonara, Cerafina, and Johnny back in time.

2007 Feb 14, Wed. Whalejet, Elrod 402. Portland, Oregon.

"What happened?" Jonara asked.

"We went back in time to the Elrod 402," Johnny said.

"But how?" Jonara asked. "The Water Ruby doesn't take me back in time, it only scans. And we're not scanning Grandma Eva anymore."

"But her dancing triggered this event," Johnny said. "Did you feel anything unusual with the candleholder?"

"It vibrated," Jonara said.

"The candleholder sent us back in time?" Cerafina asked.

"Yes, in a way," Johnny said. "The Moissan Ruby scanned Mummy Eva's dancing and linked with the candleholder. Using this link with the Moissan Ruby, the candleholder projected us back in time to this moment where I visited your mother, Jonara."

"Happy Valentine's Day!" Johnny the younger said as he met Evanita in the visitors' room of the Elrod 402 detention center.

"Johnny," Evanita said. "You're here. You brought me roses."

Evanita greeted Johnny with a flat, nonemotional tone. Her limb movements were uncoordinated and jerky, and her skin was pale.

"We're in the rose capital of the world," Johnny said. "And you deserve the best."

"They are the best," Evanita said.

Evanita hugged and kissed Johnny. Johnny immediately realized Evanita was on medication. She felt like a robot.

"Ms. Haughf is working very hard at getting you out of here," Johnny said. "Hang tough for a few more months."

"Johnny," Evanita said. "Do you love me?"

"Of course I love you!" he said. "I brought you flowers, didn't I?"

"Yes, and they look beautiful, from what I know about roses," Evanita said.

"But not as beautiful as you," Johnny said.

"Are you just saying that to make me feel better?" Evanita asked.

"No, of course not. What's wrong?" Johnny asked.

"Hug me again," Evanita said.

The younger Johnny hugged Evanita and held her tight.

"I wish I could remember what a hug is supposed to feel like," Evanita said. "Johnny—you're one of my few escapes from this detention hell. And I don't feel right, Johnny. I'm not the nice, clean girl you used to know. I feel impure."

"What are you talking about?" Johnny the younger asked.

"Take your stone," Evanita said. "Use it to read me."

Johnny the younger took the Moissan Ruby, placed it around his neck, hugged Evanita, and trembled.

"Keep your Moissan Ruby behind you," Johnny the older instructed Jonara. "We don't want bad feedback with the other Moissan Ruby."

Jonara placed her Moissan Ruby behind her. Johnny the younger scanned Evanita, and his happy expression sobered up.

"They have you on two drugs—chlordiazepoxide, trade name Librium, and carbamazepine which could be Tegretol, Epitol, Carbatrol, Equetro—"

"It's Tegretol," Evanita said.

"The first is a sedative, the second a mood stabilizer," Johnny said.

"Then I'm a druggy," Evanita said.

"No, of course not," Johnny said.

"My body doesn't know the difference. I could have gotten these off the street for all it knows. I'm a druggy," Evanita said. "I want to cry. The drugs won't let me cry. They won't let me be happy. They won't let me channel my anger. I can't be angry. I can't be anything. I feel dead inside, Johnny, just moving from one room to another. I'm dead."

"Hang on," Johnny said.

"What happens when I get out of here?" Evanita asked. "What happens when I go off the drugs? Will I be able to go off the drugs?"

Johnny the younger looked Evanita directly in the eyes.

"You'll be able to," Johnny said. "But there will be withdrawal symptoms. Going off chlordiazepoxide means anxiety attacks, especially at night. It means the shakes and possibly increased depression. Lack of sleep for sure."

"And the other one?" Evanita asked.

"You could get rebound mania," Johnny said, "and you could go into seizures."

"That sounds bad. It doesn't feel bad because I can't feel how bad it is," Evanita said. "But it sounds bad."

"It won't be easy. But I'll help as much as I can," Johnny said.

"Johnny? Is there a God?" Evanita asked.

"Good Lord, what kind of question is that?" Johnny asked.

"A simple one. A question people have asked since the beginning," Evanita said.

"In the beginning, there was nothing. God said, 'Let there be light.' And there was light," Johnny said.

"That's from Genesis, I know," Evanita said. "Someone wrote that down. Someone made up those words."

"But they have some relevance, don't you think?" Johnny asked.

"Do they? They're part of an Abrahamic religion," Evanita said. "To follow them is to follow Judaism, Christianity, or Islam. But this excludes other religions and other views."

"You sound like a logician," Johnny said. "When did you start thinking like this?"

"When they put me on the drugs," Evanita said. "Before the drugs, I would look at someone, and I would feel a connection to a kindred spirit. Now when I look at someone, they're nothing more than a biochemical machine with working parts. Even their psyche is something governed by their brain and metabolism. I see no souls in people, Johnny. They're all machines to me. Machines!"

"But we're not," Johnny said.

"Deep down I know that, but only because I learned it before I went on the drugs. I keep wondering—if I'd always been on these drugs, would I have ever believed in God? Would I have ever believed in souls?"

"Probably not," Johnny conceded.

"Something else. People who believe in God now seem to be whack-jobs. I can reason through every superstitious or emotional element of their belief system. It all looks completely flawed to me," Evanita explained. "I never dared to think like this before the drugs."

"The drugs are creating a wall between you and humanity," Johnny said.

"You're right. It is like a wall. Because now that I've reasoned people are only biochemical machines, I too am just a biochemical machine. And never have I felt so alone."

"So you do have some feelings," Johnny said.

"It's the only one I have left—loneliness—like I'm one person in the vast universe, and life itself has not been invented."

"Then you are the 'nothing' before God created light," Johnny said.

"Another thing. People say, 'God,' but what can that mean? Really? Is he an old man with a beard?" Evanita asked. "That's absurd."

"It's a primitive caricature," Johnny said.

"Is God a man or woman? Singular or plural?" Evanita asked.

"Both. Neither. Specialness," Johnny replied.

"I know what God is. God is a magical wildcard used as a catch-all when human intelligence cannot reach understanding," Evanita explained.

"Who told you that?" Johnny asked.

"No one. I reasoned it out. I never could before. But the drugs—they've done something to me. I can see this new line of reasoning. And it's perfectly believable, more believable than a God or religion," Evanita said.

"That's always the danger sign," Johnny said. "Does your reasoning say that the drugs have affected your reasoning?"

"Logically speaking, yes," Evanita said. "I know they have. But who's to say if the drugs let me see things clearly or have simply blocked off what I believed before."

"I would say they have blocked it off," Johnny said. "Your emotions are stuffed in a box somewhere. You know they exist because you remember having them."

"But they could be gone forever," Evanita said. "That's what I see right now. Because I never had this sense of logic before. Now I have it. Even if I go off the drugs, I may carry this logical reasoning with me. It could supersede what I felt before."

"Yes, it could," Johnny said. "If you allow it."

"Are you religious, Johnny? Do you really believe in God?" Evanita asked.

"You know I'm a Baptist," Johnny said. "There are two beliefs I hold dear—I believe in God, and I believe in the words of John 3:16, that belief in Jesus will give me everlasting life."

"Literally?" Evanita asked.

"Of course not literally," Johnny said.

"There, you see? You've deviated. Religion is a collection of deviations and deceits," Evanita said.

"Not everlasting mortal life. Everlasting immortal life. But why do you call religion a deceit? Is this more 'rational' reasoning?" Johnny asked.

"Yes," Evanita replied.

"God isn't literal," Johnny said. "Never was. There's no singular or plural to God."

"How do you know? What evidence do you have?" Evanita asked.

"Evidence-based support is something used in science and research papers," Johnny said. "Keep this in mind—careful choice of evidence can be submitted to support almost any concept one wishes to advance."

"Isn't that what religion does? Isn't that what you're doing now? Giving testimony to advance religion on me?" Evanita asked.

"You almost sound paranoid," Johnny said. "I didn't think that was a side effect of your medication. But maybe paranoia is a side effect of hard-core logical reasoning. I never thought of it that way."

"What about the evidence of God? Where is it?" Evanita asked.

"Some say it's all around us, that you simply have to open your eyes. Trees, birds, clouds, the sunrise—these are all—"

"Biochemical and chemical machines," Evanita said.

"So you believe," Johnny said. "But think of this—water is not singular or plural, is it? Oh sure, there are the waterways of the world. But if you add one part water to another part water, do you have two waters? No, you have water. The same with air. Water and air—they permeate, they exist, they flow. Energy too. Water, air, energy, God. Do you see the progression? When you get up to the God level, odd technicalities like singular or plural don't make much sense, do they? Yet singular and plural are absolutes for a straight, logical-reasoning biochemical machine. Absolutes are walls. The drugs in your body have created those walls. The walls can be brought down in your body. Others are not so lucky. And that's the best I can do to explain about God. I believe Jesus gives me everlasting life in a metaphorical sense for my time here on Earth and possibly more. It's good not to expect too much. But after I die, who knows? I do have a sense of spirits in people, but I don't worry too much about what happens to spirits after we die. Worrying about death is an unhealthy obsession. Are you worried about death?"

"I'm not worried because I don't feel anything," Evanita said. "But I see no difference in value between continuing to live for another day or simply dying right now and getting things over with."

"Yes, that's another danger with the straight biochemical line of reasoning. No value placed on the sanctity of life," Johnny said.

"Oh I see value in life," Evanita said. "Plants grow and produce value by exchanging carbon dioxide for oxygen and by providing a food source. Animals provide value as food to other animals."

"And people? Do you see value in people?"

"Very little," Evanita said. "People aren't a food source for other animals. They are consuming the planet. Almost seems pointless to continue the species."

"Humans are pointless, yes, that's what the drugs have led you to believe," Johnny said. "Yet we are here. So what do we do?"

"Get me out of here for one thing," Evanita said.

"You are trapped in the walls of this detention center, in the walls of your drugs, and in the walls of your spiritual search," Johnny said.

"Spiritual search? That ended when I failed my Coming-Of-Age ceremony," Evanita said.

"Did it? Are you sure?" Johnny asked.

"You know it did. You even recited off the different churches I tried. Don't you remember? When we were at Cerossi Café?" Evanita asked.

"I do remember," Johnny said.

"I started with Broadway Unitarian," Evanita said.

"By Broadway Bridge," Johnny said.

"Next I went to Saint Stellan Catholic Church, and that went bad," Evanita said.

"Across from Steel Bridge," he continued.

"I attended your sister's funeral at Barnseed Baptist Church," Evanita said.

"Quite a ways from Burnside Bridge," Johnny said.

"And Sharon found the intruders at Morris Synagogue," Evanita said.

"A bit east of Morrison Bridge," he said.

"Then Sheila started dating Davino Vagatti. She attended his church meetings at Hothrane Zoroastrian Church," Evanita said.

"Leading from Hawthorn Bridge," Johnny said.

"And the meeting at the rose garden with the Arkham Atheist group," Evanita said.

"Whose main building is just a few blocks from Marquam Bridge," Johnny said.

"And my search ended with that," Evanita said.

"But that's not the end. Do you remember what I said after Marquam?" Johnny asked.

"You said something, but I don't remember what," Evanita said.

"I named two more bridges," he said. "Ross Island Bridge was next."

"That's something else—you linked churches with bridges then, and you're doing it now."

"It's a predictable pattern," Johnny said.

"What's so predictable about searching churches?" Evanita asked.

"It's the search for identity. It happens quite often to people, most especially at your age. That's one reason why the Unitarians have the Coming-Of-Age ceremony. It gives people like you the opportunity to explore your convictions and find your identity," Johnny said.

"You speak like a Unitarian, but you're Baptist. How do you explain that?" Evanita asked.

"I'm Baptist. That's part of my identity, and I've chosen to keep it. I don't push it on others," Johnny said.

"But my mother is pushing Unitarian on me," Evanita said. "Just like her mother pushed Catholicism on her. My mother changed, so I must change."

"Be careful," Johnny said. "The creed, 'I must change' is itself a fixed stance. Changing for the sake of change is no better than doing nothing just because that's the way it was always done. But the identity you choose, the faith or lack thereof, is of your own doing. Don't do what the petty atheist does."

"Are you calling me a petty atheist?" Evanita asked. "Because I say I don't believe in God at this moment?"

"No," Johnny said. "A petty atheist doesn't believe in God, not because of experience or rationalization, but because he or she chooses to be the opposite of one or more religious groups. Someone says she believes in God, so the petty atheist says she doesn't believe. Someone says love thy neighbor as God loves you, and the petty atheist says not to love thy neighbor, because there is no God, no God is love, no love of thy neighbor. It's the opposite game. Don't play it."

"What about the Bible? The flaws?" Evanita said.

"That's another example. A petty atheist will say that since there are flaws in the Bible, there was no Jesus, and no God. But take any book written by people. You can find all sorts of flaws if you like, even owner's manuals for devices. If there's a flaw in the manual, does that mean the device doesn't exist?"

"That's silly. I buy a television, the user's manual has a flaw, so what? I still have the television, and it works," Evanita said.

"Exactly. But the petty atheist would say that since the manual has flaws, the television doesn't exist," Johnny said. "Yet you know better."

"For a television," Evanita said.

"But if you read the manual, you can tell what parts are right and wrong," Johnny said.

"Because I have the television as evidence," Evanita said. "What evidence do I have of Jesus or God?"

Johnny paused.

"I have you, don't I?"

"I think the factual accuracy of stories is less important than the main concepts being taught," Johnny said.

"Then I might as well treat the Bible as a philosophical work," Evanita said.

"You could. Different people derive different things from the Bible and other religious texts. But that gets back to what I was saying about identity."

"And the bridges? What church was Ross Island Bridge?" Evanita asked.

"That was Cerossi Café," Johnny said.

"That's not a church," Evanita said.

"Nor is the atheist group," Johnny said. "But all of these bridges tell you something, don't they?"

"Like what?" Evanita asked.

"Let me ask you. What is a bridge?" Johnny asked.

"What do you mean? I know what a bridge is. A bridge is a bridge," Evanita said.

"Cute. But if you follow the rules of logical reasoning, you cannot use a word to define the same word. It's a circular definition, and it leads nowhere."

"A bridge creates a connection between two sides," Evanita said.

"So is a button a bridge?" Johnny asked.

"No, of course not," Evanita replied.

"A button connects two parts of clothing," Johnny said. "Think about a bridge. Is a bridge just a support structure of steel and concrete?"

"Yes," Evanita said. "It can be empty and still be a bridge."

"It can be empty. It can be full too. A button can't be empty or full, can it?" Johnny said.

"This is getting strange," Evanita said. "Why are we talking about empty and full buttons?"

"Because of your state right now," Johnny said. "It's easy for you to see things in the world as forms of simple attachment, like the button. But in reality, attachments are more like bridges, with a flow between the two contact points. The flow is what gives us our soul and our reason to live. If you think of the world in terms of buttons, then the binding is shallow, and you begin to think of things as disposable and of little value. A bridge gives us deep binding, and we hopefully cherish connections a bit more than with the button."

"You still didn't answer me about the Ross Island Bridge and Cerossi Café. If the café isn't a bridge, what is it?" Evanita asked.

"I've been wondering that myself," Johnny said. "What do you suppose happened back there at the café?"

"You mean the fire and the strange effects?" Evanita asked.

"Yes."

"I'm not sure. The colors were chasing each other. No, they appeared to be chasing each other. It was an optical illusion. Different materials put out different wavelengths of light. I imagine the café owners rigged up the fire to burn different gasses to produce the different colors, using a computer program to give the illusion of shape and movement," Evanita explained.

"That sounds like a scientific explanation. But do you have evidence?" Johnny asked.

"Other than my own eyes, no. But it seems the rational conclusion," Evanita said.

"It does seem the rational conclusion, doesn't it? Yet I know for a fact that the rational conclusion is not correct. I know this stone around my neck is tied to the café. Did you notice everything was crimson, cerise, or violet at the café?"

"Come to think of it, yes," Evanita said.

"The stone often puts out a cerise or crimson light," Johnny said. "There's something special about the café—it's like a portal or bridge to somewhere else, but it's not religious. Spiritual, maybe, but not religious."

"But you can't prove it," Evanita said.

"No, I can't," Johnny said.

"So how can anyone believe you?"

"They probably won't," Johnny said. "But there are enough strange things about the café and my stone to tell me that conventional science cannot explain it, and something is definitely there, no matter what anyone says about it. And it's just as valid and powerful as the other churches, and the atheist group."

"Are you saying the Cerossi Café is linked to God?" Evanita asked.

"No. That would be guessing. And I won't do that. But I have a feeling we'll find out in time," Johnny said.

"A feeling isn't much to go on," Evanita said.

"It's all I have," Johnny said.

"What about the last bridge—Sellwood Bridge?" Evanita asked. "Is that also part of the café?"

"No, it isn't," Johnny said. "But it is the beginning."

"The beginning of what?" Evanita asked.

"The beginning of you. And the end. And the middle," Johnny said.

"You're not making any sense," Evanita said.

"It marks the end of your childhood spiritual journey. When you reach Sellwood, you'll complete your Coming-Of-Age ceremony. It's also where you were conceived, or very close," Johnny said.

"My father!" Evanita said, and for the first time since she'd taken the drugs, she felt a little (but just a little) excitement.

"Yes. And no," Johnny said.

"You're speaking in riddles. Did you know my father?" Evanita asked.

"It's not that easy to answer," Johnny said.

"It's a simple question," Evanita said. "Did you know my father?"

"Technically speaking, no," Johnny said. "But my answer is very misleading, only because the question is misleading."

"It's not a misleading question," Evanita said.

"It's just as misleading as asking if there is a God. If you ask me if I've met God, I'd give the same answer."

"Then there's no God. And you never met my father," Evanita said.

"But I know both your parents," Johnny said.

"One of your statements is a lie," Evanita said.

"Based on the way you see the world, yes," Johnny said. "The same eyes that see a flawed statement also see the lack of God. So to explain further is futile at this point. But I will say this—in the beginning, there was nothing, God created light, and there was light, God created you after a descent from Sellwood Bridge, and there was Evanita."

"You know what I think? I think you're speaking in riddles to confuse me. I think that's the religious method to confuse all rational thought," Evanita said.

"You're giving me another wall," Johnny said. "It's only a riddle for now. As you learn more, you'll understand."

"Ms. Carson," called Ox-Two. "Your time is up."

"Keep the stone, Johnny," Evanita said. "Someone might steal it here. I have girls hounding me for things."

"This way, Ms. Carson," Ox-Two said.

Johnny and Evanita hugged. Johnny kissed Evanita, but she did not respond.

"Goodbye," she said.

Johnny waved back. Ox-Two escorted Evanita from Whalejet back to Redjet. On their arrival, several Oxians surrounded the jet.

"You can't go inside," said Oxia.

"Why?" Ox-Two asked.

"Riot in progress," Oxia said.

"My things are in there," Evanita said.

"Yes. That's what's causing the riot," Oxia said.

"Huh?" Evanita asked.

"The girls are fighting over your possessions. They seem to think you have something special. Do you?" Oxia asked.

"Calico and the stone," Evanita muttered. "She told everyone."

"What was that?" Oxia asked.

"No, not one," Evanita said.

"The girls haven't found anything in your room," Oxia said, who now turned to Ox-Two and said, "Take her to isolation and strip-search her. She could be carrying drugs or weapons."

"No!" Evanita said.

"Cooperate, and you'll be released from isolation in a few hours, Eve Carson. Fight, and you'll stay for weeks," Oxia said.

"Let her fight," Ox-Two said. "This will calm her down."

Ox-Two produced a syringe filled with medication from a case. She motioned to jab it into Evanita's arm, but Evanita quickly complied.

"Okay, okay, let's go," Evanita said.

"That's better," Ox-Two said as she placed the syringe back in a small case.

Ox-Two escorted Evanita to Grenjet and led her inside.

"Isn't this the jet under construction?" Evanita asked.

"It's for girls who need mental reconstruction," Ox-Two laughed.

Ox-Two led Evanita to a room where Ox-Five sat.

"Remove everything from your pockets and place them in this container," Ox-Five said. "They'll be returned to you."

Evanita didn't have much in her pocket—a quarter, a tube of lip balm, and a facial tissue.

"Ah-ah," Ox-Five said. "Throw the tissue away. It's unsanitary and should never go in your pocket."

Evanita threw the tissue away.

"Stand in the corner and remove your clothes," Ox-Five said.

Evanita removed her clothes and felt ashamed, despite being medicated.

"Lift your arms and turn around," Ox-Five said.

Evanita complied. Ox-Five placed disposable latex gloves on her (Ox-Five's) hands.

"Remain standing," Ox-Five said. "Spread your legs apart."

"What?" Evanita asked.

"You heard her," Ox-Two said. "Spread them."

Evanita moved her legs apart. Ox-Five wheeled a small mirror between Evanita's legs and directly below her torso. Ox-Five looked in the mirror.

"Nothing here," Ox-Five said.

Ox-Five returned the mirror to its original spot against the wall. Evanita moved to put her clothes back on.

"Wait," Ox-Five said. "Time to inspect your clothing."

Ox-Five prodded and tested all parts of Evanita's clothes, pulling out pockets and checking inside the shoes.

"She's clean," Ox-Five said. "You may put your clothes back on."

Evanita dressed.

"Back to Aldojet you go," Ox-Two said.

"Aldojet?" Evanita protested. "But I live in Redjet."

"I'm being nice. I'm supposed to keep you in isolation for two hours. Instead, I'm taking you to your new home. Do you want to spend those two hours in isolation?" Ox-Two asked.

"No," Evanita said.

"Then Aldojet it is, Eve Carson," Ox-Two said. "Whatever is left of your things will be brought to your new room."

Ox-Two led Evanita to Aldojet—the yellow-colored jet containing drug offenders.

"This is your new room, Room A111. This jet is under lockdown until further notice," Ox-Two said.

"Where's my roommate? Shouldn't she be here too?"

"She will soon," Ox-Two said.

Ox-Two locked Evanita's new room. Aldojet was eerily quiet compared to Redjet. The girls on Redjet were always yelling, fighting, or stirring up some commotion. But as far as Evanita knew, there was no one else but her on Aldojet. In fact, the jet was heavily populated, but the girls were also heavily medicated to keep them quiet. Evanita looked out her window in hopes of seeing what was happening at Redjet, but Oranjet blocked most of her view. She was able to see Calico on the grounds at one point. She handed a large bundle of Evanita's things to Ox-Two in a laundry basket. Calico had several scratch marks on her face, a ripped shirt, and a bandage wrapped around her bleeding right arm. After handing off the things to Ox-Two, she sat on a bench, whipped out a pipe, and smoked tobacco. The Oxians turned a blind eye to Calico's smoking. Ox-Two did not walk over to Aldojet but instead disappeared into Cafederijet.

About ten minutes later, someone unlatched Evanita's door. In popped Tara Tushenne, also known as Mac-Two.

"Boy, what a rough day it's been," Mac-Two said. "I see they moved you in here."

"Mac-Two," Evanita said as she stood up and faced Mac-Two. "What are you doing here?"

"I live here," Mac-Two said.

"You can't! This is for detention girls," Evanita said.

"They didn't tell you?" Mac-Two asked.

"Tell me what?" Evanita asked.

"That in Aldojet and Oranjet, staff are allowed to live onsite and mentor detention girls. It's part of the 24-hour therapy plan," Mac-Two said. "Didn't I make you one of my girls? Yes, I did. And since we'll be spending lots of personal time together, you can start calling me Tara."

Tara walked over to Evanita as if to kiss her. Evanita backed up.

"Why don't you try calling me Tara?" Mac-Two said in a soft voice.

"I prefer calling you Mac-Two," Evanita said.

"That's so formal and sterile," Mac-Two said. "I'd much prefer we became very close friends, Eve."

"Eve is not my real name," Evanita said.

"I know. Your name is Evanita Carreña. But you left that name outside the gates. Inside here, you're Eve Carson. Whatever you do will be under that name, and when you return to the outside, you will become Evanita Carreña again, and everything under Eve Carson will remain inside this compound—everything you say, and everything you do. So why the inhibitions? Let yourself go in my arms."

Mac-Two attempted to embrace Evanita, but Evanita ducked under Mac-Two's arms and slipped around to the side.

"Hard to get, eh?" Mac-Two asked.

"Please, I...I..."

"You're at a loss for words. I have that effect on women," Mac-Two said.

"Daddy, can't we help Mommy?" Jonara asked.

"Not this time," Johnny said. "She must resolve this problem on her own. To interfere will only make things worse."

"Think, Evanita, think!" Evanita muttered.

"Come on, Eve! Share a little love. Let's get attached at the hip. I don't ask for a long-term commitment, just a chance to have a little fun."

"That's it!" Evanita said.

"That's what?" Mac-Two asked.

"You see me as a button on a sweater," Evanita said, "to fasten or unfasten whenever you like."

"There," Johnny said to Jonara. "Your mother is making a breakthrough."

"What's wrong with that?" Mac-Two asked. "Or are you the kind of girl who likes zippers instead. Zippers are much faster.

It's much easier to slip out of clothes and into something sexy with a zipper."

"But it's all so empty," Evanita said. "Where's the love? Can you feel the love?"

"It's making love," Mac-Two said.

"But it isn't love. After the thrill is over, what do you have?" Evanita asked.

"A good night's sleep," Mac-Two said.

"And that's it? Where's the spiritual exchange? The spiritual bonding?" Evanita asked. "Where's the bridge between two people that keeps us healthy and balanced?"

"What kind of talk is that?" Mac-Two asked. "What have you been reading?"

"I'm just trying to—" Evanita started.

"No, I know what you're doing. You're one of those goody-two-shoes, aren't you? Or you're pretending to be one. Or maybe you feel you're cheating on Calico. Is she your real lover? Is she? I'm ten times the woman she is. And I can show you," Mac-Two said.

"You don't understand," Evanita said.

"Oh I understand," Mac-Two said, now losing her politeness. "How frustrating. I put in a good word for you, and you get frozen feet on me. I've had enough. I'm taking a cold shower."

Mac-Two closed herself in the bathroom, turned on a stereo, and jumped into the shower where she began singing to the music. Evanita stared at the bathroom door for a moment while lost in thought. She didn't notice that her dorm's door lock was being picked. The door opened, and before Evanita could react, a detention inmate walked up to Evanita from behind, twisted an arm behind her back, and held a razor blade to the underside of Evanita's jaw at the top of the neck.

"One peep out of you, and I'll cut your vocal cords," said the girl. "Do you understand?"

Evanita nodded yes.

"Good girl. Smart girl. Give me some Librium," she said.

"I don't have any Librium," Evanita said.

"I said, give me some Librium!"

The girl made a small cut into Evanita's neck. Evanita felt the blade burn, and she wanted to scream, but she muffled her painful response as best she could.

"That's right. Don't scream for Tara. Don't scream for the Screws. It's just you and me," the girl said. "You're new in Aldo-jet, aren't you?"

Evanita nodded yes.

"My name is Shark. You and I are going to be best pals. Look at me," Shark said, and she turned Evanita's scared head toward her own.

Shark had scars all over her face from being cut. She cut a small part of her face (until it bled), took a blob of her blood, and smeared it on Evanita's cut neck.

"We're blood sisters, now. And we have a pact. When the Barians give you Librium, you don't swallow, see? Each night I'll come looking for protection payment. You give me the Librium, and I'll protect you. You don't give me Librium, and slick! across your neck with a razor."

"Who...who...are...you...protecting me from?" Evanita stuttered.

"From me, of course," Shark grinned. "Now, no grousing on me, see? No one likes a narc. I'll know if you do, trust me. I have lots of friends, including that Calico girl of yours. Heh, heh, heh. I have to leave now, but don't forget what I told you. Oh, here's a going away present."

Shark backhanded Evanita across the face. A ring on Shark's hand pushed into one of Evanita's teeth and chipped it off. Evanita fell to the floor, holding the broken tooth in her hand as blood oozed from her neck and mouth.

"Toodles!" Shark said in mock friendship.

Shark stamped her feet twice on the floor to punctuate her visit, and she left.

The three returned to the Texas restaurant where Eva and Anna had just finished their flamenco dance. The patrons responded in applause, and the two sat down with the three.

"I'm ready for dessert," Eva said. "What about the rest of you?"

"Oh, I must rest a momento," Anna said.

Jonara, Cerafina, and Johnny looked at one another with sour expressions on their faces.

"I think we've lost our appetites," Johnny said.

"What? You thought our dancing was that bad? Of all the nerve!" Eva said.

"No, it's not that. It's something else," Johnny said.

"I don't care. Oh well. There's nothing in this world that can't be remedied with a little wine," Eva said, and she took a big slurp of wine from her glass. "You proved that with my thyroid. I'll have to remember to swish and swallow wine more often. Just dumping it down one's throat misses out on essential nutrients."

"Mummy Eva," Johnny said. "Have you thought about what sort of funeral ceremony will be held for Geneva?"

"What do you mean?" Eva asked.

"I mean this—she's Catholic, and you're Unitarian. Will she be buried under a Catholic ceremony, or a Unitarian?" Johnny asked.

"I'm surprised you have to ask that," Eva said. "My mother made her funeral arrangements years ago. Seems that's one thing Catholics love to do—obsess with death. She has everything picked out—the church, the time, the songs, her casket, her plot—everything. It will be a Catholic ceremony, of course. I'm left out of these decisions. I always have been. But this is the last time Mother gets to preempt me. After Saturday, I only have to sell the house, and I'm done."

"Grandma?" Jonara asked.

"Yes Jonara?

"Do you love Nanna Geneva like a button or a bridge?" Jonara asked.

Eva's eyes perked up for a split second. Then she realized where Jonara got her question from.

"Johnny," Eva said, and she gave Johnny a knowing look.

"I didn't say anything to her quite like that," Johnny said. "I mean, I said something years ago, but not to Jonara."

"She got it from you," Eva said.

"She may have overheard," Johnny said.

"She got it from you," Eva repeated.

"Okay, okay," Johnny said. "She got it from me."

"Why are you pouring your nonsense riddles of buttons and bridges into my granddaughter's head?" Eva asked.

"It was research," Johnny said. "It...I...you...she...the button...like...well...you know."

"What am I going to do with you?" Eva asked. "I leave you at the table for a moment so I can perform a simple flamenco dance, and you corrupt my granddaughter! Well!?"

"It might be true," Johnny said.

"It is true! Does Evanita know about this?" Eva asked. "No, don't answer. I know the answer. Evanita is in a coma, so you decided to indoctrinate Jonara while her mother is unable to keep Jonara on the straight and narrow. Yes?"

"Yes...I mean no...I mean...something...the other...I meant to say..." Johnny stumbled.

"Never mind. Let's skip dessert and go back to the hospital. We need to visit Evanita."

"Yes," Johnny said. "That's a good idea. I'll pay for the—"

"I'm getting this tab," Eva said, "since I enjoyed it the most."

"And you ate the most too," Jonara said.

"Jonara!" Johnny said.

"For once I don't mind," Eva said. "Come along. Let's get going."

CHAPTER 15:

Getting Their Legs

2023 Oct 5, Thu Afnoon. Corpus Christi Hospital, Texas.

"I will stay home and watch house," Anna said as the party left the Texas restaurant.

"Are you sure?" Eva asked.

"Yes, Miss Eva. The dancing tired me out," Anna said.

Eva drove to Geneva's house and parked the car.

"Thank you for coming along, Anna," Eva said.

"Thank you for lunch," Anna said.

Anna left the car, and Eva was about to leave when Jonara stopped her.

"Wait," Jonara said. "I ate something bad. I have to go to the bathroom."

Jonara ran inside Geneva's house.

"We might as well wait inside," Eva said.

Eva, Cerafina, and Johnny exited the car and waited in the living room.

"Oh, you change mind?" Anna asked.

"No, we're waiting for Jonara," Eva said.

"I fix you some tea," Anna said.

"Thank you," Eva replied.

Eva, Johnny, Cerafina, and Anna enjoyed tea and cookies while they waited for Jonara. Ten minutes later, Jonara emerged from the bathroom with a smile on her face.

"Feel better?" Johnny asked.

"Yeah," Jonara said.

"All right. Eva, are you ready to—" Johnny started, but Eva was out cold.

"She's sleeping," Jonara said.

"Let her rest," Johnny said. "She's been through a lot. She can visit Evanita later."

"What about us? Do we have to wait?" Jonara asked.

"No, we don't. Anna—let Eva know we went to the hospital to visit Evanita."

"Yes, Mr. Johnny," Anna replied.

Johnny drove Jonara and Cerafina to the hospital. Johnny parked in the hospital's parking lot, and the three went inside the building and down the hallway to Evanita's room. As they entered her room, they saw a nurse massaging Evanita's legs with a leg-wrap device to improve circulation.

"One moment," said the nurse. "I'm almost done. There. You may visit her now."

The nurse left.

"Johnny?" Evanita said.

Johnny went over and gave her a kiss.

"You've come out of your coma!" Johnny exclaimed.

"Johnny," Evanita said. "You're my husband."

"Yes, yes!" Johnny said as he kissed Evanita on the cheek.

"I'm still pregnant," Evanita said. "I had a dream I gave birth to a boy, and it was all over. But it's not."

"Mommy!" Jonara said.

"Jonara! My daughter!" Evanita said.

Jonara ran to Evanita with a hug.

"Mommy," Jonara said. "This is my friend, Cerafina."

"Cerafina," Evanita said. "You look familiar, but we've never met, have we?"

"No, ma'am," Cerafina said.

"Do I know your mother or grandmother?" Evanita asked, still a bit groggy.

"Do you know the Ancona family?" Cerafina asked.

"No, I don't," Evanita said. "Still, it's like I had a dream many years ago and saw a girl like you. Strange."

"It could have been an echo from the Moissan Ruby," Johnny said. "Sometimes it reads people, and you aren't aware of the reading on a conscious level."

"Could be," Evanita said. "Johnny—I have a bad case of heartburn. Can you ask the nurse to get me an antacid?"

"You don't have heartburn," Johnny said. "You have preeclampsia. I read the doctor's report. And your heartburn is actually your liver in distress."

"I need to move a little," Evanita said. "My arms have been in this position—ow, ow, ow! Cramp!"

Evanita's left arm cramped up. Johnny massaged it vigorously to ease the cramp.

"Oh, it let go," Evanita said. "I don't understand. I've never had an arm cramp before. I didn't think they were possible."

"Your body is under great strain, Evanita," Johnny said. "It's important you rest as much as possible and do nothing to strain yourself."

"Good idea," Evanita said.

"Daddy, can we help Mommy?" Jonara asked Johnny. "Like we did with Grandma Eva?"

"Let's sit around Evanita's bed," Johnny said.

"Johnny," Evanita asked. "Tell me something. Who is my father?"

Johnny looked down in somber thought, but he did not answer. Instead, he motioned Jonara to begin. Jonara, Cerafina, and Johnny each held onto Evanita while Jonara activated the Moissan Ruby and candleholder with the cell phone.

1940 Oct 23. St. Christopher's Abbey. Girona, Spain.

"What happened, Jonara?" Johnny asked. "We're in Spain."

"I don't know. We jumped," Jonara said. "Did somebody jump or make a sudden movement?"

"The baby kicked me," Evanita said.

"That caused the time shift," Johnny said.

"Look!" Cerafina said. "Chalina is wearing some sort of nun's clothing."

"She's not a true nun," Johnny said. "More likely a nun in training. Or she's a sister."

"Sister Charlene," said a sister. "How is the little Geneva toddler doing?"

"Very well, Sister Francis," Chalina said. "See how she walks?"

Geneva toddled along the floor under her own power and balance.

"She has strong legs," Sister Francis said.

"She'll make an excellent sister, won't she, Sister Francis?" Chalina asked.

"She cannot be forced into the order," Sister Francis said. "But she is welcome to pursue an education here as long as she likes."

"That's very kind of you," Chalina said.

"It's our duty to take care of and educate the underprivileged," Sister Francis said. "Remember this when you pray, Sister Charlene."

"I will," Chalina said.

"Remember our country too," Sister Francis said. "Franco and Hitler are meeting today to decide Spain's role in the war. Pray that war does not come to Spain again. Too many have died during the Civil War."

2007 Feb 17, Sat am. Room A111, Aldojet, Elrod 402. Portland, Oregon.

"What happened?" Jonara asked.

"The baby kicked me again," Evanita said. "Oh God, I remember this day. I was up all night. Couldn't sleep. I was off the Librium and Tegretol for three days. I gave them to Shark so she wouldn't beat me up."

"Get up, Eve Carson," Tara Tushenne said. "Oh, you're already awake. What's wrong? Why are you shaking?"

"I...didn't...sleep," Evanita the younger said. "I had horrible visions...all night."

"You poor thing!" Tara said. "I'll call the doctor."

"No," Evanita the younger said. "Please, don't do that, Mac-Two."

"You know you can call me Tara," Tara said. "I want us to be friends."

"I know...know...what you want," younger Evanita said.

"Here, sit on the floor with me," Tara said.

"I feel like...like...the world is crushing me!" younger Evanita cried.

"Shhh," Tara said.

Tara pulled Evanita out of bed and onto the floor where Tara held Evanita in a side-by-side hug.

"We'll pull you together," Tara said. "Just sit next to me and breathe. No, don't sit with your legs like that. Here, try the lotus position. Fold your legs with the top of your feet resting on your thighs. Good. Now hold your hands together like this. Very good. Now breathe like I do. In, out, in, out."

Younger Evanita sat and held her hands like Tara. She emulated Tara's breathing.

"I'm...still...shaking," younger Evanita said.

"Just concentrate. Breathe. Let go of your attachments to anxiety, to stress, to people, to the world. Repeat the following words—truthfulness, benevolence, forbearance. Truthfulness, benevolence, forbearance. Say them, Eve Carson, say them."

Both older and younger Evanita said simultaneously, "Truthfulness, benevolence, forbearance."

"Ow!" the older Evanita said as she received another sharp kick in her abdomen.

1942 Jan 20, Thu. Jaffa, Palestine.

"Congratulations, Fantina, it's a boy!" the doctor said.

"This is my grandmother giving birth to my father in Jaffa, Palestine, before it became part of Israel," Johnny said.

"I didn't know he lived in Palestine," Evanita said.

"He did for a little while, but not long. He moved to the United States later."

"Do you have a name for your baby?" the doctor asked.

"Yes," Fantina said. "Aromani Karrano di Pindos."

The doctor cleaned up Aromani, placed a blanket around him, and placed him in Fantina's arm.

"You may have visitors now," the doctor said.

"Please show my father in," Fantina said.

Samouel entered the delivery room.

"Father. Come see your grandson, Aromani Karrano di Pindos," Fantina said.

"He has your eyes," Samouel said.

"And your stubborn chin," Fantina grinned.

"How are you holding up, my daughter?" Samouel asked.

"Very well," Fantina said. "There's a New Zealand soldier outside my room to protect us from harm."

"The New Zealand Army has been very kind to us," Samouel said. "God has blessed them. They have shielded us from much suffering. There are many harms in this world, Fantina, many harms."

"I thought we left them behind us in Greece," Fantina said.

"There are some people here in Palestine who would rather we leave and not come back," Samouel said, "and others who go too far and make their feelings known through violence."

"Why don't we go back to Greece, Father?" Fantina asked.

"We can't," Samouel said. "The Nazis are rounding up Jews as we speak and shipping them to concentration camps. And there's an evil rumor that senior German officials are meeting today in a little Berlin suburb named 'Wannsee' to discuss the fate of our people."

"God decides our fate," Fantina said.

"But there are those who would see us exterminated from this earth," Samouel said. "The Nazis are one such people."

"Are there others?" Fantina asked.

"Only those who are jealous of our success," Samouel said. "Bigotry and jealously are great vices of little men with great potential for evil."

"How long are we safe in Palestine, Father?" Fantina asked.

"Ow!" Evanita called as her baby kicked.

1947 Jul 9, Wed. Girona, Spain.

"We're back in Spain," Jonara said. "In Girona."

"Grandma Geneva," Evanita said. "I remember seeing her birth when I was at the Elrod 402. Look, she's carrying a basket of clothes."

"Sister Charlene," Geneva said. "I finished folding the clothes."

"Very good, Geneva. You're a good helper," Sister Charlene said. "Please, sit down. I have something to tell you."

"Sister Charlene has the same clothes as the other sisters," Cerafina said.

"It appears she's a full sister, not just a novice," Johnny said.

"Sister Charlene, I heard the other sisters say something. They said today is voting day," Geneva said. "What are they voting for?"

"General Franco drafted a resolution stating that Spain is a monarchy," Sister Charlene said. "And the people are voting for or against it."

"What does monarchy mean?" Geneva asked.

"It means 'kingdom.' Spain will be a kingdom and could have a king and queen."

"Will Franco be king?" Geneva asked.

"I don't know," Sister Charlene said. "Alfonso XIII died six years ago, and some of his sons have renounced their claim. Juan Carlos is heir to the throne, but I doubt Franco will give up power to him. Franco likes power too much."

"How long will Franco run our country?" Geneva asked.

"I don't know. Maybe a few years, maybe longer," Sister Charlene said.

"It was much longer," Johnny said. "He ruled until his death in 1975!"

"Geneva, are you happy here?" Sister Charlene asked.

"Yes, Sister Charlene," Geneva said.

"Are you telling the truth? To lie is a sin," Sister Charlene said.

"I know. I am telling the truth. I like my studies and helping in the abbey."

"Well, I have some good news that will make you even happier. We found your grandfather. He lives in the mountains, in a town called *Carreña*. I had a suspicion your family is from Carreña, Geneva Carreña. It's quite common to take the name of a town as a last name."

"My grandfather?" Geneva asked.

"Yes. You'll be leaving here tomorrow. Your grandfather will pick you up with your belongings and take you back to Carreña," Sister Charlene explained.

"Carreña? But I want to stay here," Geneva said.

"You have a devout heart, but you belong to your family. If you would like to become a sister, you may rejoin the abbey when you are eighteen," Sister Charlene said.

"Please, Sister Charlene, don't make me go. I beg you to let me stay. Sister Francis says the outside world is horrible, and people have no money. These walls are a layer of protection, and—"

"You cannot use these walls as a security blanket forever, Geneva. You must face the world," Sister Charlene said. "And you must live with your family. They are yours, and you are theirs."

"Even if it's miserable?" Geneva asked.

"Ow," Evanita said as she was kicked again.

1947 Jul 18, Fri. Haifa, Palestine.

"Look, Aromani, do you see? It's the Mediterranean Sea," Fantina said as five-year-old Aromani stood next to her at a Mediterranean port in Haifa, Palestine.

"The sea, the sea!" Aromani shouted.

"It's so hot," Fantina said. "I can barely breathe. Can you breathe, Aromani?"

"I can breathe, Mommy," Aromani said.

"We're going to watch a special ship arrive today, the *Exodus 1947*," Fantina said. "But I'm worried. It looks like a war zone around us. So many people."

"Where's Grandpa?" Aromani asked.

"There he is," Fantina said. "Over there with his friends next to that pier."

"What's he holding in his hand?" Aromani asked.

"That's a motion picture camera," Fantina said. "Grandpa is going to film the *Exodus 1947* as it arrives."

"Will Grandpa get in trouble?" Aromani asked.

"Of course not. It's just a camera," Fantina said.

"Joshua's daddy says the British are following our boat, that our boat is broken. I punched him in the eye for that," Aromani bragged.

"You shouldn't punch your friend in the eye," Fantina said.

"But he's wrong, isn't he?" Aromani asked.

"The *Exodus 1947* will dock. And when it does, the immigrants will reach freedom. We must believe this," Fantina said.

A group of boats came into view from the west.

"Look at all the boats, Mommy," Aromani said.

"It's the *Exodus 1947*," Fantina said. "It's surrounded by British boats. Oh, the *Exodus* has been to Hell and back. The British did it! I thought the British were the Allies. They're supposed to help us."

The *Exodus 1947* docked. Passengers in their sweaty and dirty condition left the boat by walking down the gangplank. Instead of being allowed to stay in Palestine, the passengers were immediately escorted to British ships.

"The British are taking them away," Fantina said.

"Mommy, look at Grandpa," Aromani said.

"I don't believe it," Fantina said. "He's fighting with a British officer over the camera. The officer won't let Grandpa keep the camera or film."

"Punch him, Grandpa, punch him!" Aromani yelled.

Kick!

2007 Feb 24, Sat am. Room A111, Aldojet, Elrod 402. Portland, Oregon.

"Let's do our morning exercises, Eve. We'll start with *Buddha showing a thousand hands*," Tara said.

The two stood next to each other and performed what appeared to be arm-stretching exercises intermixed with a return of the hands to the abdomen as if praying. Slight knee bending and ankle lifting accompanied their exercise.

"I hear your boyfriend is going to visit you this afternoon," Tara said while stretching.

"Yeah. He and I are having an argument," Evanita replied as she also stretched.

"What about?" Tara asked, still stretching.

"God," Evanita replied, also still stretching.

"Oh, he's the one," Tara said.

"He's very convincing," Evanita said. "But I've figured out how to counter his arguments."

"It's amazing how many people still cling to their superstitious beliefs of a deity in this modern age," Tara said. "This nation has the highest percentage of believers of any developed country."

"I know," Evanita said. "But I have to let go of my attachments—let go of the beliefs others push on me."

"That's good," Tara said. "Part of Falun Dafa says to let go."

The two finished their stretching.

"But letting go is for the exercises, Eve Carson," Tara said. "When the exercises end, you go back to the attachments you feel are true, good, and enduring."

"Sometimes I don't know if I can be Johnny's girlfriend anymore," Evanita said.

"You know there's always a place for you with me," Tara said. "You and I think a lot alike."

"Except I don't like girls," Evanita said.

"You don't have to like *girls* like that. Do you call all houses your home? No. You find one you like, you call it home, and you make it yours. I'm not all girls, I'm a home. Don't you want to make a home with me?" Tara asked.

"You're a good friend, Tara. But someday I want children. Women aren't meant to have children with each other. We're not designed that way," Evanita said.

"Designed? As in intelligent design? A male creator? Who decides if I can write my name on paper? I was never designed to do so, but I do. Who decides if I can ride a bicycle? The intelligent designer? Who decides if I'm a prisoner or an employee in a prison? What does the creator say about that?"

"That's all nonsense talk," Evanita said.

"Yes, harking back to a creator to hide behind a wall and deprive oneself of life is what you are attempting to do," Tara said.

"That's not what I meant," Evanita said.

"But that's what conditioning has trained you to say," Tara said.

"Now I know who distracted you from God," Johnny said to the older Evanita.

"Let's not start that again," the older Evanita said. "Ow!"

1948 Apr 25, Sun. Jaffa, Palestine.

Fantina rushed into a fallout shelter with Aromani and Samouel. Jaffa was under mortar attack by the Irgun, a militant Zionist group.

"Rabbi Evenstein!" Fantina yelled. "Rabbi Evenstein!"

"Child!" the rabbi said.

"Jaffa is under attack by the Irgun! We'll be killed by our own people!" Fantina said.

"We must leave this city," Rabbi Evenstein said.

"Leave our ancestral land? After the UN gave us part of Palestine on November 29th of last year?"

"And the fighting started the next day," Rabbi Evenstein said. "But the UN did not give us Jaffa."

"But they will, won't they?" Fantina asked.

"Maybe. Right now, we're in Arab territory, and that means danger—from both sides. Fantina—the city is evacuating," Rabbi Evenstein said. "We must leave."

"Why is it once I make a good home, it becomes a war zone? First Greece, and now Palestine," Fantina said.

"The British are pulling out of Palestine," the rabbi said.

Rabbi Evenstein motioned a fair-skinned man to come over. As he drew near, Fantina recognized him.

"Pierce Wilkinson!" Fantina said. "I thought New Zealand pulled out years ago."

"We did, at least most of us," Pierce said. "I came back to help you escape this violence."

"Pierce is coordinating an escape party tonight," Rabbi Evenstein said.

"We'll receive a British escort until we're far enough west in the Mediterranean to avoid attack," Pierce said.

"The British? They're the new Nazis. They deported our brothers and sisters on the *Exodus 1947*," Fantina said.

"Fantina," Rabbi Evenstein said. "We must trust Pierce. New Zealand and England are allies—Britain will not harm us if we're onboard a New Zealand vessel. But you must not say anything against the British to draw suspicion. Otherwise, we'll have the same fate as the *Exodus 1947* ship, and I don't want us stuck in some internment camp until old age takes us all."

That night, Fantina, Aromani, Samouel, Rabbi Evenstein, and many others left the port city Jaffa in Palestine for New Zealand with the aid of Pierce Wilkinson. The New Zealand ship was escorted several kilometers west of Jaffa before departing, leaving the New Zealand ship on its own where it navigated through the Suez Canal and down the Red Sea toward New Zealand.

"Will we be turned around once we reach New Zealand, like the *Exodus 1947*?" Fantina asked Rabbi Evenstein.

"No. The British will not disturb us," the rabbi said.

"The Red Sea," Fantina said. "I never thought I would see it."

"There's something about the Red Sea that sings to the very core of our faith," Samouel said. "Moses led our people into freedom by parting the Red Sea, now our Anglican friend is leading us to freedom."

"We could have stayed behind," Fantina said. "We could have moved to one of the Jewish-designated parts of Palestine."

"Yes, we could have," the rabbi said. "You are a mother with a young child. Your father is old and needs no additional stress. I do not wish to see your family suffer. The price has been paid. Raise Aromani in peace as a good Jewish person. Enjoy your father's company. God be with you always."

Kick!

1950 Sep 7, Thu. Carreña, Spain.

"Oh, what a tough day at the coal mine," Martin Sixpence said. "Is dinner ready, Geneva?"

Martin Sixpence, Geneva's British grandfather, arrived home from work.

"Yes, Grandpa," Geneva said.

"Let me guess—trout and beans," Martin said.

"Yes, good guess," Geneva said.

"I'm tired of trout and beans," Martin said. "Can't you find something else?"

"I'm sorry, Grandpa. Trout is all I catch in the mountain stream," Geneva said. "And we always have good bean harvests."

"I can't eat fish the rest of my life," Martin said. "I'm going outside for a smoke."

Geneva rushed worriedly to the window and watched her grandfather. He lit up a cigarette and walked around the woodpile to a covered-up hutch.

"Please don't find it, please don't find it," Geneva prayed.

"Geneva!" Martin called. "Come out here!"

Geneva rushed outside. Martin had removed the covering to the rabbit hutch.

"What is this?" Martin asked.

"Please, grandfather. I found this lonely bunny rabbit, and I want to keep her as a pet," Geneva explained.

"Now Geneva, I've told you over and over again that a rabbit is a pest, not a pet. You can't keep one here," Martin explained.

"Please, grandfather, please!" Geneva begged.

"Geneva, do you know what these rabbits represent? Cave-ins and death to us miners. They burrow under us wherever we go. Did you listen to the radio today?" Martin asked.

"Yes, I did," Geneva said.

"Did you hear about the coal mine in New Cumnock in Scotland?" Martin asked.

"Yes, Grandpa," Geneva replied.

"It collapsed. Thirteen miners died," Martin said.

"Did rabbits cause the collapse?" Geneva asked.

"It doesn't matter. When a coal mine collapses, men die. When rabbits dig too many tunnels, machines and support structures collapse into the ground along with the mine. Now you don't want to kill innocent men, do you?"

"But this bunny rabbit won't burrow under your mine. She'll stay here. I'll take care of her. Please, Grandfather, please," Geneva said.

"Get rid of the rabbit before you go to bed tonight," Martin said, "and I won't punish you. But if this rabbit is here tomorrow, it's no dinner for a solid week, do you hear?"

"Yes, Grandpa," Geneva said.

Martin and Geneva ate trout and beans. Martin remained silent the rest of the evening, being disgusted by both the recurring dinner, and the fact a rabbit was living rent-free on his property.

The next morning, Geneva awoke early to feed her rabbit. She slipped three fresh carrots into the hutch through the chicken-wire-covered sides. The rabbit ate the carrots as if starved for days. Geneva said something in Catalan to the rabbit, an apology for not visiting the rabbit more often. A fog rolled down from the early-morning mountain. Geneva left the hutch to gather wild grass for the rabbit. She returned to the hutch with grass and fed it to the rabbit. A door slammed at the house. Her grandfather, Martin Sixpence, stormed from the house, yanked Geneva away from the hutch, and burst the hutch open. He pulled out the rabbit and started strangling her.

"Curse you undermining varmints!" Martin screeched.

The moment of distress drove the calming comforts of Catalan from Geneva's cognizance. Consequently, Geneva's Castilian Spanish spewed through her speech.

"*Mi conejo!*" Geneva shouted.

Geneva lunged for Martin's hands and knocked the rabbit free.

"Get in the house!" the man ordered.

"*Mi conejo.* Run away. Don't look back. Run free, *mi conejo!*" screamed Geneva.

Geneva fell into tears as Martin dragged her back to the small mountain house. The fog cleared, and the rabbit slipped into early morning shadows. Geneva took refuge in her bedroom. She stared out the window and whispered:

"*¿Dónde está mi conejo?*"

Martin stormed into the house, into Geneva's bedroom, and slapped her across the face. He tied her to a chair and left her there.

"You're not my grandpa, you evil Anglo Nazi. I hate you! I hate you forever!"

"I'll deal with you after work," he said.

After Martin Sixpence left, Geneva worked the knots loose. She packed her things, including her *viola de gamba* and her mother's diary. She hitchhiked from Carreña to Girona where she called for and met Sister Charlene.

"I ran away," Geneva told Sister Charlene.

"You ran away from home? You must go back," Sister Charlene said.

"No. That was never my home. And that can't be my grandpa. He has no heart. I want to be a sister. I want to join the abbey," Geneva said.

"You can't be a sister until after you're eighteen years old," Sister Charlene said. "However, I'll talk to Mother Superior in the morning and see what we can do. Meantime, come in. You can sleep in my chamber tonight."

"Ow," Evanita said after a kick.

1955 Oct 26, Wed. Upper Hutt, New Zealand.

"We're going for a train ride to Featherston today," Fantina said to Aromani, who was now a boy of thirteen years. "The government is closing down the Rimutaka Incline in a few days, and I want you to see what it's like before they do."

"Who cares?" Aromani asked.

"I think you should know," Fantina said. "You should know what it's like to see the end of an era and the beginning of another. The Rimutaka Tunnel is complete and will be opened on November 1st. When that happens, the Rimutaka Incline will be shut down forever."

The two boarded a passenger car in Upper Hutt and proceeded toward Featherston.

"Are you sure this is a train?" Aromani asked as the train moved along. "It looks like a bus."

"This isn't a cargo train, it's a Wairarapa railcar made especially for passengers. That way, we can go much faster than a cargo train," Fantina said. "Look, we're going up the Rimutaka Incline. See the center rail? It's called a Fell center rail. It gives cargo trains extra traction to pull themselves up the incline or extra traction to brake on the way down. Without the extra traction, the cargo trains couldn't get over the mountain."

"We're going slow," Aromani said.

"Going up the mountain slows us down," Fantina said. "But look out the window. Isn't the scenery beautiful?"

"Yeah. How will people in the tunnel be able to see the scenery?" Aromani asked.

"They won't," Fantina said. "There's a tradeoff between time and beauty. The tunnel is quicker, but there's nothing to look at except mountain walls. The incline is slow yet beautiful."

"Speed is more important," Aromani said. "Isn't it?"

"I'm afraid for this rail line, yes," Fantina said. "This incline is also more expensive. The cost for fuel, brake pads, and maintenance is too much for the government. The tunnel will make travel cheaper."

"Cheaper," Aromani said. "Cheap speed."

"Don't forget this day, Aromani," Fantina said.

"It's just a train ride," Aromani said.

"It's more than that," Fantina said. "Different periods in history have train rides like this—the old, beautiful ways are discarded in favor of the cheap and speedy ways. But who can stop it? The government can't afford the incline anymore, and it's dangerous."

Aromani turned on his portable radio and listened to the news. The broadcaster announced that Sadako Sasaki died the previous day from atom bomb disease.

"What's atom bomb disease?" Aromani asked.

"Well," Fantina said, "it's like this. An atom bomb detonates, and it makes little bitty particles that zap through people's bodies. This is radiation. Radiation damages tissue and cells. The more radiation, the worse the damage."

"But the damage heals, doesn't it? When I scrape my arm, it heals," Aromani said.

"There is some healing, but there is permanent damage too. What does the radio say about her death?" Fantina asked.

The two listened as the radio listed the cause of death as leukemia.

"Cancer of the bone marrow," Fantina said. "Radiation causes cancer. What a terrible way to die. Her world was peaceful and quiet until the atom bomb dropped. Then it changed her world forever into something ugly until she died. How tragic. Is there anything else on the radio about her?"

"No," Aromani said. "Just something about Ngo Dihn Diem proclaiming Vietnam a republic, and that he's now the president."

"That's an example of change. But the question is—what will the change be? Oftentimes we don't know until it's too late. Always treasure the good you see each day. Next week it could be gone."

"Like this train ride?" Aromani said.

"Yes," Fantina said. "There's something I want you to have. It's a family heirloom, an emergency candleholder for celebrating *Shabbat*. I had it inscribed so you would al- 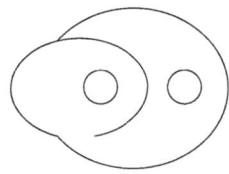 ways remember who you are and where you come from. It says,

'Aromani, son of Fantina di Pindos.' Remember three things always—you are my son, you are Jewish, and you are from the Pindus Mountains in Greece. Promise you'll remember?"

"I promise," Aromani said.

Kick!

1956 Apr 7, Sat. St. Christopher's Abbey. Girona, Spain.

Sister Charlene and Geneva worked feverishly in the infirmary at St. Christopher's Abbey. Many children had succumbed to polio and were forced to live temporarily in iron lung machines.

"We have more polio patients, Geneva," Sister Charlene said. "The epidemic is getting worse."

"I wish someone would invent a medicine to cure polio," Geneva said.

"There is no cure, but there is a way to prevent it. The Salk vaccine came out last year," Sister Charlene said.

"Well I wish the vaccine would get distributed around here," Geneva said. "Why can't we treat people with the latest medicines?"

"The Franco regime has taken a deep toll on our society," Sister Charlene said. "While I admire his devotion to the Catholic Church, the economy has suffered greatly from his regime. But keep your hopes up, Geneva. Already there are signs of Franco's grip loosening. Today on the radio, I heard that Spain has relinquished its protectorate in Morocco. Morocco is getting her legs. She's independent and free."

"When does Spain get her legs? When does the economy improve?"

"It already has," Sister Charlene said. "Franco made a deal with the United States three years ago—the Americans may have military bases in Spain in exchange for economic aid. Things are improving, Geneva, things are improving."

"Then why do I feel so terrible?" Geneva said. "I have a headache, and my muscles are sore."

"You've been working too hard," Sister Charlene said. "Perhaps you should rest for a little while."

"And I feel like throwing up," Geneva said.

Sister Charlene's eyes lit up.

"Geneva, have you been wearing your facemask constantly?" Sister Charlene asked.

"Well, mostly," Geneva said. "But sometimes it's uncomfortable, and I have to remove it to adjust it."

"In here? Did you remove it in front of the patients?" Sister Charlene asked.

"Only for a moment. I didn't think it would hurt anything," Geneva said.

"Oh child! You've put yourself at risk for polio. You must be tested at once. This could be serious," Sister Charlene said.

"I'll be all right soon. I just need some rest," Geneva said.

"Don't be disobedient," Sister Charlene said. "Report to the doctor at once."

Kick!

1956 Apr 14, Sat. St. Christopher's Abbey. Girona, Spain.

A week after her first symptoms, Geneva now lay in an iron lung machine as polio ravaged her body.

"How do you feel?" Sister Charlene asked Geneva.

"I can't feel my legs," Geneva said. "I'm paralyzed. This is the worst feeling in the world. I want to die."

"Pray for strength," Sister Charlene said. "Pray for a speedy recovery."

"What good is recovery if I can't walk again? I could be stuck in this machine forever! What kind of life is that?" Geneva cried. "Why did God invent polio?"

"We are tested on this earth, Geneva. Be strong. Life is a precious gift, not something to be taken for granted," Sister Charlene said.

Kick!

1956 Dec 12, Wed. ISIS Meeting. Montgomery, Alabama.

"The meeting went well," Jane said to Alina Zavuski.

"Look at all the women," Evanita said.

"It's an ISIS meeting," Johnny said. "The International Sapphonic Illumination Society. They discuss women's issues and rights."

"Yes, it went well," Alina said with disappointment.

"Then why do you sound so sad?"

"I am failure, Jane," Alina said.

"What? That's not true. You've helped thousands of women," Jane said.

"Do what? Read and talk, read and talk," Alina said. "But I look at newspaper at Civil Rights leaders—Rosa Parks, Coretta Scott King, Dr. Martin Luther King Jr., Claudette Colvin, Jo Ann Robinson, E.D. Nixon, and many others. They organize boycott. They make progress. What I do? Sit in chair. Hide in secret and talk. Petunia right. Time for action. Negroes boycott for rights, what do women do? Women stay home while men work. Women cook and clean while men earn money. In 1940s, I make big progress when men at war. Men came back. Women lost progress. What now? I have nothing."

"Stay here and keep teaching the women. We need you," Jane said.

"No. Time for Alina to go other place," Alina said. "I sit too long in chair. I—how do you say in America—must get my legs."

"Name the city," Jane said. "Roberta and I will pack our bags and follow you."

"No, you not follow Alina," Alina said. "I should have left sooner. Why idea not come to me sooner? Answer under nose. Kaila had answer. I not act. I slow."

"What are you talking about?" Jane asked.

"Kaila. You remember Kaila's story?" Alina asked.

"Yeah. She was kidnapped. They were going to sell her in Lebanon," Jane said.

"But other women to be sold in United States," Alina said.

"Which I find hard to believe," Jane said.

"Easy to believe. Women sold for sex. Very old business," Alina said.

"And?"

"And I hear on radio something disturbing. Japan now member of United Nations," Alina said.

"That's great news," Jane said. "Why does that bother you?"

"Because of Japanese history. Comfort women. Japan forced women into prostitution—first their own, then Korean, and Taiwanese. Maybe others."

"That's all over," Jane said. "We beat the Japanese."

"Man's war over. Woman's war in progress," Alina said. "South Korean women were comfort women for Japanese. Now they comfort women for American soldiers."

"It can't be true," Jane said. "It would be in the news, and people would protest."

"People cannot respond to what they do not know. Old Soviet trick," Alina said.

"This is not the Soviet Union," Jane said. "We would never do that."

"Then you believe world is what news tells you, no? You like ignorant Soviet citizen believing everything in *Pravda*," Alina said.

"How dare you!"

"Jane. You good person. But you naïve American. My ISIS contacts tell me about abuse in South Korea. Pleasure city set up around American military base. City called *kijich'on*. Many cities like this. Women forced to give sex to American soldiers. Abuse of women same, only nationality of male abuser different. If women not submit, women raped and murdered. Japan first, America second. I must help. I go to Korea. I say again. Male Korean War over. Female Korean War still in progress. I go help."

"Then let me come with you," Jane said.

"No. Too dangerous for naïve American woman. You have Roberta. Raise her well. You working on civilian pilot license.

Maybe join Women in Air Force. WAF. Good training school at Lackland Air Base in San Antonio, Texas. Finish training. Put to good use. Help women."

From inside Evanita, a kick!

1957 Feb 4, Mon. St. Christopher's Abbey. Girona, Spain.

"Happy Birthday, Geneva," Sister Charlene said.

Geneva sat in a wheelchair and pushed her chair to the table where Sisters Charlene and Francis stood before a birthday cake along with several other recovering polio patients.

"You're eighteen years old," Sister Francis said. "Make a wish and blow out your candles."

"I wish I could walk again," Geneva said out loud, and she blew out the candles.

"You're supposed to keep the wish a secret," Sister Charlene said.

"It doesn't matter," Geneva said. "I'll never walk again. And since I can't walk, I can't do chores, and I can't be a sister."

"Not true," Sister Francis said. "In fact, we have a birthday present that will change your life."

"A magic potion to cure my legs?" Geneva asked.

"No," Sister Charlene said. "Nothing like that. But something that will let you walk again. The sisters in the abbey collected some money together, and we picked the gift. Here."

Sister Charlene passed a large box wrapped in decorative paper to Geneva.

"It's big," Geneva said. "What is it?"

"Open it and see," Sister Francis said. "It's a surprise."

Geneva ripped off the decorative bow and the pretty paper, revealing a plain, brown, cardboard box. She opened the box, and hidden inside among sheets of tissue was a pair of leg braces and forearm crutches.

"Is this a joke?" Geneva said. "I can't wear these braces."

"Why not? We'll help you attach them," the sisters said.

"But I don't know how. I could fall. My legs aren't strong enough. And what good would it do?" Geneva asked.

"You must learn to walk. Now hold still while we attach the braces," Sister Charlene said.

The sisters attached the leg braces, and each took a forearm brace and placed it on each of Geneva's arms.

"Grip the handles firmly," Sister Francis said.

The sisters helped Geneva to her feet and kept her from falling over.

"Now walk," Sister Charlene said.

"I can't. I don't know how," Geneva said.

"Lean forward a little with your forearm crutches," Sister Francis instructed. "No, that's too far. Oh, you're falling."

Geneva fell forward onto Sister Charlene. It took both Sisters Charlene and Francis to aright Geneva.

"You see?" Geneva cried. "It's pointless."

"Nonsense," Sister Francis said. "You simply need some practice."

"Think of yourself as a boat rowing forward," Sister Charlene said, "or as a gallant four-legged horse. Your forearm crutches go first, then your legs, followed by your crutches again. Just try it!"

Geneva placed her forearm crutches in front a bit. She pulled her legs up to her crutches but did not swing them far enough forward. Her forearm crutches were stuck, she could not reextend them forward again, and she fell over. Crash!

Kick!

2007 Mar 17, Sat am. Elrod 402 Campus. Portland, Oregon.

"You like to run, don't you Eve Carson?" Tara asked.

The younger Evanita and Tara Tushenne ran lap after lap around the Elrod 402 campus, running on the track next to the inner fence underneath the aircraft tails.

"I could run forever," Evanita said.

"Another two laps, and we have to get ready for morning chores. This is St. Patrick's Day, and we've got lots of green food to prepare for lunch and dinner."

"We won't be cooking all day, will we?" Evanita asked.

"If we're quick, we can quit by noon. Why? Are you expecting him again?" Tara asked.

"Yeah. Johnny's coming to visit me," Evanita said.

"And you think you can convince him there's no God, is that right?" Tara asked.

"I don't think I can convince him, but I'm going to give it a good try."

The two finished their jogging, cleaned up in their room, and worked quickly all morning in Cafederijet cooking corned beef, Irish stew, cabbage rolls, green French fries, green rice, green cookies, and homemade green-tea ice cream. The two finished cooking by 1 pm. Evanita cleaned up and changed clothes for a second time that day, and she sat down for a moment when Ox-Two knocked at the door.

"Your visitor is here," Ox-Two said.

Ox-Two escorted Evanita to Whalejet, where Johnny waited for her in the visitors' room.

"Johnny, Johnny, I'm so happy to see you!" Evanita said.

Evanita gave Johnny a big hug and kiss.

"Wow!" Johnny said. "You've changed since I last saw you."

"I'm not on the drugs anymore," Evanita whispered in Johnny's ear, and as she did so, she licked Johnny's ear.

Johnny squirmed away.

"Hey, that tickles!" Johnny said.

"I just felt like doing that," Evanita said. "I wanted to see your reaction."

"Like I said," Johnny said. "You're not the same girl. Quite lively this time around. But how can this be? You were on Librium and Tegretol the last time I saw you. Did they change your meds?"

"Scan me," Evanita said.

Johnny shook his body and touched Evanita. Scanning her body, he found no abnormal drugs.

"You're clean," Johnny said.

"Shh. Not so loud. The staff doesn't know. They think I'm still on the stuff," Evanita said.

"Huh?"

"I pretend to take it and instead give it to another detainee," Evanita said.

"Is that legal?" Johnny said. "What if you get caught?"

"I won't. I'm good at faking," Evanita said. "But I've been thinking a lot about what you said on Valentine's Day."

"Oh?"

"Yeah. That story about the bridges. That's another trick religions do—make up analogies to constrain thinking into a narrow path," Evanita said.

"That's not what I intended," Johnny said. "I was only trying to show—"

"There's more," Evanita interrupted. "A bridge is nothing more than walls in parallel with the flow, whereas a wall is perpendicular to the flow. Your bridge analogy is nothing more than a twisted wall. And that's what religion does—it twists the truth for the convenience of feel-good-ism."

"Now wait a minute," Johnny said.

"But a bridge is a trap too. You should have figured that out. Walls create traps—they keep things out, they keep things in, and they keep flow going in one direction. There are no side streets on a bridge. One is always forced to the destination. What about freedom, liberty, democracy? Does God believe in democracy? No. Men created God before democracy was invented. Men believed in the Kingdom, in a male King, and the royal hierarchy. Many kings proclaimed themselves divine and made themselves into gods to be worshiped. Some people, like the early Jews, found a way to break free of the divine mortal King, but to do so, they had to supersede the earthly, royal god by creating their own abstract god, one that was not of this world and so could never be attacked or superseded. This is how Jews got out of worshiping the local kings."

"Evanita!" Johnny said. "If we didn't have bridges, you would complain that the shoreline is a trap, that if only we had bridges to—"

"Further," Evanita interrupted, "those who did not have a desire to supersede the local-city-state-king-as-god model did not create an abstract god, and so they didn't. Example—China."

"Huh? That's terrible reasoning," Johnny said.

"Is it?" Evanita asked.

"Do you still see people as biochemical machines? If you're off the drugs, you should feel connected again. You must be off the drugs, considering the way you greeted me," Johnny said.

"I am attached to people, and I love you very much. But I also perceive this feeling as a biochemical reaction to chemical and sensory stimuli. My emotions blocked this perception before, the drugs let me see it for the first time, and now I've kept the perception after going off the drugs. Because I went to the place of perception, I know it exists, and I can draw on it—even when emotions threaten to twist clarity of thought. And that's what religion is—emotions clouding perception. The bridge is a trap. Religion is a trap. There is no God."

"Okay, okay, okay!" Johnny said. "I'll grant you that some elements of some religions abuse God. When a man shirks responsibility by having twenty children without the means to support them and claims it's God's will—yes, that's God abuse. When someone claims God told him to do something, and he does it, and it's evil, yes, that's God abuse."

"What about when someone says the devil made him do something evil. Is that Satan abuse?" Evanita asked.

"Satan abuse? Satan abuse! Something about that phrase is all wrong, worse than wrong. Can Satan be abused? Nothing is more evil than Satan. But if Satan is abused, the person abusing Satan is more evil than Satan himself."

"Or herself," Evanita said.

"Are you saying Satan is a woman?" Johnny said.

"I'm saying religious literature has heavily blamed women for evil. A man is tempted to cheat on his wife after looking at a pretty woman. Does he take responsibility? No, he says the pretty woman is evil. And he says she has no soul."

"Men don't say that," Johnny said.

"Not today, but they used to. Why? To shore up their own weak character. So how is it a woman at one time had no soul, was not even a real person, but today she has a soul. Is this God's work?" Evanita asked.

"No, it's man's poor perception," Johnny said.

"There. My proof stands," Evanita said.

"But this is no better than the petty atheist who says that if the Bible has flaws, there is no God. People have crude perceptions of the world. Yes, it's true. They thought the world was flat until only a few hundred years ago. It had nothing to do with religion. It had to do with perception based on available evidence."

"Evidence? Suppression of evidence is more like it. What about Copernicus? Galileo? They knew better. They had evidence. What did the evidence get them? Religious persecution," Evanita said.

"Yes. Some religious views at times are crude," Johnny said.

"You call forcing a man to recant his belief of a spherical Earth as a crude belief? It was flat-out wrong. And barbaric," Evanita said.

"God forgives you," Johnny said.

"Are you speaking for God? That's another thing religion does. People call upon the supposed power of God to coerce others into a bridge and send them to the other side where their rhetorical repertoire is predefined."

"Goodness Lord Almighty!" Johnny said.

"Johnny—humans aren't the only ones who can love and hate. Look at all the pets in the world. Dogs and cats are loyal to their masters. They love, hate, and fear like people do. Often masters think their pets are like people. These pets are mammals—advanced biochemical machines. What religion is required of them?"

"But we can reason," Johnny said.

"Because we have advanced symbolic processing. Nothing more. And one side effect of symbolic processing is the creation of the super symbol, the abstract infinity, the trump, the über, the deity, the God. But why have that? Why have the über? Because life is driven to compete for something better. By definition, animals consume—there is no peaceful generation of food as in the plant kingdom. And we're animals too. We must eat. It is in the nature of animals to fight for resources—land, water, air, food. And so it is with people. The drive keeps us alive, otherwise, another animal takes over. Evolution has programmed us this way; evolution has bridged our synapses into competitive compulsions, to attain something higher. Fuse this need for something higher with the symbolic processor that has a symbol for the über, and we have religion—the drive to compete with God to attain the ultimate über, Heaven."

"No religious person will ever tell you they compete with God. People look to God for help," Johnny said.

"Not compete against God. Compete against others using God as a teammate. Johnny—scan me right now. Scan me for oxytocin," Evanita said.

Johnny scanned Evanita. Evanita planted a big kiss on Johnny, and he recorded her levels.

"Well?" Evanita asked.

"Your oxytocin levels spiked up. That's natural. Oxytocin, besides inducing labor, gives people a feeling of bonding," Johnny said.

"It's the love chemical," Evanita said. "Now scan me again. What are my oxytocin levels?"

"Your levels are up, but not spiked as they were when you kissed me," Johnny said.

"Now chase my hands," Evanita said.

Evanita moved her hands rapidly and in random directions in the air in front of Johnny. Johnny chased her hands with his.

"Catch my hands. Catch them," Evanita said.

Johnny chased, and worked, and finally caught Evanita's hands with his.

"What are my oxytocin levels now?" Evanita asked.

"They're up again. That's strange," Johnny said.

"It isn't. Competition is also a sort of bonding. So is hate," Evanita said.

"I don't get it," Johnny said.

"People have a drive to compete and attain above others in the animal kingdom, including other humans. They 'work' with

God—chase him or whatever, but this work is their so-called 'personal relationship' and gives them a sense of connection with God. But it's illogical. If there were a God, why would he grant favors to one person over another?"

"He grants favors to the righteous," Johnny said.

"But isn't it true that each person feels she or he is righteous, that she or he is somewhat better and more deserving than her fellow human?" Evanita said.

"Yes. Disproportionately so at times, but yes."

"That's the God factor—the delusion of superiority over another as a result of chasing God and gaining a sense of competitive superiority—an evolutionary trait programmed into people by natural selection. What do you say to that, Johnny Pindus?"

"Who have you been talking to?" Johnny asked.

"You doubt I can think of this on my own? That just proves what I was saying—you think you have a superior level above me. Your God factor made you say that."

"I always thought I had free will," Johnny said.

"How can you? There is no free will on a bridge," Evanita said.

Johnny sighed.

"So what now? Do you feel superior to me now that you've seemingly reasoned everything out?" Johnny asked.

"No, I don't. I feel like the kid who's discovered on her own that there is no Santa Claus. I wish there were a Santa Claus. It would be nice to have free presents every Christmas. It would be nice to enjoy childhood forever. But it didn't work out that way for me. There is no Santa Claus, and the North Pole is melting. People invent myths to occupy their brains, to distract themselves from the horrors around them in life. The drive to compete results in loss or death for someone or something. That's the ugly reality. Myth softens the blow, and why not invent an all-powerful God to save us all from that fateful moment when instead of us feeding on death, death feeds on us? Isn't that the promise of the afterlife?"

"There must be *more* than our lives on Earth," Johnny said. "Otherwise, what's the point in living?"

"Evolutionary competitive compulsion," Evanita said.

Kick!

1958 Oct 21, Tue. St. Christopher's Abbey. Girona, Spain.

Evanita, Jonara, Cerafina, and Johnny appeared outside on the grounds of St. Christopher's Abbey. A group of paraplegic boys and girls played soccer by swatting the ball with their forearm crutches.

"The days are getting colder, Sister Charlene," Sister Francis said.

"I want them to play football as long as the weather permits," Sister Charlene said.

"Geneva has adjusted well to her leg paralysis," Sister Francis said.

"I'm very proud of her. She was ready to give up on life over a handicap. I told her to pray for strength, and she did. God hears those who pray to him," Sister Charlene said.

"Look at Geneva," Sister Francis said. "Look how she maneuvers the football around those girls."

"She has help," Sister Charlene said. "Geneva is passing the ball back and forth among her teammates. See how Wooton, Reading, and Swanbourough support Geneva?"

"They are an extension of her legs," Sister Francis said. "A handicap means nothing when you have the support of teammates."

"I think Geneva has learned this lesson," Sister Charlene said. "Have you reviewed her application? She's ready to take her temporary vows."

"It's under consideration," Sister Francis said. "I'm concerned about how little time she has spent as a noviate. She could learn more before moving on. Her handicap has slowed her progress."

"You were just saying how a handicap means nothing when you have the support of teammates. Is the devotion to God any different?" Sister Charlene asked.

"No one is handicapped in the eyes of God," Sister Francis said.

"I do hope she can take her temporary vows before the next Pope is chosen," Sister Charlene said.

"Are you suggesting we are slower than the Vatican?" Sister Francis said.

"Geneva submitted her papers on the same day Pope Pius XII died—on October the 9th. Today is the 21st. In two days, a fortnight will have passed," Sister Charlene said.

"I'll expedite the process," Sister Francis said. "Geneva has a good heart. God will choose the right religious devotion for her."

"Thank you, Sister Francis," Sister Charlene said.

Kick!

1959 Mar 15, Sun. Montgomery, Alabama.

The four arrived in the Dakari house where Quadri played with his four-year-old adopted son, Marcus. Quadri stood on his knees while pretending to box Marcus. Marcus wore boxing gloves while Quadri wore training mitts.

"Keep your gloves up and your chin down," Quadri said. "Dance on your feet back and forth. Good. Jab, jab, cross. Hook, hook, uppercut. Keep your gloves up."

The front door opened, and in stepped Dr. Jelana.

"Mommy!" Marcus said.

"Hey, Marcus!" Dr. Jelana said. "How's my little prizefighter?"

Dr. Jelana knelt, and Marcus hugged her.

"And how's my big prizefighter," Dr. Jelana asked as she stood.

"Holding up," Quadri said as he hugged Dr. Jelana.

"Did your agent schedule any fights?" Dr. Jelana asked.

"No," Quadri said. "And I think it's time to move out of the South. I'm blocked no matter which way I turn."

"Oh, things will turn up. They have to," Dr. Jelana said.

"How was the play?" Marcus asked.

"It was wonderful. Kaila and I had a nice time in New York," Dr. Jelana said. "Kaila was nice enough to drive us to the airport and back, but she's too tired to stay. She had to go straight home."

"What was the name of the play?" Quadri asked.

"My dear, Quadri. I've told you a hundred times. You must pay attention to your wife," Dr. Jelana laughed. "It was a Broadway play called, *A Raisin In The Sun.*"

"Oh, now I remember," Quadri said.

"I know where your mind is," Dr. Jelana said. "Boxing. Even now, you're boxing with little Marcus."

"He's already learning the basics," Quadri said. "He will make a fine boxer. And he won't have his skin color as a barrier."

"Don't say things like that, especially not in front of him," Dr. Jelana said. "I don't want Marcus thinking skin color makes a difference in this world."

"It's not the entire world that has this problem," Quadri said, "unless the world is the Deep South such as Alabama."

"Quadri, please!"

"I wanna be like Mommy and Daddy," Marcus said. "I want suntan. Can I have suntan, Mommy?"

Dr. Jelana's eyes lit up in surprise.

"Marcus, it's time for bed," Quadri said.

"But I want to stay up with Mommy," Marcus said. "She can give me suntan."

"We'll talk about it in the morning," Dr. Jelana said. "Goodnight, Marcus."

Dr. Jelana gave Marcus a kiss on the cheek. Quadri took Marcus upstairs and tucked him in bed for the night. Quadri returned downstairs where he found Dr. Jelana making a mixed-fruit drink with ice.

"He's been saying things like that since you left for the play," Quadri said.

"Saying what?" Dr. Jelana asked.

"How he wants a suntan like we have," Quadri said. "And he believes you can give it to him."

"With xanthotoxin?" Dr. Jelana asked. "Now how could he know about that? He was only an infant when I gave it to him for our trip to Africa. He couldn't have remembered anything from that young age."

"There might be another way he knows," Quadri said.

"Uh oh. Now comes the confession. You told him. Darn it, Quadri, I told you I don't want Marcus thinking there's anything wrong with having white skin."

From upstairs, the sounds of a boy screaming echoed through the house. Kay, now three, ran downstairs and jumped into Dr. Jelana's arms.

"Marcus scared, Marcus scared," Kay said.

"He's been doing that every night since you left," Quadri said. "I'll settle him down."

Quadri left for the kitchen and returned with a bar of chocolate.

"What's that for?" Dr. Jelana asked.

"I told him if he eats enough chocolate, he'll get a suntan like us," Quadri said.

"That's silly. Why are you filling that boy's mind with foolishness?" Dr. Jelana asked.

"Because it gets him to sleep," Quadri said.

Quadri disappeared upstairs with the chocolate bar. Marcus stopped screaming.

"Let's go upstairs, Kay. Time for you to go back to sleep," Dr. Jelana said.

"What if Marcus screams again?" Kay asked.

"I have a feeling he won't," Dr. Jelana said.

Dr. Jelana carried Kay upstairs and tucked her into bed. On exiting Kay's room, Dr. Jelana met up with Quadri, and the two returned downstairs.

"So that's how Marcus gets chocolate out of you—he screams until you give it to him. I go away for a few days, and the house falls apart," Dr. Jelana said.

"No, Marcus thinks he's going to die," Quadri said.

"What? Where did he get an idea like that from?"

"One of his friends on the playground told him that. Said Marcus has atom bomb disease, and that's why his dark color is all gone. Says Marcus will turn all red and splotchy and die," Quadri said.

"Did you explain to Marcus he's a white boy?" Dr. Jelana said.

"I did. But he doesn't understand. Everyone around him has dark skin, except for him. He doesn't understand that some people have white skin naturally," Quadri said. "He's scared to death. He calls himself The Ghost, and he doesn't want to go to kindergarten in the fall. He's afraid he'll get all the other students sick and make their skin turn white."

"That Marcus has a wild imagination. I'll talk to him in the morning. Wow. I'm tired! I'm glad Kaila gave me a ride home. I could have never made the drive myself."

Marcus screamed again. Kay ran downstairs and jumped into Quadri's arms.

"Save me, Daddy, save me!" Kay begged.

"I'll go up," Dr. Jelana said.

Dr. Jelana went upstairs and entered Marcus's room.

"I don't want to die," Marcus cried.

"You're not going to die," Dr. Jelana said.

"Look at my skin, Mommy. I have atom bomb disease," Marcus said.

"No. You're fine," Dr. Jelana said as she held Marcus.

"Chocolate doesn't work. My skin is white. I'm sick," Marcus kept repeating.

Dr. Jelana continued to reassure Marcus, but he continued repeating he had atom bomb disease.

"I'll tell you what," Dr. Jelana said. "Tomorrow, we'll put you under the black light and 'treat' your skin. Then you'll be better."

"Promise?" Marcus asked.

"I promise," Dr. Jelana said.

Dr. Jelana tucked Marcus into bed and closed his bedroom door behind her. She returned downstairs to find Quadri alone.

"I tucked Kay into bed again," Quadri said.

"Thank you," Dr. Jelana said.

"So what are we going to do about Marcus?" Quadri asked.

"He's scared out of his mind," Dr. Jelana said. "He really thinks he has a disease because his skin is white. I don't think he'll be able to function in fall kindergarten class if he doesn't calm down."

"You're the doctor," Quadri said. "Aren't you going to prescribe him something?"

"I hate to start him on chlordiazepoxide so early," Dr. Jelana said.

"What's that?"

"It's a new sedative," Dr. Jelana said. "It calms anxiety, fear, and eliminates compulsive behavior."

"Sounds perfect. Give me some too," Quadri said.

"The long-term effects aren't known," Dr. Jelana said. "But my suspicion is that it's highly addictive. And with anything that's addictive, increased dosage is required to achieve the same effect. Withdrawal means all symptoms come back stronger. I don't think I can risk it. An alternative is seeing a child psychiatrist, but I don't know what Marcus's condition would be classified under. What would treatment be? I would guess gradual desensitizing to the fear. I think I know what to do, then. I'll put him on xanthotoxin again and give him black light treatment. His skin will be as dark as ours, and he won't complain. Then gradually over the years, I'll reduce his xanthotoxin dosage. His skin will lighten, but it will occur at a slow rate, and I can rationalize with him what's going on. I will have to take bloods tests to watch his liver levels, but the risk is less than with a chlordiazepoxide sedative. That's my prescription."

Kick!

1962 Apr 7, Sat. St. Christopher's Abbey. Girona, Spain.

Sister Francis sat behind a desk, and a knock sounded against the door.

"Come in," Sister Francis said.

Sisters Charlene and Geneva entered the room.

"Please sit down," Sister Francis said. "First, congratulations Sister Geneva on taking your solemn vows yesterday. It is quite a serious commitment you have made to God, and we are all very proud of you."

"Thank you, Sister Francis," Geneva said.

"Second. Have either of you heard of *Hermandades Obreras de Acción Católica*, also known as HOAC?"

Geneva shook her head, no.

"I have, Sister Francis," Sister Charlene said. "They are a Catholic worker's brotherhood group, organized to support workers' rights in Spain. HOAC is a branch of Catholic Action."

"Yes, it is. As you know, affairs of state move slowly. Coal miners in Asturias launched a small strike yesterday and a much larger strike today. HOAC has been supporting them," Sister Francis said.

"Coal miners on strike?" Geneva asked. "Is my grandfather—"

"Yes, he's one of the strikers," Sister Francis said. "The reason I've called you two here today is to inform you both of your transfers to Asturias."

"What?!" Geneva asked.

"Sister Charlene, you don't look surprised," Sister Francis said.

"You obviously know I'm a member of HOAC, and I support them any way I can. I will go to Asturias and do what the Church asks of me."

"The workers on strike will lose wages. They will need food and other provisions to sustain them during the strike. We have been asked to help," Sister Francis said.

"Who asked? Franco?" Geneva asked.

"Bite your tongue, Sister Geneva. These strikes are technically illegal, and Franco is angered by them. No. The Catholic Church in Spain is becoming split—those who support Franco, and those who support social change. More are siding for social change as days go by. We are in a *Spanish Miracle*, an economic boom most of us have never seen before. The coal miners believe they deserve better working conditions, so they go on strike. We will help them. Geneva, you are from Asturias. It's time you return home but under the Church's umbrella. You will help grow food and make supplies for the striking workers and their families."

"I want to stay here," Geneva said. "I like St. Christopher's Abbey."

"The abbey is wonderful, yes. But our devotion to the Church requires us to travel and help the lives of others. This is your first travel assignment, Sister Geneva. And there will be more," Sister Francis said. "Before you ask, this assignment is not my idea. Mother Superior has ordered it herself. You will stay at St. Renata's Abbey in Carreña, Asturias province. I have your transfer papers here. Pack your things tonight. You will leave in the morning."

"Yes, Sister Francis," Sister Charlene said.

Geneva nodded her head slightly in affirmation. Sisters Charlene and Geneva were nearly out the door when Sister Francis called Geneva back.

"Sister Geneva," Sister Francis said. "Do not let your handicap hinder you. The sisters at St. Renata will give you all the support you need."

"Sister Francis, about my grandfather. He and I didn't—" Geneva started.

"Shh. Say no more. You belong to God now. You will do his work. No one can harm you, not even your grandfather," Sister Francis said.

"Thank you, Sister Francis," Geneva said.

A bus carried Sister Geneva, Sister Charlene, and other sisters from Girona to Carreña. On reaching the town, the bus turned east onto an upward sloping mountain path and proceeded for one kilometer until it could go no farther. The sisters exited the bus with their belongings and climbed the last dozen meters to a medieval castle built into the mountainside. The castle faced south toward Poo de Cabrales.

The castle was surrounded by a moat with water renewing from the mountain. The front entrance was at the southern-most tip and consisted of a large, oblong barbican leading to the outer wall. Four cylindrical towers connected the outer wall segments. The towers and wall were topped with parapets of crenellations and merlons, allowing medieval guards to take cover and fire weapons from above. There were no medieval guards, but occasionally Geneva thought she saw one out of the corner of her eye only to realize it was a bird.

A drawbridge lowered, and the sisters crossed the moat to the barbican. Sister Rosa, an elderly woman, welcomed the newcomers and led them through the main gate into a chamber surrounded by murder holes. The newcomers shook with anxiety.

"Do not worry, no harm will come to you," Sister Rosa said. "This castle is not haunted. The sisters of St. Renata have been running it since 1492."

Sister Rosa led the newcomers from the chamber through a passageway into the outer ward—the area between the outer wall and the inner wall.

"The outer ward is where we keep animals and grow stores of food for the abbey," Sister Rosa said. "I will give you a tour once you are settled. But first, I will lead you to the inner ward."

The inner wall was circular with six towers of smaller diameter than the outer wall towers. Sister Rosa led the newcomers through the inner gate and into the inner ward. A sharp turn to the right, and Sister Rosa led the group to their rooms. The newcomers settled in quickly and only had time to use the garderobes and drink water before Sister Rosa had them on tour again. Sister Geneva had a little trouble keeping up with her forearm crutches and leg braces, and she often fell to the back of the group. Sister Rosa showed the newcomers all aspects of the inner ward—the other sisters' rooms, the stores room, the kitchen, a dining/study area, the workshop rooms, the library, and the infirmary. At the center of the inner ward lay the great hall—a keyhole-shaped room filled with tables and chairs. An altar stood at the north end close to the mountain face. The mountain face itself was not visible but instead was covered over with wood construction. The inside hall, as was the entire castle's stonework, was made of tightly fitted limestone blocks. The north wall was tall and bore a painting of Jesus as he ascended into Heaven while his apostles watched from below. A series of confessionals were located at the east and west ends of the north wall.

"We hold church service in the great hall," Sister Rosa said. "And we use it for other things such as plays, super workshops, social events, and large dinners. This is an open abbey, meaning we often invite a few hundred people to visit from nearby villages for religious events."

There was one additional building on the tour—the gristmill. It was shaped like a parallelogram and was located in the outer ward on the northeast corner of the castle. Water from the mountain face directly above fed down into the mill and provided mechanical power for grinding flour and corn meal. A recent addition of electrical generators to the water wheel provided electricity to the inner ward. The water from the water wheel then ran off into a culvert through the outer wall and flowed into the moat. The same culvert carried waste water that had flowed from the inner ward along a ditch between the mill and the mountain. With Geneva's handicap, she was assigned work in the gristmill where harvested foods were converted into preserved foods. While some harvest foods came from the outer ward, most came in through the front gate. Sisters went out each day through the front gate with processed food and returned with donated food from the nearby villages—Carreña, Poo de Cabrales, Asiego, Inguanzo, Las Arenas, Arangas, Rozagas, Puertas, Berodia, Pandiello, La Molina, Canales, Ortiguero, and Salce. There was one food the sisters had no need to bring in for processing—it was so equisitely produced by the villagers that no further refinement was possible—Cabrales blue cheese. However, the sisters did bring in Cabrales blue cheese as a special treat after successfully completing a penance.

After a month of working in the gristmill, Sister Rosa rewarded Geneva by giving her a special tour of the great hall.

"You are a hard working woman, despite your handicap," Sister Rosa said. "Sister Francis at St. Christopher's wrote me of your polio, and I want to help."

"What help is there? My legs are paralyzed for life," Sister Geneva said.

"Sister Geneva. Doesn't it seem odd that a castle would be built on this particular mountain peak? Haven't you wondered?" Sister Rosa asked.

"It does seem strange. The Picos de Europa are to the south. They are much taller and grander. To the north is a tall mountain ridge before reaching the Atlantic Ocean," Sister Geneva said. "Yes, it does seem strange to have a castle built on a low-lying mountain between two larger mountain ranges."

"Yet between those mountain layers is something special," Sister Rosa explained. "This low-lying mountain, as you call it, was not chosen at random. There are caves. Secret caves, known only to the sisters of St. Renata. We call them, *Las Cuevas de la Curación*—The Caves of Healing. They have been known to purge disease from the sick and bring life back to dead limbs."

"Will this magic cave restore my legs?" Sister Geneva asked.

"The caves are not magic. Magic is of the occult, and we do not believe in such things. But the caves provide healing of a sort. Remember, God heals in mysterious ways—often not the way we expect. But he bestows gifts far beyond our simple requests for aid. Come, follow me."

Sister Geneva followed Sister Rosa into the east confessional against the great hall's north wall.

"Sit for a moment," Sister Rosa said.

"I've never sat on the priest's side of a confessional. Why are there two chairs?" Sister Geneva asked.

"For just this purpose, so that a leader, myself, and a follower, you, can sit here and reflect on past sins and future hopes," Sister Rosa said. "Reflect for a moment quietly. You need not tell me anything."

"Something seems very familiar about this," Evanita said.

"It should," Johnny said. "This is where your Grandma Geneva took you before we were married. This is the site of the second accident."

"The second accident? What was the first?" Evanita said.

"The River Wood and Battery fire," Johnny said.

"Oh," Evanita said. "I guess that was an accident."

"You were in a coma!" Jonara said. "I saw everything."

"You did? How?" Evanita asked.

"Nanna Geneva's diary," Jonara said. "Cerafina knows too."

"Grandma Geneva showed me a diary before she died," Evanita said.

"It's the very same. She recorded many things from the past," Johnny said. "The diary bestows power to certain people for visiting the past."

"Which past?" Evanita asked.

"The past as recorded in the diary," Johnny explained.

"We're not using the diary now," Evanita said.

"No. We're using my dad's candleholder. There are relics in different families—relics built with Norway white spruce, Norway Crimson King maple, lignum vitae, and some form of flax or flaxseed oil. Some relics allow visits to the past, others—especially musical instruments—allow visits to the future."

"Why the special woods?" Evanita asked. "What's the connection?"

"That's a question you asked before, and Grandma Geneva answered. You lost that knowledge in the second accident," Johnny said.

"Tell me now. Tell me everything," Evanita said.

"I'm hesitant," Johnny said. "You didn't handle the information well the first time around. I'm not even sure if bringing you along on these visits to the past is such a good idea. I can't tell you everything so quickly. But there is something special in these Caves of Healing."

"Are you ready?" Sister Rosa asked Geneva.

"Yes."

Sister Rosa tapped on the north wall several times, and a doorway seam appeared where previously the wall was smooth.

"Where did that come from?" Sister Geneva asked.

"This is the entrance to *Las Cuevas de la Curación*. Follow me," Sister Rosa said.

Sister Rosa opened the secret door, and the two entered a short passage. Evanita, Johnny, Jonara, and Cerafina followed along.

"I hear water," Sister Geneva said.

"Just a little farther," Sister Rosa said.

The passageway opened into a brilliantly lit chamber filled with crystals of white, blue, green, and yellow, with an ever-changing rainbow effect of lights. The lights danced around as if on fire, but no flames or smoke filled the air. Additional passageways extended into different directions from the chamber. Clean water cascaded down a crystal rockface into a clear pool.

"One of our sisters is a geologist. She has studied these caves her entire life. She says the caves are composed of strontianite and celestine. Those are minerals containing strontium carbonate and strontium sulfate," Sister Rosa said.

"But what does it mean?" Sister Geneva said.

"Step into the first part of the pool. It's quite shallow, I assure you," Sister Rosa said. "But take your shoes off first."

Sister Geneva sat on a crystalline ledge and removed her shoes. She hobbled with her crutches and paralyzed legs to the edge of the pool. She placed her left foot in and removed it.

"It's warm," Geneva said.

"How do you know?" Sister Rosa asked.

"I can feel it," Sister Geneva said. "I can feel it? I can feel it!"

"Yes, Sister Geneva. You can feel the pool!" Sister Rosa said.

"But I can't move my legs. And I can't feel the dry cave floor," Sister Geneva said.

"One thing at a time. Place your feet in the pool again," Sister Rosa said.

Sister Geneva placed her left foot followed by her right foot into the pool. The water was warm and swirled around her feet and ankles. Suddenly, her feet felt like tree roots extending into the pool. She sensed the precise dimensions of the pool and realized it drained into the water taps of the gristmill.

"The water we use in the mill—it comes from here," Sister Geneva said.

"Yes, that's right," Sister Rosa said. "The minerals fortify our processed food. Many people find relief from their ailments with our food."

"This is scary," Sister Geneva said, and she jumped out of the water with her own legs providing propulsion.

"You jumped out of the water!" Sister Rosa said.

"I did!" Sister Geneva said.

Geneva tried to walk on the dry cave floor without her forearm crutches, but she stumbled and fell over. Sister Rosa helped her to her feet.

"I don't understand," Sister Geneva said. "When I'm in the water, I feel power in my legs, but once I leave the water, the power is gone, and my legs are paralyzed again."

"The water contains dissolved minerals, some of which are strontianite and celestine. But there's something special about these minerals. They seep into the flesh and provide strength," Sister Rosa said.

"How's that possible, Daddy?" Jonara asked.

"Scan the crystals," Johnny said. "What do you read?"

"They're like Sister Rosa said. I read strontium, carbon, sulfur, and oxygen. But there's something strange about the strontium. It's like—no wait, yes, no, kinda like strontium, but then it isn't, but it can't be anything else."

"You're reading the radioactive isotopes of strontium," Johnny said.

"Radioactive?" Evanita asked. "Is it safe? Radiation causes cancer."

"Relax, Evanita," Johnny said. "Don't worry about the isotopes. They happen to be safe isotopes of strontium."

"I don't know. I want to get out of here," Evanita said. "Let me go."

"It's happening again," Johnny said. "You're getting yourself worked up over the strontium."

"My legs," Evanita said. "I feel like my legs are on fire. They're burning. I'm in the factory fire again. I have to run. I have to run away, anywhere, everywhere. Johnny, make it stop. Johnny!"

"Jonara," Johnny said. "Break!"

"*Peliko!*" Jonara said.

The four returned to Evanita's hospital room. Evanita kicked her legs as if they were aflame.

"My legs are on fire!" she screamed.

Evanita's heart raced. Two nurses rushed in and forced Jonara, Johnny, and Cerafina out of the room and down the hallway. Moments later, Dr. Reegen rushed in and injected something into Evanita's IV drip line. A few minutes after that, Evanita settled down and fell asleep. Dr. Reegen reemerged from Evanita's room and found Johnny, Jonara, and Cerafina still in the hallway.

"I'm going to have to ask you three to leave the hospital," Dr. Reegen said.

"Is Mommy okay? Can we see her?" Jonara asked.

"Evanita is in serious condition. Your presence triggered a myocardial infarction. Fortunately, we were able to treat her in time and save her heart tissue. But I can't have her undergoing any further stress. Please, leave the hospital now. Evanita needs complete rest if we are to save her and the baby."

"I want to see Mommy," Jonara said.

Dr. Reegen motioned to a security guard. The security guard walked forward and took Jonara by the arm.

"Let's go, Jonara," Johnny said.

"No. I want to see Mommy!" Jonara said.

The security guard dragged Jonara down the hallway and out the hospital door with Johnny and Cerafina following behind.

"Call the hospital and get visitation permission before coming back," the security guard said, and he closed the door on Jonara's face.

"Well, that does it for today," Johnny said.

"Let's sneak back in," Jonara said while the three stood outside the hospital doors.

"And do what?" Johnny asked. "We went in thinking we could help your mother, but we made things worse."

"And I know why. I should have said something in Miramish to cure her," Jonara said.

"Why didn't you?" Cerafina asked.

"Because everything happened so fast. We were in one time, and then we jumped to another. I had no time to think," Jonara said.

"I think it's best you didn't chant anything. Sometimes a chant backfires, like when you tried destroying the boxing arena," Johnny said. "Come on. Let's go home to Nanna Geneva's house."

CHAPTER 16:

A Primary Tooth

2023 Oct 5, Thu Eve. Geneva Carreña's House. Corpus Christi, Texas.

"Thank you for letting me spend the night with Jonara," Cerafina said to Johnny and Eva.

"Don't stay up too late," Eva said.

"We won't," Jonara said. "Goodnight."

"Goodnight," Eva and Johnny said.

Jonara and Cerafina walked upstairs to Jonara's guestroom.

"I'm sorry about your mother," Cerafina said.

"I wish I could have helped her," Jonara said. "But like I said, everything happened too fast."

"Maybe you can do something now," Cerafina said. "Are there some words you can say to help her with her legs?"

"I've never tried from a distance," Jonara said. "Ow."

"What's the matter?" Cerafina asked.

"One of my baby teeth is loose," Jonara said, "but only a little. The permanent tooth is pushing up under it, and the baby tooth doesn't want to move. It's stuck in my gums."

"Wiggle it out," Cerafina said.

"I've been wiggling it. And every time I wiggle, it hurts. It really doesn't want to come out," Jonara said.

"Maybe you can say a chant to make it come out," Cerafina said. "Why don't you try?"

"Okay," Jonara said. "Hmm. What should I say?"

"How about something like, 'Tooth in the day, tooth in the night, wiggle out now, wiggle out bright'," Cerafina suggested.

"Wiggle out bright?" Jonara asked.

"I just made it up. What would you say?" Cerafina asked.

"How about, 'Baby tooth that now is loose, come out quick or I'll pull it with a noose'," Jonara said.

"You gotta work on meter and rhythm," Cerafina said.

"Strange. I had no problem before. Why am I stumbling now?" Jonara asked.

"Maybe because you're chanting on yourself instead of on something else. It's like cutting something with a knife. It's easy when you cut an apple, but to cut your own flesh, that's scary," Cerafina explained.

"It is scary," Jonara agreed.

"Maybe you should get some information on the tooth first. Then you could decide how to get it out," Cerafina said.

"I wonder if I should pull it out now," Jonara said. "What if it bleeds too much? Nanna Geneva's wake is tomorrow evening, and I don't want to look like someone from the crypt."

The two paused in thought for a moment. Jonara's cell phone rang.

"Caller ID says it's Almarita," Jonara said. "Should I answer?"

"Of course," Cerafina said. "She's your friend. Relax. Don't be so nervous."

"Hello?" Jonara said.

"Joni! It's me! Allie! Your bestest friend! Or at least, your former bestest friend. How the heck are you?" Almarita asked.

"I...am...fine," Jonara stuttered.

"You sound nervous. Are you afraid of me after last night?" Almarita asked.

"Last...night? What was...last...night?" Jonara stuttered.

Cerafina felt compassion for Jonara. Cerafina sat on the bed behind Jonara with her legs crossed and combed Jonara's hair. Jonara's voice relaxed and steadied.

"Don't you remember the conversation we had? When you told me about dating Cerafina?" Almarita asked. "And I told you to date and dump guys when you're on the road? The short leash?"

"The short leash, yes, I remember," Jonara said with more confidence.

"You sound better," Almarita said. "Did you try the short leash on a guy?"

Cerafina combed and curled Jonara's hair in Cerafina's fingers, playing with the smooth and silky texture.

"Mmm. No, no short leash," Jonara said.

"Huh? Jonara, are you smoking something?" Almarita asked.

"No! You know I'd never do that," Jonara said.

"Then why is it you went from a nervous wreck to a relaxed coolie?"

Cerafina started massaging Jonara's neck.

"Lower," Jonara blurted without realizing what she'd done.

"Lower!" Almarita said. "Who's there with you?"

"No one," Jonara said.

"What you really want to say is, 'That feels good, Cerafina. Do it some more.' Am I right?" Almarita asked.

"Allie!"

"Joni! You're so transparent. You know that, don't you? She's massaging your back, right?" Almarita asked.

"My muscles hurt. It's been a long day," Jonara said.

"I bet. More experimenting, is that right? Well, this obsession will only end in misery. I warned you last night, but you didn't listen. You've gone to the dark side," Almarita said.

"We're still friends, aren't we?" Jonara asked.

"If you were any of my other friends, I'd end it right now. But it's not that easy. We have a history, you and I. Our mothers have a history."

"I know," Jonara said.

"So we're connected, whether we want to be or not," Almarita said. "Cerafina is almost like family to me. Her dad and my Aunt Shelia dated for a while. That's why your relationship with Cerafina is so weird. It's almost incestual."

"It isn't," Jonara said. "Cerafina and I haven't done anything immoral."

"Hmm. Not quite," Almarita said.

Cerafina took the cell phone from Jonara.

"Almarita? This is Cerafina."

"Oooh. The other woman! I'm so scared!" Almarita mocked.

"Look. Jonara is stressed out about her mother, grandmother, and father. Give her a break, will you?" Cerafina asked.

"Oh, he, ha! You're kicking me around now! I should have known Jonara would set her dog on me," Almarita said.

"Jonara has nothing to do with this. I took the phone from her," Cerafina said.

"*Jonara has nothing to do with this*," Almarita mocked. "That's bullcrap. I know it, you know it, and she knows it. Jonara has everything to do with it. She *is* the reason."

"You know, Almarita, if I didn't know better, I'd say you were jealous of me," Cerafina said.

"Hah! Joni tried that line on me last night. You can't rattle my cage that easy."

"You think in black and white," Cerafina continued. "Set a goal, leash a man, accomplish goal, life is satisfied and over. You wouldn't know what to do with love if it bit you in the ankle."

"Who are you to talk, you lesbian wanna-be? You're a thief from a family of thieves. Your mother stole Davino from my Aunt Sheila. You're stealing Joni from me."

"That's absurd, and you know it. My father divorced his first wife over the affair with your Aunt Sheila. And Sheila ended her relationship with my father, not the other way around. But tell me this, All-ie! Did your Aunt Sheila really love my father?" Cerafina asked. "Or was that another example of your family holding a man on a tight leash? What about the leash you have on Jonara?"

"Stop it," Almarita said.

"Is it fair to Jonara? You want to give her love, but you can't. It's not in your family's nature. My mother loves my father, and I love Jonara. Now then, are you going to deprive Jonara of that joy? Or are you going to subject her to the leash and keep her emotions in check?"

"Stop it! You're a jealous lesbian who's poisoned to the soul," Almarita said.

"At least I have a soul. Do you?" Cerafina asked. "Listen to this!"

Cerafina gave Jonara a loud, smacky kiss on the lips with the cell phone closeby. Jonara's eyes lit open in the excitement, and she wasn't sure whether to fight Cerafina or enjoy the moment.

"What do you think of that?" Cerafina said into the cell phone, but her only reply was silence.

Almarita disconnected the phone call. Cerafina looked at the cell phone briefly. "Call ended," displayed on the screen.

"She hung up," Cerafina said.

Jonara threw her hands on her head, and her eyes rolled around as if her skull were about to explode.

"It's not working," Jonara said, and she fell into a nervous twitch.

Cerafina tried combing her fingers through Jonara's hair again, but Jonara's hands were in the way.

"No," Jonara said, and she pulled away. "I have to think. I can't be caught between my two friends."

"I'm trying to help," Cerafina said.

"I know. It's just...I'm so confused. My emotions are running all over the place—with Almarita, you, my family, and this tooth that keeps holding on while my permanent tooth pushes on it. I just wish everyone would leave me alone. Leave me alone!"

Jonara ran down the steps, out the front door, and into the night. She left everything behind—the Moissan Ruby, the Aromani candleholder, even her shoes.

Johnny walked into Jonara's bedroom where Cerafina remained sitting on the bed in shock.

"What happened?" Johnny asked.

"She's having a nervous breakdown," Cerafina said.

"She needs to let off steam, is that it?" Johnny asked.

"Yeah," Cerafina replied. "I think I should go home. Spending the night with Jonara was too much for her."

"No, you don't have to go. She needs a friend," Johnny said.

"She has one. Almarita Foster. I'm in the way," Cerafina said.

"Please stay the night. She'll be back," Johnny said.

"Thank you no, Mr. Pindus. I best be going home now," Cerafina said as she gathered her things together.

"Can I give you a lift home?" Johnny asked.

"I'll walk, thank you. I need a good cry before I get home," Cerafina said.

Cerafina walked briskly down the stairs with Johnny following. She was prepared to bolt out the door but had enough stamina to turn back and speak to Johnny.

"Thanks for everything," she said as tears started running down her face.

Cerafina bolted out the door and ran down the sidewalk as she lost emotional strength and slipped into torrential tears.

"Dammit!" Johnny said after he closed the door. "Not again!"

"Mr. Johnny, Mr. Johnny. What I do? What you need?" Anna said as she came running from the kitchen.

Johnny stared at her for a moment.

"Where's Miss Eva?" Johnny asked.

"She took her sleeping pill. She's sleeping like a baby. Should I wake her?"

"No, no, no," Johnny said. "Let her sleep."

"How I help you?" Anna asked.

Johnny patted Anna on the back.

"Get some rest, Anna. Get some rest," Johnny said.

Anna looked at Johnny in surprise, but she didn't heed him. She returned to the kitchen and worked on some muffins for the next morning's breakfast. Johnny walked upstairs and into Jonara's guestroom. He found the Moissan Ruby and Aromani candleholder on the floor. He reached for them and held them tightly in his hands, so tightly that his hands turned white.

"With all my strength I would destroy you both if it would bring peace to the Carreña family," Johnny said.

Johnny's hands shook with rage, and he traveled back in time.

1989 Dec 3, Mon. Page Street Clinic Building. Portland, Oregon.

Johnny appeared in MacNessi Dental during the beginning of lunch break. Roberta had just finished an amalgam and was cleaning up. Eva stepped into the treatment room.

"This is the conversation," Johnny said. "I've seen it too many times before. How I wish it would end and never come back."

"I was beginning to think you'd never show," Roberta said. "Where were you all morning? I've been running around doing double duty to cover for you."

"I just came back from the doctor," Eva said.

"Oh? Something wrong? You could have warned me this morning," Roberta said.

"I'm pregnant," Eva blurted.

"What!?" Roberta said.

"I'm pregnant. It's true, I'm expecting a child," Eva said.

"I knew it!" Roberta said. "Morning sickness and bad hair for the last two months. But how could you do it, Eva, after everything we've been through? You walk in here four hours late, make me bust my butt for you, and you have the nerve to say you're pregnant? What have you been doing? Sleeping with men behind my back? Well I guess it's over then."

"No, it's not like that!" Eva said, nearly in tears.

"Who do you think you're fooling? I know how the birds and bees work. Well? Who is he? Or don't you know? Too many to choose from? Or was it that Marcus Cracbern, as if he hasn't done enough already. Figures you would sleep with him. You worked for him and snuck out with him. You said you loved me. That was a lie, wasn't it? Wasn't it?!"

Eva slapped Roberta. Roberta slapped Eva back. Eva fell into tears, but Roberta's eyes went afire.

"So what do you want from me, Eva?" Roberta asked. "You want to determine the father? Go get a paternity test. Then sue the bastard for benefits. That's what your kind does. You want an abortion? Go get one. You want sympathy? Go look it up in the dictionary between *swastika* and *syndrome*."

"I don't know who the father is!" Eva cried. "I haven't slept with anyone!"

"You're pathetic," Roberta said. "Get out of my clinic. I never want to see you again, you lying breeder!"

Johnny returned to the present in Geneva's house.

"I never want to see you again, you lying breeder," Johnny repeated.

Johnny smashed his fists through the bedroom window. The glass shattered. He threw the Moissan Ruby and Aromani candleholder through the open space and sent them flying through the outside air, across the yard, and into the bushes. Anna rushed in to find a broken window and Johnny's hands bleeding.

"Mr. Johnny! Your hands are bleeding something awful! Come into the bathroom quickly. I clean and bandage you up!" Anna said.

In the time it took for Anna to clean and bandage Johnny's wounds, his rage dissipated. Anna begged him to go to bed, but instead, he walked outside the house and stood in the back-yard, alone, and began to cry in his odd sort of way. Johnny cried like a person hiccupping in slow motion. He did not wail or gush with tears, he simply let out a periodic, prolonged, hic-cup-like sound in his throat, as if an awful bit of food were lodged and could neither be swallowed nor coughed back up.

Jonara had run to the Corpus Christi Hospital. She snuck into the building and down the hallway where her mother stayed. The door to Evanita's room was closed. Waiting until no one would notice, Jonara opened it as quietly as possible and closed it behind her. She tiptoed to the far side of Evanita's bed in hopes of remaining undetected from medical personnel.

"Mommy," Jonara whispered.

Evanita did not move. Whether asleep or sedated, Jonara wasn't sure. Jonara shook Evanita's arm gently, but Evanita did not stir, nor did Evanita snore or indicate she was in some sort of restful sleep.

"You must be in a very deep sleep," Jonara said. "I wish you could hear me. I wish I could tell you what's happening. Mommy, wake up."

Evanita did not wake. Jonara placed her hand on Jonara's abdomen and felt the baby kick lightly.

"Little baby inside," Jonara said. "Can you hear me? The world is a scarey place out here. Enjoy the protection you have inside Mommy. It won't last forever."

Jonara worked at her loose primary tooth, but still it would not yield.

"If I could just get rid of this tooth, I might feel a bit better," Jonara said. "But I'm afraid to do anything more than wiggle it."

Jonara drew her hand across Evanita's abdomen, and the baby inside seemed to react.

"I will only know this feeling of carrying a child if I love a man," Jonara said. "Loving Cerafina is a dead end. It's unfair. Why can't she be a boy instead of a girl? But then she wouldn't be Cerafina. Why can't I have both?"

Evanita gurgled and mumbled. A display screen showed her brainwave activity increasing.

"She's waking up," Jonara said.

The levels on the screen increased, and a red light started flashing. A few seconds later, the door opened suddenly. Jonara ducked quickly and hid under Evanita's bed.

"Time for your tranquilizer," the nurse said. "You must be kept asleep. Don't want you overexerting yourself."

The nurse attached a slow-drip medication to Evanita's IV line. The brainwaves subsided, and Evanita's mumbling stopped.

"Good," the nurse said, and he left.

He closed the door behind him.

"If I stop the medicine, Mommy will wake up," Jonara said. "But then the little red light will flash, and the nurse will come back. How can I stop it? Oh, I should have brought the Water Ruby and candleholder with me."

Then an idea hit Jonara. Could she try without the Moissan Ruby and Aromani candleholder? There was only one way to find out. Jonara tightened a clamp on the line delivering medication. The medication drip stopped. Evanita began regaining consciousness, and the brainwave levels on the display increased. Jonara spoke:

Miramish	Translation
Liani opeifu feifa	Scans of show
Ishu fenaigeshi kiru.	In brainwaves here.
Feifo galudi rialu,	Show levels low,
Kelofo fieshu feluana derotu.	Keep red light clear.

The brainwave levels increased on the scanner and approached the red-light level.

"Why didn't it work?" Jonara whispered to herself. "Of course it didn't work. I don't have the Water Ruby and candleholder. But wait—how did I know the Miramish words to say? Unless..."

Jonara repeated the chant with one hand over her navel and the other touching the brainwave scanner. The scans returned to a lower level, falsely indicating that Evanita was in deep sleep. Evanita mumbled as she slowly regained consciousness.

"It worked. But how?" Jonara asked herself.

Jonara lifted her shirt and looked at her navel. A faint glow echoed around her navel, as if there had been some sort of tattoo of the half-face or possibly some strange characters. But the glow faded, and her abdomen appeared normal.

"Jonara," Evanita mumbled. "Jonara. Is that you?"

"Yes, Mommy," Jonara said. "I'm here."

"The doctors," Evanita said. "They did something to me. They drugged me. I feel like...like...when I was at the Elrod. I was drugged. What did Tara teach me? Buddha and a thousand hands. Thousand hands."

Evanita stretched her arms and made motions similar to the Falun Dafa she had once learned at the Elrod 402.

"This pregnancy will be the death of me, I fear," Evanita said.

"Don't say that, Mommy. Don't talk about death," Jonara said.

"Jonara. There's something unusual about our family. Good or bad, I don't know. I never figured it out. Like my father. I learned who my father was once. But I can't remember. Like a fog. Your grandma—my mother—Eva—she won't tell me. Your parents love you, Jonara. Johnny and I are your parents. You know we love you," Evanita said.

"I love you both too," Jonara said tearfully.

"Jonara. You must find out who my parents are. Eva is my mother. Find my father. Find out who you really are. You shouldn't go through life wondering. Life shouldn't be lived in a fog. Find out who you are. Live the person you are, not something else. Live, Jonara, live," Evanita said.

"Mommy. I don't know how to say this. I...I...someday I want to have children," Jonara said.

"That's wonderful. I hope things go well with you. Not like your poor suffering mother. There should be an award for every woman who brings a child into this world for all the suffering she endures. A purple heart or something," Evanita said.

"But...what if I can't?" Jonara said.

"Don't worry," Evanita said. "If you have children, you have children. If you have problems, maybe a fertility doctor can help. But that's years away. Don't worry about the future, Jonara."

"What if...what if...what if I'm a...lesbian?" Jonara cried.

"Come here," Evanita said, and she stretched her arms out. "Give your mother a hug."

Jonara hugged Evanita.

"You are my daughter. You'll always be my daughter, and I'll always love you. You are what Mother Nature made you. Treasure the gifts she bestows upon you. Be Jonara, nothing else. Promise me?"

"I promise," Jonara cried.

"You have lots of time to learn about yourself. Enjoy your youth, Jonara. Don't waste it with worry. There's more than enough suffering in the world to go around, especially as you get older."

"But if I'm a lesbian, I won't be able to have children!" Jonara blurted.

"Shhh. Easy, Jonara. Easy. There's time to think about that later. Don't take the world on your shoulders. Please, be at ease," Evanita said.

Evanita held Jonara's head to her side. The Miramish chant on the brainwave scanner subsided, and the device began displaying more accurate information. The levels rose until a red light flashed indicating Evanita's consciousness. The same nurse as before walked in.

"I thought I put enough medication in the—you again!" he said after seeing Jonara. "You're not supposed to be here. Did you tamper with that clamp? Out, out!"

The nurse opened the clamp and allowed medication to resume dripping into Evanita's IV line. Evanita slipped back into sleep.

"Mommy!" Jonara cried.

"Come on, you. You've caused enough trouble for today," the nurse said, and he pulled Jonara's arm.

"I love you, Mommy!" Jonara said as the nurse pulled her into the hallway.

The nurse dragged Jonara to a utility closet and closed the door behind them. He held her arms behind her back and forced her face against a mirror.

"Listen you," he barked. "You keep out of this ward, see? That woman is mighty sick, and I'm tired of you pesky kids running around and stirring up trouble."

"Let me go!" Jonara said.

The nurse slammed Jonara's face into the mirror several times.

"And no backtalk," he said. "You kids need to learn respect. The woodshed is sorely missed in the modern age. At least then a kid could get a proper whipping."

The nurse escorted Jonara out of the utility closet, down the hallway, and forced her out of the hospital.

"Don't come back unless you're with a parent, don't come back today, and have your parents call for visitation permission."

"But my mother is my parent!" Jonara tried to say but by that time, the nurse had left, and a security guard gave Jonara an evil eye.

Jonara walked back to Geneva's house. She gritted her teeth, and as she did, something strange happened. Her primary tooth which had clung so strongly to her gums popped out of her mouth. Then she understood. When the nurse slammed her face against the mirror, he jarred the tooth loose.

"My childhood is ending," Jonara said as she looked at her loose tooth.

Jonara arrived in Geneva's yard and threw her tooth in the bushes—ironically the same bushes where Johnny had thrown the Moissan Ruby and Aromani candleholder. She didn't realize this at the time. Jonara was tired. She went upstairs to her room and was shocked to find glass scattered everywhere. She thought of waking Johnny or Anna but was too tired to think. She went downstairs, turned the television on to a low audio level, and fell asleep to old reruns. It was the first night during her visit she didn't travel back in time.

2023 Oct 6, Fri Morn. Geneva Carreña's House. Corpus Christi, Texas.

"Jonara, are you going to get up? It's noon!" Eva said.

"What?" Jonara said with groggy eyes. "I feel like I just went to sleep."

"We've been up since six-thirty this morning," Eva said. "We ate breakfast, went to the hospital to visit your mother, came back, and now we're ready to go out for lunch."

"You saw my mother?" Jonara asked.

"Yes. She's doing much better today," Eva said.

"That's because she's heavily tranquilized," Johnny said.

"Each day she holds on gives her baby more time to develop and risks fewer problems once the C-section is performed," Eva said.

"I want to see Mommy," Jonara said.

"Um, no," Eva said. "The hospital staff told us about you sneaking in last night. Except for going out to eat, you're grounded again."

"Daddy?" Jonara said.

"I have to agree with her on this one," Johnny said. "I know you were upset last night, but the hospital staff said you fought them pretty hard."

"I didn't fight with anyone," Jonara said.

"The attending nurse said you kicked, screamed, broke glass everywhere, spilled cleaning liquid, ran down the hall, broke a—"

"It's a lie!" Jonara said. "All of it is a lie! The nurse hurt me! He shoved me against a mirror in a closet."

"That's not what the hospital staff said. Who are we supposed to believe?" Johnny asked.

"I thought you knew me better than that," Jonara said. "Use the Moissan Ruby. Scan me. You'll see I'm telling the truth."

Johnny looked at Eva, and Eva returned the gaze.

"Your father got rid of that relic and the candleholder," Eva said.

"What?!" Jonara said.

"See his bandaged hands? He broke the window last night in frustration. That's when he got rid of those relics," Eva said.

"Frustrated? About what? Daddy, we have to find the Water Ruby and candleholder. We must!" Jonara said.

Johnny was about to say something but paused.

"They're too stressful," Eva said.

"But we helped you with your cancer," Jonara said. "The Water Ruby and candleholder have the power to heal."

"It just seemed that way," Eva said.

"Daddy!" Jonara said.

"Maybe they helped," Johnny said.

"Maybe?! That's not what happened," Jonara said.

"Jonara. Your father and I have agreed that now is the time to stop relying on these relics. They may seem to help in the short term, but in the big picture, they only add more stress. Come along. Let's get lunch," Eva said.

"No. I'm staying here," Jonara said.

"Jonara! I'm your grandmother. Stop behaving like a child! Get up from that couch and come to lunch with us," Eva ordered.

"No. It's not fair. I don't want to eat at no stinking restaurant," Jonara said.

"Oh leave her be," Johnny said. "Anna can watch her."

"Very well," Eva said. "But I want you to dump that attitude of yours, young lady. It gets old fast."

Eva and Johnny left. Anna brought a plate of muffins, sandwiches, and juice.

"They told me everything about last night," Anna said. "I'm sorry for you and your mother."

"Forget it," Jonara said as she munched into a muffin and slurped down some juice.

"You were overly tired last night," Anna said. "You haven't been sleeping well, and you got cranky. That's all. You feel better today, no?"

"No, I mean yes," Jonara said. "That's strange. I do feel better."

"Your tooth is gone, no?" Anna asked.

"Yes again," Jonara said.

"Food good for you. Make you happy," Anna said. "Tonight important. Your Nanna Geneva's wake."

"I completely forgot about her," Jonara said. "Where are my manners?"

"And tomorrow is funeral," Anna said. "Did you forget that too? Miss Geneva was a fine lady. I miss her. Everyone miss her."

"Oh come on," Jonara said. "Give me a hug."

Jonara and Anna hugged.

"I still have no job after this one. Economy not always good for housekeeper, especially Hispanic housekeeper," Anna said. "I pray I not get deported."

"You're legal, aren't you?" Jonara asked.

"I have immigration papers, yes. But American government could always take away. I could be sent back," Anna said.

"I'll talk to Daddy. Maybe he'll take you on as a housekeeper. But it means moving to Portland," Jonara said.

"Hmm," Anna mused.

"What's wrong with Portland?" Jonara asked.

"No sunshine. Anna need lots of sunshine. Good for health," Anna said.

"I've never heard that before. Everyone I know says sunshine is bad. Causes skin cancer. Oh well, doesn't seem to mean much to me now," Jonara said.

"What you mean by that?" Anna asked.

Jonara thought about all the things that had happened to her in the few days she'd been in Corpus Christi.

"It's hard to explain," Jonara said. "Maybe someday I'll figure it out."

"Well, you eat and drink as much as you like. And watch anything on TV. I make you happy," Anna said.

"All right, Anna," Jonara said.

Jonara ate her fill of muffins, sandwiches, and juice. She turned on the television and searched for something to watch, but nothing appealed to her. Bored, she left the living room and entered Geneva's music room. She looked at the piano and thought of Cerafina. She almost shed a tear but checked herself and looked for something else to do in the music room. There was Geneva's viol, but again, that reminded her of Cerafina. What else did Geneva have? Jonara searched through the different cabinets and found an old-fashioned oboe.

Jonara looked closely at the oboe. The two middle-body sections were crimson, like the Norway Crimson King maple wood found on the other family musical instruments. The bell and top section were white like Norway white spruce. Lignum vitae was used in the joints between sections. The reed and staple seemed ordinary enough, being made of cane and cork-covered steel respectively, and the oboe was finished in flaxseed oil. Looking farther still, she saw two engravings inside the bell—a small carving of the half-face symbol, and the word, "MacNessi."

"Good god, this is Jane MacNessi's oboe!" Jonara said aloud. "But how? Daddy said it was destroyed. No, he said it was lost. But then how was it found? Who found it? Nanna Geneva? And why didn't she tell anyone? Maybe she did. But she didn't tell Daddy. I wonder if it still works. What am I saying, I don't even know how to play the oboe."

"Then maybe I can help," said a familiar voice.

Jonara turned and saw a fourteen-year-old girl standing in the doorway. She wore a tight-fitting flower-patterned dress, her curly hair was silky and pulled up in back, she had several flowers in her hair, and she had done her face up in makeup. She held something behind her back.

"Cerafina?" Jonara asked.

"I'm sorry. I shouldn't have offered to help. I've helped too much," Cerafina said.

"Cerafina, I—" Jonara started to say in excitement.

Jonara was happy to see Cerafina and was on the verge of dancing a jig of joy with her, but Cerafina was in a somber and apologetic mood.

"I just came by to say goodbye," Cerafina said. "I have no business meddling with your life. You came down here to help with your grandmother's affairs, your mother is ill, and I can only think of my selfish desires."

"But Cerafina," Jonara tried to interrupt.

"I know. I deserve to be yelled at, screamed at, kicked around, and beaten," Cerafina said.

"Wait," Jonara said.

"And as a peace offering, I brought you this vase of fresh flowers," Cerafina said as she produced the flowers from behind her back. "I hope someday you can find it in your heart to forgive me."

Cerafina handed the flowers to Jonara. Jonara tried to say something, but for once she was speechless. She placed the flowers on a side table and stared at them. A mixture of wonderful and powerful emotions welled up in her, and she knew that if she looked back at Cerafina, she was going to explode.

"I don't blame you for not speaking to me," Cerafina continued. "I deserve it. I don't even deserve to be looked at. I know saying sorry isn't enough. It never is. But this is the best I can do. I guess I'll go now. I'll leave you alone for good. Goodbye, Jonara."

While Cerafina spoke those last words, Evanita's words to Jonara kept circling in Jonara's mind, "You are what Mother Nature made you. Treasure the gifts she bestows upon you."

"This is it," Jonara thought. "Mother Nature is kicking in."

Jonara jumped up and at Cerafina. Cerafina backed up in surprise and lifted her arms to block what she thought was an attack from Jonara.

"Don't hurt me, don't hurt me," Cerafina said. "I'm sorry."

Jonara brushed Cerafina's arms away, wrapped her arms around Cerafina's torso, and kissed Cerafina deeply. Cerafina squirmed for a moment, unsure of what to make of the moment, but Jonara held fast against Cerafina and held her kiss with Cerafina until Cerafina stopped resisting and completely understood Jonara's intentions.

Finally, Jonara released her kiss. Cerafina's eyes opened, but she seemed starved for oxygen. Her legs went limp, and she started to fall.

"Whoa," Jonara said, and she helped Cerafina to a chair.

Jonara pulled a chair up beside Cerafina and held her upright.

"What happened?" Cerafina said. "I came to apologize, and I blacked out."

"This is what happened," Jonara said, and she gave Cerafina another kiss, although the duration was short enough such that Cerafina did not black out again.

"Jonara? Are you sure? I mean, you're not feeling sorry for me, are you?"

"I am what Mother Nature made me," Jonara said. "I'm treasuring the gift she gave me. And that gift is Cerafina Ancona Vagatti."

"But I thought you wanted children and all that. What about Almarita? Lordy, I need some air," Cerafina said as she fanned her face with her hand.

"I'll worry about that later," Jonara said. "But right now, I love you. I'm saying it to you now, Cerafina. I...love...you!"

"This is going to need many Our Fathers and Hail Marys with all the confessing I'll need to do," Cerafina said.

"Then don't confess. Is love a sin?" Jonara said.

Cerafina held Jonara's hands tenderly.

"Yes it is. At least those who don't have love believe so," Cerafina said. "Aren't you afraid, Jonara? You're only thirteen, and I'm fourteen. I know we've had this conversation before, but you dropped the L-bomb on me. Things are different. I am attached to you. Okay, I'll say it. I love you too, Jonara Carreña Pindus. Now I've dropped the L-bomb. What are we going to do?"

"What other people do when they love each other—keep loving each other. There are no laws for love," Jonara said.

"I know, I know. I don't understand anything anymore," Cerafina said.

"You were the one making advances last night," Jonara said.

"I know," Cerafina said. "I did that to make Almarita jealous."

"You mean you didn't enjoy it?" Jonara laughed.

Cerafina nudged Jonara in the shoulder, and the two had a good, hearty laugh where they relieved quite a bit of tension.

"So I have a girlfriend," Cerafina said.

"And so do I," Jonara said.

"Well, well, well. What will my family say about this? I'm heir to my grandmother's estate, but I won't have any children. That's going to upset her."

"Ah, ah, ah," Jonara said. "Enjoy what Mother Nature gave us. Don't worry about the future."

"Yeah. I guess there's always the sperm bank. But I wish there was a way we could have each other's kids. That would be the ultimate," Cerafina said.

"You know," Jonara said, "I never thought that would be possible, but I just had a funny feeling in my navel, as if something or someone were telling me we could have each other's children."

"Okay, I think the love potion is a little too strong right now," Cerafina said.

"No really. Maybe some strange cloning thing. It might be possible," Jonara said.

"Well, like you say, we don't have to worry about that now," Cerafina said.

"Do you really know how to play the oboe, Cerafina?" Jonara asked.

"I do. You know, now that we're girlfriend and girlfriend," Cerafina said, "I think we should invent pet names for each other. You know, like in any other relationship."

"Did you have one for me already?" Jonara asked.

"I was thinking, 'Buttercup,' after your hair," Cerafina said.

"Buttercup? Then I should call you Dahlia," Jonara laughed.

"I was serious," Cerafina said. "But if that's how you'll react, maybe I should call you 'Goldenrod'."

"Okay, two can play that game," Jonara grinned. "Your next name is Black-hollyhock."

"Fire-lilly," Cerafina laughed.

"Black-tulip," Jonara joked.

"Okay, okay, I see how this is going," Cerafina said.

"I think I have a name for you," Jonara said. "Cherry."

"Cherry?" Cerafina said. "Then I'll call you Jelly Bean."

"Absolute silliness," Jonara laughed.

Jonara held a hand to her abdomen and another to Cerafina's abdomen.

"You are my *shalifa*," Jonara said.

"What is *shalifa*?" Cerafina asked.

"It means 'pleasureful love' in Miramish," Jonara said. "As in, 'I love ice cream.' I'll call you Shalifa."

"Am I like ice cream?" Cerafina asked. "What flavor?"

Jonara giggled.

"I have one for you," Cerafina said. "What's the Miramish word for *ammunition*?"

"Hah, hah, hah. Very funny," Jonara said.

"No, I'm serious. You're like my secret weapon," Cerafina said.

"Really?"

"Yes, really!" Cerafina said.

"It's *shenuka*," Jonara said.

"I like it, my Shenuka, thank you," Cerafina said.

"You're welcome, my Shalifa," Jonara said.

"Shenuka," Cerafina said.

"Shalifa," Jonara replied.

"Shnuki, Shnuki, Shnuki!" Cerafina giggled.

"Shlifa, Shlifa, Shlifa!" Jonara giggled back.

The girls laughed again, and when they stopped, Jonara pondered the oboe.

"So how do I play it, Shlifa?" Jonara asked.

"You need a reed, for one thing, Shnuki," Cerafina replied.

"Here's the case," Jonara said.

"Good. There are reeds in here. We need to soak them first— at least for a few minutes," Cerafina said.

"Soak them in what, Shlifa?" Jonara asked.

"Regular water is fine, Shnuki," Cerafina said.

Jonara dashed off to the kitchen and returned with a small glass of water.

"Always soak the reeds by themselves, Shnuki. Don't soak the staple," Cerafina said as she placed the reeds in the water. "Now I must warn you—playing the oboe is more difficult than the piano or viol. Getting the reeds to vibrate just right takes lots of practice, otherwise the oboe sounds like a dying duck."

After a minute, Cerafina removed the reeds from the water and placed them in the staple which in turn she placed in the oboe.

"This is a very unusual oboe," Cerafina said. "It's of baroque design, and it looks very old, but it's been heavily modified. Extra keys have been added. And there are lots of very small pegs I can twist—I've never seen that on an oboe or any kind of wind instrument. I'm not quite sure how to play it yet, but I'll try it out and see."

"Wait, Shlifa," Jonara said. "May I try the reeds by themselves?"

"Yeah sure, Shnuki," Cerafina said.

Jonara held the double reed to her mouth and blew. It sounded like a duck flatulating. Both girls laughed.

"The double reed is difficult to master, Shnuki," Cerafina said.

Cerafina placed the reed and staple in the oboe and played through the arrangement of keys and holes. Water came out of the bell.

"What the?" Jonara said.

"Looks like water," Cerafina said. "What's that doing in there? Water is bad. This oboe could be ruined."

"Maybe not, Shlifa. The oboe's just a little rusty," Jonara said.

"Strange metaphor for an oboe. I'll try it again," Cerafina said.

Cerafina blew through the oboe. A little more water came out, but as Cerafina continued to blow, less water came out until nothing but air came through. Jonara brought a roll of paper towels from the kitchen, and the two cleaned up the water. With that complete, Cerafina tested the different keys and tone holes for tuning accuracy.

"Well I'm sorry to say, Shnuki, but the oboe is out of tune," Cerafina said. "That doesn't surprise me. I've heard that old woodwinds warp over the years causing distortions of sorts, and I suppose tones will drift. I'm sure the water didn't help either."

"What about those little pegs, Shlifa? Maybe they can help," Jonara said.

"Tuning pegs? I wonder. But they're too small for my fingers. Shnuki—is there a tool in the oboe case?" Cerafina asked.

"Maybe this?" Jonara suggested.

"Hmm. Let me try," Cerafina said.

Cerafina twisted a few pegs, played, and twisted a few more.

"Okay, I think I understand," Cerafina said, as she quickly went through the pegs and tuned the oboe.

"Wow, Shlifa, it's like you've done this before," Jonara said.

"It does feel that way. Maybe it's because I've worked with so many musical instruments," Cerafina said. "Now the question is, if this is a magical oboe, what is the best way to—"

"Oh just play it, Shlifa," Jonara said. "I'll hold onto you. Let's see what it does."

"Okay," Cerafina said.

Jonara sat next to Cerafina, placed one hand around Cerafina's waist, and placed the other over her own navel with the expectation of invoking a Miramish chant. Cerafina played the oboe. The room swirled, and the two found themselves in the Caves of Healing. The crystals glowed just as brilliantly as before, but all evidence of the sisters of St. Renata was absent—no Roman Catholic chairs with crucifix symbols or anything suggesting a Catholic presence.

1492 Jan 1. The Caves of Healing. Carreña, Spain.

"Shnuki," Cerafina said. "We're in the Caves of Healing."

"It looks different," Jonara said. "Look at the people. What are they doing?"

"I can't tell if this is the present or past," Cerafina said. "These musical instruments have shown us the future."

"This is the past, Shlifa," Jonara said. "I can feel it."

"When?"

"January 1st of 1492," Jonara said.

The two watched several people hauling in woods of Norway Crimson King maple, Norway white spruce, and lignum vitae. Others brought in flaxseed oil, yet others brought in tools, tables, and chairs.

"It looks like a woodshop," Cerafina said. "They're building things here."

Several women gathered together and stood in the shallow pool as the workers continued bringing in supplies and dipping wood in the water. One of the women in the pool was dark-skinned. She resembled Dr. Jelana and wore a white and green headscarf with a crescent symbol. Another woman resembling Fantina wore a necklace with the Star of David. A third woman resembling Jane MacNessi wore a robe with a simplified (and not-too-proportional) orbital diagram depicted on her upper left chest, the diagram showing the sun at the center orbited by the planets Mercury, Venus, Earth, Mars, Jupiter, and Saturn. A fourth woman resembling Geneva wore a necklace with a crucifix. A fifth woman resembling Cerafina's mother wore a headscarf with a fravashi symbol (of the Zoroastrian faith).

"Something's wrong," Cerafina said. "I can't breathe."

"How can you talk if you can't breathe, Shlifa?" Jonara asked.

"I can breathe, but it's difficult, Shnuki," Cerafina replied. "I can't play the oboe anymore."

The cave scene faded and was replaced by Geneva's music room where Cerafina struggled to play the last notes. Jonara felt something twisting around her leg and was horrified to see a rope wrapped around like a boa constrictor. She reached to dislodge it, but Cerafina muffled a cry for help. Jonara looked up and saw another rope writhing around Cerafina's neck.

Jonara chanted:

Miramish	**Translation**
Vapa opeifu lioila,	Rope of woe,
Leko til e vifo!	Let go!

The ropes did not release their grips.

"Let go of the oboe," Jonara said.

"I can't," Cerafina said.

One rope entangled itself around Cerafina's arms and the oboe—binding her hands and fingers to the instrument.

"Shnuki, help!" Cerafina called.

Jonara ripped at the rope and loosened it enough to slip the oboe from its grip. Jonara dropped the oboe to the floor and slid it away from them with her foot. The ropes loosened their grips immediately and fell limp as if nothing had happened.

"Thank you, Shnuki," Cerafina said as she unwrapped herself.

"I don't understand, Shlifa," Jonara said. "None of this makes sense. The viol took us into the future, but this oboe takes us to the past. And this rope. Why did it attack us? And my Miramish chant. Why did it fail?"

"Shnuki, you always spoke Miramish with the Water Ruby before," Cerafina said.

"Except for one other time. Last night at the hospital, I did a chant without the Water Ruby, and it worked for a little bit. The skin around my belly button glowed for a little bit too. But that was it," Jonara said.

"Then it worked only one time. You had an afterglow from the Water Ruby because of your prior use. But that faded. Maybe with more use of the Water Ruby, you'll develop a longer lasting charge in your abdomen, kinda like a battery," Cerafina explained. "But as for the rope, I think I understand a little. Legend says some oboes were used for charming snakes, or for making ropes act like snakes. This oboe seems to have that power. We'll have to be careful if we use it again."

"And the past? Why the past, Shlifa?" Jonara asked.

"I don't know, Shnuki," Cerafina replied. "But did you notice all those woods in the cave were the same woods used in these musical instruments?"

"There's a connection. There must be," Jonara said. "They were getting ready to build things out of those woods. And they dipped them in that strontium water."

"That cave could be the source for all these relics—the diary, the Aromani candleholder, the *viola de gamba*, and this oboe," Cerafina said.

"But not everything. My daddy found the Water Ruby in the Willamette River," Jonara said.

"And Dr. Jelana's duavisha came from that mountain in Eritrea," Cerafina said.

"What's the answer?" Jonara asked.

"I don't know, Shnuki. But I think we found the root source, the primary place where most of these things came from. And we know the oboe is one way to reach that source. What are you doing, Shnuki?"

Jonara unrolled the paper towel a bit and fashioned a headscarf over Cerafina's head.

"I thought I'd see how you look with a headscarf," Jonara said. "Kinda like the women we saw."

"You're so silly," Cerafina said.

"And you're so cute, Shlifa," Jonara said, and the two exchanged a kiss.

CHAPTER 17

The Last Leg

2023 Oct 6, Fri Afnoon. Geneva Carreña's House. Corpus Christi, Texas.

"I'm powerless without the Water Ruby, Shlifa," Jonara said. "I need to find it."

Jonara dashed upstairs to the guestroom where she had stayed. Cerafina followed at a more controlled pace. Glass remained scattered in the bedroom from the broken window.

"I know it was here," Jonara said. "Where did I leave it? Ow, my teeth hurt."

"I don't see it anywhere," Cerafina said as she helped Jonara scour the room. "What's wrong with your teeth, Shnuki?"

"I don't know," Jonara said. "It's strange. Now that my baby tooth came out, it's like my other teeth are fighting for the empty space."

"You mean your permanent tooth is hurting? The one coming up in place of your baby tooth?" Cerafina asked.

"No. The teeth next to where my baby tooth was. They're shifting or something. It's like, when I bite down, my teeth don't meet where they did before. And I feel something else, like my baby tooth is not really gone, like it's some strange sort of limb extending way out of my body."

"Where is your baby tooth, Shnuki?" Cerafina asked.

"I got mad last night. I threw it in the bushes," Jonara said.

"What bushes?"

"Here, Shlifa. Look out this broken window. I could throw my tooth from here and it would land in the bushes," Jonara said.

The two looked out the broken window, stared at each other, and said simultaneously, "The Water Ruby!"

"I bet he threw it in the bushes," Jonara said.

"You know he did! Come on, Shnuki! Let's find it before someone else does!"

The two rushed outside and searched through the bushes.

"I found your tooth, Shnuki," Cerafina said.

"He threw the candleholder out too," Jonara said.

"Did he?"

"Yeah, I found it under this leaf," Jonara said.

Jonara held the candleholder to her belly button and said:

Miramish	**Translation**
Shupo shai Moishiana,	Find the Water Ruby,
Feifo tilesh e thoisha.	Show its face.
Lalito nau di	Lead me to
Tilesh e pereishaolu beresha.	Its resting place.

The candleholder pulled violently from Jonara's abdomen. She summoned all her strength to keep a grip on it, and it pulled her arm deep into the bushes. Cerafina watched as Jonara appeared to dive into those bushes.

"Shnuki!" Cerafina yelled.

Jonara landed in the underbrush with the Moissan Ruby squarely before her face.

"Show *its* face, not *my* face!" Jonara said.

The candleholder released its grip. Jonara grabbed the Moissan Ruby, and with the help of Cerafina, she extricated herself from the bushes.

"I'm a mess," Jonara said as Cerafina helped brush twigs and leaves from Jonara's hair and clothing.

"But you're a cute mess, Shnuki," Cerafina said.

Cerafina finished cleaning off Jonara and kissed her lightly on the cheek.

"That's my seal of approval," Cerafina said.

Jonara smiled.

"Let's go back inside," Jonara said. "I want to know what happened after Nanna Geneva went into the Caves of Healing."

The two returned to the music room and sat in chairs next to each other (the same chairs where they once played the oboe).

"Wait," Cerafina said. "I want to put the oboe away. It shouldn't sit on the floor like that."

Jonara retrieved the case, and Cerafina took the oboe apart. The two placed the oboe parts into the case, and Jonara returned the case to the cabinet from where it came.

"Good," Jonara said. "Now we can start."

"How will you go back to the cave, Shnuki?" Cerafina asked.

"With the Water Ruby and candleholder, of course," Jonara said. "Do you doubt me, Shlifa?"

"It's just...well...doesn't the candleholder only tap memories of those it comes in contact with?" Cerafina asked.

"We went back to the 60s with my mother. How do you suppose she was connected to that?" Jonara asked.

"I don't know. Never mind. Let's go back in time," Cerafina said.

Jonara shrugged her shoulders and spoke:

Miramish	Translation
Aromani Lanudaku Thorithua	Aromani candleholder
Nia fapo opeifu kail,	I ask of you,
Dhaubieloko rau vaka	Transport us back
Di Lamaila veni,	To May seven,
Muipa kinida-avu.	Nineteen sixty-two.

The room swirled, and the two arrived in a salt desert with the wind blowing fiercely.

"This isn't right," Jonara said. "Something's wrong."

"We could be anywhere, in any time," Cerafina said.

"I should have mentioned a place," Jonara said. "I'll try again."

Miramish	Translation
Goko rau di	Take us to
Shai Paugi opeifu Hauthaola.	The Caves of Healing.

The two returned to Geneva's music room as if nothing had happened.

"Nothing," Jonara said.

"We need a catalyst," Cerafina said.

"A what?"

"Something to get us started," Cerafina said.

"I used a Miramish chant, Shlifa. What else is there?"

"Your Nanna Geneva's diary, for one. Or did you forget about it, Shnuki?" Cerafina asked.

"I did forget! What's wrong with me, Shlifa? That's how I got started in the first place."

"Do you still have it?" Cerafina asked.

"Yeah. It's upstairs under the pillow, unless someone took it. I'll get it right now."

The two raced upstairs, found the diary under the pillow, and returned downstairs to the music room.

"Turn the pages. Hurry, Shnuki!" Cerafina said with impatience.

"I'm going as fast as I can," Jonara said. "Here it is. Look, she recorded that day in her diary. 'Sister Rosa showed me the Caves of Healing for the first time'."

1962 May 7, Sat. St. Renata's Abbey. Carreña, Spain.

"Look, Sister Rosa. I can stand without using my crutches," Sister Geneva said.

"The water strengthens bones, muscles, and nerves. You are healing, Sister Geneva. You would have healed over the course of several years by eating our food, but your need is most immediate," Sister Rosa said.

"I can feel the dimensions again. It's like my legs are connected to the cave, like a radio. The cave is talking to me," Sister Geneva said.

"You are not the first to report this effect," Sister Rosa said. "You are being enlightened."

Sister Geneva laughed. Sister Rosa lifted an eyebrow in apuzzlement.

"One of the sisters told a joke in the inner ward," Sister Geneva said. "Strange that I can hear that from inside this cave."

"You'll find you can learn a great deal from the world by standing in these waters," Sister Rosa said.

"Oh that's wonderful! The villagers in Carreña love our food. They're enjoying some wine and blue Cabrales cheese. This is better than television. I can reach out to any happy place and enjoy the fun," Sister Geneva said.

"Sister Geneva—I must warn you," Sister Rosa said. "The pool shows many things, and some are dark. There are evils in this world unimagineable—evils that would never reach public awareness. Be careful where you tread. The devil corrupts people wherever the heart is weakest."

Geneva bent her knees and stared at her reflection in the pool.

"I can bend my knees," Sister Geneva said.

Geneva walked in the pool under her own leg power.

"I can walk," Sister Geneva said.

Geneva sensed a jogging marathon in the United States.

"I want to run," Sister Geneva said. "I want to enter a marathon in the United States."

Geneva walked deeper into the pool, and the waterline crept up to her thighs.

"Be careful!" Sister Rosa said. "Do not go any deeper into the pool."

"I'm swimming in Australia," Sister Geneva said. "At Sydney. On Bondi Beach."

Geneva walked farther into the pool until the water reached her neck.

"It's warm," Sister Geneva said. "People are swimming and laughing."

"No!" Sister Rosa said. "Come back!"

"Ugh!" Sister Geneva said.

Something pulled her under.

"Shark!" Sister Geneva said as she bobbed up briefly.

Jonara and Cerafina had been standing and watching, but when Geneva went under water, Jonara's legs buckled under her, and she fell.

"Shnuki!" Cerafina called.

"I can't get up," Jonara said.

"Your Nanna Geneva's in trouble," Cerafina said. "You're in trouble! You have to save her. Quick—chant something!"

Miramish	Translation
Shai kerafika kilo teshunei:	The task is this:
Zhupo Dzheneva	Save Geneva
Veletu shai keraishoka!	From the shark!

Jonara regained her stature. Sister Geneva returned to the surface and swam until her feet touched bottom. She walked to the pool's edge, wavered for a moment, and stumbled quickly onto the dry cave floor to a chair where she sat in complete exhaustion. Geneva breathed heavily.

"Sister Rosa, Sister Rosa," Sister Geneva struggled to say.

"Shh. Regain your breath, child," Sister Rosa said.

Geneva sat for a minute or two, closed her eyes, and swallowed heavily between breathing stretches.

"I saw...evil," Sister Geneva said. "Horrible things. People being tortured because...because they had a different faith. Because they were Buddhists. They were...tortured by Roman Catholics!"

"Shhh," Sister Rosa said. "There are those who obsess and twist the word of God, who wrongly commit heinous crimes in the name of the Church. They undermine the Church and God, Sister Geneva."

"I must help them," Sister Geneva said. "I must right for the Church what others are wronging."

"God has spoken through you," Sister Rosa said. "And I know of the place you speak."

"You do?" Sister Geneva said.

"Yes."

"Where?"

"Vietnam," Sister Rosa said.

Geneva bit her lip. It was a bitter pill to swallow.

"I have always complained about Franco's regime," Sister Geneva said. "My eyes have been shielded from other miseries. Now I know. Please, Sister Rosa, I must be transferred to a missionary in Vietnam."

"It is a difficult thing for me to do," Sister Rosa said. "Not that I have the authority. I may submit a request, of course. But Vietnam has many challenges. Your life will be in danger from many people and many sides. You might not return to Spain. Think carefully, Sister Geneva. I'll wait a week while you consider this transfer. If after that time you still wish to go, I'll submit the request to Mother Superior."

"Thank you, Sister Rosa."

"The Caves of Healing are very helpful or very dangerous," Sister Rosa said. "Many have been helped by its curative properties. But some, like you I fear, have received instructions beyond any ability to dissuade. I'll pray for the salvation of your corporeal body and immortal soul. May God bless and protect you always."

Geneva stood up, and as she did so she clicked her heels against the cave floor. Jonara and Cerafina shifted in time.

1963 May 2, Thu. Birmingham, Alabama.

Jonara and Cerafina arrived in Birmingham, Alabama. The town was bustling with black demonstrators against segregation.

"We're in the thick of the Civil Rights Movement, Shnu," Cerafina said.

"Shli, look. There's Dr. Jelana, Kaila, and Quadri," Jonara said. "They're demonstrating with everyone else."

Then without warning, hundreds of black children appeared from different streets. They had skipped school, met briefly at the Sixteenth Street Baptist Church, and joined the demonstrators a few at a time. Jonara and Cerafina were amazed at how unified the children were, singing songs like, "We Shall Overcome," and other freedom songs.

"Children!" Jonara said.

"I think I read about this," Cerafina said. "I wonder if—"

"Nothing left to wonder about. There's eight-year-old Marcus and seven-year-old Kay joining the demonstrators. Marcus's skin is dark. Dr. Jelana must have kept him on the xanthotoxin."

"I never liked watching the old videos of these events," Cerafina said. "And I'm afraid to watch them again."

"So far so good," Jonara said. "Everything is peaceful."

"That's how it always starts out. Then tension builds," Cerafina said. "Why do you think this city was called 'Bombingham'?"

Then it happened. Bull Connor, the leader of the Birmingham Police Department, began arresting the children. The police hauled the children away in paddy wagons, but more children came. The police used school buses, but still more students came. The police could not keep up and used squad cars to haul away students, and still more came! Running out of equipment, the police resorted to using fire trucks. And still the students came. Kay marched with Marcus during this time, and the two managed to avoid the first rounds of capture but could not avoid the many white people spitting and hurling insults at the two. Marcus could not believe people of any color could be so vicious. He vowed to do whatever he could to stay out of jail.

"Like dodgeball, Kay," Marcus kept repeating to her. "Don't let them hit you with the dodgeball."

What Kay or the Birmingham police didn't know was that Marcus had stolen the duavisha from Dr. Jelana. She had hidden it in a jewelry box shortly after returning from Eritrea and had forgotten about its existence. Marcus found the duavisha shortly before the May 2nd demonstration and had been experimenting with it. He learned that placing it in his navel with denture adhesive gave him power of use, and in doing so he developed a strong affection for the ghostly image of Nekara the Red, as if she were an aunt. "Aunt Nekara," he would call her, and when she appeared to him, he yielded to her as an authority figure and did as she commanded. Nekara did not issue commands haphazardly. Marcus would summon her upon need, and she issued instructions on how to satisfy that need. For this he expressed gratitude, but Nekara was no loving spirit. Her intentions on ensnaring Marcus's psyche were kept to herself.

To a lesser degree, Marcus developed a brotherly affection for Kay as if she were his sister. In fact, as far as Marcus knew, she *was* his sister. Neither Dr. Jelana nor Quadri had told either of them of Marcus's true ancestry. But this affection resulted in requests from Nekara to help his stepsister.

"Those two," a white police officer said to another as he pointed to Marcus and Kay.

The police officer allowed his dog to advance upon Marcus and Kay. Marcus held a couple of fingers over his navel. The duavisha remained hidden under his shirt, and while holding his fingers over his navel, a ghostly image of Nekara the Red appeared next to him, as if she were there to guide him.

A white woman prepared to spit toward Kay. To their delight, the police paused to witness the event created by the white woman. Nekara saw this development and quickly instructed Marcus to say, "Repel."

"*Luparzde*," Marcus said, and as he did so, he pointed his finger slightly at the white woman—enough for the command to know its target but not enough to draw attention.

The white woman spat. A puff of wind caught it and blew the saliva back onto her face.

"Ugh," she uttered.

Marcus smiled. However, the police did not enjoy this outcome and resumed their advance with their dogs on Marcus and Kay. Marcus looked at Nekara, and she instructed Marcus to say, "Skip us."

"*Fnirsk rau*," Marcus said.

The dogs jerked their leashes to the side and led the police away. The police stared through Marcus and Kay as if they weren't there.

"I was scared," Kay said. "But they are gone. We are lucky."

"He spoke the foreign words," Jonara said.

"And we saw Nekara the Red," Cerafina said. "Shnu—Nekara is linked to the duavisha. There's no question about it. And Marcus is using it."

"I know. I want to stop him, but I've had bad luck with anything connected to Nekara," Jonara said.

The police arrested children and adults until their jails had filled. The day swirled with gray before Jonara and Cerafina. They drifted and found themselves in the Dakari home. Marcus sat in a small room by himself, at least at first.

"Aunt Nekara, appear to me," Marcus said. "*Darl Nekara, opliarsne dir nau.*"

Nekara the Red appeared to Marcus.

"We have visitors, Marcus," Nekara said as she motioned her eyes toward Jonara and Cerafina. "They were with us at the demonstration today."

"I don't see anyone," Marcus said.

"They are here," Nekara said. "But they have no power. You have power, Marcus. I will teach you. There are two things you must do. Push humans to express their hatred, and call humans to share this hatred with the world, so that the world may feed. Your world feeds on hate, Marcus. It always will. Remember that. Now, say your prayers."

Marcus knelt before Nekara the Red and said the following:

Non-Miramish Language	Translation
Shorlyek orp Elesh,	Humans of Earth,
Pulasp kairsh kutarlyek,	Draw your swords,
Dhark e kifiaishsk shair elesh	And divide the earth
Ishe avu.	In two.
Voshasre kairsh guafirt,	Love your kind,
Dhark hemeru kairsh guafirt.	And only your kind.
Kaifst lor mirshyek,	Hate all others,
Yanu.	Amen.

"You are evil," Jonara said to Nekara the Red.

Nekara the Red smiled, and she spoke to Jonara.

Non-Miramish Language	Translation
Aluka, Dzhonara.	Hello, Jonara.
Vivoan kaish krufk brekasle,	Before your week completes,
Nia kifiaishsk e kail velt Serafina.	I divide you from Cerafina.

Nekara the Red broke into maniacal laughter.

"No, wait," Jonara said. "*Lutepo* (Reject), *lutepo, lutepo!*"

"Your Miramish tricks don't work on me, Earth girl," Nekara said. "*Tikaushkiatsh* (Get lost)!"

The world swirled in gray. Jonara and Cerafina left the Dakari house and reappeared atop a building in Birmingham the following day.

1963 May 3, Fri. Birmingham, Alabama.

"Shnu," Cerafina said. "We're way up here, but the children are protesting way down there."

"I'll try to get us down there," Jonara said, and she chanted:

Miramish	Translation
Shekito rau veletu	Move us from
Teshunu voritaolu daupa.	This building top.
Dhaku tienu di arithiama,	And down to street,
Derausha, dhaku dorishokata.	Dog, and cop.

"*Lushairsk* (Revoke)," Jonara and Cerafina heard from a distance.

"That sounded like Nekara the Red's voice," Cerafina said.

"She's blocking me, Shli. I can't change our location," Jonara said.

"Shnu—can you understand what Nekara says when she speaks that foreign language?" Cerafina asked.

"You know what? Yeah, I can. And I don't know why. It's not Miramish, but I understand it."

"Can you speak it?" Cerafina asked.

"No, I can't. I don't understand that either, Shli," Jonara said.

Jonara and Cerafina watched helplessly as firehoses shot water into protesters—adults and children—ripping their clothing, throwing them over cars, tumbling them down roads, and pinning them against buildings. Other protesters threw rocks and bottles, and the police responded with attack dogs.

"*Peliko* (Break)!" Jonara yelled. "Get us out of here!"

"*Lushairsk* (Revoke)," repeated the voice from a distance.

"She's going to force us to watch this depravity," Cerafina said.

The two watched in horror as Bull Connor forced his hatred machine onto the demonstrators.

"I never realized it was this bad," Jonara said. "Don't these white people feel ashamed of what they are doing?"

"They're programmed to hate," Cerafina said. "It's brain-washing."

The two sat on the rooftop and watched as the events continued for hours. At 3 pm, the attacks stopped, the world swirled, and the two jumped ahead a month in time.

1963 Jun 7, Fri. Bong Son, South Vietnam.

Jonara and Cerafina appeared in an army medical center housing the 1st New Zealand Services Medical Team. The team trained Vietnamese nurses, treated civilian war casualties, and handled other accident cases. Aromani Karrano di Pindos, a New Zealand Army medic, finished treating a soldier's trench foot and prepared to take his dinner break.

"We're in Vietnam," Jonara said. "That's Aromani—Fantina's son."

"He's much older now," Cerafina said. "I'd say at least twenty years old."

"He's twenty-one," Jonara said.

"Shnu," Cerafina said. "Do you remember the prayer Nekara made Marcus say?"

"It was awful," Jonara said. "But I don't believe Nekara had anything to do with the conflict in Birmingham. People can be bad all on their own."

"But she made Marcus think he helped incite the white people to express their hatred," Cerafina said.

"She's deceitful," Jonara said.

"If we could warn Marcus," Cerafina said.

"Do you think Nekara would let us, Shli? Do you think Marcus would believe us over Nekara?"

"Probably not," Cerafina said.

"We can try," Jonara said, "when we get a chance."

The sun was setting. Aromani was excused for his dinner break. He pulled out a letter from his mother, Fantina, and read it privately.

"My dear son Aromani. One train ends and another begins. Remember the train ride we took to Featherston? I'll never forget that scenic ride. A week later, the train ride closed. Another week, and your grandfather passed away at the impressive age of 95! I continue to visit his grave once a week. You must remember your family as you toil through your tour in Vietnam. And remember your people. We are proud Sephardic Jews, and we are spreading out through the world. Remember us when you celebrate Shabbat. This little candleholder, of which I have inscribed, comes from our ancestors who lived in Carreña, Spain. Keep it always. When you are alone and have no Jewish companionship, use the candleholder to celebrate Shabbat. Only God need know your identity. We have suffered too much at the hands of jealous people. Let them vent their hatred elsewhere, but not on you. I love you always, my dear son. Fantina."

Aromani sat in a corner, placed two small candles in his candleholder, and lit them. He prayed quietly for a few minutes.

"Captain Pindos?" a voice said.

Aromani blew out the candles, hid the candleholder from view, turned around, and faced a brown-haired American officer with a Catholic sister.

"Colonel Gracer," Aromani said to the American officer. "Welcome to the 1st New Zealand Services Medical Team. How are things at the Tan Son Nhut Air Base?"

"As best as can be expected," Colonel Gracer said. "Saigon is farther from the action than Bong Son. Except for Buddhist protests and pagado raids, we don't see the action you do."

"I hope you never do," Aromani said.

"I'm with you there. This is Sister Geneva. She's assisting us at the air base with American casualties. Sister Geneva, Captain Pindos."

"Nice to meet you," Geneva said.

Aromani paused for a moment as he stared at Geneva's habit and clothing.

"Nice to meet you," he said after a delay.

"Sister Geneva is a nurse from St. Renata's Abbey in Spain," Colonel Gracer said. "She'll be helping us transport your American patients back to Tan Son Nhut Air Base. She is a fully qualified nurse, but she is a civilian. Give her every assistance possible."

"Sir?" Aromani asked.

"I realize this is unusual allowing civilians in our group. But we are short-staffed. The Catholic Church has agreed to lend us aid," Colonel Gracer said. "As an extension of goodwill, we've accepted."

Aromani looked at Geneva with suspicion. Could he trust a Christian? Some Christians had persecuted his people over the course of two thousand years while others had helped his people such as Christian Allies liberating Nazi concentration camps during the war. Where was Geneva in that spectrum?

"I'm giving Sister Geneva a tour of your New Zealand facilities," Colonel Gracer said. "When you finish with dinner, report to me. Sister Geneva is on loan to you for the weekend, and I would like you to brief her on her duties. It's good for her to work with different medical teams. Sister Geneva and I will return to the air base Monday with the American casualties."

"Sir," Aromani said. "If Sister Geneva is hungry, I would like her to eat with me. I'll finish giving her the tour."

"Sister Geneva?" Colonel Gracer asked.

"That's an excellent idea," Sister Geneva said.

"Very well," Colonel Gracer said. "I leave her in your care. I will follow up with you after chow."

"Let me show you the food line," Aromani said.

"Thank you," Geneva said.

The two grabbed trays, got food and drink, and sat down. Aromani noticed Geneva's slight limp, though Geneva needed no leg braces nor crutches.

"You're Jewish, aren't you?" Sister Geneva asked as the two sat down.

"What?" Aromani asked. "Why do you say that?"

"You were burning two candles," Sister Geneva said. "I saw. Is that a Shabbat candleholder? It's quite small."

"It's a gift from my mother," Aromani said. "I am Jewish. Sister, there is a story that Christians blame Jews for the death of Jesus. Do you blame me for his death?"

Geneva paused in thought.

"There is a strong anti-Semetic stance among some Christians because of that, yes," Sister Geneva said.

"I see. And you?" Aromani asked.

"I don't blame Jews for anything. We owe our heritage to the Jewish faith," Sister Geneva said. "Christ was meant to be crucified. It was God's plan. Each person had a part. Peter denied Christ three times. And the Romans crucified him."

"Peter was a Jew, was he not?" Aromani asked.

"Yes, and so was Jesus," Sister Geneva added. "Yes. Blaming Jews for the Crucifixion is illogical. I do what I can to enlighten other Christians."

Aromani paused in thought again. He was at first anxious about Geneva's religion, but he felt more at ease after her explanation.

"Sister Geneva, I could not help but notice your limp. I do not mean to pry, but I am a medic. Did you hurt yourself? Do you need medical attention?" Aromani asked.

"I had polio," Sister Geneva said. "My legs were paralyzed. They've recovered somewhat so I can walk, but I can't run."

"That's a shame," Aromani said.

"That I had polio or that I can walk?" Sister Geneva joked.

The two laughed.

"I didn't know a nun could have a sense of humor," Aromani said.

"Well, technically I'm not a nun. I'm a sister. But thank you, I try to keep morale up," Sister Geneva said.

"Is everyone from Spain like you?" Aromani asked.

"Just the normal people. Those in power aren't so nice," Sister Geneva said. "Spain has been under the regime of Generalísimo Francisco Franco since 1936 by some accounts and

1939 by others. Some provinces held out against him longer than others. But things are improving. Spain's economy is booming, and we are slowly getting some freedom back, though not as quickly as we'd like. I suppose someone from New Zealand wouldn't understand what it's like to live under a regime."

"You're right, I don't," Aromani said. "But my mother tells me stories about Greece in the old days—during the Italian-Greco War. She left Greece when the German Nazis took over in 1941."

"Where did she go?" Sister Geneva asked.

"To Palestine. That was before it became Israel. I was born in Palestine. But as I got older, things became violent. So we moved to New Zealand."

"Interesting story," Sister Geneva said. "But why New Zealand?"

"It was the New Zealand Army who took my mother and grandfather from Greece to Palestine in the first place. My mother and grandfather were good friends with the New Zealanders, so when they decided to move, the New Zealanders helped," Aromani said.

"I see. How do you like New Zealand?"

"It's beautiful," Aromani said. "I love it. My mother says it's not as beautiful as the Pindos mountains—that's where she's from in Greece, but I've never been to Greece, so I don't know."

"Greece is your homeland then," Sister Geneva said.

"Yes. Both of my parents are Greek," Aromani said. "Father died before I was born."

"Oh I'm sorry," Sister Geneva said.

"I hear you sisters take on new names when you enter the convent," Aromani said.

"Most of us do. I did not. I use my first name," Sister Geneva said.

"What is your last name?" Aromani asked. "Oh I'm sorry, I don't mean to be rude. It's not like I'm asking you on a date or anything."

"I understand," Sister Geneva said. "My last name is *Carreña*. I was born in Girona, Spain, in the Catalonia province. My family comes from Carreña, Spain, in the Asturias province."

"You are named after the city of your family?" Aromani asked.

"Well, Carreña is more like a village. Coincidentally, St. Renata—my abbey—is in Carreña. Actually, it's a little east of the village, but close enough. Yes, I think I am named after Carreña."

"My mother says our family is from Carreña," Aromani said.

"Really?" Sister Geneva asked.

"I don't know if it's true. Her last name is Karrano, not Carreña," Aromani said.

"Well, there is no Karrano in Spain," Sister Geneva said. "So most likely 'Karrano' is a variation of 'Carreña'. My, it is a small world! But you are Jewish. The Jews were expelled in 1492. If your family is from Spain, they left before then."

"Expelled?" Aromani asked.

"It's a sad story. Spain became Roman Catholic and expelled the Muslims and Jews," Sister Geneva said.

"I see. And do you agree with that decision?" Aromani asked, now becoming a bit defensive.

"Of course not. It was a horrible thing," Sister Geneva said. "I'm on this earth to do God's work, not create misery through bigotry."

"I'm with you there, Sister Geneva. I'm glad we have something in common," Aromani said.

"We do indeed," Sister Geneva said. "And if your family is from Carreña, we may even be distant relatives."

"Now that would be incredible indeed," Aromani said. "My family history says we left in 1492. Strange. There's an interesting parallel between 1492 Spain and modern day Vietnam."

"Oh?"

"President Ngo Dinh Diem runs Vietnam. He got into office after his brother rigged the elections in 1955. Diem is pro-Catholic and would do anything to make the rest of the country Catholic."

"It does sound much like Isabella and Ferdinand's Spain of 1492, and it also sounds like Franco's Spain today," Sister Geneva said.

"But in Vietnam, the Buddhists were not expelled as they would have been in the Spain of 1492. The Buddhists stayed. And they are protesting the religious inequalities. Diem promised reforms, but they are nonexistent. I think Diem is stalling."

The scream of a man echoed through the halls and carried into the cafeteria. Aromani and Geneva finished their dinner and rushed to the medical bay.

"I'm sorry, but I'll have to give you a tour a bit later," Aromani said.

"I understand. Injury has no schedule," Sister Geneva said.

Aromani led Geneva down the hallway. Within a few seconds, the two arrived in the medical bay.

"Restrain him!" Colonel Gracer shouted.

Two medics worked to restrain an American soldier who'd jumped up from his bed and was running and screaming around the bay. Aromani, Sister Geneva, and three other medics ran after the American soldier.

"I can't stand it anymore," the soldier yelled. "Let me out of here!"

The medics and Geneva caught the American soldier and pinned him to the ground.

"Hold him steady," Colonel Gracer said as he reached to inject the soldier with a syringe.

"No shot, no shot!" the soldier begged. "That's how they get you. That's how they control your mind and turn you into a tree root."

"What is he talking about?" Jonara asked Cerafina.

"He's delusional," Sister Geneva said.

"Combat fatigue," Colonel Gracer said. "He'll be all right in a moment."

"Sister, please! Give me Absolution!"

"Hold strong," Sister Geneva said. "We are helping you."

"Give me my Last Rite so they can't capture my concrete pillow," the soldier said.

"He's cracked," Cerafina said.

The medication circulated in the American soldier's body, and he loosened his grip on the medics. He fell limply into twilight consciousness.

"Help him back to bed," Colonel Gracer said.

The medics and Sister Geneva lifted the man to his bed.

"I don't understand," Aromani said. "I just treated this patient's feet for trenchfoot before I broke for dinner. He was as peaceful as a lamb."

"Combat fatigue is like a time bomb," Colonel Gracer said. "It can go off any time. Fortunately, he is not in the field. The results could be disastrous. Captain Pindos—keep this man sedated until we're ready to leave."

Colonel Gracer's attention was drawn to another American. The medics dispersed. Aromani wrote something on the soldier's chart and proceeded to give Geneva a tour.

"It's not generally known that American soldiers are here. They have been arriving under the guise of 'flood relief worker'. Then they go in as a 'military adviser'."

"Flood relief worker? Military adviser?" Sister Geneva asked. "Why the deceit?"

"Deceit," Aromani echoed. "Yes, that's the word for it. This conflict is all about deceit. Who can explain that?"

"It's the devil's work," Sister Geneva said.

"That's one religious thing I'll agree on, Sister Geneva," Aromani said.

"Excuse me," Colonel Gracer said as he approached the two. "Sister Geneva, do you have any training in dental care?"

"I have a diploma in dental hygiene," Sister Geneva said.

Aromani's eyes opened in amazement.

"You are impressive," he said.

"Good," Colonel Gracer said. "I need to perform an emergency root canal here, now. No time to wait until we reach the American air base. And the New Zealand dentist is busy with another patient."

"I'll be happy to help," Sister Geneva said. "The rest of the tour will have to wait again, Captain."

Aromani entered a small office and dialed the telephone.

"Yes, Colonel Gracer and Sister Geneva made it safely," Aromani said. "Yes, they did tell me that. You do? Yes, I can accompany them to Saigon. Will do."

The world swirled with grays as Jonara and Cerafina left the medical base.

1963 Jun 8, Sat Afnoon. Bong Son, South Vietnam.

Sister Geneva entered the Cathedral of All Saints in Bong Son. It was late afternoon, and Saturday evening Mass would soon begin. A confessional was open, and Sister Geneva felt the urge to enter.

"In the name of the Father, and the Son, and the Holy Ghost, Amen," Sister Geneva started. "Bless me Father, for I have sinned. It has been a month since my last confession. I wish to say that I have had misgivings of the Roman Catholic Church since coming to Vietnam, and I question my faith. I see Diem's government giving favoritism to Catholics while at the same time he raids and destroys Buddhist pagodas. Father, does the Church condemn other faiths? The Church blames Jews for the Crucifixion. And I'm a sister. I took a vow to support the Church dogmas. But in my heart, I can't support a church who blames Jews and raids pagodas. Father, I detest my faith. This is my sin."

The priest paused. Geneva heard a strange clicking sound and realized the priest was loading his revolver.

"Father?" Sister Geneva asked.

"Hush, child," the priest said. "Do not speak so loudly. The walls have ears. Have no fear of me, I am simply preparing myself for the unfortunate."

"Is that a revolver I hear?" Sister Geneva said.

"Yes. Priests in Vietnam are equipped with protective measures. It's necessary to preserve the work of Christ."

"But Father!" Geneva protested.

"Hush child. Do not speak to others what you have said to me. For your own protection, find a way to rekindle your faith in the Church," the priest said.

"But how?" Geneva asked.

"For your penance, say ten Our Fathers, ten Hail Marys, and attend daily Mass with all your devoted heart. Make your

Act of Contrition, child," the priest said, and as Sister Geneva recited the Act of Contrition, the priest gave her Absolution with the following Latin words:

"*Dominus noster Jesus Christus te absolvat; et ego auctoritate ipsius te absolvo ab omni vinculo excommunicationis et interdicti in quantum possum et tu indiges. Deinde, ego te absolvo a peccatis tuis in nomine Patris, et Filii, et Spiritus Sancti. Amen. Passio Domini nostri Jesu Christi, merita Beatae Mariae Virginis et omnium sanctorum, quidquid boni feceris vel mail sustinueris sint tibi in remissionem peccatorum, augmentum gratiae et praemium vitae aeternae. Amen.* Go now and sin no more."

The priest flicked his wrist and in doing so closed the chamber to his revolver. Clack! The world swirled, and the two girls found themselves in the United States.

1963 Jun 8, Sat. Morn. Lackland Air Force Base. San Antonio, Texas.

"Sir," Lieutenant Colonel Jane MacNessi said. "Request permission to fly the next aeromedical evacuation mission to Tan Son Nhut Air Base."

"Request denied," the officer said.

"Sir, may I request the reason?" Jane asked.

"The Air Force is not equipped to handle female airmen in Vietnam at this time," the officer said. "Nor is the WAF authorized to fly missions."

"Sir. I am qualified to fly. I passed the same tests as the men," Jane said.

"This is not my call," the officer said. "The decision is from high up."

"Sir, I love my country. I wish to serve," Jane said.

"I know, Lieutenant Colonel MacNessi. You are a good officer. Continue studying here and work your way up the ranks. Should women be allowed into Vietnam, you'll be ready."

"Yes sir," Jane said.

Jane watched as a C-135 Stratolifter took off from the runway and headed west—eventually to land at Tan Son Nhut Air Base near Saigon in Vietnam.

"I should be flying that craft," she said.

Jane slammed her fist into her thigh in frustration. The world swirled and carried Jonara and Cerafina back to Vietnam.

1963 Jun 11, Tue Morn. Saigon, South Vietnam.

Jonara and Cerafina sat in the back seat of a car driven by Aromani with Geneva in the passenger seat.

"What did you say her name was?" Sister Geneva asked.

"Dr. Alina Zavuski," Aromani said. "She requested we meet her here in downtown Saigon. She worked in Korea in the '50s and came down here to Vietnam a couple of years ago. Sometimes she helps us train Vietnamese nurses at the New Zealand medical base in Bong Son. But I don't understand why she's so far south today. She doesn't normally come to Saigon."

"What does she look like?" Sister Geneva asked.

"She looks like—that woman standing on the corner. That's her," Aromani said.

Aromani parked the car. Sister Geneva and he walked from the car and met Dr. Zavuski near a group of Buddhist monks.

"Thank you for coming," Dr. Zavuski said. "Did you bring your camera?"

"Yes, it's here," Aromani said, and he produced a camera from a case.

"Good. Something dramatic will happen," Dr. Zavuski said. "Diem's government has oppressed Buddhists too long. Buddhists have special message for Diem, that no matter how brutal he becomes, he can never control Buddhist soul. There—see for yourself!"

A Buddhist monk stopped his car in the intersection. The hood went up. A swarm of Buddhist monks encircled him as he sat in the middle. His name was Thích Quảng Đức, and history was about to be made. A fellow monk poured a liquid atop Thích Quảng Đức as he remained sitting in the road. The monk left the gasoline container not far from Thích Quảng Đức.

"Why is that one monk pouring water on top of the other? Is it a baptism?" Sister Geneva asked.

"This is no baptism," Dr. Zavuski said.

Thích Quảng Đức prayed for a moment, lit a match, and dropped it. The "water" jumped into flames. Sister Geneva screamed.

"Jumping Jehoshaphat, we have to stop them!" Aromani cried.

Aromani ran to break through the ring of monks, but they successfully repelled him. The fire roared. Sister Geneva turned away.

"Human flesh burns easily, but soul is impenetrable," Dr. Zavuski said. "Look how he burns! And yet he remains sitting without flinching."

"How can you talk about this? It's insanity!" Sister Geneva yelled.

Thích Quảng Đức continued burning. The smell of burning flesh permeated the air.

"What a horrible smell!" Sister Geneva said. "I want to throw up."

"Throw up if you must," Dr. Zavuski said. "Purge yourself of poisoned food forced down your throat."

"But why, why?" Sister Geneva asked. "Why is life so carelessly thrown away?"

"Thrown away? No. Life seeks freedom above all else. When freedom denied, life finds it anyway. Animal caught in foot trap will chew its leg off for freedom. Captive rhino will thrust horn against enclosure until he is free or dies. Buddhist monks forced into captivity. They not yield mind or spirit."

"All because of this?" Sister Geneva said as she removed her habit.

"You are Roman Catholic. I see this troubles you," Dr. Zavuski said. "Reality of world not pretty. Diem is Catholic and pushes Catholic religion to exclusion of others. People are evil, not faith."

"Isabella, Ferdinand, Franco, and Diem," Sister Geneva said. "I can't stand it!"

Geneva threw her habit to the ground. She ripped off her religious symbols—a necklace with a crucifix, a rosary in her pocket—anything—and threw them to the ground. She ripped at her clothing. And she cried.

Police and ambulance workers rushed to the fiery scene but could not break through the circle of monks. The fire raged on, and Thích Quảng Đức's body fell over. He never once flinched or yielded his spirit to the flames.

"Spirit that does not yield to consumption of fire will never yield to injustices of Diem," Dr. Zavuski said.

Aromani gave up his effort to break through the circle. He returned to Geneva and Dr. Zavuski.

"What happened, Sister Geneva?" Aromani asked. "Were you attacked?"

"Take me back to the base," Geneva said. "I'm no longer a sister of the Catholic Church. I want out."

"I go with you," Dr. Zavuski said.

The three entered the car. Aromani and Dr. Zavuski closed their doors with care. But for Geneva, it was different—slam! With the door slam, the world swirled into gray. Jonara and Cerafina found themselves in Texas.

1963 Aug 17. San Antonio, Texas.

"I think this is Jane MacNessi's house," Jonara said. "I've seen a photo of this house before."

"Mommie!" called Roberta as she had half a foot out the front door and held onto a large suitcase. "The dorms are open today. I want to move in and make new friends."

Roberta placed her luggage in the car and with impatience began running around the house.

"She grew up!" Cerafina said. "She looks like a woman now."

"She is a woman," Jonara said. "She's the woman in the photo Grandma Eva has on her desk."

"Here," Jane said as she followed behind. "Don't forget this."
Jane handed Roberta a heavily-modified baroque oboe.

"The family oboe!" Roberta said. "Are you really going to let me take it to Wayland Baptist University?"

"This is the same oboe we have!" Jonara said. "Shli! This is Roberta's oboe! It's for sure!"

"And yet it's in your Nanna Geneva's house," Cerafina said.

"I really don't understand it," Jonara said.

"You may change your mind and join the university band," Jane said. "You did so well in high school band."

"I don't think they'll let me play with this," Roberta said. "I used a modern oboe in high school band. And I don't think it's safe to tote this baroque oboe around anyway. Someone might steal it."

Mother and daughter entered Jane's car. Jonara and Cerafina sat in back as Jane drove to Wayland Baptist University— also in San Antonio.

"I love the oboe," Roberta said. "But I'll have to work hard and focus to get through predental school."

"You'll need a study break from time to time," Jane said. "And the oboe will remind you of home and your family."

"It's such an unusual oboe too," Roberta said. "What did you say it's made of?"

"It's made of Norway white spruce, Norway Crimson King maple, and lignum vitae. It's finished in flaxseed oil," Jane said. "The reeds are just plain cane reeds."

"Such an odd collection of woods," Roberta said.

"It's an old Celtic family heirloom from Europe," Jane said. "Story goes the wood was harvested in the 1400s, and the oboe was built later."

"Is it from Ireland?" Roberta asked.

"No," Jane said.

"Scotland?"

"No," Jane repeated.

"Then how can it be Celtic?"

"The Celts once inhabited much of Europe. Slowly they were pushed west. This oboe came from either France or Spain," Jane explained.

"I could be a French red-head?" Roberta asked.

"Maybe. Or Spanish. I never learned which."

"I want to take a quick look at the oboe," Roberta said.

Roberta took the oboe out of the case and assembled it. She wet the reeds on her tongue and played. The world swirled. Jonara, Cerafina, and Roberta appeared in the Caves of Healing in 1492 much as Jonara and Cerafina had visited before with the women wading in the pool with assorted wood. A beautiful woman in a long robe stood on the pool-water as if it were frozen, but it wasn't. She had a long, flowing robe and flowers woven in her hair. She spoke something to the women wading in the shallow end.

"The woman in the robe is walking on water," Cerafina said.

"Who is she? She has blue streaks through her hair. She doesn't look like she's from Earth," Jonara said.

The vision faded, and the three returned to Jane's car. Roberta stared at the reeds.

"There's something in these reeds," Roberta said. "How old are they? There must be a fungus growing in them. I had a strange vision I was somewhere else."

"I don't know," Jane said. "I've never opened the case."

"She had the same vision we did," Cerafina said.

"I think the oboe works differently than the viol," Jonara said. "The viol shows different parts of the future. This oboe always shows the same past event."

"It's linked to the caves," Cerafina said. "It must be."

Roberta blew through the reeds once more, but they were too dry, and Roberta created a "clinker" sound. Jonara and Cerafina jumped to another time.

1963 Sep 13, Fri. Birmingham, Alabama.

Jonara and Cerafina appeared in Marcus's room in the Dakari house. Marcus was preparing for sleep with the help of Nekara the Red.

"They are here again," Nekara said. "But do not pay attention. We have work to do. Now, Marcus, what is it you wish to see in this city?"

"I want to see white men hate. I want them to show their hate. I want the world to know what they are," Marcus said.

"Very good," Nekara said. "Place the *duavirt* in your navel."

Marcus placed the duavisha in his navel. Jonara and Cerafina watched Marcus. Instead of affixing the duavisha to his navel with denture adhesive, he sewed the surrounding skin over his navel, trapping the duavisha.

"Now," Nekara continued, "say this prayer, and your wish will come true."

Nekara spoke the following:

Non-Miramish Language	Translation
Feirsf yuarnu noshkyek tesh kaift,	Show white men their hate,
Narzge tilen dargalist ishe parfp.	Make it energize in drama.
Flifst plornyek dir tshunu fidal,	Bring people to this event,
Dhark friorsk shair luvanirt.	And witness the result.

Marcus repeated the non-Miramish words, and although he recited the first line correctly, he mispronounced words in the second, third, and fourth lines:

Non-Miramish Language	Translation
Feirsf yuarnu noshkyek tesh kaift,	Show white men their hate,
Narzge tilen diagalist ishe piarfp.	Make it explode in eternity.
Flifst plornyek dir tshunu vibal,	Bring people to this bomb,
Dhark briorsk shair luvanirt.	And accumulate the result.

Nekara broke into evil laughter.

"Why are you laughing, Aunt Nekara?" Marcus asked.

"Do you know what you said? You did not repeat my words exactly. You said, 'Show white men their hate, make it explode in eternity. Bring people to this bomb, and accumulate the result.' You've condemned people as victims of bombs—forever! Hah, hah, hah!"

"No!" Marcus said.

"It cannot be undone. The chant is sacrosanct," Nekara said.

"Please, Aunt Nekara. Fix the chant. I didn't mean it."

Nekara laughed hysterically. She stomped her foot onto the floor and disappeared. The world faded into gray.

1963 Sep 15, Sun Morn. Birmingham, Alabama.

Jonara and Cerafina reappeared in the Dakari house two days later.

"Quadri?" Dr. Jelana called. "Let's take a drive this morning. It's been a long year, and now that the worst conflicts with the police are over, I'd like to see the neighborhood."

The family of four gathered in the living room in preparation for the drive. Nekara the Red appeared to Marcus. Only Marcus, Jonara, and Cerafina could see her.

"Today is the day," Nekara said. "Your wish comes true today. And you will get to see it."

"No!" Marcus muffled.

"What's that?" Dr. Jelana asked Marcus.

"I wanna stay home," Marcus said.

"No, sugar, we need to get out of the house today. We've been cooped up in here every Saturday and Sunday all year. We need some air," Dr. Jelana explained.

"Please stay home, please!" Marcus begged, and he pulled on Dr. Jelana's leg.

"Marcus," Quadri said. "Don't be rude to your mother. If she says we're going for a drive, we're going for a drive."

The four exited the house and entered the car. Dr. Jelana drove the family up and down streets and parked near Kelly Ingram Park.

"Let's get out and take a walk," Dr. Jelana said.

The four got out and walked in the park.

"Seems like ages ago when the attack dogs and firehoses were unleashed on colored folk," Dr. Jelana said. "How things have improved."

"Some," Quadri said. "But more needs doing."

"Isn't it a nice park?" Dr. Jelana asked.

The four approached a corner of the park at 6th Avenue and 16th Street. It was 10:21 am, and Nekara the Red appeared to Marcus.

"Look at the church across the street," Nekara said. "The home of Birmingham Civil Rights. Blood will be on your hands. Behold the fruit of your words."

"No!" Marcus shouted.

A split second later, a bomb exploded near the back-steps of the 16th Street Baptist Church. Dr. Jelana and Quadri dropped to the ground, pulling Marcus and Kay with them. A few seconds later, they looked up and watched people running out of the church. Police and firefighters arrived seemingly within seconds. They ran to the back of the building and dug through debris until they could get into the basement where they pulled out four girls—Addie Mae Collins, Denise McNair, Carole Robertson, and Cynthia Wesley—dead.

"Blood is on your hands," Nekara said to Marcus.

"That's a lie," Cerafina said. "The 16th Street Baptist Church bombing was set off by the KKK—Robert Chambliss, Bobby Cherry, and Tom Blanton were convicted. And they most likely had help. Marcus had nothing to do with it."

"They are here, Marcus. They say others set off the bomb. They are right. Others set off the bomb. But your curse pushed them into doing it," Nekara said.

Marcus buried his head in the ground and cried.

"You're lying to him," Cerafina said. "You're making Marcus believe he is responsible. He's not. The white men are programmed racists."

Nekara smiled. Marcus continued to cry.

"Where there's hate, there's misery, and I feed on misery," Nekara said with more laughter as she disappeared in a bright flash.

2023 Oct 6, Fri Afnoon. Geneva Carreña's House. Corpus Christi, Texas.

The girls returned to Geneva's music room. Jonara fell into tears.

"I can't handle it," Jonara said. "So much hate and misery. And that Nekara is the worst."

"Shh," Cerafina said. "I'm here with you, Shnuki. I love you. Hold onto that."

Jonara fell into Cerafina's chest. Cerafina kissed Jonara lightly and caressed Jonara's back.

"When I flew down here from Portland," Jonara sobbed. "I was mad at Daddy for lying to me about things. But I know why people tell lies. The truth is too painful to bear. It hurts, Shlifa. It hurts right here."

Jonara pointed to her abdomen. Cerafina took her other hand and held Jonara's by her abdomen.

"I have a feeling this is what growing up is about," Cerafina said. "Learning the cruel reality of life. But we'll suffer them together, Shnu—you and me. I know I'm only fourteen and you're only thirteen, but I know deep down in my heart I want to spend the rest of my life with you. I don't know what that will mean when we're older. I really don't. But I can't let you tear yourself apart over the past."

"I'm scared, Shli. The past isn't just the past," Jonara said. "I'm afraid of the future. I'm afraid it will be a repeat of the past, that I'll suffer injustices just like the people we've seen. History will repeat, Shli. It will."

"Look at me," Cerafina said, and she turned Jonara's face to hers and dried Jonara's tears, saying, "I want you to know that you're not alone! We're not alone!"

"We're not? What are you talking about?" Jonara asked.

"I think I know why you're so upset. Each upsetting thing in the past is because someone hates someone else because that someone else is different. You and I are different. We love each other. Some might call us sick lesbians. I don't care about words. I care about you. And we're not the only ones like this in the world. Many women are happy couples. And things aren't as bad today as they used to be. Society is more accepting of female couples. We might have to hide in the closet for a few years, but when we come out, people will be accepting. Most of them, at least."

"There's still one thing we can never do. We can never have each others' babies," Jonara said. "It's not fair. It really isn't."

"I know. You've said this before. But you also said you have a funny feeling that maybe someday we could. Do you still feel that way?" Cerafina asked.

"I don't know anymore, Cerafina," Jonara said.

"You called me by my name. Are you distancing yourself from me?" Cerafina asked.

"Of course not. It's just...I don't know. I'm exhausted," Jonara said.

"I know just what you need," Cerafina said, and she gave Jonara a deep kiss.

Jonara closed her eyes, and she went a little limp.

"Jonara?" Cerafina asked. "Jonara, wake up. I didn't mean to suck the breath out of you. C'mon, Jonara. This isn't funny. Jonara!"

Cerafina started to panic. She shook Jonara violently. Then Jonara opened her eyes suddenly.

"Gotcha!" Jonara said.

"Oh, you!" Cerafina said, and she pushed Jonara away.

Jonara nudged Cerafina, and Cerafina nudged back. Then Jonara tried giving a bigger nudge to Cerafina, but Cerafina stood up and stepped away. Jonara chased after Cerafina, and Cerafina ran around the music room. Cerafina tripped over a chair, and Jonara tackled her and kissed her. The room spun, and the two went back in time.

1963 Sep 29, Sun. Tan Son Nhut Air Base. Saigon, South Vietnam.

Jonara remained on top of Cerafina. The two looked and saw Colonel Gracer chasing Geneva around Colonel Gracer's room. Geneva still had a bit of a limp, and Colonel Gracer didn't have to work too hard in the chase.

"You can't catch me, Andrew," Geneva said.

"I will too, Sister Geneva," Colonel Gracer said.

"I'm not a sister anymore," Geneva said. "I'm just as single and free as you are."

Jonara stood up, and she helped Cerafina to her feet.

"They're flirting!" Jonara said.

"Wow!" Cerafina said. "Love strikes fast when you leave the convent."

Colonel Gracer caught Geneva and held her in his arms.

"Not fair. You took advantage of my handicap," Geneva said.

"You're beyond perfection," Colonel Gracer said. "I can't think of anything about you that's handicapped."

Geneva blushed.

"Marry me," Colonel Gracer said.

"So soon? Why we've only known each other for—"

"A year now. I never told you how I felt because that religious outfit of yours prevented me. Now I can tell you. I love you more than anyone or anything on this earth," Colonel Gracer said, and he kissed her.

"Yuck!" Jonara said.

Cerafina looked at Jonara in surprise.

"Wow!" Cerafina said.

"Wow what?" Jonara asked.

"Shnu—we kiss each other, and that's fine. When you see them kiss, you say 'yuck'?" Cerafina said.

"Yeah. That's strange. I shouldn't say, 'yuck', should I? I never used to before."

"That was before you became a sappho," Cerafina grinned.

"No, that's not...I mean...hey!" Jonara stumbled.

"You know it's true, Shnu! And I can prove it," Cerafina said.

Cerafina gave Jonara a deep kiss while Colonel Gracer kissed Geneva.

"Now tell me truly, was that a 'yuck' or a 'yum'?" Cerafina asked.

"Yum," Jonara said. "Yummy, yummy, yumminess! And that's the first time you kissed me in the past."

"I want to have a baby," Colonel Gracer whispered to Geneva.

"I do too," Geneva said.

Jonara stomped her foot on the floor, and the two returned to Geneva's music room.

"What happened?" Cerafina said.

"Every time I hear someone talk about having a baby, I get jealous," Jonara said.

"Hey, relax!" Cerafina said. "Let's grow up first."

Jonara walked to the diary and tapped her fingers on it. This action triggered a reaction, and the two went back in time yet again.

1964 Jun 27, Sat. Randolph Air Force Base. Universal City, Texas.

"Shnu!" Cerafina said. "Look!"

"Nanna Geneva is getting married on an Air Force base," Jonara said. "Look how pregnant she is! She's ready to pop!"

Geneva and Colonel Gracer stood before the chaplain.

"Do you, Geneva Carreña, take Andrew Gracer, as your lawfully wedded husband, to have and to hold, from this day forward, 'till death do you part?" the chaplain asked.

"I do," Geneva said.

"And do you, Andrew Gracer, take Geneva Carreña as your lawfully wedded wife, to have and to hold, from this day forward, 'till death do you part?" the chaplain asked.

"I do," Colonel Gracer said.

"By the power vested in me, I now pronounce you husband and wife," the chaplain said.

The two kissed, and Colonel Gracer's Air Force friends and family clapped.

"I wish I had family to see me married," Geneva whispered.

"That's okay," Colonel Gracer said. "I love you all the same."

The two kissed again.

"Yuck," Jonara said.

Cerafina laughed and laughed. She laughed so hard that the two traveled into the next day.

1964 Jun 28, Sun. Gracer and Geneva's New House. San Antonio, Texas.

"I don't want you going back to Vietnam," Colonel Gracer said.

"Is that an order?" Geneva joked. "I'm not military, you know."

"It's a request," Colonel Gracer said. "The air base is no place for a baby. Diem was murdered back in November, and the country is unstable. I want you safe here in the United States. I've invited some friends from church to check on you while I'm gone."

"If it's unsafe for me, it's unsafe for you," Geneva said.

"What?" Colonel Gracer said.

"Request a transfer," Geneva said.

"You're joking," Colonel Gracer said.

"I'm not," Geneva said. "Request a transfer to another air base."

"We get married, and you start making demands already," Colonel Gracer grinned.

"That's a demand?" Geneva replied. "I'll show you what a demand is."

The doorbell rang.

"Get the door," Geneva said. "That's a demand."

Colonel Gracer opened the door and led two red-headed women into his home.

"Jane and Roberta!" Jonara exclaimed.

"Come in, come in," Colonel Gracer said. "Geneva—this is Jane MacNessi and her daughter, Roberta MacNessi. This is my wife, Geneva."

"How do you do?" three women asked each other.

"Jane is a Lieutenant Colonel in the WAF. Roberta is studying dentistry at Wayland Baptist University," Colonel Gracer said.

"Are you Baptist?" Roberta asked.

"I, uh, am not sure what I am," Geneva said. "I used to be Roman Catholic."

"The nice thing about being Baptist is we don't have a laundry list of requirements to worship. Just believe in Jesus, and everything else falls into place," Roberta said.

"Well, I do believe in Jesus," Geneva said.

"You'll have to come to Bible study sometime," Roberta said. "There's always a new passage to discuss. Oh, I'm sorry, I didn't think about your pregnancy. Is this your first baby?"

"Roberta!" Jane said. "I'm sorry. My daughter forgets herself sometimes."

"It's quite all right," Geneva said. "Yes, this is my first child. And you're right—I won't be running around town anytime soon. My ankles and calves need a good rest."

"Then we can bring Bible study here!" Roberta said.

"Roberta, it's rude to force ourselves on a new acquaintance," Jane said.

"Bring your Bible study over anytime," Geneva said. "If you can put up with a screaming baby when the day comes, then I don't see why not."

"I love babies," Roberta said.

"Be careful with that idea," Jane said. "Make sure you're settled and done with school before you get serious baby ideas."

"Oh Mommie!" Roberta said.

"Oh Roberta!" Jane said back.

"I see Geneva is in excellent hands. I'm so glad we have Jesus smiling with us," Colonel Gracer said.

"Oh!" Roberta said. "Is that a cello in the case?"

"A cello?" Colonel Gracer asked. "I thought that was a guitar."

Geneva laughed.

"It's a very old musical instrument," Geneva said. "It's a *viola de gamba*. Here, I'll show you. Ooo! On second thought, Andrew, would you bring the case to me?"

"Of course, Geneva," Colonel Gracer said.

He got up, picked up the case, opened it, and gave it to Geneva.

"Thank you," Geneva said. "You'll notice this instrument has an unusual composition of woods."

"Mommie!" Roberta said. "It's...it's..."

"Just like the oboe," Jane said. "Miss Gracer, that viol."

"Please, call me Geneva," Geneva said.

"Geneva. We have an oboe with strange woods like yours. Is your viol made of Norway white spruce, Norway Crimson King maple, and lignum vitae with a flaxseed oil finish?" Jane asked.

Geneva stared at Jane and probed her.

"Do we know each other?" Geneva asked. "Where is your family from? You're Celtic, that I see. We have Celts in Spain. Are you from...dare I ask...the Asturias province?"

"I don't know," Jane said. "I know we're not from Ireland or Scotland. Family rumor says we're from France, possibly Spain."

"You must bring your oboe over. I would like to take a look at it. When you play, do you get...visions?" Geneva asked.

"Yes!" Roberta shouted.

"Oh, y'all are pulling my leg," Colonel Gracer said. "Did you meet already? Yeah, you must have met at the wedding. You planned this joke on me, didn't you?"

"Roberta and I couldn't make the wedding, sorry," Jane said. "Roberta had a prior commitment at the university."

"It's summer," Colonel Gracer said. "School is out."

"I'm taking summer school classes. I want to get my degree as quickly as possible," Roberta said.

"Well, good for you," Geneva said. "And Andrew, no, this is the first time I've met the MacNessis. Jane, Roberta—I bet you two get this reaction if you let outsiders know about the power of your oboe."

"All the time," Roberta said. "That's why we don't talk about it to strangers."

"But you're no stranger," Jane said. "It's like we've known you for hundreds of years."

"Since 1492?" Geneva asked.

Jane shook a little.

"I got a shiver," Jane said. "And I don't know why."

"This is the second time you've claimed to meet someone from Carreña," Colonel Gracer said.

"I never said the MacNessis are from Carreña," Geneva said.

"Who was this other person?" Jane asked.

"Is he Jewish?" Roberta asked.

"He is a *he*," Geneva said. "And he's Jewish. How did you know?"

"The oboe told us," Roberta said.

"Now I've heard everything," Colonel Gracer said. "A talking oboe? I need a drink."

Colonel Gracer left the room.

"I think we better keep these discussions to ourselves in the future," Geneva said. "But his name is Captain Aromani Karrano di Pindos. His family is from Carreña, Spain. That's where my family is from, but I was born and grew up in Girona. Captain Pindos is in a similar situation. His family is from Carreña, then Greece. He was born in Palestine before moving to New Zealand. He's serving as a medic in South Vietnam."

"And to think I've been begging my superior officer to fly aeromedical missions to Vietnam," Jane said. "It's like fate or something."

"Or something," Geneva said. "Captain Pindos has a small candleholder he uses—"

"To celebrate Shabbat," Roberta said. "And it has a symbol on it—a half-face symbol."

"No," Geneva said. "The candleholder *is* a half-face symbol— like the one in this viol. Look inside!"

Geneva passed the viol to Roberta.

"Mommie! It's the same symbol as on the oboe!" Roberta said. "It's creepy!"

Colonel Gracer returned with a bottle.

"Who wants to play cards?" he asked.

"Cards?" Geneva asked. "All I see is a bottle of wine. And only one wine glass. Have you forgotten your manners?"

"I didn't think you would want any in your condition," Colonel Gracer said to Geneva.

"Not for me. Our guests," Geneva said.

"Oh. Would you ladies like some wine?" Colonel Gracer asked.

"Yes, please," Jane and Roberta said.

"My apologies then," Colonel Gracer said. "I'll be right back."

Colonel Gracer returned to the kitchen while Geneva inspected the wine bottle.

"What kind is it?" Jane asked.

"Albariño. From Cambados, Spain," Geneva said.

"Wow," Roberta said. "I didn't realize your husband had a taste for good white wine."

"I didn't either!" Geneva exclaimed.

Colonel Gracer returned to the room with two additional wine glasses.

"Andrew," Geneva said. "About the wine."

"You don't like it?" he asked.

"No. I didn't realize you knew anything about white wine," Geneva said.

"I don't, really," he said.

"Mr. Gràcia," started Roberta. "I mean, Mr. Gracer. We were wondering why..."

Roberta's voice trailed off as all three women noticed Colonel Gracer's reaction of recognition.

"Andrew?" Geneva asked. "Is your last name really Gracer?"

Colonel Gracer hesitated as if trying to find the right words to explain.

"That's a 'no'," Roberta said.

"Shh," Jane said.

"How did you know?" he asked.

"We didn't," Geneva said. "Roberta made a slip of the tongue. I thought you were an American."

"I am," he stammered. "Now don't get upset, Geneva. I know you had your heart set on an American man. I am American, but not by birth."

"I don't understand," Geneva said. "You sound like an American."

"Very close," Jane said.

Geneva's eyes lit up.

"Your last name is *Gràcia*?" Geneva asked. "As in the Gràcia district of Barcelona? Is that where you're from?"

"Look," Colonel Gracer said. "What if I am Spanish? You know how the old country is with Franco. One can't do things as freely without risking repercussions. America is different."

"I do know how the old country is, and apparently so do you," Geneva said.

"Are you angry at me? I had hoped this moment wouldn't come," he said.

"Of course I'm not angry. I love you," Geneva said. "I just wish you would have told me before. But I'm glad. I feel like I know you better now. You don't have to hide behind that wall anymore. We can talk about whatever you feel like—America, Spain—anything."

"What I don't understand is how a Spaniard who likes white wine from Spain's west coast is from the east coast," Roberta said.

"How do you know so much about white wine and Spain?" Jane asked.

"I'm in college. Origins of alcoholic products is mandatory study," Roberta grinned.

"We need to have a talk about that—later," Jane said.

"That is a good question," Geneva said. "Andrew?"

"Because I'm not really from Barcelona. I mean, I am, sort of," Colonel Gracer said.

"This is confusing," Geneva said.

"My family is from a little vineyard just outside Cambados in Galicia with generations upon generations of wine cultivating for hundreds of years. There were many happy times from what I've heard. Then it happened. The phylloxera plague. My family got hit in 1880. They struggled to get by with other crops, but things weren't the same. My family blamed the Catholic Church for everything. We were big supporters of the Republicans, but in 1936, the Nationalists took over Galicia. I was about ten years old at the time, and I moved with the family to the Gràcia district in Barcelona, which at the time was still controlled by the Republicans. We changed our last names to *Gràcia* in hopes we wouldn't be tracked by the Nationalists. At that time, we joined the Spanish Baptist Convention. My family is Christian, but we couldn't support Spain's Catholic Church."

"So you became a Baptist," Geneva asked, "because your family hated the Church?"

"I became a Baptist," Colonel Gracer continued. "That's where I learned American English—one of the Baptist missionaries held English classes. I practiced by reading the Bible and attending Bible study—all in American English. But the Spanish Civil War took a toll on Spain. The Nationalists took over Barcelona, and some of the Baptist missionaries returned to their countries. One particular American missionary offered to help my family immigrate to the United States. And that's how I ended up in San Antonio."

"You didn't hear me, did you?" Geneva asked.

"Yeah, I did. But you're Catholic, or at least you were. Probably still are and have feelings for the Church. Heck, you were a sister. I'm sorry. I was afraid you'd react badly. That's why I didn't want to say anything," Colonel Gracer said.

"Come here," Geneva said.

She hugged and kissed Colonel Gracer.

"Those were tough times for everyone. I don't hate you. I love you," Geneva said.

"But I never forget my family or where they're from. So I drink Albariño from Galicia when I think of home," Colonel Gracer said.

"I think that's wonderful," Geneva said. "Now, let's do something fun. Where are those cards?"

Roberta placed the *viola de gamba* in its case and handed it to Colonel Gracer. The women agreed to play cards, and that ended the discussion of Spain for the evening.

"So what were you women talking about when I was in the kitchen?" Colonel Gracer asked. "More voodoo superstition?"

"We were talking about…" Geneva started.

"The news," Jane finished.

"Yes," Geneva continued. "The Vatican condemned the pill last Thursday. I'm so glad I'm not subservient to those rules anymore."

"Good for you!" Jane said.

"Groovy!" Roberta added.

"Wait," Colonel Gracer said to Geneva. "Does that mean I can't get ten or twelve babies out of you?"

The three women laughed and laughed. Then Colonel Gracer laughed too, revealing he'd been joking. He knocked his wine over accidentally, and the world swirled into gray again for Jonara and Cerafina.

1964 Jul 2, Thu. San Antonio Hospital. San Antonio, Texas.

"Push, Mrs. Gracer," the nurse said to Geneva.

"Ugh! This baby is too big and will never come out!" Geneva said.

"It'll have to come out," the male doctor said. "It can't stay inside."

"We're here," Jane said as she held Geneva's left hand.

"We'll stay with you until the end," Roberta said as she held Geneva's right hand.

"I hope it's a good ending," Geneva said. "Doctor—give me something for the pain."

"We could give you a twilight drug," the doctor said. "But it might deprive the baby of oxygen and cause brain damage."

"Is the baby a boy or girl?" Jane asked.

"Mommie!" Roberta said.

"If it's a boy, give him the twilight drug. If a girl, no drugs," Jane joked.

"You know, Jane, if I didn't know better, I'd say you have a thing against men," Geneva said.

"I know she does," the doctor said. "But as to the baby's gender, it is a girl."

"Then quit calling her an *it*," Jane said.

"Ugh!" Geneva said with another contraction.

"The baby is crowning," the doctor said.

"I'll crown you if you don't get this baby out of me!" Geneva said.

"Just push," the doctor said.

"I've been pushing all along. Someone else can push for a change. I'm going on strike!" Geneva said.

"It's almost over," Roberta said. "Just pretend you ate a big dinner and have to go to the bathroom."

"Well, it's the biggest bathroom push I've ever had," Geneva said. "Ugh!"

"That's it," the doctor said. "The baby is out."

The doctor cut the umbilical cord. A nurse took the baby, cleaned her up, bundled her in fresh cloth, and gave her to Geneva.

"My little girl," Geneva said. "You're the most beautiful person in the world."

"Do you have a name for her?" Roberta asked.

"Andrew wants to call her Beatrice Argantia Gracer," Geneva said.

"Yuck!" Roberta said.

"Her initials will be BAG," Jane said.

"Oh that won't do," Geneva said.

"Name her after yourself," Roberta said. "That's what I would do."

"You have a point there, young lady," Geneva said. "I'll name her *Eva Carreña.*"

"You mean, *Eva Gracer?*" Jane asked.

"Oh yes. What am I thinking? Eva Kelicacha Gracer," Geneva said.

"I just wanted to share something interesting with you," Jane said to Geneva. "Roberta's birthday is August 9, 1945. On that day, the Americans dropped the second atomic bomb on Japan."

"You're a bomb baby!" Geneva joked to Roberta.

"But earlier this day, Lyndon Baines Johnson signed the Civil Rights Act into law," Jane said. "Eva is a Civil Rights baby!"

Roberta and Jane clapped. The air stirred into colors with each clap. Jonara and Cerafina found themselves back in Geneva's music room.

"Oh where is that girl?" Eva's voice bellowed through the house. "It's time for the wake."

Jonara and Cerafina looked at each other in surprise.

"I found her," Eva called through the house as she opened the door to the music room. "She's in the music room with Cerafina."

"Cerafina?" Johnny called back. "I thought—"

Johnny appeared in the doorway.

"Oh," Johnny said. "They're being friendly."

"Jonara—what have you been doing all afternoon? Don't you see it's late? We have to get going. Your Nanna Geneva's wake starts in twenty minutes."

"I'll go home," Cerafina said.

"No, wait," Jonara said. "Why don't you come along?"

Cerafina looked at Eva and Johnny. Johnny nodded his head in affirmation.

"Come along, Cerafina," Eva said. "Jonara needs all the support she can get. I only wish her mother could attend."

CHAPTER 18

Smoke, Rain, Fire

2023 Oct 6, Fri Eve. Candlewood Catholic Church, Corpus Christi, Texas.

Eva drove Geneva's car to Candlewood Catholic Church with Johnny sitting in the front passenger seat, and Jonara, Cerafina, and Anna squished in the back seat.

"Now I want to prepare you for this wake," Eva said. "There's going to be Catholic stuff. Just play along with it. We need to get through this evening so we can bury Geneva tomorrow. The dead cannot wait for the living."

"Why don't we postpone the funeral until my Mommy is better?" Jonara said.

"No. We can't have a dead family member lying around for weeks on end," Eva said. "It's been almost a week since she died, and that's long enough."

"What are you afraid of? Nanna Geneva can't hurt you anymore," Jonara said.

"That's enough, young lady," Eva said. "I want no crazy talk during the wake. And if someone gets up and talks about old Spain, I want you to ignore them."

"Franco," Jonara said. "You don't want to hear about Franco."

"I said that's enough!" Eva yelled. "It's time we bury the dead and everything else along with them. The old days are over. Let's get on with the present."

"Mommy liked Nanna Geneva. She would want to hear about old Spain. Why don't we wait?" Jonara begged.

"I told you that's enough," Eva said. "Too many questions get asked that are better left buried."

"Like Mommy's father?" Jonara asked. "You're afraid Mommy will ask you that question, aren't you? Why the deceit, Grandma, why?"

Eva pulled the car over to the side of the road quite suddenly. She parked, got out of the car, yanked Jonara out behind the car, held her firmly by the shoulder, and gave her sharp words.

"You want to stir up trouble? Go ahead," Eva said. "See where it gets you. You don't know how the world works, little miss smartie. If you want to get along with people, you shut your mouth before things get ugly. And they're about to get ugly. Your mother is going to die."

"No!" Jonara said defiantly.

Eva slapped Jonara across the face.

"I'm a medical professional," Eva said. "And you're an emotional girl. Your mother won't survive her pregnancy, see? And when that happens, what do you think will happen to you? Oh, you hadn't thought about that, had you? That's right—it's easy to run off at the mouth, but who picks up the pieces? Your mother always did that. Now she'll be gone. Who will pick up after you? Your father? He has hydrocephalus. His brain ventricles are filled with cerebrospinal fluid, and his brain has been squeezed into a paper-thin layer against his skull. It's inoperable. Oh yes, his days are numbered. So what will you do then? Who will pick up the pieces after you? You could live with me. No, you're becoming rebellious. You wouldn't like that. Run away? Then what? Who will pick up after you then? You'll have to take care of yourself and learn about the world the hard way. Then you'll see where mouthing off gets you."

"Lies! All lies! Like Santa Claus and God!" Jonara said.

Eva slapped Jonara across the face even harder. Jonara broke into tears.

"This family is hanging from a fragile rope, Jonara, caught between a cliff and a fierce wind," Eva said. "And I won't let you sabotage what's left of it. Now shut up and get in the car!"

Jonara returned to the car and buried her feelings—a mixture of hate and sadness. Was this her thanks for helping Eva with her cancer?

"Meanie," Jonara thought to herself. "I should have let her die."

Cerafina sensed Jonara's thoughts, turned to Jonara, held a finger to her lips, and nodded her head, "No."

"Don't be hateful," Cerafina whispered in Jonara's ear.

Cerafina placed her hand on Jonara's thigh. Jonara in turn placed her hand atop Cerafina's and let slip a small smile from between the boiling layers of incensed emotions.

The group arrived at Candlewood Catholic Church, which was constructed to double as a funeral home. Friends of Geneva had already arrived, but prayers had not yet begun. Eva signed the guest book and immediately walked over to a corner where she found some old friends. Johnny signed and sat in a corner. He looked exhausted. Anna, Jonara, and Cerafina signed next.

"Let's visit Geneva," Anna said.

The three walked up to Geneva's casket. Geneva was dressed in her Third Order of Saint Dominic robe. She had a rosary in one hand and a prayer card in the other. Anna reached out to touch Geneva but withdrew her hand quickly and walked away from the casket in tears. Jonara looked next.

"I always check for breathing," Jonara said to Cerafina. "I guess I want to be the first to say Nanna Geneva is still alive. But she's not moving."

"She looks so peaceful," Cerafina said. "But she's wearing a robe from the Third Order of Saint Dominic. She must have done a lot of Catholic charity before she died."

"Which I don't understand," Jonara said. "She gave up the Church back in 1963. I wonder what brought her back?"

Jonara continued staring. A cold hand pressed on her shoulder.

"Why is your hand so cold?" Jonara said as she turned to Cerafina.

But Cerafina wasn't there. She had walked over to the flowers.

"Who touched me?" Jonara asked, but her voice was weak, and no one heard her, at least she didn't think anyone had.

A mist and fog descended on Jonara. A figure appeared in the mist and approached her.

"Nanna Geneva?" Jonara called.

The figure grew near, and as it did, Jonara recognized the shape.

"Nekara the Red!" she said.

"You are under my dominion now," Nekara said. "Yes. I agree with you. You should have let Eva die."

"Cerafina!" Jonara called.

The mist cleared, and Jonara returned to the church.

"Cerafina!" Jonara called again.

"What is it, Shnuki?" Cerafina replied as she rushed from the flowers to Jonara's aid.

"Something happened," Jonara said. "Did you see a strange fog in here?"

"No, I didn't," Cerafina said. "But I was looking at the flowers. Did you go on another journey without me? And you're in church too. Jonara, how could you leave me behind?"

"It wasn't like that," Jonara said. "I wasn't trying to go anywhere. I saw the devil, Shlifa. She came out of the mist. She...I...she..."

"Relax," Cerafina said. "Was it Nekara the Red?"

"Yeah, it was," Jonara said.

"What time did you go to?" Cerafina asked.

"I didn't. I didn't go to a place or time. It was just fog and Nekara. That was it. She said I was under her dominion," Jonara explained.

"Don't believe her. You know she's full of deceit."

"But what if she's right?" Jonara said. "She knows more than me."

"Does she?" Cerafina asked. "Isn't that the genius of deceit—to appear more knowledgable than those who are deceived?"

"Yeah, I guess you're right," Jonara said.

"Come here, Shnu, I want to show you something behind the flowers," Cerafina said.

"Okay," Jonara said.

Cerafina led Jonara behind the bouquets of flowers. They acted as a privacy wall, obscuring all but Jonara's and Cerafina's feet from view of the others. Cerafina gave her a deep kiss, and Jonara's eyes lit up in excitement.

"You kissed me in church! At my Nanna Geneva's funeral! Right next to her casket!"

"Is there a crime in love?" Cerafina grinned.

"I don't know...but somehow expressing love in church seems blasphemous," Jonara said.

"Then let's blaspheme a little more," Cerafina said.

Cerafina hugged and kissed Jonara intimately.

"No, no more," Jonara said as she pulled away. "We could get caught. And what we're doing seems disrespectful."

"But it's exciting!" Cerafina said. "I've never kissed a girl in church before. It's so spiritual."

"Okay, okay, just control your hormones for a moment there, Shli," Jonara said. "What do we do about Nekara?"

"I think it was stress," Cerafina said. "And that's why I brought you back here—to help you let go of that tension."

"Yeah, but you started a different kind of tension," Jonara said.

"I did? I thought it was just fun," Cerafina said.

"I felt something down deep, something building. It felt...wrong," Jonara said.

"Hmm. We'll have to explore that later," Cerafina said.

"We're too young! We're illegal!" Jonara said.

"I like illegal!" Cerafina replied.

Before Cerafina and Jonara could continue their conversation, the priest entered the room and called the group to attention. He instructed them to take seats, and the people did. Jonara and Cerafina appeared from behind the flowers. Eva saw them and gave them a disapproving look.

The people seated themselves, and the priest began with prayers—the Glorious Mysteries on the rosary. Eva, Johnny, and Jonara did not say the rosary. Cerafina did. The rosary had a chant and rhythm to it. A small fog descended over Geneva's casket, and the dark figure appeared—standing next to the casket with a hand on it.

"Nekara," Jonara whispered.

Cerafina continued reciting the Hail Mary but looked at Jonara with a puzzled expression.

"Go away," Jonara whispered.

Only Jonara could see Nekara, who was now walking from the casket to the priest. She made a hand gesture against her abdomen, and with the other hand, she touched the priest. A red and green fireball engulfed the priest—only visible to Nekara and Jonara. The priest, unaware of anything metaphysical, continued leading in prayers. Jonara broke out in a cold sweat and shivered. Cerafina placed her arm around Jonara just as Nekara drew Jonara back in time, pulling Cerafina back in time as well.

1968 Jan 31 Tue. Saigon, South Vietnam.

"Do you know this place?" Nekara asked.

"Release me at once," Jonara said.

"You have no power here. You're under my dominion, as I said before," Nekara said. "Look at the U.S. Embassy. The Viet Cong are attacking it now. So much for America's propaganda machine of body counts and kill ratios."

"Stop! I command you to release. *Peliko, peliko, peliko!*" Jonara commanded.

"As I said before, your Miramish tricks don't work on me. My people broke from the Miramish eons ago. Look at the Viet Cong. Witness their hatred of Americans. 'We are beginning to win this struggle. Territory is being gained. We are making steady progress.' Recognize those words? Do you *feel the rain?*"

"No. Huh? Rain?" Jonara said.

"The Success Offensive," Cerafina said. "The U.S. effort to pacify the American public who realized the Vietnam War was a mistake. Some say this type of rhetoric is *rain*. People who believe this deceit *feel the rain*. People who blindly follow this deceit to perform some controversial act without question are *running in the rain*. People who are in the know and wish to perpetuate the deceit at the expense of others are *happy when it rains*."

"Thank you, Cerafina," Nekara said. "You'll make a good follower in my domain."

"Cerafina, why are you helping her?" Jonara asked.

"Sorry. The Success Offensive is part of our American history," Cerafina said.

"Yes, isn't it though?" Nekara said. "Killing for the sake of killing. Blindly taking orders. And telling your citizens you are making steady progress. Look at the steady progress, Jonara."

"I know Vietnam was bad. You don't have to show me," Jonara said. "*Nia giashoko kail* (I curse you)!"

Nekara laughed.

"This attack by the Viet Cong is the Tet Offensive," Cerafina said. "But why bring us here?"

"Hmmm. Colonel Gracer," Nekara said. "Unfortunately, he was caught up in the attack. He died. Oh well, your Nanna Geneva will have to do without. But it could have been stopped. Explosions and bombs. Damiriak women have the power—you know—to go back in time and change a few things committed by the naïve."

"Lies," Jonara said. "I saw how you tricked Marcus."

"Is it a lie what you did for Axon in the Pindus Mountains?" Nekara asked. "You didn't think I knew about that, did you? What about when Fantina performed surgery? And all the other times you intervened in history, hmm? You don't know how it works, but I do. I can teach you. You can become powerful and teach these men a thing or two. Isn't that what you want?"

"You're the devil," Jonara said. "The devil always has a price."

Nekara laughed.

"The devil? Religious folklore? But your devil is a red-skinned man with horns and a pitchfork. I'm a leader of women. No, wait, you don't know about us, do you? Typical Earthlings. You think the universe revolves around you, that you are everything."

"You tricked Marcus," Jonara repeated.

"A young boy who wanted power," Nekara said.

"But he didn't cause the 16th Street bombing. Those men did," Jonara said.

"So? What's it to you? He's a boy. Control men before they control you. When you have knowledge, you can trick them into doing anything."

"You sound like my friend, Almarita," Jonara said.

"Oh, so you're used to having friends like me," Nekara said. "You Earth girls are easier than I thought. A revolution will take no time at all to organize."

"Be careful, Jonara. She could be lying," Cerafina said.

"Could be. But how can you know for sure? And what can you do? I'm more powerful than you'll ever know," Nekara said.

"You have no power over me," Jonara said. "I'll sit in a trench of flames before I submit to your will."

"You already have," Nekara said. "By openly defying me, you have bonded with me in a twisted way. Oh, hate is like love with the poles reversed. You've fallen into the oldest trap in the cosmos. Behold!"

1968 Mar 16, Sat. My Lai, Vietnam.

"I love helicopters," Nekara said. "Don't you? Cerafina, you're the history buff. What kind of helicopter is this?"

"It's an American craft. A Hiller OH-23 Raven," Cerafina said.

"Don't answer her questions," Jonara said.

"They seem harmless enough," Cerafina said.

"Yes, information is harmless, isn't it Cerafina?" Nekara winked and grinned. "Propagate *information* in the proper way to the proper people, and you will achieve your goal of spreading hate and violence."

"Stop it! You're a hate-monger," Jonara said.

"Among other things," Nekara said. "Cerafina, care to take a guess as to what's happening?"

"Well, these helicopters were used to see what was going on, for quick flights here and there, and to transport the occasional hurt person," Cerafina said. "This one has three American soldiers. There are two gunships nearby—they look like Hueys.

But the helicopter we're in is much smaller than a Huey. We're just hovering over this village."

"Yes, we are. Things are waiting to happen," Nekara said.

"What things?" Cerafina asked.

"Don't ask her anything," Jonara said to Cerafina.

"Wait—I think I remember the strategy of these Vietnam operations. One helicopter hovers over a village to act as bait and draw enemy fire," Cerafina said. "Then ground troops and gunships take out the enemy."

"Yes, and you are the bait," Nekara said.

Ground troops held their position. Vietnamese civilians left their homes and headed out for the morning, feeling completely safe.

"Nothing going on here," the pilot said on the radio. "Hey guys, I'm going to go get some gas. I'll be back in a little bit."

"Leaving for fuel is hardly what I call violence," Jonara said. "So you've failed. This American pilot is just doing his job."

"Just doing his job. Just following orders," Nekara echoed. "Yes! The hallmark of the hatred machine is just following orders!"

The pilot landed his OH-23 Raven elsewhere, refueled, and headed back for the village.

"This is the most peaceful and boring journey in time," Jonara said. "And where are my relatives? I don't know anyone here. This vision is a waste of my time."

"Yes, a waste," Nekara said with sarcasm. "The lives of people we don't know are a waste. A waste. They're not people. They're animals. Grunts. Trolls of the earth. Pests, vermin, and throwaways. Get the bulldozer out—it's time to re-pave."

"You're insane," Jonara said.

"Only because you don't see. But since my narrative bores your short attention span, I'll give you music to fly by."

Nekara broadcast music into the Raven that only Jonara, Cerafina, and Nekara could hear. It was the 1995 single, *Only Happy When It Rains* by the rock group *Garbage*.

"That wasn't created until 1995," Cerafina said.

"And it's completely out of place," Jonara said.

Nekara laughed and said, "You'll see."

The pilot returned to the village where he had been hovering forty minutes earlier.

"Those Vietnamese who were walking on the road are dead, sir," said a crewman.

"Excellent!" Nekara said. "The hatred begins. Kill the innocent. Kill your fellow soldier. We feed on hate, Jonara. Feed on it with me. Share this bread of death at my dinner table. Aren't you happy when it rains?"

"Oh, this better not be what I think it is," Cerafina said.

"Oh yes! It is exactly what you think it is!" Nekara grinned.

"There are some wounded down there," Thompson said.

Thompson dropped a green flare to mark the position of the wounded, signaling a medevac should transport them out. The OH-23 Raven circled about the area.

"Oh, this can't be," Cerafina said.

"Oh but it is!" Nekara celebrated with glee. "Look at the pilot's name tag."

"Thompson," Cerafina said. "And his crewmembers are Colburn and Andreotta."

"It's 0900 hours, and the male beast is rising for the day!" Nekara said. "But we can stop it. Quick, Jonara—issue a Miramish chant to stop this. You know what to say. Do it, and I'll chant in my language with you. We can stop the carnage that's unfolding. We can *save* those defenseless women and children."

"No," Jonara said. "It's a trick. You're trying to trap me the way you did Marcus."

"But he was male. You're female. Females have powers in my world to prevent tragedies," Nekara smiled. "What do you say, is it worth a try?"

"This isn't a game!" Jonara said.

"Hmm. Just remember, you could have prevented this. Blood is on your hands."

"It isn't. You pulled that line on Marcus. It won't work with me," Jonara said.

"It looks like a bloodbath down there! What the Hell is going on?" Thompson said.

"Oh, Thompson is jealous they started the massacre without him," Nekara said.

"Now that is a lie," Cerafina said.

"It wasn't a massacre?" Nekara laughed.

"You twist everything," Jonara said. "Thompson isn't jealous. He's in shock."

"It looks to me like there's an awful lot of unnecessary killing going on down there," said Thompson. "Something ain't right about this. There are bodies everywhere. There's a ditch full of bodies. There's something wrong here."

"They would have heard something on the radio if the Viet Cong had attacked," Nekara said. "But that's not how men fight dirty wars. Silence is golden. The American ground troops are *running in the rain.*"

"There was nothing on the radio," Thompson replied. "No call for medevacs—nothing. Why the silence? Why are people running from their houses? Those houses have bomb shelters. How did they get in the ditch?"

"There is a wounded girl down there," Nekara said. "See how she waves about? She will die. Quick—perform a Miramish chant and save her."

"From what?" Jonara said. "There's no enemy here."

"Don't question—just do!" Nekara said.

"Oh," Thompson said. "We've got to get some help for this one."

"Who will kill the girl?" Nekara asked. "Will it be the unseen enemy? Or will it be you, Jonara?"

"Stop it!" Jonara said. "You're trying to scare me. There is no enemy."

"I got a wounded civilian here. Can you all help her out?" Thompson called to the ground troops.

"There, you see?" Jonara said. "The ground troops will help her out."

"Oh they'll help her out, all right," Nekara laughed.

The helicopter hovered ten feet above the ground, sending air and debris all about. Thompson lifted the helicopter in the air to clear room for the ground troops to save the girl.

"Pow!"

"He killed her!" Jonara said. "The ground troop guy killed that girl!"

"With an M-16 on automatic setting," Nekara said. "He *helped* the girl."

"Radio communication doesn't work. This is not what I intended to do," Thompson said to his crew.

"There is a Vietnamese woman down there," Nekara said. "Do you see her? She's pleading for her life. No weapons to defend herself. Quick—perform a Miramish chant and save her."

Jonara did nothing. The American soldier on the ground kicked the woman to the ground and shot her at point-blank range.

"Oh, too bad," Nekara laughed. "You didn't save her. Tough luck. Aren't you proud to be American?"

Thompson saw movement in a ditch filled with dead civilians. He landed the helicopter by the ditch and accosted an American sergeant on the ground.

"Hey, there are some civilians over in this ditch. Can you help them out?" Thompson asked the ground-based American sergeant who had participated in the massacre.

"Help them out of their misery is more like it," said the sergeant.

"You bastard! Quit joking around. Help them out," Thompson said.

"Okay, Chief, we'll take care of it," said the sergeant.

"Okay," Thompson said.

"Oh this is wonderful!" Nekara said. "Don't you like it when Americans on the opposite side of the fence come in contact with each other? One side *feels the rain,* the other side is dry."

A Second Lieutenant approached Thompson.

"What's going on here, Lieutenant?" Thompson asked.

"This is my business," the Second Lieutenant said.

"What is this? Who are these people?" Thompson asked.

"Just following orders," the Second Lieutenant said.

"Orders? Whose orders?" Thompson asked.

"Just following—" the Second Lieutenant said.

"But these are human beings, unarmed civilians, sir," Thompson said.

"Look Thompson, this is my show. I'm in charge here. It ain't your concern," the Second Lieutenant said.

"Yeah, great job," Thompson said sarcastically.

"You better get back in that chopper and mind your own business," the Second Lieutenant said.

"You ain't heard the last of this!" Thompson said.

Thompson returned to the helicopter.

"Beautiful," Nekara said. "A classic demonstration of your American Mr. Stanley Milgram and his 1961 experiment."

Nekara laughed again.

"Who's Milgram?" Jonara asked Cerafina.

"Yes, Cerafina, tell us about Milgram," Nekara said. "But first, watch the ground below. You don't want to miss the ground troops *running in the rain*."

"Stop it with the stupid rain analogies. And quit playing that song. You're blaspheming *Garbage*," Jonara said.

Thompson returned to the OH-23 Raven. The helicopter took off, and as it cleared the ditch, machine-gun fire echoed from the ground.

"My God, he's firing in the ditch," Andreotta said as the sergeant executed the remaining living Vietnamese.

"Oh that was fun," Nekara laughed. "Now Cerafina, tell us about Mr. Milgram. Hurry before the next bloodshed comes along."

"In 1961, Nazi war criminal Adolf Eichmann went on trial for war crimes, crimes against humanity, and other charges. Eichmann was the master architect of the Holocaust," Cerafina started.

"Not the whole history book," Nekara said.

"This trial triggered a ghoulish question in the mind of psychologist Stanley Milgram, which went something like this: Was there any sense of morality among Eichman and his accomplices in the Holocaust?"

"And?" Nekara said. "What did Milgram discover?"

"That seemingly ordinary people will inflict large amounts of pain on others in the name of following orders from an authority figure. The willingness to inflict pain increases substantially if the act of inflicting pain is compartmentalized into pieces—with each person only performing a part of the act. This allows the person to satisfy his desire to be obedient while deferring his responsibility of the immoral act to that of an accomplice."

"Excellent, Cerafina! I will make you my minister of propaganda yet!" Nekara said.

"The Nazis used this method to create their Final Solution—their act of genocide that murdered millions of Jews," Cerafina said.

"Every good Nazi hates a Jew," Nekara mimicked. "Jews aren't people anyway. They're rats. As explained in the timeless German movie, *The Eternal Jew*."

"That was racist propaganda," Jonara said.

"But effective," Nekara said. "These American men are the same. They see the Vietnamese as no better than rats. Beat, rape, and slaughter. It's a timeless human tradition you should be proud of. Every good regime needs a Stanley Milgram program to grease the bigotry machine and maintain its paralytic grip of power."

Jonara felt hatred brewing in her.

"Men did it," Jonara let slip from her lips.

"Ah hah!" Nekara said. "Yes! Men did the killing. Men raped the woman. Men! Hate men! Kill men everywhere! Defer responsibility to men. Take none yourself. Compartmentalize! Like Milgram's experiment. Excellent! But don't take responsibility. Don't take it. No. Let no blood fall on your own hands."

"No, no, no!" Jonara said. "No blood is on my hands. And there are good men in this world."

"There are? Like your boy Thompson here?" Nekara asked. "Your American leaders feel differently."

"Another lie!" Jonara said.

"Um," Cerafina said. "In this instance..."

"Don't say it," Jonara said.

Nekara laughed.

"You know Cerafina is right. And I'm right. Look—more glory to come!" Nekara said.

The helicopter flew to another part of the village. American soldiers from the same 2nd Platoon, C Company pursued ten civilians. The civilians, including children, ran for their lives toward a bunker.

"They have fifteen seconds to live," crewmember Colburn said to Thompson, referring to C Company's advance on the civilians.

"Not if I can help it," Thompson replied.

Thompson landed the OH-23 Raven between C Company and the fleeing civilians.

"Y'all cover me!" Thompson said to his crew. "If these bastards open up on me or these people, you open up on them. Promise me!"

The crew—Colburn and Andreotta—trained their M60 machine guns on C Company.

"Neighbor against neighbor. American soldier against American soldier. Why, this is better than the Hatfields and McCoys. And the action is so far from home. What do Mommy and Daddy know about it? They're too busy swallowing that American Success Offensive rhetoric from your government. They're *feeling the rain* while their children are *running in the rain*. Oh the splendor of it all! I love America! If only your boys had tactical nukes like government-boy, happy-when-it-rains Mendel Rivers wanted. They could nuke each other."

"Damn you, Nekara," Jonara said.

Nekara laughed. Thompson confronted the American platoon leader.

"Hey listen, hold your fire. I'm going to try to get these people out of this bunker. Just hold your men here," Thompson said.

"Yeah, we can *help* you get them out of that bunker. With a hand grenade!" said the platoon leader.

Nekara froze the moment in time.

"There's going to be a big bloodbath here, Jonara," Nekara said, "unless you chant something immediately to stop it. You allowed that girl to be killed and the woman too. Stop the fight, and you condemn it. Don't stop the fight, and you condone it. Condemn or condone?"

"Don't play that game," Cerafina said. "She's using a dichotomy to force you into one of her directions."

Jonara opened her mouth as if to chant something. The first words slid off her lips, and as they did, Cerafina turned Jonara's head toward her own. Cerafina gave Jonara a deep kiss and held the kiss until Nekara ran out of patience.

"Ugh! Human love! How revolting!" Nekara grumbled.

The moment unfroze, and Thompson resumed his mission.

"Just hold your men here. If you fire on these people when I'm getting them out of the bunker, my people will fire on you!" Thompson said.

The platoon leader backed down.

"Another disappointment," Nekara said. "I hate it when the sun comes out and restores clear thought."

"You lied. Nothing would have happened," Jonara said.

"You don't know that. I might have spared them," Nekara said. "Yes, I spared them. I did your job. You didn't follow orders."

"You? Never!" Jonara said. "You're twisted beyond words!"

Thompson walked to his OH-23 Raven with the eleven civilians hiding behind him from C Company's threat.

"I got a little problem down here," Thompson radioed to his low gunship Huey.

"What do you want me to do?" the Huey radioed back.

"I'd like for you to land and get these people out of this area," Thompson said.

"Okay, sure thing. No problem," the Huey radioed back.

The Huey gunship (UH-1 Iroquois helicopter) landed nearby and evacuated half the civilians. He flew a number of miles away and landed.

"Run away," the gunship pilot signaled the civilians.

The gunship returned shortly thereafter to evacuate the second half, as if the gunship were a medevac. He repeated the evacuation with the second half. Thompson remained on the ground for ten minutes in a standoff with C Company. When the gunship left for the second and last time, Thompson reentered his OH-23 Raven and lifted off.

"Well, let's make one pass over the ditch again," Thompson said.

Andreotta saw more movement in the ditch. Thompson landed the OH-23 Raven again, and Andreotta trudged through a hundred dying and dead bodies.

"Help us, please!" many pleaded—clinging onto Andreotta as dearly as they clung to their failing lives.

Andreotta's heart weighed heavily from the physical and emotional strain of the many hands pulling down on him. Overwhelmed, Andreotta did the best he could.

"I can't help you," Andreotta said to them. "You're too bad off."

Andreotta pulled a boy out of the ditch, returned from the ditch, and placed the boy across Thompson's and Colburn's lap. Thompson piloted his OH-23 Raven to a hospital and gave the boy to a nun.

"I don't know what you're going to do with him," Thompson said to the nun. "But I don't think he's got any family left."

"So Cerafina," Nekara said. "What was the death toll?"

"No, I won't feed your appetite," Cerafina said.

"That's right," Jonara said. "We're done with you."

"Done? Oh no, no, no. You're under my dominion until I decide otherwise. Let's see—over 500 civilian deaths of which 179 were children less than two years of age. Don't believe body-count stories of 200, 100, or less. Governments always shift body counts in their favor. They are the *house*—as in gambling. And the house always wins. Oh yes, no weapons found in the village. You've got to love the body count and the kill ratio, don't you?"

"You don't have any humanity in you. Thompson is a hero. And his crew too. You can't prove otherwise," Jonara said.

"Let's take a look at that, shall we?" Nekara said.

1969 Oct. An American Military Office Room.

The three appeared at a military base with Thompson receiving an award.

"It's been a year and a half since the operation," Nekara said. "Your high-quality U.S. Army covered up the massacre for that length of time, but a leak got out. A leak is fun too. Try it sometime. Stirs the beehive quite nicely."

"Shut up already!" Jonara shouted.

"Oh Jonara, how I enjoy your emotional outbursts of hatred toward me! So becoming! But now the cover-up begins. It rains again. And it starts with buying Thompson's silence with a medal."

"For rescuing civilian children from a bunker between Viet Cong forces and advancing friendly forces, and for the rescue of a child caught in intense crossfire, your sound judgment has greatly enhanced Vietnamese-American relations in the operational area. For this, I award you the Distinguished Flying Cross," the officer said.

Thompson accepted the award slowly and reluctantly.

"So," Nekara said. "Your boy Thompson isn't such a hero after all. He accepted an award in a cover-up. He's *feeling the rain*. No wait, I used the wrong metaphor. He's *happy when*—"

"Stop it! You're impossible! And this can't be true! Thompson wouldn't be part of a lie!" Jonara said.

"Cerafina?" Nekara asked.

"It is true, but something's not right. I think he got rid of it," Cerafina said.

"Get rid of an award?" Nekara asked. "For enhancing Vietnamese-American relations? For rescuing a child caught in a one-sided cross-fire between Americans and the Viet Cong who were not there?"

"Yeah, I think so," Cerafina said.

"How can you know for sure?" Nekara said. "He could have made that up and told the world later. Another cover-up over a cover-up."

"Cerafina's right. Why would Thompson threaten to shoot his fellow American soldier only to accept an award later?" Jonara asked.

"But he did accept the award," Nekara said. "He could have refused it immediately. But he didn't. He is guilty of—"

"Of nothing!" Jonara said.

"Of being the only one guilty in the massacre," Nekara said.

"Lies!" Jonara said.

1969, Late. Capitol Hill.

"Why are we on the steps of Capitol Hill?" Cerafina asked.

"There's a closed-door investigation in progress. The public is not allowed in," Nekara said. "Cover-ups are always best handled in the deepest and darkest recesses of evil. Black thunderclouds make the best cover for evil."

Nekara salivated and rubbed her hands with anticipation.

"At this moment, Thompson is being grilled for ordering his crew to open fire on American soldiers if innocent Vietnamese were further attacked," Nekara said. "No one in the public knows his suffering. Without public support, his suffering will consume him. Excellent."

"That's not true. The public did learn about him. And eventually, he was praised a hero," Cerafina said.

"Cerafina, why bother? She'll just turn it around on you," Jonara said.

"Yes. Let's start the turning around," Nekara said. "Eventually. Yes. How many years? Thirty? That's why evil is superior to good. Evil is so quick, so instantaneous. Much evil can be accomplished before Good even becomes a first thought. Yes, Good takes too long. Let's look at the knee-jerk reaction."

The world swirled ahead in time a bit. Nekara picked up a newspaper.

"Read it," Nekara said to Jonara.

"No," Jonara said. "It's a lie."

Cerafina picked up the newspaper.

"It's not a lie," Cerafina said. "Now I remember. I'm sorry, Jonara."

Cerafina turned quickly to Nekara and said, "And I won't read it either."

"But I will," Nekara said. "This is what your Granddaddy-of-the-War-Hawks Mr. Lucifer Mendel Rivers has to say, 'Hugh

Thompson is the only American who should be prosecuted over My Lai for ordering his men to fire upon American soldiers if they continued to shoot unarmed Vietnamese civilians'.".

"His name was *Lucius*, not *Lucifer*," Cerafina said.

"Lucius or Lucifer—anyone pedaling war is my kind of man!" Nekara said.

"Well, your man Lucius died in Birmingham, Alabama, from a heart attack a year later," Cerafina said.

"A tragic loss to your government, no doubt," Nekara said, "for a Civil Rights hero."

"He wasn't a Civil Rights hero," Cerafina said. "He was a white segregationalist like many other whites in Birmingham of his day."

Jonara stared at Nekara with seething anger.

"You don't like twisted facts, do you Jonara?" Nekara asked. "But it's so fun to do. Your government does it without mercy. That's why I like them so much. And you're part of that government, Jonara, as the people who elect officials into office. That's why I like you."

"I don't want you to like me," Jonara said.

Nekara laughed and laughed. Jonara lifted a fist and prepared to chant something else.

"No, Shnuki, no!" Cerafina said.

"That's right, Shnuki," Nekara said. "Don't stand up for what you believe in!"

"That does it!" Jonara said. "No one but Cerafina calls me Shnuki!"

Jonara leapt at Nekara and throttled her neck.

"Why must you show me these miseries of the world?" Jonara demanded.

"Open your eyes," Nekara gasped. "Your family has no monopoly on misery. The world is a smorgasbord of evil ready to be consumed. Enrich your palate!"

Jonara tightened her grip on Nekara's neck. Nekara choked. Her face turned dark and expanded, as if she were a balloon filling with unventable air. Her face became pitch-black, and little white specs of light peppered it and moved across from right to left. Her face lightened a little and swirled in colors of blue, violet, pink, and orange. Her mouth opened, and a beaming bright light shone through and nearly blinded Jonara. Smoke poured from Nekara's nostrils and ears—filling the air with a dark haze. Jonara coughed on the stench-laced smoke and could barely keep her grip on Nekara's neck.

"Jonara, Jonara!" Cerafina called. "Come back. This is the moment. Come back to the living!"

Cerafina grasped Jonara's head and kissed her deeply. Jonara broke away and continued choking Nekara. Cerafina pulled Jonara's entire body against her own, hugged Jonara tightly, and kissed her deeply again.

Jonara released her grip. Smoke continued to encircle them, but its aroma changed into something more pleasant—incense one might burn at a ceremony. Cerafina released her hold on Jonara, and Jonara opened her eyes. The smoke cleared, and Jonara realized she was in a church.

2023 Oct 7, Sat. Candlewood Catholic Church. Corpus Christi, Texas.

A day had passed. Jonara was no longer in the visitation area as she was on Friday but rather was in the very last pew of the main church area where a funeral Mass was in progress. The priest had taken a moment to cense. He had been walking up and down the aisles swinging the thurible (censer). He walked to the casket and swung the thurible three times over and around Geneva's casket.

"What happened?" Jonara whispered. "I was at the wake, and now I'm here."

"You're back, Shnu!" Cerafina whispered, and she gave Jonara a quick hug. "You went catatonic on us. You didn't say or do anything after the wake. Eva put you to bed. I helped you wake up and dress for the funeral. You had us all scared!"

"I had this really bad vision," Jonara said, "that you and I were in Vietnam."

"The massacre? The helicopter? And Nekara the Red?"

"Yeah!" Jonara said.

"I was there too."

"What was the last thing you remember?" Jonara asked.

"Nekara said something about a smorgasbord. You choked her. That was it. The priest was burning incense at the wake. I tapped you on the face, but you didn't respond. You froze. If I didn't know better, I'd say you were on a bad LSD trip."

"There was more," Jonara said. "I choked her all night long. I saw stars in her face and the sunrise. Then you kissed me and broke the vision."

"I kissed you just now while the priest spread incense around. I figured no one would see us with the smoke," Cerafina said.

"This has never happened before," Jonara said.

"What if you get stuck again?" Cerafina asked. "It could be days, weeks, or years!"

"You'll just have to kiss me again," Jonara grinned.

"I hope that works. I tried kissing you last night and early this morning, and it didn't work. Only now with the incense did you snap out of it. Jonara—do you think Nekara has something to do with it?"

"She said I was under her dominion. I don't believe it," Jonara said.

"Well, something's going on. We have to be careful," Cerafina said. "What if I take on the primary duty of reading the diary or wearing the Water Ruby?"

"No," Jonara said. "They belong in my family. I have to do it. And I won't risk making you catatonic. I couldn't live with myself."

"You couldn't live with yourself? What about me? Can I live with you being catatonic the rest of your life?"

Jonara paused in thought.

"Yeah. We're girlfriends. We look after each other," Cerafina said.

"I don't know what to say," Jonara said, "except I have to find out who my mother's father is, why these relics are special, and something else—Nekara said something about her women. What was it she said? Damiriak women. She kept talking like she wasn't from Earth."

"I think it's an illusion created by our minds and these relics," Cerafina said. "It's getting dangerous. I think we should put them away."

"I can't," Jonara said. "My mother is dying, and maybe my dad is too. I've got to find out my family ancestry. I've got to. Shli—please support me in this. Don't turn your back on me. I need you now more than ever. Will you stand with me?"

"You know I will," Cerafina said. "I may not like it, but I'll stand with you."

CHAPTER 19

Hemorrhage

2023 Oct 7, Sat Afnoon. Candlewood Cemetery. Corpus Christi, Texas.

Jonara watched as workers lowered Geneva's burial vault into the grave. The priest had said the last prayers, and some of the attendees had already departed. Eva motioned that it was time to go.

"Another minute," Jonara said.

Johnny stalled Eva for that minute.

"What are you thinking?" Cerafina asked.

"That I'm in shock. That something has changed, and I should feel it. But I don't," Jonara said. "I should be sad about Nanna Geneva. I see people crying, but I'm not."

"I think I know why," Cerafina said.

"Why?"

"You're worried about your mother," Cerafina said. "The larger pain blocks out the smaller."

"I *am* worried about her," Jonara said. "I can't stop thinking about her. I've got to help her somehow, Shli. I've got to."

"The doctors are doing everything they can," Cerafina said.

"But it's not enough. Grandma Eva says my mommy is going to die, that the preeclampsia will take her life," Jonara said.

"She could be wrong," Cerafina said.

"I'm hoping. But she's a dentist—she knows about medicine and that kind of stuff. What if she's right? If you had a chance to save your mother from dying during childbirth, would you?"

Cerafina paused.

"Well?" Jonara insisted.

"Depends. If she were having a boy like Leo, I would have second thoughts," Cerafina joked.

"That's not funny!" Jonara said.

"Lighten up. It was a joke. Maybe Leo could die but Mamma could survive," Cerafina added.

"You're sick. What is it about death that makes people say sick things?" Jonara asked.

"People cope with death in different ways," Cerafina said. "It's too stressful to endure all alone—as *you* wish to do."

"I don't."

"Do."

"Don't," Jonara said. "I'd give my life for my mother."

"No, don't pull the Christ act on me. One Christ was enough. Don't punish yourself like this," Cerafina said.

"I'm going to try again," Jonara said. "I'm going to save my mommy if I can."

"With the Water Ruby? The candleholder? It didn't work before."

"The candleholder didn't work. But the diary might. I should try that next," Jonara said. "If I don't try, I'll never know. If my mommy is going to die anyway, then there's nothing to lose."

"Except yourself," Cerafina said. "And that bothers me."

"You said you would stand with me," Jonara said. "Will you help me again?"

"Yeah," Cerafina said, and she gave Jonara a hug.

Cerafina wanted to kiss Jonara too, but there were too many people watching. Cerafina simply winked at Jonara, and Jonara winked back. This then became their code indicating they were mentally kissing each other.

The five (Eva, Anna, Johnny, Jonara, and Cerafina) departed the cemetery for lunch followed by a return to Geneva's house.

"Now the real work begins," Eva said. "Let me see—where do we begin? Most stuff will have to be thrown out, of course. And then there's the—"

"Wait!" Jonara said. "Mommy should be here so she can pick what she wants to keep."

"Most of this stuff is junk," Eva said. "I've seen it all my life, and I'm tired of it."

"That's not fair. Daddy—can't we bring Mommy here to pick what she wants to keep?"

"No, Jonara, she's too sick to leave the hospital," Johnny said.

"Jonara—I thought we discussed things already. Do you understand?" Eva asked.

Jonara returned a defiant stare.

"Don't get on my bad side, young lady."

"Maybe Jonara and I should go for a walk," Cerafina suggested.

"No!" Jonara said.

"That's a good idea, Cerafina," Eva said. "Jonara? Go out for a walk with your friend."

"But!"

"That wasn't a request, young lady. Now move!" Eva ordered.

"Come on," Cerafina said. "Oh wait, I left my hair brush in the music room."

"No you didn't, it's—" Jonara started to say, but Cerafina covered Jonara's mouth.

Eva, Johnny, and Anna did not see the mouth-covering maneuver, as they were engrossed in determining what should be sold in an estate sale, what should be donated, and what should be tossed out. Cerafina led Jonara to the music room.

"Sorry, Shnu, but I had to do that," Cerafina said.

"Your hairbrush isn't in here," Jonara said.

"I know, but the diary, oboe, and *viola de gamba* are. What do you think your Grandma Eva will do with them when she finds them?"

"Throw them out," Jonara admitted. "You're right. I should trust you more."

"We can't just carry these things out—they'll see us. So let's take the viol, oboe, and diary with us through the window," Cerafina said.

"And break the glass?" Jonara asked.

"No, silly, we'll open the window and close it behind us. You really are out of it, aren't you, Shnu?" Cerafina said.

"Yeah. I'm glad I have you helping me."

The two did as Cerafina described—they opened the window, carried the musical instruments and diary with them, and closed the window behind.

"We'll keep the instruments at my house for safekeeping," Cerafina said. "I know a special place in the basement where no one will find them. And we'll carry the diary to the hospital."

"Are you sure you want to go to the hospital with me?" Jonara asked.

"Of course," Cerafina said. "I said I'd stick with you, didn't I?"

"Yeah, you did. Thanks, Shli," Jonara said.

Cerafina said, "You're welcome," with a quick kiss on the cheek.

Later, at Corpus Christi Hospital.

"She's asleep," Jonara said as the girls entered Evanita's room.

"Are you sure you want to do this, Shnu? I could read the diary. Maybe that will keep Nekara away," Cerafina suggested.

"No, I want to," Jonara said.

"Okay."

"I'll sit on my mother's right side like this so I can touch her head and right arm. You sit next to me and touch my right hand," Jonara said. "You can hold the diary open, but don't read it."

"Okay," Cerafina said.

"The diary says this, 'It was time I took Eva to Spain so she could see where her mother was born'."

1970 Jul 3, Fri Morn. Birmingham, Alabama.

Jonara and Cerafina appeared in a boxing arena with fifteen-year-old Marcus fighting bouts against a competitor—both with gloves and headgear.

"Marcus!?" Jonara wondered. "What about my family?"

In Marcus's corner was his father and trainer, Quadri Dakari. Quadri cheered Marcus on. Jab, jab, cross, hook, hook, uppercut.

"Impressive, isn't he?" said a familiar voice.

Jonara and Cerafina turned around to see Nekara wearing a boxing outfit.

"You're no boxer," Jonara said.

"Oh, I'm one of the best at feints and punches," Nekara said. "And I'm a good trainer, too. See Marcus up there? He has the *duavirt* sewn into his navel."

"Why do you call it that?" Jonara asked. "It's a *duavisha.*"

"*Duavirt* is how we say it in my language," Nekara said. "Behold. The knockout begins."

Marcus connected two successive combinations. His competitor dropped his gloves, buckled his knees, and froze in place, unable to respond. Marcus continued the assault with left, right, left, and right. The referee did not intervene until the competitor fell motionless to the canvas.

"Marcus killed him," Jonara said.

"Unfortunately not," Nekara said. "I can't allow that for Marcus yet. I need him for future things. Placing him in detention now would defeat that. And I do not accept defeat."

"Quit shoving us around," Jonara said.

"Punch me," Nekara said. "I want to box with you. Punch me right here."

Nekara pointed to her chin.

"Don't do it, Jonara," Cerafina said.

Jonara stood in place.

"Scared?" Nekara asked. "Yes, of course you are."

"Cerafina, wake me up," Jonara said.

Cerafina reached over to kiss Jonara, but Nekara threw a glove in between them.

"Not so fast," Nekara said. "Look at the blood on that poor defeated boy's face. Isn't it gruesome? Makes you want to watch more—like your ancient gladiator contests. Blood is so addictive, don't you agree?"

Instead of Jonara, Cerafina threw a right cross to Nekara's face. Nekara bounced back for a moment but regathered her strength and prepared to retaliate against Cerafina. Jonara took the initiative and kissed Cerafina. The arena swirled, and the two returned to Evanita's hospital room.

"Unk," Evanita moaned in her sleep.

Cerafina felt a kick from Evanita's abdomen.

"The baby is kicking again," Cerafina said.

Jonara placed a hand to her mother's forehead.

"My mother is burning up," Jonara said. "She has a high temperature."

"Are we causing this?" Cerafina asked. "Your mother suffered a lot the last time we were here."

"I think if we take breaks like we did just now, it'll be fine. She'll have time to get a little strength back," Jonara said. "Look at the clock on the wall."

"Only ten minutes have passed. Neither of us went catatonic for very long," Cerafina said.

"Good. Let's try again," Jonara said, and she read more from Geneva's diary.

1970 Jul 3, Fri 3 pm. Manchester Airport, England.

Jonara and Cerafina appeared in the airport just behind Geneva and six-year-old Eva.

"What do you mean, you won't honor my tickets to Barcelona?" Geneva said to the Dan-Air manager. "I paid the full amount for these tickets."

"I'm sorry, Ms. Geneva. Those tickets are counterfeit. Whoever sold you those tickets had no authority or affiliation with Dan-Air."

"You people better get your act together. I've been waiting in this airport for two days while you've been leading me on, making me think you would honor my two tickets to Barcelona. And now you've decided not to? What kind of customer service is this?"

"We took it up with management. At first they said 'yes', but now they say 'no'," the Dan-Air manager said.

"Who's your manager?" Geneva asked. "I want to speak to him. Or her—what's your name again?"

"It's on the nametag," Ross said. "I'm Ross. My advice to you is to return to the States, or purchase another set of tickets from Dan-Air to Barcelona."

"Return to America? I came all the way over here to celebrate my daughter's sixth birthday in my birthtown of Girona, Spain. Do you know anything about Girona?"

"It's in Spain," Ross said.

"It was one of the last cities to resist Franco's army in 1939!" Geneva said.

"I'll remember the history lesson," Ross said.

"You'll remember a lot more after I'm done suing your airline!" Geneva said.

Geneva walked off in a huff—pulling Eva behind her.

"I'm sorry, Eva. I wanted to celebrate your sixth birthday in Girona. But someone deceived us in the States. I should have known the deal was too inexpensive to be real. I don't have enough money to buy more tickets to Spain. I'm sorry. It looks like we'll have to return to America."

"But you promised, Mother!" Eva protested.

"I know, darling, I know," Geneva said. "Tell you what. When we get home, I'll have a big birthday party for you. You can invite everyone from school."

"But my birthday was yesterday! It's over!" Eva cried. "I spent my birthday in this boring airport."

Eva wailed with tears. Geneva buried her face in her hand.

"Ah yes. A mother-daughter experience gone wrong," Nekara said from behind Jonara.

"Where did you come from?" Cerafina asked.

"Misery and death have the same scent. I can smell them from years away," Nekara said.

"Go away, Nekara. We don't believe your lies anyway," Jonara said.

"I'm not here to feed you lies but to feed on death," Nekara said.

"There's no death here," Jonara said.

"There will be. And you can't stop it," Nekara said.

Nekara disappeared from view.

"Damn that Nekara," Jonara said. "Why can't she spend all her time with Marcus and leave us alone?"

"She's enriching her palate," Cerafina said.

"That's not funny," Jonara said.

"Sorry," Cerafina said.

Eva stood up and grabbed her shorts.

"Potty," Eva said. "Potty."

"All right. We'll find you a potty," Geneva said.

Geneva led Eva around and for some reason had difficulty finding the restroom.

"What is it with these British places? Everything is backward or haphazardly thrown together," Geneva said. "Okay, Eva, this looks like a restroom. Let's see."

Geneva opened the door. It was not the restroom but instead a utility room. Inside, she caught Ross in a sexual situation with another male. Geneva quickly slapped her hand over Eva's eyes.

"Mr. Ross!" Geneva protested.

Ross pushed Geneva out carefully to prevent his exposure to the public, and he closed the door.

"Well I never!" Geneva said.

Geneva looked around the airport and found the loo. Moments later with Eva relieved, she exited the loo and saw Ross attending the Dan-Air counter. She approached him.

"Mr. Ross!" Geneva said. "You should be fired! Not for who you are, but for what you're doing on company time. Instead of getting your jollies, you should be resolving my ticket problem!"

"Shhh," Ross said. "Not so loud."

"I'm going to get louder if you don't do something. I'm going to explain to your co-workers the real reason you can't get my ticket resolved. You're resolving personal matters!" Geneva threatened.

"Please, Ms. Carter," Ross said in full nervousness.

"The name is Carreña! Geneva Carreña! And this is my daughter! Eva Carreña! And you better get us on the next plane to Barcelona or else!" Geneva threatened.

"What happened to Gracer?" Cerafina asked. "Wasn't that her husband's name? Wasn't that Eva's last name?"

"Looks like Nanna Geneva went back to Carreña for herself and Grandma Eva," Jonara said.

"I can't," he begged. "It's full. There's another flight, but I—"

"This flight, Mr. Ross!" Geneva ordered.

"Yes, of course," he scrambled. "Just don't tell anyone. I'll get fired. Please, don't come back to this airport after this. I beg you."

"Stop begging and get us on that plane to Barcelona!" she ordered.

"Follow me," Ross said.

Ross led Geneva and Eva to cargo processing. Jonara and Cerafina followed behind. The face of Nekara briefly appeared as a bobbing ball next to Jonara.

"Now comes the fun part. Witness what men do for personal entertainment," Nekara said.

"Where's that music coming from?" Cerafina asked Jonara.

"You like it?" Nekara said. "It's a song by Depeche Mode called, *Never Let Me Down Again*. It's so appropriate for the moment."

"Hardly," Cerafina said. "That song wasn't released until 1987. You're 17 years out of time."

"If I say it's appropriate, it is!" Nekara said, and she vanished from view.

The music continued playing until the song reached its end.

"She's getting on my nerves," Jonara said. "I wish we could get rid of her."

Ross led Geneva and Eva to a Dan-Air cargo box. The box had rounded corners, was tall and wide enough to hold two people, and was triple-walled.

"What's this?" Geneva asked.

"Your transport to Barcelona," Ross said.

"This box? It looks like an oversized icebox. Stop wasting my time. Get me on that plane!" Geneva ordered.

"I'm telling you, this is the way on. You and the girl get in the box, and I'll load it on the plane into freight hold number three," Ross said. "It's perfectly safe. My friend and I have used it for free rides around Europe. It's exciting what can happen when the altitude is high."

"You're kidding," Geneva said.

"Look," Ross said, and he opened the door.

Inside were padded walls covered with posters of attractive men in swimming trunks.

"I don't want to hear any more about high altitudes," Geneva said. "This is disgusting. What's the padding on the walls for? And why are the walls so thick?"

"We don't like being heard. And the ride gets bumpy. But for you, it should be smooth," Ross said.

"Is it sanitized? Will we get a disease or something?" Geneva asked. "And how do we get out in Barcelona?"

"Here," Ross said as he approached with blankets. "I'll cover everything up with these blankets. You won't have to see anything or touch anything. Perfectly clean. But I'll leave the peephole open. When you get to Barcelona, wait until the box is unloaded and the way is clear. Then open the door and sneak out."

"Sneak out," Geneva said. "I can't believe it."

"It looks like fun," Eva said.

"Look, lady, I'm putting myself out on a limb for you," Ross said. "This kind of stuff could get me fired."

"Seems that's your favorite expression—getting fired," Geneva said. "Very well. This will be the last time I fly on this plane."

"It will be the last time anyone flies on this plane," Nekara said as she popped her head briefly into Jonara's and Cerafina's view.

"Go away," Jonara said.

"Do you know why Ross likes high-altitude flights?" Nekara asked. "Physics. Decompression makes the balloon expand."

"Physics," Jonara said as she shafted her finger into Nekara's head.

Nekara disappeared like a balloon being popped.

"She's disgusting," Cerafina said.

"Tell me about it," Jonara replied.

Geneva and Eva sat in the box. Ross closed the door.

"Test it," Ross said. "Can you open the door?"

Geneva opened the door and closed it.

"Don't forget," Ross said. "Wait to be unloaded before getting out. You don't want anyone to see you."

Ross loaded the box on a small utility vehicle and signaled a cargo handler to take the box to the plane—a De Havilland Comet 4B with identifier G-APDN. As directed, the handler loaded the box onto the airplane in freight hold number three against the rear pressure bulkhead.

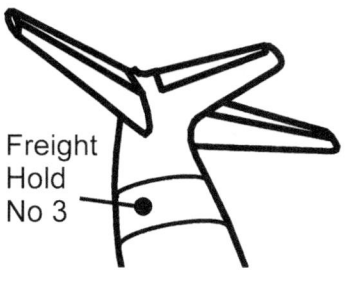

"Wait!" Geneva yelled from inside. "Someone needs to stamp our passports for customs!"

The walls were too thick, and no one heard Geneva. Jonara and Cerafina walked back to the terminal where passengers now boarded Flight G-APDN.

"Now what?" Cerafina asked.

"You get on the Comet, that's what," Nekara said, appearing out of nowhere and fully in their view.

"No," Jonara said.

"That's your automatic response to me, isn't it Jonara?" Nekara asked. "Really, you must learn to enrich your vocabulary. But I'll save you the bother of wondering what to do next. Here—let's ride on the plane to Barcelona."

Nekara placed her hand to her abdomen, made a finger signal, and the three appeared on the De Havilland Comet.

"You can't force us to stay here," Jonara said. "Cerafina— let's get out of here."

"Are you sure, Jonara?" Nekara asked. "Your grandmother and great-grandmother are on this flight. Don't you want to see if they survive or not?"

"Survive? Of course they survive. They have to. My life is based on them."

"Up to this point, Jonara. Up to this point," Nekara said.

Cerafina disappeared.

"Where's Cerafina?" Jonara asked. "What have you done with her?"

"It's not what I've done," Nekara said. "It's what you haven't—or won't—do."

The airplane took off from Manchester Airport and flew toward Spain.

"Cerafina, wake me up," Jonara said. "Cerafina!"

"She can't hear you," Nekara said. "She's home studying her piano music."

"Whatever your game is, Nekara, it won't work. Cerafina is sitting next to me in the Corpus Christi Hospital with my mommy," Jonara said.

"Are you sure? Look at the window. I'll show you what's happening on October the 7th, 2023," Nekara said.

Jonara looked at the window. Cerafina was at home playing the piano. Her hair was unkept, and she labored over the piano. A boy about her age walked up behind her and whispered something in her ear. It wasn't Leo. She stood up, turned around, and hugged him.

"That's her boyfriend," Nekara said.

"It's a lie. She doesn't have a boyfriend. I'm her boy...girl...it's all a lie," Jonara fumbled.

"Look at the window again at Evanita's hospital room."

Jonara looked in the window. The room was empty.

"Look again. Your house. Your grandmother's house. Your great-grandmother's house," Nekara said.

Jonara looked. All three houses had different people living in them.

"More lies. That could be anything," Jonara said.

"But it isn't. Scan the images with your *moisharn*—what you call the Water Ruby," Nekara said.

"How do you know about that?" Jonara asked.

Nekara laughed. Jonara scanned the images, and the Moissan Ruby confirmed them as true.

"You've tricked the Water Ruby!" Jonara said.

"No trick, Jonara," Nekara said. "A *moisharn* never lies."

"But you do," Jonara said.

"When it pleases me. But telling the truth is more pleasing in this instance," Nekara said. "You hold your life in your hands—and the lives of your grandmother and great-grandmother."

"What are you talking about?" Jonara asked.

"It's 4:08 pm," Nekara said. "You have almost two hours to decide."

The De Havilland took off from Manchester Airport and gained altitude. All seemed well. The airplane settled into flight, and the passengers expressed no apprehension. Nekara started to sing.

"On top of Montseny, all covered with snow. I lost my directions, and descended too low!" Nekara laughed.

"Stop it!" Jonara shouted. "I can't stand you anymore. I'm getting rid of you!"

"Better not!" Nekara said. "You need me!"

"Bullcrap!" Jonara shouted.

Miramish	Translation
Zhaipo Nekara vaka	Send Nekara back
Di shai kiutha	To the abyss
Veletu tolu sha bilefio.	From where she came.
Zhaipo Nekara vaka	Send Nekara back
Dhaku firopo shash	And rid her
Veletu teshunu varila!	From this plane!

Nekara held a finger signal over her abdomen on one hand and waved goodbye to Jonara on the other hand.

"You'll ask for me before it's over," she said as she faded into nothingness.

"I hope you never come back," Jonara said.

Nekara's laugh echoed in the distance.

"Cerafina, wake me up!" Jonara said.

Nothing.

"*Peliko!*" Jonara said, but again nothing. "*Peia elifa lerifa ilofa keia orifa!* (P-e-l-i-k-o!)"

No change. Jonara shook the Moissan Ruby.

"Show me Cerafina," Jonara said.

An image of Cerafina at home playing a piano duet with her boyfriend appeared in the airplane's window.

"No, it can't be true," Jonara said. "But this is the Water Ruby. It never lies. Show me Mommy. Show me Evanita Carreña Pindus."

The airplane window swirled with grays. Jonara spoke again:

Miramish	Translation
Feifo nau	Show me
Ivanita Karenya Pinedosa!	Evanita Carreña Pindus!

The windows continued to swirl in grays.

"Dammit!" Jonara said, and she spoke:

Miramish	Translation
Feifo nau Iva Karenya!	Show me Eva Carreña!

The window showed six-year-old Eva with Geneva in the freight box at the rear of the airplane.

Miramish	Translation
Feifo nau Iva Karenya	Show me Eva Carreña
Ishu shai kelosha	In the year
Avu-dint avuda-iri!	Two-thousand twenty-three!

The window showed a sign for Arbúcies Municipal Cemetery in Spain, followed by two tombstones—one with Geneva's name and the other with Eva's—both with death dates of July 3, 1970.

"Dead? Today? WHY???" Jonara cried.

"They chose this path, as did you," Nekara's head said as she appeared for a moment and disappeared.

A stewardess heard Jonara shouting and came over to check on her.

"We have to stop this plane," Jonara said.

"I'm sorry. Is there a problem?" the stewardess asked.

"We're going to crash!" Jonara said. "We have to turn around and return to Manchester."

"Is this your first flight?" the stewardess asked. "I can tell it is. Children often get frightened by airline flight. Here, I'll bring you something to drink. It will help you sleep."

"No, I don't want to sleep," Jonara said. "You're not paying attention. You have to turn around now!"

The stewardess signaled to another stewardess who picked up the plane's phone and spoke with someone. After a moment further, the stewardess hung the phone on the switch hook and joined the discussion with Jonara.

"We have a nice place for you to rest in back," the second stewardess said. "There are no windows and nothing to see that can frighten you. You'll be perfectly safe. I assure you."

"No, no, no!" Jonara yelled.

Jonara jumped out of her chair and bolted for the pilot's cabin, but a third stewardess blocked her path and grabbed hold of her arms. Jonara struggled and nearly got through, but the two stewardesses behind caught up with her and helped drag her to the back. A fourth stewardess opened a bathroom door. The first three pushed Jonara into the bathroom, and the fourth one locked it.

"Let me out, let me out!" Jonara pounded on the wall.

The stewardesses left her and returned to work. Jonara looked at herself in the mirror. Her eyes were red with dark patches under them. She turned on the water and held her hands below.

"Please, someone help me," she said.

"Did I hear someone call me for help?" Nekara said as she appeared in the mirror.

"I don't want your help," Jonara said. "This is all your do-ing."

"Oh no. Real evil is better than fiction. I could never develop a tragedy like this," Nekara said. "Behold your ending."

Jonara watched in horror as an image of the De Havilland Comet plowed through a grove of beech trees on a mountain slope, exploded into fireballs, and disintegrated on impact. A 125-acre swath of leveled trees was all that remained.

"Please, it can't be," Jonara said.

"It is. Oh, you humans care not for the past. You only have to check your history books to know this outcome is real," Nekara said.

"Then my grandma and great-grandma shouldn't be on this flight," Jonara said.

"Neither should you. But the three of you insisted on flying this plane," Nekara said.

"I insisted on nothing. You dragged me here," Jonara said.

"So you say," Nekara said, and she disappeared.

"Jonara, you fool," Jonara said. "Just make a Miramish chant and wish this accident away."

Miramish	Translation
De Havilaneda Kometa	De Havilland Comet
Fuifo ishu aula derotu.	Fly in air clear.
Sheluko kaish e marina	Stay your course
Raupo ishu Bareselona, lolifa.	Land in Barcelona, dear.

Jonara paused and said:

Miramish	Translation
Feifo nau Iva Karenya	Show me Eva Carreña
Ishu shai kelosha	In the year
Avu-dint avuda-iri!	Two-thousand twenty-three!

The mirror showed Geneva's and Eva's tombstones in the Arbúcies Municipal Cemetery with a death-date of July 3, 1970.

"Damn it, dammit, damn it all to pieces!" Jonara cried.

She fell to the floor and wept.

"I can't stop it. I can't. It's all over. What a stupid way to end. Stupid!"

"How far we've fallen!" Nekara said as she poked her head through the mirror. "It was only four days ago I had your father on the bathroom floor of an airplane whimpering like a beaten dog. Now it's your turn. Like father like daughter."

Jonara beat her fists against the floor.

"Oh you humans give up so easily," Nekara said. "Don't you realize you have no power to stop an indurated event?"

"I already know that!" Jonara yelled.

"Oh let's see—another twenty minutes? No, less. You've seen the result. What a shame you're locked in here with no windows, so far in the back of the plane. You'll miss out on a glorious front-row view when the plane plows into the mountain. No windows, all wondering, and not a friend in the world. Goodbye, Jonara. I'm sorry you couldn't entertain me with more misery, but I have a tight schedule. Evil doesn't wait for the helpless."

Nekara disappeared.

"Help me, please!" Jonara cried.

Nothing.

"*Feifo dauna* (Show time)," Jonara said.

The mirror showed 1753 hours.

"This is your pilot speaking," called a voice over the intercom. "We have just passed the Spanish frontier and will be arriving at Barcelona in about fifteen minutes. Please attach your seatbelts, and thank you for flying Dan-Air."

"Not even a bloody seatbelt," Jonara said. "Wouldn't do any good."

Jonara stared at the mirror.

"I'll never know who my mother's father is. I'll never know about 1492," Jonara said.

A strange sort of calm and resignation came over Jonara. Images flashed in the mirror of her past—playing with toys, seeing Almarita at school, her mother, her father, her other family, the visit in Corpus Christi, the adventures in time, Cerafina, and Nekara the Red. Strangely, she felt nothing. It was as if she were looking at a slide show of the ancient world.

"Even Nekara doesn't hurt me," Jonara said.

Jonara half-expected to see Nekara show her evil face, but she didn't.

"So this is the end," Jonara said. "Then let it be. The end. The beginning. It's all the same. *Yufipa muida-avu* (Fourteen ninety-two)."

Jonara felt herself in two places at once—the bathroom of the De Havilland Comet, and the Caves of Healing where the different women stood in the pool. It was a scene she witnessed before, and now she stood in the pool with the women. In the deeper part of the pool was the beautiful woman she'd seen before—standing on water as it were. A crimson-cerise light emanated from her.

"Felifia?" Jonara caught herself saying to the woman in the deep.

Jonara didn't know how she knew the woman's name, but she accepted it.

"Are you God?" she asked.

Felifia said nothing, but instead held out an arm as an offering to lead Jonara away.

"It's my time to go," Jonara said. "I'm ready."

A sense of warmth traveled up through Jonara's legs from the pool. Knowledge of the Earth's history flowed through her. Again, she felt no emotion—images of past peoples, their successes, and their failures flashed before her eyes, yet she felt no remorse or reward. It was a rite of passage, that there was nothing left hidden for those who travel beyond forever. And in that splash of knowledge, she watched Flight G-APDN in its final minutes with a strength extending from Felifia such that Jonara felt no fear and no agony.

Legend:

    ATC: *An Air Traffic Controller*
    Pilot: *Pilot of Flight G-APDN*
    DN: *Radio call sign of aircraft Flight G-APDN*

  1757 Pilot: "Passing Barcelona FIR boundary. Leaving 160. Estimating Point Berga 01."

1759	ATC:	"DN. Contact Barcelona Approach on 119.1 Mhz."
	Pilot:	"Barcelona approach DN."
	ATC:	"DN. Turn left heading 140."
	Pilot:	"Turn left onto 140. Present level leaving 130. Estimating Sabadell 07."
1800	ATC:	"DN. Confirm estimating Sabadell at 07."
	Pilot:	"Sorry, 05."
	ATC:	"Roger then cancel my last transmission. Proceed heading to Sabadell."
1801	Pilot:	"Barcelona approach DN. Out of 100 for 90."
	ATC:	"DN Roger. Have you DME on board?"
	Pilot:	"Negative, sir."
	ATC:	"Roger DN. Continue descent down 60."
	Pilot:	"Roger. We are leaving 90 for 60."
1802	ATC:	"DN. Turn now left heading 140."
	Pilot:	"Left onto 140 leaving 85 for 60."
	ATC:	"Confirm passing Sabadell now."
	Pilot:	"In about 30 seconds."
	Pilot:	"Barcelona, DN. Passing Sabadell."
	ATC:	"DN Roger. Radar contact. Continue descending down 2800 feet, altimeter 1017, transition level 50."

The Moissan Ruby indicated to Jonara the aircraft was not passing Sabadell as the pilot thought, and Barcelona's radar contact was of a different aircraft. Flight G-APDN was in fact a few minutes away from the cloud-covered Peaks of the Needles in the Montseny Mountains near the city of Arbúcies, forty miles northeast of Barcelona Airport, with the target mountain peak having an elevation of 3840 feet.

1803	Pilot:	"Roger. Cleared further down to 2800 feet on 1017, transition level 50."
	Pilot:	"Barcelona. DN requests the duty runway."
	ATC:	"DN. Duty runway 25."
1805	ATC:	"DN. Altitude."
	Pilot:	"DN is passing 4000 feet on 1047."

1807   ATC: "DN. Confirm if on course."
               Static.
        ATC: "DN. Confirm if on course."
               Static.
        ATC: "DN. Do you read?"
               Static.

Toothpicks. That's what the beech trees looked like to Jonara. Toothpicks disappearing under the mowing of a model airplane made of blood and fire. The image changed from color to black and white. Blood and fire sloshed along the toothpicks, creating a backwash of death. Seven crew—all dead. One-hundred and five paying passengers—all dead. The mountain shrank, or Jonara ascended in the air. The fire that was once a large fireball shrank into a seemingly small campfire. Felifia extended her hand farther to Jonara, and Jonara slowly extended hers. But she looked back for a moment—where were Geneva and Eva?

"Family," Jonara said. "Where is my family? They must join with me."

Felifia motioned her hand to smoke rising from the cave pool. Jonara followed the smoke into the pool and back to Earth where she descended to the aircraft wreckage at ground level. A mixture of debris confused the view, but she saw something that caught her attention—the rear fuselage between the rear bulkhead and the first parts of the tail was intact.

"They were next to that bulkhead," Jonara said. "They could have survived. They must survive."

"You cannot stop it," echoed in Jonara's mind from Nekara.

"I can't stop it, but maybe I can change it," Jonara said. "If only I could change it."

Jonara ascended up the line of smoke back into the Caves of Healing where Felifia reextended her arms to Jonara. Nekara's head appeared in the cave and said:

"No. The event is indurated. You cannot stop it."

Felifia turned her attention toward Nekara, placed a hand against her (Felifia's) abdomen, made some hand signals, and with the other hand pointed at Nekara. Nekara screamed and shrank into darkness. Felifia looked at Jonara, and a great smile of happiness and satisfaction grew on her face. She nodded, "Yes" to Jonara. Jonara returned to the bathroom floor of the De Havilland Comet.

    1805 ATC: "DN. Altitude."
          Pilot: "DN is passing 4000 feet on 1047."

The aircraft screamed toward the beech trees on the Montseny Mountains. Jonara placed a hand on the aircraft's fuselage and yelled:

Miramish	**Translation**
Kisheluako!	Indurate!

Time slowed. As the aircraft plowed through the trees, low rumbles of imploding thunder carried through the aircraft. Jonara could not see outside or into the passenger area—she was blind to the collision. Then something changed. She wasn't just in an aircraft ready to die. She was back in the boxing arena with fifteen-year-old Marcus landing hooks and uppercuts on her jaw. She was at the 16th Street Baptist Church when the bomb exploded. Vietnam during the massacre. The Helrod. War in the Pindus Mountains. Bombs in Palestine. Calico Shepherd beating up the German and Russian girls. The River Wood and Battery fire. Cerossi Café. The Thach maneuver. The Nationalists closing in on Girona in 1939. The Jewish and Muslim expulsion of 1492.

"*Fipato* (Expel)!" Jonara shouted.

A tree gashed open the fuselage next to Jonara. The aircraft slung back and forth and sent Jonara through the hole and into the mountain snow. Jonara looked up, and the aircraft was in one piece! There were other gashes in the fuselage, but the aircraft survived and did not catch fire. Passengers and crew exited the craft, including Geneva and Eva.

"Thank you, Felifia," Jonara said.

Geneva received a concussion on her head and was disoriented.

"Is this Barcelona Airport?" she asked in total confusion. "Baggage boy, which way to the terminal?"

"Look at the snow!" Eva said. "I want to go sledding!"

There was no baggage boy, of course. Eva ran away from the aircraft, and Geneva pursued.

"Wait for your mother, Eva," Geneva called.

Geneva caught up just as they reached a steep slope. They fell to the snow, and Jonara did too. The three slid like human sleds and gained speed down the mountain, going faster and faster. Jonara felt as if she'd left her stomach back on the mountaintop, and her heart anticipated the final impact at the mountain's base.

"It was a trick," Jonara said. "Some last finger of death by Nekara. We won't die in the airplane crash. We'll die from hitting the bottom of this mountain."

The three slid off a cliff and went airborne. Jonara flailed her arms around wildly to get her orientation but could not. The images of Marcus boxing her skull to a pulp filled her brain. The drastic altitude change tore at her tissues, and blood poured out of her mouth and nose. Her vision went dark with red, and at the moment she expected impact, she opened her eyes.

Crash!

Jonara fell from the chair in Evanita's hospital room to the floor. Or was it Evanita's room? Jonara stood up and saw an old man bleeding to death.

"He's hemorrhaging to death!" Dr. Reegen said as he rushed in.

"What's that girl doing here?" asked a nurse.

"Get her out!"

A nurse pulled Jonara to her feet, and Jonara glanced back to see the man bleeding profusely from his lower abdomen.

"Where's Mommy!?" Jonara screamed.

The nurse pushed Jonara out of the room and slammed the door closed.

"Where's Mommy!?" Jonara yelled again.

Jonara looked around. Where was Cerafina?

"Cerafina?" Jonara called, but Cerafina did not respond.

The doctor ripped open the old man's door and hauled him on a gurney down the hallway, yelling something about getting the man into OR (operating room). Jonara ran after, but a nurse tripped her up. Jonara landed flat on her face and hit her forehead on the floor. Smack!

Jonara stood up in a daze. She felt different. Why? She didn't know.

"Where's Cerafina?" Jonara asked calmly, as if nothing had happened. "Where's Cerafina?"

A nurse saw Jonara.

"She's in shock. Restrain her," a nurse said in reference to Jonara.

Jonara did not respond at first, but when a nurse grabbed her by the arm, Jonara felt an intense need to run. She ran out of Corpus Christi Hospital, down the street, and up to the front door of the Vagatti house. Out of breath and panting hard, she knocked.

"Yes?" said Davino Vagatti as he answered the door.

"Oh Mr. Vagatti," Jonara said. "I'm so glad to see you. I need help."

"I'm sorry, do I know you?" Davino asked.

"Yeah. I'm Jonara."

Davino shrugged his shoulders to say he didn't understand.

"Jonara Pindus. You took me to the hospital a few days ago. Uncle Fostero? The group of THEY? Remember?" Jonara asked.

"I'm sorry. You are confused. I see you have a bump on your head. There's a hospital down the street. I'll call an ambulance."

"I know there's a hospital down the street. No, don't call an ambulance. I'm okay. Can I see Cerafina?"

"You know my daughter?" Davino asked.

"Of course! I'm her best friend, you could say. We've been hanging out this past week," Jonara said.

Davino's eyes lit up in surprise.

"Cerafina," Davino called. "There's a girl here. She claims you know her, that you two have been hanging out all week."

Jonara heard Cerafina's laugh from inside, but the laugh gave her the shivers. It was as if Cerafina had heard a funny joke with the joke being on Jonara. Davino left the front door and returned to his business.

"Well, well, well, so you're my friend, are you?" Cerafina asked as she arrived at the front door.

"Shlifa—please don't joke around with me. I'm really tired, and I need a friend right now," Jonara said.

"Shlifa? Who's that? My name is Cerafina. And how did you know about me? I've never seen you before."

"Shli, please! Not now! Don't you remember when we were in my great-grandmother's music room and kissed?" Jonara asked.

Cerafina's face turned hostile.

"What kind of gag is this?" Cerafina barked. "Who the hell are you? Did that jerk Greg Dannerstadt at school put you up to this?"

"What's wrong, my love?" asked a teenage male voice from inside.

"Some two-bit whore of Dannerstadt's is calling me a dyke," Cerafina said.

The male appeared in the doorway. Jonara recognized him as the one Nekara showed her while Jonara was on the De Havilland Comet. A wild thought that Nekara had changed something finally materialized in Jonara's brain, but she refused to accept it. Could this be Cerafina's boyfriend? How? What had Nekara done?

"Listen, you hussy," the boy said. "Tell that crap-for-brains Dannerstadt he's looking to get his family jewels kicked to China. Get it? Now scram!"

The boy slammed the front door onto Jonara's face, breaking her nose. It bled. Jonara stood motionless and cried—her tears rolled down her cheeks and mixed with her nose blood. Cerafina quickly lifted a curtain in the living room and saw

Jonara standing on the front doorstep. Cerafina ran to the front door, opened it as if a tornado had blown it open, and kicked Jonara squarely in the abdomen. Jonara toppled backward off the front porch and landed on the front sidewalk with her back.

"Get off my property before I call the police!" Cerafina threatened, and she slammed the front door.

Jonara, now deeply in pain, rolled over slowly and crawled to the edge of the property. When she reached the public sidewalk, a pair of red and black shoes greeted her. She looked up and saw...Nekara. Nekara laughed insanely.

"Kiss my shoes," Nekara said. "Kiss my shoes, and all will be better. Refuse, and spend the rest of your life crawling on all fours."

Jonara shook with such misery that she could barely keep her posture. The Moissan Ruby didn't activate, which surprised Jonara considering how badly she shook. In utter despair, she lifted her head and dipped it over like a cat dipping her head down for a drink of water.

"With tongue," Nekara added.

Jonara moved her lips down toward Nekara's shoes and extended her tongue in a final surrender of her soul to the devil. Just as her tongue was about to touch Nekara's shoes, Nekara disappeared. Jonara retracted her tongue. She remained in place and stared at the dirty cracks in the sidewalk where Nekara once stood.

2110 Dec 28, Sun 7 pm. 376 Grey Road, Hamilton, New Zealand.

"Oh, it's past dinner!" Jonara said. "I wondered why I got so hungry. You're welcome to stay, of course. No, wait, you have other editing to do, don't you?"

"Yeah, we do," Kristi said. "Today took longer than expected. I didn't realize you remembered so much from the past."

"Of course, Kristi. No one forgets something like that," Jonara said. "Although I wonder if I left out any details. I'll have to think about it tonight. Are either of you interested in a slumber party? No wait, what am I talking about. I'm a hundred years old! I can't act like a teenage girl. I guess I got caught up in the story of my youth. Funny how that changes a person, if only temporarily."

"We'll be back tomorrow," Kristi said. "Now you will remember us, won't you?"

"Of course," Jonara said. "I remembered you today, didn't I?"

"Well," Kristi said, "after a bit of prodding you did."

"Oh. Hmm. I must drink more coffee when I get up in the morning," Jonara said. "Here, let me show you the way out. I wouldn't want you to get lost in my old mail and papers."

"Thank you," Kristi and Margaret said.

Jonara led Kristi and Margaret to the front door.

"There. Come visit me again. Come at Easter too," Jonara said.

"We'll see you tomorrow. Sleep well tonight," Kristi said.

"Goodnight," Margaret said.

"Goodnight!" Jonara replied.

The story continues in book three, Imperative Birth.

APPENDIX A:

Characters

Kristi Fernandez
Television journalist for Channel-A news interviewing Dr. Jonara Carreña Pindus in 2110 at Jonara's home. Kristi is nearly nine months pregnant with her wife's child. She is married to Margaret McAleese.

Margaret McAleese
Television camerawoman capturing video and audio of Kristi's interview with Dr. Jonara Carreña Pindus. She is married to Kristi Fernandez and is the other biological mother of Kristi's unborn baby.

Jonara Carreña Pindus
Daughter of Johnny Pindus and Evanita Carreña. Jonara is the primary character in book two. She travels back in time with the help of her Nanna Geneva's diary. She has a good friendship with Cerafina Vagatti and a straining friendship with Almarita Foster.

Evanita Carreña Pindus/Eve Carson
Daughter of Eva Carreña, granddaughter of Geneva Carreña, mother of Jonara Pindus and wife of Johnny Pindus. Evanita starts book two as a patient in the hospital in Jonara's present and a prisoner at the Elrod 402 in Jonara's past. Evanita is given the role name of Eve Carson while in the Elrod and is initially a roommate of Calico Shepherd in Redjet but later becomes the roommate of Tara Tushenne in Aldojet.

Johanidan (Johnny) Reginald Pindus

Johnny is born to Aromani Pindus and Deladi Sweets in 1981. He is Jonara's father and Evanita's husband. Johnny finds the Moissan Ruby in the Willamette River when he is eight years old.

Valeria Pindus

Johnny's older sister. Provides a home for Johnny when he is eight years old.

Eva Kelicacha Carreña

Eva is born on July 2, 1964 to Geneva Carreña and Colonel Gracer in San Antonio, Texas. She barely remembers her father and later grows up in Corpus Christi, Texas. Eva's intelligence drives her to pursue a career in dentistry. She graduates with a medical degree from the University of Texas Houston. She moves to Oregon and receives a pediatric dental degree from the Oregon Health and Science University. She practices dentistry at the Page Street Clinic building and specializes in treating low-income families.

Eva never marries but gives birth to an only child, a daughter named Evanita in June of 1990. Eva keeps the knowledge of Evanita's biological parentage a secret from Evanita for most of Evanita's childhood.

Eva believes in equal rights for women, and that men are the root cause for almost all problems women have.

Eva has straight, shoulder-length black hair, brown eyes, and an olive complexion that could suggest her place of origin as southern Spain, Armenia, or the Middle East. She is at least five feet, eight inches in height. She enjoys a variety of French wines and is an accomplished ballerina.

Geneva (Nanna) Carreña

Born February 4, 1939 in Girona, Spain to Margene Carreña and François Vallan. Evanita's grandmother and Jonara's great-grandmother. Owns house in Corpus Christi. Dies in book one. Eva, Evanita, Johnny, and Jonara stay at Geneva's house pending her funeral.

Anna
Geneva Carreña's housekeeper.

Davino Vagatti
Father of Leo and Cerafina. Davino works in an oil refinery. He moves from Portland, Oregon to Corpus Christi, Texas, is divorced from first wife after having an affair with Sheila Stout. His second wife is Marina Ancona.

Cerafina Vagatti
Daughter of Marina Ancona and Davino Vagatti. Good friend of Jonara Pindus. Shares many journeys back in time with Jonara.

Sheila Stout
Daughter of Sharon Stout. Has affair with Davino Vagatti. Later gets involved with Adrian Cracbern.

Almarita Foster
Daughter of Claire Stout Foster, granddaughter of Sharon Stout. Jonara's friend in Portland.

Adrian Cracbern
Son of Marcus Cracbern. Air Force pilot. Marries Sheila Stout.

Mr. Chuck Harbuck
Owner of a shrimping business. Competitor to Marina. One of his boats is stolen by Leo Vagatti.

Jan Haughf
Lawyer at Haughf Telly Law Firm. Jan represents Eva Carreña.

Vadafa, Biorna, Tioma
Powerful women from Cerafina's future.

Nekara the Red
Powerful woman who has a link with the *duavisha*. She attacks Jonara, Cerafina, and Johnny when the three attend a Margo

dinner on a boat in Rome, Italy circa 1955. She antagonizes Jonara.

Mr. Ross
Airline manager for Dan-Air in Manchester, England.

Greg Dannerstadt
Cerafina's classmate of ill repute.

Elrod 402

Fronka Nordekter/ O Grammeni
Chief Administrator of Elrod 402.

Arfella Beffenstein
Chief architect of the Elrod 402 facility.

Oxia, Ox-One, Ox-Two, Ox-Three, Etc.
Security personnel at Elrod 402 in order of rank. Department name is Oxi.

  Oxia is interested in giving privileges to Evanita in exchange for a sexual relationship. Ox-Two and Ox-Three make deals with Calico—supplies to Calico in exchange for inside prisoner information.

Baria, Bar-One, Bar-Two, Bar-Three, Etc.
Health personnel at Elrod 402 in order of rank. Department name is Bari.

Dazia, Daz-One, Daz-Two, Daz-Three, Etc.
Education personnel at Elrod 402 in order of rank. Department name is Daz.

Dialytika, Diali-One, Diali-Two, Diali-Three, Etc.
Sanitation personnel at Elrod 402 in order of rank. Department name is Dialytik.

Macron, Mac-One, Mac-Two, Mac-Three, Etc.
Cafeteria personnel at Elrod 402 in order of rank. Department name is Macro.

Tara Tushenne
Begins as Mac-Three, promoted to Mac-Two after existing Mac-Two has nervous fit. Tara is attracted to Evanita and offers to help Evanita if Evanita will reciprocate this love. Tara becomes Evanita's second roommate in Aldojet (where Calico is Evanita's first in Redjet).

Fiori Sheppe (Calico Shepherd, Cal, Cali)
Evanita's first roommate at the Elrod 402. Calico has a variant of Turner's syndrome with a mixture of XX and XO chromosomes. She has a medium height, wide stature, shield-shaped chest, clubby arms, pigment patterns on her skin, a webbed neck, a wide and square face, a blue eye, a half green and half yellow eye, and hair with shocks of white, black, blond, and red. Calico is very strong and resistant to disease.

Calico has deals with Ox-Two and Ox-Three to obtain goods such as tobacco, chocolate, and coffee. In exchange, she provides information on other detainees.

America, Pre-1970

Jane MacNessi O'Leary (Janna, Janie)
Born November 3, 1923. Roberta's mother. Trudy's friend. Married to John (Jack) O'Leary. Jane is strong, has red hair, and is of Celtic descent. She graduates from Mary D. Bradford High School in 1942. She marries Jack O'Leary in July of 1942.

John (Jack) O'Leary
Born 1921. Jane's husband and Roberta's father.

Trudy Hansen Sheppe
Born 1924. Calico Shepherd's grandmother. Friend of Jane MacNessi. Married to Wilton Sheppe (born 1916).

Arbutus (Arbie) Hansen Knoxberger
Trudy's sister. Married to Arnold Knoxberger. Arnold dies during World War II afterwhich Arbie reverts her last name to Hansen.

George Henrock
Jane's and Trudy's boss at Daschwirk in Kenosha, Wisconsin.

Joe Henrock
Spring training coach for the All-American Girls Baseball League. Works with Trudy and Jane to determine aptitude during spring 1944 tryouts.

Petunia
Racine Belle player during 1944 season.

Mum
Racine Belle player during 1944 season.

Jeff
Security guard at Daschwirk.

Jim
Crib manager at Daschwirk.

Bill
Machinist at Daschwirk.

Hank
Floor cleaner at Daschwirk.

Mr. Grundle
Jane's boss at Daschwirk after George Henrock dies.

Dr. Alina Zavuski
Russian atheist. Owner of a special barn in western Racine County with an underground room for feminist meetings.

Grandmother of Dr. Antonina Zavuski. Alina goes to South Korea to help women who are victims of American soldiers. Later, she works in Vietnam until 1975 when the communists take over.

Pete
Television deliveryman. Mum and Pete install a GE Model 901 projection television at Jane and Jack O'Leary's house.

Father O'Riley
Marquette admissions counselor.

Theodore Cracbern
Husband of Alice Cracbern and father of Marcus Cracbern. Co-pilot of the Rainbow Vortex B-47 bomber. Takes film footage of the Operation Castle Bravo thermonuclear test on March 1, 1954 and flies suicidally toward the blast. Dies of cancer later in 1954.

Alice Cracbern
Wife of Theodore Cracbern. Has only one child with her husband, a son named Marcus. Dies while giving birth.

Marcus Theodore Cracbern/ Marcus Margo/ Marcus Dakari
Son of Theodore and Alice Cracbern. Born December 1, 1954. Is raised by Dr. Jelana Margo, takes her last name, and later takes the last name Jelana's husband, Quadri Dakari, until Marcus is eighteen years old, at which time he drops Dakari as his last name and goes by Marcus Cracbern.

Dr. Jelana Margo
Born in 1924 to Isha Jelanaka and Amiri Margo. Is a doctor of obstetrics and gynecology at a Montgomery, Alabama hospital. She delivers Marcus Cracbern to Alice Cracbern. After Alice's death, Jelana adopts Marcus and raises him. Jelana marries Quadri Dakari, a successful boxer from Asmara, Eritrea.

Kay Margo Dakari
Born December 1, 1955 to Jelana Margo and Quadri Dakari in Montgomery, Alabama.

Nurse Kaila Baker
Dr. Jelana's assistant who helps deliver Marcus.

Lashanda Madison
Isha and Amiri Margo's neighbor. Her husband dies from a Ku Klux Klan lynching.

Larry Madison
Lashanda's husband, neighbor of Isha and Amiri Margo. Is hung by the Klan.

Justino
The Margos' tour guide in Lisbon. Kaila and Justino go out on a date to see the movie, *Les Amants du Tage* (*The Lovers of Lisbon*).

Quadri Dakari
Boxer in Asmara, Eritrea, Africa. Father is Italian, mother is full-blooded African.

Aman Kwen
A boxer in Asmara, Eritrea who Quadri defeats.

Hakim
Quadri's trainer.

Spain, Pre-1970

Margene Carreña
Geneva's mother. Gives birth to Geneva in Girona, Spain, as the Spanish Civil War ends.

François Vallan

Geneva's father. François is from France.

Father Mendez

Marries Margene Carreña and François Vallan in 1939 in Girona, Spain.

Garcia Delgato

A witness at Margene's wedding. Garcia is a homeless drunk.

Chalina Darconejo/Sister Charlene

A witness at Margene's wedding. Chalina is a waitress.

Sister Francis

A Roman Catholic sister at St. Christopher's Abbey in Girona, Spain.

Martin Sixpence

Geneva's maternal grandfather. Leads a coal-mining operation in Carreña, Spain.

Sister Rosa

A Roman Catholic sister at St. Renata's Abbey in Carreña, Spain.

Greece/New Zealand, Pre-1970

Fantina Karrano di Pindos

Born 1900. Jewish Aromanian living with her father in Samarina, Greece in the Pindus Mountain range. She has white hair and fair skin. She nurses Axon Dendritous back to health. Fantina marries Axon and has a baby—Aromani Karrano di Pindos. Fantina flees Greece and settles first in Palestine and later in New Zealand.

Axon Dendritous
Johnny Pindus's grandfather. Axon is a Greek soldier fighting in Greece against the Italians. Axon and company fight on skis. Axon dies in 1941 during Germany's invasion of Greece. Axon is an Eastern Orthodox Christian.

Samouel Karrano
Born 1860. Fantina's father. Samouel is Jewish and believes everything in his life should be strictly kosher.

Karla Karrano
Ancestor of Samouel Karrano, Fantina, and Johnny Pindus. Karla lives in Carreña, Spain until 1492 when Jews are forced to leave during the Spanish Expulsion. In that year, Karla emigrates from Spain to Athens, Greece.

Kailos Karrano
Born 1798. Fantina's great-grandfather and Samouel's grandfather. Fights in the Greek War of Independence. Settles in Pindus Mountains and builds cabin where Samouel and Fantina live.

Rabbi Evenstein
Marries Axon and Fantina. Arranges Fantina's and Samouel's escape to Palestine.

Aromani Karrano di Pindos/ Captain Pindos/ Aromani Pindus
Born January 15, 1942 to Fantina Karrano di Pindos and the late Axon Dendritous. He spends his first years in Palestine, moves with his family to New Zealand, and serves in the New Zealand Army in Vietnam. There he meets an American, Deladi Sweets, and marries her under the last name of Pindus. He completes his tour in Vietnam and immigrates to the United States where the two live in Portland, Oregon. He is the father of Valeria and Johnny Pindus.

Pierce Wilkinson

Member of the New Zealand Army. Escorts the Karrano family and Rabbi Evenstein from Greece to Palestine in 1941, and the Karrano family with Rabbi Evenstein from Palestine to New Zealand in 1948.

Colonel Andrew Gracer/ Andrew Gràcia

American Army medical officer. Doctor and dentist. He marries Geneva and has Eva with her. Dies during the Viet Cong's Tet Offensive.

Timeline

1492 Jan 1
Female ancestors of families MacNessi, Margo, Carreña, Ancona, and Karrano meet with Felifia in the Caves of Healing of Carreña, Spain as part of a final ceremony before most are forced to leave Spain for religious reasons.

1939 Feb 4
Margene Carreña gives birth to Geneva. Geneva's parents—Margene and François—die. Geneva is raised by Chalina and Catholic sisters.

1940 Oct 23
One-year-old Geneva walks in St. Christopher's Abbey. Franco and Hitler meet to decide Spain's role in World War II.

1940 Oct 28
Battle of Pindus begins between Greeks and Italians.

1940 Dec 16
Axon leads his Greek military company on skis in a charge against Italians. Axon crashes into a cabin at the bottom of a slope.

1940 Dec 19–23
In Samarina, Greece, Axon awakes in a cabin owned by Fantina di Pindos and her father—a Jewish family. Fantina nurses Axon back to health by treating wounds and singing.

1940 Dec 24
Axon awakens from his coma. Fantina and her father celebrate the beginning of Hanukkah.

1941 Mar 22
Samouel Karrano leaves Fantina in Samarina to fight the Italians with the Greek Army.

1941 Apr 6
Germany invades Yugoslavia.

1941 Apr 13 Sun
Germany invades Greece. Samouel's and Axon's company retreats to Samarina.

1941 Apr 15 Tue
Rabbi Evenstein marries Fantina Karrano di Pindos to Axon Dendritous in a Jewish ceremony.

1941 May 3 Sat
Fantina travels to Athens with her father, Samouel, to witness Axon's death. Fantina, Samouel, and Rabbi Evenstein leave Greece for Palestine.

1942 Jan 20 Thu
Fantina gives birth to Aromani in Jaffa, Palestine.

1943 May 30
Jane MacNessi and Trudy Sheppe watch the Racine Belles women's ball team compete against the Kenosha Comets.

1943 Sep 1
Kenosha Comets win second round championship.

1943 Sep 3 Fri
Jane receives a raise to eighty-cents an hour and tickets to the Kenosha Comets–Racine Belles championship series.

1943 Sep 5 Sun
Racine Belles win All-American Girls Softball League championship over Kenosha Comets in three straight wins.

1944 Spring
Jane and Trudy try out for the All-American Girls Baseball League.

1944 May Sat
Jane, Trudy, Arbie, Mum, and Petunia play Sheepshead at Arbie's home in Racine, Wisconsin. The following Monday, Jane is assigned to the Minneapolis Millerettes as a pitcher. She declines the offer and remains employed at Daschwirk.

1944 Dec (mid)
Jack O'Leary returns home to Jane on Christmas leave from the European war theater. Jack shows signs of battle fatigue. Drunk after a night on the town, he rapes Jane.

1945 Aug 6
Jane is pregnant and goes into labor, but the labor stops before her baby is born. The United States drops an atom bomb on Hiroshima, Japan.

1945 Aug 9
Jane gives birth to Roberta MacNessi—a 6-pound 5-ounce 19-inch-long baby girl. The United States drops an atom bomb on Nagasaki, Japan.

1945 Oct
George Henrock, Jane's boss at the Daschwirk factory, dies of a heart attack. Henrock is replaced by Mr. Grundle. Mr. Grundle fires Jane for being a woman to free up a position for a soldier returning from the war. Jack is hired at Daschwirk and performs Jane's job at almost double the wage.

1945 Dec
Jane separates from Jack and moves herself and Roberta in with Arbie. Trudy moves in with Jack and has an affair.

1947 Mar 21 Fri
Arbie and Jane work in the cafeteria at Kefer Toothe Company in Racine, Wisconsin. After work, Arbie, Jane, and Roberta take a ride in Arbie's new car—a 1947 Studebaker Champion convertible—to Dr. Alina Zavuski's barn in western Racine County.

1947 Jul 9 Wed
Eight-year-old Geneva helps with errands in St. Christopher's Abbey in Girona and is told she is to move in with her grandfather who lives in Carreña.

1947 Jul 18, Fri
Five-year-old Aromani Karrano di Pindos witnesses the arrival of the *Exodus 1947* in Haifa, Palestine.

1948 Apr 25
Jaffa is under attack by Zionist militants. Pierce Wilkinson arranges safe passage to New Zealand for Fantina, Samouel, and Aromani.

1948 Aug 16 Mon
Babe Ruth dies.

1948 Aug 17 Tue
Kenosha Comets defeat Springfield Sallies in Kenosha after Chet Grant's inspirational speech about George Gipp and Babe Ruth. Jane is a member of the Comets team while Arbie is a Sallie.

1948 Aug 27 Fri
Jane's last at-bat with the Kenosha Comets against the Springfield Sallies. Jane and Arbie eat in a Kenosha restaurant and discuss Jack's television and Arbie's education.

1948 Oct 8 Fri
Jack O'Leary invites co-workers to his house to watch the World Series on his television. The television malfunctions. Jack blames Jane.

1948 Oct 9 Sat
Jane attends her last ISIS meeting in Racine. Mary Margaret McBride is the topic for discussion.

1948 Oct 10 Sun
Jack O'Leary receives delivery on a $2100 General Electric Model 901 projection television. Jack and his friends watch the World Series followed by the Green Bay Packers football game against the Chicago Cardinals.

1948 Oct 11 Mon
Jane applies for admission to Marquette University but is surprised to find her bank account is overdrawn. Jane leaves Jack after discovering he funded his projection television with her savings. Jane agrees to move to Montgomery, Alabama with Dr. Alina Zavuski.

1948 Dec 31 Fri
Jane, Roberta, and Alina celebrate the new year in Montgomery, Alabama.

1950 Sep 7 Thu
Geneva's grandfather, Martin Sixpence, attacks her pet rabbit in Carreña, Spain. Geneva leaves her grandfather for St. Christopher's Abbey in Girona.

1954 Mar 1
Operation Castle Bravo 15 megaton thermonuclear test on Bikini Atoll in the Pacific Ocean. Theodore Cracbern attempts suicide by flying a B-47 bomber (named Rainbow Vortex) toward the nuclear blast.

1954 Mar 2

Jack O'Leary visits Jane MacNessi while she is repairing the Rainbow Vortex B-47 bomber. Jack takes Roberta shopping. While trying on shoes, Roberta is exposed to X-rays from a pedoscope.

1954 Dec 1

Marcus Cracbern is born.

1954 Dec 19 Sun

Dr. Jelana, Kaila, and Marcus visit Dr. Jelana's parents' house for dinner. Neighbor Larry Madison dies at the hands of the Ku Klux Klan.

1955 Feb 25

Isha Margo, Amiri Margo, Dr. Jelana Margo, Marcus, and Kaila Baker begin their journey to visit Asmara in Eritrea, Africa.

1955 Feb 26

Isha, Amiri, Dr. Jelana, Marcus, and Kaila land in the Azores.

1955 Feb 28

Isha, Amiri, Dr. Jelana, Marcus, and Kaila land in Lisbon, Portugal.

1955 Mar 2

Isha, Amiri, Dr. Jelana, Marcus, and Kaila land in Rome, Italy.

1955 Mar 3

Isha, Amiri, Dr. Jelana, Marcus, and Kaila take a boat ride in Rome. Nekara the Red sings in the band. Nekara attacks Jonara, Cerafina, and Johnny.

1955 Mar 5

Jonara, Cerafina, and Johnny travel to Asmara, Eritrea, Africa in hopes of finding the Margo party.

1955 Mar 6
Jonara, Cerafina, and Johnny find the Margo party. Quadri Dakari defeats Aman Kwen in a boxing match. Kaila is kidnapped by slave traders. Quadri, Hakim, and Dr. Jelana search for Kaila.

1955 Oct 26 Wed
Fantina and Aromani take one of the last overland train rides from Upper Hutt to Featherston in New Zealand.

1955 Dec 1
Kay Margo is born in Montgomery, Alabama.

1956 Apr 7 Sat
Geneva contracts polio at St. Christopher's Abbey while tending to polio patients.

1956 Apr 14 Sat
Geneva is in an iron lung machine while enduring polio.

1956 Dec 12 Wed
Dr. Alina Zavuski holds her last ISIS meeting in the United States and informs Jane she plans to help abused women in South Korea.

1957 Feb 4 Mon
Geneva celebrates her eighteenth birthday in a wheelchair. She receives leg braces and crutches as a gift.

1958 Oct 21 Tue
Despite her paralysis, Geneva plays soccer at St. Christopher's Abbey.

1959 Mar 15 Sun
Quadri first teaches four-year-old Marcus to box. Dr. Jelana arrives home from a *Raisin In The Sun* play.

1962 Apr 7 Sat
Geneva is transferred to St. Renata's Abbey in Carreña, Spain to prepare food in support of a coal miners' strike.

1962 May 7 Sat
Geneva is introduced to the Caves of Healing.

1962 Jul 10
Operation Dominic Sunset thermonuclear device tested at Kiritimati (Christmas) Island in the Pacific Ocean.

1963 May 2 Thu
The Dakari family participates in the Civil Rights march in Birmingham, Alabama. Marcus begins using Nekara's language with his duavisha stone. Marcus communicates with and learns from Nekara.

1963 May 3 Fri
Birmingham Civil Rights demonstration. Bull Connor sets dogs and fire hoses on demonstrators.

1963 Jun 7 Fri
Aromani meets Geneva at a New Zealand medical base in Bong Son, Vietnam.

1963 Jun 8 Sat
In Vietnam, Sister Geneva questions her faith before a priest during confession. In San Antonio, Texas, Jane is denied permission to fly a C-135 Stratolifter to Vietnam.

1963 Jun 11 Tue
Dr. Zavuski, Geneva, and Aromani witness self-immolation in Saigon, Vietnam.

1963 Aug 17
Jane takes Roberta to Wayland Baptist University in San Antonio, Texas.

1963 Sep 13 Fri
Marcus, under the direction of Nekara, mispronounces a chant and throws a curse on the world.

1963 Sep 15 Sun
The Dakari family witnesses the 16th Street Baptist Church bombing.

1963 Sep 29 Sun
Colonel Gracer and Geneva become intimately involved.

1964 Jun 27 Sat
Colonel Gracer and Geneva marry in Universal City, Texas.

1964 Jun 28 Sun
Geneva meets Jane and Roberta MacNessi.

1964 Jul 2 Thu
Eva is born in San Antonio, Texas.

1968 Jan 31 Tue
Colonel Gracer dies from the Tet Offensive against the U.S. Embassy in Saigon, Vietnam.

1968 Mar 16 Sat
My Lai massacre.

1969 Oct
Thompson receives award and throws it away.

1969 Late
Congress investigates My Lai massacre.

1970 Jul 3 Fri
Nekara the Red gives Jonara and Cerafina a difficult time while witnessing this day in history. The two first appear in a boxing arena and witness Marcus in his bouts. The two then travel to

Manchester Airport, England. Geneva and Eva board doomed Dan-Air Flight G-APDN from Manchester to Barcelona.

1989 Dec 3 Mon

Roberta and Eva have a falling out at MacNessi Dental over Eva's pregnancy.

2006 Nov 18 Sat

Geneva visits Eva in Portland. Eva calls the military and the Catholic Church "emotion predators." Evanita is transferred from Portland Detention Center to Elrod 402. Evanita meets Calico Shepherd.

2006 Nov 19 Sun

Evanita attends first church service at Elrod 402 and travels back in time to witness her Grandma Geneva's birth.

2006 Nov 20 Mon

Eva appears in Multnomah County Courthouse as plaintiff against Fronka Nordekter regarding abuses against Evanita. Evanita spends entire day mopping and cleaning. Evanita refuses sexual advances from Oxia.

2006 Nov 21 Tue

Johnny visits Evanita at the Elrod 402 and heals her broken legs and other wounds.

2006 Nov 22 Wed

Oxia introduces Evanita to the Helrod—an H-shaped pole structure for disciplining girls. Evanita works in the cafeteria and reads Mac-Two's psyche driving Mac-Two insane. Evanita suffers injuries including head trauma from Mac-Two. Mac-Two is thrown out of Elrod 402. Mac-Three (Tara Tushenne) is promoted to Mac-Two. Evanita undergoes surgery to remove a brain clot. Later in the evening, she is released to her dorm room. She falls unconscious while watching a Helrod punishment event. Calico revives her and takes her to Redjet where Calico forces Evanita to do Calico's laundry.

2007 Feb 14 Wed
Johnny visits Evanita for Valentine's Day. The two have a religious argument.

2007 Feb 17 Sat
Evanita begins Falun Dafa exercises with Tara to ward off withdrawal symptoms from taking Tegretol and Librium.

2007 Feb 24 Sat
Evanita and Tara perform Falun Dafa and discuss relationships and religion.

2007 Mar 17 Sat
Evanita and Tara run laps around the Elrod 402. Johnny visits Evanita, and the two have another argument about religion.

2023 Oct 4 Wed
Jonara and Johnny eat breakfast across Nueces Bay Causeway and discuss the Moissan Ruby. Johnny shows Jonara the Aromani candleholder. Jonara and Cerafina play Geneva's white *viola de gamba* and use the Moissan Ruby to travel back in time. Cerafina attempts to open Geneva's car trunk in the hospital parking lot. Cerafina retrieves the diary. Jonara travels back in time with Cerafina, and later with Johnny. Jonara begins using the Aromani candleholder and Miramish to help people.

2023 Oct 5 Thu
Jonara, Cerafina, and Johnny visit Eva in the hospital and fight her thyroid cancer. Later, Eva dances the flamenco in a restaurant. Cerafina initially spends the night with Jonara at Geneva's house. Jonara's primary tooth is loose. Cerafina and Almarita have a fight through Jonara's cell phone. Cerafina and Jonara have a fight. Jonara tells Evanita that she (Jonara) is a lesbian.

2023 Oct 6 Fri
Jonara discovers the MacNessi oboe in Geneva's music room. Cerafina and Jonara make up and begin calling each other pet names. Geneva's wake. Jonara becomes catatonic.

2023 Oct 7 Sat

Jonara revives from her catatonic state while attending Geneva's funeral Mass. Geneva is buried in Candlewood Cemetery. Jonara and Cerafina return to Evanita's hospital room. Nekara alters time. After Jonara's hospital stay, Cerafina is no longer with Jonara but is instead at home. Jonara goes to Cerafina's house and finds her with a boyfriend. Cerafina does not remember Jonara and becomes hostile.

2027 Dec 24

Cerafina has argument with Hank and Jean-Jacque on the Verona Ancona megayacht.

2027 Dec 25

Cerafina uses hand signals to choke her half-brother, Leo. Cerafina attends a meeting on the spaceship Velita where she learns she is to be killed.

2110 Dec 27 Sat

Kristi Fernandez's and Margaret McAleese's first day of interviewing Jonara Pindus at Jonara's home in the vicinity of Hamilton, New Zealand.

2110 Dec 28 Sun

Kristi Fernandez and Margaret McAleese interview Jonara Pindus for a second day at Jonara's home in New Zealand.

www.ingramcontent.com/pod-product-compliance
Lightning Source LLC
Chambersburg PA
CBHW070339030726
47504CB00001B/1

* 9 7 8 1 9 3 5 8 1 6 0 2 7 *